Men of Sorrows

Smugglers of the Marsh

A Novel

Mary-Elizabeth Thomas

Bloomington, IN Milton Keynes, UK

authorHOUSE®

AuthorHouse™
1663 Liberty Drive, Suite 200
Bloomington, IN 47403
www.authorhouse.com
Phone: 1-800-839-8640

AuthorHouse™ UK Ltd.
500 Avebury Boulevard
Central Milton Keynes, MK9 2BE
www.authorhouse.co.uk
Phone: 08001974150

Author's Note: 'Men of Sorrows' is a work of fiction based on researched facts and not an historical text book. I have sometimes invented characters or situations for the benefit of the story and I have sometimes changed the dates of certain events. Where possible I have used the names of the real people involved, and given my interpretation of the events that have been chronicled in the archived materials.

First published by AuthorHouse 1/8/2007

Printed in the United States of America
Bloomington, Indiana

This book is printed on acid-free paper.
ISBN: 978-1-4259-6175-6 (sc)

Acknowledgements

This book owes its existence to the many people who supported me and believed in its potential while I was researching and writing it during a difficult time of my life. So my everlasting thanks are due to: Jean Campbell, Jackie Jermin, Rebecca Boulton, Ray Rose, Liz Gedge, Mary Gerard, Robert Williams and my super family – John Scott and Vivien Jones, Tony Thomas and my wonderful children and their partners – Lucy and Ian Russell, James Thomas and Louise Williams – always remembering my Mum who knew and supported my work.

Thanks are also due to the patient and painstaking staff of the Centre for Kentish Studies, Maidstone, the staff at the London Museum, the staff at Guildhall Library and and the staff at the London Metropolitan Archive.

The letter written by Will in Chapter Forty Three is based on a letter written by Lord Kildare of Carton (1730, London), correspondence held by Public Record Office for Northern Ireland, reference D/3078, MIC541

Some of the text from the trial of Arthur Gray is taken from the Old Bailey Proceedings online (www.oldbaileyonline.org, 17 June 2003) 20th April 1748, trial of Arthur Gray ((t17480420-23) consulted 13/07/04

Map by Tony Thomas

Artwork by Louise Moore

"he was ....
a man of sorrows and acquainted
with grief"

from *Messiah*
George Frideric Handel
composed 1741

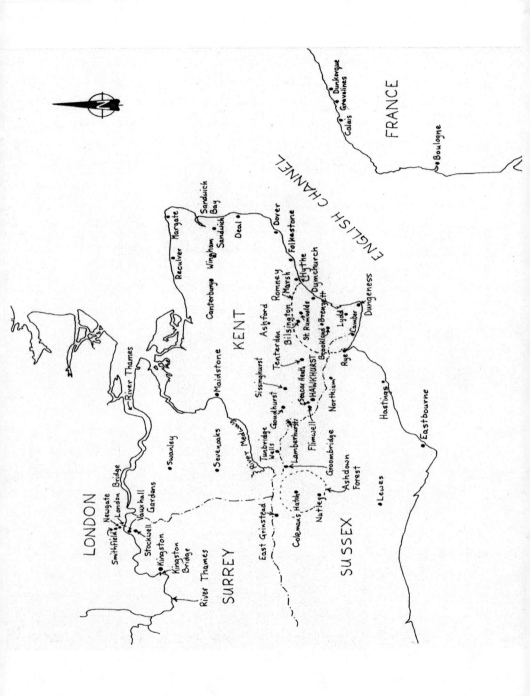

Part one

1713 - 1738

Baptismal records, St Lawrence's Church Hawkhurst, Kent

December 27th, 1713

Lucas, son of John and Hannah Webb
Arthur, son of John and Mary Gray
Thomas, son of John and Elizabeth Kennard
Bethlehem, daughter of John and Jane Stone

CHAPTER ONE

The 'Angel' Alehouse, Hawkhurst, Kent, February 1719

'Come and kiss your mother goodbye,' the man said abruptly.

The child seemed to hesitate. 'Where's she going? Can I go with her?' He glanced at the shape on the bed. 'Will she take the new baby with her?'

With an impatient movement, John Gray grasped the child by the arm and swung him over to the bedside. 'She's already gone. Now kiss her cheek and get gone yourself. Lizzie Kennard and Hannah Webb will see to her now.'

The boy peered at his mother's face and then obediently kissed her cold white cheek. 'Goodbye, mumma,' he said. 'I will try to be a good boy.' The child turned to look at his father. 'Will we keep my new brother?'

His father ignored him and looked again at his dead wife's face before he left her to be laid out by the two women who were waiting in the back room. The fever had left Mary's face white and ravaged and death had already started to work its blueness and stillness over her features. He could still make out something of the calm beauty she had possessed, in the line of her brow and the fine line of her nose. He had known her all his life and had been her husband for the last seven. Yet she had always seemed apart from him, remote, even in their most intimate times together. He wondered, as he looked at her still face, if he had ever really known her, if he had ever known what she thought. Death made her more remote yet. Now he would never know her. Any secrets she had from him would go with her to the grave. Time

5

had taken her, her body was given up to corruption, her soul – well he didn't know about that. Mary had always seemed half out of this world anyway with her knowing smile and secret eyes. Arthur had a look of her sometimes, John Gray thought – not in his features, no he had none of Mary's dark colouring or delicate build – no, not in features, but in his ways.

Arthur, like his mother, even though he was only five, had a way of looking at his father that made him feel uncomfortable, made him feel he was prying, made him feel that Arthur knew something that his father didn't.

The mewling of his week-old second son in the other room brought John Gray back to the present. He wiped his hand across his face and took one last look at his wife. With a sudden movement, he lifted the tankard he was holding and poured the rest of the small beer down his throat. As he turned to walk out of the room, he saw that his son was standing in the doorway, his blue eyes looking anxiously up at his father. John Gray walked out of the room and his son followed him.

Two women were sitting at the table, drinking beer from the jug, chatting quietly. Arthur went to look at his new brother, lying in the old wooden cradle that had been brought out five times, but only used for himself and now for this new baby. Two other brothers and a sister had been born but had flown heavenward to God as soon as they entered the world, according to Parson Saunders. The Parson said the same thing about babies almost every Sunday that Arthur could remember as he sat on the hard wooden bench in the big church at the end of the road, clasping his mother's hand – there were nearly always babies being given back to God's keeping. He wondered why God sent the babies at all, if he wanted them back so quickly. Arthur wondered too, how they could be in heaven since he knew they were in the churchyard. He had forgotten exactly where his brothers and sister were because there was no marker for any of them, but there was a corner of the churchyard where all the babies were put. He sometimes went to sit there in the summer. He thought it was sad that they were hidden in the dark earth, especially when the sun was so warm beating down on his head and all the birds were singing and the grass smelt clean and sweet underneath him.

Arthur looked at his dark-haired baby brother again, sticking its small fist in its mouth and looking back at him with wide surprised eyes. Arthur put his finger in the baby's hand and smiled as the tiny fingers clasped it. 'Good little brother,' he whispered. 'Don't go back to heaven, stay with me.'

'Earth's hard as iron. They can't dig the grave deep enough yet,' Hannah Webb said, looking up at John Gray. 'Who are you going to put the baby to, John?'

He looked round and answered dully, 'Dunno. Thought it would die. It might yet.'

Lizzie Kennard peered at the baby. 'Oh no, never say so! He looks right enough.'

'Martha Allen,' the other woman suggested. 'Her youngest died not more than a week ago. She was still suckling. Perhaps she could barmaid for you, as well as suckle the baby, now Mary's gone. Amos hasn't had much labouring work this winter. They would be glad of a few extra pennies. Shall I ask her for you, John?'

John Gray grunted and nodded his assent.

'What'll you name him, John?' Lizzie Kennard asked. 'He should be William, shouldn't he? After Mary's father? With Arthur being called for yours?'

He shrugged his shoulders. 'William Durrant didn't do nothing for me. But it's as good a name as any, I suppose.'

He looked at the baby with an expression of discontent; another mouth to feed and now he had no wife to do women's work, nor to share his bed and give him comfort of her body. There was Arthur to look after and this other child, if it lived. He didn't really care either way. He went to pour himself some more beer from the jug, but walked instead into the bar room and came back with a bottle. He poured the clear liquid into another tankard and put it to his lips. The smell of cheap Geneva filled the room.

Churchyard, St Lawrence's, Hawkhurst, February 23ʳᵈ 1719

In the end the ground remained iron-hard and with heavy falls of snow on consecutive nights, the grave could not be dug for four days. The villagers who attended the funeral were huddled in their threadbare coats against the icy blasts of the wind swirling sleet into their faces, all anxious to remain only as long as was necessary.

They heard the words familiar to each of them, so often did they gather at the churchyard to hear them. Even Parson Saunders, who enjoyed the melancholy aspect of a burial, was hurrying over the words, his great bulbous nose red with cold and a drip hanging off the end of it. He held the prayer book open but scarcely looked at it. If his flock was familiar with hearing the words, he was certainly familiar with saying them.

'Man that is born of a woman hath but a short time to live and is full of misery. He cometh up and is cut down, like a flower; he fleeth as it were a shadow and never continueth in one stay. In the midst of life we are in death: of whom may we seek for succour, but of thee, O Lord, who for our sins art justly displeased?'

He nodded at John Gray at this point and he, in response, threw down the clump of frozen earth he held in his hand. He shook Arthur's arm and the boy copied his father throwing his small clump which landed with a gentle thud on the wooden coffin six feet below. Arthur continued to gaze at the rough wood as the Parson's words droned on above his head.

'Forasmuch as it hath pleased Almighty God of his great mercy to take unto himself the soul of our dear sister here departed, we therefore commit her body to the ground,'

Was his mother also his sister then, Arthur wondered to himself? And how could she be everyone else's sister? He knew one of the babies sent from God had been his sister and she was lying in the ground now with the other babies. He looked down into the dark earth again and the wooden lid of the coffin. He wished his mother wasn't in it. He sniffed and looked back up to Parson Saunders, whose black cloak was flying out behind him in an icy gust of wind. He was bringing the service to a close.

'Lord, have mercy upon us,' he chanted. He looked expectantly at his flock, who responded dolefully,

'Christ, have mercy upon us,'

With a final *'Lord, have mercy upon us,'* the Parson snapped the prayer book shut, cast a fierce eye on John Gray and his son and then on the rest of the mourners and turned on his heel.

Arthur looked across the grave and saw his three particular friends. The four children had all been born within a few weeks of each other. He glanced at Beth Stone and her mother. Beth was wearing a scarlet cape, billowing in the sudden blasts of the wind, showing the rabbits' fur lining. Her nose was pink with the cold and Arthur could see tears sparkling on her eyelashes and wondered why she should be crying.

Tom Kennard and Lucas Webb stood next to her in front of their mothers, clasping their hats tightly and fidgeting with cold. Lucas mouthed something silently to Arthur and then grinned. Arthur couldn't make it out but grinned back anyway. Hannah Webb, seeing the children's glances, gave her son a little shake and pushed his hat down firmly on his head.

Satisfied that they had done their part in commending the spirit of Mary Gray into God's keeping, the small crowd dispersed, Arthur hurrying to keep up with his father as they made their way across the churchyard into the road and back to the *Angel* alehouse, where the new baby, abandoned while his mother was buried, cried alone.

CHAPTER TWO

Summer 1722, Bazenden's Wood, Hawkhurst

'But I don't want to play mothers and fathers, Beth,' Arthur said exasperatedly. 'That's a girl's game.'

They were sitting in a clearing in Bazenden's Wood at the bottom of Highgate Hill. Tom Kennard had said there was a badgers' sett in the earthy bank and though the boys had poked sticks down the holes, there had been no sign of any creatures and they decided the badgers must have abandoned it.

Tom and Lucas Webb were now engaged in climbing the big elm tree under whose branches Beth Stone and Arthur were sitting watching Will who at three and a half, had grown from placid baby to placid toddler. He was happily playing with two old tin soldiers which Beth's mother had given him.

'But you don't have to do anything much,' Beth protested. 'I'll be the mother and Will can be our baby and you can just come in and pretend to sit and eat the supper I've prepared for you.'

At that moment several twigs and one heavier branch dropped from the tree narrowly missing Arthur. He looked up to see Tom Kennard's freckled face grinning down at him.

'Nearly got you,' he said.

Arthur grinned back at him. 'Nowhere near.'

Beth looked up too. 'Oh Tom, would you like to play mothers and fathers and be the father? Arthur won't.'

Tom Kennard hung on to his branch and looked down at Beth. 'Might do,' he said. 'Watch out! I'm coming down.'

With that, he inched further along the branch which bowed down as his weight bore onto the narrowing stem and dropped the five feet or so, landing in a pile of last autumn's leaves. Lucas, higher up, scrambled down and joined them.

'Will is our baby,' Beth explained and turned to the toddler. 'Come in now, Will and have supper. Your father has come home.'

Will looked round, but carried on playing.

Beth tutted and picked up her skirts. 'I'll have to bring you in and you must go to bed early.' She stepped over to Will and hauled him up holding him round the waist, his head at her shoulder. 'Now eat your supper. You'd better eat it all up.' She placed an imaginary plate in front of him but Will was engrossed by a butterfly that was fluttering around his head and his eyes were crossing as he tried to focus on it.

'He's a great big baby for you to have,' Lucas said laughing.

Tom Kennard peered at Beth. 'Do you know where babies come from, then?' he asked her.

She met his gaze. 'Of course I do. They come from God,' she said calmly.

Tom Kennard, who had four older brothers and sisters, guffawed. He made the shape of a big belly in front of him with his hands and waddled round Beth, piping in what he imagined was a girlish voice, *'God has given me a baby. It come from God, but I ain't sure how it got there.'*

Beth looked puzzled and stared at him, while Arthur and Lucas laughed uncertainly. 'I don't know what you mean, Tom,' she said. 'But I don't think you should say that about God.'

'Babies come from there, Beth,' he said, eyeing the lower part of her body.

Beth looked down at her skirts. 'Where?'

Tom laughed nervously and pushed his hand towards her skirts pressing a little above her knees. 'There, from your you-know-what!'

Beth stepped back away from him, her cheeks pink. 'God puts the baby in the mother's belly,' she said.

Tom laughed again and raised his eyes heavenward. 'With a bit of help from a man's yard,' he declared. 'From his pintle! From his cock!'

The other two boys laughed nervously. Beth picked up her skirts. 'I'm going home,' she said and started walking away.

'Wait a minute, Beth,' Tom Kennard called. 'Are you a virgin?'

Beth, only knowing the word in connection with the Blessed Virgin thought it must mean a holy female saint. 'No of course I'm not,' she said decisively continuing on her way, her cheeks burning. Arthur wanted to go after her, but didn't want to miss anything that Tom might say. He could tell from the way Beth's shoulders sagged, that she was feeling uncomfortable. Tom burst out laughing.

'What's funny?' Arthur asked him. 'What is a virgin?'

'It's any woman who's never opened her legs for a man,' he replied. He called out to Beth's departing back, 'You've seen calves and lambs born, Beth! You've seen how they come out. How do you think they get in?'

Arthur wasn't sure himself. It was true; he had seen many animals being born. Surrounded by farmland it would be difficult to avoid, but he had never associated the haphazard dropping of animals in the fields, with how babies came to be inside their mothers in the first place. Did they have to *open their legs to a man* first, as Tom had indicated?

'Is that right what you said?' Lucas asked Tom. Tom put his arm on his friend's shoulder and started whispering in his ear. Lucas started to grin and Arthur became anxious to know what was being said. 'What is it, Tom? Tell me too. Go on.'

Tom grinned and pressed his mouth near Arthur's ear. Arthur listened with guilty excitement, but also some disbelief. 'But how do you know all that, Tom? I think you're making it up.'

Tom licked his thumb and crossed his heart. 'Strike me dead if I'm lying! Anyway, I seen it. Kat Lambert showed me in Tulhurst's barn. I had to pay though. A farthing for the top half and a farthing for the bottom half. A half penny for each place if you want a feel.'

'Will she show us? Will you ask her for us?' Arthur asked. Kat Lambert was a big tall girl of nearly thirteen; he would be quite nervous of asking her himself.

'Pay me a half penny an' I'll ask her,' Tom bargained.

Arthur looked at Lucas. 'A half penny to ask her for me and Lucas?' he negotiated.

Tom Kennard spat on his hand and held it out to Arthur. They shook hands and Arthur and Lucas dug in their pockets to find a farthing each.

Tulhurst's Barn, Hawkhurst

Word had got round of the event that was to take place in the barn a couple of afternoons later and a queue of more than ten lads had formed. Kat had set up an area partitioned off by some hay bales and a screen of old sacking and her friend, Sal Turley seated herself before it, ready to collect the money. Arthur had had to bring Will with him again and Lucas was minding his youngest sister. For another farthing, Sal had agreed to mind them both and the two toddlers sat in another little enclosure of hay bales playing with a ball Lucas had brought with him.

Arthur was towards the back of the queue behind Tom Kennard who had earned himself a free look by providing Kat with her young patrons. Some of the Hawkhurst boys, Pete Tickner, Billy Bishop, and Sam Terrell were all present as well as George and Tom Kingsmill and Bernard Woollett, who had walked all the way from Goudhurst.

Kat was nothing if not economic with her business and the boys were quickly in and out, grinning and giggling. If she thought they were ogling too long, they got a quick slap round the head and Sal helped push them out.

Billy Bishop, a big lad of eleven came out, his hand clapped over his mouth, even his ears pink with embarrassment and a guilty pleasure. His other hand was held over his privates, Arthur noticed and he was making an up-and-down gesture with his fingers.

'Your turn, Arthur,' Sal called, bored. 'What are you paying for? A look or a feel?'

His mouth went dry. 'A look,' he croaked.

'What?' Sal asked. 'Cat got your tongue?' she quipped. 'Kat got your tongue? It's a jest. Get it?'

He nodded, bewildered. 'A look,' he repeated.

'Top or bottom, or both?' she asked.

'Both,' he answered and Sal called over to Kat, 'Just a look, this one, top and bottom.' She put the money in a knitted purse. 'Go on then,' she said to Arthur. 'What are you waiting for?'

She gave him a brisk push through the sacking and he saw Kat sitting on a hay bale. She stood up. She had taken off her stays and chemise and thrown them onto a broken barrow at the side and had loosed the lacing at the front of her gown. She casually undid the lacing and pulled the two halves of her bodice apart. Arthur stared mesmerized at her rounded breasts, fuller and larger than he had imagined and tipped with small pink nipples. His eyes went from one to the other but with a quick movement, Kat pulled the lacing together, before he had looked as long as he would have liked. She pulled up her skirts to her waist, presenting Arthur with a view of her long legs encased in rather grubby stockings with leather garters and her long white thighs and to his surprise, a triangle of dark hair where they met.

'That's it!' she said, dropping her skirts and sitting back down. 'Next one, Sal,' she called.

'No, wait!' Arthur said, hastily.

'Wait? I don't wait. Your time's up. Go on.'

'I want to touch,' he explained. 'Can I?'

Kat shrugged her shoulders impatiently, as she stood. 'Make your mind up, Arthur. You have to pay another half penny for the top and bottom again. Have you got enough?'

He dipped in his pocket, praying silently that he had and drew out three farthings holding them out to Kat. She shook her head. 'No. That's not enough. You're a farthing short.'

Arthur sighed and looked up at her.

'You ain't got enough, Arthur.'

'Wait. I've got three farthings, ain't I? And it costs me two of them to touch you down there,' he said, getting bolder. 'Yet there's only one place down there. And two up here. Really you should only charge me one farthing for down there and a farthing for each of those.' He indicated her breasts now hidden behind the loosely tied bodice.

Kat raised her eyes heavenward. 'Can you hear this, Sal? Look, Arthur, when you're older, you'll understand it's what's down here-,' she said, pointing between her thighs 'that men pay for and a good bit more than a farthing!'

Arthur looked at her not quite understanding.

She suddenly laughed. 'I'll tell you what, though. You can touch me below for the halfpenny and you can touch just one of my titties instead of both of them, for your other farthing.' She laughed again. 'Hear that, Sal?' she called out. She pulled up her skirts again to her waist. 'Just the flat of your hand, mind! No fingers poking, nor anything like that.'

Arthur nodded and peered again at the top of her thighs. He held out his right hand and very gently laid it against the short springy hairs, feeling the warmth of her body under his palm. He was aware of her powerful, female scent, heady and unnerving but he still couldn't work out how a baby could get in or out of that mysterious place. There seemed to be no entrance and he didn't dare separate his fingers, but simply pressed with the flat of his hand.

'That's enough,' Kat declared and dropped her skirts. She pulled her bodice apart again and her bare breasts jutted in front of him. 'Which one do you want to feel?' She moved one shoulder forward and then the other, offering him a choice. Her breasts bounced gently, rippling almost as if they were filled with water. Arthur peered at them both and pointed to her left breast.

'All right then,' she agreed. 'No pinching, neither. Just a squeeze.'

He held out his right hand again and saw how it shook slightly. He hoped Kat wouldn't notice. He pressed his palm against the breast. Her skin was the softest he had ever felt and warm. He pressed it harder trying to flatten the breast against her ribcage but it simply splayed out wider. He felt her heartbeat under his fingers and her nipple harden under his palm. He drew in his breath.

'Time's up. That's it,' Kat said, shaking him off as she started to pull her bodice together.

Just then there was a commotion at the door of the barn and shouts and voices.

'Quick, Kat!' Sal called, as the sackcloth partition was pulled down and Parson Saunders stood there with a well-dressed gentleman standing behind him.

'May God forgive you, Katherine Lambert! For you are as the whore of Babylon!' the Parson pronounced fiercely.

Kat, her dark curls tumbling round her face, had clutched her bodice in front of her, but she suddenly laughed and let the two halves fall apart, her breasts swinging forward, her hands on her hips. 'Pardon me, Parson Saunders,' she said, smiling. 'But you and your friend will have to wait your turn.' She burst out laughing. 'Get the money and run, Sal,' she cried, swinging round to grab her undergarments and waved them in Parson Saunders' face as the two girls dashed out of the barn.

The other boys had already fled; even Lucas had grabbed his baby sister and run, leaving only Arthur, his emotions a mixture of excitement and guilt and Will playing happily amid the straw.

'The devil has made you his own,' Parson Saunders said wrathfully to Arthur, his great red face seeming to tower above him.

The other man approached. He did not seem angry but looked at Arthur keenly. 'How old are you, lad?'

Arthur looked from him to Parson Saunders before he replied. 'Eight last birthday, sir.'

'So young and already an instrument of Satan! Fornicating with the harlots of Babylon,' the Parson pronounced. 'It's scandalous, Thomas, is it not?'

The other man looked at him and then glanced down at Arthur again.

'The Devil makes work for idle hands, it is true, Parson,' he said, mildly. 'Yet I think you may judge too harshly. If a boy this age is capable of fornication, I should be very surprised to hear it.' He turned to Arthur again. 'Well boy, you've heard the charge. Have you fornicated with these girls who have just run off in such a disgraceful manner?'

Arthur shook his head. 'I don't know what it means. I only looked. And touched a bit.'

'But was there contact, boy? Was there carnal knowledge?' The Parson's questions thundered out. Arthur shook his head again. Perhaps touching was the sin, perhaps touching was fornication.

Thomas Lamb looked at the Parson. 'Leave it there, eh, Parson? Which of us, as a boy, hasn't tried to look at a maid if we could? And some of us still look, eh, Saunders?' he asked. 'I thank God for my eyes, yes and thank Him for making so many pretty women for us to look at.' He turned back to Arthur. 'What do you do all day, boy?' he asked.

Arthur looked up at him shrugging his shoulders. 'Nothing much. I do a bit at harvest time and we've been picking apples, but they've finished now.'

Lamb looked across at the Parson. 'You see, it proves the point I have been trying to make. Don't you agree?' he asked. 'These boys, what are they, eight, nine, ten years? – have nothing to do. If there's no apprenticeship for them, nor yet no schooling, what else will a young mind turn to, but trouble and naughtiness, especially if there are saucy young maids to tempt them.'

The Parson looked down at Arthur. 'Can you read, boy, or write?' Arthur shook his head. 'But I can add up and take away.'

Lamb smiled. 'Well Parson, are you with me in this? A small school, just a few boys to start with, mind, no more than ten. I daresay we could engage a schoolmaster for less than twenty pounds a year.'

Parson Saunders shook his head doubtfully. 'I'm not yet convinced of the benefit. A more rigid process of employment of children might be a better answer. But if you're to put up the money, I will engage to help select the boys for you. I am familiar with most of the families and know who might benefit and who might not. This boy for instance, is already turned to the Devil's path. Who knows what plans and artifices he might devise if he were able, by reading, to discover how others have turned evil to their advantage?' He pulled out a pocket watch and observed it. 'I have a funeral to prepare for. And calls to make on Mary Lambert and Margaret Turley to chastise them for letting their daughters run wild.' He looked fiercely again at Arthur. 'If I thought your father would beat you for it, I would tell him but he will be far gone in liquor this time of day.' He brushed past Arthur and left the barn.

Arthur went to pick Will up, relieved that he wasn't going to get a beating. As he made to go, Lamb caught his sleeve. 'You say you can add up and take away, lad. Prove it.'

Arthur holding Will's hand, thought for a moment. 'Kat let me feel her below her skirts for a halfpenny and above for a halfpenny. That's four farthings. But I only had three. So I asked her to let me touch below for two farthings and let me feel one titty for my other farthing!' He hurried out, dragging Will after him, not able to stop himself from laughing. Lamb started to frown and then pursed his lips as though trying to hide a smile.

'Saunders may be right about this boy. He may go to the Devil. Or he may fly as high as he chooses!'

CHAPTER THREE

Christmas Day 1723, Rye

Beth Stone remembered the Christmas of 1723 as one of the happiest of her childhood. Her mother's sister, Ann, was pretty and full of laughter and her Uncle Richard Austen a kind and jovial host. Beth and her parents, her uncle, aunt and cousins Nicholas and Francis, slipped across the pathway into St Mary's Church in the morning and entered the Austen family box. The Rector, Edward Wilson had chosen for his text, *'Train up a child in the way he should go and when he is old, he will not depart from it,'*.

Richard Austen had invited his kinsman Thomas Lamb and his wife to join them for Christmas dinner. The Lambs were an important family in Rye and Richard Austen, now a Freeman of the town, often mixed with significant men.

The bells rang out as they left the church. When they got home they were greeted by the smell of a wonderful Christmas dinner with a fine roast goose dressed with buttered parsnips; a plum pudding and syllabubs and a plate full of sugar mice which Beth's cousin Francis would have eaten all by himself if his brother had not grabbed a handful and shared them with Beth. Richard Austen chided his younger son for being greedy and Thomas Lamb quoted the verse from the morning sermon.

'You may think your father is being hard on you or unkind, young Francis, but you will know, if you paid attention this morning that he is providing you with a pattern for living, so you do not grow up to be a grasping adult.' Mr Lamb had such a way of speaking that Francis could not tell whether he was being teased or chided.

Beth, who was an attentive and retentive listener, had thought about the verse. 'But Mr Lamb, what if there is no one to train the child? How would he know which way to go? And if he went the wrong way, it would surely not be fair if he was punished for it?'

Thomas Lamb looked at the little girl with interest.

'Well, John Stone, you seem to have a biblical scholar in your family,' he said to Beth's father seated opposite him. 'I'm sure, Beth, that you can't be referring to your own situation? For I'm certain that your mamma and papa train you in exactly the right way?'

Beth shook her head. 'Oh no, Mr Lamb, I'm thinking of someone else. I have a particular friend, two particular friends who don't have a mother, and their father – well, I don't think he pays them much attention at all. So how will Arthur know which way to go?'

John Stone grunted. 'Two ragamuffin sons of a former alehouse keeper,' he explained to his brother-in-law and Thomas Lamb.

'I imagine then that you're talking about Arthur and William Gray, John?' Thomas Lamb said nodding at Ann Austen as she offered him more tea from an elegant silver tea pot.

'Then you know the family?' Richard Austen asked, surprised.

Thomas Lamb paused before answering. 'Oh, I am familiar with most of the Hawkhurst families by now. Since I bought my land in Hawkhurst I have got to know who owns what and who leases which parcel of land. And I used to sup at the *Angel* when John Gray ran it with his pretty wife.'

'God rest her soul,' Beth's mother, Jane Stone said solemnly. 'I think that had she lived, perhaps John Gray would not have fallen into drunkenness the way he has. She was always a gentle, kindly sort of woman.'

'Amen to that,' Thomas Lamb said swiftly and added, 'the younger boy Will, is much like her.'

'Unfortunately the elder boy seems more like his father,' John Stone said gruffly.

'I think that's a little unfair, John,' his wife put in. 'He may seem a little wild and rough in his manners but he's a hard working lad and takes good care of his young brother.'

'You always see the good in people, Jane, even when it ain't there. For my part, I'm prepared to wager he'll follow his father's path before long,' John Stone answered.

'I have observed the elder boy a little,' Thomas Lamb acknowledged. 'Perhaps you know I am one of the governors of the charity school which opened this summer in Hawkhurst?'

'My dear, you are far too modest.' Mrs Lamb interrupted her husband. 'Thomas put up more than half the funding for the school,' she explained to the guests around the table. 'He likes to hide his light under a bushel, but I will not.'

Her husband nodded and continued. 'Parson Saunders and I questioned each child closely to decide who might benefit from schooling and who might not. I partly agree with you, Stone – Arthur may follow John Gray's example and become a good-for–nothing drunkard. Indeed one could hardly blame the boy if he did – remembering your text, Beth, – for what example does he have before him each day, but drunkenness and sloth?'

John Stone nodded but Lamb continued, with his elbows on the table and his fingertips pressed together. 'However, I did say I only partly agreed with you. For I think if he does not follow John Gray's path, then he might become something quite remarkable indeed. He has cleverness and a quickness – but his greatest gift, as far as I can tell, is his endeavour. I don't know what else to call it. But once he has chosen a path, he will follow it to the end, of that I have no doubt whatsoever.'

Mrs Lamb, who had been following the conversation with interest, suddenly spoke.

'Children are such a blessing. It pains me to hear of parents who don't appreciate them. This Mr Gray – having lost his wife, you would think he would find blessings in his two sons and look to them for comfort instead of looking to find it in a bottle. Mr Lamb and I have never been blessed with children – it has been a constant sorrow to me.' She seemed lost in her own thoughts for a while.

Thomas Lamb looked at his wife across the table and then reached over and patted her hand. 'That's why we take comfort in the friendship of folk such as yourselves,' he said, nodding at the two couples, 'for we can partake a little in the joy you have in your children.'

The Austens' little housemaid arrived at this point bearing a large fruit cake, decorated with holly on a pretty blue and white plate and the table became merry again, as Ann cut the slices and her husband handed them round. The rest of the conversation was given over to more frivolous subjects. The two boys, Nick and Francis vied with each other for their pretty cousin's attention and Mr Lamb told such funny stories in his droll way, describing people he had met going about his business and mimicking their voices so well that everyone laughed.

Towards three o' clock in the afternoon, Francis, looking out of the parlour window announced excitedly, 'It's started to snow, mamma. May we go out and play snowballs?'

His mother stood behind him holding back the heavy curtain as she peered out. 'It's almost dark, Frankie,' she pointed out.

'Oh mother, do let us,' Nick pleaded coming to join them.

Richard Austen stood up. 'What say you all to a walk before dark, eh?' He patted his stomach. 'I think I should walk off some of your excellent goose, Annie.'

'To say nothing of that delicious plum pudding,' Thomas Lamb laughed. 'I'll join you, Austen. What about you, Stone?'

Beth's father nodded. 'Aye, I have no objection.'

'Then you must all forgive me,' Mrs Lamb said. 'If you do not object, Mrs Austen, I shall remain seated on your comfortable sofa.'

'Then I will keep you company,' Ann said swiftly, knowing her duty as hostess.

'Oh no, my dear,' Mrs Lamb protested. 'I am sure you are as keen as the children to be out in the snow. You look so young, you seem little more than a child yourself!'

'I will keep you company, Mrs Lamb,' Jane Stone offered. 'Indeed I would much rather stay in the warm.'

The walkers wrapped themselves up well in greatcoats, capes, hats and mufflers and set off for their stroll around the quiet streets of Rye. Lights were burning at the windows in the homes of rich and poor alike, the setting sun casting the last of its rays over the streets with their sprinkling of snow. As they walked down to the Landgate, they looked out to sea.

'Look, father. A boat,' Nick said.

'My, what it is to have young eyes,' Thomas Lamb exclaimed. 'But yes, even I can see the lights cast from it. Now what boat comes into Camber bay on Christmas night, Austen?'

'I reckon it's a smuggling cutter, Thomas,' Richard Austen said peering into the rapidly falling darkness, his hand on his elder son's shoulder. 'If we could see round to the shore I am pretty certain we should see the answering lights from the company of men on the beach.'

'How exciting, Richard!' Ann declared. 'Do you see them, Beth?'

'But shouldn't we call out the Watch, father?' Nick interrupted.

'What would the Watch do?' Beth enquired, standing next to her aunt and straining her eyes to see. She thought the cutter looked a pretty little boat. She had just been able to make out its white sail before the gathering darkness obscured it.

'The Watch would shoot 'em all,' Nick said drawing an imaginary pistol out of his pocket.

'Nonsense, Nick,' his father retorted. 'It's not up to the Watch to catch smugglers. And the Watch isn't armed. It's the Riding Officers' duty to patrol the shore and then they have to call in the Dragoons to help them. The nearest ones to us are Captain Pelham's militia in Lydd and most likely, like all sensible men, they are at home enjoying their Christmas. This is probably why the smugglers have chosen tonight to land their goods.'

'Well I wish them joy of their booty, Richard,' Thomas Lamb retorted. 'For they will spend the rest of the night in the snow and cold in wet boots and damp coats, driving their horses over the Marsh. I know where I would rather be, eh, Stone?'

John Stone nodded slowly. 'Each man must do as he sees fit, I dare say.'

Richard Austen clapped his brother-in-law on the back. 'And none of us will argue with that, brother.'

The four adults turned to walk back to the house in Church Square and the inviting fire in the parlour, Nick and Francis following; but Beth remained a while, her hands on the stone wall, gazing out at the scene in the distance. The moon appeared through the clouds and momentarily lit up the little cutter, with its network of ropes leading to the shore, where hidden from her view, a company of men worked, cutting the precious cargo free from the ropes and loading it onto a column of waiting horses before they disappeared across the dark expanse of the Marsh. The little cutter heaved round and slipped silently away back across the Channel whence she had come.

Beth couldn't know then, the effect that another landing on another Christmas night, on this same beach, would have on her life and the lives of those around her.

CHAPTER FOUR

Hawkhurst, Summer 1724

When Beth was putting her music sheets away after her lesson on the spinet, her mother came back into the room and drew out a small piece of paper from her sleeve. She sat on the wooden settle and patted the seat next to her.

'What is it mamma?' Beth asked. 'Something good?'

'Something I think you will enjoy, my darling. My sister Ann has sent up a letter with the carrier from Rye. You will remember Mr Thomas Lamb with whom we shared Christmas at your aunt's?'

Beth nodded.

'Well, James Lamb his brother is going to be made Mayor and he has invited your uncle and aunt and your father and me to the elections and to the refreshments afterwards. Mayor-making! It will be an exciting day, Beth. Your cousins Nick and Francis will be there and I think that now Nick is nearly twelve, he's old enough to look after you while your father and I attend the official business. I went once the year before you were born. Your aunt had only been married a few months to your uncle Richard – you know she married very young at just sixteen and she invited me to Mayor-making Day. We had such fun! There are fairing stalls selling things you can't imagine and all the shops and houses decorated and everyone so gay and happy. And what you will enjoy best of all, is when the new mayor throws the hot pennies.'

'Throws the hot pennies, mamma? What does it mean?' Beth asked, already entranced at her mother's description of Mayor-making.

'I think it's because the town of Rye could mint its own coins, or some such thing. But what happens is, the pennies are polished like gold and heated up and then the Mayor holds them in a blanket or a similar piece of cloth and flings them into the crowds and all the children may snatch them up and keep what they can. Only they are very hot, so you have to be careful. Though Annie was sixteen and a married woman, she couldn't help but join in. How Richard teased her.'

Jane Stone smiled, remembering the happy day.

'Will we ride there, mamma?' Beth asked.

'No, I think your father will take the wagon. It's been a dry summer – the roads will be good.'

Beth swung herself down from the settle. 'If we're going in the wagon, can I ask Arthur and Will to come with us?'

Jane Stone frowned. 'It's a kind thought, Beth. But I don't know if John Gray will let them. Isn't Arthur still at the charity school?'

Beth nodded. 'He still has a place, but he doesn't go every day. You know he goes to chop wood in Goudhurst for a penny a day when he can. But he would enjoy the Mayor-making. Perhaps he could snatch lots of the hot pennies. And little Will would like the fairing stalls, mamma. Can I ask them? Oh please say I can.'

Jane Stone laughed. 'You may mention it to them and I'll go and see John Gray. Now finish putting your music away, Beth and wash your hands ready for supper.'

Beth, with a clean apron on and a red ribbon tied around her thick brown hair, set off down the hill towards Hawkhurst Moor and the charity school for ten boys which had opened last summer. She knew they came out at five o clock and she waited at the gate. Sure enough the doors swung open as the church clock struck five and the boys spilled out, their slates and books tied up with leather straps.

'Hello Lucas,' she said to one of them. 'Is Arthur coming out?'

The fair haired lad with an honest open face smiled at her. 'Hello Beth,' he said, stopping at the gate. 'Well, he won't be out yet. He's got another beating to get first. He missed Friday and old Penfold is hopping mad. He missed twice last week. Penfold says he'll tell the governors again.'

'Oh Lucas, that's unfair. He goes to chop wood at West's in Goudhurst.'

'I know that, Beth,' Lucas said, rubbing his chin. 'But it don't make no difference. Penfold says he's taking the place of a boy who really wants to learn.'

'But Arthur does want to learn. He's really clever. He learnt his letters last year and he can add numbers in his head as fast as anything,' Beth protested.

Lucas nodded. 'Aye, he has me beat there, that's for sure.'

Beth twirled a strand of her hair in her fingers, looking thoughtful. 'Now you've told me this, I don't know what to do, Lucas. I was going to ask Arthur and Will to come with us to the Mayor-making in Rye next Monday. But I wouldn't have him get another beating for all the world. What do you think?' she asked, looking up at him.

Lucas grinned. 'I think if you asked him to go to the Bogeyman's lair he would follow you there, Beth. He's sweet on you, that's for sure.'

Beth blushed prettily and smoothed down her apron. She didn't know if it was true, but it would be very agreeable to have an admirer. 'I'll ask him and see what he says.'

Lucas turned back to the school gate. 'Now's your chance, Beth. Here he comes.' He shouted across to the sturdily-built lad with light brown hair and blue eyes who appeared at the oak door of the school. 'How many, Arthur?'

Arthur approached Lucas and Beth and sniffed. His eyes were red, but neither of his companions said anything.

'Ten across each hand.' He dropped his slate and held out both hands. Beth gasped in horror to see the fine red weals criss-crossing each other, across the back of his hands, with little drops of red where the switch had drawn blood. His hands shook slightly.

Beth clapped her hands across her mouth and then asked, 'Does it hurt terribly, Arthur?'

'No,' he lied. 'Just stings a bit. After three or four, you don't notice any more.'

He picked up his slate and started walking along the road, Beth picking up her skirts and walking alongside him, Lucas trailing behind.

He turned off back to the smithy where his father had his business, calling goodbye to them both.

'Arthur, I had come to ask you something but I don't think I will, now. I don't want your poor hands to be beaten again.'

'What was you going to ask me, Beth?' he said, smiling at her.

'I was going to ask you if you would like to come to the Mayor-making in Rye on Monday. Oh, Arthur,' she said breathlessly, 'it will be such fun, if only you could come and Will too. We're going in my father's wagon. My mother is going to ask your father if you can come. And they toss pennies for all the children to pick up. Perhaps you would get enough so you wouldn't have to chop the wood and you could go to school and not get beaten.'

He looked at her excited face, her grey eyes meeting his, her curls shining in the sunlight.

'Could your father not write you a note?' Beth asked.

Arthur shrugged. 'He can't write.' He turned into a row of small cottages. 'Will's with Mrs Kennard today. I have to pick him up.' He opened the little white gate and went round the path to the back of the house.

Lizzie Kennard was gathering in her washing from the line. 'Oh hello, Arthur, Beth,' she said, smiling. 'Will's inside. There's milk and oatcakes on the table. Help yourself. I shall be within in a moment.'

They found Will sitting on a high stool, a cup of milk on the table in front of him, crumbs of oatcakes around his mouth and down the front of his old jacket. He smiled when he saw Beth and Arthur. 'Saw the puppies today, Arthur,' he said, picking up another cake. 'Can we get one do you think?'

'Where would we put a puppy, Will? Have sense,' Arthur said, but not unkindly, helping himself to milk and oatcakes. 'Dad would like drown it anyway,' he added.

Jane Stone stepped into the backyard of the shabby house at the end of the Moor, where John Gray rented two garret rooms for himself and his two boys. She had known John Gray all her life. He had always been something of an idler but when he had married Mary Durrant it had seemed he might make something of himself after all; and when they took over the *Angel* it was a good enough business for a few years. But he started drinking with his customers and then carried on after they had left. Within a year of Will's birth and Mary's death, the *Angel* had been sold on, at a loss and the new buyer gave up trying to restore it to any economic stability. It had now reverted back to a dwelling place, its customers gone to the *Six Bells*, the *Oak and Ivy* or the *Royal Oak*, the other alehouses in Hawkhurst. John Gray now scraped a living by delivering yarn to housewives who made a little money by spinning or weaving. The Grays' living seemed precarious and it could not be many months, Jane thought, before John Gray ended up in the workhouse and the two boys were sold into apprenticeships. Maybe it would be better for them she thought, for they might at least be sure of a meal a day and the prospect of being able to learn a trade.

She found John Gray outside his lodging, sitting on a broken bench in the yard smoking a pipe.

'Good day to you, John,' she said brightly.

He looked at her but did not rise and said nothing but simply nodded.

She approached him, noticing his bloodshot eyes and the shabby coat he was wearing. 'How are you, John?'

'Alive, ain't I?' he said.

She paused a moment before speaking. 'I've come to ask you if you will let John and myself take your two boys to Rye on Monday. For the Mayor-making.'

'Why would you want to do that, Mis' Stone?' he asked.

She shrugged. 'They would be companions for my Beth,' she replied carefully. 'We would take care of them, you know. And they would enjoy it.'

John Gray grunted and sucked on his pipe. 'Why should they have enjoyment?' he mused. 'Sooner they learn life is harsh, the better.'

Jane Stone said nothing and waited for him to speak again.

'Rye?' he asked.

She nodded. 'Come, John,' she said bracingly. 'I remember a time when you and Mary danced near every night for a week at haymaking back in '11 or '12. You had enjoyment then.'

'Times change,' he said shortly. 'Mary's long gone.' He seemed thoughtful and added, 'and all her secrets with her.'

Jane Stone gave a short laugh. 'What secrets, John?'

'If I knew that, they wouldn't be secrets, would they? Anyway, what woman don't have secrets?' He blew out the smoke.

'My Beth tells me there has been some trouble with Arthur missing school. I would willingly write him a note to take, John.'

He took another drag on his pipe. 'I don't know what he must needs go to school for. He don't need readin' and writin'. He needs to be out working more.'

Jane Stone seated herself carefully on an old wooden barrel opposite John Gray. 'Listen, John. Arthur did well to impress the charity governors enough for them to offer him a place. He must have answered their questions well.'

'Huh,' he sniffed disparagingly. 'Parson Saunders and Thomas Lamb deciding who's good enough for their charity and who ain't! They only want boys to be able to read the Bible, so they're sure of knowing their place. *"The poor are always with you"*. I remember that from my Bible.' His eyes looked cold and hard and Jane felt she might be making matters worse.

'You could come too, John.'

He looked surprised, but said nothing, continuing to draw on his pipe. 'How would you be getting there?' he asked at length.

'The wagon,' she replied.

He put a hand to his face and rubbed the stubble. 'Rye, eh? All right, Jane Stone,' he agreed, as if it were he doing her a favour. 'Happen I will.'

'But why you must ask John Gray, is beyond me,' John Stone exclaimed when his wife told him he would now be carrying three extra passengers to Rye. 'It's bad enough we're to take his ragamuffin sons, but him also?'

'I don't think he'll let them come now, unless we take him too,' she said, fetching a rich butter sauce from the range. 'You know Beth is fond of both boys.'

'That girl has too tender a heart,' he retorted, tucking a brocade napkin over his shirt and helping himself to roast fowl.

'Can a girl ever have too tender a heart?' Jane asked him, taking her seat and pouring her husband some wine.

'If it means she is forever offering kindness to the likes of the Grays, then, yes she can. I hope you ain't thinking of serving them up as a suitable dish for the Lambs?' He put a morsel of the fowl in his mouth.

'Thomas Lamb told us that he used to drink at the *Angel*, so he knows John Gray already,' Jane Stone countered.

'Yes but that was before he became the drunkard he is now. But Lamb's brother, the new Mayor, he don't know him. He will judge him on how he appears on the day. I only hope John Gray may not shame us by association.'

'John Gray won't accompany us to the election, or to the Mayor's refreshments,' his wife explained.

Her husband carried on eating. 'I don't object to the way you have dressed this bird,' he said after a moment. He looked into his wife's blue eyes. 'I give in to you too often.'

'You leave me alone too often,' she retorted.

'Not this again, Jane,' he declared, a flush of annoyance colouring his face. 'I go to London to look after our interests.'

'Can't Robert ever go? Why must you have the care of your brother's business? The bulk of the estate is his.'

'And he unmarried and all his estate likely to come to me,' her husband replied.

'Couldn't Beth and I come with you sometimes to London, then?' she asked, putting her hand over his.

He slid his hand away, ostensibly to pour himself some more wine. 'Not to London, no. Your place is here. I will take you all to Rye, but the next day I'll go up to town.'

She nodded slowly. 'For how long?'

He cut himself another piece of meat. 'Oh, perhaps for a week or so,' he said.

'Upon business?' Jane asked, doubtfully.

'Yes, Jane,' he assented, thinking of the dark-haired beauty living in a discreet house off Hanover Square, with whom he had been transacting at least part of his business these many years. 'Upon business.'

CHAPTER FIVE

Mayor-making Day, Monday 28ʰ August 1724, Rye

Arthur, his young brother Will and Beth allowed themselves to be pushed along with the throng of merrymakers up the Landgate and towards Longer Street. All the shop fronts were decorated with greenery and ribbons and most had set up stalls outside, displaying all their wares: leather slippers, silk stockings with elaborate embroidered clocks, gilt-framed mirrors, ribbons, laces, caps and garters, little carved wooden figures and glass marbles that Will could only stare at; as well as the usual meats, fish and vegetables.

There were stalls with jugs of foaming milk and plates of buttered wheat and barley. All the inns and alehouses had thrown open their doors to attract customers, but also to keep cool air blowing through when it got progressively hotter as the sun climbed higher in the cloudless sky.

Arthur bumped rather heavily into someone coming the other way. He looked up ready to beg pardon, to see it was only another boy admittedly about six inches taller than he but not more than twelve or thirteen, he guessed.

'Watch where you're going,' the boy said crossly, looking down at Arthur. He had a handsome face with dark eyes and shoulder length dark curly hair. He wore a linen shirt of a rich cream, a soft leather waistcoat and he had a curious neckerchief of painted silk round his neck; he wore them with an air.

'I beg pardon, then,' Arthur replied and then turning to Beth and making sure Will was still behind them, said, 'Come on, you two.'

The youth stepped in front of Beth however and nodded slightly.

She looked up at him and smiled. 'Perhaps you could tell us what time the Mayor throws the hot pennies?' she asked.

The handsome lad looked into Beth's face noticing her smooth cheeks and the way her thick brown hair picked up the sunlight and glinted with gold. Though she was tall, taller than the lout she was with, the youth thought, she was still a child for her chest under her laced gown was flat, but in two or three years she would be enough to tempt any man. She also looked familiar to him and he wondered if he had met her before. She was obviously not local or she wouldn't have had to ask about the coin throwing.

'Oh, about half before three this afternoon,' he said. 'But it's only for children. I shan't go. I've other things to do.'

Though Beth had been looking forward to the coin throwing, she didn't want to appear childish, so she asked the youth, 'What then? What will you be doing?'

He shrugged his shoulders. 'I might go rabbit shooting,' he said carelessly. 'Want to come?' He flicked her cheek with his forefinger.

Beth looked across at Arthur doubtfully but Arthur's face was full of interest. 'Have you got a gun then?' he asked.

The youth nodded. 'Yes. Stoopid! How else am I gonna shoot 'em?'

'I would quite like to try it,' Arthur admitted, 'but I ain't got a gun.'

The older boy tutted. 'I might let you try mine. Who are you all anyway? I ain't seen you before, have I?' he asked.

Beth, remembering her manners introduced herself. 'I'm Bethlehem Stone and this is Arthur and Will Gray. We've come down for the Mayor-making from Hawkhurst. My mother's sister is married to Mr Austen who is a relative of the Lamb family. You know that Mr James Lamb is going to be elected the new Mayor.'

The youth nodded, eyeing Beth with interest on hearing of her social connections. He jerked his head in Arthur and Will's direction. 'And are they related to you or the Lambs?'

'Oh no,' Beth replied. 'But they're my friends.'

The youth bowed slightly to Beth and ignored Arthur and Will. 'I'm Jeremiah Curtis,' he said. 'Come with me, then. We'll pick up my gun and go down to Playden Fields.'

Will pulled on Arthur's hand. 'Shall we see the pennies tossed, though, Arthur?' he asked, a worried expression on his small face.

'Shut up, Will,' Arthur said dismissively. 'You want to see the gun, don't you?'

They followed Curtis a few yards up the road and he turned into a handsome house with leaded windows in two square bays. He hurried up the stairs, Beth and the two boys following behind him. Taking a key from his pocket, he unlocked the door which gave into a very spacious square room at the front of the house overlooking Longer Street. There was a large high bed with crimson drapes, wardrobes, chests, a table and several chairs. The bed was unmade and there were clothes strewn over the floor, scattered papers and a few coins on the table and a fine chiming clock on the mantelpiece.

'Do your parents live here, too?' Beth asked, curious.

'My mother died last year. It's mine now. I rent it,' Curtis answered, going to one of the wardrobes and pulling out a long gun. He placed the fowling piece on the bed and dived amongst the items on the floor of the cupboard to find a box of lead shot, which he transferred to his pocket.

Arthur was silent as he looked around the spacious room, which was more than twice the size of the rooms he shared with Will and his father, and wondered how the youth made enough money to pay his way on his own.

Ten minutes later, they had made their way out of Rye against the crowds who were coming in for the festivities, along the London Road. They turned off into the meadows at Playden. Curtis led them to a grassy bank and stretched out full length on his belly. 'You have to be quiet,' he ordered. 'Don't let the baby cry.' He nodded towards Will.

'Ain't a baby,' the young boy said.

'Hush Will,' Beth said. 'Lie next to me and watch out for the rabbits.'

Arthur had noticed enviously Curtis's easy handling of the gun as he loaded and cocked it. After a few minutes, a small brown rabbit appeared about fifteen yards beyond the bank and then another. Curtis aimed carefully and fired, but missed, the shot landing harmlessly in the grass a good two feet to the side of the first rabbit. Arthur felt pleased that the youth had missed, but said nothing. The rabbits disappeared and they waited again until two more reappeared, whiskers twitching but unaware of any imminent danger. This time Curtis's shot found its mark and the rabbit fell at once. Beth swallowed rather hard.

'Do you want to try?' Curtis asked her.

She shook her head. 'I think I would rather not, Jeremiah,' she replied. 'But Arthur will, I'm sure.'

Arthur nodded and switched places with Beth so he was lying next to Curtis, who showed him how to load and cock the gun. 'Don't touch the trigger until you have the rabbit in your sight, Gray. The gun throws a little to the left so you'll have to compensate for that if you can, though beginners aren't usually any good, anyway.'

They lay silently waiting for the rabbits to reappear and as soon as one did, Arthur immediately aimed and fired. The rabbit dropped to the grass. Arthur laughed and punched his fist in the air. 'Yes!' he said, delighted.

Curtis sneered and said, 'Beginner's luck.' However when Arthur had bagged another two, he took the gun back from him.

'Go and pick the rabbits up,' he said sullenly and Arthur scrambled over the bank, Will following him over to the patch where four small bodies lay. Arthur picked them up by their hind legs.

Will's face puckered and his lower lip trembled. 'Are they all dead?' he sniffed. 'Don't want the bunnies to be dead.'

'Oh shut up, Will,' Arthur snapped.

'Yes, don't cry Will,' Beth said. 'You like rabbit pie, don't you? How do you think they get the rabbits?' Though her eyes were dry, her voice was a little unsteady as she thought of her scarlet cape with its lining of rabbits' fur.

'Don't want rabbit pie no more,' Will cried. Beth drew out her handkerchief and wiped Will's tears taking his hand, for Curtis was already striding back across the meadow to join the road back into Rye, Arthur following with the rabbits slung over his shoulder.

When they got into the town, the heat was more noticeable for it was almost midday and the yellow sun beat down from a cloudless sky. Curtis turned to Arthur saying, 'What do you want to do now? There's a butcher in Middle Street will pay you for the rabbits. I can't be bothered today. I don't need the money, anyway.'

Arthur hesitated. He wanted the money, but didn't want to be on the receiving end of Curtis's beneficence.

'There's plenty of food to buy on the fairing stalls,' Curtis said. 'We can go and eat it in Drake's Shed; it's an old deserted building down on the Strand. Then you can go to your penny throwing this afternoon.'

Beth smiled at him. 'What a good plan. Don't you think, Arthur?'

Arthur nodded reluctantly.

They met Beth's cousins, Nick and Francis, in Middle Street. The boys had fidgeted all through the long election ceremony, and were glad to get out of the stuffy town hall and into the fresh air. A half hour later Curtis led them into Drake's shed, a high wooden barn with straw on the floor. It had evidently been in use as a repair yard at some point for there were pieces of broken furniture, carts with missing wheels and some sawn timbers scattered on the floor. It was cool and shady inside and they all found places to sit.

Arthur sprang up. He had been thinking of Curtis's words about selling the rabbits and having bought food for him and Will, was left with only two pence in his pocket. 'I think I'll go and see that butcher, Curtis,' he said casually.

Curtis nodded, uninterested.

'Bring us back some cakes, Gray,' Francis said, as he had a sweet tooth.

'Oh yes, Arthur,' Beth agreed. 'They had honey cakes on the stall near the church.'

'Keep an eye on Will, then. Will, stay here,' Arthur ordered looking at his little brother who was sitting on the straw floor next to Beth, finishing off his plain pudding.

Arthur wandered back out into the bright sunlight feeling the heat of the sun on his head. He had never felt out of place with Beth, though he was aware, who could not be? – that her circumstances were so different from his own. She and her parents lived in a fine house. He didn't know whether they owned it or rented it, but it had a garden and Beth had her own room. There was a room full of books and a professor came all the way from Tunbridge Wells to teach Beth the spinet. Arthur attended the charity school in Hawkhurst now and again but Beth had a governess who came to the house twice a week to teach her.

Her mother Jane was always kind and polite to Arthur and Will; and Beth's father, though of uncertain temper, had never treated him unkindly. But meeting Beth's aunt and uncle, and her cousins in their fine linen shirts and with silver buckles on their shoes, had made him aware of his own shabby clothes. Most of them were passed down from his father and altered to fit him by Hannah Webb or Lizzie Kennard, the village women who sometimes came in to do a bit of housekeeping for them; the clothes were then passed down again to Will. Jeremiah Curtis was another mystery to him. He hated the way Curtis treated him and was suspicious of his motives and angry at the way he seemed to have engaged Beth's interest, with little or no effort.

Sighing heavily, he turned into Middle Street and found the butchers, at the sign of the '*Stuck Pig*'. Despite his best efforts at haggling, the butcher would give him no more than four pence for the rabbits, saying they were so full of shot it would take him half a day to remove it. Arthur reluctantly agreed but at least he now had sixpence to spend or save as he chose. Stopping at one of the stalls in Middle Street, he saw a display of plates of cakes and sugar treats. It was a popular stall and there was a large and good-natured crowd queuing. The stallholder was joking with a great fat woman who was buying a bagful of honey cakes. The plate on the end at the front was filled with sugar candies. Looking around him swiftly, Arthur dipped his fingers into it and grabbed a handful, his arm hidden by the press of bodies.

Someone came up behind him and put their hands heavily on his shoulders. He jumped, thinking he had been seen taking the sweets. He turned round, smelling the spirits and looked up into his father's bloodshot eyes. John Gray was swaying as he held onto Arthur. 'Come here, son,' he said thickly. 'Ain't you going to have a cup of ale with your old dad?'

Arthur sighed. 'I was going back to see Beth and her cousins,' he explained but his father cut him short and cuffed him rather clumsily round the ear.

'No, come in the alehouse first, boy. How much have you got on you? Come on, turn out your pockets.' He thrust his hand into Arthur's coat pocket as he spoke. His clumsy hand caught the loose seam and ripped the pocket, the coins tumbling onto the cobbles. His father stooped down and picked up the four pence that Arthur had been paid by the butcher. His other twopence was luckily in his shirt pocket.

'That'll do, boy, that'll do me just fine. Go on then. Go and find your friends and leave your old father on his own.' He stumbled back through the threshold of the inn, leaving Arthur running his hands through his hair in exasperation at the injustice of life.

Making his way slowly up Middle Street, Arthur was surprised to find Will sitting in the road, ignored by and ignoring the passers-by, intent on what he was doing. Arthur could only say angrily, 'what do you think you're doing Will, you stupid baby? I told you to stay where I left you.'

Will looked up at Arthur. 'You said you'd come back an' you didn't,' he said accusingly.

'Oh shut up, cork brain,' Arthur commanded, his anger at his father spilling out at his brother. 'And get up Will! You shouldn't sit in the road; there could be dog shit or anything there.' He bent down and pulled Will up roughly by his arm. 'Now come on. Keep up with me,' and though he still felt cross, he waited until Will had caught up with him and then took hold of his hand and held it tightly.

When they got to back to Drake's shed, it took a moment for their eyes to get used to the darkness after the bright sunshine outside.

'Where've you been, Gray?' Nick asked. 'Did you get anything to eat?'

Arthur looked round and saw Nick and Francis sitting high up on some wooden chests. A face appeared between them and Arthur saw, with annoyance, that Beth was up there with them. Curtis was sprawled on his back, his fowling gun propped beside him, on the ancient wreck of a small rowing boat that lay hull uppermost on the straw-covered floor of the shed.

'Why didn't you look after Will?' he asked, accusingly, of all of them.

'Didn't come here to nursemaid your little brother,' Curtis said, sounding bored, his hands clasped behind his head.

'I'm coming down,' Beth said and swung round dangling her legs over the end of the crates, still about six feet off the ground and showing her bare legs and feet and a few inches of lace petticoats.

'Be careful, Beth,' Arthur exclaimed reaching out his arms, as she lowered herself precariously and dropped the full height. He caught her in his arms where she remained for a moment or two, looking rather surprised and then swung herself out of his hold.

'I'm sorry Arthur. I didn't think that Will would go after you. I thought he would stay where you left him.' She held out her hand, smiling at the small boy. 'You are a naughty boy, Will! Where did you go?'

Will came up and took her hand beaming at her. 'Went with Arty,' he said simply.

She laughed and ruffled his hair. She turned to look at Arthur. 'Well, did you get us anything to eat?'

Arthur dug into his pocket. He pulled out a piece of linen and Beth's eyes lit up as she opened it.

'Sugar candy,' she said delightedly, picking one up and putting it in her mouth. She took another.

Curtis sat up and looked across at her and Arthur. 'Is that the best you could do, Gray?' he asked.

'Suppose you go and get something then, Curtis?' Arthur suggested. Curtis slid himself off the hull and came over to Arthur helping himself to one of the candies.

Nicholas and Francis by now had also swung themselves off the crates and dipped their fingers into the small pile of sweets and very soon they were all gone.

'Can I come with you to buy something?' Will asked Curtis, grasping the older boy's hand and looking up at him.

Curtis shook his hand out of Will's grasp. 'No, I don't bother with babies!' he said, sneering.

Beth was pulling her shoes on and looked from Curtis to Will. She was enjoying being the focus of the four boys' attention and Curtis's rather offhand manner appealed to her. All the same, Will was a favourite of hers and she hated to see the way the boy's face dropped when Curtis shook him off.

'Come with me, Will,' she said taking his hand. 'I shall buy you something from the fairing stalls.'

Will, aware that he had won some sort of victory, held Beth's hand tightly and walked out of the shed with her, Nicholas and Francis following close behind, Curtis strolling slowly and Arthur at the rear, despondent and if he but knew it, lovesick.

An hour later, they were all tightly packed in Church Square for the coin throwing. The sun was beating down on the townspeople gathered for the occasion. The lucky ones had gathered early and were standing under the shade of the great yew. The new Mayor and the freemen of the town were assembled at the Old Cross at the south door of the churchyard.

'I can't see, Arty. What's happening? Has he thrown the pennies yet?' Will asked.

Arthur shook his head. 'Naa. Come here then, Will, I'll lift you up,' he said as he bent down and hoisted Will up holding him round the waist.

Excited chatter broke out as two great braziers were carried out and set on a small platform. On them were placed two pans of the pennies which had been shone and polished. As the town clock chimed the half hour, two of the Town Sergeants in their gorgeous red robes took the pans off the heat and poured the pennies into a square of cloth. The new Mayor in his finery, sweating under his large hat and scarlet cape, held the four corners of the cloth and swung it over his head, releasing it when it was at its apex and a shower of the shiny pennies was scattered all over the grassy bank. All the children dived after them. The coins were burning hot and half the fun for the children was trying to gather as many as possible without burning their fingers.

'Ow!' Beth yelled, as she scooped a handful and then dropped them as they were so hot; Will was not fast enough to get any but Arthur scooped up as many as he could rapidly transferring them to his pockets. After a few minutes, all the coins had been collected and the children's excited chatter died down as the crowd began to disperse.

Arthur noticed Beth's parents in the crowd with several other grown-ups and, to his alarm saw that one of them was Thomas Lamb, one of the governors of the charity school, before whom Arthur had often appeared to try and justify his frequent absences. Beth went over to them and Arthur could see her explaining something to them and laughing and showing off the two coins she had managed to keep hold of. She looked round and called Arthur and Will over.

'Aunt Ann, Uncle Richard, this is Arthur and Will Gray, from Hawkhurst.'

Arthur reluctantly approached the adults.

'Are you enjoying yourself, young man?' Beth's aunt asked him. He could see the likeness between her and Beth's mother. Beth's mother was pretty enough, Arthur thought, but Ann Austen was much younger and very beautiful with golden hair, brown eyes and a mouth which turned up at the edges so it seemed she was always smiling. If he had a mother, he would like such a one as this, he thought.

'Yes, thank you, ma'am,' he answered. He nodded his head politely to John Stone and also to Mr Lamb who stood beside him. Arthur held his breath as he waited for the inevitable comment on his presence here when he should have been at school. For a moment he wished his father was there to speak on his behalf. Although he looked around for John Gray, he knew it was pointless for he would surely be in one of the inns; and for half a moment he thought how pleasant it would be to have a mother, father, aunts, uncles and cousins all happy together on a summer's day.

Arthur took a chance and looked up at Mr Lamb; better have it out now than have it hanging over him the rest of the day. 'I ain't at school, sir,' he said, defiantly.

Mr Lamb looked down at him and though his mouth was stern, his eyes were twinkling. 'A statement beautiful in its obvious truth,' he replied.

'Arthur is here with his father, Thomas,' Jane Stone exclaimed, smiling at Mr Lamb and touching his arm. 'And at my invitation. He surely can't be punished for that?'

Lamb nodded and looked at Beth. 'And what do you say, young Beth? I'm sure you have an opinion. Let me hear it.'

Beth looked from Arthur to her mother and then at Mr Lamb. 'I hate to see Arthur's poor hands when they have been beaten,' she said, fiercely, 'and though I know it will hurt dreadfully, you had better beat mine because I asked if Arthur and Will could come with us today.'

Lamb smiled at her solemn face and addressed himself to Arthur. 'Well, Gray, here is a dilemma for you. This young lady stands as your advocate and has expressed herself willing to receive the punishment you deserve. What say you?'

There was a pause before Arthur answered. 'I shan't ever let anyone hurt Beth,' he said quietly.

Lamb, who had been enjoying himself immensely at this interchange, realised that there were deeper emotions here than he had thought. He remained silent for a moment comparing the little girl with her pink cheeks and thick brown hair and the promise of a serene womanhood to come, with the boy who stood next to her, sullen and stocky, his face remarkable only for his clear blue eyes. Not for the first time, Lamb found himself wondering what the boy's future might hold.

He cleared his throat and gave a short laugh. 'Well, since Beth invited you, and Beth and her parents were invited by Mr and Mrs Austen who were invited by me and I was invited by my brother, the new Mayor, – I think we may safely tell Penfold your schoolmaster, that your being here today was at the instigation of the Mayor of Rye himself! I do not think Penfold will find himself justified in giving you a beating, Arthur.'

Arthur smiled broadly as Lamb laughed again and the rest of the adults joined in. Beth, relieved that Arthur wasn't going to suffer having his hands beaten when he returned to school the next day, tugged on her mother's hand. 'May we go and look at the fairings now?' she asked.

Jane Stone nodded. 'Mind you all stay together then, love,' she said, kissing her daughter. 'And Beth, remember Nick has charge of you all. He is the oldest. He has charge of you and Will, also,' Jane Stone called out to Arthur as the children began to leave. Arthur turned round and looked over his shoulder, giving a tiny nod of his head to Beth's mother though she could tell by his expression that he had not the least intention of placing himself under Nick's command.

'What shall we do now?' Beth asked. They were sitting on the low wall watching the boats, the heat of the afternoon shimmering around them. Will had fallen asleep in the shade by the wall at Beth's feet clutching the little carved wooden horse she had bought him; the older boys having taken off their coats and neckerchiefs had rolled up their sleeves and kicked off their shoes.

'I should like to try for some more rabbits, Curtis,' Arthur said, anxious to try and make some more money.

'Oh no, Arthur,' Beth protested, 'it's much too hot to walk all that way again. Besides, Will is fast asleep. I'd rather stay here. There's a nice breeze from the water.'

'I might let you try for some more, Gray,' Curtis said lazily. He raised his eyebrows to Nicholas and Francis. 'What about you and your brother, Austen?'

Nicholas shook his head. 'No, we'll stay here.'

'Leave your coats here,' Beth suggested. 'I'll mind them for you. And I promise to mind Will this time.'

'Meet us back in Drake's shed,' Curtis said. 'I'll bring us some wine and cakes. About six? Oh, Beth, I bought something for you.'

She looked across at him as he pulled out something from his pocket. It was one of the little rectangular mirrors which she had admired on one of the fairing stalls, with a gilt frame and etched into it in small writing across it, was a little verse:

How sweet was to sit in the maze,
Amid the bright choirs of the fair!
Their glances diffus'd such a blaze,
I thought beauty's goddess was there!

Beth looked at it, entranced, glancing at her reflection in it and then reading the verse again. She looked up at Curtis and half smiled, not quite knowing what to say. He stepped towards her, bent his head down, drew her towards him by her shoulders and kissed her full on the lips. Beth, who had never been kissed by any male except her father or her uncles, stood stock still, her arms by her sides, not sure whether she liked this or not though she was aware of her cheeks becoming pink and warm.

Francis started to laugh, but Arthur felt furious. It would never have occurred to him to kiss Beth but as soon as he saw Curtis doing it, he realised that it was precisely what he wanted to do himself.

The two boys set off back to the meadows, Curtis's fowling piece held in the crook of his arm. Neither of them spoke as they walked together, until they reached the meadows and Curtis held the gun out to Arthur. 'Go on then, Gray.'

Arthur easily remembering how to load the gun, was soon ready but the rabbits seemed reluctant to come out or perhaps they too were dozing in the cool of their burrows. Curtis lay on his back, his hands shading his eyes, sucking a piece of grass, while Arthur lay on his belly, watching carefully for his prey.

'So, this Beth Stone – what does her father do? Does she have brothers and sisters?' Curtis asked.

Arthur shrugged. 'No. She's the only one. I don't know what her father does. He goes up to London to look out for his business, but I don't know what it is. Her Dad's brother has a lot of land up where we live.'

'And what about your father, Gray? Does he own land?'

Arthur shook his head. 'No,' he said simply. 'He used to run an alehouse but-,'

Though he hated the life his father led, he was too proud to confess it to this sneering youth. 'He ain't so well, now,' he finished. 'He can't really work no more. What about you then, Curtis?'

Curtis exhaled through his teeth. 'I told you, my ma died. I don't know who my father is, except he has a lot of money.'

A shot sounded as Arthur let off the gun and he watched the rabbit drop instantly. The afternoon drifted on. Arthur shot another two rabbits. Curtis dozed. After another half hour with no sign of any more rabbits, Arthur got up.

'I'll take these back to the butchers then, Curtis.'

Curtis drew out a watch from his shirt pocket. 'It's half before six, Gray. I'll go back to my place and see you at the Shed, then.'

They walked back into Rye. It was still thronging with people who had been working all day and were now intent on enjoying the fine evening either in the streets or in the taverns. Curtis stopped off in Longer Street and disappeared into the house.

Arthur carried on to the butchers, but discovered that he had put up his shutters and closed for the day. Deciding that he would take the rabbits home and give them to Hannah or Lizzie to cook, he made his way to the Strand and Drake's shed.

He noticed a few members of the Militia in the town and wondered idly why they were there. When he got to the shed he found that the great door had been pulled shut. As he pressed his shoulder to it, the door creaked and swung open. Adjusting his eyes to the relative darkness, he quickly noticed that another cart had been pushed in and wheeled to the back. It had all four wheels, unlike the other wrecks there and was covered in tarpaulin. Arthur stepped slowly over to it, looking round, dropping the rabbits. He lifted up a corner of the tarpaulin and saw in astonishment that it was filled with oilskin bags, sealed and tied. He started to pull the strings at the top of one of them.

'Now you just stay right where you are and don't be doing nothin'' you might regret!' a deep voice said menacingly.

Arthur spun round to see in a dark corner to his left, a man standing in the shadow, holding a long carbine which was pointed straight at him. He had a dark-coloured neckerchief fastened round the lower part of his face and a hat pulled down low over his forehead, so Arthur could only make out his deep-set dark eyes. His heart started racing and he felt the sweat forming in his armpits and palms.

'What are you doing here, boy?' the man asked.

'I just come here to meet my friends, s... sir,' Arthur stammered, looking down the barrel of the gun. 'I don't mean no harm.'

'And what time are your friends coming here?' the man questioned, pointing the gun straight at Arthur's heart.

'Six.'

'Fuck!' the man cursed. 'Look boy, you get sixpence if you do a small job for me or the butt of my carbine round your head if you don't. So what's it to be?'

'Whatever you want me to do, sir,' Arthur said, thankful to be given the option.

'Then help me move these pieces of wood over my cart there, so it's all covered up and no one's any the wiser it ain't been here months.'

Arthur nodded quickly and started helping the man carry the wood, laying it on and over the cart and propping some up beside it. They stepped back as the man seemed satisfied and Arthur had to admit, it now looked like any other piece of junk that might be found in the deserted shed. Just then, they heard voices outside and the door was pushed open. Three of the Militia men, armed and booted, pushed their way into the shed.

Arthur's companion hastily pulled down the neckerchief so his face was revealed and stepped closer to Arthur putting his arm around his shoulder, his hand gripping him tightly, warningly.

'What's going on here? Identify yourselves,' one of the soldiers ordered.

'Hold up there, Captain,' the man said jovially. 'Joe Gardener and my boy Tom, at your service, Captain.'

'What are you doing here?' the senior soldier asked. Though he was only a corporal, he had no objection to being addressed as 'Captain'.

'We've been rabbiting, ain't we, Dad?' Arthur said quickly, indicating the rabbits at his feet. 'Is it a crime sir?' he asked the soldier innocently. 'Ma will give you what for,' he added looking up at his new 'father'.

The man rubbed his face and smiled ruefully. 'Aye, she would that. But it ain't a crime surely, Captain? If it is, I never heard it. We was on common land.'

The soldier sniffed. 'No it ain't a crime. But what are you doing in here?'

The man drew out an earthenware bottle and held it up. 'Just stopped off somewhere cool and quiet for a sup of ale before we go home.'

The soldier, hot and tired with his thick coat buttoned all the way up to his neck, prodded at a couple of the old crates nearby. The door was pushed open again and Curtis stood there, a look of surprise on his face at the scene before him.

'There you are, Jack,' Arthur said quickly, willing Curtis to play along. 'We thought you was never coming. This is my cousin, sir,' Arthur said to the soldier. 'Jack Gardener.'

The soldier nodded, bored by this domestic scene. 'Well, we'll leave you to it. What's in that basket, lad?' he asked Curtis.

Curtis opened it. 'Cakes and wine.'

'Just as your aunt asked you to fetch home from the fairing stalls,' the man said. 'We'll be on our way home then, officers, as soon as we've refreshed ourselves.'

The soldiers nodded, turned on their heels and left the shed, their voices fading as they made their way up the Strand.

Arthur, Curtis and the man remained still and unmoving. Then the man let out a sigh and rubbed both hands over his face. 'Mother of God, that was close,' he declared. 'Too bleedin' close!'

He propped his carbine up against the wall and clapped Arthur on the back. 'And it ain't often I meet such a quick-thinking lad, no indeed.' He dipped into his pocket and drew out a few coins. 'There's a shilling for you, boy,' he said to Arthur. He handed a sixpence to Curtis. 'And half that for your friend here.'

'What's going on here?' Curtis asked.

Arthur shrugged his shoulders. 'I dunno. What is in the cart?' he asked the man.

Curtis immediately looked interested. 'What cart?'

Arthur nodded in the direction of the hidden cart and Curtis went over to it, pushing his hand through some of the pieces of wood to feel the tarpaulin. He lifted it and let out a low whistle. 'That's tea, ain't it? And uncustomed, I reckon.'

'I reckon you have the right of it,' the man nodded.

'Then my silence is worth more than this sixpence. That's what the Militia were looking for, ain't it?' Curtis asked.

The man nodded. 'But I hope you ain't thinking that I'll pay you any more than sixpence for keeping your mouth shut?'

Arthur had been listening in astonishment. He knew smuggling went on, but he had never been this close to it. The tea must have been brought in on one of the smuggling cutters and laid up here for safe keeping. Arthur knew that his own father acquired some of his liquor from the Free Traders, and complained about the cost even though it was much less than it would have been, had he purchased it through a more orthodox route.

Though Curtis had been calculating a quick pay off for his silence, Arthur was thinking much longer term, and wondered if there was any way he might become part of this illicit but apparently well-paid occupation.

'You said, I was quick thinking?' he asked the man, who nodded. 'Then let me join you.'

The man frowned and then burst out laughing. 'Damned if I don't just let you,' he said. He rubbed his face. 'What about your friend there?' he asked indicating Curtis. 'Am I buying his silence or his future services too?'

'It's up to you, Curtis,' Arthur said, feeling that at last he had an advantage over him.

'What would you pay us? And who are you, exactly?' Curtis asked.

'I pay you nine pence for each run, a shilling if you can ride. And when we shake hands, I'll give you my name.'

Arthur looked from Curtis to the man and held out his hand. The man shook it and then held it out to Curtis who hesitated for a moment. Then he took the man's hand and shook it also. The man smiled and said, 'John Grayling is my name.'

'Jeremiah Curtis,' Curtis stated.

'And I'm Arthur Gray,' said Arthur laying his hand over the top of Grayling's and Curtis's and though he couldn't know it, he was forming one of the most far-reaching associations of his life.

Towards ten o' clock, Curtis and Arthur, Beth and her cousins and a very tired Will, met with the adults as they came out of the new Mayor's handsome house. It was a balmy, beautiful clear night, with thousands of stars and a bright crescent moon throwing a silvery light onto the streets of Rye.

Jane Stone turned round saying to Arthur, 'Do you know where your father is? He must come with us now if he wants to be carried back to Hawkhurst.'

Arthur cast his eyes down. 'I think he's still in the *Mermaid.*'

No one said anything. They stopped at the *Mermaid* and Stone and Austen went in. Mr Austen came out. 'He went to the *Two Brewers* apparently, some time after eight. He's probably there still.'

Sure enough, when they reached the Landgate and went into the alehouse opposite, the two men came out a few moments later having located John Gray.

'Thomas, I think we may need your assistance. He's somewhat in liquor,' Richard Austen said and Arthur, shamefaced, wished himself anywhere but here, as the three men came out a few minutes later with his father between them, dead drunk, cursing and swearing and flinging his arms about. Arthur, with Will tugging at his coat, was acutely aware of Beth's discomfort, of Curtis with his usual sneer and of Nicholas and Francis's curiosity.

His father vomited suddenly at their feet. 'Fuck you all! Fuck the lot of yers,' he slurred.

'Quiet sir or the Watch will be out for you!' Lamb said, stepping out of the way of the vomit.

'Fuck the Watch!' John Gray declared.

They finally got him the short way to the wagon and hauled him in where he lay full length on his front. The adults paused to say goodbye. Curtis nodded at Beth, ignored Arthur and turned back into town.

As they were waiting to get into the wagon, Arthur drew Beth a little way away from the others round the far side of the large elm tree. 'Beth,' he said softly.

He wanted to tell her of the events in Drake's Shed. He still felt the excitement at the pit of his stomach and felt alive with the possibility of being able to make enough money to keep Will and himself and even their father from falling into the desolation of utter poverty. Even more, he felt the excitement of having outsmarted the soldiers, not by any show of strength, but by John Grayling's and his own quick wits.

But as soon as he looked at Beth, he could only think of how jealous he was of the way she seemed to favour Curtis over him.

'What is it Arthur? You've acted strangely all day.'

'When Curtis kissed you – did you object?'

Beth bristled. 'Why do you ask?'

'You didn't look as if you objected,' Arthur said crossly and then added, 'would you mind if I kissed you?'

She looked uncertain, a little shy. 'I don't know, Arthur.'

He put his hands on her shoulders as he had seen Curtis do and pressed his lips to her mouth, closing his eyes. Her lips tasted sweet, of the honey cake she had just eaten and he could smell her female smell, warm and heady. He pressed his lips harder to hers, feeling his own body unexpectedly tighten and harden.

She quickly pulled away.

'That's enough, Arthur,' she gasped and hurried back round to the wagon, taking her father's hand as he helped her up.

CHAPTER SIX

Dungeness, Late September 1724

'Come on you two boys,' Robert Bunce said encouragingly, clapping a huge hand on each of their shoulders. 'John Grayling wants you to learn all you can tonight.'

He took his eyes off the little boat out a few hundred yards off shore and looked at the two youths he had been told to keep an eye on. Grayling had taken both of them on a few weeks ago and thought them 'promising'; that was all Bunce knew.

'What've you learned already, eh?'

'Not to blab,' Arthur said readily.

Bunce nodded. 'Aye, that's rule number one, I guess. Don't let no one know, who don't need to know.'

Arthur found himself eager to learn everything this older man had to tell him. This was more exciting than answering old Penfold's boring questions and he felt he wanted to be all over the beach, in all places at once, listening to the men's comments, watching the various tasks they had well in hand. He and Jeremiah Curtis were sitting on some unloaded kegs, in a little shelter in a trough of pebbles, comfortably out of the wind. Robert Bunce wore his greatcoat collar turned up and had a hat pressed down low on his forehead and a long woollen muffler wound round his neck. As the men worked, they discarded their outer clothes for it was warm work and essential to work quickly when loading the heavy casks and kegs and oilskins.

Arthur wished his coat was thicker but for the first time in his life, he was glad that his father's cut-down coat that he was wearing came

down nearly to his feet and kept his legs warm. He would know better
next time. He would wear two sets of clothing like the rest of the men.
He had never been out at night on the sea shore before and hadn't
known how cold the wind could be, blowing straight off the sea with no
windbreaks on this open, barren beach. The tide pushed the pebbles
up into troughs forming bands of shingle, the smaller pebbles falling
on top of the large stones and providing a shelter to sit in, though
Arthur could see it made the men's work harder, having to haul the
cargo up and over the troughs. As their heavy boots crushed the only
plants that were able to survive here, Arthur could already recognise
the pungent smell of the sea kale as it mixed in with the salt air.

Though he knew that he had so much to learn, he already felt at
ease. There was a feeling of enthusiasm, of adventure, being part of this
band of men all willing to take a chance and make a push for a better
living. He breathed in the cold night air deep down into his lungs. It
was the smell of excitement; exhilarating, life-affirming. Being out at
night, with the stars above, the pebbles crunching under his feet, the
sound of the surf rolling in, the lamps on the little boat bobbing on
the waves, made him feel glad to be himself, glad to be Arthur Gray
out with a smuggling gang, able to make a living and for the first time
in his life to see a way ahead and a purpose to his learning.

'What might pose a danger to us, Curtis?' Bunce asked the older,
darker youth.

Jeremiah shrugged. 'The Dragoons?' He had one eye on the little
boat out at sea.

'No, the Dragoons won't come out unless the Riding Officer puts
in his request,' Arthur corrected him.

Bunce smiled. 'That's right. And what else do you know about a
Riding Officer?'

'He keeps his movements secret, like we do,' Arthur replied.

'And is he armed?' Bunce asked. Arthur looked doubtful. Bunce
answered his own question. 'Yes, he is. And likewise so are we. See
them men standing every fifteen yards or so, flanking the beach?
They have weapons. Might be a simple stave, or a hanger with a sharp
blade, or a carbine. Some of us who have been soldiering might have
a musket or pistols.'

'Does anyone ever get shot?' Curtis asked, interested.

'Upon occasion, as a last resort,' Bunce said carefully. 'They are used more in the way of warning the officials off, if you see what I mean. We got weapons and we might use 'em. That's usually enough to keep the Riding Officer in the other direction.'

'How long will it take us to unload?' Arthur asked, watching the men on the shore going about their business, some of them carrying the goods in from the surf and others carrying them onto waiting horses and wagons.

'Depends on the tide, the wind, whether you're working on a pebble beach or sand. Pebbles can slow you down 'cause they're hard to walk upon, but wet sand can be the same. A good team can unload, in ideal conditions, about five hundred tubs ashore in twenty minutes. And, 'fore you ask me, I'll be asking you – what's a tub?'

'A half anker,' Curtis replied before Arthur had a chance.

'Which is about four gallons,' Arthur put in.

'Right you are, young Gray. And Curtis too. You're both learning fast. French brandy comes in half ankers. Stuff we get from Holland comes in whole ankers. That's how you can tell the difference. And this is unlowered spirits, right? Undiluted. Strong stuff. We sometimes dilute it with sugar water. Or *let it down*, you might hear that phrase used - to sell it on but that's done inland. Our business is to get it off the boats soon as we can and on to the horses or wagons. Sometimes we spike it, or peg it. That means we taste it to make sure it's good stuff. See the men over there?' Robert Bunce jerked a thumb towards the rough track above them. 'You'll see 'em loading six or seven half ankers to a horse.'

Arthur was beginning to realise how much was involved in planning just this one night's activity. He was becoming more and more thankful that he could add up quickly in his head.

'I suppose we need to know how far the safe houses are, how long it will take us to get there?'

'Exactly so,' Bunce nodded 'But it ain't just safe houses we use – there are ditches and churches and vaults and barns and stables and hayricks all over the Marsh we can call on and on all the routes inland.

So you gotta know all them too. Now, look at that dear little boat out there and tell me what you can about her.'

Arthur and Jeremiah both stood up to peer out to sea but it was difficult in the light of the half moon to pick out much more than her general shape and the number of lamps she was carrying.

'Is she a lugger?' Arthur suggested.

'No, that's a cutter. She's the *Old Molly*, built at Folkestone by Benedict Marsh on the Sandgate Road, sails and ropes come out of Nathan Bennet, Back Street. I used to live in Folkestone myself 'fore I was married, so I know the place well. Your cutter is fast with one mast and a straight running bowsprit.'

Arthur sighed. Would he ever be able to learn all this?

Curtis was beginning to look bored.

'*The Old Molly*, she's safe here, we got deep seas,' Bunce was saying, standing up to look at her. 'Your lugger is your best boat in shallows, she's got a shallow keel and a broad beam. She can come in really close. Luggers come in on the Goodwin Sands; you should see a Deal man handle one in them shoals they got there. But we got just one cutter tonight, carrying four, five tons maybe.'

'But who owns the boat? The Captain?' Arthur enquired.

Robert Bunce laid a finger at the side of his nose. 'Ah, now you're asking. Depends how successful you are as a Lander. That's what we call the boss of a gang. If you can afford it, you owns yer own boats. And has 'em made just how you wants 'em.'

'How much money do they make?' Jeremiah Curtis asked, pulling his coat tighter about him as the wind whipped up.

'Depends on what you do. The Lander, he makes the most and quite right too. I don't know what he makes, but I seen John Grayling's house in Hastings and very fine it is. You lads, you're the very bottom of the rung. There's the crew to pay, there's the regulars in the gang who might be batmen looking out to protect us, or tubmen who do the loading, then there's labourers and fishermen who may come in just to help run or store, there's the farmers whose barns and outbuildings you might use to lay your goods by, there's the horses to be driven or rode, there's the clergy who might give you a lend of their vestry, or a farmer of his haystack. There's the bagman who collects the money, there's your agent in France, there's your quill driver who writes out your orders and makes sure you bin paid. Can you write?'

Arthur nodded, grateful for the first time that he could.

'Well there you have me beat,' Bunce said, 'cos I never learned. Only my name can I write and can't read a single thing.'

'But who puts up the money?' Arthur asked realising this was a much bigger business than he had at first thought. He had assumed Grayling was of the same standing as a farmer or a yeoman, but was beginning to understand that he ran a much larger and more complex organisation than he had ever imagined.

'Ah well, you're talking of the shadowy men, we call 'em *Venturers*, cos they venture to put up the money to start with. But you won't never get to meet them that's for sure. They like to remain in the shadows, put up the money, take a lot back, nearly most of the profits it seems. But there's still plenty for us.'

'And where do we run goods to?' Arthur questioned.

'Ain't you seen' em being run?' Bunce looked down at his eager face, illuminated in a shaft of moonlight. Arthur nodded.

'We run 'em all over the Marsh all through Kent and up through Sussex,' Bunce explained, 'but most of the money is made in London. Ever been there, boys? No? Well, maybe one day. It's a sight to see. All the dealers come to buy. But you don't need to be knowing much about that. You won't be running up to London, not yet a longwhile. We're running into Lydd tonight, storing some there and taking the rest inland. And here's the boss himself come to see how you're shaping up I expect.'

John Grayling came up to them. 'Alright Robin?' he asked Bunce, cocking his head at the two boys.

'Yep, I should say so,' Bunce replied.

'Stuffed full of facts, are they?'

Bunce nodded. Grayling looked at his two newest recruits. 'You lead your horses to Lydd and unload 'em at the *George*. Now, you lodge in Rye don't you, Curtis? Then you take Gray with you. He can't be going back to Hawkhurst tonight. Gray, you stay with Curtis whenever you must lodge overnight at Rye in future.'

He started to walk up the beach, the two boys following. Robert Bunce went over to the line of horses to collect his mount ready for the run inland.

'Can I ask you something, Mr Grayling?' Arthur said after a few steps.

'You won't never learn less you do,' he replied looking straight ahead at his men finishing off the loading.

'How do you know what will make a profit?' Arthur asked.

Grayling turned to look at him. 'Well, it's a good question and I would say that the answer is Politicks. Government puts a duty on something that most men want and most men will try to get it cheaper, without paying that duty. It's human nature, ain't it? We used to make all our money from running wool to France cos the Government taxed it so high, it used to be worth our while to run fleeces over to France. The French weavers would sell it back to our merchants cheaper than they could buy it from our own people. Now the bloody Irish are selling to the French cheaper than we can, so we have to look elsewhere. Spirits and wine always make a profit and this year, the Government has gone and put a duty on tea. And what does every housewife in the land want for breakfast but her pot of tea? So I reckon we will make more guineas there than all the spirits and wine put together.'

'From the tea?' Arthur asked, surprised. It seemed a very ordinary commodity to him.

'Tea don't sound so exciting as spirits or wine,' Curtis agreed doubtfully.

'It don't need to be exciting,' Grayling explained. 'So long as it's something that everyone wants, you can be sure the Government will put a duty on it. And thereby makes a living for us Free Traders. And that's your first lesson in Politicks, boys. If the Government makes something illegal or expensive, you can bet your mother's soul, it's something everybody likes and wants. Tea is easy to carry and pound for pound will give us a better return, you mark my words. That's enough learning for one night, I reckon. Now here's Larry Jockey. You do what he does, follow him into Lydd and help him unload the horses and then you can make your way to Rye. You both be back at the *George* in Lydd next Wednesday sennight for we have another run then.' He dug his hand in his pocket. 'Nine pence each, boys. As I said, it becomes a shilling when you're experienced enough to ride inland. Which I am hopeful of your becoming in a trice.'

CHAPTER SEVEN

Jew's Cut, Dungeness, Autumn 1725.

The clouds which had been scudding across a black sky, momentarily cleared and the thin line of the crescent moon lit up the activity going on all around. A small cutter lay out at sea, its sails flapping gently. Arthur who was huddled in a trough of pebbles with some of the other men, saw the now-familiar network of ropes leading from the cutter to a tub boat and then onto the shoreline. Twenty or so men were occupied pulling in the ropes and cutting free their cargo. Another twenty busied themselves carrying the barrel-shaped wooden kegs and oilskin bags from the shoreline to the beach where a line of horses and ponies stretching back to the sea road, stood, ears alert to the men's muffled calls. In the inky distance, individual men were posted every twenty yards or so, some with a long carbine slung over their shoulder, others standing with their weapons resting over their forearms. Since they had been running tea this last year, they had been making two or three runs a week; it seemed that Grayling was indeed right – the tea merchants took all they could bring over.

A big man swung a keg from his shoulder and landed it with a soft thud on the wet sand at Arthur's feet. 'Dutch or French?' he asked the boy.

Arthur looked up at the man. It was John Turner, big and tough. Arthur wouldn't like to get on the wrong side of him. He glanced at the keg in front of him. He had seen many such by now and knew at once by its size it was Dutch and said so. The man laughed under his breath. 'So you have learned something, then. Now, has you ever tasted it? Could'ya tell the difference?'

Arthur shook his head.

'What? Nearly twelve and not tasted the Dutch?' John Turner thrust a hand deep into his greatcoat pocket and pulled out an earthenware bottle. 'We've untapped one of the kegs,' he said jerking his head back towards the boat. 'Taste it then, boy. That's unlowered spirits. Blows yer brains out – blows mine out, anyway.'

Arthur reached out and took the proffered bottle. His tongue recoiled as the fiery liquid swilled into his mouth. He swallowed it quickly and coughed as the fumes drifted up his nose and into his eyes.

The man gave a short laugh and took the bottle back. 'Keeps the night air out, dunnit, lad?'

Arthur still coughing, nodded and wiped the back of his hand across his mouth.

He put his hand into his breeches pocket, pulling out a sugar candy wrapped in a piece of old linen. He pushed the sweet between his lips, sucking it against the roof of his mouth to get rid of the foul taste of the Dutch spirits and wondered not for the first time, what made adults prepared to pay so much for it and what his father found in it that he must needs spend all his income on it, while his two boys sat with hungry bellies at the table.

He shrugged. Though he didn't understand its attraction to men like his father, he knew he should thank providence that men did want hard liquor, for it was making him a living. He thought to himself that the nine pence that he had earned for tonight's work, would soon join the pile of coins that was hidden behind the back of the skirting board in the room he shared with Will - and it meant bread, cheese and enough to buy meat which Hannah Webb would cook for them. Maybe there would even be enough to buy another carved wood animal for Will's collection. And most importantly he would buy a red ribbon to give to Beth for whom, since he had kissed her on Mayor-making Night, he had developed a feeling so overwhelming that the mere touch of her hand could set his heart bounding and his mind racing with thoughts that he knew from Parson Saunders' ferocious sermons, would send him straight to hell.

He shifted his position slightly trying to rub some warmth into his cold limbs, watching the last of the cargo being loaded onto the horses. His shoulders felt stiff and cold, for the driving rain had soaked right through his greatcoat and he could feel his shirt wet from his neck to his waist.

He and Curtis had been on many runs now over the past year and Arthur felt he was becoming a useful member of the gang. He felt uncomfortable around Curtis though. Arthur could cope with his sneering manner though it irritated him; but he hated the way Curtis took short cuts, not loading the horses with the right number of half ankers or oilskins and he always seemed to manage to avoid getting wet when it was their turn to haul the tub lines in, standing in the cold sea water.

It was the same tonight. Arthur's boots were wet from standing at the shore line, helping carry the kegs ashore. When the goods were loaded and the men and horses that were running goods inland had disappeared over the flat eerie plain that was Dungeness and then onward across the Marsh, the rest of the gang made their way into Rye where Arthur would reluctantly have to share Curtis's lodging.

It was the custom for the men to end the night in one of the inns in Rye. This night they had started at the *Dolphin* and then moved onto the *Red Lion* but Arthur, tired and wet, had fallen asleep in one of the wooden chairs near the fireplace in the *Dolphin* and when he woke, he realised all the other gang members had gone.

Harriett Marshall, one of the barmaids came up to him and ruffled his wet hair.

'My word, Arthur, you've got yourself wet tonight,' she said smiling. 'What can you have been up to?' She looked around the bar room. 'I think all your friends have gone. I expect you're hungry. I'll fetch you some buttered wheat, what do you say to that?'

He nodded and watched her make her way into the taproom. By half past midnight the alehouse was almost empty and Harriett came back up to him. 'You'll have to make your way off, now Arthur. Who are you lodging with tonight?'

He shook his head. 'I'm supposed to stay with Jeremiah Curtis.'

She looked at him clicking her tongue. 'I know you don't get on with him. Perhaps I can do better than that.' Harriett went off to have a word with the landlord and came back in a few moments. 'He says you can sleep in the kitchen. If you curl up next to the range, you'll be cosy. There's an old blanket hung over the door in there you can use.'

It was warm enough by the range and he had company in the form of a sandy-haired mongrel who hung around the taproom, and curled up on Arthur's feet sharing the warmth. Arthur preferred the dog's company to Curtis's.

CHAPTER EIGHT

Late autumn 1725, Hawkhurst

'So do you think your mother would agree to lend me her mare?'
Arthur asked Beth. They were up in Upper Willow Pite Field near where
Beth's uncle, Robert Stone lived in a strange and dark old house.

Beth pursed her lips. 'I'm not sure. I don't know if she really
approves of what you do. I don't mean to hurt your feelings, Arthur.'

'Oh it don't bother me, Beth. Your mamma, well, she don't have
to worry about money, does she? It ain't quite the same for me. But I
ain't asking for the mare to ride when I'm with the gang, am I? I should
just like to borrow her now and again to ride over the Marsh and get
to know the routes better. Sometimes at night I don't have the faintest
idea of where we are. There are ditches and dykes and great troughs
of water and one farm looks just like any other.'

Beth looked worried. 'If there's any chance of your falling in a
ditch or some such thing, I'm sure my mamma will lend you the mare
to help you make sure you know the Marsh better.' She took his hand
with both hers. 'I couldn't bear it if you got hurt.'

He looked into her grey eyes and swallowed hard, then bent forwards
and pressed his lips to hers, pulling her closer to him by her shoulders.
Whenever he kissed Beth, he thought how Kat Lambert had casually
revealed herself to him and tried to imagine Beth unloosing her stays
and offering him her breasts to feel or even lifting up her skirts and
letting him feel her most private place with his hands and fingers and
his own burning flesh. Then he would try and banish the ideas for he
felt perhaps Beth might read his thoughts and she would be offended

or even frightened. He reluctantly pulled away from her, hoping she hadn't felt the hard ache in his breeches as he held her so close.

'Shall we go and call on my uncle?' Beth said, her cheeks pink, her curls a little dishevelled.

'Old Robert Stone?' Arthur asked. 'He's a bit strange, ain't he?'

Beth shook her head. 'I think it's just that he doesn't like people. I wouldn't call on him if I were on my own. I've only been inside his house once. Let's see if he will invite us in.'

They took the path through the woods that led eventually to Stone's house. It was an old timbered building nearly two hundred years old with small mullioned windows and a high-pitched roof whose tiles looked as though they were sloping to one side. In fact the whole of the house had an uneven look to it and it stood right on the edge of the woods, the trees and shrubs growing close beside it, their branches embracing some of the windows and a thick and dark green ivy had scrambled all the way up one side of the house.

They stood in the little porch and Arthur tugged the bell. There was no response and he pulled it again.

'Perhaps we should, go, Arthur,' Beth whispered when just at that moment, the great door was pulled open and Stone's manservant stood before them.

Beth looked up at him. 'Good afternoon,' she said politely. 'I wonder if my uncle Stone is at home? Would you tell him, if he is at home, that his niece Bethlehem has come to call on him?'

The manservant, tall and thin, said nothing but bowed his head slightly and ushered them in to the small, square dark hall. There were stained glass windows set high up on both sides and the small amount of sunlight that penetrated, made coloured patterns on the flagstones. The only furniture was an old dark oak settle, a small table and a long case clock whose ticking seemed to fill the room. Though it was very warm outside, it was cool, cold almost indoors.

After a while, the manservant came back. 'Mr Stone regrets he is unable to receive you at the moment. If however you would like to wait in the kitchen, I will bring some refreshments for you and Mr Stone will be able to give you a few minutes of his time after that.'

Arthur looked across at Beth, wanting to laugh. Beth however rose to the occasion, nodding graciously and picked up her skirts to follow the servant across the hall and into the kitchen at the back of the house. This was a lighter, more welcoming room and they sat across the table from each other and waited for the manservant who told them his name was Doust, to make a pot of tea in a beautiful silver tea pot and serve it to them in blue and white china cups with slices of a seed cake.

When they had finished and Arthur had eaten his third piece of cake, the door opened and Robert Stone came into the room. He was a good deal older than his brother, Beth's father and was dressed in the style appertaining to the last quarter of the last century, with a frock coat with very wide skirts, a long, elaborate waistcoat and a full wig. He made a stately bow to which Beth curtsied and Arthur hurriedly nodded his head.

'Are you well, Bethlehem?' he asked at length.

'Yes thank you, Uncle,' she said in a small voice. 'I've brought my friend, Arthur Gray.'

She turned to Arthur, who tugged at his neckerchief and bowed from the waist. Robert Stone inclined his head with a thin smile.

'And your parents, niece? They are well?'

'I thank you, sir, they are both very well.'

'And the refreshments, they were to your liking?' he asked waving a hand in the direction of the table.

Beth and Arthur both nodded. 'Very much to our liking, Uncle, thank you.'

He nodded again and bowed. 'Thank you for calling, child,' he said and turned and left the room.

Beth and Arthur looked at each other and hurried out of the kitchen, through the hallway, leaving Doust to close the door behind them and then they gave way to the laughter that had been rising in them both.

'Well, he is a strange one, that's for sure,' Arthur exclaimed. 'Come on Beth. We can run all the way down from here. Race you to your house.' They set off at a tearing speed down the pathway through the fields and woods and back into the village to Beth's house.

They found Jane Stone baking in her kitchen. She was a little doubtful at first on hearing Arthur's request to borrow her mare but when Beth pleaded and explained it would not be used for running goods, she relented and said he could borrow the mare twice a week if she was not riding Cassie herself.

'But aren't you at school any longer?' she asked Arthur who was enjoying milk and cakes at her table.

He shook his head as his mouth was full and when he had swallowed, replied, 'No, Mrs Stone, I've done my two years; Penfold's been trying to get rid of me for ages since I never attended every day anyway. But I've learned to read and write and add up and take away and I can say my catechism in my sleep. Besides, I'm learning more now than ever.'

He was about to explain the finer points of a run to Beth's mother, but thinking about it, decided it was best left unsaid.

He was most grateful to her for the loan of the mare and he spent two days a week crossing and recrossing the Marsh, discovering the tiny villages and churches dotted all about. He got to know which farmers owned which land and which ones were helpful and which ones were hostile, although these were a minority. He discovered all manner of safe refuges and the different signs that were used to let the local people know the pertinent details of a run; this could be simply the way a gate was tied, a cloth attached to the sail of a windmill, the number of cows left in a certain field or a similar apparently innocuous sign. Old Penfold would have had nothing to complain about with regard to Arthur's enthusiasm or aptitude for his new education.

CHAPTER NINE

Early September, 1727, the Grays' rented rooms, Hawkhurst Moor

In two years Arthur had grown tall and muscular through carrying and handling the heavy weights of the kegs and oilskins and at nearly fourteen, looked at least a couple of years older.

He returned from a run early one morning. As he climbed the stairs to the two rooms, he heard his father shouting and Will's voice, piping and shrill. He pushed open the door. His father was slumped as usual at the table, the smell of spirits strong in the room. Will was sitting on a stool in the corner. They both looked at Arthur as he entered, his father's eyes hostile, Will's bright with fear and red-rimmed. His face was tear-stained and there was a red mark on his cheek.

'What's happened?' Arthur asked quickly. 'Will, come here.'

Will ran to his brother's side and Arthur put a hand on his shoulder. His father looked at his elder son and took another swig of gin. 'Spoilt brat,' he said nodding at Will.

'Will?' Arthur said, looking questioningly at his brother. Will's chest was heaving with emotion. 'He took my collection, Arthur. He's sold them to a pedlar. All my animals,' and his face crumpled again.

Will's collection was his precious set of little carved wooden animals, which had started with a horse Beth had bought him at the Fairing Stall in Rye on Mayor-making Day. Arthur had found a shop in Hastings one morning that sold them and had bought Will a couple more on his birthday and Beth had asked William Colvill, the local carpenter to fashion another. Will's horse was joined by a pig, a cow and a dog. He kept them in a little box and gave them all names. He was deeply attached to them and wove stories in his head about them and their doings.

Arthur patted his shoulder and hugged Will to him, feeling his small body shake, as he clutched the empty box. 'I suppose it was for that,' Arthur said contemptuously nodding at the flagon of gin on the table. 'Don't I bring you enough?'

'No. Not enough,' John Gray yelled, getting unsteadily to his feet.

'What pedlar? Where's he gone?' Arthur asked.

John Gray shrugged his shoulders. 'Dunno. Kilndown? Lamberhurst? He's too big for games, anyway,' he said looking at Will.

'He's only eight,' Arthur said defensively. 'What did you hit him for?'

'I was trying to stop him getting all the shillings,' Will cried.

'What?' Arthur said, immediately fearing the worst and looked at the open door into the tiny room he shared with Will and where, behind the skirting board, all the proceeds of his activities with John Grayling's gang were hidden. Now he was working with the gang on every run and riding goods inland, John Grayling paid him three shillings a run and Arthur had kept his father and Will in food and clothes and had still saved nearly twenty pounds.

He dashed into the room, going to the skirting and found the board pulled away from the wall and the hole empty. All the nights he had spent out in the cold and rain, leading horses across the Marsh through the night mists, carrying kegs and sacks, sometimes up to his knees in mud and ditch water, avoiding the Riding Officers, cuffs and curses from the men, came swimming in front of his eyes. He stormed back into the room where his father backed defensively.

'Where is it? Where is it?' he spat the words out, fiercely. 'Where's my money?

John Gray laughed and tapped his waistcoat pocket. 'Found a new home, it has.'

Arthur lunged towards him. 'You thieving, fucking bastard!' he yelled, pushing his hand into his father's coat. John Gray, taken by surprise was caught off balance and fell heavily against the cupboard behind him, knocking the chairs and table flying in all directions, sending splinters of wood everywhere. Will, his eyes wide open in astonishment and fear and amazement to hear his brother swear at their father, shrank back against the wall.

John Gray managed to right himself and with the advantage of his height smacked his fist, with all his force, across Arthur's face. Arthur saw it coming however and ducked at the last minute, only catching the tail end of the blow. He took advantage of his position and keeping his head low, rammed into his father's belly. They both rolled onto the floor and once they were down, the advantage was Arthur's, for John Gray's body had grown soft and weak through drink and idleness. Arthur realised that for the first time in his life, he had more strength and more agility than his father.

He pushed his hand into his father's jacket, feeling the weight of the bag of shillings and ripped the pocket out with the bag inside. He rolled away from his father, picking himself up quickly, his breath coming in great heaving sighs. He went and stood by Will, waiting for his father to get up. He did so and looked across the room at his sons. Then he blew out his breath in a contemptuous sigh and brushed past them.

'Don't ever hit Will again,' Arthur hissed through his teeth as he passed. John Gray stopped and looked at Arthur. He raised a hand in Will's direction and the boy instinctively shrank nearer to his brother. Arthur stepped forward, clenching his fist, his eyes meeting his father's, his expression a challenge. 'Don't hit him again. Not ever,' he said menacingly.

John Gray shrugged his shoulders and stumbled unsteadily across the room and through the doorway. The two boys heard his uneven steps as he made his way down the stairs and out.

Arthur paused for a moment and exhaled. 'Come on Will, let's get this place cleared up. And then I'll get on the Lamberhurst Road, to see if I can find that old pedlar.'

They righted the table but two of the chairs were beyond repair. Arthur put the bag of money in his coat pocket. 'I'll take you to

Hannah Webb,' he said to Will. 'Best you're not here when he comes back.'

He left Will drinking milk and eating apple tarts at Hannah's. Then he set out for Beth's house, wondering if her mother would let him borrow the mare. He let himself in the gate and walked around the path to the back, but the windows were open and he heard music and realised that Beth would be in the middle of her music lesson. He stood listening, marvelling that she was able to make the tinkling notes so well and then remembering the urgency of his visit, hastened round to the back door and was let in by Ruth, the little house maid.

'Is Mrs Stone at home?' Arthur asked, looking round the neat kitchen and smelling the delicious aroma of baking cakes. She shook her head nervously, touching her cap. 'Mistress has ridden to the Wells.'

'Oh,' Arthur said, disappointed. 'And I don't suppose Mr Stone is here?'

She shook her head again, 'No Master Arthur, he's gone to London with the carrier.'

'Well I'll see Beth, then,' he announced and stepped cautiously into the hall and tapped on the parlour door. The music stopped and Arthur heard Beth's voice at the other side. 'Arthur,' she said surprised, opening the door. 'What do you want?'

Arthur noticed the pink flush rise to her cheeks. Her thick brown hair tumbled about her shoulders and he couldn't help but notice how the tight lacing at the front of her gown forced her small breasts into prominence.

'Goodness, what has happened to your face?' she said and put her hand up to his jaw where his father's blow had made contact. The touch of her fingers muddled his thinking and for a moment he stood there savouring her closeness and the touch of her flesh on his. He pulled himself together. 'I came to see if I could borrow the mare, but Ruth says your mother has ridden her to Tunbridge Wells.'

'Yes, that's right. Is something wrong, Arthur?' she said.

He nodded and looked into the room to see Professor Rolfe standing by the spinet. 'I'm keeping you from your lesson, Beth,' he said awkwardly, not wanting to discuss his family matters in front of the music teacher.

'Professor Rolfe,' Beth said, in her assured way, turning to the older man. 'I'm afraid I have an urgent matter to attend to. I shall practise extra hard before next week, I promise.'

Since Beth was obviously not going to return to the instrument, the Professor had no option but to bow graciously and make his way out.

'Now, tell me Arthur,' she ordered urgently as soon as the Professor had left the house.

'I need to get on the Lamberhurst Road as soon as I can. My Dad has sold Will's collection to a pedlar and I mean to get them back if I can. It sounds foolish now only you know how he cares for them.'

Beth looked anxious. 'Not the animals? Oh poor Will. I know he is so fond of them. Oh Arthur, do hurry and try and get them back. There's only my father's horse here but come with me and I'll help you saddle him.'

Arthur looked doubtful. Borrowing Jane Stone's mare was one thing, for she always had a kind word for Arthur and had let him ride Cassie on many occasions before but John Stone had a changeable temper and could be sullen; Arthur was unsure how he might react to his horse being taken without his knowledge but Beth was already across the hallway and opening the side door which led out to the small stable at the back of the house.

He lifted the saddle easily off the wall and between them they hoisted it over the horse's back and Arthur reached beneath to fasten the girth.

He straightened up and turned his back to the horse's flanks, looking at Beth. Their eyes met. He lowered his head and brushed his lips against hers, his hands on her shoulders and then when she didn't protest, he slipped them down tracing the line of her collar bones. He felt the quick rise and fall of the upper swell of her breasts under his fingers. With thoughts of chasing after Will's animals almost forgotten, he saw the heap of fresh straw behind her and wanted to lower her gently down; he wanted to untie her laces and reveal her breasts completely; he wanted to lift up her skirts and find relief in her body from the tightening hardness in his loins, instead of fumbling with himself in the dark as he did when he thought Will was safely asleep. She seemed to sway a little and then she pulled away and said breathlessly, 'Really Arthur, you must hurry. Quickly!' She looked pink and a little startled.

He reluctantly let go of her and led the restless horse out into the yard. He was a large beast, snorting and blowing as soon as he felt the saddle on his back.

'Be a good boy, Achilles,' she said. 'You will be careful with him, won't you, Arthur?'

He looked down at her and smiled. 'Don't worry. I'll be back in an hour or so.'

He flicked the reins and the heavy horse made off. Luckily the past few weeks had been dry and the track was dry and firm. It would not do for the horse to lose his footing, he thought and then smiled ruefully to himself, thinking he was probably on a wild goose chase. His father was not very clear which way the pedlar had gone. He was likely sitting in an inn even now, miles in the opposite direction, with Will's wooden toys tucked into his wicker basket ready for sale at the next pedlary fair. Achilles had a lumbering gait and wasn't particularly fast. However it was a pleasant sunny afternoon and it had been one of the warm and bright Septembers that were often hotter than July.

Arthur thought back to the fight he had had with his father. He didn't regret the fight, but unfathomably, he regretting swearing at him. The thought of his father hitting Will made his anger rise again. Maybe Will was young for his age and should have stopped playing with his wooden animals long ago. He thought of himself at Will's age. At eight and a half, Arthur had been caught out in Tulhurst's barn, paying his halfpennies to look at the mysteries of Kat Lambert's naked body. He smiled at the memory of the Parson's wrathful explosion and Thomas Lamb's more measured response.

His thoughts went back to his schooling. Though he hadn't thought much of it at the time and had probably attended for only half the time he was supposed to, he was grateful now for the chance he had been given to learn to read and write and to make quick calculations in his head. Most of the men in the gang couldn't read or write more than their own name and he realised he had the advantage over them, as he took on more and more work with Grayling. Grayling often carried notes on him and would refer to them during a run.

He pulled himself up with a start for while he was daydreaming he had hardly noticed that he had ridden through Kilndown and was approaching Lamberhurst. As luck would have it as he came up to the *Chequers Inn* he saw, tethered outside, a horse that could only belong to a pedlar with baskets and packages and brightly coloured cloth bags all hanging from the saddle. The horse had a nose bag strapped to it and was crunching noisily. Arthur tethered his horse next to it and paused for a moment before going in.

Arthur remembered that he had brought his bag of money with him, after wresting it from his father. He should have left it with Beth or with Hannah Webb for safekeeping. Better safe with them, than with him out on the road here. But it was too late now. He straightened up and went into the inn. He asked for some beer and noticed the pedlar straight away sitting by himself in a corner, a bowl of soup in front of him and a piece of bread and cheese at his side. His heart sank as he looked more closely at the pedlar. He was a big man with a mean face, dark piercing eyes and a sour expression. Taking a deep breath, Arthur went over to him and stood facing him. The pedlar looked up.

Arthur said nothing but indicated the chair opposite him; the pedlar shrugged his shoulders and carried on lapping his soup noisily. Arthur sat down. 'Good afternoon, sir,' he said.

Again the pedlar ignored him.

'I believe you've travelled through Hawkhurst?'

The pedlar looked up. 'So what if I have?'

'I think my father might have sold some objects to you by mistake,' Arthur said pleasantly enough. The pedlar carried on noisily lapping his soup, then wiped the bowl with a hunk of bread. He gave a short laugh. 'By mistake was it?'

Arthur gave an uneasy smile. 'He sold you some wooden animals that belong to my young brother. I'm willing to pay you whatever you gave for them.'

The pedlar nodded. 'Them's good pedlary,' he said. 'Easy to sell again. I'll get a good price. I don't believe I want to sell them to you. Maybe I'll keep 'em and give 'em to my own boy. You may as well get on your way.'

'Well how much do you want?' Arthur asked. 'You must want to sell them at some stage. Surely that's how you make your living?'

'And what do you think you know about how I make a living?'

Arthur sighed. This was becoming much more difficult than he had imagined. It would be easier to go to Hastings and find the shop that sold them. 'A shilling,' he said defiantly.

The pedlar held up his tankard to his lips, sitting back in his chair. 'No deal.'

Furious, Arthur got to his feet and went back out to his horse. He looked again at the pedlar's horse, laden with other items and thought for a moment of taking some as payment in kind. But what would he want with old pots and pans, or wooden combs? He kicked up a stone and wondered whether to go back inside and tackle the pedlar again. Just then he looked up, hearing horses approach and was surprised to see John Grayling mounted on his white mare, flanked by Thomas Holman and Larry Jockey and some of the other members of the gang, escorting several loaded horses. Grayling was directing them round to the stables at the back when he saw Arthur.

'Well, if it ain't young Gray! You look as if you had dropped a guinea and found a farthing. What are you doing here?'

Arthur looked at the men and horses and understood they were running goods on their way to London. Many of the inns and alehouses on route were safe houses and Arthur realised the *Chequers* was probably one of them. He shrugged his shoulders. 'Trying to get something off a pedlar he won't sell me.'

'Oh yes?' Grayling said, dismounting but not really interested.

'My father sold him something belonging to Will, my little brother.'

Grayling had noticed the pedlar's horse and said with more interest, 'Well, then it looks to me like you've got yourself involved with Joe Croucher. Big man, is he, with shifty eyes?'

Arthur nodded.

'It should be easy enough to persuade him, I think. Is he within?' he asked, jerking his head to one side. 'Let me tether my horse, then and we will have ourselves a conversation with Mr Croucher.'

Grayling went in and saw Croucher at once. Croucher looked uneasy when he saw Arthur come back in with John Grayling especially as Holman, Jockey and several others soon followed.

'Good day to you, Joe,' Grayling said amicably sitting down next to Croucher. Thomas Holman sat the other side. 'This lad here tells me he wants to buy something that you won't sell him. Is that right?'

Croucher seemed to sink back in his chair. 'I never knowed the boy was one o' yourn, Grayling. How was I supposed to?'

He looked across at Grayling and then up at the band of men surrounding him. He reluctantly picked up the bag at his feet and snatched the wooden animals out.

Grayling picked up the carved dog and looked at it curiously. 'It's a well made piece, I grant you, Joe. But not hardly worth all this trouble. Gray here wants them back and I've no doubt you're going to sell them back to him, aren't you, Joe?'

Croucher said nothing but then reluctantly pushed them towards Arthur.

'What did you offer for them, Arthur?' Grayling asked.

'A shilling,' Arthur responded.

'Oh? Good as they are, I don't think they are worth that. Let's say ten pence. We don't want no one saying that there's been any thieving going on, do we? So Arthur, pay our friend Joe here his ten pence and he can be on his way.'

Croucher stood up, snatched up the coins Arthur had flung on the table, wiped his hand across his mouth and made for the doorway. Arthur followed him out and watched him approach his horse. The pedlar mounted and unloosed his reins. He looked at Arthur, pressed his heels into his horse's side and rode off. Arthur watched him go and then turned back to Achilles.

Grayling came out.

'Thank you very much, John,' Arthur said. 'My little brother will be very happy to get them back.'

Grayling waved a hand dismissively and then nodded towards Arthur's borrowed horse. 'Is that your mount?'

Arthur nodded.

'Well, if it ain't a lucky day for both of us,' Grayling exclaimed. 'I'm two horses and two men down and Holman's has lost a shoe. We had a run of bad luck, just past Flimwell. Two of the horses got the staggers. Have you ever seen it, Arthur? Queerest thing you ever saw in a horse. Even blowin' tobacco smoke up their noses didn't cure it. Savage and Turner have stayed behind. We've double loaded two of the horses. But I see this horse of yours looks like he could carry a good weight. You come with us. We're running up to Stockwell.'

Arthur shook his head. 'No. I can't. He ain't my horse. I've only borrowed him. I have to get him back.'

'Well, borrow him for a bit longer.' Grayling looked suddenly stern. 'It ain't all my boys I take to see Stockwell, Arthur, especially not one as young as you. I've scratched your back Gray, now it's my back has got an itch.'

Arthur looked resigned. He would rather face John Stone's wrath than John Grayling's. He nodded at his boss. 'Yes, of course.'

Grayling clapped him on the back. 'That's the spirit lad. Knew I could rely on you. Now that's settled, have you tried the kidney pie, here, Arthur? Goes down a treat with their cider.'

They went back into the inn and Arthur joined the rest of the men for their meal. When they had finished they reloaded the horses.

Arthur slung some oilskins of tea and a couple of kegs of spirits over Achilles leaving just enough room for him to mount up. They set off on the London Road. Arthur had never been further than Sevenoaks and looked about him with interest as they followed the London road from that pretty little town on into Swanley. It was still a fair day and they passed a few other travellers, wagons and carriers. If anyone knew they were carrying uncustomed goods, no one had anything to say about it.

Towards five, they approached the little village of Stockwell. It seemed a pretty enough place with a green and several fine houses round it but further towards Lambeth, they came to a much busier area with a wider thoroughfare and several large buildings. These were all very similar, most of them two-storeyed and newly built in red brick and with windows only on the second floor.

Grayling led his men through a bricked archway into a courtyard and a man in a leather apron came out at once to greet him. They obviously knew each other well and the men led their horses through another arched entrance where the stables were located and where there were several wagons and carts being unloaded. Grayling hailed and shook hands with another man, tall and rather elegant and wearing a large rose in his buttonhole. James Brooksey, who had been riding next to Arthur, turned to him. 'That's Thomas Moreton, runs the Groombridge Gang. See that flower, that's his trademark if you like. All the gang leaders have a particular one. With Grayling, it's his long hair and his red muffler; Ned Henley from Folkestone wears the uniform of the Irish militia and his men call him 'Captain'.

Grayling came back with Moreton and to Arthur's surprise introduced him to the other Gang Leader.

'So you're running with this old rascal, eh?' Moreton said laughing looking down at Arthur. 'Well you won't go far wrong. First time up here, John tells me? Look and learn, Gray. Look and learn.' He doffed his hat slightly to Grayling. 'Are you staying up here, John? I've got my boy with me. We went to St Bartholomew's fair yesterday. You could visit with your lads.'

Grayling thought for a moment and then said, 'Why not? I ain't been for years. Tom? Larry? Will your wives let you stay out another night? Jockey, you and the boys can go and bespeak some rooms when you've unloaded and I'll take young Gray here to have a look round. We'll see you at the *Robin Hood* later.'

Grayling led Arthur to a door at the side of one of the courtyards with a little outbuilding attached. It had a small window hatch giving out onto the courtyard. The man sitting inside got up when Grayling tapped on the window and came out with a bunch of keys. They exchanged greetings and the man selected one of the keys and let them both in the main building. Arthur was amazed to see it. It had a high pitched roof, supported by colonnades, limewashed walls and row on row of storage racks from floor to ceiling, all numbered. There was the dry, slightly sweet smell of tea in the building and it was stored in thick canvas bags as well as wooden chests.

'Is this all uncustomed tea, then?' Arthur whispered in amazement.

Grayling laughed. 'No. That's the beauty of it, Arthur; this is a bonded warehouse. It's all mixed up now with a custom stamp on every bag and chest. I'm not saying how that came to be,' he said, laying a finger at the side of his nose. 'The Manager knows which of it came in by us and others like us and which of it came in by the more orthodox route. Once it's here, we can't be touched for any wrongdoing. Most peoples' tea comes in the back door, even those whose tea is poured in the noblest houses in the land. When all's said and done, Arthur, every man likes to pull the wool over the Government's eyes when he may. Would you rather pay seven shillings for your pound of bohea, or two shillings?'

Arthur nodded slowly, amazed again at the size of the smuggling operation. 'And are all these warehouses just for tea?' he asked.

Grayling led him through a connecting door into another equally impressive room. 'No, there's wine, arrack, cambric, silk, china, all manner of things. All the tradesmen come here to buy. We got more warehouses up Kingston way, mainly tea and spirits there, but Stockwell is well placed for us, running up from our bit of the coast. Now lad, let me introduce you to the Master of the Warehouse, Thomas Batson.'

Thomas Batson turned out to be an extremely fine gentleman. Arthur noticed he had large silver buckles on his shoes, his coat and hat that were hanging on a peg in his office looked to be of the finest material and his linen shirt was extremely white and neatly pressed. He had a large gold watch chain hanging across his waistcoat which was of a bottle green with very fine embroidery and he wore a signet ring on his little finger with a stone in it that kept catching the light and which Arthur was sure, was a real and very large diamond. He greeted Grayling with the utmost cordiality which was extended to Arthur and joked about what they might be expected to see at St Bartholomew's Fair.

'There's sure to be something to your taste,' he said. 'Wild animals, acrobats, sideshows, freaks, whatever you fancy. Be sure to watch your pockets, though. There's all manner of villains to be found there.'

At length Grayling and Batson parted company and Arthur went back with his boss to pick up their horses. Arthur's head was reeling with all he had seen and heard about this part of the business. And the more he heard, the more drawn he became.

As they rode slowly up Kennington Park Road, towards the *Robin Hood*, Grayling slowed his horse down as a gibbet came into view. The tall gaunt structure looked out of place in such a pleasant green lane and it seemed to cast a chill over the landscape.

'What's that wooden handle at the top?' Arthur asked solemnly, full of a morbid curiosity.

Grayling cast him a dark look. 'That's the swivel, lad. That's how they attach the culprit once he's been hanged and his body's been tarred and hung in chains.'

The hairs at the back of Arthur's neck and on the backs of his hands stood on end. They both looked in silence, then Grayling kneed his horse and they set off.

The next morning Arthur drew Grayling aside and explained he was carrying a large amount of money. Grayling rubbed a hand over his face. 'That's not a very good idea at all, Arthur, not at all. And it ain't no use leaving it here for we may not come back this way. No the best thing to do is to hang it between your legs and draw it tight under your balls.'

Arthur looked worried and started to protest but Grayling interrupted him. 'Safest place, ain't it? You might not notice anyone stealing it out of your pocket, but you will for sure notice if someone's hand slips up between your balls. Unless it's a pretty little girl and you want her to, that is.'

He showed Arthur how to make a girdle around his waist with a piece of stout cord and tying the rope securely round his purse, passed it between his legs and tied it up in front. Though it was not particularly comfortable and Arthur imagined he would be in some difficulty when he wanted to relieve himself, at least he could feel the purse all the time and it was true, no one would meddle with it without his knowledge.

They set off still on horseback crossing London Bridge with all its stalls, shops and houses and wonderful views over the great river; though Arthur found the smell almost unbearable.

Once over the bridge they made their way through Cornhill, Threadneedle Street and westwards towards Smithfield when the noise and general hubbub and the increasing crowds showed them they were approaching the fair. They made their way through the throng down Magpie Alley to the *Magpie* tavern where they stabled their horses and the other men took a drink or two before making their way on foot back to the fair. Several of them wanted to watch a prize-fight but Arthur standing a couple of rows from the back, soon tired of it. They were two great hulking men, stripped to their breeches, their hair tied back. Soon, blood and spittle and teeth were flying and because they were so evenly matched, Arthur thought it would only be decided by whoever tired first.

He wandered off intending to take a look at the acrobats' sideshow and on his way there, bumped into a tall man. He looked up and saw with astonishment John Stone, equally surprised, staring down at him. Neither spoke and then Arthur noticed the woman standing beside him and holding his arm and smiling. She was tall and had a mass of very dark hair, a wide red mouth and large brown eyes. She was dressed in a fine gown with much wider panniers than the Hawkhurst women wore, and the low cut laces at the front of her gown displayed a fine bosom with a patch of a crescent moon, Arthur noticed, on the upper curve of her right breast.

Arthur might at first have thought that she was just some woman John Stone had met by chance, though he would never have thought John Stone one to visit St Bartholomew's Fair at all. Stone looked so discomfited that Arthur became suspicious. Stone put his hand on Arthur's shoulder and smiled. 'What are you doing here, Arthur?' he asked pleasantly, just the faintest hint of unease in his voice.

Arthur, aware that John Stone's horse was stabled a few streets away in the stables of a tavern that even Grayling acknowledged was frequented by some very unsavoury types, cleared his throat before replying. 'Well, sir, I, that is – I had some business here, unexpectedly.'

Stone nodded. 'Yes, yes, so have I. Indeed.'

'What a coincidence, John, your meeting someone you know. Aren't you going to introduce us?' The woman smiled down at Arthur as she spoke.

Stone looked distinctly uncomfortable and mumbled, 'Arthur Gray, an acquaintance of mine.'

'From Hawkhurst?' she asked.

He nodded. As Stone seemed reluctant to introduce the woman to Arthur, she smiled at him and holding out her hand said, 'Mrs Gresham. How do you do, Arthur?' and tucked her hand back in Stone's arm.

Arthur nodded and looked back at Beth's father, dawning realisation that this lady was more than a chance encounter. He turned as if to go. John Stone reached out and touched his arm and then let his hand drop. 'Goodbye then,' he said.

Arthur spent the rest of the afternoon wandering around the Fair, the purse of money hanging between his legs growing decidedly uncomfortable as the day wore on. Towards three, he was relieved to come across Grayling who had decided it was time to return and gathered all his men from the beer tent; and they made their way westwards towards the *Magpie*.

Arthur went into the necessary house at the back to untie the cord from his middle and flexed his thighs, rubbing his balls and his cock. As soon as he touched himself, he thought of Beth and how he had trailed his fingers over the swell of her breasts after they had swung the saddle up on Achilles' back in the stable yesterday morning. He frantically pulled on his stiffened flesh, ashamed and yet powerless to stop himself once he was in the grip of such a yearning ache, scared in case anyone should come in and discover him. He stifled a groan in his throat as he shuddered to his climax, half leaning against the rough wooden door. He hastily wiped himself on his handkerchief, placed the leather purse back in the inside pocket of his jacket and went back inside the *Magpie*. The gang at last saddled up and made their way through the hot dusty streets, back across the bridge and were soon in the leafy villages of Surrey, passing through Lambeth and Stockwell again and from there back into their own county out onto the London Road towards Sevenoaks.

Arthur rode straight to Beth's house, dismounted and went to the kitchen door, meaning to ask Ruth the housemaid or Beth to open the stable gate to let him return Achilles. Ruth opened the door and let him in and both Beth and her father appeared coming in from the passage way. Before Arthur had time to respond to Beth's cheerful greeting, John Stone had walked across the kitchen and put his arm on Arthur's shoulder and led him outside. 'Well, Arthur, did you enjoy the fair?'

Arthur nodded. 'Very much, sir,' he said and couldn't resist asking, 'Did you?'

Stone looked uncomfortable, as if he was about to make a sharp retort. But instead he clapped Arthur on the back.

'See here, Arthur, you're not a boy any longer, are you? You're a young man, fifteen is it? What? Not fourteen till November? You should know that Mrs Gresham, the lady I was with, is an old friend of mine. I've known her many years, before I was married to Beth's mother, in fact. But you know what women are?'

Arthur didn't know whether to nod or shake his head.

'Beth's mother, my dear wife, wouldn't understand this. She would take all sorts of silly notions into her head. You know how easily they get hold of the wrong end of the stick.' He smiled at Arthur. 'I'm sure you will understand it's better if you don't say anything about this. Better you don't say anything about having seen me at all in fact. You wouldn't want Beth upset in any way, I'm sure. Or Mrs Stone. So,' he said, holding out his hand. 'Shall we shake hands on it?'

Arthur, willing enough, took his hand and shook it. 'I came here to return your horse,' he explained.

Stone looked surprised 'Return my horse?'

Arthur nodded. 'I borrowed him yesterday. It's a long story. I meant no harm. Mrs Stone was away from home and I asked Beth.'

'Where is he now?' Stone asked.

'Outside the front of your house. I only came in to ask someone to open the stable gate,' Arthur explained.

Stone paused for a while. He had thought Arthur had come round so hurriedly to make mischief. 'Well, this is strange. I bought a new horse in London yesterday. That's why I went up by carrier. Achilles is all very well for slow journeys but he's a lumbering great beast. I've bought another, so why don't I say that you may borrow Achilles if I'm not using him? That will also be an understanding between us, as well as the matter of Mrs Gresham, eh?'

Arthur raised his eyebrows in surprise. 'That's very kind of you, sir and thank you very much.'

They went inside.

'Not at all, boy. Not at all. I'm glad we've got that cleared up. Now here's Beth come to see you and ask you about your adventures no doubt and here's my dear wife too.'

'Arthur, I'm so glad you're home safe,' Beth exclaimed, coming over to him. 'But where on earth have you been? You've been gone a day and a half.'

'Now, Beth, it don't do to go troubling a young fellow about where he has been. And I know all about Achilles and there's no harm done. In fact I've said your friend can make use of him when I don't need him, now I have Duke.'

Beth looked from her father to Arthur. This was a surprising turn of events. She took Arthur's arm.

He smiled down at her. 'I must get back, Beth,' he said. 'I must take Will his animals.'

'Oh, Arthur did you get them?' she asked, taking his hands. 'How clever you are. Is that what you've been doing all this time?'

Arthur looked at John Stone and at Beth's mother. 'No I went to Bartholomew's Fair, as well.'

'What? How is this? You mean you've been all the way up to London?' Beth asked, wide-eyed.

'Bartholomew's Fair?' Jane Stone declared. 'I've often heard it spoken of, but I've never been. What's it like, Arthur?'

She turned to her husband. 'You could have taken Beth and me to London. If only I had remembered the Fair takes place at this time of the year. I'm sure Beth would have enjoyed it. You too, John. I've heard there is something there for everyone. Is there Arthur?'

Arthur turned almost imperceptibly towards John Stone.

'Oh I reckon so. I reckon anyone could find something to please them at St Bartholomew's Fair.'

The warm and sunny September turned into a cold, blowy October. Arthur made sure he brought enough smuggled gin from the smuggling runs to satisfy even John Gray's need. Arthur had apologised to his father for swearing at him.

'It was wrong of me, Dad and I'm sorry for it,' he had said awkwardly one evening soon after his return from London. John Gray, having downed near enough a whole bottle of French brandy, was feeling at peace with the world. It was gin that made him pugilistic. He looked up from the chair he had slumped in and gazed at his elder son with bleary eyes.

'What's a curse or two, son, eh? Come 'ere.' Arthur had reluctantly gone over to him and his father motioned for him to lower his head. Arthur kneeled down and John Gray hauled himself up and put his face near Arthur's. The smell of spirits was pungent. He unexpectedly kissed his son's cheek. 'You're a good boy. If only-,'

Arthur drew his head away. 'If only what, Dad?'

John Gray fell back heavily in his chair. 'Nothin',' he said and closed his eyes.

Later that month a death was announced in a letter coming by carrier from Rye to Jane Stone from her sister. Ann Austen's husband, Richard had died unexpectedly after an illness of only two days. He had gone to bed complaining of a sore throat, had seemed a little feverish the next day and his wife had found him dead beside her the following morning. Nick and Francis, their two sons, were brought back from their school in Hastings and Beth and her parents went down for the funeral. Jane Stone and Beth stayed on a month to be company for Ann Austen, a young and pretty widow at only thirty one.

Two months later at the beginning of December another letter came by carrier to Jane Stone. On Christmas Eve Ann was to marry William Pix, the young brother of Thomas Lamb's attorney, Jeffery Pix who was also his friend and kinsman. William was only twenty four and the owner of a large farm at Northiam just outside Rye. Jeffery Pix, who attended the wedding, had now acquired through his young brother's marriage, a couple of step-nephews; childless himself, he had offered a place in his successful law practice in Chancery Lane to Nick as soon as he had finished his studies. William Pix insisted the boys carried his own surname as well as Austen. The fine house that the Austens had owned in Church Square was rented out and the income settled on Nick and Francis and a portion on Ann herself. The new Mrs William Pix, coming out of St Mary's Church on her young husband's arm, had done well for herself and her boys and Arthur was even more aware of the yawning divide between his position in life and Beth's with all her rich and well-connected relations.

CHAPTER TEN

Early February – 1729, Dungeness Beach

'God's truth!' John Grayling swore as two of his men tripped over the lengths of rope along the shore and dropped the heavy kegs they were carrying. 'Get your arses up, you two! We've two tons to unload tonight and tide's turning in half an hour.'

From a distance a little farther up the beach Arthur, holding the reins of a horse looked at the scene being played out on the shingle lines of the shore. Tonight's run was not going according to plan; that was obvious. The cutter was late coming in and the beach party had been waiting since eight o' clock. It was now past ten – a cold clear night, good for landing but it also meant that the large company could easily be picked out in the moonlight if there were any Revenue men about. Which wasn't likely, Arthur thought. They wouldn't take on thirty men who were armed with steel tipped bats and pistols.

Although they might do, he thought to himself, *if they knew how many of them were drunk!* Arthur had been amazed at the amount of drink now being consumed by the men. It was common enough to take a flask or two of spirits out on a run – God knows it was a cold enough business on a night like tonight. But having sat on the shingle for over two hours, most of the men had settled down to steady drinking.

When the cutter was finally sighted and the tub-boat had been dropped bringing the tub-line to shore, instead of hauling in and cutting free the pairs of kegs attached to it, men staggered all over the beach, some falling into the surf, cursing as the cold water hit them and others dropped the heavy crates and boxes instead of carrying them straight to the horses and wagons further back near the sea road.

Arthur hated to see the clumsiness that spirits wrought in a man. He had seen the effects of hard drinking in his own father to know the damage it could bring to a man and those around him. Drink had made his father stupid, unreasonable, unable to work or to be relied on or respected. Drink had lost him his business and his home and made him reliant on his two sons. The money Arthur brought home and the small amounts Will earned doing odd jobs paid for the two increasingly shabby rented rooms and their food and clothing.

He looked about him again and made out John Turner and Larry Jockey trying to haul up a heavy crate, with no order to what they were doing; one dropping it as the other tried to lift and then both pausing to take another swig.

Beams from the lanterns cast lights all over the beach. It was bitterly cold holding the horses, exposed to the wind. Arthur pulled his old greatcoat tightly about him and wrapped his muffler several times round his neck. The greatcoat was his father's and fitted him in its length, although the width was too big for him. The muffler was his own, given to him last birthday by Beth. He smiled at the memory.

'Here you are, Arthur,' she had said smiling up at him. 'I knitted it myself. Do you like it?'

He had unwrapped it carefully and Beth, impatient had unfolded it for him and reached up to put it round his neck, laughing. He had put his arms on her shoulders and kissed her lightly on the lips, the smell of her, soapy and clean, as arousing as the touch of her mouth. Then with all the embarrassment of his fifteen years, he changed back from would-be lover to boy and said casually, 'S'alright, I suppose,' in case she should guess his fierce pride that she had made something for him with her own hands.

She looked disappointed and stepped back as Will, now nine, clamoured for her attention. 'Let me see it,' he shouted and pulled it from Arthur, wrapping it round his own neck.

Beth had laughed as the two ends brushed the floor. 'You need to be a little taller, Will,' she had said.

'Huh, he'll always be a little scrap, him,' his brother jested.

'No I will not. Will I, Beth? Will I?'

'You will very likely be taller than your brother,' Beth stated calmly. 'Your dad says your mother was tall – you'll likely take her build.'

Will looked at his older brother with satisfaction. 'See? Beth says I'll be taller than you.'

'So you might,' Arthur agreed, 'unless I knock your block off first,' and he lunged at Will who screamed delightedly and wrestled his brother to the ground....

'What are you up to?' John Grayling asked bringing Arthur back to the present with a jolt. 'Take your mare down and load her up, you can't stand here all night dreaming.'

'Ned Savage posted me as lookout,' Arthur replied, stung by the implied criticism. 'He said I was to take my horse last, when we've unloaded. Though who knows when that will be? Look at Jockey and Turner, fallen over in the sand. We'll still be here tomorrow morning at this rate!'

'That's enough from you, young'un,' Grayling said, secretly agreeing with the youth, but not stupid enough to give him any delusions of knowing better than his elders. 'You stay put then and keep a lookout. Happen we might come back at daybreak. We're losing the tide and wind's changing.' He cursed under his breath pulling his hat further down on his head and stamped off, his steel-tipped boots crunching the shingle as he went.

Arthur watched him in discussion with several of the men near the water's edge and then saw one of them jump into the tub boat and start rowing out to the cutter. The remainder of the unloaded cargo was strapped onto the horses. Some men were mounted but most of the horses were led up the beach to the rough road beyond. This still left fifteen or so horses, Arthur's borrowed mare included with nothing to carry. He frowned as he saw a figure approaching him. Arthur's heart sank as he saw it was Jeremiah Curtis, now nearly eighteen, tall and lean and with an almost constant sneer on his handsome face. Although Jeremiah took part in many of the runs, he always seemed to have plenty of money of his own and now rented a second large room at the house in Longer Street.

'Come on Gray. Don't stand there like an idiot. The run's abandoned till daybreak. Anyone already loaded is on their way. Grayling says you're to lodge with me. We'll come back at six in the morning.'

Arthur nodded reluctantly. He would have to return to Rye instead of making his way inland with the goods if all had gone according to plan. He couldn't cross back into Rye with his horse using the ferry so it meant leaving her, probably in Snoad's Barn at East Guldeford.

'We're going to the *Red Lion* first. You better hold your liquor, Gray. You don't want to be rolling in the ginnels like your old man.'

Curtis never lost the opportunity to belittle Arthur or rub him up the wrong way. 'You can stable that fat old mare at the barn and collect her tomorrow. I'll see you back in town,' and Curtis turned towards the road, turning up his collar against the wind.

Arthur sighed and began to lead the mare up the shingle, after dousing his lantern. He would rather be on his way home but as it was the custom for all the men to meet up in one of the alehouses after a run, if they weren't involved in riding or driving the goods, he prepared to trudge the three miles back into Rye. There were a few other men also walking their horses, but Arthur kept his distance. There was an acknowledged hierarchy and Arthur knew that even after nearly four years with the gang, he was still the youngest member and was therefore at the bottom of it.

There were lights twinkling in the town and the alehouses were doing good business on such a cold night. He made his way along the Landgate and then down Longer Street before slipping in the side door of the *Red Lion*. The bar room was thick with smoke and the smell of cheap spirits and beer. A cauldron of stew hung over the fire in the back room, its smell wafting into the bar and making Arthur realise how long it had been since he had eaten.

'Here's the stripling thinks he can organize us better,' Thomas Holman called out, taking a swig from his tankard. Some of the older men were becoming jealous at the way Grayling had taken Arthur and to some extent, Curtis, under his wing. Grayling often asked them to help decipher the letters and bills that came over on the boats. Curtis though was careful to keep in with the men and would always join in drinking with them after a run.

'Don't approve our drinking, does he?' Holman added. He looked round at his companions who all laughed.

Jeremiah Curtis was of course already seated at the table, a bottle in front of him. 'Think you could do it better, don't you Gray?' he asked smiling but his tone was hostile.

Arthur shrugged and answered, 'Stands to reason we'd work quicker if we were all sober.'

John Turner slammed his tankard down onto the table. 'Oh, *stands to reason*, does it?' he mimicked. 'Being sober don't keep a man warm at night, do it?' he asked. 'When you've been out nights more than twenty years, you can talk about being sober.'

'Aye, we was all owlers running wool over to France before you was born,' Larry Jockey put in. 'Don't try and tell us how to suck eggs.'

Jockey's words reminded Arthur that most of these men had been involved in smuggling wool out of the country to France, long before it had become more profitable to run goods in. 'I don't mean to,' Arthur protested, 'I just think-,'

'*Just think*? *Just think*? You wanna '*do*', not '*think*'!' Turner argued, his red face just inches from Arthur's, across the table.

'Oh, Gray does a lot of thinking, don't you Gray?' Curtis goaded. 'Thinks Beth Stone will be his girl, for one thing.'

One of the men guffawed. 'The little Stone lass? Related to the Pix family now ain't she? Got ideas above your station there. Mind you, I wouldn't mind nailing that one. I know something would wipe that '*better than you*' look off her face.'

'Aye, your fat arse sitting on it,' Turner said and all the men laughed.

In one movement Arthur sprang up and landed his fist on John Turner's chin. It wasn't a hard punch but it had the element of surprise and Turner was knocked back in his chair. He sprawled to the floor, his tankard knocked out of his hand and the beer spilled out as it went flying and soaked his neighbours. John Grayling, who was one of them, sprang up and grasped Arthur by the collar over the table and hit him hard across the face with the back of his hand. It was Grayling's habit to wear a steel ring on his forefinger and this caught the skin at the edge of Arthur's eyebrow and a trickle of blood ran down his face. 'Out, go on, get out before you cause any more trouble! What's got into you, lad? Go and cool off! And mind you're back at six tomorrow morning.'

He swung him round and pushed him towards the door, his hand on the flat of Arthur's back between his shoulder blades.

Meanwhile the men were picking their comrade up off the floor. Arthur took one look back and then hurried down the steps into the cold night air. He ran down the street, around the corner and then paused for breath, leaning back against the wall, his heart hammering against his ribs. He dug into his pocket for a handkerchief and wiped it across his eye, wincing as he made contact with the cut.

'Bloody fool!' He swore at himself because John Grayling could easily have thrown him out of the gang and then where would he be? Besides, John Turner wasn't known as 'Cursemother Jack' for nothing and Arthur reckoned Turner would want to get even at some point. He rubbed his cheek where Grayling had hit him and reflected he had probably got off lightly for now. He heard footsteps and turned anxiously to see who it was.

Jeremiah Curtis appeared around the corner. 'Gray, you should learn a lesson. Some things are worth fighting for and women ain't one of 'em, not even a ripe little muff like Beth. No woman's worth it.'

'What do you know about women, Curtis?' Arthur sneered.

'Well at least I've had a few,' he responded, 'and Stone is next on my list. What she needs is a good fucking, a good roll in the hay, skirts up and legs apart.'

Arthur looked at him for a moment, his fists clenching. Then he relaxed them. 'Fuck off, Curtis,' he said and pushed past him up the street.

Without really thinking where he was going, he found himself tripping up the step into the taproom of the *Dolphin*. The smoke from the men's pipes and smell of the tallow candles almost choked him after the cold fresh night air. He was still smarting from the drubbing John Grayling had given him. Arthur hated to be made a fool of, especially when he was so sure he was right. It wasn't right for them to talk about Beth like that, but he was a fool to have risen to the bait. They were always talking like that, about the women they had had, or would like to have. It was a dangerous game to play with these men. They were mostly rough and tough and Grayling had a job on his hands keeping them in order. The other men might be older than Arthur was, but who was to say they always knew best? It could not be denied that when they were drunk, they were clumsy and slow. Surely it made sense to have them sober? Arthur calculated they could have shifted the load almost twice as quickly if they were working at full efficiency.

'Hello Arthur. You haven't been this way for a time. Thought you were always at the *Red Lion*. Isn't their ale to your taste no more?'

Arthur looked up from the corner seat he had occupied to see the barmaid, Harriett Marshall, smiling teasingly at him. He smiled back. 'Got thrown out,' he said sheepishly.

'Ooh you must have upset someone. And looks like you came off worse.' She gently touched his reddened cheek. 'You can tell me about it,' she invited. 'Want some ale?'

He nodded and she went back to the bar, returning with a jug and two tankards, a hunk of bread and some yellow cheese. She pushed the wooden plate in front of him. 'I've an idea where you've been. Oh, I know how you like to keep it secret,' she said. 'Ned Savage was in here. He said that all hadn't gone according to plan. So I'll guess you've been out all evening without a bite to eat, wherever it is you might have been, if you want to play your cards that close to your chest.'

Arthur nodded and Harriett sat down opposite him. He wasn't sure if she was teasing him but all the same, it was nice to have her attention. He liked the way her thick brown hair escaping from her cap, swung in tendrils across her cheeks. Her face, which could sometimes look quite pinched, was transformed when she smiled. Arthur knew that her husband Samuel had died last winter and that Harriett, as well as working at the *Dolphin* now also took in washing. He noticed that her hands were red and chafed as she put the food and drink in front of him.

'Go on then, eat up,' she commanded.

Arthur quickly tore off a hunk of bread and bit into the cheese realising again just how empty his belly was. Harriett watched him sympathetically as he washed the first few mouthfuls down with a swig of beer and then she took a sip of her own. 'Well, do you want to tell me about it? Why did you get thrown out? Did you cheek the landlord? I wouldn't have thought John Beaver's a man to take offence, nor to belt you one.'

Arthur shook his head, his mouth full and then said, 'No, he didn't throw me out. We all went back to the *Red Lion*. It was John Grayling who clouted me. I punched John Turner. He said something, well, something rude about Beth, you know? They were all drunk. I shouldn't have done it but I couldn't help it. And John Grayling thinks I cheeked him, but I didn't, not really.'

'I know you're keen on Beth Stone, but you shouldn't mind what they say, you know, Arthur. Men will say anything when they've had a few – take my word for that. Still, John Grayling is a fair sort of man, I should think, though no grown man wants to take advice from a lad, even one as big as you,' she laughed. 'How old are you now, sixteen?'

'Fifteen last November,' Arthur said.

Harriett looked thoughtful.

'I would have thought,' Arthur went on, 'that doing the thing properly would be to everyone's advantage. We could unload more quickly, with less risk. We lost the tide and probably half the cargo, so now we have to come back tomorrow morning and run the goods inward in daylight. It's not worth going home tonight.'

'Are you staying with Jeremiah Curtis again?' Harriett asked.

Arthur nodded.

'He's a strange one, that one. And I take it you don't want to?'

Arthur shrugged his shoulders. 'Bloody, bloody shithead!' was all he said, and then added, 'I beg pardon, Harriett.'

Harriett smiled and got up. 'Drink up, Arty, I'll bring you another.'

It was past midnight when the last of the drinkers had been persuaded to make their way home and Arthur was still sitting in his corner, his head comfortably light from the ale and his belly satisfied not only with the bread and cheese, but with the remains of a cold rabbit pie Harriett had brought him. Used to living with his father and Will, it was a pleasant change to be waited on by a pretty woman and Harriett's soothing words did much to salve his bruised ego.

Arthur heard Harriett call goodnight to Thomas Beane, the *Dolphin's* landlord and then she came up to him, a thick woollen shawl round her shoulders. 'Come on Arthur, you can stay with me. I've two rooms in Watchbell Lane, not a step away. The children are in my other bed, but there's a chair you can sleep on.'

Arthur nodded and let Harriett take his arm. She was as tall as he was, but she was thin and hardly seemed substantial at all as they stepped out into the night.

The house where Harriet rented two back rooms on the ground floor was a tall narrow building in a row of six. She unlocked the front door with a key she pulled out from a ribbon round her neck and put her finger up to her lips. 'Shhh, don't wake the children.'

She led him down a black hallway. At the end were two doors facing each other. She quietly opened one and Arthur peering in as his eyes got used to the light of one candle on an old chest, could just about make out a low bed at the end of the room, the three small shapes in it being Harriett's two daughters and her son. Although the tallow candle gave out the usual animal fatty smell, the room was full of linen hanging on lines criss-crossing the room, which smelt nicely Arthur thought, of soap. The embers of a fire were dying in a grate at the other side of the room.

'I always leave a candle in the room for them. Mrs Swan upstairs keeps an eye on them for me, in exchange for her washing,' Harriett said, as if she was ashamed at leaving her children here alone night after night.

Such a thought never even entered Arthur's head, familiar as he was with his own father's careless custody of himself and Will. He suddenly felt a well of affection and respect for Harriett because she was anxious that he shouldn't think ill of her.

'Here's the chair for you,' she said unnecessarily, indicating the one in front of him. 'I'll bring you in a blanket and a pillow.'

She disappeared into the room opposite. Arthur took off his greatcoat and hung it over the back of the chair trying not to make any noise. At home he would normally throw a pillow at Will to wake him up if he came in late and Will, roused from his slumber would mutter crossly and roll over back to sleep at once not even waking when Arthur got into bed beside him and put his cold feet on the backs of his brother's warm legs. However Will was almost ten and not likely to make a fuss, whereas Arthur knew Harriett's children were much younger, besides which two of them were girls who would very likely cry if he accidentally woke them.

There was a small sound at the doorway and Harriett came back into the room. She came up to Arthur holding a blanket and pillow in front of her and Arthur noticed she had undressed and put on a nightgown. Her pale bare feet showed at the hem and though it had long sleeves, it was cut low in front and Arthur saw her thin chemise just covering her breasts, underneath it. He felt embarrassed but also excited at the presence of a grown woman in front of him wearing so little. He was reminded of Kat Lambert who had let him feel her soft warm breast in exchange for a farthing all those years ago. Harriett held out the blanket and pillow which he took and which he in turn held in front of him.

'Well, Arthur.' She gave a shy laugh and said softly, 'Good night,' kissing him on the cheek. She drew back her head quickly and then as quickly again thrust her face towards him and kissed him on the lips. Arthur clutched the blanket and pillow tightly but pressed his lips against Harriett's with equal pressure and then felt her hands on his shoulders. She took the bedclothes from him and dropped them to the floor at the side, stepping closer to him and pressed her body against his. Arthur, roused at once with all the vigour that only fifteen-year-old boyhood could produce and hardly able to believe what might be about to happen, put his arms around her but she was already pushing him towards the door.

'Not in here,' she whispered and before he knew it, she had backed him into her room opposite and closed the door. There was no candle and only the faint gleam of moonlight from the one small window. He could hardly see, but Harriett, familiar with the room, took his hand and led him to the bed, lifted the covers and got in pulling him on top of her, her hands already impatient with his shirt and breeches. Arthur, confronted for the second time in his life with a woman's naked body not only compliant but eager for his touch, hardly knew where to begin. His own body led him to the right place and his uncertainty was guided by Harriett's experienced hands and mouth, so it seemed that almost before it had begun, it was over and Arthur lay panting on top of her, unwilling to move until she said, 'Roll over, Arthur, you're squashing me.'

He lay on his back, not sure what to do, his mind still reeling from the experience of doing with a woman, what he had up until then, only done with himself. 'Shall I go next door?' he asked.

Harriett laughed and propped herself up on one elbow, looking at him in the shaft of moonlight. 'No my dear, not unless you want to.' She touched his lower lip with her forefinger. 'Don't you want to do it again?'

Arthur raised his eyebrows in the dark. 'I dunno. I think so. Am I supposed to?'

She laughed again, pulled the blankets up and nestled against him. 'You can do whatever you want, Arthur.'

Given such a generous invitation, Arthur availed himself of it most of the night until before dawn, Harriett gently pushed him away laughing softly. 'I need some sleep, Arty, even if you don't. Ain't you got to be back at Dungeness at six? And you don't have to go on nailing me as if there's no tomorrow. I'll be here next time you're in Rye.'

CHAPTER ELEVEN

The 'Ship in Distress' alehouse, Rye, late August 1729

John Turner emptied the last of the brandy down his throat and wiped his sleeve across his mouth. He pushed the empty plate away from him and pulled his heavy pistol out of his pocket and laid it on the table in front of him. It was an old brass and wood piece from the *Tower* armoury. And he had killed a man with it once. Back in the year 02, he thought. Or was it 03? What did it matter? The man had been a Marsh farmer who had objected to Turner and Holman shearing his sheep and taking their fleeces over to France to sell to French wool merchants. Though he hadn't been involved in a run involving wool for many years, he still thought of himself as an Owler. They were good days, he reflected – two or three men could run forty fleeces or more over the channel in a night and come back with gold in their pockets. Now it needed thirty, forty, fifty men a time to manage the business these days and it was becoming a young man's job. Turner sighed. He was fifty one. 'Don't need no lads telling me my business,' he mumbled to himself and hearing the church clock strike twelve, looked out of the window into the daylight in the Strand to see if there was any sign of the fellow he had asked to meet him there.

Jeremiah Curtis stepped into the doorway of the *Ship in Distress* and looked round for the bulky figure of John Turner. He didn't particularly like Turner but he said he had a proposition to put to him. Curtis had agreed to meet him there. Besides, he had an eye to Becky Sadler, one of the barmaids. He had nothing else to do that afternoon and Becky, with her plump shoulders and tumbled brown curls would spread well on his bed, Curtis thought. Seeing Turner, he ambled in and sat down opposite him. Turner didn't speak but nodded his acknowledgment and raising his eyes to Becky, ordered a couple of drinks. Neither man spoke until Becky had brought the drinks and they had taken a couple of mouthfuls.

'Don't think you have much regard for Gray?' Turner said at last.

Curtis said nothing.

'I reckon he has too much to say for hisself. Been rattlin' me all year,' Turner stated, picking up his pistol and putting it back in his greatcoat pocket.

'So?' Curtis asked, eyeing him keenly. 'You gonna shoot him?'

Turner laughed. 'No, no. Ain't doing no shootin', Curtis. Think he needs a lesson, though.'

'What's this got to do with me, Turner?' Curtis asked, already sounding bored.

'Need you to tell Gray to be at a certain place at a certain time, is all. Now, are you up for that or not?'

Curtis shrugged his shoulders, straining his neck to look through into the taproom where Becky was bending over pouring a drink, giving him an interesting view of her bosom as she leaned forward. 'What's in it for me, Turner?'

Turner jerked his head in the direction of the taproom. 'Like what you see, do you?'

Curtis looked back at the older man. 'Maybe.'

'She's a plump little pigeon. Coos nicely when she's plucked, if you get my drift.'

Curtis raised his eyebrows. 'And?'

'And she's my pigeon, Curtis. She owes me some money and what with the interest I charge her, it don't seem like she'll never pay it off, so she pays me any way she can. Knows she could be locked up for debt if I was to hand this piece of paper over to one of the Jurats,' he said, referring to the law keepers of Rye and tapping his breast pocket. 'But she can be yours for a couple of afternoons – and all you gotta do is tell Gray there's a get-together before the next run.'

'Call her over,' Curtis said, indicating Becky.

Turner caught her eye as she was going back to the bar and she came over. He drew his chair out and patted his knee. She obediently came and sat on it, putting one arm round his shoulder. He cupped her chin more firmly than was necessary and then kissed her hard on the mouth.

'Not here, Jack,' she said, nervously, looking over to the landlord.

'Becky girl, you like the look o' Curtis here, don't you?'

She looked at the dark-haired youth, half smiling but said nothing.

'I want you to be friendly toward him when he asks you to and we'll say that's this week's payment accounted for, unless you happen to have the money?'

She shook her head. 'You know I'm already behind with my rent.'

'Well, then, my girl, here's the answer for you and no one is asking you to do nothin' you ain't done before, eh?' He turned to Curtis, jigging the girl up and down on his knee. 'She's a cosy armful and does what she's told. Not got much conversation. Makes most sense when she's on her back,' he added, talking about the girl as if she wasn't there. He tipped Becky off his knee and pushed her towards Curtis. He caught her and drew her down to him with one hand, brushing his palm lightly over her bosom as he did so and then pushed her back up. It would add a certain piquancy to know he had got her as part of a deal. It made her his goods.

She adjusted her lace. She smiled with her mouth but her eyes looked lifeless.

'Very well, Turner. You've got a deal. I'll take her off your hands for a couple of days.'

Turner spat on his hand and held it out to Curtis. 'All you got to do is tell Gray to be in Turkeycock Lane without fail next Wednesday night, half before eight and wait there. Tell him Grayling has something to tell some of us about the next run, only some of us, mind. Let Gray think he's one of the chosen few. He's so cocky he won't resist that. And he mustn't fail. Think you can do that?'

'Oh yes,' Curtis replied coolly. 'I can do that.'

'It's a deal then. And Becky's yourn Wednesday night til Friday.'

'Til Saturday,' Curtis countered.

Turner frowned and then nodded. The men shook hands and the deal was made. Curtis went over to Becky before leaving, whispered in her ear and pinched her cheek. It left a red mark and she put a hand up to her face as she watched him walk out of the door. She glanced back to Turner to see that he was looking at her closely.

'But what's it about, Curtis?' Arthur asked the next day. He had stayed the night in Rye with Harriett. They shared a bed with comfort and familiarity now and he always slept well after their lovemaking, Harriett curled up in front of him, her thin hips tucked up against his belly, his arm thrown across her small breasts. He still thought of Beth as his girl and wished she would do what Harriett did with him. But Beth was still only fifteen and if he went too far with her, if he tried to cup her breasts under her stays, she would pull away, disconcerted and uncomfortable; leaving Arthur cursing himself for his over-eagerness and all the more desperate to see Harriett again – Harriett who was always pleased to see him and took the trouble to show him how a woman liked to be pleased, as well as demonstrate how many ways a woman might please her man. He put away the thoughts of Harriett and Beth and looked again at Curtis.

'Grayling don't usually call a meeting before a run.'

Curtis shrugged. 'Grayling will tell us on Wednesday, I guess. It's something to do with the next run, that's all he said.'

'But Turkeycock Lane? Why there?' Arthur asked, as they sauntered down Longer Street.

'Grayling don't care to talk about it in the *Red Lion*, or the *Mermaid*. Maybe he wants to use Town Ditch as a hiding place for run goods. Your guess is as good as mine.'

'And we're all to be there?'

Curtis shook his head. 'No, not everyone. Just a few of us that he depends on. I'll be there but I may be late. I've already told Grayling. But don't fail, Gray. I think there's something big about to happen.'

Arthur nodded. 'All right. I'll be there.'

The following Wednesday, Late August, 1729, Turkeycock Lane, Rye

Arthur leaned his shoulders against the wall, his hands in his pockets and wondered what could be so urgent about the next run that he must wait here to hear it. He heard the town clock strike the half hour and then the hour and was about to give up when he heard footsteps and voices coming round the end house of the small terrace and saw John Turner, Larry Jockey and Thomas Holman approaching. He knew instantly that something was amiss and at the back of his mind realised that Curtis had helped set him up. Arthur had known that Turner would want to get his revenge for being punched at the *Red Lion* earlier in the year and knew that this was the moment when he would be required to pay for his actions. The men looked grim and uncompromising. He looked around quickly but there was a dead end behind him and he realised he was trapped. The three men spread out in front of Arthur and Turner said unpleasantly, 'Well, Gray, I believe we have a reckoning, you and me.'

Arthur looked defiantly at him. 'Come on then, Turner, just you and me.' He looked nervously at Jockey and Holman. He might stand a chance against Turner alone, simply by being more agile for the men were all in their fifties, but he knew that he couldn't hope to compete against the three of them.

'Oh, it will be just you and me, Gray, with Holman and Jockey holding on to you, just in case you thought you might run for it.'

Realising that he wouldn't stand a chance if he was held down, Arthur suddenly darted to his left in the gap between Turner and Holman but Holman gripped his coat and tugged it round, bringing Arthur to a sudden halt. Holman grasped his left arm and twisted it up painfully behind his back. Larry Jockey did the same with his right arm and Turner stood two feet in front of him, as Arthur struggled between the two men. He became aware that he would not be able to escape their hold and stood still for a moment meeting Turner's gaze.

He thought perhaps Turner had changed his mind, for he simply stood there. Arthur relaxed slightly and let out his breath. Just at that moment, the big man swung his right fist up punching hard in Arthur's belly just below his rib cage. Arthur doubled up in pain, groaning, but his two captors swung him upright again so that Turner's left fist came crashing into Arthur's jaw setting his ears ringing and the taste of blood in his mouth. Turner's right fist quickly followed his left, catching Arthur's temple and the socket of his left eye leaving him unable to see and feeling the blood running down his face. Then another hard blow to his belly knocked the wind out of him and he struggled to catch his breath. Though the blows to his face were acutely painful, it was the punches to his belly that did most damage, leaving his legs shaking, his mind given over only to blotting out the pain. After that, he lost track of the blows.

'That'll do, Jack, eh?' Larry Jockey said uneasily, feeling the youth go limp in his grip.

'Aye,' Holman agreed. 'He'll have learnt his lesson.' He let go of Arthur's arm and Jockey did the same. Arthur slumped to his knees, unhearing.

Turner, his face red and sweating, looked down at him. 'There's just one more thing,' he said, digging into his greatcoat pocket and unstopping the flask he had drawn out. 'Needs to acquire a taste for the spirits, don't he?'

He pulled Arthur's head up by grabbing hold of his hair and forced the mouth of the bottle between his lips. Arthur instinctively spat it out but Turner got behind him and pinched Arthur's bleeding nose, forcing the bottle into his mouth again. 'That's right, boy. Swallow it down or stop fucking breathing. It's up to you. You'll soon get a taste for the unlowered stuff!'

Jockey, uncomfortable at hearing Arthur's gasps and coughs as the undiluted brandy went down his throat and spilled down the front of his shirt and coat, now covered in blood, said with some alarm, 'That's enough Jack. We don't want no killing done. He's only a lad after all.'

Turner seemed not to hear and continued to tip the spirits down the boy's throat, until Holman made a sudden movement and went to grab the bottle from him.

'Larry's in the right of it, Jack,' he said pulling the bottle away.

Turner turned to face him clenching his fist and Holman instinctively shifted his head back.

Turner laughed unpleasantly. 'That's right Tom, best keep out of my reach, eh?' He let go of Arthur who slumped forward onto his face. Turner looked down at him. 'Reckon he'll think twice now before he lashes out at his elders and betters, eh?'

He moved to go but then thought better of it and turned back. He stood looking down at Arthur's limp body. Then with a vicious movement, he kicked Arthur in the ribs, his heavy boot slamming into his unresisting victim. Holman and Jockey were standing silently waiting for Turner to finish and then all three men hurried away, as in the distance the town clock chimed the half hour. Larry Jockey looked over his shoulder as they turned into Conduit Hill, to see if there was any movement, but the prone figure they had left behind gave no sign of life at all.

Rachel Tourney sighed as she carried the two large buckets over her shoulders in the heavy wooden yoke. For some reason the pump in the yard at the back of the handsome house she worked at was not working and for the past two mornings she had had to start her day by going to the pump at Town Ditch at the bottom of Conduit Hill and carrying the heavy buckets full of water back to the house.

She was just about to turn to go along to the pump when she heard a dog barking in Turkeycock Lane. She wouldn't have thought more about it, but the dog didn't stop; it carried on barking constantly, almost keeping to a rhythm. She looked up to the end of the lane. Yes there he was, she had noticed him around here before, a sandy-haired mongrel with a tattered ear but a friendly face. She had seen him stealing scraps of meat from the butchers in Middle Street and hanging around the *Dolphin*. He seemed to be standing over a pile of rags. Rachel put the buckets down and walked slowly towards the dog.

'What is it then, boy?' she said soothingly. 'What's there?'

As she got nearer, she stopped in her tracks as she realised the shape was a man. She could smell the spirits on him but also the smell of vomit and at first she didn't know if he was dead drunk, or dead. She looked more closely and her instinct told her he was still alive. The mongrel had stopped barking and was looking at Rachel expectantly, wagging its tail.

'Oh I don't think we want to stay here boy,' she said nervously. 'Come away from the nasty man.' As she spoke there was a shudder and a groan from the body lying in front of her and she stepped back, wondering whether to go and fetch the Constable and then realised he wouldn't be at his work yet.

With determined steps, she hurried back along the street and up Conduit Hill, the dog watching her go as if he knew she was fetching help. Robert Spain, her employer's house servant would be up by now, Rachel thought. She enjoyed a bantering, easy-going friendship with him which she hoped would develop into something more with a little encouragement. He was open and honest and had been about a bit. Robert would know what to do.

Five minutes later, Rachel was back in Turkeycock Lane with Robert. The man on the ground hadn't moved and the dog was still sitting next to him.

'God have mercy, Rachel, he's had a skinful ain't he?' Robert exclaimed, smelling the brandy. He bent down to touch the man's shoulder to turn him over. As he did so, both he and Rachel gasped in horror to see the beaten face, one eye swollen and closed and a dark bruise over his jaw. There was dried blood around his nose and mouth, as well as stains down his shirt and coat, a mixture of brandy, blood and vomit.

Rachel turned quickly away, put her hand to her mouth, retched twice and was sick, her breaths coming fast. Robert ignored her as he slipped an arm beneath the shoulders of the unknown victim.

'Leave off, Rachel and go and fill one of your buckets. Be quick,' he snapped.

Glad of something to do, she rushed away to collect the bucket she had left at the corner of the street and hurried to the pump swinging the handle quickly.

When she returned, Robert had propped the fellow up against the wall and said over his shoulder as she approached, 'Here, tip it slowly over him. That might bring him round.'

Rachel did as she was told, upending the bucket. At first it seemed to have no effect but as the steady stream of water poured over Arthur, he coughed twice and then groaned and tried to open his eyes.

'Why, I know who this is,' she said, recognition dawning, for her best friend was Harriett Marshall and a couple of months ago Rachel, calling unexpectedly early one Sunday had disturbed her friend and her young lover in bed. The young man, embarrassed, had quickly dressed and gone on his way. Though his face was battered and the features distorted, the water had washed away the filth from it and Rachel recognised him in astonishment.

'His name is Arthur Gray,' she said. She knew from Harriett's rather hurried explanation that he was concerned with the smuggling gangs and she immediately assumed this punishment he had taken was somehow connected.

'Well, someone is not very pleased with him, Rach,' Robert exclaimed.

'He's only a lad, Robert, not more than sixteen I think. But don't fetch the Constable. I don't think he would want the law involved,' Rachel explained, setting down the bucket and stooping down to look at Arthur more closely.

Robert cocked a knowing eye at her. 'How come you're familiar with him?' he asked. Before she could answer, Arthur tried to speak but his tongue was swollen, bitten with the first punch Turner had thrown and his lips were bruised where the bottle had been forced into his mouth, so his speech was unintelligible.

'All right there, my lad,' Robert said and turned back to Rachel.

'He's a friend of Harriett's,' she explained. 'That's how I know him, but he's not from here – comes from Hawkhurst I think. But truly, Rob, what are we going to do with him? Surely he needs the surgeon fetched? Can we take him to Harriett's?'

'No,' Robert said decisively. 'We'll take him back to Lamb's. He's in London, isn't he for a few days yet? And with Mrs Lamb at her sister's for the month, we'll be safe. I think someone is bound to see us if we try to convey him all the way to Harriett's rooms in Watchbell Lane. You fill the buckets as usual and I'll slip through the back alleyways and you let me in the garden door. We'll lay him in the spare garret room and no one need know he is there.'

With that, he hoisted Arthur to his feet and though he groaned as Robert's arm went round his bruised and injured torso, he managed to stay on his feet as he was half dragged down the empty street, the dog who had been his unexpected saviour, following at their heels.

All went according to plan. Even carrying Arthur aloft up the three flights of stairs was achieved without mishap. Between them, Rachel and Robert managed to divest Arthur of his clothes discovering that his chest and back were a mass of black and blue swollen bruises. There was a particularly bad wound with the skin broken over the ribs on his left side, where the steel cap of Turner's boot had caught him. Rachel took his clothes down to the kitchen intending to soak the stains out of them later on and raided the kitchen for some goose grease which was all she knew of to put on cuts and bruises.

She carried up with her a jug of milk and managed to get some of it between Arthur's swollen lips before they lowered him back down on the pillows. The little garret room at the top of the house was becoming very warm. Robert threw open the window and immediately the cooling air blew into the room. The crying of the seagulls out at sea and the sounds of the busy town coming to life soon lulled Arthur to the healing sleep his body needed.

He awoke ten hours later to a great hubbub outside the garret door. The door was thrown open and a finely dressed gentleman, whom Arthur even in his drowsy state immediately recognised as Thomas Lamb, came in. Just behind him Robert and Rachel and Mrs Peppiat, Mr Lamb's housekeeper, all talking at once, were trying to cross the threshold.

'Good God,' Lamb exclaimed seeing Arthur lying in the little bed, his face bruised and swollen. 'What in the name of heaven is going on here?'

'I knew something was going on sir, when Tourney here starts soaking a man's clothes in the kitchen thinking I was gone off for the afternoon. You bring shame to this house, girl, bringing your lover here,' Mrs Peppiatt declared, rounding on Rachel.

'Indeed, sir, he ain't my lover. That's not it at all,' she protested to her employer with an anxious look.

'No,' Thomas Lamb said with a decisive nod. 'I don't believe he is but you may all get back to your work and leave me to find out from this young man what he is doing in my house.'

With that, he ushered them back down the stairs, closed the door, drew up a chair and sat opposite Arthur. He had been shaken when he saw the youth, recognizing Gray at once in spite of the appalling injuries to his face. He knew well that the lad ran with the smugglers. He looked at him thoughtfully for a moment, before laying his hand over Arthur's saying, 'Well, Arthur Gray, if I'm not mistaken? What befell you, lad?'

Arthur, who had struggled up on his elbows when the room was invaded by so many unexpected visitors, sank back down on his pillows drawing his breath in sharply as the pain in his ribs stabbed. 'I don't remember, sir,' he said thickly, his head still spinning from the effects of the brandy that Turner had forced down his throat, as well as from the beating.

'Come lad, you can do better than that,' Mr Lamb said encouragingly. 'My man tells me you stank of spirits. Is that it?' Arthur remained silent and then Lamb said quietly and with some feeling, 'Arthur, I think and very much hope that these wounds did not come from falling whilst you were in liquor.'

Lamb's eyes held the youth's and after a few moments, Arthur said with difficulty, 'A man thought I had done him an injustice and sought justice from me.'

'And the brandy?' Lamb asked. 'Had you been drinking that before he sought this justice from you?'

Arthur shook his head. 'That was part of his justice,' he said. 'He forced unlowered brandy down my throat until – well until I didn't remember no more.'

'And this is the truth, Gray? On your mother's soul?'

Arthur looked quickly up at the older man at the mention of his mother. 'On my mother's soul, sir, I swear it's the truth.'

Thomas Lamb looked thoughtfully at Arthur and knew instinctively that he was indeed telling the truth and felt relieved and justified that his faith in the lad's integrity had not been misplaced. 'And the man who meted out this '*justice*'? Is that the end of it?'

Arthur nodded and tentatively put a hand up to his bruised jaw and mouth. 'I hope he feels we're quits now.' He tried to laugh but the pain in his side wrenched a gasp from him and the older man noticed how he had paled.

Lamb pulled back the bedclothes to his waist. 'Merciful God,' he gasped, visibly shaken, looking at the bruises covering Arthur's chest and abdomen. He noticed how the youth's body shook slightly with the effort of each indrawn breath. 'What sort of injustice can you have done to deserve such a punishment?' He dropped the sheet back and stood up going over to the window, rubbing a hand over his face. A fishing boat out at sea bobbed gently on the waves.

'Look here, lad,' he said gently. 'I know who you run with and I don't expect names from you. But I am going to fetch my surgeon Halley, to you. Don't worry,' he added, putting up a hand as Arthur raised his head to protest. 'I'll furnish him with a story to raise no suspicions. But you may have broken ribs, or worse. Are you bringing up blood?'

Arthur nodded. 'But I think it's coming from my mouth, not from my belly.'

'Well, Halley will know,' Lamb answered. He turned back to the bed and sat down again next to Arthur. 'You're to be thankful my pump isn't working, Gray. For if young Rachel Tourney hadn't gone to fetch water, you might even now be lying dead in Turkeycock Lane.'

Arthur glanced at him through the one eye he could open, wondering how much Thomas Lamb knew about his connection with Grayling's Gang. 'It's good of you, sir, but I don't know why you're showing me such kindness.'

Lamb's eyes met his gaze and he paused before answering. 'Let's just say that I do it for the kindness I have for someone who is close to you.'

Arthur tried to think what he might mean but his head started to throb and the great pain in his side soon stopped him from thinking about anything at all, apart from how he might bear it. Thomas Lamb looked again at the youth, his expression both compassionate and pensive and then hurried out of the room calling to Robert Spain to fetch Halley with all haste.

CHAPTER TWELVE

January 1730

A hard winter in '29 and '30 forced a lull in Arthur's activities with the gang. Deep falls of snow across the Marsh made it difficult to run the goods, the horses and men often getting stuck in drifts. Four horses were lost when they fell into a dyke hidden by snow, weighed down by the kegs they were carrying. Their whinnies of distress caused even the most hard-hearted of men to turn away with regret at their inability to help the beasts out. Less runs completed meant less money for everyone and it was a bleak Christmas for most of the men.

In January a fever swept though the village, taking its toll on old and young alike. Arthur returned home one morning and met Hannah Webb coming out of the house where he and his father and Will still rented the two rooms. She looked in now and then and did a bit of cooking and cleaning. Arthur noticed she had red-rimmed eyes.

'What is it, Hannah? What's wrong?' he asked.

'Oh Arthur, this dreadful fever, ague, they're calling it. Lizzie's boy, your friend Tom Kennard took it yesterday and-,' she pulled out her handkerchief, 'poor lad died this morning.' She sobbed freely, the tears welling up again as soon as she mopped them away.

Arthur could barely take it in. Tom was only a few weeks older than he was; they had played together and only drifted apart when Arthur and Lucas Webb were offered places at the charity school and Tom went to work on his uncle's farm. He felt his own eyes pricking with tears. He could say nothing.

'Sal Piper, Sal Turley that was and her newborn, both of them gone and her poor husband beside himself with grief. And your friend Beth-,'

Arthur's heart almost stopped. 'Not Beth!' He could hardly say the words. He felt the world spinning around him, unreal. *'Please God, not Beth, not Beth!'*

'No, not her, Arthur but her father, not likely to last the day, so they say.' She wiped her eyes again. 'I'm sorry to be the bringer of such bad news. I must get away. I told Lizzie I would help lay her boy out.' She wept again, patting Arthur's shoulder as she turned down the gravel path, her shoulders sagging with grief.

Arthur watched her go and then let himself in the back door and sat on the bottom step putting his head in his hands. Tom Kennard, dead. And Sal, who had been best friends with Kat Lambert, the enterprising girls who had made a bit of money out of young boys' curiosity. Sal with her quick tongue who always seemed so fit and strong. She had been married about this time last year, Arthur thought and remembered seeing her in the autumn, proud and happy in her pregnancy. Now she and the baby were both gone. And Beth's father, John Stone, likely dying. Arthur didn't know what to do. He wanted to be with Beth, wanted to put his arms round her and keep her safe from any of the bad things that life could hand out. He didn't know if he would be welcome at her house at such a time.

He stood up decisively and went back out making his way up the hill to Beth's house. He went to the back door and tapped on it looking through the window at the side to see if anyone was about. The door was quickly opened and Ruth, the little housemaid answered it, her face white and drawn. He heard Beth's voice call out anxiously, 'who is it, Ruth? Is it Mr Young the surgeon?'

'No Beth,' Arthur replied stepping into the kitchen.

'Arthur,' she exclaimed, a catch in her voice. 'You shouldn't have come, but I'm so glad you're here. You must know about my father?'

He nodded, stepped across the room and took her in his arms. She rested her head on his shoulder and said nothing for a while but he could tell by her shallow breathing that she was struggling to control her tears. 'How is he?' he asked gently.

She shook her head. 'Not well. I don't know, really. My mother won't let me see him in case I take the fever from him. She wants me to go to my aunt Ann.'

'If there's danger then you must go,' Arthur said forcibly. 'I'll take you there.' He pulled her close to his chest again.

She shook her head and said in a small voice, 'I want to stay with my mamma.'

Just at that moment they heard footsteps on the stairs and Jane Stone appeared, her cheeks pallid and a frozen expression on her face. *'The Lord giveth and the Lord taketh away. Blessed be the name of the Lord,'* she said quietly. Her face remained expressionless. Beth turned in Arthur's arms to look at her.

'Oh, you're here, Arthur?' the woman said calmly. 'That will give comfort to my Beth.'

Beth pulled herself out of his embrace and made to run over to her mother but Jane held up her hand to keep her away. 'No, don't touch me, child. I don't know how the fever is passed on.' She seemed calm, unmoving and almost serene. 'Ask Ruth to bring up some hot water to the bedchamber. I will wash and have her burn these clothes.'

She turned to Arthur. 'Will you do me the kindness of fetching Parson Saunders, Arthur? Will you tell him that John Stone, that- that John Stone has died and his wife, his widow that is – would like him to pray over his body?'

Beth burst into tears and again went to run to her mother but Arthur caught her arm and pulled her back to him. He rocked her in his arms whispering in her hair. 'It's all right, Beth. I'm here. I'll look after you.' His eyes met Jane Stone's over Beth's head as he stroked her hair. She looked as if she was about to speak but instead turned slowly and went back upstairs.

The following Sunday, Arthur and Will attended the funeral service for all four who had died. They had managed to get their father there also, before he had drunk too much and they sat towards the back of the church as Parson Saunders gave the sermon for the four departed. Arthur thought how his life had been touched by all of them. John Stone, of uneven temper, taking care of his elder brother's interests and more besides, in London in the hope that he would inherit and now here he was in his coffin, dead before the older man.

He looked at Robert Stone curiously and thought about the day he and Beth had called on him. He hardly ever came into the village, still preferring to live an almost hermit-like existence in his strange old house beyond Slip Mill Lane in the thickly wooded area and hardly ever spoke to anyone. Though he stood next to Jane Stone and his niece, it was Jane's brother-in law, William Pix, who supported her with his arm around her shoulders, his wife and two step-sons next to him. It was the first time Arthur had seen Nick and Francis since the visit to Rye for Mayor-making six years ago. Nick, nearly seventeen, was due to start working with Jeffery Pix in his attorney's office when he finished his time at university. He had grown tall and thin, with the same fair floppy hair that he had had when Arthur last saw him. Francis, shorter and darker had grown quite stout, his sweet tooth giving him a round face and podgy hands. Their mother, Ann, was still a beautiful woman not looking her thirty four years, her golden hair dressed neatly on the back of her head with little curls over her forehead giving her a girlish appearance. Beth was standing tall and straight next to her mother, listening to the service intently. Arthur didn't think she would find much comfort there. The parson had chosen a text from Ecclesiastes as the corner stone of his sermon said for all four souls: *'A good name is better than precious ointment; and the day of death better than the day of one's birth.'*

Poor Robert Piper, Sal's husband, sobbed loudly and continuously, weighed down by grief, leaning heavily upon his elderly father who held his arms tightly round his son. When the coffin was carried past him, he ran his hand gently along it, his last physical contact with his wife and tiny son. The Kennards were all present; all Tom's older brothers and sisters as well as his parents and the two little sisters. They all held hands as Tom's coffin was lowered into the ground.

Three more died the following week, but they were old folk whom Arthur hardly knew. He could not associate the grief he had felt for Tom and to some extent Sal and the grief on Beth's behalf for her father – with the deaths of these old people who had lived their lives and might have lingered in a more painful death than the relatively quick one which the fever had brought.

The fever brushed its hand over the village and left it as suddenly as it had come. The only person to take the fever and get better from it was Tom Carswell, one of Will's schoolfellows, a small quiet boy, the only surviving child of his queer, elderly widowed mother. He was at death's door one moment and the next morning he sat up and asked for bread and jam and a cup of hot milk.

Bitter cold January gave way to a mild February with none of the winds or snow it often brought. The Marsh looked green and fresh and the early windflowers pushed their heads up through the dark soil and the hardy Romney Marsh ewes dropped their lambs early. The sea kelp on Dungeness sprung up into life and the calm seas gave plenty of opportunities for many cutters to make their way from Boulogne and Dunkerque to the companies of men of Kent and Sussex waiting on the beaches to land their cargoes; the shillings Arthur earned quickly accruing to an extent which surprised even him.

And in a quiet house in London just off Hanover Square, a dark haired woman sat at her window and wondered why John Stone, her lover of many years, had neither visited nor made contact with her.

April 1730

Arthur was walking with Beth up in the Frythe Woods, north of Hawkhurst and along a pretty tract of bluebell woods known as the Upper Wish on Seacox Heath.

They stopped and looked at the wonderful view of the woodlands of Kent and Sussex spreading beneath them, calm and peaceful in the quiet April evening, the sun still warm on their bare heads and arms. They had walked in a companionable silence. Since her father's death, Beth had seemed more of a woman and less of a girl. Both she and her mother had started to rely on Arthur to help with jobs about the house that needed a man's strength or height.

'This would be a good place to have a house,' Arthur said at length, gazing over the scenery. 'Close enough to the town but peaceful. You wouldn't be bothered by people up here.'

She looked across at him. 'Are you bothered by people, Arthur? You seem at home in a crowd.'

'Oh I like a crowd well enough, but it's nice to be up here alone – alone with you, that is, Beth.'

He looked into her face trying to read the expression in her calm grey eyes and the half smile on her lips. He pulled her slowly towards him running his hands up to her shoulders and then pressing his lips to hers. He had kissed her many times but it was never quite like this with the pressure of her mouth equal to his. Then in response to his questing tongue, she opened her mouth and he tasted her lips and tongue, sweet and enticing. He drew her down to the mossy bank and buried his face in her neck, inhaling the clean soapy smell he always found so arousing. He began untying the laces at the front of her gown and paused looking into Beth's eyes. Finding no resistance, he ran his palms over the upper swell of her breasts and then searched under her skirts and petticoats until he felt the silky softness of her thighs and the gentle roundness of her buttocks as he slipped a hand beneath her, drawing her to him.

He struggled to undo the lacing of her stays, but eventually they were cast aside and there was only the fine lawn of her chemise between them. He took the hem and gently lifted it up the length of her body. Beth raised her arms and drew it off, laying it on the grass next to her and then she remained still, half smiling up at him, as Arthur struggled to remove his own clothes. He didn't want to take his eyes off the swell of her breasts, the nipples rising as they were exposed to the air, and he laid a hand on her small flat belly flat trailing his hand to the mound of dark hair where her thighs met and where Arthur was longing to press himself.

She was shy but she didn't shrink from his touch and he felt the lines and contours of her body with a kind of wonder, often drawing his head away to look at her. She was as beautiful as he had dreamed she would be, her naked body as alluring as he had imagined from the moment he had first kissed her on Mayor-making day six years ago.

She whispered his name as she lay under him and when he could no longer hold himself back, she gave a small gasp when he breached her inner softness. He wanted so much to bring her pleasure but lost himself in his own delight. He shuddered as he felt her small movements under him. She lay still and soft beneath him, a little uncertain whether it was over, her hands clasped round his neck.

He looked down into her eyes, kissed her mouth and sighed. 'Oh Beth, I do love you so.'

CHAPTER THIRTEEN

July 1730, Hawkhurst

Will, coming out of school at five, swung his books above his head, the old leather strap threatening to break and fling them all asunder if it did so. Will wouldn't have minded. He hated school. His school mate Jim Cook felt the same and both of them wanted to leave and start working with Arthur. Jim's cousin, Ben Raven lived in Rye and also worked with Grayling's men. Most of Will's schoolfellows had fathers or brothers connected with the gang, if not by taking part in the runs, then by receiving some of the cheap goods that were run. Apart from two of the lads whose fathers were in crafts that they could follow and William Sturt who wanted to be a soldier, all the boys expected to have some work with the gang when their brief time at school was finished. Neither Will nor Jim could see the point of endless days spent listening to Penfold, or repeating parrot-fashion algebraic formulae or the catechism when Parson Saunders visited, when they both felt their futures lay with the gangs.

'Coming out birding this evening?' Jim asked, as they made their way along the Moor. 'There's a pair of Stone Curlews I seen in Marlpit Fields meadow.'

Will nodded. 'I'll see you about seven. I'll have to get back before nine, though. Arthur's out again tonight, down at Bulverhythe same as last night. I'll have to stay in with my Dad.'

Jim nodded. He knew that John Gray's erratic behaviour meant that one or other of his sons had to keep an eye on him until he fell in a drunken stupor on his bed for the night.

But when Will got home and made his way up the two flights of stairs, there was no sign of his brother. Normally Arthur got back from a run in the morning and went straight to bed, getting up some time in the afternoon. Will found his father asleep in a chair.

He shook his father's arm hesitantly. 'Dad!' There was no response. He tried again.

This time John Gray lifted his head from his chest and opened one eye. 'Whassamatter?' he slurred.

'Where's Arthur, Dad? Has he been back?'

Gray looked at his younger son and then closed his eyes, shaking his head. 'Naaa.'

Will looked round to see if there was any sign that Arthur had come back and gone out again but everything was as it had been this morning. He left his father sleeping and went back downstairs and out into the road. He almost bumped into Jim Cook coming from the other direction.

'Have you heard, Will?' Jim looked worried.

'What?'

Jim paused, looking closely at Will before answering. 'One of the men got shot!'

Will stared at him. 'Who? Who got shot?'

Jim shook his head. 'He didn't say.'

Will took Jim's arm and gave it a little shake. 'Who didn't say, Jim? I can't make sense of it.'

Jim paused and took a deep breath. 'The carrier come up from Hastings. Says there was a shooting at Bulverhythe. Is that where they were?'

Will nodded. He felt his legs weaken as though they were going to bend under him and he put his hand on Jim's shoulder.

'He didn't know who it was,' Jim continued. 'Man's dead though. Shot through the head. What'll you do, Will?'

Will stared back at Jim. 'I dunno. What can I do?'

Then he knew what he would do. He would go and tell Beth. She might know how they could find out more. He started off up the road, looking back at Jim over his shoulder. 'I'll be at Beth Stone's if you find out anymore. You come and tell me straight away, right?'

Jim nodded.

Beth was in the garden at the back of her house standing on a little wooden ladder, her upper body hidden amongst the branches of an apple tree. Ruth was standing below holding a basket and put the apples in as Beth passed them down to her. Ruth saw Will first and called up to Beth. She pushed a couple of branches aside and smiled at him.

'Hello Will, would you like to help? Some of the best apples are right at the top of the tree and neither of us can reach. Perhaps you could knock some of them down with a pole? Will? Will?'

She clambered down the ladder and ran over to him, taking his hand, looking at his white face. 'What is it Will? It's Arthur, isn't it? Oh, tell me Will.'

He shook his head. 'No. Yes. I don't know. One of the men has been shot dead!'

He suddenly burst into tears. Beth took him in her arms, her chin resting on the top of his head. She couldn't speak for a moment, waiting for him to tell her more. She felt her own heart racing.

Will, embarrassed at his tears, pulled away from her and dipped in his pocket for a handkerchief. He wiped his eyes. 'I'm sorry, if I frightened you. That's all I know. The carrier came up from Hastings. He didn't know any more. What should we do?'

Beth looked at Will's frightened face. Will was relying on her strength as she relied on Arthur's. But she couldn't think beyond her own fear.

'Should we ride down to Hastings, Beth?' he asked.

'I think we should go to your house. That's where word will come if – if there's any news, that's where word will come. I'll just run in and tell my mother and then we'll go back.'

Will nodded, feeling better now that this trouble was shared with Beth and she had taken charge. She and Will sat on the grassy bank outside the house, not talking, just waiting.

Towards nine as the setting sun sank lower and lower, they heard a solitary horse making its way up the road. Will ran forward. Beth couldn't bear to look. Then she heard Will's cry. 'It's him! It's Arthur. My brother's alive.' She picked up her skirts and ran after Will, both of them falling into Arthur's arms as he slid from the horse, tired, dishevelled and shaken by the events of the previous night, but alive.

Sitting in Jane Stone's kitchen with a plate of cold beef, bread and cheese and a large tankard of ale before him, Arthur explained briefly what had happened. It wasn't for women's ears, he thought and he tried to make as light of it as he could. The Riding Officer for Bulverhythe must have been tipped off, for he was there waiting with two Dragoons. There was an exchange of fire and Tom Catt, one of Moreton's men, working out of Groombridge, had been shot. But there was a rumour that the two Dragoons had themselves already been indicted for murder.

The run had been quickly completed, the goods temporarily laid up in safe houses, ready to run onwards when things had calmed down.

Arthur ran a hand over his face 'That's it, really,' he said. He looked at his audience and half smiled. 'I'm tired, I need to go home.'

Jane Stone had listened in horror. She suspected her daughter was in love with Arthur but Beth had not confided in her mother. Jane noticed how Beth followed every word that Arthur spoke, her eyes never leaving his face.

Will, thankful that Arthur was now safe, was aware that his feelings were a mixture of a morbid thrill at his brother's description of a close brush with violent death, shared equally with an exhilaration at the picture Arthur unconsciously sketched of the excitement and comradeship that came from working with the gangs.

As Arthur stood at the door ready to go, Jane Stone went to her kitchen cupboard to give Will some of the cold beef which they hadn't eaten leaving Beth and Arthur alone for a moment.

Beth looked up at him putting her arms round him tightly and kissed him pulling his head down to hers. 'I'm so glad that you're safe. I couldn't bear to lose you,' she said, her voice shaking a little.

'Beth, I don't want this trouble to be yours,' Arthur stated quietly.

She looked up into his eyes again. 'This trouble is mine,' she said. Then as Will came up she let her arms drop.

Arthur looked down at her, surprised and moved at the depth of the emotion in her voice.

He walked back with Will and they fell into bed. Will with the ease of childhood, dropped off to sleep quickly but Arthur lay on his back, thinking. Though his body was weary, his mind was racing and he couldn't stop reliving the events of the night.

About sixty men, both Hawkhurst and Groombridge Gang members were working together, along a wide expanse of the beach. When they were a mile inland, Catt and one other of the Groombridge men had become isolated, when one of their horses went lame. They had all heard the shot and come running, but it was too late and Tom Catt lay face down, his blood and brains spilling out onto the rough track, his own pistol still in its holster, unloaded and unfired.

The two Gang leaders had worked together quickly. The local Justice was knocked up by Moreton himself and a deposition made. The Justice seemed to be on good terms with Moreton and frowned when he listened to the story and issued a warrant for the two Dragoons. Catt's body was taken before the surgeon in Hastings and then carried home by his companions to his wife in Frant.

There had been no lookouts, or not enough, Arthur thought and what was the point in taking a weapon if it wasn't loaded? Though Arthur admired the way Grayling and Moreton managed large companies of men, he thought he might do things differently if he was in charge. He wouldn't split the men into such small groups of ones and twos. Their strength lay in their numbers. If you carried weapons they should be ready for use, he reflected and then wondered, if he himself had been carrying a pistol, could he have turned it on another man? Could he have cocked it and feeling the smooth brass trigger with his forefinger, squeezed it to fire its lead ball into another man's body?

He looked across at Will, snoring lightly, his face half illuminated by a shaft of moonlight. Arthur turned on his side and closed his eyes but it wasn't until the pale pink fingers of the dawn brushed across the sky that he fell into a dreamless sleep.

CHAPTER FOURTEEN

August 1730, Hawkhurst

Arthur was walking up the Moor when he noticed a woman coming towards him. She wasn't one of the local women and she was dressed much finer then they were accustomed to. The lace at her bosom and elbows was very white, her dress was of silk and not of the cambric that the local women wore and her mass of dark hair gave her an exotic look. He passed her by wondering who she was and as soon as he passed, he realised he had seen her before. He thought again and remembered the dark haired woman on John Stone's arm at St Bartholomew's Fair. Mrs Gresham.

He turned round and she turned at the same moment, recognition also dawning in her eyes. He bowed slightly and she smiled and came up to him.

'I can't remember your name, but I remember your face. Though you have certainly grown.'

'Arthur Gray,' he said politely. 'And I remember your name, Mrs Gresham. I didn't expect to see you here.'

She said nothing for a moment and then took his arm. 'Is there an inn with a private parlour where I might have some conversation with you? I know no one else here,' she said looking round her. 'And I have lately heard some news which I confess, though I was expecting it, has upset me.'

He offered her his arm. 'The *Royal Oak* is only a step or two away,' he said, wondering what she might wish to discuss with him.

He settled her into the back parlour and the landlord brought a pot of coffee. She took a sip and then began her explanation.

'I didn't know until half an hour ago that John Stone was dead.' Though her voice was steady he noticed that her hand shook a little as she sipped the coffee from the dainty cup. 'I hadn't heard from him since January; up until that time, I was used to hear from him or see him every fortnight or so. I don't know how much you know.'

She looked at Arthur anxiously before continuing. 'John Stone and I have been very close friends for a long time. I left matters for a few months, but I could not believe he would simply end our - friendship so suddenly and without word. I came down by my coach this morning and went to the Parson, believing he would know where I might find John.'

She put down her cup and drew out a fine lace handkerchief pressing it to her mouth. 'He informed me in the barest of terms that John had died in January and I could find him in the graveyard. Your Parson Saunders is a man who does not mince his words.' She was silent for a moment trying to collect her thoughts and Arthur assumed, trying not to weep in front of him. 'I've not come here to cause any trouble, but I would like to know who has handled his affairs.'

Arthur, worried that this woman meant mischief for Beth and her mother, said quickly, 'Do you know that John Stone had a wife and a daughter?'

She met his eyes. 'I've known of them these many years. Is it his widow who is managing his affairs? If it is, I wouldn't approach her. I hoped there might be a male relative or an attorney?'

Arthur looked at her directly. 'What do you want, Mrs Gresham?'

'Only to speak to John's man of business – to know simply if he left any provision for me, or any memento that I might remember him by.'

'If he had, wouldn't you have been contacted by now?' Arthur asked.

She looked away and then stood up. 'I don't know,' she said simply. 'I don't know what to believe. But if you will not help me, I shall be on my way.'

Arthur, who up until then had decided it would be the best thing if she went away, suddenly changed his mind. 'No, wait. There is someone. Robert Stone, his older brother. I believe he handled everything. But he's an odd fellow and doesn't like strangers.'

She gave a short laugh. 'I'm not afraid of strangers and as I said, I've not come to make trouble. Where might I find Robert Stone?'

'Did you say you have your own coach?' Arthur asked.

She nodded.

'If you will take me up with you, I'll direct you to his house and wait for you.'

She nodded and put her hand on the door knob. Arthur stepped forward and opened it for her waiting for her to pass.

She smiled up at him as he looked into her dark eyes. 'You're very gallant,' she said, her wide silk skirts brushing against him as she passed.

Two hours later, Arthur who had been waiting in the coach outside the strange rambling house, reached to open the door as he heard Mrs Gresham come out of the entrance porch. To his surprise he saw Robert Stone himself escorting her out. She climbed in and the coachman pushed the door shut and scrambled up to his place.

'I hope your encounter wasn't too unpleasant, Mrs Gresham?' Arthur asked.

She smiled, sitting back amongst the plush squabs. 'Now where had you the idea that he would be unwelcoming? He was most gracious and accommodating to my wishes. He is going to write to me and says he will wait upon me in London when the matter is ready to be dealt with.'

Arthur looked puzzled. 'He ain't going to make you known to Mrs Stone and Beth is he?'

'Oh no,' she said, looking out at the passing countryside on the short way back to Hawkhurst. 'We both wish to keep everything confidential - I shan't come back this way, I think.'

CHAPTER FIFTEEN

Wednesday 17ʰ October 1731, afternoon

It was a perfect autumn day. The early mist which had been hanging in the air when Arthur had gone to his bed at six, had lifted and the sun shone in a clear sky. He got to Beth's house to find her already waiting outside at the back gate. He took her in his arms, savouring the fresh smell of her skin and her hair as it swung about her face as they kissed. They started walking back along Hawkhurst Moor, swinging their hands.

'We loaded three tons of tea last night,' he said. 'And look.' He dipped his hand into his pocket and drew out a small remnant of silk, handing it to Beth.

She took it in her hands and turned it over. 'French silk?' she asked. 'It's very fine. Look at the sheen on it, how it catches the sun.'

He nodded. 'It's from Lyons.' He pronounced it in the English way. 'I wondered if you or your mother wanted some?' he asked. 'We're bringing more bolts of silk and cambric next time.'

Beth looked uneasy. 'I wish you didn't do it, Arthur.'

'What?' he asked, laughing.

'You know – smuggling.' She looked uncomfortable. 'I had a letter from my cousin, Nick,' she said. 'He says it deprives the country of revenue.'

Arthur looked annoyed. 'Just the sort of thing an attorney-in-training like Nick, would say. Beth, if you went to France you could buy a pound of tea for two shillings. If you bring that same pound of tea back over here, the Government will want to take five shillings out of your purse for it. Now where's the reason in that? Why should the Frenchies drink their tea cheaper than us? And what does the Government do with that five shillings? I swear I don't see a penny of it.'

She looked bemused. 'I don't know who has the right of it, Arthur but that's not why I don't like you doing it.' She paused and then added shyly, 'It's because you might get hurt. How could I bear that?'

He stopped walking and drew her to him. 'Don't worry about me, Beth. I can take good care of myself.'

She changed the subject, turning into Henshill Lane. 'I need to go to Rowlands Farm to get a jug of milk. My mamma wants to set a junket. I wager I'll get there before you,' she said laughingly, and set off down the hill at a run.

Arthur followed and easily beat her and they arrived out of breath and laughing. They entered the cool dairy with its white-tiled walls and copper jugs set on large long tables. The three dairy maids were there and Beth went up to one of them, a pretty fair haired girl whose stays were laced tightly, showing off her neat bosom to Arthur's evident pleasure.

'A jug of milk please,' Beth said, a frown of annoyance on her face as the girl came out from behind the table and brushed too closely against Arthur to fetch one of the jugs.

'It's Sarah Allen, ain't it?' he asked, watching as she leaned forward and carefully poured the creamy milk from one of the large pails into the jug. He remembered that her mother had looked after Will when he was a baby and had worked in the *Angel* with his father until it was sold. She nodded and then turned to smile at him. She fixed a cork lid into the jug and took Beth's two pence from her.

'Goodbye then, Arthur,' Sarah called out as Beth and Arthur left and she and the two other maids giggled together at some private joke.

'Will and my father are both out,' Arthur said as they approached his house, 'and Lizzie Kennard has been already, she won't call again.'

Beth said nothing but followed Arthur up the two flights of stairs to the two garret rooms nominally still rented by John Gray although for many years now it had been Arthur's money that secured them. He set the heavy jug on the table and took off his greatcoat, went round the table to where Beth stood and pulled her quickly towards him. He swept her up in his arms laughing at the look of surprise on her face but her ready response to his kiss indicated that she was as well pleased as he was to find the house to themselves on such a pleasant afternoon.

He quickly removed his clothes leaving them in a pile on the floor and lay on the bed watching Beth undress. She stepped out of the heavy gown and the light panniers she wore, untying the ribbon laces at her shoulders and then came over to the bed and turned her back towards him so he could undo her stays which he found arousing and enticing. She rolled down her stockings and hung them over the chair with the rest of her clothes and stood in her chemise before him. He held out a hand to her and she stepped towards the bed.

He lay stroking her hair, their legs still entwined, their breathing now slow and relaxed after their exertions.

'Arthur?' she asked, her voice a little uncertain.

'Hmm?' he replied.

'Do you ever think of the future?'

He laughed gently. 'What future?'

She turned onto her stomach, propping herself up on both elbows facing him, her hair a cloud around her face. 'Our future.'

He looked into her eyes and touched her cheek. 'Of course I do. You know I do.'

She ran her fingers through her curls. 'And we'll be together?'

'Beth, you know we will-.'

'But I mean, together like this,' she interrupted. 'As a couple,' she added shyly.

'What's brought this on?' he asked and then added, 'We'll get married one day.'

'But when, Arthur? I worry sometimes-.'

'What do you worry about, sweetheart?' he asked, stroking her hair. 'Tell me.'

She slowly turned around and slipped out of bed going over to the chair where she had neatly folded her clothes. 'I worry that I might have a baby,' she said diffidently, pulling her chemise back over her head.

Arthur glanced quickly at her breasts and her flat belly exposed while she had her arms above her head, struggling into her chemise. 'You ain't pregnant, are you?' he asked quickly. 'I always try to be careful, you know that.'

She nodded and turned to him. 'But I don't want to always have to be worrying if a baby comes. I should like to have our children, Arthur. When we're man and wife. If that's what you intend.'

He hastily got out of bed struggling into his breeches and took her in his arms. 'And do you think I don't want that, Beth? Didn't I ask you to marry me that first time we lay together in the Upper Wish? But I haven't saved enough money yet. How could I ask you to come and live here? What a villain I should be.' He gave a short laugh.

She looked down at the floor. 'But we needn't live here, Arthur. We could live with my mother. Our house is big enough. I have a small allowance, you know.'

He let go of her and looked at her, puzzled. 'Are you serious, Beth? You can't think I would ever live off you and your mother and what your father left you? Besides I'm sure your mother don't approve of my business.'

Beth was struggling into her gown. 'But you don't have to run with the gangs. You don't have to work for John Grayling. Nick writes to say there's an opening for-,'

'For what?' Arthur asked, tight-lipped.

She tossed her head and met his gaze. 'For a clerk,' she said defiantly. 'Jeffery Pix is thinking of opening a second office in Rye as he has done so well in Chancery Lane. I wish you would consider it. You'd be safe. I hate it when you're out all night and I lie awake never knowing whether you will come safe back. You're sometimes late, or gone for days at a time. That time you were beaten by John Turner and I didn't hear from you for days - and when you disappeared with my father's horse, when you went chasing after Will's toys. Don't you know the agony I go through, wondering if you've been taken by the King's Men, or are lying in a ditch somewhere? Don't you know I nearly died when news came that one of you was shot? I prayed it was not you and when I heard it was Catt, I thanked God, *thanked God,* for taking someone else and sparing you.'

Arthur raised a hand to touch her face and comfort her and then dropped it. He could not account for his feelings. He was unable to give any credit to her suggestion of working as a clerk and was angry to think that her cousin Nick was making himself busy in his affairs and writing to Beth of them.

But he also scarcely ever gave any thought that Beth might be worrying about him while he was going about a business which, he had to admit, for all its dangers, made him feel alive and gave him the only chance he could see of escaping from the poverty into which many of his peers seemed prepared to fall without making a push to escape it. He planned marriage to Beth in a few years when he had established himself as one of the senior members of Grayling's men and he could provide her with a life suitable to her upbringing, as well as providing for Will and his father.

She had struggled into her clothes and was tying her laces awkwardly behind her back. He went to help but she shrugged him off and sniffed. She knotted up her hair quickly and then snatched up the heavy jug of milk.

'Don't go like this, Beth. You must see we can't marry yet. I do love you but I won't drag you down.'

She was at the door and crossed the small landing.

'Shall I see you tomorrow as usual, at St Lawrence's?' he asked urgently, chasing after her. He saw her disappearing down the stairs and turning at the next landing. 'Beth?'

She put her hand on the newel post and looked up at him. 'I don't know. Perhaps,' she said and hurried down the stairs.

St Lawrence's Churchyard, Hawkhurst, Thursday 18th October 1731, late afternoon

Arthur took his greatcoat off and hung it over one of the gravestones. The October sunshine was surprisingly warm on his shirtsleeved arms and the trees all around the churchyard still hung on to their leaves, which were just beginning to turn gold and red, yellow and bronze. He didn't know if Beth would turn up after their disagreement yesterday. He thought to himself that it had been their first serious argument and it made him feel unsettled and unhappy.

He hadn't realised because he had never felt like this before, how necessary Beth was to his comfort and well-being. Each time he saw her he had felt the same feeling inside him, pride that she had chosen to be with him and comfort that she was in his world at all. All the worries he had - if a run had gone badly, if he had had to bite his lip to stop himself from trying to tell the old hands how to do their jobs better or if Will was being tiresome, or his father was drunk by mid morning – all his worries seemed to fade into the background as soon as he saw Beth.

He wished he had made himself clearer to her yesterday. He wanted to marry her more than anything in the world, to be sure she would be at his side for ever. But their situations were so far apart. What could he offer her? Two rooms at the top of the house he shared with Will and his father? Even if he rented another, how could he expect Beth to settle into such a life? Beth, with her quick mind, her love of music, her collection of books? Surely she had seen the sense of it overnight? Surely Beth could understand that he could never be so beholden to her mother by living off her or taking a lowly position in her step-uncle's office? If she would wait, he would be able to offer more. He would build a fine house up at Seacox Heath, as he had vowed to do.

He was so lost in his thoughts that he hadn't noticed Beth walking up the road, in a gown of palest blue, her hair tumbling over her shoulders, glinting gold. He held out his arms to her, worried in case she wouldn't return his embrace but she stepped into his arms returning his kiss and as always rousing his desire as he felt the closeness and warmth of her body. 'Sweetheart, I'm so pleased you've come.'

She smiled up at him, dipping into the lace at her neck and pulling out a scrap of paper. She waved it in front of him. 'Look, Arthur, you'll never guess what it is.'

He snatched it playfully from her and held it above his head. 'Is it important then?' he teased, relieved that she seemed to bear no ill will from their argument.

She laughed as she tried to retrieve it. 'Yes, it came to my mother from Jeffery Pix, the attorney in London who is my Aunt Ann's brother-in-law. It was brought this morning. Let me read it to you.'

Arthur felt a stab of anxiety in his gut, but said lightly enough, 'It's in a fine hand, Beth. I believe even I could make this out. Shall I read it?'

'Yes,' she said a little uncertainly. 'Why not?'

Arthur started to read out loud and then the smile died on his face as he continued the rest silently. Holding up the letter, he read a sentence from the middle of it.

'I hope you will indulge us when we beg the pleasure of Mrs John Stone's and her daughter's company for a visit in Chancery Lane, London, for the mutual enjoyment of our families'.

He handed it back to her, his face grim. 'Is this Nick's doing? You surely won't go?'

'Arthur, I knew you would be awkward. But please don't spoil my pleasure in this. It's very kind of Mr Pix and his wife to invite my mother and me.'

'Well I can see why your step-uncle William has a kindness for you - his wife and your mother are sisters. But his brother Jeffery Pix doesn't owe you anything. You're not related to him. You hardly know him,' Arthur said fiercely.

'But he's connected to my family now. He and his wife have no children. They've liked having Nick stay with them. I think they like having young people around.'

'Huh, I'm sure it was Nick who persuaded him to ask you.'

Beth exhaled, trying to keep her voice even. 'Arthur, I hoped for better from you than this, this - pettiness.'

'I don't see why must you go and stay with them,' Arthur said petulantly.

'I told you. It's a great kindness; even more so because he has no compulsion to offer it, beyond the fact that it will give pleasure to my mother and me.'

'I'm sure your mother will accept. She and your aunt are probably planning for you to marry Nick or Francis,' he suggested scornfully.

'So what if they are?' Beth asked, her breathing shallow and quick with emotion.

'Would you?' Arthur countered.

Beth's grey eyes blazed in rare anger. 'Why not?' She tossed her head in a gesture Arthur knew so well. 'You say you won't marry me.

You know I don't like you being involved with the gangs, but you won't give it up.'

'But you know how it is with me, we went over this yesterday. I can hardly support Will, my father and myself, let alone a wife. My Dad drank all the profits from the alehouse years ago. Working with the gangs is the only way I'll ever make enough money for us. If I don't do it, I'll never be able to marry you.'

'We've talked round in a circle now,' Beth said exasperated. 'You don't have to work with them. You're clever. You could do anything.'

'What? Become a lawyer like your cousins? I don't have a father with guineas enough to buy me a place. But, I'm forgetting. I ain't quite fine enough for that, am I? But I can be their clerk, doing their fetching and carrying for them.'

Beth shook her head. 'So you'll stay with them, with Grayling, Curtis and the rest?'

'I have to.'

'And that's your final word?'

He lifted a hand and then dropped it by his side. He nodded. 'It has to be.'

'But you'll be imprisoned if you're caught. Who would look after Will and your father then? Or perhaps you've in mind that Will would take over? A boy of twelve?'

'I won't get caught. Everyone is on our side. You don't understand just how big this business is or how many men in high places take the uncustomed goods we bring in – who would turn me, or any of us over to the King's men?' Arthur asked, his stormy blue eyes meeting Beth's grey ones.

'Who knows?' she asked with a little impatient movement of her head. 'I know you all ride armed. Catt was shot, wasn't he? I'm sure he thought he was safe. It only needs one of the Officers to fire.'

'Beth, Beth, don't speak so. Things are different now. The Officers know there are too many of us now for them to have any chance against us. By the time they'd called the Dragoons, we'd be long gone. They let us be because their heart isn't in it. When Catt was shot, he was with only one other man, isolated – we don't work like that now, you know that. We stick together, work in a big group, we have lookouts and the Officers know if it ever came to a shoot out, we could outgun them.'

'There's no point in talking to you about it.'

She flounced off, picking her way over the long grass.

'Oh Beth, don't go. Stay with me,' Arthur called out.

She turned round, facing him, the swell of her breasts rising and falling quickly, 'So you would like me to stay? You don't want me to go?'

'Beth, love,' he replied, taking two steps to her side and grasping her hands, 'of course I want you to stay.'

He pulled her closer to him and she let her forehead be kissed but as his mouth sought hers, she pulled her head away. 'So if I stayed, you would go on working with the gang?'

Arthur nodded, his lips on her neck.

'And we would go on being sweethearts?'

He nodded again, his lips caressing her throat.

'But we won't be married?' she asked.

Arthur pulled his head away. 'Oh not again! It's not fitting for me to even ask you at this time.'

She struggled quickly out of his embrace and he didn't have time to duck as she slapped him hard across his face, catching him off balance. 'So I'm good enough to be your whore, but not to be your wife. You've an odd sense of what *is* fitting, Arthur Gray!'

Arthur put a hand to his cheek and goaded by fear of being without her, jealousy of losing her to her cousins and guilt that he wanted her to forego this pleasure, flared up. 'If it ain't to your liking Beth, go and marry one of your cousins then!'

'Well, Arthur, maybe I just will,' she flung at him and turned on her heel, the last of the autumn sunlight turning her hair to gold as she hurried along the churchyard path towards her home.

CHAPTER SIXTEEN

Goudhurst, Late 1731

George Kingsmill had been courting Sarah Fishenden all summer. She lived in Horsmonden, the village next to his. Her brother, Peter, was a chandler and had two men working for him and was set to do well for himself.

George didn't think he was in love with Sarah but her black hair and eyes and the swing of her hips as she walked, set his loins on fire. They met on Sunday mornings when he wooed her with a passion bordering on frenzy. She would not give in to his pleas, his whispered promises, though she let him kiss her, let him unlace her simple cotton gown and let his hot hands find a cool resting place in her bosom. But as soon as he tried to pull up her skirts she would roll away from under him giggling, leaving him trembling, sweating, and desperate for relief.

'Not till I'm your wife, George Kingsmill,' she would scold, tossing her head and setting her hands behind her back to draw tight the laces once more and restore her bosom to its rightful place, with the lace tucked across the upper softness of her breasts.

It was after one of these abortive attempts to consummate his passion that he came across Sarah Allen, the plump little dairymaid, as he rode up North Road in Goudhurst on his way home. Though Sarah Allen lived in Hawkhurst, on Sundays she usually visited her brother Joseph who had married a Goudhurst girl last year and now worked with his father-in-law who was a sawyer.

George drew his horse to a halt in front of her, taking off his hat and bowing low over his horse's neck.   'Good day to you, Sarah.'

She stopped and slowly looked up at him, silhouetted as he was against the late afternoon sun. 'Hello George,' she said smiling. 'Where are you going?'

'Oh, I'm just idling about,' he said.

'The devil makes work for idle hands,' she retorted. 'If you'd been at church this morning, you'd have heard Parson Finch tell us so.'

He laughed. 'I don't need Parson Finch to tell me that,' he said. 'Well, Miss Sarah, that's a fetching cap you have on. Turn around, go on. Let me see if the back is half so pretty as the front.'

Sarah blushed and bit her bottom lip. 'Get on with you, George Kingsmill!' she said but nevertheless slowly turned round and met his gaze again as she came to face him.

'Where are you going?' he asked, liking the way some of her hair had escaped from her cap and was curling round the back of her neck.

'Back to Hawkhurst,' she said.

'Well, I'm idle, as I've told you. I'll carry you, Sarah. It's foolish for me to ride single when we're going the same way.'

'What reason would you have to ride to Hawkhurst, George?' she asked looking up at him from under her lashes.

'Oh I can always find business in Hawkhurst,' he replied. 'Though it's reason enough to ride with such a comely girl as you.'

She chose to ignore this compliment, but couldn't stop a rosy blush creeping into her cheeks. 'How can I ride cross-saddle, with you mounted?' she asked.

'Well you get up and I'll lead you.'

Thus it came to be that every Sunday after spending the morning with Sarah Fishenden in Horsmonden, George came home to Goudhurst, picked up Sarah Allen and carried her back to Hawkhurst. After a couple of times, she agreed to sit in front of George on the saddle, his arms tight about her waist as they rode. George made an excuse about Sarah's father not being likely to approve of him, as he had something of a reputation as a young hothead; and thereby got her agreement to let him drop her off at Tulhurst's barn a little way out of Hawkhurst. No one was aware of their liaison. George would turn his horse round and return to Goudhurst going back to the small house on the Cranbrook Road which he shared with his brother Thomas and their sister Rose who kept house for them.

On the sixth occasion, having dismounted at Hawkhurst, he and Sarah lingered for a while at Tulhurst's Barn and George took her in his arms to kiss her goodbye. Her soft pink lips melted under his. He led her into the barn and they half-fell, half-sat on some soft bales of hay where she let him go as far as his other Sarah did and then further still and instead of meeting laughing but definite resistance as he lifted up her skirts, he was met with soft yielding flesh and little cries of pleasure.

By the end of February she had missed her monthly course and was sure she was pregnant. The next Sunday she told George. The following Sunday though she waited in the usual place for him, he never came and she walked all the way home on her own, her stays beginning to bite into her waist. Her father asked her what was amiss as she arrived home, mud around the hem of her dress and a high colour from her exertions. She said nothing and went to her room.

In the middle of the next week she went back to Goudhurst and approached the Kingsmills' lodging with some apprehension. A tall handsome woman answered the door and Sarah knew from her likeness to George, in her dark hair and eyes, that she must be his sister.

'Beg pardon, ma'am,' she said politely. 'Is George Kingsmill here?'

Rose Kingsmill looked at her in a not unfriendly way. 'No, miss. Who's asking?'

'I'm Sarah Allen. I'm a friend of George's. I have some – some business with him.'

Rose stepped outside and looked up and down the quiet street. 'You'd best come inside,' she said, smoothing down her apron. People who had 'business' with either of her brothers usually wanted to place an order for smuggled goods.

She showed Sarah into the kitchen where she was in the middle of baking. 'It's probably my brother Thomas you should speak to,' she said having offered her visitor a chair. 'He's out, right now. But he's looking after most things while George is away. Or you could try Bernard Woollett.'

'Away?' Sarah asked, ignoring Rose's last remark, a lurch in her stomach making her feel suddenly nauseous.

Rose laughed. 'Our Georgie-boy's got himself engaged to Sarah Fishenden, Horsmonden way. At last! Don't know what she did to make him come about but whatever it was, it worked. So that's how come he's not here. He's gone to stay with her for a time. Helping her brother out, he's a tallow chandler and he's a man down right now.'

Sarah heard Rose's voice and her own heartbeat hammering in her ears.

'Are you quite well there, miss?' Rose's question seemed to come from a long way off.

Sarah felt the bile rise in her throat and she put a hand to her mouth, praying that she wouldn't be sick. She nodded and said weakly, 'Yes. A little warm.'

Rose nodded looking across to the open fire. 'It's unseasonal mild for this time of year and it gets so hot in here when I bake'. She poured a tankard of beer from the jug on the table and offered it to Sarah. 'So was it anything particular you was wanting from George?'

'Tea,' Sarah said at length. 'A bag of tea.'

'A whole bag?' Rose asked, raising her eyebrows. 'Well you should know. I'll be sure to tell Tom. Where should it be dropped off? What's your direction?'

'Henshill Lane, Hawkhurst,' Sarah said, wondering how her voice could sound so calm when her heart was pounding against her ribs, with the sweat under her chemise trickling down the small of her back.

'Hawkhurst?' Rose said, surprised. 'I wonder you didn't ask one of the Hawkhurst men. Still, you know your business I suppose. I expect Pete Tickner or Arthur Gray will drop it off for you. Arthur lives up near you.'

She paused, waiting for Sarah to get up. 'Well, one bag it is then,' she said with an air of finality and her visitor stood up and made her way out.

As soon as she was outdoors, Sarah dashed to the alley at the end of the street and came to the backyard of the *Chequers* which was thankfully empty. She sank to her knees and retched twice and vomited holding onto the small wooden gate, her heart pounding, and her whole body bathed in sweat. Her body was shaking and it was a full five minutes before she rose from her knees. She turned to the pump and swung the handle a couple of times, holding her mouth under the flow of water, rinsing the bitter taste from her mouth, the cold water on her cheeks bringing her jarred senses to some kind of order.

CHAPTER SEVENTEEN

Hawkhurst, March 1732

Arthur could tell from the pink in the morning sky that it must be about half past six. His mind was not easy. Nothing was going well, not the business, nor at home where his father and Will were both difficult in their different ways.

This was the third run of the week and though he had been on horseback each time, he had been assigned to work with a different group of men on each occasion and all of them chose different routes to run the goods from Dungeness inland. Grayling had posted Savage, Holman and Turner in charge of each group. Although Ned Savage had been well organised, dropping the goods off in a logical order, Thomas Holman and John Turner had no such order and they kept having to double back on themselves in order to deliver the goods, criss-crossing the Marsh. They often had to dismount where they drove themselves too near the cuts and dykes and were frequently up to their knees in water. An uneasy truce existed between himself and John Turner and Arthur made sure he kept his mouth shut, even if it was obvious Turner was making mistakes. He didn't want to give him any more cause for another kicking or beating.

As for his father Arthur sighed, he was surely drinking himself to death. He seldom ventured up before noon, the smell of spirits already on his breath. Arthur had given up trying to hide the flagons of Geneva from him.

Then there was Will, who had put on a sudden spurt of growth, all arms and legs, grown gangly and thin, his voice sometimes a boy's and then the cracked bass of a youth. He had finished his schooling last year and was plaguing Arthur to be allowed to go on some of the runs, though Arthur set him to study his books while he was out. He didn't know what Will got up to most of the time. Last autumn it was true, he had picked up some work on the surrounding farms but thought it a poor way to earn money and would rather be holding horses, or even acting lookout for the gang.

Will and his particular friends, James Stanford and Jim Cook were running wild, Hannah Webb had told Arthur. At present, as far as Arthur could work out, it was just boyish pranks but without a firm hand it could turn into villainy.

As Will got bigger, the bed that both brothers shared seemed even smaller and Will complained that Arthur's heavier weight over the years had caused the thin mattress to dip down on his side so Will was always rolling into the middle, to both their discomfort. Arthur had thought for some months now that he should make some effort to rent more rooms, perhaps on the ground floor so that his father wouldn't stumble up and down the stairs. He could just afford it he thought, but supposed Hannah and Lizzie would want more payment to look after bigger premises. What he needed, he reflected, was a wife and this made him think of Beth, whom he hadn't seen or spoken to since she walked away from him last October.

He knew she had gone to stay as she had been invited, with Jeffery Pix and his wife in London. Then he had heard that she and her mother had stayed on with her mother's sister, Ann Pix, in Northiam. Even though he had made several drops there and he had ventured near the farm where her aunt and uncle lived, there had been no sign of Beth.

At first he had been so angry with her for going away that he hadn't realised he was missing her. But then her absence became an acute pain which dragged his spirits down and made it impossible for him to find pleasure in anything. He thought he would go mad with the physical longing he had for her. Then he drove himself half-crazy thinking he had forgotten what her voice sounded like, especially when he was out at night on a run, walking or riding across the dark Marsh, his concentration gone, thinking only of how much he missed her.

He had been sharp with Will and his father, snapping at them for the slightest thing but then, as he realised how bleak his life was without Beth, he became sad and withdrawn, with hardly a word for Will and was coldly polite to his father. He tried to accustom himself to the fact that he had lost her and lived in daily dread that word would come of her betrothal to her cousin and that he would live his life, empty and hollow, his love for her pointless and his plans for their life together nothing but a shallow dream.

Trying to cast aside the thoughts that made him feel so miserable, he turned into Henshill Lane and dismounted with the last bag of tea to be delivered slung over his horse. He was about to leave the oilskin in the back porch at the bottom of the three steps when the door opened and looking up, he recognised the Allen daughter who worked at Rowlands Dairy. She was about a year older than he was, short with a voluptuous figure and pretty plump shoulders. Her bosom was full and rounded as he could clearly see looking up at her. 'Hello,' he smiled. 'It's Sarah isn't it?'

She smiled back, white teeth showing as her full pink lips parted. 'Hello Arthur. I didn't know if you would remember me,' she replied.

'Wouldn't forget you.' He smiled and indicated the bag of tea. 'This yours?'

She looked at it and then frowned. 'Oh is a bag that much? I didn't think it would be so big. Is it very heavy?'

'Not for me,' Arthur said swinging it up on his shoulder. 'You couldn't lift it though, a little thing like you. Where do you want it? Reckon this should last until Christmas unless you drink a lot of tea.'

'You better bring it in,' she said, 'if you don't mind, that is. My father's away and my grandmother's an old body. I doubt she and I could lift it between us.'

He followed her into the kitchen and put the bag on the table. He heard a frail voice calling from another room and Sarah popped her head round a door across the hallway. He could hear an exchange of voices, the querulous voice of an old lady and Sarah's rather high-pitched but not unpleasant voice. When she came back into the room, Arthur thought once again how pretty she was, not beautiful like Beth of course, but she had a nice round face and pink cheeks and her dark blonde hair hung in waves to her creamy shoulders.

If Arthur had been wiser in the ways of women, he would have known that she had rubbed her cheeks and bitten her lips to redden them while she was in the other room, as well as tucking the lace of her chemise further down her stays so that there was more of her full and pretty bosom on show. All Arthur knew was that it felt good to be standing in her kitchen in the early morning of a fine March day.

'How much do I pay you?' she asked rather nervously.

'A guinea,' Arthur said and then at the look of shock on her face added, 'You don't have to pay all at once,' disregarding all the rules of the business by so saying.

'I ... I didn't think it would be so much,' she said hesitantly.

'I can put the money in for you for now and you can pay me back bit by bit, if it's easier for you.'

'Oh Arthur, would you? How kind you are! Let me make you breakfast, that's the least I can do. Sit down here while I set things ready,' Sarah invited, beaming at him, the beginnings of a solution to her problem, not yet dawned on her, but waiting, as it were, for her to stumble upon.

It was pleasant to sit at her table, having been on horseback most of the night and Arthur was content to watch her bring plates and mugs, a jug of foaming milk, a large golden loaf, a dish of yellow butter and then he inhaled the delicious smell of eggs and bacon as she set a heavy pan over the fire.

For the next few weeks it became Arthur's habit after a run, to call on Sarah ostensibly to collect the money she owed him. She would always be up and dressed and looking as fresh as a daisy, the smell of bacon drifting from the doorway as soon as he approached. She would give him breakfast and then paid him twopence, sometimes sixpence towards the bag of tea he had delivered.

One morning, about three weeks after he had delivered the tea, they finished breakfast and as Sarah was putting the dishes into a large tin bowl, Arthur approached her from behind and slipped his arms around her waist. She paused for a moment and then turned round in his embrace, putting her wet hands up to his shoulders and turned her face up to receive his kiss.

He ached for the softness and warmth of a woman's body, after months of the gnawing hunger for Beth. Sarah took his hand and he followed her into the little bedchamber next to her grandmother's and they fell onto the bed struggling to remove each other's clothes which served to heighten Arthur's passion as the delights of Sarah's buxom body were revealed a little at a time. This roused him to such a passion that he realised, too late, that he had failed to withdraw from her at the crucial moment and spent himself inside her. Lying afterwards in her embrace, his head on her accommodating bosom, it didn't seem to matter.

A month later, Sarah told Arthur she was pregnant. Searching his face for his response, she saw at first surprise, then a resigned but not unkindly look.

'Well, Sarah, we had best have the banns read.'

And if the baby, that she said was due in December, happened to arrive in October, well she wouldn't be the first wife to produce her first child early.

CHAPTER EIGHTEEN

1732 May, the Grays' rented rooms, Hawkhurst Moor

'You must wish me joy, Will,' Arthur said as he helped himself to some stew and sat down at the table tearing off a hunk of bread.

'Wish you joy? What for?' his brother asked sopping up gravy with his crust.

'I'm getting married.'

Will looked up, his face shiny with excitement and spoke with his mouth full. 'Has Beth come back? When? When's she coming to see us?'

Their father grunted and Arthur looked across at him saying quickly to Will, 'No. I haven't seen Beth since she went away. I'm not marrying Beth. It's Sarah.'

Will looked incredulous. 'Sarah Allen? But I don't understand. Why aren't you marrying Beth? Does she know?' Will sounded hurt, shocked.

'Why would Beth be interested in what I'm doing?' Arthur asked and then as neither his brother nor father said anything, added, 'Well, is neither of you going to wish me happy?'

His father muttered and Will got up quickly pushing his plate aside and stormed out of the room.

Arthur, with a piece of bread at his lips, flung it back down on the plate and pushing his chair back, went after Will who had stomped down the two flights of stairs and into the back yard.

Arthur caught up with him, grabbed hold of his sleeve and hauled him round. 'Don't act the child, Will. I'm marrying Sarah and that's all there is to it, so you had better get accustomed to it. She'll be your sister after all.'

'Well, why have you and Beth been – why are you and Beth – oh I dunno.' Will turned away. 'I thought she would come back. I thought she would always be with us. It's horrible without her.' His voice wavered and he sniffed. 'If you would go and see her Arty, or I could p'raps? Tell her you want to marry her. She would, I know she would.'

Arthur put his hand on Will's shoulder and said more gently, 'No, she wouldn't, Will. I can't ask her. The fact is, Sarah's going to, well she's having a baby.'

Will turned back and looked up at his brother. 'What? Whose baby? Your baby?'

Arthur nodded. 'Yes of course.' He put his arm around Will and drew him back towards the house. 'So I had best start looking to rent some more rooms. We won't all fit in these.'

Will shook himself free and paced over the flagstones in the yard, kicking at stones, his hands pushed down in his pockets, his back firmly turned against Arthur. At length he said, 'You wouldn't marry her, would you, you wouldn't marry that Sarah if there wasn't a baby? You'd ask Beth.'

Arthur answered lightly enough, though his heart was heavy. 'But there is a baby, Will and I won't do Sarah any dishonour. Besides it'll be a good thing for us to have a woman about the place, supper on the table when we come home, the linen washed and folded.'

'Does my father know?' Will asked.

'Yes' he assented, 'and it will be a good thing for him to have Sarah with us. You know he's getting frailer. A woman is better at looking after people.'

Will looked at his brother again. 'You should send word to Beth, tell her. She might come back.'

Arthur met his gaze. 'Will, it's better if you forget about Beth. She'll very likely marry one of her Pix cousins and move to London and become a great lady. She's more gently born than us. It's only right she should marry in her own station. I did – I did once want to marry her, but it was stupid of me.'

'She never treated me any different, even if she is better born than us,' Will said. 'I think she's the best person I know, - well, best with you.'

Arthur laughed. 'Oh, I'm a long way off a best person, Will. Ask Parson Saunders.'

Will reluctantly turned back to go into the house. 'Huh, what does he know, Old Redbeak, the Parson?'

Friday 23ʳᵈ May, 1732, the Pix farm, Northiam, near Rye

Beth was trimming a bonnet at the table in her aunt's front parlour in the large farmhouse at Northiam. Her aunt put her head round the door. 'Here's a young man you know asking for you, Beth,' she said ushering him into the room.

'Will!' Beth said looking up and smiling. 'What a surprise! How very kind of you to call on us. You remember, Will Gray, Aunt, from Hawkhurst?'

Her aunt nodded. 'Yes indeed. We have already exchanged how d'ye do's, haven't we? How is your father, Will and your brother?'

'Both well, thank you ma'am,' Will said gruffly hoping Beth's aunt would leave the room so he could talk privately with Beth. He glanced around the room noticing its handsome proportions and a vase of flowers set on a small table in front of the window. He thought it suited Beth, to be sitting in such a fine room.

'Well, I must see to the linen, Beth. I shall leave you to your visitor.'

Beth's aunt gave Will another glance and left the room. Will looked awkwardly at Beth. She looked different to him but he couldn't think why.

Beth broke the silence by laughing. 'What a fine tall young man you've grown into while I've been away. Come and stand next to me. I think you must have my height, if not more.'

Will stepped a couple of paces towards her and found he was looking straight into her eyes instead of up at them as he had remembered. He broke into a smile. The nice soapy smell enveloping her invaded his senses, evoking memories and thoughts of her he felt ashamed to own.

'Yes you're taller than I and I even have little heels on my shoes. You must be nearly as tall at Arthur.' Her mouth felt strangely dry as she said his name and as soon as she had spoken it, Will looked uneasy. Her first thought was, '*he's come to tell me Arthur is dead. He lied to my aunt just now when she asked him how Arthur was. He's going to tell me while I'm on my own. That's why I never heard from him. He's dead. I shall die too. I can't live in this world if he's not in it.*'

'What's the matter, Will? Is something wrong with Arthur? Have you brought me a message from him? I've wondered, worried...'

'No, there's no message from him. It's just that he – that is, oh Beth! – Arthur is marrying Sarah Allen.'

Beth looked at Will for a moment, her expression unchanged. Then she turned away swiftly and kept her back to Will as she went over to the window, seeing her aunt in the yard admonishing the laundry maid as the line appeared to have broken and there was linen lying all over the muddy ground. *Not dead then? Not dead, but lost to me anyway. Marrying Sarah Allen? Forgotten me so soon?*

Trying to make her voice sound normal, she asked quickly, 'Sarah Allen? Sarah? The girl who works in the dairy in Rowlands Farm? And Arthur is to marry her?' Beth could barely put a face to the name of this girl who would change her life so completely.

Will noticed the slight tremor in her voice and said quickly, 'He's got her with child, Beth. The banns have been read. They're getting married next week. Huh!'

Beth pressed both hands to her cheeks, her thoughts in turmoil. *Got her with child? Is that all it needed to take him away from me? After always making sure he never got me with child!*

'Next week! Next week?' she exclaimed. 'But I don't understand – why have you come here Will? The marriage will go ahead-,'

'I dunno why I come,' Will groaned addressing Beth's back. 'It was stupid. I was stupid. I wanted you to marry – I wanted Arthur to marry you. I thought you would. I don't know why you went or why he let you go. I just thought if you came back, he might change his mind. He said you would marry one of your cousins and that we should forget you.'

'He believed that? He said that?' Beth turned back, tears sparkling on her eyelashes, her half-formed plans for her future crumbling around her. 'Will, I can't stop this marriage. How should I – if she's going to have a child? But how could he ever think I would marry my cousin when I, when he.... only I thought – your brother said he couldn't afford a wife, let alone a wife and child. That's what he told me. That's why I went. And I asked him if he would stop working with the gang.'

Will sniffed. 'He goes out most nights on runs with any gang that will take him, now that he needs more money. He's out with Moreton's people, Captain Harvey's Irish Gang at Folkestone, the Wingham men, anyone. I want to go only he won't let me.'

'Not you too, Will! I should think not. He puts himself at risk of imprisonment every night he's out.' Beth came back to the table, not wanting to hurt Will by wishing him gone, but needing to be alone to give way to this crushing grief which seemed to be squeezing the air out of her lungs and causing her heart to hammer at her ribs. 'Will, come and sit down.' She pulled out a chair and waited for him to be seated. 'You did right to tell me about Arthur. I just need to think, to get it straight in my mind.' She put one hand to her forehead. 'There's nothing to be done, nothing at all. Only, it's so unexpected. It's taken me by surprise. You must tell me more, so I can understand. Where will you live? Has Arthur arranged anything?'

Will grunted. 'Yes, he's rented rooms within a little way of where we are now. Only I have to share with my father now, instead of Arthur and we are on the ground floor, not above stairs. And soon we'll have a squalling baby with us!'

Beth tried to smile in spite of herself. 'Oh Will, it's hard being a younger brother. But you'll be better looked after. I don't know Sarah, but she'll surely keep a good house for you all. Your brother wouldn't bring someone you disliked into your home, you know that.'

Will pulled a face and then said, 'Will you come back, Beth? Please?'

'We were coming back anyway, my mother and I. We can't stay forever with my aunt and uncle.'

'The wedding is next Thursday,' Will announced in a dull voice and rose to go. 'You look real pretty, Beth, prettier than I even remember. Arthur must be mad.'

Beth caught Will's hand and held it between both of hers.

'Oh it's probably just this new way I have of dressing my hair. All the London ladies are wearing more curls-.' She stopped suddenly and said, 'You're a good kind boy, Will. No, I mustn't call you a *boy* with you grown so tall. You're a fine young man, then. Now, I must hurry you away if I'm to pack all my things up.'

She saw him out to the front of the house where he had tethered the horse he had borrowed and watched him make his way down the rough road which led back to Hawkhurst. When she could no longer make him out, she took two deep breaths and then, as the tears spilled down her face, she dropped to her knees holding the tether-post for support. She tried to catch her breath and give way to crying at the same time and her voice cracked on the first dry sob, rasping her throat. She cried out aloud through her sobs, 'Arthur! Arthur!' calling his name over and over, on her knees, her head bent as if she was praying to some merciless, unhearing god. She felt, as the sobs racked her frame and her voice grew hoarse, that it could not be possible to feel so much pain, so much jealousy, so much anger, so much love and still live.

Thursday 29 May 1732, St Lawrence's Church Hawkhurst

The bride and groom stepped out of the church porch into the sunlight. Some of the villagers had gathered outside on the stone path leading down to the lych gate. The giggling village children had made a bower of early summer flowers and greenery, which they held up but Arthur was too tall so he stooped in order to let them hold it over his head and Sarah's. As he looked up, the smile died on his lips for Beth stood just a few feet in front of him. Beth, whom he hadn't seen or spoken to since she turned on her heel and left him seven months ago on this same church path, was standing amongst his friends and neighbours meeting his gaze with that direct look from those calm grey eyes, the gentle breeze lifting her hair and fluttering the lace at her neck.

He knew then on the instant that it had been folly to think he would ever forget her or be able to live without her or make any sort of life that she wasn't part of. She was as necessary to him as food, as water. He didn't understand quite how she came to be there and a questioning look came into his face, at odds with the laughter and cheers of the wedding guests all around him. He felt a sudden great longing for her physically, but a feeling of great comfort that she was there at all, that she had come back into his life for whatever reason, that he could speak her name again, touch her, laugh with her. He also knew with a great certainty that whatever the future might hold, he would never let her go again; and that she, having come back, would not leave him.

Sarah, the bride on his arm, was saying something in his ear. He inclined his head to hear her, his eyes still on Beth. Beth smiled slightly at Arthur, nodded to Sarah and then turned her head away as she moved through the throng walking down the stone path, head aloft, shoulders back and the glints in her hair catching the sun and turning into gold.

CHAPTER NINETEEN

Sunday 12th October 1732, Hawkhurst

Arthur looked over the heads of the rest of the congregation from his pew at the back of St Lawrence's and easily picked out the gold lights in Beth's hair as she sat in her family pew several rows in front of him. Parson Saunders was delivering one of his ferocious sermons on the verse, *'So teach us to number our days that we may apply our hearts unto wisdom,'* and Arthur made no attempt to smother his yawns. He had been on a run last night and had got home towards three in the morning, slipped into bed beside Sarah and had slept easily until she woke him at nine to get ready for church. He had been an indifferent churchgoer before his marriage but Sarah liked to be seen doing things properly and she attended each week. Since his marriage though, this had been the one place he could be sure of seeing Beth and he willingly accompanied Sarah, usually bringing a reluctant Will with him.

He could see Beth turning her face slightly to her mother. Since her return from London, she seemed even lovelier to Arthur. She had acquired, what could he call it? – town polish. Always elegant, she now had tricks of arranging her hair, knotting ribbons or silk flowers in her curls that marked her apart from the other Hawkhurst girls. He sighed. Their meetings since he had married Sarah were awkward and difficult for them both. Though Sarah was a willing and active bedfellow, even this late in her pregnancy, he still had a physical longing for Beth. He had only to hear her voice and get close enough to her, to recognise her own special, soapy aroma and he would be lost in his thoughts of having her in his arms and in his bed again.

His wandering thoughts were brought back to the present by Sarah, who had adjusted her position so she was sitting, half leaning against him. She had backache almost continually this last month and the wooden pews were narrow and uncomfortable. Even in her loose gown and loosely tied stays, she was sighing every now and again and pressing her hand into her side.

He put his mouth to her ear. 'Why don't you go home, Sarah? No one will think badly of you.'

She turned to look up at him. She had noticed the way he had scoured the congregation looking for Beth. She shook her head. 'No. I'm all right. Perhaps you might rub my back?'

He put his hand over her thickened waist at her back and rubbed his palm over her gown. He could feel only the stiff canvas of her stays under his fingers and couldn't think it was giving her much relief. She leant her cheek against his arm but then it was the prayers and they all had to shift around to kneel down. After another half hour, the long service came to an end and they went home to eat.

When the meal was finished and Sarah had cleared away the dishes, Arthur suggested to Will that they go for a walk.

'Why don't you lie down for an hour or two?' he asked his wife. 'You look tired. I'm sure my father will lie down on his bed so the house will be quiet while Will and I are out.'

Sarah looked across at Arthur. 'Well, perhaps. I am feeling a bit tired.'

'So am I, after that boring sermon!' Will said. 'He gets worse, though, don't he, Old Redbeak? Jim Cook and Stanford reckon there's a pair of nightingales in Skippers Fields. Could we go and look for them, Arty?'

'Why not?' Arthur said and the two brothers made their way out, Arthur dropping a careless kiss on his wife's blonde curls.

They made their way up the Moor. 'There's a fair at Lydd in a couple of weeks. I saw the handbills up yesterday. Would you like to come?' Arthur asked casually.

'I should say I would,' Will exclaimed. 'I'd like a clasp knife like yours, Arthur. Do you think they might have them on one of the stalls?'

'I don't know. It's general pedlary. You never know what they might have. I'll be taking Sarah. I don't think our father will come. I wondered if you might ask Beth to come with us,' he said lightly.

Will nodded at once. 'She'll come all right. She likes a fair as much as I do. We can call in and ask her now.'

'No, you call in, Will,' Arthur suggested. 'I need to call on Larry Kemp. I'll see you outside his house.'

Will shrugged and at the top of Highgate Hill he went a few houses along to call on Beth while Arthur turned the other way to Kemp's house hurriedly thinking up a reason to call on him. Fifteen minutes later, Will came dashing along to find Arthur. Arthur could hardly wait to hear if he had been successful.

'Well?' he asked when Will said nothing.

'Well, what?'

'Is Beth coming?'

'Course she is,' Will said. 'Told her you'd tell her when and where. Come on, let's go and find those birds.'

Tuesday 28ᵗʰ October 1732, Lydd

Arthur helped Sarah up to the seat in the front of the wagon he had borrowed from Larry Kemp. He had forgotten his pregnant wife wouldn't be able to ride to Lydd so he had hastily changed his plans for riding there and now he was to drive Sarah, Will and Beth down to Lydd for the fair which was held in the afternoons of the next two days.

At the last moment Grayling had fixed up a run for the night of the 28ᵗʰ, so Arthur had to arrange to go down early in the day and had taken three rooms at the *George* so that Beth, Sarah and Will could stay there on Tuesday night while he was attending to business with the gang. Though he didn't know how far inland he was to run the goods, he was sure he would be back in time to grab some sleep and enjoy at least some of the afternoon's fair.

Sarah sat in silence next to Arthur. When he had told her of the fair, her first instinct was simply to say no. Though Arthur thought her baby was due in December, Sarah had calculated it would be born in late October as far as she could tell and she had no wish to be driven over the Marsh to a fair in Lydd. However when she learned that Beth was to be one of the party, ostensibly to keep Will company, she agreed to come. She could hardly tell Arthur the real reason for not wishing to go.

They arrived at about four in the afternoon and Arthur tooled the wagon round to the stables at the side of the Inn, leaving the horses in the charge of Humphrey Haddon, one of the servants. Stanton Blacklock the landlord knew Arthur well, for the *George* was one of the favourite haunts of the gang and they often met there waiting for a boat to come in and some of them met up after a run if they were not involved in running goods inland.

'I've put you and your missus in one of the rooms at the back,' Blacklock explained to Arthur. 'Thought it would be quieter there for your lady, as you said she was in a delicate condition. Young miss with you is further up the corridor in a neat little room, even got a mirror in it and your brother, well I hope he won't find nothing wrong with his room though it is on the small side. Just room for a bed but no more. What more does a young lad want, eh? We're pretty full up what with some of Grayling's other lads staying here too.'

It was the first time Arthur had ever had any of his family with him while he was involved in a run. The men started arriving about nine. Arthur had ordered supper in the small dining room, not really wanting Beth and Sarah to sit in the back room with the gang because, although he knew they would be polite enough while the women were present, he knew the sort of ribald remarks they would make afterwards. Some of the men were already in the bar when Sarah and Beth came out and they stood back to make way for them. Sarah who normally liked the company of men, felt heavy and awkward especially when she stood beside Beth, tall and elegant in lilac silk, her hair shining gold in the candlelight of the bar room.

Will however was in a fever pitch of excitement and begged to be allowed to sit in the back parlour with the gang members. Gathered together they were an impressive body of men, mostly big and burly, made more so by the layers of clothes they wore, all with long greatcoats, mufflers and hats; and when John Grayling arrived, with his long hair tied behind in a queue with a large black riband and a red muffler wound several times round his neck, Will felt himself indeed in the presence of a Somebody. There was much drinking, though Will noticed Arthur didn't take anything beyond a tankard of ale and the conversation was of *luggers* and *cutters* and *tublines*, most of which was beyond Will's comprehension.

Towards ten, Arthur told Will it was time he retired to bed and despite his protest, Arthur was insistent. He accompanied Will out and went to join Beth and Sarah who were sitting in the front parlour. There were a few other older patrons sitting quietly in front of a small fire burning in the grate and there was a low hum of conversation. Sarah had brought some embroidery and was sitting as close as she could to the candle in the sconce, while Beth had a small volume in her lap and had evidently been reading.

'Arthur, dear,' Sarah said holding out her hand as soon as she saw him. He came over, glancing at Beth but took Sarah's hand and sat down on the little stool in front of her.

'Will's going up to his bedchamber now and I think you should, too,' he said to both the women. 'It can get a bit noisy when all the gang gets here.'

Beth closed her book and Sarah, gathering her embroidery, held out her hands for Arthur to help her up and tucked her arm in his. He accompanied the three of them upstairs and when they were on the landing, said in a quiet voice, 'The cutters aren't due in until just after midnight and I have to do the run in as far as the Sevenoaks turnpike. I'll try and get back as soon as I can but if I'm not here in the afternoon, Will must escort you both to the fair and I'll find you there.'

'Well, I've never been to Lydd before,' Beth said. 'I think I'll go and look at the Church tomorrow. I've never seen such a tall spire and it's just a step across the street.'

'Oh, churches,' Will said disparagingly. 'I'd sooner come with you, Arty.'

Arthur smiled down at him. 'Not yet a while, Will. You must look after the girls tomorrow.'

They said goodnight and parted company on the landing, Will and Beth going to their separate rooms and Arthur going in with Sarah to find she had hung up their clothes in the cupboard on their arrival and turned down the bedcovers. The linen was clean and fresh and satisfied even her high standards. She undressed quickly and pulled on her nightshift and climbed awkwardly on to the high bed. She held out her arms to Arthur. 'Come and lie down next to me for a while before you go.'

He said nothing but did as she asked. She picked up his hand and placed it on her belly. 'Can you feel him kicking, Arthur?'

He felt the odd little movement under his palm. 'Tell him to be still and let his mother get some sleep,' he said kissing the top of Sarah's head as he slipped off the bed. He stepped down the corridor and as he passed Beth's door, he heard her singing softly. It caught at his heart for he remembered she would often sing as she went about her preparations for bed. He stood there for a moment listening and then when she stopped, he hastily stepped down the stairway into the brightly lit bar room now noisy with the mens' laughter.

CHAPTER TWENTY

Wednesday 29th October 1732 Lydd, the George Inn

Beth came out of her room the next morning soon after nine o' clock, to find Sarah in the corridor facing the wall and seemingly supporting herself up against it for both her arms were extended with her palms flat on the wall. 'Sarah?' she called. 'Is anything amiss?'

Sarah turned slowly towards her and said through clenched teeth, 'My pains have started.'

Beth slowly approached her. 'Are you sure? It's too early, surely?'

'I'm telling you, they've started,' Sarah replied crossly and then caught her breath.

Beth looked up and down the corridor, as if searching for inspiration. 'Well you had better get to your bed. Come, take my arm.'

Sarah didn't answer but took Beth's arm pressing her other hand into the small of her back. Beth pushed open the door and helped Sarah over to a chair and then turned down the covers on the bed. 'Where's your nightshift, Sarah?'

'Hanging in the cupboard,' she answered shortly.

Beth pulled open the door and instantly she caught her breath, for Arthur's clothes were also hanging up and she immediately smelt his own aroma on them. Her pain was still as acute as it was when Will had told her that his brother was going to marry the girl who now sat a few feet from her, Arthur's child big in her belly. She had to acknowledge that she was an outsider now, only a bystander at this marriage about to be sealed with the birth of a child. She set her mind firmly on the present and pulled out the linen shift. She didn't want to be in attendance any more than Sarah wanted to have her there but fate seemed to have cast them as companions in this hour.

'Can you manage to get off your gown?' she asked.

Sarah shook her head and held up one arm to indicate the side laces which Beth undid. She helped Sarah step out of her hooped gown and petticoats and loose-tied stays until she stood in her thin chemise. Beth helped pull it over her head. Unlike most of the girls in the village who came from large families and shared several to a room and were often surrounded by pregnant sisters or mothers, Beth had grown up an only child and had always had her own bedchamber, and had never seen a naked heavily pregnant woman before. She felt uncomfortable at the sight of Sarah's swollen breasts, their teats dark brown and long and her huge belly, her white skin stretched taut over it. She pulled the nightshift over Sarah's head and helped her into the bed. 'Sarah, I don't know how to help you. I don't know what must be done. I think I should go and see if I can fetch a local woman who can help.'

Sarah was breathing through another pain and said nothing.

Beth looked down at Sarah who was clutching the side of her belly. 'Is it all right if I leave you for a while?'

Sarah remained silent but nodded. Beth glanced at her for a moment and then quickly stepped out of the room. She went to Will's room and banged on the door. There was no answer and she turned the handle. It was not locked and she went in. The bed was unmade and there was a piece of paper on the crumpled sheets.

Gone birding. Didn't fancy your stuffy old church. I'll come back this afternoon.
- Will

Beth half smiled in exasperation but thought Will was best out of the situation after all. She hurried downstairs and found Stanton Blacklock, the landlord, at the cupboard under the stairs.

'Oh, Mr Blacklock,' she said breathlessly. 'Mrs Gray has started her labour pains. They've come early and I don't know what I should do. Is there a doctor or a midwife nearby could be fetched? Or your wife perhaps?'

He straightened up. 'Lord! My wife's been dead these many long years, miss. Nearest doctor, that'll be Rye but we do have a man-midwife here, that is, if Mr Gray will allow him to attend his wife.'

Beth shook her head impatiently. 'Mr Gray isn't here. Can I fetch the man-midwife? Only tell me his direction.'

'No you go back to your friend and I'll send one of the lads for him. Best get a fire lit in her room though. That is one thing I do know and make sure the windows are closed.'

Beth went back upstairs to find Sarah red in the face and panting with her exertions. She found a piece of linen and dipped it in the pitcher on the chest and wiped Sarah's face with it. 'There's a man midwife here in Lydd, Sarah. I hope you won't object to his presence—"

'Where is he?' Sarah asked, cutting Beth short.

'One of the lads is fetching him. He'll be here soon, I'm sure.'

An hour later, they were still waiting and Beth slipped out and ran downstairs again to find the landlord in conversation with the lad he had sent.

'Here's Jack come back unsuccessful. The man midwife was called to a case up at Dymchurch but Jack here has left a message with his housekeeper who says he will come as soon as he is able.'

'But I don't know what to do,' Beth retorted.

'Nature knows what to do,' Blacklock said reassuringly. 'Let nature do what comes naturally. Don't you panic, miss. Likely it will go on for hours yet.'

Beth looked up at him and was about to make a sharp retort but instead she said, 'I don't think so. And we'll need some more linen and a towel to wrap the baby in, when it does arrive.'

She followed him upstairs to the linen cupboard and Blacklock called to a little maid to go and make up a fire in Sarah's room.

By three in the afternoon Sarah's pains were coming more frequently and even more painfully. At the crest of each wave of pain her face was bright red, the veins on her forehead standing out, her grasp on Beth's wrist tight and painful. The blazing fire and the closed window made the room unbearably hot and stuffy and Beth thought she would suffocate if the child didn't come soon.

'Oh for pity's sake, when will it stop?' Sarah gasped in between pains and then as another wave of cramping pain overtook her, she clasped Beth's hand again and groaned through clenched teeth. 'Damn you to hell, George Kingsmill,' she screamed. 'Damn all men!'

Beth could hardly believe what she had heard. She tugged at Sarah's hand. 'Sarah, what do you mean? What has George Kingsmill to do with this? Tell me.'

But at that moment another shock of pain washed over Sarah and she ignored Beth's question. 'It's coming, Beth,' she screamed. 'I need to push!'

Just then there was an urgent knocking at the door and Beth, held fast by Sarah's hand, could only call out, 'A moment please! Who is it?'

'It is William Waylett, the man midwife,' a voice replied.

There was another shriek from Sarah.

'I think I had better come in,' the man's voice said.

'Yes, pray do,' Beth called urgently and turned round to face the man as he entered. He was a tall, thin man, younger than Beth had imagined, perhaps thirty or so. He placed his bag on the floor. 'Mrs Gray, I assume?' he said, nodding at Sarah.

'Oh help me,' she gasped.

He took a few moments to take out some instruments and linen from his bag and laid them carefully on the sheet at the foot of the bed. He drew up a chair at the side of the bed level with Sarah's knees and discreetly lifted the shift and peered at her. 'I have come just in time,' he announced solemnly.

He laid a hand on Sarah's belly and pushed down. She screamed and cursed but it seemed to have the desired effect, for as he pushed up her shift, Beth saw in amazement the baby's face appear between Sarah's wide open thighs. She gave another push and the baby slipped out attached to its thick purple cord. The man midwife held the baby up by its heels and slapped its back. It let out a cry and he wrapped it in the cotton towel.

'You have a daughter, Mrs Gray. A fine baby, I might add. About eight pounds I should say.'

He laid the infant on Sarah's thigh as he cut the cord and then handed the baby to her. Sarah remained half-sitting up, her legs bent at the knees, her thighs still wide open, as she took her daughter from him, her face wreathed in smiles.

'Oh Beth, look at my baby. Isn't she beautiful?' she said reverently.

Beth looked at the infant but her emotions were in turmoil. Could Sarah mean that this child was not Arthur's at all, but George Kingsmill's? Had Arthur married her, knowing that? Or, and she groaned inwardly to think it, had he married her believing this child was his? She sucked in her breath. This child was the only reason Arthur had married Sarah. She started to do her sums. It was now the end of October, which meant the child was probably conceived in February. She put her hands to her face in an agony of uncertainty. Without knowing when Arthur had first bedded Sarah, Beth could not be sure.

She turned back to Sarah. The man midwife was still working between her thighs and he said to her, 'Offer your breast to the baby, Mrs Gray. She should suck straight away.'

Sarah fumbled with the buttons at her neck and held the baby to her full round breast, pushing the nipple at the baby's mouth.

William Waylett glanced up. 'Well done indeed, madam,' he said for the baby could be heard sucking greedily.

He wrapped up some linen and said, 'Well I have finished here. Keep to your bed Mrs Gray. I understand your husband is not here; I shall make up my bill and leave it downstairs. Good day to you and to you, miss. I shall call in a few days to make sure all is well.'

'Just one moment,' Beth said, following him out of the door and closing it behind her. 'The baby, will it be all right? I know it was supposed to arrive at Christmas time.'

He laughed. 'Now, what has put that idea into your head? That baby has gone its full term, even a week or so over,' he said, 'and as I told Mrs Gray, she weighs about eight pounds. No, there's nothing early about that baby.'

Beth went slowly back into the bedroom. The heat was oppressive. Sarah was still suckling the baby, stroking its downy head. If she remembered what she had said, she showed no signs of it, for she didn't look embarrassed or guilty as she turned to Beth.

'Is there no sign of Arthur? He'll be so pleased to see our child. Could you fetch me a clean shift and a bowl of water so I'm fresh when he comes? And I have such a thirst. Is there any ale?'

Beth said nothing but went to the cupboard again. By the time she had given the bowl to Sarah, helped her change her shift and put clean linen under her, she was aching with tiredness herself and uncomfortable in the heat of the room. She longed for a wash and a change of clothes herself. She was just about to leave the room when there was a knock at the door. She opened it slowly and Arthur stood there, looking anxious and tired, stubble on his chin. Beth's heart leapt to see him and instead of wanting to tell him her suspicions straight away as she thought she would, she was suddenly desperate that he shouldn't know if he had been tricked into this marriage.

'Beth,' he said. 'Is it true? Stanton Blacklock says Sarah has been in labour.'

Hearing Arthur's question as he stood on the threshold, Sarah laughed lying back on her pillows. 'Come and meet our daughter, Arthur dear.'

Arthur turned, disbelieving to the bed. Beth, knowing she should leave husband and wife alone at this moment, slipped out of the room to make her way down the corridor into her own but not before she saw out of the corner of her eye, Sarah open up her nightgown again and getting Arthur to lift the baby to her exposed breast, began to suckle it as her husband looked on. Sarah turned her head infinitesimally to look at Beth with an expression of triumph. Then she turned back to her baby and put her hand over Arthur's.

Beth pulled off her clothes and left them in a heap on the floor, delighting in the cool room and using the cold water in the pitcher to wash herself. She caught sight of the reflection of her naked body in the old mirror standing in the corner and turned slowly to face it. She looked at her small breasts and laid a hand on her flat belly. She felt like a girl, a child almost, beside the voluptuous womanliness of Sarah's body and wondered if Arthur compared her own body with his wife's.

It was over a year now since she and Arthur had lain together, Beth thought, remembering that last afternoon before they had argued in the churchyard and she had stormed off intent on going to London, hoping her absence would make him miss her more, never dreaming he would have sought consolation so quickly and found it in Sarah's comfortable arms. Never imagining either, that twelve months after leaving him, she would have been with his wife throughout her labour, an unwilling participant in an event which must demonstrate to the world that Arthur and Sarah were truly man and wife. Pretty, buxom Sarah and their daughter were his responsibility and their welfare must now be his main concern. Beth sighed and pulled her fine linen chemise over her head.

Twenty minutes later she came out, her hair dressed and wearing a gown of embroidered linen with fresh lace at her neck. She went into the parlour and found Will sitting there.

He got up when she entered. 'What's happened? Is the baby coming? So much for our day at the Fair!'

Beth smiled at him. 'You have a niece, Will. And there's nothing to stop you having a day at the Fair tomorrow.'

'Huh,' he grunted. 'I'll bet Arthur won't come with us now. Will he?'

Beth shook her head. 'I doubt it. He won't want to leave Sarah and the little one. You and I can go.'

He nodded and sat down. 'Is it well? The baby?'

Beth nodded 'Of course. Sarah's well, too.'

'It's come early, hasn't it? I wondered if anything was amiss, that's all.'

'Yes it has come early,' Beth said flatly.

Will looked at her suddenly. 'Are you quite well, Beth?' he asked gruffly.

She smiled. 'Of course. Just a little tired, that's all.' She felt that if Will was kind to her, she would cry. She said brightly, 'I've bespoke supper. Why don't you go and eat? I'll be along in a moment.'

'Yes, I am hungry,' he assented and disappeared into the dining room.

A few moments later Arthur appeared in the parlour. He had put on a clean shirt and washed although he hadn't shaved. Beth searched his face to see what emotions were there.

'Thank you for being with Sarah,' he said awkwardly.

She shook her head. 'What else could I do?'

He sat on the chair and rubbed a hand over his face. 'I suddenly feel grown up, Beth. It makes you think, I can tell you, having a child.'

Beth looked into her lap.

'She looks a healthy baby, don't you think? I was expecting her to be smaller, coming so early.'

Beth couldn't answer for a moment. This was her opportunity to tell Arthur what Sarah had cried out at the peak of her labour pains. She opened her mouth and paused before saying, 'Arthur?'

He caught her gaze and raised his brows, saying sharply, 'What is it?'

She pressed her lips together and smiled. 'Well, look how tall and well-built you are. And although Sarah is short, she's well formed, too. I don't think it likely the pair of you will ever have small babies.'

He looked surprised and then grinned. 'No, I suppose not.'

'And have you noticed how like you the baby is? She has your nose and chin for sure.'

'Does she?' he asked. 'I must be sure to notice next time I look at her.'

November 1732, Hawkhurst

The baby was baptised with her mother's name but was always known as Sally. Sarah took to motherhood easily. She had plenty of milk and Sally was a contented baby who soon began to sleep throughout the night and was quiet and happy during the day. Arthur was particularly pleased by this as he was out on runs two or three times a week and coming home in the early hours of the morning and sometimes not until daybreak, wanted only to fall into bed. Though he missed Beth and thought about her more than he did about Sarah especially during the long cold nights walking or riding over the Marsh, there was great comfort in coming back to a warm bed, with his warm and sleepy wife in it, who never seemed to mind when he pressed his cold body against hers to take some of her warmth. More often than not, he would pull up her nightgown and press himself against her soft flesh.

For the first few weeks after Sally's birth, Sarah would not let him make love to her, but offered him her hands and her mouth. Then early one morning when Arthur had climbed in beside her, she herself pulled off her nightgown and he felt her open her warm thighs under him, her hand already reaching for him. She held him close as he was about to pull away from her and he shuddered to his peak of pleasure inside her. 'But Sarah,' he whispered. 'We don't want another baby yet. You should have let me pull away from you.'

'It's all right, Arthur,' she said, drawing his head to rest on her ample bosom. 'I can't get pregnant while I'm suckling.'

'Oh,' Arthur replied doubtfully. 'I didn't know that.' He shifted his head slightly to get more comfortable and was soon asleep.

Beth, seeing Arthur and his small family in Church the next Sunday couldn't help but feel the jealousy in her heart well up again. Sarah made a point of taking Arthur's arm, holding her baby in the other and the other mothers from the village came up and made a fuss over the baby. Sarah by giving birth, had been elevated to a sisterhood of matrons from which Beth as an unmarried girl, was excluded.

Jane Stone looked across at Arthur and Sarah surrounded by well wishers and said to her daughter, 'I don't know how they will manage in those three rooms when Sarah's father moves away and her grandmother moves in with them.'

Beth looked at her mother. 'I didn't know he was moving away?'

Jane Stone nodded. 'I understand the distant cousin on whose farm he works has died and he is to marry the widow. She doesn't want his first wife's mother living with them, so she must go to Sarah and Arthur, I suppose. But with Will and his father living there too, perhaps Arthur will have to look for more accommodation.'

Beth couldn't help but feel a little satisfaction in knowing that Sarah's housewifely skills would be taxed by having another elderly relative to look after, though she felt ashamed to admit it to herself. However even in this Sarah seemed to win, though it meant the loss of her grandmother. A week before the old lady was due to move in with the young couple, Amos Allen found she had died peacefully in her sleep. He could move to East Grinstead, knowing he had done his duty by his first wife; and Sarah, though she had loved her grandmother, gave a sigh of relief when she realised she would not have to give over the parlour as a bedroom for the old lady. Arthur and Will were no less relieved.

CHAPTER TWENTY ONE

April 1733, Arthur and Sarah's lodgings, Hawkhurst

In late spring John Gray finally succumbed to the illness which he had brought on himself, by drinking himself slowly to death. His last two weeks on earth were spent in misery. His skin became bright yellow and his water, blood red. Though Arthur fetched the surgeon to him, he stood at the foot of the bed shaking his head.

'There's nothing any man can do for him, Arthur. He knew years ago the liquor would kill him. I'm only surprised he has lasted this long. No, it can't be long now. All you can do is keep him as comfortable as you can. Get your wife to sponge his face and make him some barley water.'

Sarah had carried in a jugful of barley water she had just prepared, intending to help Arthur support John Gray's sweating body, so he could sit up, when she pressed a hand to her forehead, swayed and sank down in a faint, spilling the jug and its contents all over the floor. Arthur lowered his father quickly and stepped hastily across to Sarah, kneeling beside her and taking her hand. She looked alarmingly pale and he was just about to call for Will to fetch the surgeon back, when her eyes fluttered open.

'Sarah,' he said. 'What is it? Are you ill?'

'Unlace my gown, Arthur and let me breathe,' she said weakly and he put his hands to her bosom, untying the laces and pulling the two edges of her bodice apart. Her breasts rose and fell as she gasped in air, resting her head against the arm he had put round her. A little of her colour returned to her cheeks. She patted her stomach and smiled.

'Well, it's confirmed my suspicions, Arthur dear,' she said at length. 'You've got me with child again.'

He looked shocked and frowned. 'But so soon? Surely you told me it wasn't possible while you were suckling Sally.'

She smiled. 'There's no stopping nature, I suppose. You wouldn't have me turn you out of our bed, would you? Or refuse you my body?'

He said nothing for a moment, seeming to be lost in thought. Then he regained possession of himself. 'Come on Sarah, let me help you to bed. You must lie down, surely? I'll fetch Will to help me with my father.'

He helped her to her feet and she hung on his arm as he guided her out of his father's room and into their own bedchamber. 'When will the baby be born?' he asked as he pushed another pillow behind her head.

He had helped her off with her gown and stays and she lay in her chemise on the bedcovers, for it was a warm day for April. She stretched her arms above her head. 'I think it will come at the time of your own birthday in November. Although with Sally coming early, who can tell?' She held out her arms to him, the filmy material of her chemise moving over her breasts. 'I'm sure it will be a son this time. Tell me you're pleased, Arthur.'

He took her in his arms, his chin resting lightly on the top of her head. 'Of course I'm pleased,' he said flatly but all he could think was that in November he would be only twenty and by then he would be the father of two children, with a wife and brother to care for. He kissed her curls, promising to look in on her later as he went back to his father's room calling for Will to come and help clear up the spilt and sticky barley water.

Towards evening Arthur went back to his father to find Will sitting at his bedside. Will looked up at his brother, with haunted eyes. 'He's asking for liquor, Arthur.'

Arthur sighed. 'What harm can it do now? Go and bring one of the flagons up. There's some French brandy, if he ain't already taken it.'

A week later, Arthur and Will were standing at their father's graveside, listening to Parson Saunders deliver the familiar burial service. Sarah could not attend, as she was suffering with this pregnancy as she had in the early days of her first, with sickness and faintness.

Will took Arthur by surprise by sobbing uncontrollably as the coffin was lowered into the ground. Arthur put his arm round his brother with some difficulty as Will was now as tall as his brother. Will had never seemed particularly to care for his father, who had been a drunkard as long as Will had been alive but he seemed genuinely grieved to lose the only parent he had ever known.

Arthur looked at the coffin with mixed feelings. There was a time when he had hated his father, or was that true? He had certainly hated what he had become and resented the responsibility he had forced his elder son to bear from such an early age but mostly he felt shame. Shame that his father had been so weak to let liquor ruin his life and shame that he and his brother had had to witness it in front of so many others.

The small party of mourners made their way back to Arthur's lodging, Sarah insisting that she would be well enough to welcome them with a few refreshments. Far from looking pale and wan as he had left her, Sarah was up and dressed in a becoming gown of soft grey, her hair dressed and white lace at her bosom. Sally was gurgling in her cot in the corner of the room and the table was spread with cold beef slices, cakes, pastries, white bread and butter and jugs of tea, milk and ale.

Whatever other faults Arthur might find in his wife, Sarah had rapidly become a model housewife and the three rooms he rented for his family had never looked cleaner or more comfortable. Arthur sat Will down in one of the chairs at the table and Lucas Webb kindly attempted to draw him out of his grief, reminding him of some of the more amusing incidents from their childhood. Arthur was relieved to see his brother wipe his eyes with his handkerchief and start to laugh at one of Lucas's anecdotes as he helped himself to a large slice of Sarah's excellent seed cake.

Sarah poured out a cup of tea and took it over to Beth. 'How kind of you to come, Beth,' she said brightly.

'I wouldn't have stayed away for the world. I knew Mr Gray all my life.'

Sarah smiled. 'I wished I felt able to attend the funeral, but I've been very sick this morning.'

Beth looked at her, curious, taking the tea cup from her. 'Nothing serious, I hope, Sarah?'

Sarah beamed back at Beth. 'Well, nothing that is not perfectly natural. I'm pregnant again. Arthur is so pleased. I didn't know he wanted a family so quickly but he seems anxious for me to have our children as soon as I can.' She looked into Beth's face, her smile still playing on her lips.

Beth stared at Sarah, disbelieving, shaken. She had forgotten, or refused to think that while she was living without the lover she had become accustomed to, Arthur and Sarah were enjoying the comforts of a normal and apparently happy, married life.

November 1733

If there were any doubts about Sally's true parentage, there could be none about Sarah's second child, for Arthur showing Beth his new daughter a day after Sarah had given birth said, 'She has such a look of Will, do you see? It's just how I remember him as a baby, with dark hair and eyes. And my father always used to say Will was like my mother, so I think Rebecca will look like my mother too.'

It was not to be wondered at that Becca, as she was thereafter known, inheriting Arthur's brains and the looks of Mary Gray, very quickly became and remained Arthur's favourite child.

There was another consequence of this second daughter's birth. Sarah had been pressing Arthur to move Sally into a little bed in Will's room so the new baby could sleep in the cradle instead of sharing her parents' bed. Will, rejoicing in having the luxury of his own bedchamber for the first time in his life, went storming out when she told him.

Arthur found him in the back yard, his shoulders hunched against the cold of the raw November morning. 'Will,' he called. Will's shoulders moved expressively without his needing to speak. Arthur went up to him and put his arm around his shoulders. 'Come in Will, let's discuss this.'

'What's to discuss?' he replied. 'It's not my house. I can't stop you letting your daughter sleep in my room. You could turn me out if you wanted to.'

Arthur gave a short laugh and smiled. 'Well that ain't very likely, is it? My baby brother?'

'You've babies of your own now,' Will countered. 'I don't come first with you, Arthur. I don't come first with no one. Nor likely to.'

Arthur turned to face Will. 'No matter how many children I have, Will, you're the only brother I'll ever have. Will? Come on. When you get a wife, you'll come first and last with her, can you doubt that?' He playfully cuffed his brother's chin with his hand and then drew Will's head near his own. 'It's time for us all to move on together. I've bought the lease of a house.'

Will turned to look at Arthur, a look of surprise in his face. 'A whole house?'

Arthur nodded. 'Up at Highgate Hill where it meets the Rye Road. You know the tall, narrow house with the great holly bush by the front porch?'

'Not that one, Arty? That's just a few houses from Beth.'

'Well, as it happens, that is so. But I chose it because there'll be room enough for us all.' Arthur patted Will's shoulder affectionately.

'But Arthur,' Will stopped and turned to his brother. 'Are you sure you can afford it?'

Arthur looked at him in amusement. 'So long as the world and his wife keep drinking tea, I can afford it very well.'

CHAPTER TWENTY TWO

January 1734, Arthur's new house, Hawkhurst

They moved into the new house on one of the only days in January when it didn't snow or rain. It didn't take long to pile up their belongings onto the wagon borrowed from Larry Kemp and Will, wandering from room to room in the new house said they had better go to Tunbridge Wells to buy some more furniture. Arthur had to agree that the large rooms now at their disposal looked bare and empty with their few pieces of furniture standing forlornly in them. This shopping trip spawned another, as Arthur decided he needed his own wagon for his growing family and a trip to Ebenezer Comfort the wheelwright and wagoner, resulted in the purchase of a second-hand but sturdy wagon.

There was a small stable at the back of the house and a pretty little walled space that Sarah wanted to make into a garden. However, Arthur said firmly that half of this area would be needed to park the wagon. No matter how much Sarah protested and wept and sulked, he was insistent. Sarah stamped her foot and thrust Becca, whom she had been suckling, into his arms and flew up to their bedchamber in a rage. Arthur was equally furious. Becca, wailing in his arms, was now red-faced and protesting loudly at having her meal interrupted. Arthur had been unpleasantly surprised at how Sarah could suddenly fly into such towering rages, making everyone around her aware of her temper. He couldn't help but contrast Sarah's moods with Beth's calming presence and as he flew up the stairs after her, the thought of what he had lost through his own folly, made him speak sharply and harshly.

He laid the squalling baby down in the middle of the bed. 'Attend to your daughter, woman!' he snarled.

Her back remained firmly turned against him.

'Sarah, I won't have this.'

Becca wailed again, stuffing her small red fists into her mouth, her piercing shrieks jarring Arthur's ears. He was across the room in three steps and swung Sarah round by her arm. She looked up at him defiantly through her tears.

'Sarah, this is my house, everything in this house is mine including you and if I decide on something, that's an end to it. If you understand that, your life will be easier. Now, do whatever Becca needs. I assume she wants to suckle?'

He jerked Sarah by her arm over to the bed and pushed her down upon it, making her sit. Sarah remained there but did not move though in truth, the cries of her small daughter seemed to cause her milk to flow and she felt her chemise growing damp at the front. Arthur, fuming, looked at Sarah for a few moments and then said, 'Very well!' scooping up his daughter.

'What are you doing?' Sarah asked, frightened. He said nothing but carried Becca out of the room and down stairs. Sarah flew down after him. 'W…what are you doing, Arthur?'

'I'm taking Becca into the village and I'll find a wet nurse to put her to. Sam Terrel's wife has just had a baby, I'll ask her.'

'You wouldn't, you wouldn't dare!' Sarah cried and ran to the door before him and stood with her back to it. He said nothing but raised his eyebrows.

Sarah dropped her head. 'Give Becca to me.'

He paused. 'Is this an end to your display of temper?' he asked.

She nodded slowly.

He waited. 'And have you anything to say?'

'I'm sorry, Arthur.' She held out her arms and after a moment he laid the baby in them and watched Sarah as she carried her over to the chair, where she sat down and untying her front laces, pulled her chemise open and held the baby to her bosom. Becca's squalls began to give way to noisy suckling as she pushed her small face into her mother's warm and comforting breast.

Arthur heard Sally begin to cry as she woke from her nap in the little room upstairs. He looked towards the staircase and went out of the front door, leaving Sarah to manage both her daughters. He fetched Achilles, whom he had been given by Beth's mother after John Stone's death. He led him from the stable to the grassy bank outside the house where he had left the wagon. He soon had him harnessed up and he tooled the wagon through the narrow entrance and manoeuvred it into the space Sarah had reserved for her garden. As he was leading Achilles back into his stable, Will came in. He came up to Achilles and rubbed him between the ears.

'All right, Arty?'

Arthur nodded. 'There's a run from Hastings, tonight, Will. Do you want to come with me?'

Will could hardly believe what Arthur had suggested. He had been clamouring for years to be allowed to work with his brother. 'Do you mean as part of the gang?'

Arthur nodded as he pulled the stable door shut. 'It's up to Grayling whether he'll take you. If not, you'll have to wait at the *Anchor* and I'll come and fetch you back. We'll ride on Achilles. He can carry both of us.'

Will anxiously awaited two o' clock when Arthur had said they would leave. He spent the last hour getting dressed in two sets of clothes as Arthur had told him and came down into the parlour, self-conscious in his long greatcoat passed down from his brother, a long muffler and warm hat.

Sarah looked up from her sewing. 'What's this?' she asked, as Arthur came in similarly dressed.

'There's a run tonight,' he said shortly.

'And you're taking Will?' she asked.

Arthur nodded. 'Make sure you lock the doors before you go to bed,' he said.

She came out with them to the stable and watched in silence as the big horse was saddled up. She had seen the wagon parked up taking up most of the space in the walled area, but knew better than to say anything. Arthur was about to swing himself up when she took his arm. He turned and looked at his wife and then kissed her cheek, climbing on the horse. 'Goodbye, Sarah,' he said, putting his hand down to hoist Will up behind him and they set off into the cold January afternoon.

They reached the welcoming lights of Hastings just before five, the roads wet and heavy and Arthur was grateful for Achilles' lumbering strength. The *Anchor* stood opposite the beach and after stabling Achilles in the inn's stable yard at the back, Arthur and Will stepped into the warmth of the tavern. Arthur saw John Grayling sitting in his customary chair and went up to him.

After exchanging greetings, Arthur drew up a chair. 'John, you see I've brought Will with me. I wondered if you could try him out tonight and if he's any good, might there be a place for him?'

Grayling looked up at Will, standing tall and serious. Grayling held out his hand. 'Always willing to give new blood a chance,' he said. 'Stick with your brother and you can't go far wrong. We've two cutters tonight. Near on five tons to unload so our work's cut out for us.'

As John Grayling had advised, Will stuck close to Arthur who gave his brother a running commentary on what was happening much as Robert Bunce had done when Arthur and Jeremiah Curtis had joined as new recruits nine years ago. Arthur kept out of Curtis's way as far as was possible. Curtis had somehow insinuated his way into the men's trust; he was free with his money and always drank with them. Will openly disliked Curtis but was sensible enough not to antagonise any of the men now he was hopeful of joining the gang.

'What are you doing here, Will Gray?' Curtis asked, seeing Will on the beach standing a little way away from Arthur, as they were waiting for the tub lines to be brought in.

'Grayling says I can try out tonight to see how I do,' Will explained shortly.

Curtis looked at him disapprovingly. 'Let's hope you can keep your mouth shut and your nose clean then, boy,' he muttered. 'Don't suppose you got your own mount?'

Will shook his head. 'Arthur carried me here.'

'Oh, I see.' Curtis looked straight out to sea. 'You won't get far without your own horse. But they cost. Or are you going to wait for Arthur to hand down that old nag of his, like he hands down his clothes?'

Will remained silent. He dearly wanted his own horse, but he wasn't going to admit anything to Curtis.

'Will, come over here,' Arthur called. Will turned from Curtis and made his way over to his brother.

'Don't have much to do with Curtis,' Arthur said. 'He always tries to go one better than anyone else and it's only ever for his own advantage.'

'You don't have to protect me, Arty. I can look after myself, you know,' Will grumbled. 'I'm fifteen next month.'

Arthur looked across at Will and grinned. 'You're still my little brother. Here!' Arthur picked up a half anker of spirits which had come loose from its twin. They were normally roped together for easy slinging over a horse. He tossed it to Will. 'Are you big enough to carry this?'

Will reached out his arms and caught it though the weight of it nearly drew his arms down to the ground.

The run went smoothly and within an hour the cargo was unloaded and the first men had departed up through Hastings town and out on to the road that would lead them through Flimwell passing within a few miles of Hawkhurst and then onto the Sevenoaks turnpike and beyond that to London, which is where Arthur was scheduled this run. 'You'll have to go back to the *Anchor*, Will. I can't take you on Achilles. I'll be riding him with a full load of goods.'

Will looked disappointed but smiled anyway. 'That's all right, Arty,' he said. 'I'll get a lift home from the carrier tomorrow.'

It had come on to rain and Arthur pulled his collar up as he led Achilles up the beach. 'Have you got enough money on you, Will? You'll need to bespeak a room. And the rest of the men who aren't running goods inland will go back there to drink. John Turner and Larry Jockey - they'll drink heavily. Don't get involved with them and don't have more than a tankard of ale, but make sure you pay when it's your round. Will you be all right?'

Will nodded. 'Yes Arthur,' he said firmly. 'I'll be fine. Go on! I'll see you some time tomorrow.'

They had reached the rough track above the beach which led directly onto the cobbled road that would take them through the town.

Arthur, aware that he had never left Will out alone at night before, wanted to hug his brother before leaving him but knowing Will would be acutely embarrassed, contented himself with simply patting his shoulder and gripped it with his hand before hoisting himself up on Achilles and following the rest of the gang who were headed towards Sevenoaks with him.

Will stood watching the line of men for a while and was about to turn back when he heard the whinny of one of the horses and a curse from the man on its back, as he fell heavily from the horse on to the cobbles beneath him. The men riding before and behind the shying mare tried to move their horses away from her. She continued to rear up, hooves pawing the air as the loaded goods on her back banged and clattered against each other as they started to loosen. Ben Raven who had been injured when he fell from her, tried to curl himself up in a ball to protect himself from her flashing hooves.

Before Arthur had time to do anything, he saw Will rush past and run up to the horse. He reached up in front of it, its hooves missing his face by inches as he called to it, grabbing the reins. 'Woah, there, shh, whoa, calm down now, sweetheart, calm down.'

He carried on talking to the horse and Arthur watched as the horse's eyes which had been flashing wildly and showing nearly all of the whites, began to return to normal. She dropped her hooves and her back stopped twitching.

Ben Raven slowly unwrapped his limbs and tried to drag himself away towards the gutter. Will's mouth was near the horse's ears, one hand rubbing down her head, the other holding the reins. John Watts and Bernard Woollett came running up, as John Grayling, who had been at the head of the line of mounted men, dismounted and came over. Watts and Woollett had helped Ben Raven to his feet. He was clutching at his collar bone.

'Well, I never seen anything like that,' Grayling said to Will. 'You got a way with horses, boy, and no word of a lie.'

'Something spooked her,' Will explained diffidently. 'She just needs to be spoken to gently.'

'And gently is what you did,' Grayling acknowledged. 'What's the damage, Ben?'

Raven looked pale even under the small light from the half moon and the lanterns the men held. 'Think my collar bone's busted, John,' he said with some effort. 'Felt it snap as I put my hand out when I fell.'

'Right, John and Bernard, you take him to Richard Sadler, the surgeon in Church Street. Knock him up. He'll see to Ben here and put it on my account.'

He turned to Will. 'Well, I got a half-loaded horse and no rider for her. How about it? Think you're up to it?'

Will's face lit up. 'What ride her all the way to London, you mean?'

Grayling laughed. 'No not that far, not on your first run with us. No you can drop off the goods when we store some in Hawkhurst, that'll suit you better. I take it you got stabling for the mare til she's needed again? But you done good, lad. Now let's not delay any longer. Mount up then and get in line behind your brother there.'

They reached Flimwell a little after midnight and here the company parted. Arthur brought his horse alongside Will and reached over to pat his arm. 'You did well, brother. Put the mare in the stable and I'll see you tomorrow. Try not to alarm Sarah when you get home, Will. She's not expecting either of us back tonight.'

Will nodded and watched the line of horses continue up the Sevenoaks road while he turned in with the others down the lane that led to Hawkhurst.

Will found Sarah was up anyway when he let himself in, for Becca still woke several times in the night and he saw the candlelight under the door of the bedchamber. He called out softly, 'It's me Sarah. I'm back. Arthur's gone to London. He'll be back tomorrow.'

He heard the handle of the door turn and Sarah stood there, a warm shawl round her, Becca clutched to her breast. 'Is everything all right then, Will? Is Arthur all right?'

Will looked down at his sister-in-law. 'Yes, of course. He says he'll be back tomorrow.'

Sarah looked as though she was going to say more, but she turned back into the room. 'Good night then.'

Arthur returned at about four the next afternoon. He had been in no particular hurry to return to Sarah and though he had finished the business at Stockwell by lunchtime, he had stopped off at Sevenoaks, had an agreeable meal at the *White Hart* and looked at some of the shop fronts before setting out for home. Sarah spent all afternoon baking, whenever Becca could be laid in her cradle and Sally strapped in a kitchen chair with a wooden spoon and tin plate to play with.

Arthur returned to the smell of a beef and onion pie which tasted as good as it smelled, followed by a plain pudding with lashings of thick yellow cream. Neither Sarah nor Arthur mentioned anything about the row they had had the previous day and though Sarah was tired from disturbed nights with Becca, she turned willingly enough to her husband as he climbed into bed beside her. She helped him to pull up her nightgown, as his hands and mouth sought the comfort of her breasts and belly. As Arthur had reminded her the day before, she belonged to him.

CHAPTER TWENTY THREE

Night of Tuesday/Wednesday May 15th/16th, 1736 Jews Cut, Dungeness

Arthur quickly turned his face away as another wave broke at thigh height and splashed over his face and chest. He spat the salt water out of his mouth and blinked hard a couple of times to try and squeeze the stinging sea water from his eyes. He turned back to the shore to see Will anxiously watching him. After two years, Will had become an experienced member of the gang, noted for his way with horses.

Over the last few months, Grayling had arranged for Arthur and Curtis to take it in turns to plan and carry through some of the smuggling runs. Sometimes Grayling would come along and just observe what was going on; other times he didn't turn up at all but mysteriously seemed to know anyway just how the night's work had gone. Tonight it was Curtis's turn to lead the run.

Arthur thought it was typical of Jeremiah Curtis to place him in a lowly position as one of the tubmen, when it was Jeremiah's turn to lead the run. It was customary for the more senior members of the gang to ride the goods inland, leaving the junior members to drive the pack horses or work as tubmen. Arthur was now up to his thighs in freezing water and with a large surf, the waves frequently splashed over him completely. Not that Arthur minded this temporary demotion in itself. He had worked his way up through all the jobs in the gang and it was no bad thing to be reminded of the particular difficulties associated with any of them.

Although it had been a pleasant warm day, the night sea was still cold and Arthur was shivering as he cut free the half ankers attached to the ropes that the tub boat had pulled in and then tossed the kegs to Pete Tickner who was standing a little further in, the water only up to his knees and his legs kept dry by the oilskin waders he was wearing.

Just over an hour later the last kegs were unloaded from the cutter and the tub boat was sent back. Arthur waded out of the surf, rubbing his hands up his arms to try and get warm. Pete Tickner waited for him on the shoreline. 'Cold night, eh, Arthur?'

Arthur nodded. 'Especially if you're standing in the sea!'

They trudged up the shingle troughs, made even harder to walk on as Arthur felt the seawater squelching in his boots. 'You'll have to wait for me, Pete,' he said. 'I've got half the English Channel in my boots, I think.' He sat down on the pebbles and pulled his boots and waders off turning them upside down to see the water stream out of them.

At that moment Curtis came up. 'No slacking there, Gray,' he said. 'I've a spare driven horse. You can lead her to Brookland with the others. Your brother's got her at the moment.'

Arthur looked across at Curtis but he was already on his way back up the beach.

'I'm running the goods all the way to Stockwell tonight, Arthur,' Tickner said. 'Reckon I'll see you tomorrow. It's your run then, ain't it?'

Arthur grinned. 'Yep, my turn then.' He pulled his boots back on and hurried up the beach to find Will leading both horses. Will held out Arthur's greatcoat, which he had left with his brother so he had at least one dry item of clothing to wear for the rest of the night.

'You're soaked, Arthur,' Will said, seeing how his wet shirt and breeches were clinging to him and hearing his teeth chattering.

'I reckon I'll keep warmer walking than I would riding, Will.' He took the reins from Will and walked briskly in front of the laden horse. 'We're storing them at the *Woolpack*, ain't we?'

Will nodded. 'Shouldn't take us much more than two hours to get to Brookland. Then home on Achilles. I reckon we'll be home by six.'

They trudged over the Marsh, sticking to the rough tracks where they could and made their way out towards Brookland. There was only a crescent moon but it gave enough light, along with their half blacked-out lanterns to make out their way. The flat blackness of the Marsh seemed to stretch away into infinity after they left the lights of Lydd behind them. The silver slice of the moon occasionally shone out when the clouds parted, to light up a solitary tree dotted here and there, the thick silence broken only by the comforting sound of the horses moving and the crunch of their own booted footsteps. Occasionally a marsh animal could be heard snuffling through long grass, searching for a meal. As long as Arthur kept walking he forgot how cold he was and after two hours, he quite enjoyed being out in the fresh night air as the few lights of Brookland gleamed in the distance.

When they reached the *Woolpack* they were surprised to see Curtis standing outside waiting for them.

'What's up?' Arthur asked, expecting Curtis to have unloaded his horse and returned to Rye long ago.

Curtis looked angry. 'Fucking landlord's away,' he hissed.

'So? Martin will be here, won't he?' Arthur asked referring to the landlord's son.

'Yes, but John Cowen has taken the key to the inner store with him. Fuck!' Curtis kicked up a stone which bounced off one of the horse's flanks, making it whinny and shy up.

Arthur paused and then said, 'Oh.'

'What do you mean, *Oh*, what's that supposed to mean, Gray?'

Arthur bit his lip to stop himself from smiling. 'It don't mean nothing, Curtis. What do you want us to do?'

Curtis pursed his lips together. 'You come with me, Gray. We'll see if we can break the fucking door down.'

Arthur said nothing but raised his eyebrows to Will as he passed him, following Curtis into the side door of the inn. The inn had a couple of little bar rooms and private parlours and it was off one of these that a small passage led to a door. It was the key to this that was missing. The little door led down steps to a long passage with a large storage area at the end of it and beyond that there was another passage with steps leading up that would bring a man out, if he so wished, to a rough field some twenty yards beyond the back of the *Woolpack's* stables.

The door was much thicker than a normal door, made of heavy oak with a large iron lock.

'I wouldn't go breaking that, Curtis,' Arthur said, as they both examined it while Martin held a lantern aloft for them.

'What does your father want to take the key with him for, anyway?' Curtis asked, crossly.

'Always takes it with him,' the youth answered. 'Said there wasn't no runs expected, anyway, when he went. He'll be back tomorrow.'

'Huh,' Curtis snorted. 'Where's he gone, anyway?'

Martin grinned at Arthur. 'Dad's gone courting, Tenterden way.'

Curtis stormed out, without a word to either Arthur or Martin. They grinned at each other and Martin jerked his head in Curtis's direction. 'What's got into him, Arthur?'

Arthur shook his head and followed Curtis back outside where the men and horses were waiting.

'What's going on?' Will whispered to his brother, but before Arthur could answer, Curtis was up on his horse. 'Bring the horses to Brenzett. We'll use one of the barns there.' He dug his heels into his horse's flanks and rode off. The small party of men and horses turned round and made their way after him.

A half hour later, they were unloading their horses into the small barn just outside the village of Brenzett.

'Whose barn is this?' Will asked as he heaved the last pair of kegs off Achilles' back and passed them along the line of men who were storing them neatly at the back of the barn.

'Paul Ramsey's,' Arthur answered, lifting a heavy crate off the horse he had been leading. 'He doesn't always care to have his barn used, especially if he doesn't know about it beforehand and I don't suppose Curtis has told him.'

Curtis had already left, leaving the men to finish unloading and was on his way back to Rye. He had told them he would arrange to pick the goods up tomorrow.

'But there's another run, tomorrow,' Arthur had protested, knowing he himself was to lead it.

Curtis had shrugged. 'Can't be helped, can it?'

'But it needs eight or nine men to reload this stuff,' Arthur pointed out. 'I've already worked out my loading figures.'

'Well, you'll have to do 'em again, won't you?' Curtis had said and ridden off.

It was nearly eight o' clock in the morning when Achilles, with Arthur and Will aloft, finally plodded into Hawkhurst and they could dismount. Will led Achilles into the stable ready to rub him down and give him his well-earned food while Arthur stepped into the kitchen, to find Sarah with a tub of hot water and a pair of washing tongs, starting her linen wash. She came over to Arthur and kissed him. She wrinkled up her small nose. 'Your clothes smell wet.'

He laughed. 'If you can wait a while, you can have them to put in your tub, Sarah. I got a rare soaking last night.'

'Well take them off now and I'll put them straight in and then cook you some breakfast.' She knew how her husband and Will enjoyed the eggs, bacon and sausages she invariably cooked for them when they returned from a run. Arthur hung his greatcoat over a chair and pulled off his shirt, waistcoat, breeches and drawers and stood naked in the middle of the kitchen, leaving his clothes in a pile on the floor.

Sarah looked up at him. 'Here, Arthur, stand by the dresser. I'll dip some linen in this hot water and wash all that sea water off your back. It's left scum marks where it's partly dried.'

He turned his back to her and sighed with pleasure as the hot wet cloth, dripped warm water over his back and shoulders and under his arms. She briskly rubbed him dry with a rough towel.

He turned round to face her and pulled her to him. 'Can't you come up to bed with me, Sarah?' he asked, his hands resting at the back of her waist and pulling her into his groin.

'No I can't,' she exclaimed. 'Get along with you! Go upstairs and put your nightshirt on and then come down and I'll have breakfast ready. Go on, here's Will at the door.' She pulled herself out of his embrace smiling and briefly touched him intimately before pushing him into the hallway as Will came in the back door.

The following night, May16th/17th 1736, Dungeness Point

Will, acting as a lookout, heard the sound of horses' hooves in the distance as they crunched along the rough pebble track. There was a heavier sound which he recognised, after closing his eyes to concentrate on it, as heavy iron-clad wheels also crunching as they rumbled over the pebbles. He gave a low whistle across to Tom Dixon, the man nearest to him, who pushed his hat further down on his head as he hurried over to Will. 'What is it, lad?' he whispered.

'Horses, three at least and a wagon,' Will hissed. He had drawn his Henshaw pistol, looking gravely at Tom Dixon. 'Go and tell, Arthur,' he said to the older man.

'Sure you're safe hereabouts on your ownsome?' Dixon asked.

Will nodded. 'Be quick though.'

Dixon hurried off down the beach towards the landing party. Will, all his senses alert, looked about him. He could see Ben Raven much further away and wondered if he too had heard the approaching party. There was no cover on the beach, so there was no point in running anywhere. Will stood tall waiting for whoever it was to approach and swung his muffler round his face. He heard one of the horses approach nearer and out of the moonlight it was almost upon him.

'Who's there?' he yelled as the horse skidded to a halt two feet in front of him.

'Put up your gun! It's Tom Kingsmill,' the rider announced.

Will hesitated though he recognised Tom's voice. Kingsmill dismounted. 'Is that you, Will? Where's your brother?'

But at that moment, they both turned as Arthur and Tom Dixon trudged up the shingle. 'What's all this?' Arthur asked.

'We got ourselves a couple of trapped rats,' Kingsmill said. 'Here they come now.'

The rest of the men looked as three horses approached, followed a little way distant by a wagon drawn by another two horses. Jeremiah Curtis reined in his horse. He was leading the two others horses, their riders sitting awkwardly, blindfolded. Kingsmill pointed at the two men.

'Two Customs House officers,' he said. 'They'd seized our brandy from the barn in Brenzett and were making their way off with it. They'd loaded most of it in this handsome wagon, property of His Majesty's customs, so we brought it back with us. Caught them red-handed on the road at Old Romney, not two hours since.'

Arthur looked up at the two men and saw they had their hands tied tightly in front of them and their clothes looked dusty and stained. It would not have taken them two hours to bring the men from Old Romney to Dungeness Point. Arthur guessed Curtis and Kingsmill had dealt out some rough treatment to the two officials before bringing them back.

Arthur frowned. He had known it was a bad idea to store the brandy in Ramsey's barn. They hardly ever used it now. It was too open to prying eyes, though he was curious to know how these Customs House men had got to know about it so quickly. Curtis had already caused him difficulty by taking off eight of the men he had planned to use on running tonight's goods and now he had caused another problem for Arthur to deal with.

'Dismount, then,' Arthur ordered. The men hesitated. It was difficult to do so, with their hands tethered. Curtis reached up and roughly grabbed one of the men by the shoulder, pulling him off the horse's back. He would have fallen heavily but Will reached out to steady the man and did the same for the other. One was taller, thinner than the other, older man. Both wore their distinctive coats, proclaiming their occupation. 'Identify yourselves,' Arthur ordered. The taller man opened his mouth.

'F... Freebody Dray, Customs House officer at D... Dover,' he stammered nervously.

'And you?' Arthur said, poking the other man in the chest. The man looked as though he was trying to peer through his blindfold.

'John Derby of the same.'

'You're a long way off your patch,' Arthur commented. 'What brings you here?'

Neither man spoke. Arthur took his hanger and gently laid the sharp steel tip on the taller man's coat at his breast. 'What brings you here, I asked.'

'Information laid,' he replied, 'but I don't know who laid it, I swear.'

Arthur put a hand up to his face and rubbed it over his mouth and chin, wondering what he should do with these two men. 'What was the information laid?' he demanded.

'Keep your mouth shut, lad,' the older of the two men said steadily to his companion. Curtis pushed forward and swung his fist up, crashing into the older man's jaw. He fell heavily to his side and struggled to get up. Curtis placed a boot on his chest.

Arthur kicked Curtis' foot off with his own. 'Let him up,' he said angrily. 'You,' he commanded the older man. 'Get up to your knees and stay there. And you join him, Freebody Dray.' He pushed the younger man down, so they were both huddled kneeling painfully on the pebbles.

'Watch them close,' Arthur ordered Tom Dixon and Curtis pulled out his pistol and held it to the younger man's temple. The captive pulled his head back, catching his breath.

'Yes,' Curtis snarled. 'It is what you think it is, Freebody Dray. I will make a hole for the sun to shine through you if either of you play any tricks!'

You see a man's fear most clearly in his eyes, Arthur thought to himself, *and although he is blindfolded, the younger man shows me his fear in his hunched shoulders, his bowed head, in the tension in his upper body.*

Arthur pulled Curtis's arm and led him away further up the beach to where the wagon was. The rest of the men had approached and they all stood round the wagon. Arthur held the lantern above it and recognised the kegs as part of the previous night's aborted run. They were out of earshot of the two customs officials.

'Shoot 'em,' Curtis said. 'There ain't no witnesses, are there, just us?'

Some of the men muttered their agreement.

'They wouldn't hesitate to shoot us,' Tom Kingsmill declared. 'I don't know why you're waiting, Gray.'

'I ain't in favour of shooting men in cold blood, that's why,' Arthur snapped.

'Aye, that's right,' John Watts assented. 'Don't want indictment for murder, do we?'

There were more voices raised in agreement.

'Tom, unload the wagon and we'll drive it empty and leave it on the road somewhere. Double load some of our horses with the kegs,' Arthur said. He looked at the horses Darby and Dray had been riding.

The men were gathered round, waiting for their orders. 'Load up their two horses as well and then finish unloading here. We've still a couple of tub lines to cut free. Get to it! Let's waste no more time.'

The men turned back to the shore. Arthur went back over to the two captives. He looked around him at the moonlit beach. 'I think I must trouble you for the loan of your horses - you won't be needing them.'

The younger man raised his head in the direction of Arthur's voice thinking he meant to do away with them. 'Oh please sir, don't do it, don't shoot us, I'm begging you sir!' He caught his breath and started to sob. 'There's only me, sir, I got elderly parents and one young brother only ten! Who's to look out for them if I'm gone, sir, oh please, I beg you, I beg you!' He reached out with his tethered hands and pulled the hem of Arthur's coat to his blindfolded eyes and sobbed.

Curtis began to laugh but Arthur felt suddenly sickened by the scene, ashamed of himself. *What madness is this?* he thought to himself. *That might be me, begging for my life. What made this man choose the Custom men, and me choose Grayling's?*

'How old are you, Dray?' he asked.

Dray lifted up his head. 'Twenty two sir. And Mr Darby here sir, I know he won't beg for his life but he has a wife and two children.'

Arthur bent down and pulled the hem of his coat out of Dray's hands, thinking to himself that he was the same age as the man before him pleading for his life and that he had two children the same as the other captive.

'Take them up, Pete,' he said softly to Peter Tickner who ordered the two men to stand. They sucked in their breath. Arthur watched them, wondering what it must feel like knowing your life was in the hands of another man. He went over to Tickner. 'Signal the tub boat to come back in, Pete and put them in it. We'll board with them.'

Tickner frowned. 'What's afoot, Arthur?'

Arthur shrugged and smiled at him. 'I'll send our two friends over to France for the day. That'll keep them out of the way.'

Dray and Darby, still blindfolded and tethered, sat awkwardly in the little boat, wondering if at any moment they would be tipped out into the sea but as they approached the *Swallow*, Arthur took out his clasp knife and cut the ropes that Curtis had bound round their wrists.

'You're on your oath not to remove the blindfolds, or that's an end of you,' he said. 'But you'll need your hands to climb the ladder and board the boat.'

He stood up, the little tub boat rolling at the sudden movement and Arthur placed Dray's hands on the bottom rung. 'Go on, climb aboard.' He was followed by Darby and then by Arthur himself. Captain Ollive was waiting at the top looking puzzled.

'I've two passengers for you, Captain,' Arthur announced and then took his arm to move him out of earshot. 'Can you take them to Boulogne and send them back with the next boat coming over? Drop them off at Rye tomorrow and tell them their horses will be waiting in the stables at the *George* for them?'

The Captain gave a short laugh. 'What game is this, Arthur?'

'No game, Captain,' he replied. 'I just need to frighten them a little and keep them out of our way for a day or two. Guard them closely but see that they come to no harm.'

Arthur was already beginning to feel queasy at the pitch and roll of the cutter. 'I'll be getting back.'

The Captain nodded, knowing Arthur's dislike of being at sea.

In five minutes, Arthur was back on dry land and preparing to mount his mare. Curtis was supervising the clearing up of the beach, making sure there was nothing left behind. Arthur looked across at Jeremiah. 'Would you have shot them, Curtis? In cold blood?'

Curtis returned Arthur's gaze and nodded. 'Dead's dead ain't it, cold blood or not?'

'And earned yourself a bounty on your head?' Arthur asked.

Curtis shrugged. 'Reckon we'll all have that one day, don't you?'

CHAPTER TWENTY FOUR

Night of Wednesday 26th June 1737, Lydd

'Want you to come up to Stockwell, Arthur.' Grayling was sitting opposite Arthur at the *George* at Lydd, waiting for two cutters due in later that night.

'Thought I was going there anyway, John,' Arthur replied, putting his hand over his tankard as Stanton Blacklock brought another jug of ale over. Grayling held up his tankard and waited for the landlord to fill it to its brim. He took a mouthful and then wiped his lips with the back of his hand.

'Ah, but there's a bit more to it this time. Think it's time I introduced you to some important people.'

Arthur raised his eyebrows. He wondered why Grayling had chosen this small table to sit at with only two seats drawn up to it, a little way away from the larger tables where the rest of the men sat.

'Why do you think I've had you and Curtis trying your hand at running things these last months?'

'I suppose you're thinking of the future, John,' Arthur answered, his voice serious.

Grayling nodded. 'My future, your future. Aye, you're in the right of it. I been in this business more than forty years. Sometimes it don't seem like more than a couple of years ago, when we used to run wool over to France.'

He was quiet for a moment obviously thinking of the old days.

'The thing is Arthur, well, two things really, First is that a man of my age should start thinking of slowing down a bit, taking things a bit easier, which is what I am wishful of doing. You and Curtis are the sharpest two in the gang, you both got your strengths and you both got your weaknesses. Now that ain't a criticism,' he said holding up his hand. 'Show me a man without a fault and I'll show you a corpse. So I'd like to know I'll be handing things over to a safe pair of hands. I reckon since I knowed you both, you've learned most of what there is to know about this business. Except for the last thing and that's the most important, cos without it we wouldn't have been able to start such a business in the first place.'

'You mean the Venturers, John?' Arthur said. 'The men who put up the money?'

Grayling nodded slowly taking another mouthful of his drink. 'Before a man will put his money into your business, he's got to like you and trust you. Most men would sooner trust you with their wife than with their money. Now I've never mentioned have I, never given you any sort of clue about who might have a finger in this pie, so to speak?'

Arthur shook his head. 'No you haven't, that's for sure.'

'Well, I'm going to take you up to Stockwell and then onto one of the coffee houses to have a bit of conversation with one or two gentlemen. After that, it's up to them and up to you to make any sort of arrangements you might be wishful to make. They'll probably want you to stay a couple of days, if they like the cut of your jib.'

Arthur wondered who the Venturers might be and what they might ask him. A thought occurred to him. 'Is Curtis coming too?'

Grayling looked into the distance. 'Took him along last week.' He said nothing more.

Arthur waited. 'And?'

Grayling shrugged. 'I ain't heard nothing more. Don't know if Curtis has.'

Arthur said nothing, but wondered why Grayling had chosen to introduce Curtis first to his backers.

'So Arthur, discretion always.' He laid a finger at the side of his nose. 'No need to tell you to keep this to yourself. Now you may remember I said there was two things I wanted to talk to you about. Well the second one is this. You know as well as I do that the Government is a slippery fish and is always trying to make life for us free traders more difficult. The Act of Indemnity,' he said solemnly. 'A very bad thing, a very bad thing indeed. You do understand what it means?'

Arthur nodded. 'It means if one of our number grasses on us, he gains immunity from prosecution.'

Grayling nodded. 'Aye, so he does,' he said fiercely. 'At the present time, the rewards from staying within our band outweigh any reward that might be offered. And anyone who grasses us up knows, if he splits on us, then he and his family will be outcasts from our company. And as you well know, if you live in Hastings, or Rye, or Hawkhurst or Goudhurst or just about any of the villages hereabouts, that means being an outcast from his entire village; most folks being involved one way or another as members or customers of our business. But you can never tell what a man might do, so my advice is watch your back.'

'But is there any trouble, John?' Arthur asked, concerned.

Grayling shook his head. 'Nothin' in particular but as you know I was took last year on a false charge. Assaulting a Customs House officer! Luckily John Goddard, the local Justice has been a customer of mine for years, so as you know I was released without charge and quite right too. But it has given me to think. The penalty for resisting arrest if you're being taken, suspected of smuggling, is transportation. And there is always a Dragoon ready to swear you was resisting arrest.'

Arthur looked grim.

'Transportation! Might as well be death,' Grayling declared. 'I don't reckon there's much of a life to be made in the West Indies or America. Especially as you'd be working there seven years as a slave. But a man must confront his fears.' He paused for a moment. 'Now, where was I? Oh yes. I reckon if there's any chance at all of being taken and charged and God forbid, found guilty – then a man should start preparing for that.'

Arthur leaned forward in his seat. As more and more of the gang were arriving, it was getting very noisy. 'But how can you prepare for that, John?'

Grayling smiled and laid a finger at the side of his nose. 'What's the use of any money you might have made if you're a slave in America and your money is sitting under your bed back home? None at all. So I've started enquiring as to how I might be sending some of it abroad, as an insurance you understand. It's just a hint to you, Arthur. There's rich rewards to be made if you lead the gang. You can pretty much take what profit you choose. But that's up to you to discuss with the gentlemen I shall introduce you to. And now I do believe we have a couple of cutters to see to.'

For the first time during a run Arthur's excitement was reserved for what was going to happen afterwards. He could hardly wait for the cutters to come in and the tublines to be sent ashore. At last the cargo was loaded and the run in began, Arthur near the head of the column of men who were running the tea straight up to London.

Thursday 27ᵗʰ June 1737, London

They reached the little village of Stockwell towards seven in the morning on a bright clear day, the yellow sun rising high in a blue sky smudged with little puffy white clouds. Grayling and Arthur took rooms at the *Robin Hood.*

Grayling drew out his brass watch. 'We're meeting them at one,' he said. 'I'll knock on your door about midday then.'

Five hours later, both men made their way on horseback again towards London Bridge. 'We're going to *Jonathan's* coffee house in Change Alley,' Grayling said, as they set off.

They left Stockwell behind them and crossed the great river by London Bridge. They made their way through a part of London Arthur had never seen, through Fish Street Hill and into Gracechurch Street, a huddle of houses, shops and taverns, the air alive with the calls of street vendors; shouts and laughter coming from the open doors of the taverns, the noisy rattle of lumbering carts and in the air an overpowering mixture of smells – the earthy smell of dung, the pungent aroma of gin and ale wafting out from the taverns, the warm leathery smell of horses and the potent smell of humanity pressed together and going about their pleasure and business in the great city on a hot June morning.

Change Alley was a thriving, bustling narrow street, in some places not much wider than a passageway, tucked between the wide thoroughfare of Cornhill and the narrower Lombard Street with its tall houses and iron railings. Grayling turned his horse into the stables to the side of the coffee house, pressing a coin into the stable lad's palm and led Arthur round to the front of a tall, three-storey building with double bay windows looking onto the street. Four wide shallow steps led up to the front door which stood open.

Grayling entered the little hallway and greeted the servant who sat in a porter's chair and paid him the penny entrance fee for both of them. There were rooms leading off to the left and right and Grayling, poking his head round both, entered the room on the left. The room ran the whole depth of the house with windows at each end making it light and airy. The windows were bare of hangings but as the rooms stood higher than the street outside, no one could see in. The floors were a bare dark wood and there was an arrangement of oblong tables in a 'U' shape with wooden upright chairs and some fixed seating around the walls. Almost every chair was taken and there was a great hubbub of earnest conversation, shouts of laughter and the occasional call to one of the servants for more coffee.

The servants, all male, wore brown silk waistcoats and brown jackets and all had neat powdered wigs tied at the back with a brown riband. They were engaged in bringing coffee, Arthur noticed, in silver coffee pots on silver trays, the men drinking the rich dark brown liquid in small bowls. Arthur never had much liking for the strong bitter taste of coffee but its aroma in the room mingling with the smoke from the pipes that some of the customers were smoking, added to the atmosphere of men at business, sharp and serious, vibrant and stimulating.

Grayling's quick eyes were darting around the room and he half turned to Arthur, nodding towards the table at the back of the room. 'There are the two gentlemen we've come to do business with, one of them as you will note, well known to you.'

Arthur looked in the direction Grayling had indicated and at first only noticed a slightly built man in his mid thirties, with long black hair worn loose, a swarthy complexion, his prominent nose and dark features proclaiming his Jewish origins. Sitting next to him and much to Arthur's surprise, laughing at some joke his companion had made, was Thomas Lamb. Lamb looked up and seeing Grayling and Arthur, rose to his feet holding out his hand and shook their hands warmly. 'Good day, good day indeed Grayling. And to you too, Arthur. Let me make my good friend known to you.'

Lamb turned to his companion. 'Sampson, may I make known to you, Arthur Gray? John Grayling here, you already know. Arthur, this is Mr Sampson Gideon, a good friend of mine.'

The Jew rose from his seat and Arthur found himself looking down into a pair of dark, intelligent, slightly hooded eyes. He held out his hand and Arthur noticed what fine long fingers he had and the elegant gold ring he wore on his little finger. He had a small gold pin in his neckerchief and dark quiet clothes. There was nothing to suggest he was one of the most successful financiers in the country.

Lamb called for some more coffee and the four men took their seats. There was some small talk about the weather and the ride up from Kent and then Lamb leaned forward and said to Arthur, 'I expect you're somewhat surprised to be meeting me here, Gray?'

Arthur waited until the man servant had set the coffee pot down at the table. 'I knew you had varied business interests, sir, but yes, I am surprised.'

Lamb laughed. 'I've been connected with Grayling here for some years now to the benefit of both of us, eh John? You'd be surprised how many men of substance in Kent and Sussex are involved in one way or another with your activities. The first thing to understand though is that any transactions or discussions we have are in confidence and would be denied by myself, or-,' he added, with a nod at Gideon, 'by any other person or persons who might wish to have dealings with you at some time in the future. Nothing linking us is ever committed to paper. If anyone was to say that we had been seen in *Jonathan's* together, well, what else should acquaintances do who find themselves in London, but enjoy coffee and gossip in one or other of the coffee houses? Grayling here will tell you that sticking by those rules has done us very well these past years. Am I not right, John?'

Grayling nodded. 'Can't argue with that, sir, no indeed.'

'Grayling says he's thinking of winding down his activities and who can blame him? He has put forward one or two names of likely men he thinks might step into his shoes at some point. And your name has come up,' Lamb declared.

Arthur nodded. He understood the position at once. These men of substance were prepared to put up large amounts of money which made the whole business possible. In exchange for that, Grayling and the rest of the gang ran the risks but by doing so were able to make more money than would ever be possible in the normal run of things. He looked across at Gideon, who hadn't yet commented.

Lamb saw Arthur's glance and nodded. 'Yes, my friend Gideon here has large funds at his disposal, is that not so, Sampson?'

Gideon nodded slightly. 'Let me tell you a little of myself. I set up in business in '20 with £1500 capital I was fortunate enough to inherit from my late father. That capital has since increased somewhat and is invested mostly in landed estates but I also speculate. It means I am willing to risk putting my money into schemes which are hungry for it and which look as though they would give me a good return, either through repayment of the loan or a share of the profits.'

Lamb poured himself some more coffee and Grayling pushed his chair away from the table. 'Well, I think I will leave you gentlemen to it.'

Arthur was surprised, thinking that Grayling was going to remain at the meeting, but seeing no expressions of surprise on either Lamb's or Gideon's face, he quickly realised this had been pre-arranged. Grayling had made the introduction; it was now up to Arthur to prove his worth. They rose and shook hands and Grayling made his way out pressing Arthur's hand tightly as he shook it.

'Now, Arthur, to business,' Lamb said, as they sat down again. 'Grayling wants to cut down on his activities. What's your opinion on that?'

'I'll be sorry to see him go,' Arthur said simply. 'He's taught me all I know.'

'But what are your own thoughts about it? What would you do differently? What can you say to persuade us to back you above another?' Gideon asked, his small eyes fixing Arthur's.

'I know John limits the runs to two, maybe three a week. There's scope for more. The London warehouses take all the tea we can bring in. He was right there. He told me when I first joined the gang that our fortune would be made in tea and his words have been proved right. It's light to carry and easy to store. I believe we could run it four or five times a week, depending on tides and weather of course,' Arthur said eagerly.

'We bow to your greater knowledge of such things,' Gideon acknowledged. 'But what you say is indeed food for thought.'

'It's natural Grayling wouldn't want to be out four or five nights a week,' Lamb assented. 'But you're a young man Arthur, well placed to do so, full of energy and courage.'

'Even if John was to hand over to me and I'm not assuming that he will, or that you gentlemen will choose to back me - but if you did, there are still the men to consider. They would have to agree to work for me.'

'And you think that would be a problem?' Gideon asked.

Arthur shook his head. 'No but I would do things differently,' he answered, thinking at once that if he had sole control, he would outlaw any drinking while they were running goods, knowing how it slowed the men down and thinking that it might put some of the men off altogether. 'But that side of things would be my business,' he added.

'You have obviously been thinking about this,' Lamb said. He looked across at Gideon. 'What say you, my friend?'

The Jew placed his fingertips together in a careful motion and looked at Arthur. 'I should like to speak more with you. Perhaps you will come up again next week, shall we say next Thursday? Let us meet here again at noon?'

'Well, Arthur, shall we see you?' Lamb asked.

'Yes indeed sir,' he said. Gideon and Lamb rose and Arthur realised the meeting had come to an end. They all shook hands and Arthur made his way out.

Lamb turned to Gideon. 'He's a fine fellow, ain't he?' he said.

Gideon looked up at him. 'You're fond of him, I think, Thomas?'

Lamb slowly nodded. 'Indeed I am. His life has been closely tied up with mine in many ways.' He looked thoughtful for a moment and then added brightly, 'Now what gossip is to be had in the *Gentleman's Magazine*?' and summoned one of the servants to bring him a copy.

CHAPTER TWENTY FIVE

Saturday 29th June 1737, Arthur's house, Hawkhurst

Ever since Arthur and Curtis had been taking it in turns to organise some of the runs for the gang, Arthur and Will had gone through the figures together. It was easier working in a pair so that one of them could calculate the purchase price while the other worked out the profit to be made on all the items once everyone had been paid off.

Then Beth had called round by chance one afternoon to bring over to Sarah some spare plums her mother had sent round. Sarah happened to have taken Sally and Becca to Goudhurst to play with their twin boy cousins for the afternoon. Beth laughed when she saw Will struggling over the figures and sat down at the table with them.

'No Will, you must do it this way – add this column of single figures, then carry them across,' – she took the quill from his hand and as their hands touched, their eyes met, their heads close together. Arthur felt a queer stab of jealousy. He had said nothing though and Beth stayed for an hour obviously enjoying the challenge of the calculations, her handwriting much neater than either his or Will's. When they had finished, he sent Will off to find Joanna, the little housemaid he had taken on to help Sarah, to bring them some tea. 'Would you do this for me on a regular basis, Beth?' he had asked, taking her hand.

She had looked across at him, saying nothing.

'It would be once a week for that week's activities when I'm in charge of the run. There's no danger, Beth. We burn the papers once the run is complete. I wouldn't suggest it if I thought any harm might come to you.'

She half smiled. 'I never thought you would place me in danger, Arthur. And yes, I will help you and Will.'

From then on, she came round each week and she, Arthur and Will would sit round the large table in the room Arthur used as his study, going over the figures. Even if Arthur wasn't in charge of the run, he asked Beth to come anyway, simply for the pleasure of having her in his home, hearing her laugh, inhaling her closeness.

On his return from his meeting at *Jonathan's*, he called round at her house, pleased to find her alone. 'Do you agree that it looks promising, Beth? The fact that they want to see me again?'

Beth looked up from the figures for the run the following Monday night, which Arthur had brought round with him. 'Yes, it looks to me as if they want to discuss it further. But what was it like, Arthur, in the coffee house? I've read about them, *Galloway's, the Cocoa Tree, the Smyrna.* Were there any women there?'

Arthur laughed. 'Not even the servants, Beth. No, it was a cross between an alehouse and a schoolroom, I suppose. Everyone was going about their business. I didn't have time to pay attention to anyone else apart from-,' he almost mentioned Lamb's name and only just stopped himself. Better to keep quiet, he thought to himself; not that he didn't trust Beth. But Lamb and Gideon might not choose to work with him and then there would be no point in telling her. He would wait and see what the following Thursday would bring.

He got up to go back home, gathering up the papers and putting them inside his coat pocket. He held out his hands and took both of Beth's in his. He bent to kiss her cheek and then slipped his arms around her, pressing her to him. He felt her heart beating against his chest and her breath warm on his shoulder. This was as much of her as he could have. It was never enough and it was also too much.

CHAPTER TWENTY SIX

Friday 5ᵗʰ July 1737 Vauxhall Gardens, London

On the agreed day, Arthur had ridden up to Stockwell alone, having taken his usual room at the *Robin Hood*. He supposed he could have stayed somewhere nearer, but felt uncomfortable not being familiar with north London. He had no idea where Thomas Lamb stayed and he didn't ask him. They were to meet, not at the coffee house this time but at the *White Horse* in Covent Garden where they had discussed all manner of topics, not even mentioning the smuggling gang.

Arthur discovered that Gideon possessed a powerful intellect, moved in Government and financial circles, moving money effortlessly from one market commodity to another and his word was held to be one of the securest in London financial dealings. Gideon mentioned Sir Robert Walpole, Lord Hardwicke and the Duke of Newcastle, almost in passing and though Arthur knew that Walpole was First Lord of the Treasury, he needed Lamb to explain that the other men were two of the most powerful members of the Government. Their meal stretched into the afternoon and on into the evening when they strolled along to the *Piazza* for supper, where the discussion finally turned to the complex details of how the smuggling runs were financed. Arthur was numbed for a moment at the figures that were being spoken of.

'Don't think in hundreds, Gray, or even in thousands, but in tens of thousands. The beaches you control are the nearest to France and therefore the quickest to bring the goods over. If you're willing to run four or five times a week and can raise enough men and horses, there are tens of thousands of pounds to be made,' Gideon had said.

'You'll need to speak French, Arthur,' Lamb had urged. 'You want to know what the warehouse managers are up to on the other side. If I remember, French wasn't one of the subjects Penfold taught.'

Arthur shook his head. 'French, though! I don't know if I could.'

Lamb looked closely at him. 'Get Beth Stone to teach you. You're close, I believe? She speaks it very well.'

Arthur wondered how Lamb seemed to know so much about him and Beth.

'We reckon you have another year to wait, Arthur,' Lamb explained. 'That will give you time to prepare your accounts, get your men together, take a few trips over to France and see the lie of the land. I think that you can rest assured that Gideon and I have agreed to support you over any other.' Lamb was helping himself to some more of the partridge pie, one of the many dishes set out on the table in front of them.

'You may contact me through my attorney,' Gideon said, 'and nearer the time we will discuss the exact amount to be involved. I imagine an initial investment of five thousand pounds might suffice.'

Arthur's mind reeled. Though he knew that whole cargoes were sometimes worth two or three thousand pounds, he could not imagine what it must be like having that amount of money at one's disposal.

Towards ten in the evening, Lamb rose to his feet, Gideon choosing to walk the short distance to his home and Lamb showing Arthur how to summon a hackney carriage. He haggled with the driver who agreed to take Arthur back to Stockwell for three and sixpence, which Arthur thought excessive but which Lamb said was a fair price for a journey across the river at night.

On Friday morning they met again just before midday and Lamb and he were invited to Gideon's home in Leicester Fields off the Strand. They parted at five. That evening, his two hosts had promised to take Arthur to Vauxhall Gardens and he had gone back to the *Robin Hood* to change before returning to meet them at Westminster Stairs. He had made a great effort to dress carefully and was wearing his best frock coat, waistcoat and stockings that Sarah had carefully folded for him and packed in the wicker basket set across the back of his mare, when he had left Hawkhurst early on Thursday morning.

Gideon pressed a roll of banknotes into Arthur's hand. 'Here, enjoy yourself, my boy,' he said smiling.

'Ain't you coming in, sir?' Arthur asked. 'Or you, Mr Lamb?'

Lamb shook his head. 'Oh no, lad, I've been here many times. You don't need us to show you round. You'll find what you're looking for, or maybe what you don't know you're looking for. Every young man should come to Vauxhall at least once in his life.'

'Yes, my friend is right, Gray,' said Gideon. 'I'll bid you goodnight here and I hope you will think over what we have spoken of. We shall speak again soon.'

With that, both men shook Arthur's hand and went back through the throng to take the ferry back to Westminster, leaving Arthur to discover the delights himself. He watched them disappear. They were an odd couple - Lamb, now well into his sixties with iron grey hair but still upright and maintaining his fine appearance in a light brown wool coat and yellow tabby brocade waistcoat; Gideon, smaller, slight almost, clad entirely in black, his dark eyes as Arthur now realised, not missing any trick.

When Arthur could no longer see them he turned back and wondered what entertainment he might find in the famous Gardens. He paid his shilling to one of the men in the boxes who gave him his ticket. The Gardens were surrounded by walks planted with trees and Arthur began to see why it was thought to be such a marvel for all the trees were illuminated with little coloured lights. He allowed himself to be carried forward by the throng and found that there were boxes which he gathered were for the accommodation of supper parties and in the centre of the quadrangle there was an orchestra tuning up.

He found a refreshment box and bought a plate of ham and a glass of champagne. He wandered up grottoes and along arbours, then realised these were almost exclusively peopled by courting couples and quickly went back to the tree-lined avenue to find some entertainment. He discovered that the Gardens were frequented by people from all walks of life from the very highest lords and ladies, elegant in satin and lace, the women with jewels sparkling at their throat and arms and even in their high powdered wigs; the gentlemen making Arthur feel shabby indeed even though he was wearing his best frock coat and white silk stockings, for their coats were of the richest satin and brocade and their waistcoats a wonder of embroidery and fit.

However there was also some very low life indeed and he saw poor street walkers in the shabbiest of gowns hardly covering their stays, accompanied by some rogues and thieves he would be hard pressed to be civil to.

He carried on walking towards the back of the Gardens where there were fewer crowds and put his head round the door of one of the larger boxes. It had a tented front and looking in, Arthur smelt a sweet, almost sickly odour. There were about a dozen or so people seated around who looked at him curiously and towards the back Arthur found a flapped entrance from the tent into the rear area. He approached this and immediately the two men who had been standing at either side, came together blocking his way. Neither spoke but one of them held out his hand. Arthur put his hand in his pocket and pulled out a banknote and offered it to the man. He took it in silence but still barred his way and it was not until he had laid out another two banknotes that the men parted and let him through.

After the bright illuminations outside, it seemed very dark and he had to strain his eyes to see anything at all. At first he thought he must have paid his way into a bawdy house for the first sight to meet his gaze was a woman lying on several large cushions, her stays undone and the silk gown pulled down to her waist, her bared breasts full and enticing, her long dark hair tumbling over her plump shoulders. However her male companion, who was fully dressed, merely lay beside her occasionally stroking her forearm. Arthur then noticed an odd pipe contraption at their feet, with a little burner beside it and he realised the smoke from this was giving the room its sickly sweet odour. As his eyes got used to the dim light, he made out more people. Two girls lay next to each other, the one naked from the waist up, the other from the waist down, embracing and kissing each other and a few feet away from them a couple were in the act itself, the woman's legs clasped tightly round her companion's waist, his bare buttocks white, his breeches awkwardly round his knees. Arthur turned round, wanting to sit and watch while he decided what to do next, for his head felt suddenly light.

A hand tapped his shoulder and he turned round to see a woman smiling up at him. Her hair was dressed high on her head, unpowdered, a mass of auburn curls with thick ringlets hanging onto her shoulders. She had large violet eyes and dark lashes and her mouth was full and red. She was smiling at him and Arthur's eyes were drawn to what even he could tell, was a magnificent gown of emerald silk, lace at the low cut neckline and diamonds sparkling in her hair and at her wrists and a long string of pearls at her throat.

'Well, you're a fine specimen,' she said, laughing and her voice sounded like water babbling over stones. She stepped up to him and put her hands behind his head, drawing him down to her and kissed him, pushing her tongue deep into his mouth. As she kissed him, she lowered herself backwards onto a pile of cushions, pulling Arthur with her. His arms encircled her pulling her against him, his knee pushing between her thighs. She laughed and touched him in his groin. 'Plenty of time for that, my darling. But try this first.' She picked up one of the oddly-shaped pipes and presented it to his lips. 'Go on, angel, inhale deeply. It will take you to Paradise.'

He did as he was bid and the first inhalation seemed to set his blood on fire. He inhaled again and a third time and then breathed out deeply and laughed. All his senses seemed on fire. The colours in the tented room sprang into life; he had never seen such rich reds, or deep blues or bright, bright yellow; it was as if he was looking into the sun itself. The music coming from the orchestra a third of a league away, suddenly boomed around his head and he could pick out every note. His auburn-haired companion, who was lying next to him, now rolled over onto his chest and smiled down at him. Somehow there were two of her and then four and then eight and they all floated up to the ceiling above him smiling with such a benign kindness that Arthur felt all was right with the world, and he felt a great love as well as lust for this flame-haired beauty who seemed to surround him.

He reached out for her. She caught his arms and then he felt the pipe back in his mouth and he inhaled again. This time he seemed to float out of his own body to join hers and looked back down to see himself lying on the cushions, with the auburn haired woman lying on top of him. He seemed to hover there for a while and then was vaguely aware of being moved. He thought he must be outside again for there were now thousands of lights and a mass of people. He felt a great affinity with the crowd and held out his arms to them. He heard voices but couldn't tell what they were saying; only catching snatches of conversations. The woman was next to him; he could smell her scent and her curls were tickling his chin. He thought he must be in a carriage but finer than he had ever been in for the squabs under him were soft and silky and the equipage so well sprung, he felt as if he was flying. He sensed he was leaving the cold night air and that he was inside again. He thought she was helping him up flights of stairs and then felt a soft mattress under him. He felt her fingers at his clothing and saw his wallet in her hands. He laughed. 'Yes have it,' he mumbled. 'Have it all. It's for you.'

She laughed too, a rich warm laughter that seemed to reverberate inside his head. 'Oh I don't want your money, my angel. It's only your body I want tonight.'

He became aware of her naked body moving on top of him and reached up to touch her. Her skin was like finest silk. He clutched a handful of her hair and pulled it to his face. Her curls enveloped him, her rich perfume filling his nostrils, the pearls around her throat hanging down and tickling his chest. He assumed she was making love to him but he couldn't really tell. His whole body felt on fire and more alive than it had ever been.

Arthur opened his eyes and tried to focus but could not and so closed them again. A few minutes later he tried again and realised he had died and was somehow in heaven for above him were clouds of purest white and a sky of heavenly blue. Amongst the clouds were cherubs and angels draped in silk with outstretched loving arms and faces of indescribable beauty. Then there was a movement above him and he saw the face of the woman from the previous night, her mass of curls like a red halo round her head. So had she died with him and were they both now in heaven?

'How are you my darling?' she asked smiling. He became aware of his body lying prone under hers and shifting his gaze, saw white walls and the top panes of a large window.

'Were you admiring my ceiling?' she asked. 'It's a copy of the painted ceiling in the King's bedchamber at Hampton Court by Signor Verrio. Did you think you was in Paradise, my angel?'

She smiled again and then moved out of his sight. But Arthur could not reply, for she had taken him in her mouth and he felt her curls on his belly, the weight of her pearl necklace sliding over his thighs. She was bringing him to the point of pleasure so quickly that he could only reach out and touch her hair. He closed his eyes and moaned and gave himself up to his gratification.

She quickly pulled away from him and straddled him, lowering herself onto him; he was helpless as he reached the critical point of his pleasure and spent himself inside her, a groan wrenched from his throat. He wanted to cling onto her but she dislodged herself and walked across the room away from him. He struggled to his elbows, his head spinning as he looked around him and was amazed to find himself in a room of such proportions as he had never been in. The bed on which he was lying was as wide as a man's height with hangings of a cerulean blue. When he put his feet to the ground, they sank in a carpet that was as soft as velvet. He put his hand to his head as it swam and then stood unsteadily. The woman had seated herself, still naked, at a large dressing table and was brushing her hair.

'Who are you?' he asked.

She looked at his reflection in the mirror. 'Nell Villiers,' she laughed. 'That is, Lady Eleanor Villiers. Do you like my little house?'

Arthur looked around the room again, stunned by its magnificence. 'Where are we?' he enquired, stumbling unsteadily to one of the huge sash windows and looking down at the beautiful grassed square outside.

'Grosvenor Square,' she replied. 'Horribly expensive, but fortunately my husband is extremely wealthy.'

Arthur sucked in his breath, feeling immediately vulnerable at this casual mention of her husband and he with no clothes on and no sign of them and no very clear idea of where Grosvenor Square might be. 'Your husband?' he said alarmed.

'Lord John Villiers. I should like to introduce you but he is unfortunately in Ireland or some such place. He will be desolated not to have met you.' She sounded perfectly serious as if he was at some tea party she was hosting.

An odd thought entered Arthur's mind. 'Do you know Samson Gideon and Thomas Lamb?'

She looked at him over her shoulder. 'Samson Gideon I have heard of. Who has not? But not the other. Why do you ask?'

'They didn't put you up to this?' he asked. 'God, my head feels thick!' He put his hand up to his forehead and supported himself on one of the elegant chairs at the window.

'No one puts me up to anything,' Nell replied, putting down her hairbrush. 'I had a mind to have you in my bed as soon as I saw you. Now, won't you tell me your name?'

'Gray,' he replied. 'Arthur Gray.'

'And what do you do, Arthur Gray? What brought you to Vauxhall with a pocket full of banknotes?'

'I work with a smuggling gang,' he said simply. 'In Kent.'

She laughed her tinkling laugh. 'How delightful. You must be successful for it obviously makes you a deal of money. Now, are you staying in London for long? Shall I have your company for a few days?'

He shook his head 'No. I must go back now. If you would tell me where my clothes are?'

'I haven't the faintest idea,' she replied. 'I can't remember where I took them off you. They're probably next door.' She tugged a pulley on the wall. A moment later, to Arthur's embarrassment but not at all to Nell's, a young maidservant entered the room. 'Would you find this gentleman's clothes, Martha and press them and then bring them back? And bring me my chocolate.'

The girl bobbed a curtsey and left the room, seemingly unaffected by the sight of her naked mistress with her lover.

'I take it that was your first time with the poppy?' Nell asked him.

He looked perplexed.

'The poppy! Opium!'

'Is that what it was?' Arthur asked, one hand rubbing his eyes. 'My first and my last I should hope – with all respect to you, ma'am,' he added hastily.

She eyed him up and down. 'What a shame you must go. I own it would have been fun to have kept you for a few more days. Come let us say our goodbyes.' She stood up and walked slowly over to him, with a languid movement that Arthur found mesmerising. She put her arms about him and began planting kisses, feather light, on his mouth and up and down his torso.

A few minutes later there was a tap on the door. She detached herself from him. 'That will be Martha with your clothes.' She opened the door and took the pile of neatly pressed clothes and handed them to Arthur who began to struggle into them, as Nell sipped her chocolate from a silver mug.

'Now remember, Arthur Gray, if you're ever in London be sure to come and see me. I shall always be pleased to see you. What can I give you to remember me by? A piece of jewellery? Some silver? No, I have it. One of John's waistcoats. You have his build. Come through here to his dressing room.'

Arthur obediently followed her to another equally magnificent room where she threw open the door of a large cupboard where her husband's clothes were hung. She drew out a beautiful waistcoat.

'It's quite his favourite,' she said, displaying the blue silk with its exquisite embroidery of flowers and humming birds for Arthur's inspection. 'It's Spitalfields silk, woven to fit with no seams. Even the pocket flaps were woven in the one piece. I believe there isn't another like it in the country. Let me find some stout paper to wrap it in.' She opened drawers and doors in a large, finely engraved cabinet that stood as tall as Arthur and at length drew out a large piece of waxed paper. She folded the waistcoat and wrapped it up, holding the parcel out to Arthur.

'Ma'am, I can't accept this,' he protested but she pressed it into his hands.

'I should count it a great rudeness if you refused it, Arthur Gray. Now I shall show you out. You may have my carriage to take you where you will.'

'I left my horse at Stockwell.'

She laughed her rich laugh again, her red curls bobbing and bouncing. 'I have no clear idea where that is but I'm sure my coachman will find it'.

They went back through to her bedchamber and she picked up a dressing robe of pink satin and ivory lace, casually wrapping it round her, though she did not fasten it. She led him down a magnificent stairway into a large hall.   She kissed him again full on the mouth. 'Well, I wish you Godspeed and all luck with your gang. Perhaps if I am ever in Kent I shall meet you.'

'I don't think our paths are likely to cross again, ma'am,' he said with a bow and then feeling there was too much to say to attempt any of it, he stepped out into the street.   The coachman had let down the step and Arthur climbed up into the carriage.   A liveried flunkey shut the door and the coach sped on its way.

CHAPTER TWENTY SEVEN

Friday July 19 [th] ***1737, Arthur's house, Hawkhurst***

Arthur looked again at the waistcoat hanging in the wardrobe. He took it out and laid it on the bed. It looked as out of place in the bedchamber as one of the humming birds embroidered on it would look perched in the apple tree in the garden surrounded by all the brown thrushes and sparrows. He had tried it on that morning, Sarah curious as to how he came by it but eventually accepting his explanation that it was a gift from one of the important men he had been to see.

She was petulant and inclined to be quick-tempered for she was in the first months of pregnancy and she followed him round asking him several times why he hadn't brought her anything back, reminding him she wanted some fresh items for the new baby. She was anxious for Arthur to buy another cot instead of using the heavy old cradle that had been used for both Sally and Rebecca as well as for Arthur and Will long before.

'It was business, Sarah,' he had said. 'Not a shopping trip. For heaven's sake, let that be an end of it,' and then she had started to cry and he must take her in his arms and dry her tears consoling her with a promise of a bolt of French silk from the next run.

She allowed herself to be comforted and sat on his lap but for the rest of the day she was in a low mood and Arthur was still out of temper with her when Will came into the house, towards five in the evening, Corker the dog, at his heels. Corker, a black and white mongrel of uncertain parentage, had been acquired by Will as soon as he decided to move out of Arthur's home soon after his eighteenth birthday six months ago. Though he rented a couple of rooms in a low pitched house in Stream Lane, he spent a great deal of his time at his brother's house and when Sally and Becca heard Corker's barks, they came running in from the garden screaming with delight and clamouring for Uncle Will to pick them up.

He scooped them up, one under each arm and spun them round, until one of Becca's flying feet dislodged a vase from the beauset and it fell to the floor, luckily landing on the thick rug and not breaking. It was enough to break up the domestic interval though and Sarah scolded Will for his clumsiness and gathered up her daughters whisking them away to the kitchen. Will noticed the waistcoat on the table straight away and picked it up reverently, with a low whistle.

He was now an inch taller than Arthur as Beth had predicted all those years ago and though he was taller, he was two stones lighter, of a much finer build than Arthur. Beth teased him because he had a predilection for fine clothes and accessories and held accounts with tailors at Hawkhurst and at Tunbridge Wells.

'This is fine indeed, brother,' Will said. 'Where did you come by this?'

'It was a gift, from my trip to London. A long story and not one I'm inclined to go into. Anyway it didn't fit me. I've taken it to Bill Collshaw, the tailor and he says it's too fine to be making any bigger. It's made without seams you see and there's nowhere to add anything to it.'

'So it is,' Will exclaimed. 'I've never seen anything like.' He was pulling off his own waistcoat. 'Can I try it, Arty?'

Arthur nodded and Will eagerly pulled it on. It certainly looked better on Will than it had done on Arthur, but it was baggy at the back and therefore did not hang right. Will was very taken with it, stroking the exquisite softness of the silk. 'It could be made smaller though,' Will said encouragingly.

Arthur shook his head. 'That would spoil the whole point of it, Will.'

Arthur thought that a chance encounter between Will and Nell Villiers' husband, however unlikely it seemed, would be catastrophic if Lord John Villiers happened to notice a man wearing his favourite waistcoat which had been specially woven to fit him.

'No, I'm going to return it, Will,' he announced. 'I was uncomfortable with it from the start,' which was true indeed.

Will reluctantly started to take it off as a voice in the hall told them Beth had arrived. Both men turned to greet her as she came into the room, fresh and cool in lavender linen. The whole story of the waistcoat, at least the whole story that Arthur was prepared to give, had to be told again and Beth took it in her hands marvelling at the exquisite work of the embroidery.

'I'm no needlewoman at all,' she said 'but I've never seen work like this. It's sewn so fine you can't tell the front of the embroidery from the back. Will it not seem very ungrateful to return such a lovely thing, Arthur?' she asked.

Arthur took it back from her and began to wrap it in the waxed paper Nell had folded it in. 'No, for the person who gave it to me knew I was reluctant to take it,' he said carefully. 'Now,' he added as he pushed some papers into a pile on the table, 'to work!' for Beth had come to do the weekly bookkeeping with them.

Two hours later, the three were sitting companionably round the table, Beth's rows of neat figures laid out upon the paper calculating the outlay necessary against the orders received and Will's less neat ones showing the profit to be made against each item and a separate sheet showing the preferred route from sea shore to ultimate delivery all the way to Stockwell and beyond across the Thames. The first night's run was to be from Folkestone and Arthur dictated to Will, 'The Pilgrims Road, all the way to Maidstone, crossing the Medway at Aylesford, from there on to London and using the Lambeth ferry for the spirits.'

'Yes, the Pilgrims Road,' Beth said tapping at the map they had spread out in front of them. 'It's a good straight run in. And if you need a safe house, the *George* at Aylesford will answer.'

Arthur smiled at her; sitting next to Beth, laughing with her, feeling completely at home with her, enjoying her easy mastery of a technical point - he could almost imagine that she was his wife, sitting here in the parlour enjoying this cosy intimacy. At that moment, Sarah who had come into the room a few moments before with some embroidery, said, 'You was used to say the Pilgrims Road was too slow in a wet summer,' and the illusion of the moment was shattered.

Arthur, still cross with her for her petulance in the morning, said coldly, 'Sarah, you're welcome to listen to our plans for the run but I don't think you can have anything of value to say to its execution.'

Sarah tossed her head. 'I'm sure I have as much right as Beth or Will to say anything I like in my own house.'

Will and Beth looked at the table, uncomfortable to be drawn into this domestic tiff.

'How can you compare your opinion on the subject with Beth's? Or my brother's?' Arthur asked angrily, with a fury that seemed all out of proportion to Sarah's "crime". 'Especially in your present condition, with your only conversation new cradles and baby jackets!'

Beth and Will sat in mortified silence. Sarah tried to keep her head up and maintain her eye contact with her husband, but she could not hold it and with a sob she turned to go out of the door. Arthur was up in a flash though and grabbed her sleeve and swung her back into the room.

'No, Sarah, we will not have one of your flounces,' he said angrily. 'Apologise to our guests for this outburst and then bring us some refreshment as is your place and duty as their hostess and which is a task you *are* equal to.'

Sarah was shaking her head and catching her breath as she tried to talk. 'Oh ......Arthur ... oh.....don't treat me.......so!' She was searching frantically for a handkerchief in her sleeve and found it but Arthur shook her arm and it fell to the floor. Will quickly got up and picked it up, handing it to Sarah.

'I'm waiting, Sarah,' Arthur said coldly.

'Indeed, Arthur there's no need-,' Beth started to say.

'Indeed there's every need,' he interrupted her.

'I'm s...sorry...,' Sarah sobbed at length. 'I'm s...sorry...to you both....Will...and ...Beth.'

Arthur held onto her sleeve for a moment, and then dropped his arm. Sarah hurried from the room and they heard her sobs as she ran into the kitchen.

Will gathered his papers together and said uneasily, 'Well, I think we have done all we can. I'll take myself off.'

'Sit down Will,' Arthur commanded. 'You'll have your refreshments. It's bad for Sarah to think she can get away with her childish behaviour.'

Beth got up quickly. 'I'll go and see if I can help with the tray,' she declared and before Arthur could say anything she had slipped out of the room down the corridor into the kitchen.

Sarah had set a tray on the big oak kitchen table and a pan of water was boiling on the range.

'Which cups do you want us to use?' Beth asked as normally as she could, not looking at Sarah's red eyes.

'The green and white,' Sarah said in a small voice. 'There are some almond cakes in the little box by the jug of milk.' She sniffed and quickly wiped her eyes on her apron.

'Ah, these are my favourites,' Beth said warmly, taking the lid off the box. 'You make them very well. I've no doubt Will and I will do justice to all of these.'

Sarah had got up as the pan of water began to boil and taking a thick wad of cloth, went to pick it up.

'Oh let me do that,' Beth said, going to her assistance.

'No, it's very well,' Sarah replied, carrying it over to the table and setting it down beside the large silver tea pot.

'Then let me at least carry the tray in,' Beth protested but Sarah, wiping her eyes with her apron said, 'No, Arthur will expect me to be bringing it,' and she picked up the heavy tray and carried it into the parlour.

Will sprang up at once ready to take the tray from her but she took it to the table and poured the tea into the cups passing them round and set the cakes on a little porcelain plate. She sat upright at the table next to Will.

He valiantly kept a small conversation going but as soon as he had finished his tea, he pushed back his chair saying, 'Where's that dratted dog of mine? Here Corker!' He stood up. 'Has he stolen his way up to my nieces' room, do you think, Sarah?' he asked and whistled calling, 'Here, boy.'

From above them, Corker's paws could be heard tapping across the floorboards and down the stairs. His black and white face appeared round the door, tongue hanging out and tail wagging. Will put his hand down to the dog, saying, 'Good boy,' and bent to kiss Sarah.

'Beth, will you take my arm? I'll walk you home.' This was something of a long standing joke as Beth's house was only four away from Arthur's, but it helped fill an awkward moment and the goodbyes were said.

Sarah went back to collect the tray. 'I'll leave this for Joanna in the morning. I think I shall go to my bed.' She looked across at her husband's back. 'Good night.'

He nodded and went back over to the table.

Two hours later he went up to bed. Sarah, who had not been to sleep, lay silent in the moonlight watching her husband get out of his clothes and slip in beside her. He turned his back to her and she lay still beside him. She waited for a moment and then with a deliberate movement, she pulled up her nightgown and turned towards him pressing her breasts and her swelling belly against his naked back using the only skill she knew to make peace with her husband. She put one hand on his hip and, when he didn't move or say anything, slipped her hand further round his body stroking the skin at the top of his thigh. He lay unmoving for a moment and then grunted and shifted round onto his back giving his contrite wife easier access to his body.

The following morning, he sat at his table, pen and ink in front of him and a piece of thick cream paper at his right hand.

Dear Nell, he wrote, or should it be *Dear Lady Eleanor,* or *Dear Eleanor?* He decided on *Dear Nell, Thank you very much indeed for your kindness in giving me the Waistcoat here enclosed. I am too fat for it and my tailor says it is impossible to enlarge it. By returning it, I mean no offence and thank you again for your genorocity, gennerecity –* he crossed it out and wrote, *kindness. I am Madam, your most obedient servant, Arthur Gray.* He read it through and copied it painstakingly out on a fresh piece of paper and enclosed it in the parcel.

He thought nothing more of it but just before Christmas, the carrier brought a small parcel to the house. Sarah, eight months pregnant and liable to flare up at the least thing, demanded to open it with him, but he would have none of it and slipped into the dining room, pulling the door firmly shut behind him, deaf to Sarah's snivels.

He opened the box and amidst the straw wrapping was a small object wrapped in linen. He emptied it out and a silver pocket watch fell onto the table. He picked it up, marvelling at its workmanship and intricate face and turning it over saw that engraved on the obverse was **A.G. from E.V. 5th July MDCCXXXVII.** There was a letter tucked around it and he unfolded it and read:

Dear Arthur, It is not that you are too fat but that you have more mussles than my husband – she can't spell any better than I, Arthur thought, surprised *– though perhaps your tailer had the right of it when he said it was impossible to alter. I am enclozing another gift. I have spent many hours wondering what a member of a Gang of Smugglers would Need and at length decided on the enclozed item. Which at least may enable you to be on Time when you collect your booty. The watchmaker tells me to tell you three things – it is by de Duillier and Debaufre - it uses rubies as bearings – it is one of the first in the country to use Graham's cylinder escapement. I said Never mind all that, will it tell the right time he said Madam by my life its precision is a Wonder of Modern Science. Thatt it will be of more use to you than the Waistcoat is the wish of your friend, Nell Villiers.*

CHAPTER TWENTY EIGHT

1738 January, the George Inn, Lydd

Arthur reined in his horse and made his way into the *George*. There weren't as many horses in the stables as he would have thought. Certainly Grayling's bay mare wasn't there and it was unlike him to be late. He stepped into the taproom and saw Ned Savage sitting at a table, with Thomas Holman, George Chapman, Sam Austin, Peter Tickner and the Kingsmills. No one else was there. He went over to the table. Although there was a general hum of conversation the men seemed subdued. 'What's all this, then?' he asked Ned Savage. 'Where's everyone else?'

Ned Savage looked up at him, his face drawn. 'Ain't you heard, Arthur?'

Arthur pulled up a chair and sat down, flinging his hat on to the table. 'I've ridden from Sevenoaks. I've heard nothing. What is it?'

The rest of the men seemed reluctant to say anything. Ned Savage looked across at Arthur. 'It's Grayling. He's been took this afternoon, in Hastings. He's in Lewes Gaol.'

Arthur's jaw dropped. He could say nothing.

'When you was late, we feared you'd been took as well,' George Chapman put in.

Arthur was shaking his head. 'I can't believe it. Who took him?'

'Customs Officer brought the Militia with a warrant to his house,' Savage explained.

Arthur looked round at the men's dejected faces. 'On what evidence? Do we know?'

'On information laid against him,' Tom Kingsmill put in. 'We've got a traitor amongst us. And won't I know what to do if I get my fucking hands on him! You're related to John Collier, the fucking Surveyor General, Holman. Who says it wasn't you?'

Holman raised his head, shaken by this accusation. His distant cousinship with the man who was in charge of all the Riding Officers for Kent and Sussex was often commented on and a sore point with Holman. There were general voices in agreement, the tone of the men's voices getting harsher and more discordant.

'Don't be such a fucking idiot, Kingsmill,' Arthur said severely. 'What would it profit Holman to grass up Grayling? What does it profit any of us to lose him?'

Thomas Kingsmill met Arthur's gaze. 'You're next in line, Gray. Reckon you got more to gain than any of us.'

Arthur returned Kingsmill's gaze. 'If any of you think it was me, say so now and be done with it.'

The men looked into the tankards of beer, silent. Kingsmill looked away.

'Right,' Arthur said after a moment. 'Let's think how we can best deal with this, instead of fighting amongst ourselves which is just what Collier's men want us to do. I take it Grayling was charged under the Act of '36?'

The men all looked at each other. 'Does nobody know?' Arthur asked.

They all looked blankly at him. 'Well, first things first. There are two cutters waiting, due in about an hour.'

'Are we still going to do the run?' Sam Austin asked.

'Yes Sam, we're still going to do the run. Are you armed?'

The men nodded, but looked uncertain.

'Look, we know there aren't enough preventive men about to stop us as a group, especially as they know we're armed.' He took out his watch. 'Will and the rest of the men should be on their way to Jews Cut already. We'll ride out there now as planned and wait for our cutters.'

Though the men were nervous and jittery, the run was completed without any mishap and the goods were run straight inland.

As soon as Arthur had heard the news about Grayling, he knew he must go and see him in Lewes Gaol, a miserable, dank, foul-smelling place, laying a little way outside the town. As he had thought, a little cash went a long way and he was soon being led down the long dark flagstoned passages towards the cell where Grayling was kept. The construction of the passages and stairwells, lit here and there by lamps, caused some voices to carry and others to echo and at times it sounded as if there were half a dozen voices behind Arthur and the gaoler, whispering and then fading away. Arthur thought it wouldn't be a pleasant place to walk unaccompanied at night.

They passed many cells, the prisoners hands outstretched at times, making as if to grasp at Arthur's legs and body as he passed. A curse from the gaoler silenced most of them but some were full of bravado, challenging the gaoler to do his worst.

'You're gonna get the worst, Walters, worser than what I can give you,' the gaoler shouted back at one such. 'You'll be dancing from the end of a rope this time next week. And good riddance.' He spat on the floor as he spoke.

They approached a small cell at the end of the passageway. 'Away from the door, there,' the gaoler called out and Arthur made out Grayling's head through the little square iron-framed window in the heavy door.

'You get locked in with the prisoner,' the gaoler said to Arthur, 'or I comes in with you. Up to you.' The gaoler waited holding the heavy keys aloft.

Arthur hesitated for a fraction of a second as his mind turned over the thought of being locked in a cell. What if the authorities had been expecting him to visit Grayling and he had walked into a trap? He dismissed the thought. 'No. Let me in alone with him.'

The gaoler nodded. 'You call me when you want to come out. If only it was that easy for the rest of these bastards, eh?' he chuckled to himself, turning the key and pushed the door open. Arthur walked in and the door clanged shut behind him. He heard the sound of the key being turned.

'John,' he said, holding out his hand to Grayling who had risen from the small uncomfortable-looking chair.

'Well, it gladdens my heart to see you, Arthur, so it does. I was relyin' on you to come. Here, sit down on this chair, lad, while I sit on what they call a bed.'

'By God, John, how has this come to pass? The men are saying someone informed on you.'

Grayling nodded. 'That's how it looks. For I was taken outside my own house and for evidence they brought Ursula, my bay mare round from my own stables with four half ankers slung over her. You know as well as me, Arthur, that I never carry tubs to my own stable. You know brandy can only come over officially in sixty gallon casks. I may as well advertise my trade in the weekly paper! No, they was planted there by someone who knew my movements. Three militia men's word against my own. And here I am banged up facing transportation.'

Arthur rubbed a hand over his face. 'But you ain't without influence. Can't you call in a few favours?'

Grayling smiled and sighed. 'I fear I've called nearly all of 'em in, Arthur. Called many of 'em in, when I was took two years ago. But listen, lad. I've known these last two years, since they passed that bloody Act of Indemnity that we was all running risks. It means we're all at the mercy of each other. I had some good advice from Gideon and I've laid up some cash for myself in America. Reckon that's where I'm headed. Heathen, wild barbarians live there no doubt. But I don't intend to serve seven years as a slave! I'm fifty nine now. I've had a plan in mind these last two years, as I told you something about. I reckon if I survive the passage, I'll find a pot of gold waiting for me. But I need you to run a few errands for me. Will you do it?'

Arthur felt a lump in his throat. 'As if you have to ask me, John. All I have, has come through you.'

Grayling held up his hand. 'No, I only brought out what was there, lad. Knew as soon as I seen you, you'd do well. Have you, by chance, any cash on you?'

Arthur nodded and half laughed. 'In a purse tied under my balls, as you taught me.'

Grayling also laughed. 'Aye, that's a good trick. Well, if I may trouble you for some gold pieces, I shall be able to surround myself with a bit more comfort than they seem to consider necessary here.'

Arthur looked round at the small hard bed, the one candle in a holder out of reach, the bucket in the corner of the room and a small grate, high up which allowed only a little of the daylight in.

'If you go to my house and see my Margaret-,' here Grayling's voice quavered, 'she'll recompense you for whatever you lay out for me and no questions asked for she knows you are a true friend.'

Arthur had not liked to ask about Grayling's wife.

'That's the one thing that is hardest to bear, Arthur and you will know having a wife yourself.' Grayling paused for a moment and swallowed hard a couple of times. 'In the normal way of things, I would have bought a berth for Margaret on the same ship I'll be transported on. I'm in the way of knowing which Captain it might be has the transporting of me. A gift of gold will secure a comfortable cabin, not down in the hold with the rest of the poor souls. And another gift on safe arrival ensures the Captain won't take the money and put you anywhere on the voyage. There are unscrupulous Captains that will sell the same cabin over and over and all his paying guests end up in the hold anyway. But that's neither here nor there.' He shook his head. 'My Margaret has a fear of crossing the water and there's no moving her. She's a little older than me and though we have both wept over it, singly and together, she says she can't leave dry land.' He put his hands over his face. 'Forty years we been together.'

Arthur, moved and saddened, sat still. Grayling took a handkerchief out of his pocket and blew his nose. 'Well, there's no sense in crying over what can't be helped and she won't go short. There's a stash of money well hidden and we've planned she'll go and live with her sister in Devon, lest the Crown decides my property is forfeit to them.' He paused again and stared into the space behind Arthur. 'Fair distraught she was, when I was took. But not one word of censure, or no tears then. *'Just you make sure you keep your muffler and coat with you, John Grayling,'* she says, *'for I've heard tell them gaols get mighty cold in winter.'*

He wiped his eyes.

'Now Arthur, to business. The men will follow who they choose but I reckon none of them will argue with you taking over. It was always between you and Curtis and my money has always been on you. Lamb and Gideon are of the same mind as you know. Maybe some of the older ones will make a crack or two about you but none of them has the balls to take over as Lander. No, I reckon you earned your place. The rest of it's up to you. Speak to Gideon again and to Lamb and watch your back. As I said already, we're all at the mercy of each other.'

Arthur spent the next twelve days riding around Sussex, Kent and up to London meeting people he had never met before. He took with him letters of introduction that Margaret Grayling had given him, taken from a box her husband had been organising for the past two years. Though the trial wouldn't be held until the next Assizes, Grayling had arranged things as if he knew already what the outcome must be. Arthur arranged for Will and Jim Cook to take charge of the runs that still went on, while he laid the ground for Grayling's departure. He was in the saddle for half of nearly each day and never slept in the same bed two nights running. When he finally rode home, Joanna met him at the door to tell him that Sarah had given birth to her third daughter six days ago. Sitting on the bed watching Sarah suckling the fair-haired baby, he reflected and felt ashamed of himself as soon as he thought it, that Grayling's departure meant more to him at the present time, than the arrival of his own daughter.

The trial went ahead in April. Arthur attended but it was all over in a matter of half an hour. The sentence was transportation to Maryland in June of that year, on board the ship, *Gilbert,* captained by one John Magier. Grayling did not look at all surprised to hear all this and Arthur remembered that one of the men he had met and taken a letter to back in January had called himself Mr Magier. Arthur accompanied Margaret Grayling on her last visit to see her husband and waited outside the cell while they said whatever it was two people said to each other who had been together as man and wife for forty years and were about to be parted. He went back one last time in early June to make his own goodbyes and Grayling embraced him like a son and kissed his cheek before sending him on his way. Arthur couldn't remember when he had felt so low.

CHAPTER TWENTY NINE

Late August 1738, Hawkhurst then Rye

The time after Grayling's arrest, Arthur realised, was a critical period for both himself and the gang. For a time the men seemed almost like fatherless children, despondent, aimless. They needed leadership and Arthur needed to prove himself to them. They had carried on with the smuggling runs under Arthur's direction but at times the men appeared to treat his leadership as though it were a temporary thing and that Grayling would be restored to them and everything would be as it once was. Some of the men seemed to lean towards Curtis for leadership, probably because he gave them an easier time than Arthur did.

Arthur had made several trips over to France with the returning boats to Boulogne, Dunkerque and Calais. There were vast distilleries at Dunkerque and warehouses at Boulogne, built for the sole purpose of exporting to the free traders the other side of the channel. At Gravelines, the quaint little town between Calais and Dunkerque there was a colony of English men and their families, most of them old Owlers who had escaped to France to escape prosecution. Some had simply moved their families there and set up with the proceeds of their chosen trade and there were many inns and alehouses, recalling their former lives. Arthur noticed the *Shorn Sheep*, the *Home from Home*, the *Fairest of Folkestone* and the *Man of the Marsh* amongst the French taverns.

He had spent hours with Beth and her French grammar book but while he was sitting with her in her parlour or his study, with the door firmly shut against Sarah and the three small girls, he found her presence so distracting that he could hardly take anything in.

'It's no use, Beth,' he had said one afternoon as they sat in her parlour. 'I ain't ever going to ask the Captain of the ship to dance with me, am I? That's all your grammar book seems to teach. I need to know how to tell him the order is short. I need to tell the manager of the warehouse that the tea ain't up to standard or that the oilskins are badly packed or he is asking too much per half anker.'

'But Arthur, I'm not sure that I know those words in French,' Beth protested. She looked thoughtful. 'Why don't you take a notebook with you the next time you go, with a list of the words you need to know, then point to the articles in the warehouse and get the Frenchman to write down what they are and I'll be able to read it and tell you the way to pronounce it.'

He smiled down at her as he was preparing to leave. 'What a team we would make together, Beth,' he said fondly. She looked as though she was about to reply, but just then Jane Stone came into the room and the moment had gone.

Realising that it was important that he actually did learn enough at least to get by in French, he set himself to learn on his own after he had left Beth and by the summer of Grayling's transportation, he had acquired an extensive knowledge of the sort of vocabulary that would be useful to him and a rudimentary knowledge of how it should be written. Curtis looked disparagingly at Arthur when he saw him consulting his notebook, during one of the early runs without Grayling.

'Need to look at your notes, Gray? Thought you would have it all up here,' he said tapping his forehead.

'It's in French, Curtis,' Arthur answered quickly.

Curtis gave a short laugh. 'French? Oh, I learned that at school.'

'So you can order 800 pairs of half ankers of cognac, two tons of Bohea, five gallons of Hollands to be brought over on the next tide and landed at Jews Cut, can you, Curtis, in French?' Arthur asked, goaded as always by Curtis's sneering attitude.

Curtis shrugged. 'They most of 'em speak English anyway,' he said and rode off.

The trouble in the gang came to a head when during a difficult run, made more awkward by a strong surf and the turning tide, some of the men had arrived late and worse for drink. One of them in Arthur's earshot made a comment about Will receiving more money than the rest of them. It was true, but he didn't know how the man could have known it. It was unlike Will to say anything. Arthur regarded Will as his deputy and paid him as such. Will knew all the details of the runs and did the paperwork with Beth and himself and the fact that he was Arthur's brother made it all the more likely that Arthur should favour him above any other man.

Arthur got progressively angrier as the run continued, thinking of the years of training and application to details he had gone through in order to organise the simplest of runs and felt he had earned his right to lead the men and to run it how he saw fit. He rode over to Will who was supervising some of the loading.

Will looked up smiling. 'Nearly through, Arthur.' Will noticed his brother's stormy look. 'What's wrong?'

'Will, I want you to pass the word round that anyone who wants to continue in the gang is to meet tomorrow at Playden Fields, off the London Road outside Rye, two o' clock.'

Will looked puzzled. 'What is it, Arty?'

'I'm going to fix this once and for all,' Arthur said determinedly. 'Each man who's here can pass it on to anyone he knows who has ever worked with us.'

'But that could be four or five hundred men,' Will exclaimed. 'And some may be busy - the farmers and fishermen and such like.'

'Well any man who ain't bothered enough to come can forget about working with me. I mean it, Will. This has dragged on for too long since Grayling went. The men seem to be half-hearted and only want to do the easy runs and if they only turn up once a week they expect the same for the night as the men that do three or four. Well no more. I'm going to reward loyalty. Just make sure every one knows about it, Will. Two o' clock tomorrow.'

The following day dawned hot with a yellow sun high in a cloudless sky. Arthur had ridden up to Stockwell with the rest of the men. He got through the business quickly and was back in Hawkhurst by eight in the morning. He was physically tired and got into bed but his mind was racing, wondering if he had done the right thing and how many men would turn up. He would look a fool if only a handful chose to obey his command. Well, he would have to handle it as best as he could. Though he had pulled the blinds shut, the bright sun stole round the edges and filled the room with light. He lay in bed tossing and turning for an hour and then gave up, pushed the covers to one side and pulled his clothes on.

Sarah was sitting quietly in the kitchen nursing Susannah and he could hear the two older girls laughing in the garden. Sarah looked up in surprise. 'You haven't had much sleep. What's the matter?'

He went to fetch his hat. 'Nothing. I'll be out all day that's all.'

Sarah detached the baby from her breast and pulled her bodice together, laying Susie in the large cot. 'I'll make you some breakfast then,' she said trying to glean what she could from his expression.

'No I'll eat on the road somewhere. If Will calls round, tell him I'm at Beth's house and then on my way to Rye.'

Sarah bit her lip. 'Why are you going to see Beth?' she asked quickly.

He pulled his coat off the hook and looked across at her. 'It's business, Sarah. Nothing to do with you.'

'But your business is my business, Arthur,' she said, unhappily.

Arthur remembered Beth saying a similar thing to him years ago, after Catt had been shot. He shook his head. 'No, the house and the girls are your business. I thought you understood that or do I have to keep saying it?'

She was about to make another retort, but he held up his hand. 'Not now, Sarah,' he said again, more vehemently. 'I don't have time for this. I'll see you later tonight or maybe tomorrow.' He opened the door and was gone.

'Do you think I've been foolish, Beth?' Arthur asked. 'What if nobody turns up? A great fool I shall look.'

'And is that your greatest fear, that you might look a fool?' Beth questioned him, taking his hand in hers. 'I never wanted this for you, but I see that you do it well, better than other men. The men will want to work with you because they know you're successful and that they can be too. You started out with so little and look at you now and it's all come by your own efforts.'

He pressed her hand and then carried it to his lips. 'I think you know me better than anyone, Beth,' he said quietly, looking into her grey eyes. He knew every expression in them. 'I wish-,'

She put a finger to his lips. 'No wishes, Arthur,' she said softly.

He set off for Rye an hour later and urging his horse to a gallop came upon twenty or so of the gang all riding towards Playden fields. They greeted him as he approached.

'Will's gone on before,' Tickner said, as he lined up his horse next to Arthur's. 'What's all this about then?'

'You'll find out soon enough, Pete,' he said. 'A call to arms if you like,' and he dug his knees into Peg's flanks and rode ahead.

The road was choked with men on horses through Peasmarsh and into Playden, some in wagons and some on foot. He recognized all of them, some longstanding gang members, others farmers and labourers who had worked only a few times with the gang. He exchanged a few words with some of them but mainly kept his own counsel and rode alone. The gathering crowd could be heard from some distance and some of the village folk had come out of their houses to watch the constant stream of men and horses.

When he reached Playden fields he caught his breath for to the left of the road a throng of men were gathered spread out over the field, sitting, standing, and some holding their horses. As Arthur turned his mare into the fields, Will came riding up. 'Arty, did you ever see anything like it? I believe there are five hundred men here and half as many horses.'

Arthur took out Nell's watch and saw it was just on two. A rider approached from the rear and turning round, Arthur saw it was Curtis. 'Your big day, Gray,' he said shortly. 'What's your intention? Inspecting the troops?'

Peg shied up a little and Arthur drew her to order by shortening the reins. 'Maybe I am, Curtis.'

With that he nudged Peg forward into the middle of the body of men who moved back to make room for him to pass. Wondering how he could get their attention, he drew out his pistol, cocked it and fired into the air. The loud report drew an instant silence.

Arthur felt nervous. He tugged at his neckerchief and then said in a loud voice, 'John Grayling was the best Lander in the south!' There were a few nods and a low hum of agreement and the men looked up at him, waiting for him to continue. Some towards the back hadn't heard and were asking, *'What's 'e sayin?'*

Arthur found his voice. 'John Grayling was the best Lander in the south, but John has gone! I regret that. He was a good friend to me.'

His voice rang out over the ranks of men, some indifferent some interested but now all quiet, listening to his words. Arthur's voice rang out again. 'I had nothing when he took me on. I was a boy of eleven. He paid me nine pence for my first run. I thought I was a king!'

Some of the men laughed.

'I thought I was a king,' he repeated. 'And it felt good. I wanted to keep that feeling. And I have. From then on, I always had money in my pocket and food on my table and called no man 'master'. But as I said, John has left us. God keep him safe but he's not coming back. We are a good gang, the best, better than Moreton's, better than Henley's, but we can be better, faster, and richer. We can run four, five times a week.'

He paused to see how the men took this. They were quiet, listening for his next words. More runs meant more money. Arthur raised his voice again.

'There's plenty of money to be had for all of us but I'll only have men with me who I can trust. I won't have any man who is drunk working with me. I don't object to working with other outfits, sometimes it's to our advantage, but we work as one. There's no leaving till the job's done, till everyone's got their share and if I've promised men for the whole run up to London, then you go, even if it may not be our goods you're running. Is that clear? I don't want any misunderstanding on any point. And if you carry pistols or any other gun, it's got to be in good condition and loaded. If my life depends on your pistol, I want to know it's got dry powder in it and a touch hole that ain't bunged up. So if any man wants to speak out, let him do so now.'

He tugged the reins and urged Peg forward through the massed ranks of men. 'You Holman? Maybe you have something to say? Perhaps you George? Or Tom?'

Worthington, a blacksmith who sometimes worked with them on the Folkestone landings and who was standing a little in front of Arthur said, 'Thought Curtis was leading us some times. Who says it's gotta be you?'

Arthur looked down at him and then across at Curtis. He paused for a moment and then raised his voice again. 'Worthington here says he might be for Curtis. It's up to you. But one thing is for sure. A gang can't have two leaders. If you go with Curtis now, you stay with him.'

He turned to Curtis. 'What's it to be, Jeremiah? Are you standing against me?'

Curtis, a flush of annoyance on his face, steadied his horse. Though he knew he had some of the men's following, he didn't want to go head to head with Arthur so publicly.

'Are you with me, Curtis, or against me?'

Curtis frowned. 'Oh you can be king of this dunghill, Gray,' he said softly so only Arthur could hear; and then raised his hat and made an elaborate bow to Arthur apparently acknowledging his leadership to the crowd.

'Right then, if there's no gainsaying, we are now the Hawkhurst Gang,' Arthur announced.

Will started to clap and whistle and very quickly the men all joined in as Arthur rode amongst them acknowledging their applause. Towards the back of the ranks of men, Arthur saw John Turner with Jockey and Holman. He looked very hard at Turner. He remembered the blows he had received at Turner's hands in Turkeycock Lane.

'You might want to think twice, Turner. I mean what I said about no drinking,' Arthur stipulated.

Turner gave a snort, but said nothing.

Among the faces in the crowd Arthur also recognized Robert Bunce, the man who had talked him through his first landing on a starry autumn night, fourteen years before. Bunce stood up, smiling and reached up to shake Arthur's hand. 'Well done, lad,' he said. 'Very well done, indeed.'

Part two

1739 – 1745

CHAPTER THIRTY

1739 January, Flimwell

'Come for a ride with me, Beth?' Arthur asked, after they had finished the paperwork for the morning. It had been a wet, mild unsettled winter with few opportunies to enjoy a ride without the horses getting bogged down in mud. Yet this morning had dawned with no rain and a pale blue sky with a watery sun trying its best to shine.

'Where to?' she asked. 'Shouldn't you be getting home?'

'Not yet. The girls are moping about with runny noses and Sarah's in a bad mood. I need to feel the wind through my hair. Let's go up to Flimwell and we can ride through the Upper Wish. The snowdrops will be out. You know how you like them.'

Beth didn't need much persuading. She had accepted spinsterhood with a quiet acknowledgment though she sometimes wondered why fate should have cast her in this role. She couldn't help but be aware that girls in the village, who were less pretty and less able than she, had effortlessly moved into wifehood and motherhood. She enjoyed the challenge of the paperwork she did with Arthur and Will. Her life was not as full as she would have liked; she was educated, she liked to read, she loved music, but she could not fill her days with these.

There was a limit to what a woman in her position could do. If she were married, her days would be filled with the care of her husband, her household and her children. But she was not married. Her mother ran their household and with only the two of them in it, there was very little even for Ruth the maid to do. Though she hadn't approved of Arthur working with the gang at first, she saw how it fulfilled and challenged him. He had the responsibility for the welfare of hundreds of men at times and she couldn't help but be envious of the way his days were filled with different challenges. She was envious of Sarah, married to Arthur and even if he treated her indifferently sometimes, nothing could take away her status, her busy life with a home and children to look after.

They rode up the gentle hill, the woodlands getting thicker as they rode steeper and when they got to the Upper Wish, there was the wonderful view beneath them of the woodlands of the Weald.

'I'm going to ask Thomas Lamb to sell or lease me a piece of this land, Beth,' Arthur said as they sat astride their horses, drinking in the view.

She looked across at him. 'That was always your dream.'

'I can afford it now, whatever Lamb asks for it, if he's willing to sell that is,' he said.

'I think you're a favourite of his, Arthur. He seems to take an interest in whatever you do.'

'That's strange, because I could say the same about his concern for you. He has a kindness for you but you're connected with his family through the Pix's and the Austens and with he and his wife being childless, I think it's only natural. Perhaps I should send you to ask him to sell me a piece of his land.'

He wished it unsaid as soon as he had said it; the house he was going to build here if Lamb agreed, had originally been intended for himself and Beth when they were planning their future together years before.

It made his heart ache to think that he might have upset her. He reached across and touched her hand. 'Beth, you know I – you know, well, there's not a day goes by I don't think of what might have been.'

She looked away and nodded. 'I too, but there's no point, is there? We have to play with the cards life has dealt us.' She kept her face turned away from him, trying to control her emotions. 'Come on,' she said suddenly. 'Prue wants to gallop. Let's race to Flimwell.'

CHAPTER THIRTY ONE

Tuesday 31ˢᵗ March 1739, the 'London Trader' Inn, Rye

It had been fine and bright since daybreak but as Arthur walked up the Strand on his way to the *London Trader* where he had arranged to breakfast with Lamb, a fine, drenching rain started as the Church clock struck nine.

He had worked out roughly how much the materials to build the sort of house he had in mind, might cost and had added to that the cost of the labour. All he needed to secure now was Lamb's willingness to sell a piece of land and at a price acceptable to both of them.

Arthur went into the little back room, to see Lamb already seated at one of the small oak tables, a plate in front of him, and a mug of ale at his right hand. He looked up and smiled to see Arthur. Arthur sat down in the chair opposite.

'I've taken the liberty of ordering for you. Forgive me for starting before you. I have another meeting at the Town Hall at ten,' Lamb greeted him. 'I take it some cold beef and a loin of veal is to your taste? I believe there's also a dish of pullets and larks.'

'Well, I shan't go hungry, that's for sure,' Arthur said and just at that moment, Alice Gillart brought in a tray with Arthur's plate.

'Yes that's right, Alice, put it down there in front of Gray. Is there any of your apple tart, Alice? I know it ain't usual for breakfast and if my wife could bake such a tart, Arthur, I believe I should never dine away from home.'

The barmaid busied herself with plates and bowls and the men deferred talking of business until she had gone and pulled the door shut behind her. Lamb poured himself more ale but Arthur put his hand over the top of his mug.

'No more?' Lamb asked, jug poised. 'Ah well, you know best. Now what is this business you want to discuss, Arthur? Everything's running smoothly, is it not?'

Arthur nodded. 'Yes, it's going very well. In fact, it's in connection with that, that I wish to speak to you or rather put something to you.'

Lamb nodded, helping himself to a portion of pullets. 'Go on.'

'I've made a good deal of money these last years, as you know.'

'None better, lad, none better. But if you want advice on how to invest it, you'd do better talking to Gideon.'

Arthur shook his head, his fork halfway to his mouth. 'No, that ain't it. I don't want to invest. I'd rather my money was in a place where I can go and look at it every now and then.' He paused. 'Sir, I know you own the land up by Frythe Woods?'

Lamb looked up, surprised and nodded slowly.

Arthur continued. 'The portion at its southernmost border at Seacox Heath? I believe that lies within your boundary? I think the land lying next to it is leased to the curates of Hawkhurst?'

'You have done your homework Gray. Yes, it is old church land. But there's no shifting them. They won't sell to you Arthur. I've tried to persuade 'em on many occasions. What's your interest in it, Arthur?'

'Well it isn't their land I'm so interested in, only in so far as they might be my neighbours. I should like to buy or lease the land at Seacox from you. If you agree, I intend to build a house there.'

Lamb took a sip of his wine. 'This is a suggestion of some note, indeed. Have you chosen your spot, or are you talking in general?'

Arthur looked keenly at the older man. 'I've chosen a spot, Mr Lamb. There's a particular place I have in mind, just at the bottom of the Upper Wish, towards the top of Delmonden. There's a view over the woodland that is – well, it's a view I could never tire of.' He thought back to the time he and Beth had walked there and sighed.

Lamb, who had finished his meat, was cutting himself a large portion of the handsome apple tart and scooped up a spoonful of thick yellow cream. 'I had thought of building a house for myself

there once upon a time. But I shan't now. When I bought the land,
I was still hopeful of getting an heir and leaving it to him. Property
only makes sense, in a way, if you have some expectation of your heirs
and descendents living there.' He looked at Arthur thoughtfully. 'You
have children, Gray. Only daughters I know, but you have a young
and pretty wife, who has proved herself fertile. You must live in hope
of a son?'

Arthur shrugged his shoulders and laughed. 'To be honest I must
confess, it was my own comfort I had in my mind when I first thought
of this house. And the comfort of one other,' he added solemnly,
thinking of Beth. 'But that was not to be.' He stared at the wall for a
moment and then said briskly, 'So do you think we might do business
together?'

Lamb twirled the stem of his wine glass between his fingers and
thought for a moment. 'My immediate thought is this – that a sale of
land would probably suit both our purposes better than the granting of
a lease. You know Arthur, that though the world knows of our social
connection, somewhat loose though it is, through your friendship
with the Stone family and their connection with my late kinsman,
Richard Austen and also the Pix family – the world must have no idea
of any other business arrangements we have. I made this clear at the
beginning, did I not?'

Arthur nodded his assent.

'In fact, as I made clear, I would deny any more intimate knowledge
of your business that I might have gleaned simply by living in Rye and
familiarity with Hawkhurst. I think it might therefore link us too
closely if I was seen to lease you land. Whereas a sale of land could be
done through third parties; and we would share only the relationship
of neighbouring landowners. Yes, the more I think of it, that would
be the only way for me to proceed with any safety.'

He chewed his bottom lip and looked thoughtfully at Arthur again.
'I'll tell you what. I have to be in London next week. Let us meet
thereafter – send word to me in Conduit Hill on what day I should meet
you and we'll look at the land together. I may bring Hogben with me.
He measured out the land when I bought it. He'll be able to suggest a
suitable price, if I decide to go ahead. But I do not think you need be
unhopeful, Arthur.'

He pulled out a pocket watch and wiped his lips with the brocade napkin before rising. He held up his hand, as Arthur made to rise. 'No, stay put and finish your excellent breakfast. You will do justice to what I've left of that apple tart, I hope.' He held out his hand and Arthur rose anyway to shake it. Just then there was an urgent knocking on the door. Lamb opened it and Arthur looked past him to see Jim Cook standing there, his hat in his hands, the lapels and shoulders of his coat very wet, as the fine soaking rain persisted.

'Yes, Jim, what is it?' Arthur asked, a frown appearing on his brow.

Jim Cook looked somewhat anxiously at Thomas Lamb and held out a piece of paper, sealed. 'Urgent letter for you, Arthur.' He looked as if he wanted to say more, but wouldn't do so in Lamb's presence. Arthur reached out and took the paper, tearing it open and read it quickly, exhaling sharply as he did so.

'Not bad news I hope, Gray?' Lamb asked.

Arthur looked up. 'No, well, yes. But nothing to concern you, sir. Only some business that I need to attend to with some haste.'

'Then I'll leave you to it and get away to the Town Hall. Remember what I said Gray?'

Arthur nodded and shook his hand again and watched him go. He ushered Jim Cook in and Arthur sat down, pushing the plates away and spread the letter out on the table. 'When came this, Jim?' he asked, reading it again. 'It has yesterday's date on it. I take it, it came over by boat?'

Cook nodded. 'It come off the *Marie-Simone* not an hour since. She came in on the morning tide. She's waiting a little way out in the bay to take back your reply.' He waited for Arthur to tell him more.

'There's been a great fire at Boulogne, Jim. Many of the warehouses have gone up in smoke. This is from my French agent, Ducroix.' Arthur was summarising the letter to Jim as he read it. 'He's salvaged a lot but the goods are standing out of doors now, exposed to all weather. Most of the tea ain't in oilskins yet, he says. He wants me to take delivery of it straightaway. He tells me the quantities here and it will take me a while to work out the lading, but I think it could be ten or eleven boatloads. If I don't take it, he must get rid of it, probably to his Parisian buyers. But it'll take him some time to restock. If I don't take it, we'll be unlikely to get supplies from him for some two or three months.'

Jim whistled. Most of the gang relied on two or three runs a week and would be unhappy to depend on the vagaries of an English summer to pick up work labouring, where they must work for three or four weeks to earn what Arthur would pay them for a night's work. 'Ten or eleven boatloads, Arthur? Can it be done? I ain't ever seen so much run in one go.'

Arthur didn't speak for a while. He was trying to calculate how many men and horses he would need. 'We can't do it on our own,' he said half to himself. 'We would need Henley's men and more besides. Ducroix wants me to send word to him and if I want it, he'll begin to load it and ship it out straightway. If the *Marie-Simone* sails back at once, Ducroix will organise the loading this evening. That will mean a morning landing.'

Jim Cook groaned. 'A morning landing? Running such a quantity of goods inland in daylight. Can it be done, undiscovered?'

Arthur laughed, pushing his chair back from the table and reached over for his hat. 'That's what I intend to find out. Come on, Jim, we've no time to lose.'

As soon as he had read the letter, Arthur had already decided to take the goods. What Jim Cook said was true, he thought. Arthur had never heard of such a large quantity of goods being run in daylight. Perhaps that very fact would make the authorities unlikely to believe any rumours that might begin to circulate.

He would need every man, horse and wagon he could lay his hands on. And more besides. Within half an hour he and Cook had rounded up twelve of their men from Rye and they were sitting in the back room at the *Red Lion* where they were accustomed to meet. He laid the facts before them and a great hubbub broke out as they expressed their opinions, some cautious and others already asking Arthur how it might be accomplished.

'I've decided to send word back to my agent to send me everything he wants to get rid of. I've worked out that the cargo will likely occupy ten or eleven boats, depending how well they are loaded.'

There were shouts of amazement at such a quantity and several men began to question whether it was possible.

'You'll need some hundred and fifty men at least, Gray,' Curtis said calmly. 'And double the amount of horses.'

Arthur allowed himself a half smile. 'Oh I think you underestimate, Curtis. I was counting on two hundred men and perhaps four hundred horses.'

Larry Jockey shook his head. 'Can't be done. I ain't never seen anything like that number, not in nearly forty years.'

'Just because it has never been done, don't mean it can't be, Jockey. I'm going to direct Ducroix to send the boats to Sandwich Bay. The wide sandy beaches there are flat and it'll be easier to land such a vast quantity there than anywhere on Dungeness. We can still run the goods up through Canterbury and lay some up in safe houses.'

'Sandwich Bay?' Ben Raven remarked. 'Let's hope we don't lose it all on the Goodwin sands then.'

Arthur shook his head. He knew Raven was referring to the dangerous shoals, where many ships came to grief. 'Ducroix has local men from Deal to pilot the boats safely in. They know their way around the shoals. I'm going to ask Edward Henley's men to help us and that means they'll get a share. I'll ask the the Wingham men too, John Pettit's men – they're ideally placed and Henley and Pettit will be able to provide porters and carriers and most of the wagons. We won't want to bring them all the way over from Hawkhurst. But we'll use our usual men to help carry and drive the horses. Every man must be armed and there's no drinking until after we've finished. We'll run a diversion at Jew's Cut and let them think we're expecting a landing there, just to throw them off our trail. That'll tie up the Dragoons from Lydd.'

'What about the Dragoons and the Customs from Ramsgate and Dover?' Ben Raven protested.

'We'll throw a false trail for them, too. A diversion at Reculver will put them off our scent. Besides, I don't think many of them would take on such a large troop as we will be. What do you say, Curtis?'

'Oh it's a daring endeavour, Gray. I just hope it ain't a foolhardy one,' Curtis replied.

'You needn't come if you think it will fail,' Arthur retorted quickly.

Curtis shook his head. 'Oh no, I shouldn't miss it for the world.'

'As many of us as possible will put up for the night in Deal. We'll ride out from there and the Folkestones and the Winghams can meet us at Sandwich. Jim, I've scrawled a note for you to take to Will, after you've taken my reply to the *Marie-Simone*. I'll ride to speak with Henley myself. You must fly, Jim. Now the rest of you, here are the details – memorise them and make sure you all know what you're supposed to be doing.'

Arthur spread out some rough drawings and routes he had scribbled down and the men gathered round the table as he explained his plan in more detail.

CHAPTER THIRTY TWO

Wednesday 1ᵗ April 1739, Daybreak, Sandwich Bay

Arthur and Will were riding at the head of their column of eighty men as they left Deal and set out on the road for Sandwich Bay. It was a perfect spring morning; a calm navy sky with the pale rose dawn breaking and a light breeze coming off the sea. Small breakers pushed their way up the pebbled beach and some early morning fishing smacks were bobbing about at the water's edge. There was a low hubbub from the men behind and the crunch of horses' hooves on the rough gravel track. Arthur felt a stab of excitement in his stomach. This was the biggest run yet and a test of his leadership. Foolhardy, Curtis had called it. Well, they would soon know. He pulled out his watch, and checked the time. Six exactly, - the Wingham men should be well on their way and Henley's men too, should have left Folkestone some time ago.

Will looked across at him and smiled. 'It's a fine morning for it.'

Arthur nodded back at him. He tugged on his horse's reins and wheeled her round, backtracking up the line of his men, sharing a joke with one, a word of encouragement to another, before cantering up to join Will again. Arthur breathed in the fresh, clean air coming straight off the sea. It felt good he thought, to be leading his men and riding at the head of them with his brother next to him, a venture of his design in front of them, the good sun already surprisingly warm and the sea, sparkling and calm stretching out to their right.

In a few minutes they were approaching the Sandwich road and Arthur doubled back his horse again, shouting his orders at the men.

As they rounded a curve in the road, Arthur caught his breath for he could see the cutters and luggers laying a little way out, their sails fresh and white against the pale blue and pink of the sky. He counted them slowly, yes there were eleven of them waiting for his signal to begin the unloading.

'It's the *Old Molly*, ain't it Arthur?' Will said, straining his eyes to see the details of the first cutter.

'Yes, I believe she is,' Arthur agreed. 'Let's hope it's a good omen, then,' he said, for the *Old Molly* was the cutter he had unloaded from on his first run with Grayling back in '24.

Before them, Arthur could make out the bay of Ramsgate in the distance. Suddenly the peaceful scene sprang into life and activity. The tub boat appeared bringing in the tubline with the kegs attached to it by ropes, the first of the cargo. The men efficiently unloaded the oilskins and placed them on the shore in rows of twelve for easy counting. As they were unloading the first boatload, Henley's men appeared, some seventy of them, Henley at their head in his usual semi-uniform of green coat with gold braiding which caught the sun and glittered on his shoulders. He raised his hat to Arthur, indicating his two younger brothers riding behind him.

'Top o' the mornin,' he said gaily. 'And ain't it a fine one? Be Jesus, did you get any sleep at all, man?'

Arthur laughed for he had left Henley after half past one that morning and gone on from there to Pettit at Wingham, before finally falling into bed in a room at the *Magnet Inn* on the London Road just outside Deal, where Will had taken a room for them.

'Morning, Ned, Patrick, John,' he said acknowledging the three Irish brothers, all remarkably alike with their dark hair and blue eyes. 'Oh I got a couple of hours sleep,' Arthur assented. 'All well? No sign of the Winghams on the road?'

'Not yet. They'll be here,' Henley said cheerfully. 'So you want us over there?' He indicated the beach to the south west of where they were. Arthur had gone carefully over the plans late into the night with Henley.

'That's right. And the Winghams will be higher up on the beach, the first to load up and they'll post look outs for that part of the beach. They'll send their driven horses off but most of the men will stay to help us load, then we'll help you Folkestones to your share. Post your lookouts to the south and west. My men will guard the east. I'm hoping three hours, four hours at the most before we're all away.'

'Right you are, Arthur,' Henley said and held out his hand. 'Good luck.' Arthur leaned across his horse and shook his hand warmly. 'You too, Ned.'

Three quarters of an hour later the cargo from the *'Old Molly'* was laid high up on the beach, a mass of kegs and barrels, bolts of silk and lace and hundreds of oil skin bags of tea and the next two luggers, the *'Flower of Folkestone'* and the *'Two Brothers'*, were being unloaded. Most of the men were in shirtsleeves for it was hot work and the sun had now risen in a cloudless sky, remarkably warm for this first day of April. Arthur, his holsters slung low round his hips, made his way up the beach and onto the rough sea road, looking for any sign of the Wingham men.

The Winghams were late and by now should have loaded the first of the cargo onto their horses and started to send them inland. Arthur, irritated, had had to use some of his own men, men he could ill afford to spare from the loading party, as lookouts on the beach where it joined the track; which was where the Winghams should be. He had worked with Ned Henley many times. Henley was an experienced Lander, some ten years older than Arthur but he had worked with John Pettit's men from Wingham only a few times. He knew Pettit less well and was beginning to doubt his reliability when he saw the Wingham men at last making their way along the track. Pettit galloped up to Arthur, pulling his horse up sharp.

'Sorry we're late, Gray.'

He gave no reason and Arthur said, annoyed, 'Well you had better make up for lost time and get to it straightaway. Post your lookouts first and relieve my men. This is pretty much your share of the goods, as we agreed last night,' he said, indicating the goods nearest the track with a sweep of his hand.

John Pettit nodded and cantered back along his column of men, who started to dismount and turned to the beach as Pettit told them what to do.

Will came up to Arthur, wiping his brow with his sleeve. 'Are they hurrying, Arthur? The beach is getting pretty full up. Why were they so late?'

Arthur put his arm on Will's shoulder as they walked back down the beach. It was heaving with activity, the beach filling up with the unloaded cargo. Both the Hawkhurst men and the Folkestone men were unloading quickly but it was true, they would have to start spreading the goods wider as they were now only able to stack them twenty yards or so from the shoreline.

Arthur seated himself on a couple of crates and ran his hand through his hair. 'Oh, Pettit gave no reason,' he said. 'I wish we were moving more quickly.' He drew out his watch and saw with annoyance it was nearly nine o' clock. 'We should be three quarters done by now, Will.'

'Well, we have pretty much over half of the cargo off but we're behindhand in loading it,' Will remarked and gazed over the beach and at the luggers still waiting off shore.

'I'll go and tell Ned to start loading from the south- that will free up some space,' Arthur said decisively and he set off across the sand.

'Where's Ned, Bartholomew?' he asked the elder of the two Pinn brothers, who was hauling two kegs, one on each shoulder.

Pinn turned round and smiled at Arthur, nodding his head to his right. 'You'll find him up on the beach, he's further over, d'you see him, Arthur?'

Arthur looked in the direction Pinn had indicated and picked out Henley's green coat amongst the others. 'Ah, yes, I see him. How's that young wife of yours, Bartholomew?' he asked.

The man half smiled as he set the kegs down adding to the long row. 'Oh she's fair to middling, Arthur. Expecting again. We've had no luck before, lost three at birth. Who can tell?'

'Well, be sure to give her my best wishes and you too, Bar.' He set off again further up the beach. Henley was moving some of the oilskins bags of tea higher up the shore but stopped as he saw Arthur approaching.

'Ned, I think you'd best start loading onto the wagons or else we could be here all day. The Winghams have put us all behindhand I'm afraid.'

'I think you're right Arthur. Hey, Tom! James!' he called to two of his men. 'Start loading the wagons, will ye?' He looked back out to sea. 'That's the *'Two Brothers'* and the *'Night Owl'* finished. Seven luggers left.' Another two tub boats arrived at the shore line and were met by the party of men standing in the surf whose task it was to pull the ropes ashore and cut loose the cargo.

Arthur went back up the beach to spur on the Winghams whose work was slow and poorly organised. He could hear some sort of fracas as he approached and found twenty or so of them gathered round the horses, arguing and shouting. Several of the men had mounted the horses. Arthur, his anger rising, saw some of the kegs had been spiked and he looked up to see earthenware bottles being passed round. He stepped up to the man who was about to put a bottle to his lips and snatched it out of his hands.

'By Christ, you will not drink on my time, man,' he said furiously and flung the bottle across the sand, its contents spilling out, the shards of liquid spraying out in an arc of rainbow colours as they glinted in the sunlight. 'Dismount, you men! We need the rest of you to unload and remain as lookouts.' He got hold of the reins of one of the mounted horses and kicked over one of the spiked kegs. Hearing the disturbance, Will and some of the rest of Arthur's men had run up. Meanwhile more of the Winghams had mounted their horses.

'Our stuff's loaded, boys. Why wait here?' challenged the man whose bottle Arthur had snatched away.

'Aye, this is going on too long. Like as not the Customs Men will be out,' another put in.

'What's going on, Arthur?' Will asked, standing alongside him.

'These bastards are reneging on our deal, that's what,' Arthur spat the words out. Pettit had by now come up. 'Call your men to order, Pettit,' Arthur ordered.

'Denne! Matson! Get back here! You know our agreement!' Pettit shouted.

'Fuck the agreement, John!' the first mounted man called out. 'I didn't know we was goin' to be out half the day. I say we go now. Who's with me?'

There was a chorus of 'ayes' from most of the Wingham men, who had been drinking and several more of them mounted. The first man dug his spurs into his horse and started off. Arthur, at a disadvantage as he was on foot, tried to grab the reins, but the man dug his spurs harder and the horse shied up and then cantered off. Mayhem broke out as the Hawkhurst men tried to prevent the Winghams from leaving, but more and more of them swung themselves up on their horses, sometimes two to a horse, kicking out at the men on the ground. Arthur pulled out one of his pistols and fired into the air.

The men, who were already galloping away, pressed themselves flat to their horses and fired their pistols as they went. Arthur's men returned fire; he saw a couple of his men stagger and fall, to be picked up by their companions and the rest of the men on the beach came running up. Just then another pistol shot sounded from behind him and Arthur turned to see the distinctive coats of Customs House officers and a party of Dragoons riding up from the right. At this, the rest of the Wingham men mounted and galloped off, pistol shots whistling past them. Arthur noticed the Pinn brothers, Bartholomew and Michael, reluctantly climbing onto their horses. Bartholomew shrugged his shoulders as he caught Arthur's glance and galloped away.

Arthur and his men returned fire, but then he shouted 'Take cover,' and they fled back to the beach scrambling behind the crates and oilskins and finding shelter as best as they could.

There was some answering fire from Henley's men way over to the left and the Customs Men reeled their horses back, in obvious surprise at the size of the company of men and took shelter to the right behind the first batch of unloaded cargo. The firing ceased as each side retrenched and thought what their next move should be. Then Arthur and Will could only watch in dismay, as the Customs Men started to round up the Hawkhurst horses, flinging pairs of oilskin bags and kegs over them, loading them as heavy as they dared, but also drawing the wagons that the Wingham men had left behind to form a barricade at the top of the beach.

'How many of 'em do you make, Will?' Arthur hissed through his teeth.

'Sixty? Seventy?' Will suggested. 'But all armed and with the advantage of being above us.'

'Yes and we're pinned down here with the sea behind us,' Arthur said grimly.

Pete Tickner came up behind Arthur. 'Can we shoot our way out?' he asked.

Arthur shook his head. 'We're too vulnerable. Fucking Wingham men! We've wasted our bullets on them.' He rubbed a hand over his face. 'My musket is lying higher up the beach,' he said exasperatedly. 'Well, we must do something or they'll wait for the tide to come in and watch us drown. We'll have to take to the boats, some of us.'

'But they'll try to pick us off as we make our way to them,' Tickner exclaimed.

'Tickner, you've no need to tell me what's obvious. Find out how many weapons we've got between us and how much ammunition. Henley's got the best chance of getting out. His exit ain't blocked like ours. I'll try and get over to him and tell him to fetch in some more men. Pass me my coat, there, Will. It might give me more protection against their fire than my shirtsleeves.'

'But Arthur, you'll be an easy target,' Will protested. 'Let me go in your place. I'm faster than you.'

Arthur smiled rather grimly. 'No this is my job, Will.'

'But you've got Sarah and the girls to think about, Arty. Don't go!'

Arthur put his hand on Will's shoulder. 'Don't worry Will. I'll come through alright. Well, Pete,' he said, as Tickner scrambled back. 'What's our fire power?'

Tickner shook his head. 'Not so good, Arthur. A lot of the men fired off their pistols at the Winghams. Some have spare balls but a lot of their powder is damp where it's been laid on the sand.'

'Well you must give me what cover you can. Pass the word, Pete and then we'll try and keep these Dragoons occupied until Henley brings us some reinforcements.'

He pulled on his coat buttoning it to the neck and grabbed his hat pushing it low over his forehead. With one look back at Will he darted out across the sand running in a zig zag to make himself a more difficult target. A pistol shot whistled past his ear and another buried itself in the sand by his foot as he scrambled over the beach. It seemed the longest run of his life though it was perhaps only a distance of some fifty yards.

Will and Pete Tickner watched him anxiously, their men firing sparingly to keep the Dragoons as busy as they could without using up too much of their precious ammunition.

Curtis who had been well back on the beach, scrambled up.

'A dog's dinner this has turned out,' he sneered. Will ignored him, looking anxiously for any sign of Arthur. After about ten minutes, they saw Arthur start to run back towards them.

A bullet flew past and Arthur made a flying leap flinging himself down towards Will and Curtis under the low wall of crates and kegs and tossing up sand as he landed heavily and scrambled up beside them. 'Can you reload, Will?' he asked urgently.

Will shook his head. 'No, I fired both my pistols. My powder's damp. I've only my hanger to use.'

'You, Curtis?'

Curtis gave a short laugh. 'Me neither, Gray. Looks like we will have to sword fight it out of here. Though I don't fancy my hanger against a Dragoon's carbine. Thought you had this one planned down to the last detail?'

Arthur looked grim. 'Fucking Wingham men,' he said again. 'This only works if we can trust each other.' As Arthur raised his head above the crate, a bullet whistled past, carrying off his hat and grazing his eyebrow, the blood immediately coursing down his cheek. 'Holy Christ,' he exclaimed. 'I never thought they was that accurate!'

He put his hand to his brow, looking dazed for a moment and drew it away covered in blood. Will was looking at Arthur, horror-struck but Arthur clapped him on the shoulder and said, his voice only slightly unsteady, 'It likely looks worse than it is Will, don't worry. It don't hurt me at all. It's just a graze.' He grabbed his hat and looked ruefully at the burnt hole in the brim. 'Just wrap my neckerchief round my forehead for me, will you?'

He looked round at the chaos surrounding them. There was still a great pile of oilskins bags and tubs of spirits and bolts of silk in long waterproof carriers on the beach where it had been hauled up. He could see half his men using the kegs as cover. Some of them had made

a dash for the tub boats and he saw young Thomas Kemp clap a hand
to his shoulder as a bullet sounded and his two companions dragged
him to the boat and hauled him in. The Dragoons' muskets were at
their maximum range luckily and the rest of the balls bounced in the
surf sending up little fountains of sparkling seawater.

'Henley has the best chance of getting us out,' Arthur said again,
keeping his head low. He put his hand to his eyebrow and Will feared
his wound bothered him more than he admitted to. 'We're pinned
down either side now those bastards have scuttled.'

'Henley?' Curtis asked doubtfully. 'Can you trust him?'

'With my life,' Arthur replied grimly. 'I don't doubt him. He'll ride
back to Deal or Folkestone, maybe into Hythe and round up some men.
He says he can call on fifty or more and I'm sure of it.'

'Then let's hope the Custom House Officer can't match him,' Will
said.

'Not he, brother,' Arthur exclaimed bracingly. 'I'm surprised he can
call on this many. He's come out of Margate I'm sure of it. I think it's
Jarvis Cooper. If this is all the men he's got with him, it's because the
rest have gone to Reculver to our diversion. Henley has already gone
with two men on fast horses. It will take Cooper longer to send word
to Margate, than it will take Henley to get to Folkestone. Then when
we get out of here, I believe we have some business in Wingham.'

Curtis cocked an eyebrow at him. 'You going after 'em?'

'I told you, Curtis, this only works if we trust each other. I'll knock
some trust in them or blow their brains out.'

A little over an hour later Arthur heard with relief, horses approaching
from the south west and knew it was Henley's reinforcements. There
had been sporadic firing exchanged between Arthur's men and the
Dragoons and Customs Men. The Hawkhurst men could only look
on as the officials had moved more and more of the cargo from the
beach. This and the loss of some of their horses was a great misfortune.
Arthur didn't dare call it a disaster, even to himself. He was already
thinking of ways to get it all back. But for the moment, they had to
get out of this situation.

Henley's men rode along the rough track towards the Customs
Men's position, brandishing their pistols, occasionally firing into the

air. Outnumbered, the only course open to the officials was to make a tactical withdrawal. They pulled back towards their own horses, exchanged a little gunfire, mounted their horses and to the cheers of Arthur's men, rode off on the Ramsgate Road. 'God be praised,' Arthur exclaimed, standing up, watching them go.

Henley came running over to Arthur. 'Thanks be to the Holy Mother for getting us all out o' that tight spot,' he said, grinning ruefully. 'I said enough *'Hail Marys'* back there to last me the rest o' me life, so I did.'

Arthur laughed and shook his hand, then looked around at the chaotic scene left behind. 'What a mess,' he said, drawing his hands over his face. 'We'll load what we can and get out of here.'

'You don't think the Dragoons'll be back?' Henley asked, with a nod in the direction of the departed officials.

Arthur shook his head. 'No, I don't. If they had any more men, they'd have been here by now, but I ain't one to tempt Providence any more than I have to. Besides we have some wounded to take care of and then I've some business in Wingham.'

Henley cocked his head. 'So that's the way the wind blows, does it?'

Arthur met his gaze. 'I ain't leaving it like this, Ned. Without knowing we can trust each other, where shall we be? Forever expecting a knife in our backs.'

Curtis had come up to them and said, 'Exactly so, Gray.'

'Do you want our help, Arthur?' Henley asked.

'Can you spare us some of your horses, Ned and also your wagons to convey our wounded? I don't yet know how bad they are. Curtis, you might find out for me,' he said and turned back to Henley. 'I'd be grateful if you'd take them to Folkestone, Ned. Who's your surgeon?'

'We use Scrope Hamilton at Sandgate,' he said. 'He's skilful and a good man. He'll see your boys right.'

'We use Bowra at Sissinghurst, but it's a long way to drive men if they're wounded so I'd be grateful for that, Ned. But I don't want your help with the Wingham business. That's my fight.'

'Revenge is a dish best served cold, Arthur, so they say,' Henley said.

'Oh this ain't revenge, Ned, it's justice!'

It was towards five in the evening when Arthur and forty of his most trusted men rode into Wingham High Street. The fight that followed was vicious, bloody but mainly one-sided. The Winghams had no idea that they would be called to account so quickly for their actions and having drunk for most of the day, were sitting in the ' *Blew Anchor*' toasting their good fortune. Arthur and his men burst in. He specifically wanted no killing done, but he did want to teach the Wingham men a lesson they would not forget in a hurry.

The swordfight lasted no more than forty minutes and left nine of the Wingham men wounded and the *Blew Anchor* a tangle of broken chairs, tables and bottles. While thirty of Arthur's men carried the fight inside, ten others with Will in charge rounded up the Wingham men's horses stabled outside which Arthur reckoned was payment of some kind for the goods the Winghams had taken without staying until the end of the run, as had been agreed.

Arthur's men made their way out of the inn and mounted up following Will's group as the townsfolk looked on from behind their windows. They rode into Hawkhurst and divided the horses into two groups; Tom Kingsmill agreeing to find stabling for twenty in the alehouse stables of the *Star and Crown* and the *Chequers* in Goudhurst while Pete Tickner could stable another twenty at his farm towards Sandhurst. They agreed to meet the next day to make sure that each man whose horse had been taken by the Customs Men or Dragoons, was given a replacement.

Arthur had scarcely noticed the glancing cut he had taken from one of the Wingham men's swords, running the length of his inner arm from his wrist to his bicep. He had borrowed a neckerchief to bind round his wrist thinking that was the extent of the wound and he was carried along by the exhilaration of the day's events. As he rode towards home he noticed that his left sleeve was becoming wet but it was not until he dismounted that he realised anything was seriously wrong. The combined effect of having been involved in such a venture for almost thirty six hours with no more than a couple of hours sleep and the loss of blood from his head wound and latterly his arm, caused him to feel a little dizzy. Sarah came out with a lamp and as he slid out of the saddle and turned to Will, he put a hand up to his brother for support and then, to Will and Sarah's horror, collapsed at their feet.

Arthur's House, Hawkhurst, Thursday April 2ⁿᵈ 1739

He came to, hearing the carrier's wagon rumble past the house and couldn't think for a moment what had happened. Then the events of the past forty eight hours came flooding back to him and he tried to get out of bed, but as soon as he made to throw back the covers, he found his left arm bandaged and in a sling and he had to admit, hurting like the devil. He gingerly moved the covers and swung his legs out and stood holding onto the bedpost for support. He stepped over to the chest and caught sight of himself in the mirror. Though he had his nightgown on, his left arm was drawn out of it to accommodate the sling and he had a swathe of bandages round his forehead. He put his hand to his eyebrow under the bandages and winced. Just then the door opened and Sarah stepped into the room.

'Get back into bed at once, Arthur,' she scolded, putting down the tray she had brought up. 'At once!'

He stood there and she went over to him. 'Truly, Arthur, Bowra said you were to stay in bed two days and I promised him faithfully I would keep you there, else he threatened to bleed you and I know how you hate to have that done.' She took his arm and led him back to the bed.

'Bowra?' Arthur asked, a little unsteadily, surprised at how weak his legs felt. 'When was he here?'

'Last night,' Sarah answered, pulling the covers back up and plumping up his pillows so he could at least sit upright in some comfort. 'Will went off to Sissinghurst to fetch him after we carried you up here. When I saw you faint on the ground and your bloody neckerchief round your head, I thought you were mortally wounded. But it wasn't until Will took your coat off that we saw it was your arm was giving you most grief.'

She went back to get the tray, but Arthur patted the bed beside him. 'No, come and sit here, Sarah and tell me the rest. I'm sorry I caused Will to ride out again. He'd been in the saddle nearly twenty four hours.'

'You know Will can never do enough for you,' she observed. 'Bowra was here by ten, stitching up your head and your arm and gave you a potion to drink. I don't know what it was but it sent you off to sleep straight away and he has left some more of it and some febrifuge pills you must take.'

'I can't be taking pills, Sarah, I have to get up and sort out some matter with the horses today.'

He went to rise again but Sarah pushed him back down and rested her hand on his chest.

'Will has it all in hand, he says to tell you. I gave him a good breakfast at eight o' clock and he's gone off with Pete Tickner to do whatever must be done. There's nothing for you to worry about, except to get better.'

Arthur relaxed into his pillows. The bed felt very comfortable under him. He had managed to extricate himself and his men from a dangerous situation and had got some amends for the treachery of the Winghams. Will was safe; no one had been killed. They had salvaged some of the cargo and would still make a good profit. He was lying safe in his comfortable house, with Sarah his *'young and pretty wife'* as Lamb had described her, managing his household in her usual efficient way. He could imagine the wild sight he must have presented, collapsing at her feet. Some wives would have run hysterical he thought but Sarah had taken it all in her stride and hadn't passed one word of censure even though he had neglected to send word to her from Rye and the last she had seen him was two mornings ago when he set out for Rye and his appointment with Lamb. He couldn't remember when he had felt so in charity with her. 'Where are the children?' he asked.

'I sent them over to Maria, to keep the house quiet,' she said.

'Then we're alone in the house?' he asked smiling at her.

'Joanna is downstairs,' Sarah said, raising her eyebrows.

'But she's not likely to bother us?'

Sarah shook her head. 'No. Why?'

'Come here,' he said sternly, motioning her to lean forward. She looked puzzled but did so. He put up his hand to the back of her head and undid the ribbons of her lace cap pulling the pins from her hair.

'Arthur,' she protested, putting her hands to her hair. 'You're meant to be resting.'

'Oh, I shall rest. But I shall rest much better with my wife beside me. Or under me. Or maybe on top of me as I'm so poorly. Now take off that pretty gown and we'll see how well I can manage with only one arm!'

An hour later, Sarah, nestling comfortably under his good arm, told him he had managed pretty well.

CHAPTER THIRTY THREE

1739 September, Hawkhurst

Beth knocked at the door, biting her lip when there was no reply. She went round the rough path to the back and found Sarah and the three girls in the garden, Sally and Becca, the two older girls playing with their dolls and Susannah sitting on a rug. Sarah had brought a stool outside and was sitting under the shade of the elm tree with a basket of mending. 'Sarah, thank God you're in. I thought you might all be away from home.'

Sarah half smiled. 'What is it, Beth?' she said carrying on with her sewing. Sally and Becca had run up to Beth, excited to see her and were pulling at her skirts. For once, Beth was impatient with them. 'Is Arthur here?'

Sarah took a moment to answer, seeming to concentrate on a piece of needlework. 'No, Beth, I'm afraid he is not.'

'Is he on a run?' Beth asked, distracted, pushing a strand of hair out of her eyes. 'I didn't think anything was planned.'

'He's gone up to London,' Sarah said at length. 'You'll have to wait for his return, as I do.'

Beth sighed. 'Sarah, I've some trouble with my mother. She's very ill. I wanted to fetch my Aunt Ann from Northiam.'

'You mean you wanted Arthur to fetch her?'

Beth nodded. 'I know he would do me this kindness.'

Sarah said nothing, but got up from her mending.

'Has Will gone with Arthur?' Beth asked, following Sarah.

Sarah shook her head. 'No I don't think so. Is there anything I can do for you Beth?'

'Thank you but no,' Beth replied. 'I'll try and find Will.' She let herself out of the garden gate.

She had no luck either at Will's rooms in Stream Lane though Mary Munn who rented downstairs was baking in her kitchen with the door open into the hallway, saw Beth and upon her enquiring, said she thought James Stanford had called on Will in the morning and they were very likely at the *Six Bells*.

Beth hurried to the alehouse and saw John Crisford, the landlord, outside the front entrance taking delivery of some sacks of flour.

'Oh, John,' she called, breathless from her fast walk. 'Is Will Gray inside?'

He nodded taking a heavy sack on his back. 'Yes, he's here with a few others. Not often we see you here though, Beth,' he added but she had already darted in through the low door and was straining her eyes to see in the relative dimness of the small taproom. There was a bunch of men sitting round one of the large tables and with relief she noticed Will's back straight away.

'Will,' she called. He turned round at once, the smile still on his face from one of the bawdy jokes Stanford was telling. His smile died when he saw her worried expression and he stood up and came over to her. 'Beth, what's the matter?'

She unexpectedly took his arm and drew him outside. 'Oh Will, would you please go to Northiam and fetch my aunt? My mother is very ill,' and she burst into tears, leaning against him. He put his arms round her and held her to him but her moment of weakness was over and she pulled herself back wiping her cheeks with her hands. 'There, I'm well now, Will. I'm sorry. Only it's such a relief to find you. I went to Arthur but he's in London.'

'Yes, that's right,' he assented. 'He's gone up to Kingston to one of the warehouses. Of course I'll fetch your aunt. I'll be back with her in no time. But tell me about your mother. Have you fetched a surgeon to her?'

'Edward Young has been with her yesterday and today. He thinks her heart is failing. I've never known her ill.' There was a sob in her voice. 'I must get back to her.'

'Wait a minute, Beth. I have Jenny my mare stabled here,' he said, taking her arm and guiding her round to the back of the alehouse. 'I was going to Edenbridge with Stanford. Just give me a moment to fetch my hat and Corker and I'll carry you back to your house and then set out.'

He came out a moment later, his hat in his hands and Corker at his heels and Beth followed him to the stable yard. Will mounted the mare and then held out his hand to Beth and hauled her up behind him, cross saddle. Corker barked with excitement and ran behind. Fifteen minutes later, Will was cantering towards Northiam.

Beth sat next to her mother, holding her hand. She was propped up with four pillows, finding it difficult to breathe if she was any flatter. Beth had never given a thought to her mother being ill, let alone dying, as she now feared she was. She had always been well and her brown hair had no grey threads and her blue eyes were as clear as ever but as she lay in her bed, Beth noticed the veins in her neck standing out and a pulse there throbbing faintly.

'Oh Mamma,' she said, softly, touching her cheek.

Jane Stone opened her eyes and looked at her daughter. 'Child,' she said fondly. 'My dear little girl.'

'My aunt Ann is coming, Mamma,' Beth said, smiling. 'Will Gray is fetching her. She'll be here in no time.'

Jane Stone smiled and closed her eyes. The afternoon wore on. Edward Young the surgeon called in again but didn't stay long. He knew there was nothing more to be done. An hour later, Beth heard Ruth opening the door and heard Will's voice and her aunt's. She hurried to the stairway and called out her aunt's name.

'Oh my dear Beth, this is sad news, only let me see my dear Jane. Will has told me she is very ill.'

Beth went to her aunt's arms and said, tears in her eyes, 'She's dying, Aunt. Her heart is failing her.'

Will, watching from the bottom of the stairs saw the two women go arm in arm into the front bedchamber. He had a word with Ruth, the housemaid and went back outside to rub down the horses.

Will came back into the house and found Beth in the kitchen pouring out some barley water. She turned when he entered and going up to him took both his hands in hers. 'Will, it was so kind of you to fetch my aunt.'

'Oh, think nothing of it,' he said bracingly. 'But how is your mother?'

She looked down shaking her head. 'I don't think she can last very long. Her breathing is very difficult. Excuse me, Will but I must get back to her.'

'Yes of course. I'll stay here if you like, in case there's anything I can do.'

She nodded. 'You've always been kind to me, Will,' she said quietly and took the barley water upstairs to her mother.

Jane Stone knew her time on earth was not long. She felt very weary and wanted only to rest. Sometimes she was aware that she was in her own bedchamber, her body feeling heavy and tired. She knew that her daughter and sister were close by, but then she was a child again, as light as a feather, running in the fields around Hawkhurst, forty years ago, fifty years ago, seeing her own father and mother again and her little sister Annie. Then she was a bride on John Stone's arm coming out of St Lawrence's church. She smiled, in her dream. She thought of Beth's father and the first time she had held her only baby in her arms and how the solemn little girl had stared up at her that Christmas morning. *My child* she had whispered softly...

'Yes, mamma? I'm here beside you,' Beth said, a catch in her voice.

'Child, your father -,'

Beth caught her breath on a sob. 'Oh mamma, he is waiting for you. He is surely waiting for you.' She carried her mother's hand to her face and kissed it. Her mother's breathing slowed and became more laboured. Her aunt sat the other side of the bed, stroking her sister's cheek. Jane Stone sighed, seeking the green fields of her childhood again; and left to find them.

Arthur returned from London, two nights after, very late. His house was in darkness and he let himself in lighting the candle with his tinder box. He heard a door opening upstairs and looked up to see Sarah in her nightgown at the top of the stairs, carrying a candle.

She came down, smiling. 'Arthur,' she whispered. 'I didn't know when to expect you.' She went up to him and put her arms about him.

He kissed her cheek but she turned her face and kissed his mouth, touching the hair at the back of his neck.

'Don't let me make you cold, Sarah,' he said, putting her from him. 'It's raining. I'm soaked.'

'As if I mind that,' she said. 'Have you eaten?'

Arthur nodded. 'I had boiled mutton in Stockwell an age ago. I'll raid your kitchen. Only let me get out of these wet things.' He shrugged himself out of his greatcoat and pulled off his hat, passing them to Sarah. She carried them into the kitchen, Arthur following. She hung them over a chair and lit candles.

'The range is still warm,' she said. 'Have some bread and ale and I'll cook you eggs and bacon.' She knew better than to ask him about the business he had transacted in London.

'What news is there, Sarah?' he asked.

She smiled diffidently. She had no intention of telling him about Beth's mother tonight. 'Oh, Jim Cook called round to ask if you had any errands for him.' Arthur nodded. Jim was proving reliable as a gang member and also as a deputy to Will. Arthur had already decided to pay him a few shillings more for the extra work he undertook, fetching and carrying.

'And Josiah Colvill called twice. He wanted to ask you something about the windows,' she said referring to the carpenter whom Arthur had commissioned to work at Seacox, knowing this would take his attention.

'Did he? Do you know precisely what?' he asked, interested.

Sarah shook her head, breaking three eggs into the heavy iron pan. 'No, but he said he would sort it out with Daniel West, the timber merchant.'

Arthur nodded in approval watching her prepare his meal. 'I'll go up to Seacox tomorrow.'

Lamb and Arthur had come to an agreement about the sale of ten acres of land up at Frythe Woods and Arthur spent as much time as he could up at Seacox Heath overseeing the work and taking note of the progress made. For a while the site looked like a mud pool after several weeks of rain but then in early May the weather changed, bringing day after day of warm sunshine and the walls and wooden framework went up. Arthur began to look at the plans with satisfaction now he could see how well they were put into effect. He knew that he had been less than kind to Sarah over the issue of a flower garden at their present house and observing, somewhat guiltily, the simple pleasure she got out of the small vegetable patch, he included a large terraced garden in the plans and the local seedsman and gardener had made a couple of visits to discuss what might be accomplished.

He drew his chair nearer the table as Sarah carried the pan over to him. A half hour later, they went up the stairs to their bedchamber, Sarah sitting up in bed watching as her husband pulled off his clothes. She lifted the bedcovers and then with a quick movement pulled her nightgown over her head tossing it on the coverlet. Arthur got into bed blowing out the candle as Sarah's arms snaked around his neck, pulling his head to her bosom.

Will came in by the kitchen door the next morning, as Arthur was still breakfasting. Sarah was upstairs dressing the children and Arthur indicated a chair for his brother. 'You're up betimes, Will. Some beef?'

Will nodded, taking a plate from the dresser and helping himself to several slices. 'I saw your horse in the stable so I knew you were back. I thought you would be at Beth's.'

Arthur looked up, a forkful of beef halfway to his lips. 'At Beth's? Is anything wrong?'

Will looked surprised. 'Hasn't Sarah told you? Jane Stone has died. Two days since.'

A pulse throbbed at the corner of Arthur's mouth. 'No! I can hardly believe it. Sarah said nothing.' He pushed his chair away from the table, looking grim. 'Who's looking after Beth?'

Will took a sip of beer. 'Her aunt has been with her and William Pix came up yesterday. Robert Stone was fetched over but he only stayed a while. Pix has sent a carrier up to London with a message for Nick and Francis to come for the funeral tomorrow. I've been wishing you back these last two days.'

Arthur had got up and wiped his face on the kitchen cloth and was shrugging himself into his coat. He picked up his hat just as Sarah came into the room carrying a basket of linen to wash.

'Why didn't you tell me about Beth's mother, Sarah?' he asked accusingly.

Sarah looked up at him. 'It was so late when you came back last night. What could you have done?' she protested.

Arthur looked at her for a moment but said nothing. He turned on his heel. 'Are you coming, Will?' he asked and was gone.

Arthur knocked on the front door, turning his hat in his hands. To his surprise, Beth herself opened the door, her black gown denoting her deep mourning. She looked at him for a second, then her face crumpled and she buried her face in his jacket. He put his arms round her, pulling her to him, his mouth near her ear. 'Hush, Beth. It's all right. It's all right. I'm here now.'

Will, a couple of steps behind, looked at his brother's back.

Arthur, Will and Sarah sat half way back in the church at Jane Stone's funeral. The church was full, for Jane Stone had been well-liked and Beth too was liked for being her mother's daughter but also for herself. Most of the villagers were there and Beth was surrounded by her family. Her Aunt Ann and Ann's husband, William Pix, sat either side of their niece. Nick and Francis, whom Arthur hadn't seen for four or five years sat immediately behind her. In their dark wool frock coats and silk waistcoats they looked every inch the young attorneys they now were, working with William Pix's brother Jeffery. He had also come down from his successful practice in Chancery Lane with his wife, now both grown old and comfortably plump; and with whom Beth had gone to stay that fateful summer that had changed all their lives. Thomas Lamb and his wife were also present and Arthur recalled that the Pix, the Austen and the Lamb families were all related.

At the graveside, it irked Arthur to see Nick take Beth's arm. It was unseasonably cold, a soaking rain driving across the churchyard, the women's gowns getting muddy around the hems, the men wishing the service to finish so they could put their hats back on.

Back at Beth's house, Arthur tried to get a moment alone with her but she was always with one or more of her family, more often than not, Nick or Francis. He managed to corner her in the passageway and took her hands.

'Beth, I haven't had a moment to speak with you.' He spoke almost in a whisper, not wanting to be overheard. 'I haven't said how sorry I am.' He looked into her eyes wanting to say much more.

She nodded and pulled her hands away saying quickly and also in a whisper, 'I have to go Arthur. I must pack a few things.'

'Pack? Where are you going?'

She looked up at him. 'To stay with my aunt. She insists. I'll be company for her, as well as she for me.'

'But how long are you going for?'

She shook her head. 'I don't know. I hadn't given much thought to it. Maybe I'll stay until January.'

'Until January?' This time Arthur shook his head slowly. 'I don't want you to go, Beth. You can't go.'

'I don't know what to do. I don't know that I care to live here by myself. You must see what an awkward position I'm in now, unmarried and alone?'

'But you aren't alone. I can look after you -.' He started to pull her towards him but just then the parlour door opened and Nick came out. Arthur dropped his hands straight away and he and Beth sprang apart.

'Beth,' Nick said, looking from Arthur to his cousin. 'Are you ready? My mother and stepfather are ready to leave. She said you were packing.'

Beth nodded. 'Yes, Nick, I'll be only a few minutes.' She glanced at Arthur and then went upstairs.

Nick and Arthur faced each other across the hall. 'How are you, Gray?' Nick asked awkwardly, tucking a strand of his fair floppy hair under his wig.

Arthur nodded. 'Well, thank you. And you?'

'Yes, I am well. This is a sad business. I didn't know my aunt was so ill.'

'No.'

'I hope to serve Beth in any way I can. She'll need her financial affairs to be looked after. It's fortunate that I'm in a position to help her.'

'What makes you think she'll want your help, Nick?' Arthur asked, grudgingly.

'Well I think I'm her closest male relative. Until she marries.'

Arthur met his gaze and was about to answer when Beth came back down the stairs, a small basket in her hand, her cloak around her. He did not get the opportunity to have any further private conversation with her and watched her uncle hand her up to the wagon. Nick and Francis mounted their horses and set off behind.

A week later, Arthur himself set off for the Pix farm at Northiam. Apart from the months when she had left him to stay with Jeffery Pix and his wife in London, he had become accustomed to seeing Beth almost every day of his life. He felt empty and uncomfortable without her. Sarah's inconsequential conversation drove him almost to distraction and the children's chattering set his teeth on edge. 'For God's sake, Sarah, if they can't keep quiet, will you please remove your daughters from this room?' he had snapped.

'But Arthur they're only playing with their chalks,' Sarah had protested. With an impatient movement, he had gathered up the papers he had spread over the table – the calculations for the next week's run which he was attempting to work on without Beth or Will – and stormed out of the room. He sat in the taproom of the *Oak and Ivy* in a foul temper and did not return home until well past midnight. Sarah was, as usual, lying in bed awake, waiting for his return and although the wifely attentions of her mouth and hands won her his body, his thoughts were his own and afterwards he quickly turned his back to her, pretending to fall asleep, his mind racing with schemes that would surely destroy any peace of mind Sarah might have if she ever found them out.

Arthur hastily dismounted at the large farm in Northiam as Ann Pix opened the door to him, having seen his horse from her front parlour window.

'She's out with my sons, Arthur,' she explained when he enquired after Beth. 'They've ridden to Tenterden, I believe. You're welcome to wait.'

An hour later, the three cousins returned and William Pix returned from his acres; and it seemed as if even here, Arthur might not be able to have any private conversation with Beth.

'Beth is coming up to London, mamma,' Francis said as they sat round the large table while Betsy the maid poured their tea

'So you've agreed to go then, Beth dear?' her aunt asked. Nick was sitting close to Beth and passed her a tea cup, Arthur's watchful gaze noticing how his fingers brushed against her wrist as he did so, in a small caress that no one else would have been aware of.

Beth nodded. If she had been aware of Nick's touch, she gave no sign of it. 'Nick and Francis have told me that Jeffery Pix and his wife have repeated their kindness and invited me to stay two or three months with them. Your brother-in-law is so kind. But I'll come back at Christmas, Aunt and will stay with you.'

Ann Pix nodded. 'You would have been welcome to stay with us all winter, dear, but you will be better entertained in London by your cousins. I know you will mourn for your mother, Beth, as I do for my sister; but she wanted your happiness above anything. She wouldn't have wanted you to settle for spinsterhood in Hawkhurst, I do know that. I'm sure my sons will ensure you don't lack for company or diversions,' she said, looking up at her boys.

Beth nodded and sipped her tea. 'I must call back at home to pack some more clothes. I wonder, Arthur if I can ride with you back to Hawkhurst today?' she asked him, smiling.

He was looking very sullen after Ann Pix's speech but he smiled at Beth, nodding. 'You've no need to ask me, Beth.'

As soon as they set off for Hawkhurst Arthur wondered how he could prevent Beth from going away to London. As he had feared, it was obvious that Nick had a tenderness for Beth; and Arthur was sure that he would probably ask her to be his wife. Beth, alone in London with her cousins, might be tempted to agree bearing in mind what she had said about the awkwardness of her position now that both her parents were dead.

Arthur found himself gripping his reins tightly. He could hardly bear to talk to Beth in case he drove her away as he had done once before by losing his temper, but he was eaten up with jealousy and the fear of losing her again; the half-thought out plan he had been turning over in his mind these last few days, occupying his thoughts and driving his actions.

When he swung her down from her horse at her house in Hawkhurst, he kept his arms around her waist. 'Would you marry Will?' Arthur asked suddenly.

Beth looked puzzled and half smiled as if he might be joking. 'Will? Your brother?'

'Of course Will my brother. Who else would I mean?'

'Arthur what are you talking about? He'd never ask me – we aren't–,'

'But *if* he asked you?' Arthur interrupted. 'Would you?'

Beth shook her head and looked at him with her calm grey eyes. 'I've never thought of marriage with Will, Arthur, as you must surely know.'

'Well, think of it now.'

'But I think of Will as your young brother. I'm more than five years older than he,' she protested.

'But he's a man now, nearly twenty one. Those five years you are older don't signify now.'

'Has he said something of this to you?' Beth questioned.

Arthur half smiled. 'No, well - yes …he has thought of it, I'm sure.'

He let her go and took the reins of her horse to lead it to the stable. Looking at her over his shoulder, he said, 'Will has always loved you, I'm certain of it.'

The next day Arthur called at Will's rooms early and found him with his pistols on the table cleaning them with some soft wadding. 'Expecting trouble?' Arthur asked. 'Next run's not till next week, ain't it?'

Will shook his head. 'No, but my Henshaw don't always fire. The touch hole is bunged up with something. What's that you've brought?' he asked, looking at the sheaf of papers in Arthur's hand.

'Oh, just some information about the Kingston warehouses. We'll be running goods all the way up there next week.'

He sat at the table and spread the papers out. For a few minutes neither brother spoke, each seemingly engrossed in their tasks. Corker came across to Arthur and sniffed his legs and then sat beside him. Arthur absently put his hand down to the dog and stroked his ears. 'Will,' he said, not looking up from the papers. 'Why don't you ask Beth to marry you?'

Will stopped cleaning his pistol and looked across at his brother, incredulous. 'Ask Beth to marry me? Marry me?' he asked. 'Of course I would never ask her. Beth would never marry me.'

'Why not?' Arthur enquired, laying down his pen and sitting back in the chair.

'Because she - because-,' Will stopped himself and looked hastily back at his pistol. 'Because she wouldn't, that's all.'

'Well, how can you be sure? I think you should ask her. I think she'd say yes.'

Will looked back at his brother, hope in his voice. 'She can't have said something to you, surely? I would be the happiest man alive if it could possibly be true. But I can't believe -,'

'Ask her, Will,' his brother responded forcefully. 'She won't be surprised I can assure you. She's at home now but if you're going courting, you'd best be quick. Nick comes for her at noon.'

Will looked at Arthur, still not sure. 'If you're wrong about this, she'll think me the biggest fool in Christendom.'

'And I'll think you the biggest fool if you don't ask her.'

Will pushed his chair back and stood up, looking down at the table. 'I'd better put my pistols away-.'

'I'll put them away. Now go. Go on.'

Will straightened his neckerchief and pulled his waistcoat straight and went to the door. Arthur got up and followed him. As he turned, Arthur put his arms around Will and embraced him. 'Good luck then, little brother. I'll be waiting here for you however it goes,' he said and the emotion he felt showed plainly in his voice.

An hour later, Arthur who had been unable to settle to anything although he had half-heartedly carried on cleaning Will's pistols, heard the front door open. He listened again and heard Will's voice and then Beth's. Corker who had been sitting at Arthur's feet, scrambled up and started scratching at the door. The door was thrown open and Will stood there, a fine colour in his cheeks and an expression Arthur could not read on his face. Beth stood behind him looking solemn. Arthur looked from one to the other.

Will opened his mouth to speak. 'You may wish us happy, Arthur,' he burst out, with a smile lighting up his whole face. He turned to Beth, looking into her eyes. 'Bethlehem Stone has agreed to become my wife and has made me the happiest and luckiest of men.' With that, he put his arms around her waist and lifted her off her feet, swinging her around as she laughed and kissing her on the lips as he set her on the floor a little in front of Arthur.

'Ain't you got a kiss for your new sister?' Will asked gaily.

Beth saw Arthur almost wince as he said the words but he put his hands on her shoulders, saying, 'Of course I have.' He brushed her cheek with his lips, the sweet smell of her, as always, arousing and irresistible.

CHAPTER THIRTY FOUR

December 18th, 1739, Rye then St Lawrence's Church, Hawkhurst

It had been a bitterly cold winter with several falls of snow and Arthur and Will had come back from a run in early December to say that the Thames was frozen over – there were people skating and stalls set up with hot braziers roasting chestnuts with no fear of melting the thick ice.

A week before the wedding, Beth asked Arthur to take her into Rye to buy Will a wedding gift. She wanted to buy him a neckerchief pin and there was a jewel merchant in Rye who she suspected might have just the thing.

Beth had been staying with Arthur and Sarah since she and Will had become betrothed. It was a time of bitter sweetness for Arthur, having Beth under his roof and his protection. Sarah was guarded with Beth and even more demonstratively affectionate towards Arthur in her presence, putting her arms round him, sitting on his lap, touching his cheek and always making a point of retiring to bed whenever Arthur did, saying goodnight to Beth outside her bedchamber, as she followed her husband in.

It was with a sense of joy and relief despite the freezing weather that Arthur set off next to Beth, both riding carefully in the snow-covered tracks, Beth in a shimmering gown of heavy embroidered silk with a quilted woollen scarlet petticoat showing at the front and wearing a thick cape, fur lined and with a fur lined cap and hood.

They arrived at midday and stopped at the *Mermaid* for hot beef stew and spiced wine before finding their way along the shops in the Strand and Middle Street. Arthur took her elbow and guided her along the street when they bumped into Thomas Lamb coming the other way. 'What a happy surprise this is,' he said smiling at them both. 'Where are you bound?'

When they explained their errand, he turned with them into the jewel merchants and sat down on the high back chair close to the fire.

Beth chose a fine silver pin with a small ruby set in it. Arthur selected a pair of silver shoe buckles for Will and lockets for Sarah and the girls for Christmas. He had some business at the *Ship in Distress*, intending to take Beth with him and install her in the coffee parlour, but Lamb stepped up and said he would be glad of Beth's company for an hour or two and said he would bring her to Arthur at half past two.

Beth took Lamb's arm and they walked quickly towards Conduit Hill where Lamb's tall, handsome house was situated. 'Would you do me the kindness of allowing me to serve you some refreshment, Beth?' he asked. 'My wife takes a nap in the afternoon but my housekeeper makes a very creditable pot of tea, I assure you,' he said, his eyes twinkling.

'It's very kind of you, Mr Lamb,' she said, stepping into the front drawing room.

Mrs Peppiatt brought in a large tray with a silver tea pot and urn and delicate white cups and saucers. She poured their tea, curtseying as she left the room. Lamb got up and went over to a small cabinet and opening a drawer brought out a small dark leather bag.

'I should be honoured if you would accept this as a wedding gift, Beth. It belonged to my mother. By rights it should go to my eldest son's wife.' He paused and looked thoughtful but continued quickly. 'Well, I have none and therefore, I should like you to have it. We are connected through your aunt's two husbands and there are no girls in either family.'

Beth took the leather pouch in her hands, undid the drawstring and tipped out onto her lap a necklet of three rows of pearls held together with a diamond clasp. 'Oh, Mr Lamb,' she said slowly, with a female's fascination at the flash of diamonds. 'It's beautiful but I can't possibly accept it.'

'It would hurt me so very much if you refused it, Beth my dear,' he said quietly.

Beth felt the smooth shiny roundness of the pearls between her fingertips and gazed at the rainbow colours of the diamonds as they flashed in the reflected glow of the candlelight and firelight. 'Doesn't Mrs Lamb still wear it?' she asked, not looking up and letting the jewels spill over her fingers.

Lamb smiled. 'Not these many years. It needs a young slender neck to carry it off and she prefers her favourite bracelets and brooches I gave her as I climbed up in the world. Won't you put it on, Beth?' he asked indicating the mirror above the fireplace.

She stood up and approached the mirror and lifting her hair out of the way, quickly fastened the necklet, its diamond clasp in the middle of her throat just above the hollow.

Lamb stood behind her, looking at her reflection. 'It looks very well, my dear. Very well indeed. You must agree?'

Beth touched the pearls with her fingertips. 'It's so beautiful, but I can't think it's right to take it.'

'It's because it's so beautiful on you that you must take it. It will only sit here in a drawer never seeing the light of day. I absolutely insist,' he said.

She smiled at his reflection beside hers. 'In that case, dear Mr Lamb, thank you very, very much.'

Lamb nodded approvingly. 'I'm glad that it's settled then; I'll have it cleaned and give it to you on your wedding morning if I may. I hope Mrs Lamb and I may come to the church?'

Telling Arthur about the gift and Lamb's wish to attend the wedding on the way home, Beth asked Arthur if he thought she should invite Mr and Mrs Lamb to the wedding meal afterwards and the party that had been arranged.

Arthur frowned. He had never told Beth outright that Lamb was his main investor but he wondered sometimes if she had guessed. She was very sharp about such things. He was surprised that Lamb would want to come to the wedding – he was generally very careful about only being seen with Arthur and Will as if they had met by chance. Although perhaps because of his connection with Beth's family, it was not as surprising as it had first seemed.

'He's obviously fond of you, Beth. I'll leave it up to you. Sarah will need to know if two more are expected and probably wanting to stay the night. I can't think he'll want to ride back to Rye at night in such weather as we're having, especially if he has Mrs Lamb with him.'

In the end, Lamb decided himself. He sent a message by carrier to Beth to say that he alone would come to the church service but would return home immediately afterwards, the weather not being conducive to an old man and an old horse attempting the journey homewards in the descending darkness of late afternoon.

Christmas Eve 1739, Will and Beth's wedding

Will had come to Arthur's house to get himself ready for his marriage to Beth. Even Arthur who was sometimes scornful of Will's love of fine clothes, had to admit that his brother looked extremely fine in the wedding suit made by his tailor in Tunbridge Wells. He had chosen a wool suit of dark green with no collar with a close-fitting red waistcoat, white silk stockings and black shoes with the silver buckles Arthur had bought him in Rye.

Arthur fixed a Christmas rose in Will's buttonhole and patted his arm. 'Well, little brother, are you ready?'

Will smiled and nodded. 'Do I look good enough, Arty?'

'Never better,' Arthur declared, linking arms.

It was a cold, bright morning with a clear blue sky. The church path was already filled with guests well wrapped up against the cold, making their way into the church. The men clapped Will on the back, some making ribald comments and the women commenting favourably on his finery. It was dimly lit inside the church with large white candles burning and because it was Christmas, there were swags of greenery hung over the ends of the box pews and twisted around the large candles and on the pulpit.

Arthur and Will made their way to the front, Will tugging nervously at his neckerchief and twisting his hat in his hands. Parson Saunders came out of his vestry and solemnly shook both their hands. There was a low hum of hushed voices and then a nod from the verger at the back. Beth appeared on her uncle, Robert Stone's, arm. She looked calm and beautiful, in a cream gown with pale green sprigs of embroidery over the full panniers, Brussels lace at her throat and elbows, all made from bolts of silk and lace Arthur himself had ordered from Lyons. She wore Lamb's pearls around her throat and three diamond hair pins from Will tucked in her curls, glinting through the short lace veil she had on her head. The clerks started to chant the Psalm:

'*Blessed are all they that fear the Lord: and walk in his ways. For thou shalt eat the labour of thine hands: O well is thee and happy shalt thou be. Thy wife shall be as the fruitful vine: upon the walls of thine house; Thy children like the olive-branches round about thy table*'.

Arthur couldn't remember paying much attention to the wedding service when he had married Sarah; there had only been their immediate families present and it had seemed to Arthur that it was merely a way of regularising their relationship and ensuring that the baby she was carrying was born in wedlock.

Today however, he seemed to hear the words as if he had never heard them before. Would Beth be '*as the fruitful vine*' with her and Will's children '*round about their table*'? He had imagined he could bear the thought of Beth being married to another man if that man was Will. Now, his palms started to sweat as he thought about it – Beth in Will's arms, Will in Beth's arms – Beth, *fruitful as the vine*, with Will's children.

Parson Saunders' voice reached him and drew him back to the present.

'*Dearly beloved, we are gathered together here in the sight of God and in the face of this congregation, to join together this Man and this Woman in holy Matrimony; which is an honourable estate, instituted of God in the time of man's innocency. First, It was ordained for the procreation of children, to be brought up in the fear and nurture of the Lord and to the praise of his holy Name. Secondly, It was ordained for a remedy against sin and to avoid fornication; that such persons as have not the gift of continency might marry and keep themselves undefiled members of Christ's body-.*'

'The gift of continency,' Arthur thought. '*Well, that's one gift I don't have.*' He hadn't avoided fornication; he thought of Harriett and Sarah, Nell

Villiers and Beth. Then he heard Will's voice repeating the solemn words after the Parson. Arthur looked at the flagstones at his feet as he heard Beth saying the familiar words, promising to love and obey Will and keep herself only unto him.

The couple knelt together before the altar. Parson Saunders chanted, '*Lord, have mercy upon us*', and the couple made the response, '*Christ, have mercy upon us.*'

Arthur heard the droning voice of the Parson as if he was addressing him personally. '*For this cause shall a man leave his father and mother and shall be joined unto his wife; and they two shall be one flesh*'

One flesh, Arthur thought. *That is what Will and Beth have become, at my instigation, - one flesh, whom God hath joined together and no man must put asunder.*'

Parson Saunders closed the prayer book and the long ceremony drew to a close. The couple turned to face their congregation and made their way down the aisle as the clerks chanted another Psalm. As they reached the oak doors and stepped outside, the bells began to ring and the village children appeared with the bower of winter greenery, jumping up as both Beth and Will were so tall. *This is where I saw that Beth had come back to me, on the day I married Sarah,* Arthur thought to himself. *This is where she smiled at me and I knew I would always love her.*

After the wedding Lamb embraced Beth and then slipped away. Will and Beth, Arthur, Sarah and the girls, Sarah's brother and his wife and twin boys, James Stanford and his wife, Lucas Webb and Martha and their son, all gathered at Arthur's house for a wedding meal. Beth's side of the family was thinly represented; her uncle Robert Stone, almost silent and reluctant to stay and Francis Pix were the only members of her family present, her aunt's indisposition with a low fever keeping her and her husband at Northiam. Nick used the fierce winter weather with the Thames frozen over as an excuse not to come down from London.

Will drew Arthur aside, looking so happy that Arthur felt ashamed of himself for not sharing it.

'It's the happiest day of my life, Arty and due to you. I would never have guessed Beth would marry me in a thousand years if you hadn't encouraged me.' He put his arms around his brother and embraced him. Arthur hugged his brother to him but said nothing.

Beth appeared at the end of the hallway and Will held out his hands to her saying to Arthur as she approached them, 'Look at her face, Arthur. Look at her figure. Ain't I the luckiest man on earth? Have you ever seen Beth look so beautiful?' He pulled his wife into his embrace.

'Beth always looks beautiful,' Arthur said slowly and made his way into the parlour where the meal was laid out.

The main festivities of the wedding were to take place in the evening. There was to be a party in Tulhurst's barn and many of the villagers had been helping get it ready. It was hung with greenery and plenty of candles. Perhaps because it was Christmas Eve, as well as a wedding celebration, everyone seemed in a specially happy and carefree mood, the children screaming with excitement, the women in their Sunday best; even Corker wore a red ribbon round his neck. Sarah's brother Joseph had provided planks of wood from his saw mill and the carpenter, Josiah Colvill had laid them over the dirt floor of the barn to give a firm, dry footing for the dancing.

It became very warm in the barn, despite the heavy snowfall beginning outside and towards ten o' clock, it became the general opinion that the time was right to escort the new couple to their home to enjoy their first night of married life. Will good-naturedly allowed the women to twine twists of greenery about him, which was said to ensure a fruitful union. The party guests formed a laughing throng around the couple and lit their way with flaming torches from the barn along the snow-covered tracks to Stream Lane and Will's rooms. Most of the men joined in singing bawdy songs which dealt in the main with what the bridegroom would be doing to his new bride as soon as they were left alone.

They eventually reached Will's door and he picked Beth up in his arms carrying her over the threshold, to the cries and shouts of good wishes until James Stanford pulled the door firmly shut and the revelers made their way back to the barn where the festivities continued.

Arthur, at the back of the throng, turned his head once to look up at the lighted window in Will's room. He felt relieved that Beth was now part of his family, that she would never be taken away by marriage to someone else, but felt more deeply an aching jealousy, a physical pain deep in his gut that she would be sharing Will's bed from now on.

Sarah, noticing her husband looking up at the window, tucked her arm in his possessively and said, 'I wish them joy of each other's bodies tonight. I'll wager they're already naked abed. Do you remember our wedding night, Arthur?'

He paused a moment before looking down at her. 'Of course, Sarah. I'll never forget anything about our wedding.'

Will tapped on the door. 'May I come in, darling?' he asked softly.

There was no answer but slowly the door opened and Beth stood there in a filmy nightgown, her hair brushed loose, hanging over her shoulders. She opened the door wider and stepped back to let Will in. He had taken off his shirt and stockings and stood in his breeches, smiling down at her. The branch of candles on the chest of drawers next to the bed and the small fire in the grate gave a flickering, golden light to the room, which made Beth's hair sparkle and her skin gleam.

Will put a hand to her shoulder, holding his breath and then lowered his palm slowly feeling the softness and warmth of her breast under the fine cotton of her gown, the peak hardening under the glide of his palm. He let out his breath in a sigh and slipped his other hand around her back, drawing her to him and touching her lips softly with his own.

'Beth,' he said lightly, his mouth at her ear and then paused. 'I've– I've never done this before. I hope I won't disappoint you.' This unexpected and gentle admission touched her heart in a way that the most ardent lovemaking would not have and she put her arms around him, drawing his head down to hers and looked into his dark eyes.

'You could not ever disappoint me, Will,' she said slowly and pressed her lips to his. She felt his arms around her, as he picked her up and carried her the few steps to the bed.

Later as she lay in his arms, her nightgown discarded and her hair cascading over his chest, she said softly but urgently, 'Will, there's something I need to tell you.'

He shifted slightly and propped himself up on one elbow looking into her face illuminated by the candlelight, a small smile on his lips. 'No there isn't, sweetheart.'

'Yes, Will,' she insisted, 'something you don't know. Something I need to tell you.'

'I do know, darling. And you don't need to say anything,' he answered, taking her hand in his and kissing her fingertips.

'But, it's about Arthur—,' she began, afraid that if she didn't speak now, the two of them would live a lie forever.

'Arthur is my dear brother, as he is now yours.' He pressed his lips to her palm. 'I never thought you could love me, but you say that you do. It's enough for me that you say it. I love you and I love Arthur. You're the two people dearest to me in the world. You love him and I love him. He loves you – who could not love you, Beth? You don't have to tell me anything more, sweetheart. There's nothing more to say about it, ever.'

She looked up at him for a moment, wanting to say more but instead she reached up and kissed his mouth, feather light, touching his cheek with her fingertips, feeling his body respond instantly.

And nothing more was said on that topic for the rest of their lives.

Spring 1740

Will and Beth continued to live in Will's rented rooms, Arthur discouraging them from moving into Beth's old house. He felt it wasn't fitting that they should use Beth's old home and planned to build them a house near Seacox but eventually even Arthur had to agree it was foolish to leave Beth's house empty in the meantime. Will and Beth made arrangements to move in during May; but not until Arthur had arranged for Saltmarsh and Wicken, the gilders and carvers from Tunbridge Wells, to come and beautify the parlour fireplace with some intricate carving; and paid Henry and Roger Kemp, the glazier and plumber, to renew the ground floor windows and run a pipe from the standpipe into the kitchen.

Will and Beth settled into a chaotic, disorganised married life, which seemed to suit both of them. Beth, even Arthur had to admit, was an indifferent housewife. The larder was often half-empty and the floors unswept, even though there would be pots crammed with wildflowers on almost every surface, in the spring and summer. Beth ordered books from London and musical scores which she played on her old spinet usually encouraging Will to sing to her playing. Will's weakness for clothes was indulged Arthur suspected, by money from Beth's inheritance and they cut a fine figure as a couple, he had to admit as they were both so tall and wore their clothes with an easy grace.

Beth quite often forgot to organise their evening meal in time and Will, easy-going and indulgent, would kiss the top of Beth's head and suggest one of the local alehouses for a plate of stew or soup. It was at Arthur's instigation that Annie Mercer was engaged to be a house servant for them, little Ruth who had been there when Jane Stone was alive, having married her sweetheart and moved to Lewes. After Annie was engaged, the house was at least clean although never tidy. Arthur, taking Sarah's excellent housekeeping for granted, couldn't understand why Will and Beth's house with no children in it could be so untidy, while his own, with three small daughters was as neat as a pin. Arthur found no fault in Beth for any of this. If Sarah had thought that because of Will and Beth's marriage, her husband would be less attentive to Beth, she found she was mistaken. Now they were living only four doors away, the newly-married couple often called in.

Sarah felt she could not possibly compete with the invisible bond that seemed to exist between Beth and her husband and could use only her skills as a housewife and a lover to keep Arthur by her side. She never once refused him the comfort of her body and he had only to comment that he liked a particular way of dressing a fowl, or a butter sauce with a certain dish and Sarah would write it in her housekeeping journal, in her laborious and childlike handwriting.

CHAPTER THIRTY FIVE

Thursday 23rd June 1740, Arthur's house; Will's house, Hawkhurst

Arthur intended to have several hidden passages built into the new house at Seacox Heath as well as deep cellarage under it and he made use of members of the gang who worked as labourers to dig the deep foundations, rather than bring in outsiders.   Since Grayling had been betrayed and taken, there remained at the back of Arthur's mind the idea that he and Will might one day need either to hide up, or escape and there were several routes out of the house that weren't obvious to the casual observer.   He needed secure locks and latches and went to call on his old schoolfriend, Lucas Webb the blacksmith, for his advice.   Lucas came out of the smithy, glad to get away from the heat of the brazier and bellows for a while and called for Martha to bring them some ale. He took a few details from Arthur, showed him a few examples of the heavy iron he might use and agreed the job could easily be done.

The following day Arthur had arranged to meet Henry Kemp who was bringing some of the glass for the ground floor windows at Seacox and was to start fitting them while Josiah Colvill, the carpenter was also on site. Though they could have done their work in Arthur's absence, he liked to be there to oversee the work and discuss any last minute changes with them. Having secured both their services for the 23rd, he was determined to stick to the plan even though his wife and daughters reminded him of his promise to take them to the fair at Horsmonden.

'I know I said I would take you, Sarah,' he agreed at breakfast the day before, 'but that was before I knew I could only secure Kemp and Colvill for tomorrow. Will and Beth are going. I know that they planned to ride but I'll lend Will the wagon and I'm sure he'll be pleased to take you all.'

Will was happy to act as both driver and escort. He and Beth came round for supper with Arthur and Sarah the evening before the fair and Will promised to be back by half past eight the next morning. Though he tried to pretend he was doing his duty by going with them, both Beth and Arthur knew that Will loved the excitement and the crowds at a fair and would always come home with his pockets full of worthless trinkets that had seemed wonders of grace and design when he bought them.

He was disappointed therefore when the next morning, Beth, who was normally up with the lark and anxious to be up and about on such fine summer mornings as this one promised to be, rolled over in bed, begging Will to pull the curtains tightly shut to keep the sun out saying she had as bad a headache as she could ever remember. Will, all solicitude and concern, did as she asked and sat gently on the bed next to her. He put his hand lightly over hers. 'Poor darling,' he said. 'What can I do?'

'Nothing, Will,' she whispered. 'Only let me rest and I'll try and go back to sleep. But open the window wide please to let the fresh air in.'

'Are you sure the sounds in the road won't disturb you, sweetheart? I'm sure it'll be busy with folk making their way to Horsmonden,' he said, opening the catch and looking down into the road.

'Oh, I had forgotten the fair. I don't think I can go,' Beth said, turning onto her side and holding out a hand to him.

He came over to her and knelt at her side, kissing her fingers. 'Of course we shan't go, love. I'll send Annie over to tell them as soon as she gets here.'

She smiled up from her pillow and touched his cheek. 'Oh no. I'd feel much worse if I thought I'd spoiled everyone's day. I'd much rather you went. I want only to sleep all day and Annie will be here to fetch me anything I might need. Really, I'd be happier if you went. You can bring me a fairing back.'

He looked doubtful and stroked her hair. 'I don't think I should leave you, Beth. What if you needed the physician?'

She gave a little laugh. 'It's only the headache. I'm never ill. Only please go. Arthur will worry if you're late.'

He stood up. 'You must promise to send Annie to fetch Arthur from Seacox if you feel worse. He'll bring the surgeon if you need him. I'll feel happier if you promise me that. Would you like Corker to stay and be company for you?' he offered.

She smiled. 'No, take Corker with you; only don't let him get in any fights. And I promise to send word to Arthur if I need help. But it won't be necessary. Bring me up some of Sarah's delicious lemonade that she sent us away with last evening and I'll be fine.'

But by the time he had returned with a jug and a glass, Beth was lying fast asleep her cheek resting on one hand, the other hand lying on the coverlet. He looked at her for a moment, watching the rhythmic rise and fall of her breasts as she slept, set the glass of lemonade down quietly on the small table next to the bedside, dropped a kiss on her forehead and stepped silently out of the room.

'Here's Uncle Will and he has brought Corker,' Becca announced excitedly, pressing her nose to the kitchen window, as she saw Will opening the back garden gate. 'But where is Aunty Beth, Daddy?' she asked, looking up at Arthur. He came to stand next to her and then seeing it was true that Will was alone, went over to the door and stepped out into the yard.

'Where's Beth?' he asked, closing the gate and looking along the road.

Will shook his head. 'She has the headache. She sends all sorts of apologies but can't come.'

'Then are you mad, brother?' Arthur asked, annoyed with Will's apparent negligence of his wife. 'What are you thinking of, leaving her ill and on her own, for the sake of a fair? Of course you will go home.'

Will shook his head. 'That's what I thought, Arthur, but she wouldn't have it. You know how stubborn she can be.'

He followed Arthur into the kitchen, taking off his hat. 'She said she would feel worse if she felt she'd spoiled everyone's pleasure. At least I got her to promise to send Annie for you, if she needs help.'

Arthur looked slightly less cross. 'I should think so,' he said.

Sarah came into the kitchen, pretty and fresh in floral linen, a new cap trimmed with lace on her head, its ribbons tied neatly at the back of her head.

'Here's Will come to tell us Beth is unwell and can't go with you to the fair,' Arthur said to her.

Will brushed his sister-in-law's cheek with his lips.

'Unwell?' she repeated, raising her eyebrows. 'Might you have some news to tell us soon, Will?'

Will looked puzzled.

Sarah laughed. 'When a bride of six months is unwell, some folk might say there is likely to be only one reason.' She looked across at her husband to see his reaction; and felt both satisfaction and a jealous fear when she saw his face register a flush of annoyance.

'Oh no – no,' Will said, embarrassed, looking at his feet. 'Nothing like that. No. Beth would have said if it was anything like that. Not that we wouldn't be pleased. Only – no, nothing to tell as far as that goes.'

'Well, it's early days, yet, Will,' Sarah said bracingly. 'I'm sure we'll see Beth with your firstborn big in her belly before long. Wouldn't you say, Arthur?'

Arthur looked across at his wife. 'I would say it's hardly our concern.'

She gave a toss of her head, wanting the last word. 'I thought we were all one family now, that's all.'

There was a silence in the room and then the door was pushed open and Corker's nose appeared, followed by the three girls.

'Where's Aunty Beth?' Becca asked Will, grasping his hand.

He smiled down at the girls. 'Your aunt has the headache and wishes to stay in bed. She says we are to have an enjoyable day and I'm sure she'll want to hear all about it when she's better, so you must take note of everything you see. You can help me find something especially nice to buy for her.'

'Ribbons,' Sally said firmly. 'And I should like some too.'

'I should like one of those little box things like Aunty Beth has got, with all shells stuck on it,' Becca said.

'And what do you want, Susie?' Will asked kneeling down to get on a level with Arthur's youngest daughter. She stared at him wide-eyed. 'Cake,' she said and they all laughed.

'Doesn't Uncle Will look beautiful?' Becca asked, looking up at his pale green coat, with its matching satin waistcoat. 'Why don't you ever wear such pretty clothes, Daddy?' She turned to her father and he raised his eyes heavenward.

'Because I have better things to do than spend hours at my tailor's,' he grinned. 'Come, Will, the wagon is out at the front. I'll ride with you as far as Seacox.'

Beth woke from a dreamless sleep, heavy-eyed and lethargic. She lay still and slowly opened her eyes, trying to think whether it was morning or night. Then she remembered and yawned and stretched her arms above her head. She put a hand to her forehead and realised the thudding headache had left her. She pushed back the covers and stepped cautiously out of bed. Apart from feeling as if her legs were made of lead and her head stuffed with cotton wadding, she no longer felt unwell. She padded barefoot across the room and opened the door giving out onto the landing. Leaning over the banister, she could hear Annie singing to herself in the kitchen and she called down to her. She heard Annie's shoes on the flagstones and then she appeared at the kitchen door, a mixing bowl in her hands. 'Yes, mistress? I hope you're feeling better?'

'Yes, thank you Annie. What time is it?'

'Just after twelve, mam.'

'Would you make me some tea, Annie? But don't bring it up. I'll be down soon.'

She stepped back into the bedroom, slipped out of her nightgown and bathed with the cold water from the pitcher on the dressing table. Splashing the cold water over her face and body made her feel more alert and she dressed in a comfortable gown, putting on a fresh linen chemise, brushing her hair and knotting up the little curls on top in her accustomed fashion. She tied a pretty lace cap over her curls, fastening the strings behind and went downstairs. After tea and toasted bread and honey, she felt almost completely well again.

'I'll go out for a ride, Annie,' she said getting up from the table. 'What are you cooking this evening?'

Annie made a little bob. 'A beef pie, just as Mr Will likes it,' she said, Will rapidly having become a favourite, mainly because he ate heartily anything she cooked.

Swinging her straw hat in her hands, Beth went round to the stable and saddled Prue. It was a warm, sparkling day but there was a gentle breeze which just lifted the curls off her forehead and made it more comfortable than a scorching day would have been if Beth's head had still throbbed. As it was, she felt glad to be out in the fresh air and she thought that a good canter with the wind blowing through her hair and the smell of the hedgerows and trees would set her to rights again.

She set off along the Rye road but she hadn't even got as far as the *Oak and Ivy*, when she saw Thomas Kemp, also mounted, riding the other way. She knew he worked with the gang and his father and uncle were a glazier and plumber, who were doing some work for Arthur up at Seacox. It was they who had done the work in Beth's old house before Arthur had allowed her and Will to move in. She reined in her horse and called to him. 'Hello, Thomas.'

He smiled back at her, touching his hat. 'Hello Miss Beth, Mrs Gray that is. Not at the fair?'

She shook her head. 'And you neither, I see?'

He wheeled his horse round and the two mares put their heads together. 'I was off up to Seacox,' Thomas said. 'My Dad was meeting your brother-in-law there but there's been something of a mishap.'

'I hope no one is hurt?' Beth asked

'No, no. Only my Dad had loaded the windows on the wagon and the wheel come off when he was pulling out. Half the glass is broken. My Dad is hopping mad as you might imagine. Point is, he can't do no work for Arthur today. I'm on my way there now to tell him and to call on Josiah Colvill on the way to tell him there ain't no way he can do his work neither, not without the glass. Then I have to call on

Ebenezer Comfort, the wheelwright to send him back to my Dad with another wheel. I don't know if I'm coming or going, that's the truth and my Dad will be sweeping up broken glass for a month.' Thomas finished his explanation and wiped his sleeve across his face.

Beth looked thoughtful. 'Look Thomas, why don't you go to Ebenezer and I'll deliver your messages? I'm only out riding for pleasure. It seems that you'll be busy for some while,' she suggested. The route to Seacox was a pleasant enough ride if she went through Horns Lane and up Delmonden.

Thomas looked uncertain. 'It's putting a lot of trouble on you, Miss, Mrs that is,' he corrected himself.

'It's no trouble at all, Thomas,' she assured him. 'Josiah Colvill's direction is Horns Lane, isn't it? I'll take the message to him and then go up to Seacox.'

Thomas smiled. 'Fact is, Mrs Gray I'd be thankful not to be the one to tell Arthur. My Dad says he had today all planned out. I know he'll be mad but it wasn't anyone's fault.'

Beth turned her mare round and nodded across at Thomas. 'I'll make that perfectly clear to Arthur, don't worry.'

Thomas breathed a sigh of relief and they cantered together back to Highgate Hill. Thomas turned off to find Ebenezer Comfort and Beth trotted the mare round the back of Colvill's small cottage to tell him that there would be no work for him with Arthur today. She then set the mare off up the winding lane which would eventually lead up the hill to Seacox.

Arthur heard the horse's hooves and its rider dismount and assuming it was Josiah Colvill, carried on measuring the door frame with a wooden ruler. He was working in the room planned as the front parlour which would have two glazed doorways as well as a long curved bay window giving a beautiful view onto the sweeping countryside below. He looked up slowly, the charcoal in his mouth, expecting to see Colvill and looked in surprise and some concern, to see Beth standing in the frame of the doorway.

He took the charcoal out of his mouth, a frown on his brow and said urgently, 'What is it Beth? Are you ill? You should have sent Annie for me.'

She laughed. 'No, I'm very well now. I needed to be out in the fresh air and my headache is quite gone.'

He still looked worried. 'Are you quite sure, Beth?' He looked around. 'I don't even have a chair to offer you.'

'Stop fussing, Arthur. You're worse than Will. I'm perfectly well only I've brought you some news you won't like.' She stopped and looked at the empty door and window frames.

He looked anxious. 'I guessed it was so,' he said. 'Though Will thought not, but it was bound to happen. I mean, you and Will are husband and wife. It's only to be expected. I've no right to dislike your news.'

Beth looked puzzled and stared at Arthur. 'What on earth are you talking about? I've come to tell you that Henry Kemp can't bring your glass today.'

'Then you're not - you're not carrying a child?' he asked, with relief.

She frowned and shook her head. 'No, why should you think that?'

This time Arthur shook his head. 'Oh, the fact that you were unwell and Sarah saying there was likely only one reason for it. The more I thought, the more probable it seemed. Forgive me, Beth. It can't be my business to question you about this.'

He looked uncomfortable for a moment and then asked briskly, 'Now what's this about Henry Kemp?'

She ignored his last remark and looked questioningly at him. 'I should like children, Arthur. How will you feel when I have them?'

He turned away, busying himself with the ruler and his drawings. He shrugged his shoulders slightly. 'How ought I to feel? I should accept it. I shall accept it. It's bound to happen. You're both young and fit. ' He turned back. 'Now tell me where my glass is.'

Beth looked solemn but then smiled. 'There was an accident with the wagon and it's all broken. There, I've said it now and you can be angry. I met Tom Kemp riding to tell you. You must be a very hard master,' she teased. 'He was quite afraid to come and tell you lest you got mad with him. I was particularly to say it was no one's fault. And I also went to tell Colvill that there was no point in his coming here today either. Arthur, I've just thought. We can go to the fair and meet them all there. Think how surprised they'll be.'

Arthur had put both hands up to his face and drew them down over it, ignoring her last remarks.

'By all the saints,' he said slowly. 'It's taken me these three last weeks to organise them both to be here on the same day.' He looked at the window frames. 'Oh well, I may as well finish up here. No point in measuring up any more windows till Kemp has set the first ones in. Yes you're right. Perhaps we can go the fair.' He gathered up his papers. 'I tell you what, Beth,' he said eagerly. 'Come and tell me what you think of the next room. I'm planning it to be a music room.'

She laughed. 'Well, you've grown very fine! I see we shall have to call on each other and leave cards.'

He looked a little hurt. 'Well it ain't really just for music. It's the dining room, but I thought I would have it large enough for a harp or harpsichord for the girls as well.'

She laughed again but followed him out of the room they were in, through the back hallway. He pushed open another door which led into a room of handsome proportions which also had the framework for a fine bay window. They stood in the empty room looking out through the space where the windows would be. It smelt of fresh wood, the wood shavings lying in light golden piles on the floor. Spreading out beneath their view was the gentle slope where the garden would be planted out and beneath that, stretching miles into the pale blue horizon, the green woods of Kent and Sussex, bathed in the incomparable sunlight of a June afternoon.

Arthur looked across at Beth noticing her sudden silence. 'Do you remember when we first came up here?' he asked.

She nodded quickly, knowing that he was going to ask it, before he had finished the sentence. 'Your dream came true,' she said quietly.

'Not all of it, not the most important part, Beth. This house was meant for you and me,' he replied.

Beth turned to him and smiled. 'Dreams have a habit of doing that, Arthur – not quite coming true, or not in the way we want or expect.'

They were both silent then, each with their own thoughts. Then Beth said brightly, 'It's a very handsome room and I'm sorry if I mocked it.' She moved to the window space and ran her hand along the smooth wood and then yelled, 'Oh!' and pulled her hand away quickly.

'What is it, Beth?' Arthur asked urgently.

She was sucking her palm. 'Just a splinter. But it's gone in deep.'

'Let me see,' he said taking her hand without thinking and drawing her back over to the light. His face was near her palm. 'Yes, here it is. One moment. There!' He pulled the splinter out and Beth gave a sharp cry, tears springing to her eyes at the small, sudden pain in the tender skin of her palm.

'I'll kiss it better,' Arthur said and did so, in the same way he might have done if one of his daughters had fallen down and hurt herself. There was no motive of desire or yearning at first, but as he went to draw his lips away he suddenly became aware of the softness of her hand in his and the alluring scent of her flesh. He pressed his lips back to her palm and raised his eyes to hers as he did so, watching her expression. He moved his lips slowly up her arm, dropping kisses on her wrist and forearm, catching his breath at the warm softness of her skin and then with a tender gesture, he pushed the lace of her sleeve higher up her arm and planted a kiss on the soft skin at the inner join of her elbow.

If she had remained unresponsive he might have been able to stop there and they would have carried on looking at the house, reading the plans, discussing changes, perhaps continuing in a comfortable friendship like this for the rest of their lives – but she did not remain unresponsive. She gently put the palm of her other hand on his shoulder, as light as a bird. Moving his lips from her arm, he looked into her calm grey eyes and saw the welcome and love in them, just as he had seen in them ten years ago when he had made love to her for the first time, both of them sixteen, lying on a mossy bank, not very far away from where they now stood.

In a moment his lips found hers and they were raining kisses on each other, hungrily and urgently. He looked around, his arms about her, searching for something to lie on. He pulled off his coat, dropping it to the floor, lowering Beth onto it murmuring her name into her hair, kissing her throat and not allowing himself the time to unlace her gown. He urgently pulled up her skirts and petticoats, his need for her acute and immediate. He undid his breeches, feeling her hands already there, her legs clasping his, pulling him towards her. He called her name, almost on a sob, as he possessed her. Though they had not lain together like this for ten years, the years fell away; their bodies were united as if with the intimate familiarity of accustomed lovers, their passion heightened by the intensity of their hunger for one another. Arthur looked down at Beth's lovely face, as he reached his pleasure within her, watching the expression on her face as her pleasure mingled with his.

As Arthur held Beth in his arms as they lay on the floor, his coat as a pillow under their heads, he felt a great contentment in his love for her but, though he scarcely admitted it to his conscious awareness, there was a flicker at the back of his senses of fear and foreboding.

CHAPTER THIRTY SIX

October 1740, Hawkhurst

'Arthur, will you be free on the evening of Friday the fourteenth?' Sarah asked her husband, poking her head round the door of the parlour where he had a pile of papers spread out in front of him.

'Why, Sarah?' he asked absently, running a finger down a neat line of figures. He stopped and looked up at her. 'What's to do?'

She came into the room and sat down opposite him. She glanced at the papers, but knew better than to comment on them. 'My brother Joseph has sent a letter up to me. Friday fortnight is a triple celebration – it's Joseph's birthday, he and Barbara will have been wed ten years and the twins are nine years old. They're having a small supper and have asked us to go. Do say we can, Arthur.'

He frowned. 'That's the week after next. I don't know what I'll be doing then. You know I'm dependent on tides and so on. Ask me again this time next week. But there may well be a run on, so don't depend on me coming with you. Couldn't you and the girls go anyway?'

She sighed. 'I don't think so Arthur. I don't think we'd be back until after dark. I wouldn't care to drive the wagon all the way from Goudhurst in the dark. And if you're away, Jim Cook will be too so he couldn't drive us. It doesn't matter. I'll send a note back to say we can't come.' Her mouth was tight.

Arthur turned back to his papers and Sarah stood up and walked out of the room to find Beth knocking at the back door. Beth smiled and stepped in. 'Hello Sarah, I've come to do the paperwork with Arthur. Will's gone off to Maidstone to look at some horses.' She took off her cloak and hood for although she had only come from four houses away, there was a pelting rain.

Sarah looked at her swelling figure. 'You'll soon have to start lacing at the side, Beth. You're increasing at such a rate.'

Arthur had come into the room, hearing Beth's voice. Beth nodded at him.

'Yes, I know, Sarah. Will is convinced I'm carrying a large son.'

'How many months are you?' Sarah asked.

'I'm not quite sure,' Beth said, shy suddenly. 'Three or four.'

She looked at Arthur who was watching her closely. 'We'll have to work without Will, Arthur. Colonel Brotherton of the Maidstone Militia is selling off some horses and Will thinks there are bargains to be had.'

'Well, he's a good judge of horseflesh, I'll allow him that,' said Arthur. 'Come through then, Beth, there's a lot to be done. I can't get these figures to add up. Bring us some tea, will you Sarah?'

He took Beth's arm and led her into the parlour, closing the door. As soon as they were alone, he took her hands. 'Do you really not know, Beth?' he asked urgently. 'I thought women could tell.'

She looked diffident. 'I've told you before. I can't be sure, Arthur. My courses, well they're not always regular.' She put a hand up to her forehead. 'I think it's Will's.'

Arthur hastily pulled her into his arms. It felt strange to feel her swelling belly pressing against him where she had always been so flat. He smoothed her hair and held her to him for a while. He did not dare to kiss her but holding her close was enough. He put her from him as he heard Sarah approaching and Beth sat down at the table and started to study the figures.

'Well, I can see where you've gone wrong here. You've forgotten to carry the ten over from this column.' Arthur stood behind her and looked at the numbers she was pointing to. Sarah came in with a tray. Her husband and Beth were doing the paperwork, as they often did. This was one area of his life where she would never be allowed to enter.

Arthur had a successful week. The gang had unloaded over twelve tons from two cutters, the value of each cargo put at three thousand pounds. The building work at Seacox was going well, with all the windows installed and the house was likely to be ready to move into around Christmas time. Will had bought two good mounts from Colonel Brotherton and Arthur had spent a whole morning with Beth and Will finalising the accounts of the last two runs and the pile of gold pieces that Arthur had hidden away, its location unknown to Sarah, was larger than he had ever imagined.

Sarah again asked Arthur about the visit to her brother.

'Yes,' he said in answer to her question, brushing her cheek lightly with a fingertip. 'Tell Joseph and Barbara we'll join them for their celebrations.'

'Oh Arthur,' Sarah said, wrapping her arms around him and kissing him. 'I'm so pleased. I thought there was no chance of it.'

He returned her embrace and kissed her again. 'You can ask him if he has any wooden chests. You'll need to start packing things ready for the move.'

As Joseph had his own saw mill, there were always spare bits of wood being made up into chests and boxes by one or other of the lads apprenticed to him.

'I thought we would take Sally and Becca with us and ask Will and Beth to mind Susie. What do you think?' Sarah asked leaning against his chest.

He nodded. 'Yes, if we're going to be back late, it'll be easier if Will and Beth can come over here. Susie will be a nuisance if she misses her bedtime.'

'Yes,' Sarah said leaning her cheek against Arthur's arm. 'That's what I thought.'

'Are you tired, Sarah?' he asked.

Sarah looked at the clock. 'No, not at all. It is only half after nine.'

Arthur kissed the top of her curls and started to pull the pins out of her hair. 'Good,' he said. 'Let's go to bed.'

The plans for the evening with Sarah's brother did not go quite according to how they wished. Beth said she would be happy to mind Susie. Some new music scores had arrived from London and she wanted to go over them in her head before trying them out on her old spinet. Will however had planned to be in Maidstone again in the late afternoon on the 14th.

'Brotherton has a couple more promising horses,' he explained to Arthur, who had called in the day before the planned visit.

'You've three already as well as Beth's mare, Will,' Arthur said smiling.

'I know, but Beth will like another and besides, I'm thinking of getting a wagon now I've a family to think about,' he pointed out, a little embarrassed.

Arthur looked at him and then at Beth. 'Will you be all right looking after Susie by yourself?' he asked Beth anxiously.

She laughed. 'I hope I'm still capable of looking after a two year old for a couple of hours, Arthur,' she protested. 'I believe you're setting out at four? Tell Sarah I'll be round a little before then.'

'We'll be back by nine,' Arthur said.

'I'll be back soon after then myself,' Will commented.

'Susie goes to bed at about six, I think,' Arthur said. 'You'll have a quiet, peaceful evening with your music, Beth.'

Arthur's house, Hawkhurst, Friday 14th October 1740

Standing in Sarah's kitchen, Beth looked up at the clock and saw it was nearly six o' clock. She had fetched Susannah's little nightshift from her niece's bedroom and bent down to pick the little girl up. She suddenly felt a sharp pain in her abdomen which made her catch her breath. She stood still and put her hand on the dresser to support herself, the other hand over her stays, breathing shallowly to try and ease the pain. After a few moments, it passed and she sighed and breathed out in relief. Then another pain, exquisite in its intensity, stabbed at her insides. She felt a sensation of something falling away from her and another sensation of warmness and wetness, which her mind refused to acknowledge. Clumsy with pain and fear, Beth pulled up her skirts and pressed her hand against herself and stared unbelieving, as she drew her hand away and held it in front of her and saw the bright red blood glistening on her fingers.

She felt her legs give way under her and pressing her back against the wall, slid to the floor. Susannah was standing solemnly looking at her, clutching her doll.

'Susannah! Susie!' Beth cried, but then faltered. What did she want the little girl to do?

'Susannah, can you - can you go next door for me and fetch Maria? Go and fetch Maria, Susie,' she begged, trying to keep her voice calm.

Susannah looked at her smiling. 'Mia,' she said.

Beth nodded, the faintness threatening to claim her at any moment. She was aware she was sitting in her own blood. She lifted her eyes to look at the back door and then drew in her breath as she noticed the bolt she had slid across at the top of it, to prevent Susannah from going out without her knowledge. She gave a short weak laugh.

Susannah came over to her and held out her doll to Beth. 'Dolly,' she said, smiling.

Beth looked again at the door. She must reach it; she must somehow reach up and unbolt it so the little girl could run next door and bring help. She tried to draw her knees up so she could get in a position to stand but her legs would not obey her brain's frantic messages. She rolled to her side, thinking she might attempt to crawl to the table and pull herself up. Shaking with effort, she hauled herself up, her knees trembling as she knelt on them.

Susannah came up to her and tapped her back. 'Horsey,' she said delightedly, thinking her aunt was playing one of the magical games she sometimes did and tried to climb onto Beth's back.

'No, oh no, sweetheart! Not now,' Beth cried.

She lost track of time as she crawled across the kitchen floor, her bloodied skirts getting caught up in her knees as she inched across the flagstones. Losing track of time, she didn't know if it was minutes or hours later when she pressed her face against the wood of the back door, pushing her hand up to feel the cold iron of the latch. She held onto it, trying to use it to give her some leverage to haul herself up, but each time she tried, her sweating hand slipped away from it. After three attempts she gave up. She could no longer see clearly and she felt so very tired now that all she wanted to do was close her eyes and rest and give in to the sweeping lethargy that had been trying to claim her. She was aware that she was somehow propped up with her back to the door, her legs straddled underneath her. Susannah was sitting on the floor under the table and began to cry. Beth closed her eyes.

The knocking came from a long way away. She wished they would stop it and let her sleep. It carried on. She was aware of Susannah's wails and muffled voices, angry at first and then alarmed. She tried to open her eyes and somehow Arthur and Sarah's faces seemed suspended above her.

'Merciful God!' she heard Sarah's voice say and then felt Arthur's strong arms around her and his voice at her ear.

'Will she never wake?'

'In her own good time.'

'She lost so much blood. I can't bear to think of her lying there without help.'

'Hush, Will, she'll not want to see you like this.'

'Should the surgeon be fetched again?'

'He can do no more at present, Will. You heard him say so. She must rest and try and regain some strength.'

'Move that light away, Sarah. You can see it bothers her eyes.'

'How will I tell her, Arthur? I can hardly bear it myself.'

'Hush, Will, you must take control of yourself.'

'I'll sit with her, first.'

'No, you will both leave and send Annie up to me. Beth's gown is soaked through and we must change it and the linen. This is women's work.'

'No, I'll stay and help lift her. Surely she should be moved as little as possible.'

'Then let Will stay. He has the right. But it's not seemly for you to see her unclothed, Arthur. You must wait outside.'

'Has she taken anything?'

'A little barley water, nothing more.'

'She's so pale. I can't bear it.'

'Has she spoken?'

'Nothing of sense. She didn't know me.'

'Is she in pain? Does she still complain of it?'

'No, she's quiet now.'

'Surely she must wake soon.'

'She seems less restless, for sure.'

'I think she has a little more colour. What say you, Sarah?'

'A little. Perhaps.'

'I think her hand moved in mine. I swear it.'

'Let me see, brother.'

'Yes, look, her eyelids move. Oh Beth, my darling wife, yes, open your eyes and come back to me.'

'Beth!'

'She's awake. Don't try to get up, sweetheart. You're quite safe. You're quite safe.'

'That's right, Beth. Don't be anxious. You have only to lie there and get better.'

'Arthur,' Beth whispered, in a thread of a voice. 'Have I been ill?' She looked up at the unfamiliar ceiling and said, suddenly afraid, 'I don't know where I am.'

Will took her hand, kneeling beside her and brushed a hand across his eyes. 'Beth, my darling, you're in Arthur and Sarah's bedchamber. You were ill, but you're better now. There's nothing to fear.'

He kissed her hand and then buried his face in the coverlet, his shoulders shaking. Arthur, standing behind him, gripped his shoulder, while Sarah looked on. If any of the three had noticed that Arthur's was the first name Beth had called when she woke, none of them mentioned it.

Two mornings later Will slipped into the room and sat gently on the bed, taking Beth's hand. She was dozing but in a little while she opened her eyes and looked at him for a moment as if trying to recollect her thoughts. 'I'm so sorry, Will,' she said flatly. 'I lost the child.'

Will, a catch in his voice, grasped both her hands. 'Don't you ever say that Beth, do you hear me? Don't you ever say sorry to me. Except that you want them, my darling, I shan't mind if we never have children. Not if it means you may suffer like this again.' He raised both her hands to his lips and dropped a kiss on the back of them. 'When I saw you so pale and with so much blood everywhere, I thought you had been murdered.'

'I don't remember, Will. Did you find me?' she asked.

He shook his head. 'No. Arthur and Sarah came back about nine o' clock. They heard Susie crying in the kitchen and called out to you to let them in. When there was no reply, they came in the front door. Susie ran out to Sarah and they found you huddled against the back door. Arthur carried you up to the bedchamber and Sarah flew next door to ask them to send Davie for Edward Young.'

Beth nodded. 'Yes, he is very gentle. Go on, Will.'

'I arrived ten minutes later. When I saw your gown where Sarah and Arthur had taken it off, soaked with blood in a heap on the floor, I though you'd been hacked to death. And then I saw you lying here and your chemise, even your dear stockings were red with blood – oh my dear love, I thought I would go mad with grief. But Arthur knew what to do. He had used a folded sheet to staunch the flow of blood. Forgive me for speaking indelicately, sweetheart. But I truly believe he saved your life. I don't know how I can ever repay him.' He pressed his forehead against Beth's hands and after a little while, she loosed one hand and drew his head nearer hers stroking his hair.

Sarah came in a few minutes later with a bowl of water and fresh linen. Will raised his head quickly and dashed a hand over his eyes.

'I wish you will go and fetch Corker in from the garden, Will,' Sarah said. 'He's been in my vegetable patch again.'

Will rose quickly. 'Oh Sarah, that dratted dog! I'll go at once and if he's done any damage, I'll set it to rights. I'll be back later, Beth,' he said.

Sarah set the bowl down on the little table beside the bed.

'I'm putting you to a lot of trouble, Sarah,' Beth said, glancing up at her. 'I'm even sleeping in your bed. Where is everyone moved to?'

Sarah shrugged. 'We are sisters, through our husbands, aren't we? Who else should be troubled? I'm sleeping with Susie in the little bedchamber. Sally and Becca have gone with Arthur. He's sleeping with Will at your house.'

'I think Will must be glad of Arthur's company. He seems very low.'

Sarah handed Beth the bowl and the piece of linen. 'He makes too much of it. I don't mean you have not been very ill, Beth. But there can hardly be a woman in Hawkhurst who has not lost a child at some point. Babies are easy got and easy lost, after all.'

She went over to the window and looked at Will in the garden, on his hands and knees by the vegetable patch repairing the damage Corker had done. She turned back to Beth and the sisters-in-law looked at each other for a moment unwilling to speak further.

'If you pass me your nightshift, Beth, I'll take it to wash,' Sarah said, at length.

Beth recovered slowly remaining at Arthur and Sarah's house for another three weeks and even then, when she was anxious to get back to her own home, Arthur insisted that she and Will came and ate dinner every night so that he was sure Beth was getting the benefit of Sarah's excellent cooking.

Arthur tried to broach the subject of Beth's miscarriage with her when he had taken her for a gentle walk along the Rye road, enjoying the last of the autumn sunshine. 'About what happened, Beth, I'm sure it doesn't mean that anything is wrong. Will and you will have other children, you know.'

Beth didn't answer for a while and then said, 'Sarah told me babies are easy got and easy lost, you know.'

Arthur sighed. 'Sarah doesn't always think before she speaks.'

They turned to go back the way they had come and she took Arthur's arm. Looking down at her, he noticed once again how the last rays of the autumn sun turned her hair to gold. Apart from the one occasion Beth had spoken to Will about losing the baby, she never mentioned it again to him. She sensed Will had taken it very hard and found it best not to talk about it. Will thought her silence was due to her grief and carried the problem to his brother while he was up at Seacox fixing some extra wall sconces for the multitude of beeswax candles he had planned to have in each room.

'What do you think, Arty? I'm afraid to say anything in case I upset her. I hate Beth to be unhappy. Do you think I should take her up to London, or some such thing?'

'Why on earth would she want to go up to London, Will?' Arthur asked bolting up a fine ironwork sconce to one side of the massive fireplace. 'Has she said so?'

Will shook his head. 'Well, no, only I thought it might divert her. The other thing is,' he paused, feeling embarrassed. 'I don't know whether I should, well, that is, I don't know when it will be comfortable for Beth to lie with me again.'

Arthur hastily busied himself with the fitting and addressed himself to the wall. 'Surely Beth will tell you when she feels the time is right?'

Both brothers remained silent.

'So long as you're – gentle with her, Will,' Arthur said after a while.

'Of course I will be! How can you think otherwise?' Will demanded indignantly.

Arthur turned round. 'I don't think it. Here, hold this will you?' he said, handing over an iron fixing.

Will looked thoughtful. 'Do you think I should try and get her with child again, quite soon and that will make her forget what has happened this time?' He paused and Arthur remained silent.

'Yes,' Will said definitely, half to himself. 'I think that's the answer.' He handed Arthur the ironwork. 'Thank you Arty, I knew you would have the solution.'

CHAPTER THIRTY SEVEN

The day before Christmas Eve 1740, Seacox Heath, Hawkhurst

Becca had spent most of the morning since breakfast with her nose pressed up against the window pane in the kitchen. There was a light dusting of snow and small flakes were falling. As she looked up at them it seemed as if she was the one that was moving, drifting through the pale sky.

The delicious smell of plum pudding wafted its aroma not only in the kitchen but in most of the downstairs rooms; and Joanna was busy in her large apron, her face red, her sleeves rolled up as she kept topping up the pan of boiling water. Becca had jumped down from her place to snatch up some almonds that Joanna had laid out on a tin plate and in the moments she was away from her place at the window, Arthur rode up, Jim Cook beside him leading another horse loaded with packages and parcels.

Joanna looked up from her pan and out through the small panes of the window and glanced across at Becca. 'Looks like your Dad had ridden up.'

Becca rushed to the window, clambouring up on the chair and then jumped down again. 'Mamma! Sally! Daddy's here.'

She rushed to the heavy oak door, struggling with the great iron latch and pulled it open as Arthur and Jim were dismounting. She rushed out and Arthur let go of his horse's reins and scooped her up, kissing her and wrapping her inside his coat.

'Are they our Christmas presents?' she asked, struggling to pull her head out from under her father's heavy coat and looking anxiously at the boxes and packages.

'Well, they might be and then again they might not,' he teased. Just then Sarah and Sally appeared at the back door. 'Take the horses round to the stables, Jim. And be careful with those packages.'

Jim Cook grinned and led the horses away, his boots crunching on the snow. Arthur stepped into the warmth of the kitchen, his boots leaving puddles on the smooth flagstones. It was the first time he had ridden back to Seacox as his home and he had felt the pride rising within him as he and Cook had approached the house, its red brickwork looking mellow in the pale morning light, the dusting of snow on the roof giving it a homely look and the smoke rising from the chimneys, showing that it was lived in and cared for already.

Sarah helped him off with his greatcoat and hung it and his hat on the pegs in the little ante- room off the kitchen. He kissed her and Sally, teased Joanna about the daubs of flour on her cheek and sat down at the table while Sarah made a pot of tea. His two elder daughters and his wife looked at him expectantly, all wanting to ask whether he had been successful in his commission and had brought back from the London dressmaker, the gowns made up in the silks they had chosen a few weeks ago.

'Are our gowns ready, Daddy?' Sally asked at length, unable to wait any longer.

He sipped his tea without saying anything and then nodded. 'Jim Cook is unloading them now.' He looked across at his wife. 'You'll need to press and hang them, Sarah. But I don't need to be telling you that.'

'Are they pretty?' Becca asked, taking his hand and looking up at his face with a serious expression.

'Your Uncle Will must answer that, Becca. I'm no judge of such things, as your mother will tell you.' He looked across at Sarah again. 'How is the house? Does everything work? Do all the doors open and close? Have none of the shelves fallen down?'

She smiled. 'Everything works well, Arthur.'

Sarah was a born housewife and arranging linen cupboards and displaying her china, hanging the curtains and laying the rugs were activities exactly to her taste. The fact that she had moved from one house into another within a week of Christmas had not disquieted her at all.

At that moment, Jim appeared at the kitchen door laden with parcels. Arthur got up and helped him in with them and carried them all to the table.

'I fancy these three large boxes are yours, Beth's and Martha's,' Arthur said 'And these smaller ones are the girls' gowns.'

'Now don't leave them there, Arthur,' Sarah scolded. 'They'll get plum pudding or the goose stuffing on them. Jim, can you carry them into the back sitting room? Sally, go and see if Susie has woken from her nap. Then we can try them on and make sure there are no alterations to be made.'

'Oh, I was very precise about handing over the exact measurements you gave me,' Arthur said. When the girls had followed Jim into the other room, he went over to Sarah and put his arms round her waist kissing her on the cheek. 'I'm hoping the gowns will be a peace offering in some way,' he said doubtfully.

Sarah remained in his embrace but bent her head back to look up at him. 'What have you done, Arthur?'

He shook his head. 'No, it's not what I have done, but what I must do. I think I may spoil your Christmas arrangements a little, Sarah.'

She said nothing but continued looking at him, raising her eyebrows.

'There's a run for Camber bay,' he said defiantly.

'When?'

'Christmas Night,' he said quickly. 'It can't be helped, so it's no use protesting. I wouldn't have chosen the date, but it's a question of tides both sides of the Channel. If we miss the 25th, we can't do it until the 31st. '

He felt Sarah's body tighten. 'I was thinking that maybe you would like to do what you had planned for Christmas Day, on Christmas Eve instead. We could ask Lucas and Martha to come tonight, instead of tomorrow. I know Will and Beth will be agreeable. Is it much trouble to bring all the plans forward by one day? Will and I must leave early on Christmas afternoon.'

'You want to serve the goose and the plum pudding tomorrow?' Sarah asked.

'Yes, it can't make too much work can it?' Arthur observed with all the ignorance of a man who couldn't boil an egg.

Sarah twisted out of his embrace. 'Well you'd better let me get on and send Jim Cook with a note to Lucas and Martha,' she said severely.

'I know my clever Sarah will manage,' Arthur coaxed. 'Especially now she has this fancy new range and everything to hand in the new kitchen.'

She said nothing but went over to one of the cupboards and began drawing out pots and pans. Arthur, thinking he would be better out of it, went to put his coat back on. 'I'll call on Lucas myself. I was going to see Will anyway.'

Lucas and Martha were perfectly happy to start their Christmas festivities a day early and promised to arrive at about four that afternoon.

Martha was anxious to see the gown that Arthur had brought back. He had given her the silk as a token of his gratitude to Lucas for providing blacksmithing services to the gang, often at short notice and for making up the many bolts and locks on all the doors at Seacox. Lucas refused to take any extra payment for himself but was happy for Martha to have the treat of some French silk made up by one of the London dressmakers.

Will and Beth were never put out by changing plans at the last moment and Beth said they would be at Seacox that afternoon.

By the time Arthur returned, Sarah had everything in hand in the kitchen; the gowns had been unpacked and pressed and were hanging in their bedchamber. The bedchambers for their guests were made up, Sarah enjoying the luxury of having two spare rooms to offer her guests and plenty of linen to make up the beds. The girls were looking out of the window waiting for Will and Beth and greeted them with shouts of excited laughter.

'Uncle Will has another new suit, mamma,' Becca said. Arthur looked him over. He certainly looked very fine in his dark blue wool coat and matching waistcoat. But there was no time to admire Will, as Lucas and Martha and three year old Joseph arrived; and Sally and Becca whisked the little boy away into the back sitting room to show him their toys. Susie was enchanted to have a playmate just a few months older than herself and their squeals of laughter could soon be heard.

They all took their seats in the large dining room. There was still the smell of fresh paint and new wood throughout the house and Martha declared she had never been in such a fine dining room before, not even when she had visited her sister who was a housemaid up at the new house at Finchcocks, declaring the dining room there to have an unhandsome fireplace and a carpet that was commonplace. All the adults laughed, though Arthur's smile died quickly and he looked thoughtful. While Lucas was regaling the children with a funny story about trying to shoe a horse who kept butting him out of the way, Will asked his brother under his breath, 'What's wrong? There's not some trouble about the run is there?'

Arthur shook his head twirling the fine stem of his wineglass in his fingers. 'No, all's well, brother. I think I must be tired.' He smiled and Will smiled back. He could hardly tell Will that throughout supper, he could not rid his mind of the thought that he had made love to Beth in this very room last summer, that the child she had lost might have been his and that he had felt the same longing for her all evening.

After Sarah's delicious supper, the girls couldn't stop wriggling with excitement for they were to show off their gowns.

'What say you, Will? Shall we let the girls go?' Arthur asked, willing himself to join in the happy atmosphere.

Will laughed. 'I think we had better or Sally is going to wriggle herself onto the floor.'

Sarah drew back her chair and Beth and Martha followed her. The three little girls and Joseph ran up the stairs and the men were left to their brandy. A half an hour later, Beth, Sarah, Martha and the girls could be heard giggling and laughing as they came down the stairs.

The double doors were pushed open and they stood there, Becca and Sally at the front, self conscious and giggling, Susannah holding her mother's hand tightly and Beth and Martha at the rear.

The men stopped drinking at the vision of female finery in front of them. Martha's honest open face and her high colour could not do justice to the cerise silk she had chosen; and Sarah looked a dignified matron in her cream floral. Sally's dress would be too short in another month, Arthur thought and Becca looked by far the prettiest of his daughters in her dark green which complemented her fine dark colouring; and he smiled to see Susannah picking up her skirts showing her little fat legs.

But when he saw Beth in the rich brown damask with the gold quilted petticoat showing at the front which caught the candlelight and seemed to shimmer as she moved, he caught his breath. She had been perfectly right in her choice – the brown matched her hair exactly and the gold picked out the golden lights in it. She had put back on the weight she had lost after losing the child and perhaps a little more, her shoulders and bosom graceful and womanly, her height giving her an elegance which the other two women could not match. She had never looked lovelier, or statelier, he thought.

'Beth,' he said slowly. 'You look beautiful.'

No one else spoke and then Lucas said quickly, 'Aye, so you do. And so do you all, ladies. Is it not so, Arthur?'

'Yes, yes of course,' Arthur said, managing to take his eyes off Beth at last. 'You look very fine Sarah and Martha.' He collected his thoughts. 'Yes, you all look very lovely. Come here, Susie and show me your petticoats.'

Beth looked at Arthur with her calm grey eyes and then went over to Will and took his arm. Sarah smiled at Beth as she passed but as she looked at her husband, her mouth formed a hard straight line.

CHAPTER THIRTY EIGHT

Christmas Day, 1740, Seacox Heath, then Camber

A light fall of snow and a silver grey sky caused Arthur and Will to leave even earlier than planned. Christmas Day was spent quietly in comparison with Christmas Eve. They went to Church in the morning. All the women and the girls wore their new silks, though because of the bitter cold, most of their finery remained concealed beneath their cloaks. By three o clock it was almost dark and Arthur and Will saddled up their horses, wrapped themselves up well in greatcoats, mufflers and hats, Will wearing a new beaver lined tricorne that Beth had given him for Christmas and set off back through Hawkhurst. They collected Jim Cook on the way and all three made their way through Tenterden and onto the Appledore Road. It hadn't snowed again but it remained bitterly cold and they kept at a steady canter to make good time and to keep warm. They saw the lights of Lydd twinkling before them a little after six. The little street was quiet, the great spire of the Church of All Saints disappearing up into a black sky, the church empty now its last service had been held and the good folk of Lydd had gone back to the warmth of their homes to enjoy Christmas night before their own hearths.

Arthur, Will and Jim led their horses into the stables which were already nearly full. Humphrey Haddon, one of the servants at the *George* came out with a lantern, his coat buttoned up to his neck and his hat crammed down low on his head. Arthur nodded at him in acknowledgment. 'Stables are full tonight, Haddon? And not just with our men?'

'No sir, we've a party down from Dover, got on the wrong road and broke the axle on their coach. The other coach travelling in the party brought 'em all down this way. They thought they'd reached Hastings.'

'I see,' Arthur said loosening the saddle from his horse. Strangers were always bad news on a run. They could be spies for the Riding Officer or paid informants. He carried his saddle to the hooks on the wall and hoisted it up.

'There's a letter waiting for you,' Haddon explained, pushing a lock of his greasy hair out of his eyes. Arthur raised his eyebrows but said nothing. He turned round waiting for Will and Jim and then they all made their way round to the front and into the warmth in the taproom of the *George*. He saw the rest of his men gathered in the small front room where they usually met up. Stanton Blacklock greeted them cheerfully and wished them a Happy Christmas.

Arthur nodded. 'I believe there's a letter waiting for me?'

Blacklock nodded and reached behind the bar. He pulled out a piece of paper and handed it over to Arthur. Arthur broke apart the seal and carried it over to the candleholder on the wall. Will who had stepped over to his side, raised his eyebrows. 'What news?'

Arthur frowned. 'It's from Captain Ollive of the *Eliza*. She has a broken mast and can't sail. He's transferred the cargo to the *L'Aimable Virtue*,' he said hesitantly, trying to make out the French, 'and it will be captained by *Hanchette*, *Honchette*, I can't make out his name – no one I know anyway. And the cutter is coming later. I don't think she'll be in much before three in the morning.'

Jim Cook came up. 'Trouble?' he asked, seeing Arthur's frown.

A laugh went up from the back parlour which had been given over to the Dover party. They were obviously intent on making the most of their bad luck. Arthur folded the letter and put it back in his pocket. 'Captain Ollive sent this over this morning. Our landing is put back, Jim. Well,' he said, looking at them both. 'The last thing I wanted is to have the men sitting round in the bar all night but there's no choice. Keep an eye on them, Will.'

Camber beach, early Monday morning, Boxing Day, 1740

It was just before four that the '*L'Aimable Virtue*' signalled the blue flash that told the landing party she was ready to unload. Sam Austin gave the answering light and the tub boat was lowered over the side to bring the first tublines in. Bob Fuller and George Kingsmill were waiting in the freezing surf to bring the lines in, pulling the ropes held up by their cork floats so they could start cutting the pairs of kegs free, passing them quickly down the line to the rest of the men waiting to load up.

Forty pairs were quickly unloaded and the tub boat came in again with the next two lines, but as Fuller and Kingsmill ran out to grab the lines, they started shouting and Fuller turned back to the shore, shouting to Arthur. 'Line's broke, Arthur, line's broke.'

Arthur saw Fuller splashing about in the surf, trying to follow the floats and retrieve the lines; otherwise the kegs would be at the mercy of the tide. Fuller and Kingsmill were wearing the long oilskins waders they wore over their boots and up to their thighs to give them some protection against the freezing wet of the sea water. Arthur hesitated for a moment and then dashed into the freezing water, seeing Fuller up to his waist.

'Come on Curtis!' he yelled turning back to Jeremiah who had been standing right beside him. The tide was turning though and the floats and their precious cargo were bobbing further and further out of Fuller's reach.

'Damn and blast it,' Fuller cursed as a wave smacked him in the face.

'Come back in, Bob,' Arthur shouted, still a few feet behind him. He cupped his hands around his mouth and shouted to Sam Austin, trying to stop his teeth chattering.

'Signal the cutter to send the tub boat to me. I'm going aboard.' He saw in exasperation that Jeremiah Curtis was still standing at the shoreline, obviously having decided not to get himself any wetter.

He saw Austin nod; the moonlight was at least in their favour, lighting up the scene. Bob Fuller and George Kingsmill waded back to the shoreline, where Tom Kingsmill was waiting with a couple of old blankets. Arthur went back a little towards them until the waves were lapping at the level of his knees. He started shivering, clapping his arms about him trying to keep warm until the tub boat arrived. Two crew men pulled him aboard and started rowing back to the cutter.

Arthur hauled himself up the ladder and clambered onto the deck where the Captain stood waiting for him.

'Hanchet?' Arthur asked, looking at the loose-framed dark-haired man with the weather-beaten face who stood before him.

'Ah, oui, Monsieur,' he said, holding out his hand.

Arthur shook it but didn't smile. 'I take it you speak English?'

The Frenchman shrugged his shoulders and then nodded. 'A little.'

Arthur sighed. 'You've lost me forty kegs. The lines weren't tied properly.'

The Frenchman raised his eyes heavenward. 'Pardon?'

Arthur exhaled. 'Christ!' he said to himself. 'The lines, les lignes, ils sont, ils ne sont pas, propre,' he faltered.

'Ils ne sont pas propre?' the Captain asked looking surprised. 'Qu'est ce que sait que ca?'

'Le cognac, mon cognac est perdu,' Arthur struggled and gave up. 'Where's the bill of lading?' he asked

'Le bill?' The Captain seemed to understand and drew some paper out of his pocket. Arthur took it to the lantern at the side of the boat and read a few lines. It was less than a quarter of what he was expecting to receive.

'Sweet Jesus, is this all?' he demanded. 'C'est tout?'

The Captain looked at the scrap of paper and shrugged, then took the lantern from its holder and beckoned Arthur to follow him down into the hold. The timbers creaked and rasped around him as he lowered himself. It smelt damp and the flickering lights showed the small hold with a good six inches of water in it, stacked with the kegs strung together in pairs and oilskin bags, piled haphazardly on top of them. Arthur pulled a length of the rope to which the kegs were tied and flexed it between his hands along its length while the Captain watched him. The boat rolled beneath his feet. He was not a good sailor and he began to feel the rising nausea in his gut, but refused to give into it. It took him a good twenty minutes to test the whole length of the rope and he was aware that the tide was now against them.

'This one is good,' Arthur said at length. 'C'est bon.'

The Captain called an order and two of his men appeared at the entrance to the hold and dropped down. Then at a command from the

Captain, they began pulling the paired kegs up between them. Arthur started examining the oilskins, for pound for pound he would get a better return on the tea. He decided to leave the rest of the spirits. But when he started to check the seals of the oilskins he found some of them chewed and snatching the lantern again held it down to illuminate what he suspected. Rats! They scampered away from the light, but he could see they had been at many of the oilskins. If they had made the smallest hole the tea would be damp and useless to him. He knew some unscrupulous gangs would sell seawater-damaged tea, but it lost you your good name and in Arthur's estimation, it wasn't worth it.

He pulled his watch out. Ten past six. He knew the sunrise was just before eight and allowed himself until seven to check the rest of the cargo and get it overboard. He started to check each oilskin, telling the Captain which bags he would accept and which he would not.

Forty minutes later, he eased himself back up out of the hold onto the deck. It had started snowing again quite heavily, the flakes laying on the ropes and sails of the small boat. He took out his charcoal and crossed through the bill of lading and wrote roughly the corrected amounts he had accepted. He would have plenty to say to Captain Ollive at their next encounter but for the present he wanted to get off the cutter and back on dry land and get the goods away before daybreak. The two crewmen started to row him back to the shore and after a couple of minutes he put his head over the side of the boat and was sick. Though he had been freezing cold, he now felt hot and dashed a handful of seawater over his face. That and the act of vomiting made him feel slightly better and he jumped out of the boat as soon as he could and splashed through the surf. Will was waiting for him, a layer of snow settled on his shoulders and hat.

'What a night, Arthur! I've loaded everything we've got. There are just the last oilskins to load and then we can be away. But I shouldn't think we've got much more than half a ton of tea.'

Arthur nodded. 'You're right, Will. Go and mount up and get all the men to do the same. It only needs a couple of us to load this last. Load Peg with some of the oilskins will you?'

Will nodded and set off up the beach. Arthur supervised the final unloading and signalled to the cutter that it could haul the tub boat aboard and set sail back across the channel. He watched it slowly turn around and its lights were soon lost. He turned back to the shore. The last of his men were mounting their horses and apart from the hollows and tracks in the sand where the men had dragged the cargo up the beach, there was no sign that they had ever been here. Soon the tide and the snow would cover up even that evidence. He saw Peg, his mare and whistled to her. She pricked up her ears at the familiar sound and came down the sand towards him. Will was a little way off, saying something to Jim Cook. Arthur waved a hand to him reaching his other hand under his horse's belly to adjust the saddle, moving the oilskins a little out of the way so he could mount easier.

'Fuck!' he cursed as the leather girth snapped and the saddle slipped to the side. 'What else can go wrong?'

Arthur was uncomfortably aware of his wet breeches and his heavy boots squelching sea water between his toes. A short distance away on the beach the men milled around, the breath of their horses white in the bitter night air.

'What's to do now, Arthur?' Will asked bringing his horse nearer. 'Do we move inland or store the goods at Lydd?' He removed his hat and knocked it against his thigh to shake off the snow that had settled on it.

'No, I've a mind to move them in a little. I don't want to store them in Lydd now. Too many strangers at the *George* for my liking.' He jerked his head towards the line of men moving off and frowned. 'All this for half a ton of tea and most of us in trouble with our wives for being out on Christmas night!'

George Chapman rode up flashing a lantern.

'Put out your light, George,' Arthur snapped. 'We don't want to attract any attention. It's almost daylight.'

'What are we doing, Arthur?' Chapman asked. 'I've a bad feeling about tonight. Some of us ain't hardly carrying anything.'

'You're right, George. It doesn't need all of us. Keep Sam, Bob, Jim and the Kingsmills and Curtis; send the rest home. Take the goods to Tenterden and store them in our safe house. Is there a spare saddled horse? Or I must ride bareback. I don't think your mare will carry both of us, Will?'

'Aye, Jenny would take your weight,' Will said smiling and patting his mare's neck. 'But the snow's falling harder. I wouldn't have her slip for the world.'

Just as Arthur turned back to Chapman, a bullet whistled past his ear and buried itself in the sand. 'Sweet Jesus!' he said, pulling his pistol from its holster and cocking it, straining his eyes to make out the shadowy figure on horseback who had suddenly appeared out of the darkness.

A voice called out, 'Hold up, in the name of His Majesty! I suspect you are running uncustomed goods.'

'Hold fire!' Arthur called to the unknown rider. 'Give me that lantern, George.'

The men just pulling away from the beach had halted and were calming their horses. Chapman passed Arthur the lantern and he too had pulled out his pistol. Arthur meanwhile had shone the lantern full in the face of the horseman and then recognising Will's former schoolmate, called out, 'Tom Carswell, is that you? Have you run mad? For God's sake put up your pistol before you harm someone.'

'That's uncustomed tea!' Tom Carswell said waving his pistol towards the oilskin bags slung over Will's horse.

'Of course it is,' Arthur snapped. 'And some of it's for your own mother, Tom. Now put up your weapon and go home and let us get on with our business. God knows, we've had enough ill luck this night without you adding to it.'

'Get that light out of my face, Arthur!' Tom replied crossly. 'I can't see you.'

'Not till you put up your weapon, Tom. What in God's name are you doing here? It's bad enough you're a Riding Officer but your mother said you were posted up in Essex.'

'I w... was,' Carswell stammered nervously, 'but Polly's not been well and I asked to be brought back nearer home. The Camber stretch was the nearest they could offer. Collier reckoned I wouldn't have the guts to grass up my friends, but I have to, don't I?'

Arthur exhaled in exasperation. 'They don't expect you to, Tom, do they, that's why Collier don't want you working anywhere your family and friends are. For God's sake, Tom, you must be aware how often we use this beach?'

Tom hesitated and then his horse shied up. The faintest pink glow was appearing in the sky. 'Dismount, Will,' Carswell shouted suddenly. 'And drop the oilskins on the sand.'

'I'll be damned if I do,' Will replied.

'Tom, don't point your pistol at Will,' Arthur said warningly.

'I'll blow your brains out!' Carswell said to Will, a note of panic sounding in his voice.

'This is madness, Tom,' George Chapman said, steadying his own horse, which seemed to have sensed the other horse's unease. 'There are two pistols aimed at you.'

'Well drop them,' Tom insisted, trying to control his horse with his left hand while his right tried to steady the pistol still aimed in Will's direction. 'I'll shoot Will if you don't.'

Will's horse made a sudden movement forward. There was a quick burst of gunfire and three flashes in the semi darkness where the guns had gone off. Arthur, horrified, saw Tom Carswell drop like a stone from his horse and then there was a low groan to his left and he saw Will slump forward over his horse, his reins let go and both hands clutched to his side.

The rest of the men came riding back down to the beach and a great hubbub broke out, but all Arthur could think of was Will and in two steps was at his side, grabbing the horse's reins and trying to steady her, lest she tip Will off. He reached up to put his arm on Will's shoulder and Will with an effort raised his head and looked at his brother as if he were trying to bring him into focus.

'Take me home, Arty,' he said, his voice a ragged whisper. Shaking with effort, he put out his right hand to grasp his brother's wrist and Arthur felt with alarm that Will's hand was warm and sticky with blood.

A disembodied voice near Arthur's ear said flatly, 'Carswell's dead.'

Arthur turned his head slowly to see Tom Kingsmill standing next to him. 'Two shots, one in the chest one in the shoulder,' Kingsmill added.

Arthur looked at him, wondering why his brain seemed to have stopped working. 'We must... I need to get Will home,' was all he could say.

'Jesus Christ! Jesus Christ! Jesus Christ!' George Chapman was standing over Carswell's body and then dropped to his knees beside him. 'I never meant to kill you, man!'

'Kingsmill, get Chapman out of here,' Arthur said gruffly. He had pulled off his muffler and kerchief and was awkwardly trying to make a rough bandage around Will's middle.

Kingsmill nodded. 'Aye, we'll all get out and store the goods for now. Best leave Carswell where he is. Fucking traitor!' he said savagely. 'His sort is better dead.'

Arthur looked briefly at Chapman, still kneeling in the sand. 'It could have been either of us killed him, George. How can we ever know? It was Will or him. He should have put up his gun. Why didn't he put up his gun?'

Jim Cook approached Arthur and looked at Will slumped over the horse, the early morning light beginning to illuminate the chaotic scene, large snowflakes now settling thickly on men and horses. 'God!' he exclaimed. 'Not dead, is he? Not Will?'

Arthur shook his head. 'No but he's bad Jim, I have to get him home. John Bowra will come. I need to get word to him.'

It was Jim's turn to shake his head. 'No he's gone to his daughter's, Canterbury way. We took him some silk last Monday week, have you forgot? It was her Christmas box, from him.'

Arthur's brain began to work again. 'Christ! If Bowra's at Canterbury, it will take an age to bring him to Hawkhurst.'

'First place they'll look for you anyway, Arthur. Ain't it better if you lie low somewhere else for a while?'

'What? Look for me?' Arthur couldn't think what Cook meant for a moment. 'Oh, yes, yes of course. They'll be looking for me. Jim, do you know where Bowra's daughter lives?'

As Jim nodded, Arthur continued. 'You must ride there and bring the doctor to me. You make for Canterbury, go up through Ashford and I'll bring Will across the Marsh – we'll meet up at, at …' Arthur paused, trying to calculate how fast Jim could get to Canterbury and how long it would take him to get Will across the Marsh to a suitable hideaway. 'I'll get Will to St Rumwold's, meet us there. Don't fail me, Jim. I'm depending on you. Will's depending on you.'

Jim gave a quick nod of his head. 'I'll manage it. Don't you worry.' And he was gone to his horse.

Jeremiah Curtis had brought up another horse for Arthur and he swung himself up on the saddle. 'Reckon it was your ball found its mark,' Curtis said blandly. 'You was stood still, Chapman was mounted, stands to reason your shot was more accurate.'

Arthur met Curtis's gaze, his thoughts suddenly turned back to a hot summer's day many years ago when Curtis had shown him how to shoot rabbits. 'We'll never know. How can we know?'

He glanced briefly at Tom Carswell's body lying face up on the sand, where Kingsmill had turned him over, the front of his coat stained dark red and a pool of blood sinking into the sand around him. He looked ridiculously young. Will groaned softly at Arthur's side. Arthur took the reins of his brother's horse and his own, dug his heels into his horse's flanks and set off towards the Guldeford Lane which led to Brookland and the safety of the Marsh.

Arthur kept both horses at a trot as soon as they had left the sand and were on the rough track. His mind was jangling with his thoughts in turmoil – *keep Will on the horse, get Will to safety, how long will it take me to get to St Rumwold's? What if Jim don't find Bowra? Tom Carswell killed, dead, lying in the sand, Polly waiting at home for him, oh God, no don't think of that, concentrate on the road, keep Will safe. What if it was Will lying dead, Beth waiting at home for him? No! That's the road to madness; don't think that, concentrate on the road. God, forgive me if I killed Carswell. God forgive me and let Will live! God have mercy! Don't punish me by taking Will! Let me think of a psalm, a prayer!*

"Of whom may we seek for succour, but of thee, O Lord?" The words from the burial service were the only ones to come into his head. *"Lord have mercy! Christ have mercy! Lord have mercy!"* And then instead of struggling to remember the words, they flooded into his mind, unstoppable. *"Man that is born of woman hath but a short time to live – he cometh up and is cut down like a flower – in the midst of life, we are in death."*

Will was in the midst of life, is he now in death? Arthur thought panicking, hearing his own heartbeat pounding in his ears. *Cut down like a flower! Oh sweet Christ, have mercy! Have mercy, have mercy, have mercy!*

An oath from Will brought Arthur to his senses. 'Will, Will you must hold on, brother, we must keep going. I'll get you to safety Will, don't worry.'

Will remained slumped forward, just about hanging on and he turned his head to look across at his brother. The rosy dawn had lit up the sky, but the whirling snowflakes made it difficult to see. Arthur drew both horses up and lined up next to Will. He reached over and pulled his brother's collar up at the back of his neck. He looked about him and realised they were approaching the few houses and St Augustine's Church at Brookland. They might find a safe resting place at the *Woolpack*, but it was too close to Camber and too far for Jim to return with the doctor. There were no lights anywhere. Arthur urged the horses on towards Brenzett.

Will groaned again and as he moved, his hat fell off and rolled into the snow. Arthur drew up his horse and dismounted, brushing the snow off the hat as he picked it up. He felt the beaver-skin lining and sighed as he remembered how often he had scolded Will for being so particular about his clothes. As he went back over to Will, he felt a shiver of fear to see his brother looking so ill, a greyish tinge about his face, his lips blue. He touched his hand and found it icy cold and Will gave no response to the pressure of Arthur's grasp.

'Will?' he called softly and then again more urgently, 'Will!'

A slight movement and he knew his brother still lived, but only just. Arthur patted the mare's neck and said softly, 'Your master reckoned you could take my weight as well as his. Let's try you.'

He gently took Will's foot out of the stirrup, putting his own in and swung himself up behind his brother. The mare snorted and lost her footing but quickly righted herself. Arthur put his arms around Will and pulled him into an upright position as far as he could. He pressed his knees into the mare's sides and set her off at a walk, leading the other horse.

If he had a mind to it, he would have seen the beauty of the unfolding scene in front of him. The Marsh opened up ahead of him, flat, eerily quiet, beautiful. The long clump of trees far away on his left marked the road to Tenterden and beyond where the rest of his men were headed. But all Arthur was aware of was the soft crunching of the horses' hooves on the snow and their occasional whinny and constantly, the dead weight of Will against him. The sheep on the surrounding fields stood, their faces blank and stupid, their fleeces a dirty yellow against the purity of the snow.

He skirted around the few houses and tried to calculate how long it would take them to reach St Rumwold's Church. The mare was walking at about two miles an hour, it must be twelve miles from here, could Will possibly survive six hours without help? He pressed his knees again and adjusted the reins encouraging the mare to a canter. His left arm pressed against Will's side was becoming sticky and wet as the faster movement of the horse caused the wound to open and bleed more profusely. Arthur slowed back down to a walk but the blood continued running down Will's chest and over his left leg, down the mare's flanks leaving a bright crimson trail in the snow, which was slowly covered up as the flakes continued to fall. Minutes stretched to hours as Arthur walked the horses, then sped to a trot, then dropped back again to a walk, all the while clutching his young brother, willing him to live.

Four hours later Arthur saw the distinctive turret and cupola of St Rumwold's Church come into view. His left arm was clasped tightly around Will, the fingers of his right hand almost frozen into the reins. He led the horses to the clump of trees at the side of the church and slowly and awkwardly dismounted. He half dragged, half lifted Will from the mare's back and carried him to the porch of the church, manhandling him while he struggled with the great iron latch. He entered the small building and lay Will down against the wall at the back. It was not particularly warm inside, but it was a relief to be out of the snow and Arthur felt his fingers and toes coming painfully back to life. Fetching some hassocks, he placed these under Will's head and shoulders. Under his greatcoat, Will's shirt was stained dark red, his breath coming in painful little gasps.

Arthur rubbed a hand over his own face, then took out a flask and undoing it, pressed the bottle to Will's lips and tipped some over his tongue. It simply ran out again, so Arthur took two gulps himself and then put it away. He went back outside to tether the horses and on his return, sat down behind his brother, wrapping his arms round him and letting Will's back rest against his own chest. Putting his mouth near to Will's ear, he said urgently, 'Stay with me, Will, don't do this to me, don't die, don't go!'

He looked around the church, at the simple cross and altar and the great bible on the pulpit, hugged Will to him and waited for Jim and the surgeon to arrive.

He couldn't believe he had dozed off, yet the sound of horses outside roused him from sleep that was for sure. His arms around Will were soaked with his brother's blood and there was a sticky pool of it underneath both of them. He eased himself from under his brother and laid his fingers on the butt of his pistol under his greatcoat. The great oak door was pushed open.

'God's truth!' Jim Cook exclaimed as he set eyes on Arthur, whose hands and arms were covered in blood, dark stains all over his greatcoat and a trail of bloody footprints over the flagstones.

'John, thank God you've got here,' Arthur said, wiping his hand on a dry patch of his coat, to shake the doctor's hand and then thinking better of it, simply led him over to Will, who lay slumped to one side.

John Bowra lowered himself stiffly to his knees, pulling aside the blood-soaked clothing and the muffler Arthur had wrapped around Will all those hours ago. 'Arthur, I can't work on him here,' he announced having taken one look at the wound. 'We must get him to Pinn's farm. That's close by.'

Arthur shook his head. 'The Pinns have nothing to do with my business. They run with the Wingham men.' Bowra had sewn up Arthur's head and arm after the fight with the Wingham gang last year. 'They won't take us in, John.'

John Bowra rose slowly from his knees, nodding as he did so. 'Yes they will,' he said. 'Bartholomew Pinn owes me a favour. Delivered his wife of twin boys after three still births, last August twelvemonth. Wingham men! Hawkhurst men! It's all the same business, or am I wrong?' He shook his head. 'Cook, you ride there and bring Pinn and that brother of his back with a hurdle or gate of some sort. Will here can't be put upon a horse again. If there's any gainsaying, just tell him John Bowra desires his hospitality for a while.'

Jim Cook nodded and was off.

'He's very bad, I know,' Arthur said, despair in his voice, as the doctor turned back to Will. 'He's as cold as ice. I couldn't seem able to get him warm. I've ridden with him right over the Marsh since daybreak. He's my only brother, but if he's dying, John -.' He had to pause and steady his voice before continuing. 'If he's dying, I'd as soon he died here in a church than any other where, not on Pinn's kitchen table, that's for sure.'

'Dying? It's too soon to talk of dying,' Bowra said briskly. 'The fact he's so cold may be just the thing to have saved him. I've noted it before that a man don't bleed so freely in the cold. No, he's young and strong.'

Arthur's eyes looked more hopeful. 'If you save him, John, well, it won't go unrewarded-.'

Bowra held up his hand 'Ph! I help you Arthur, as you've always done right by me. Do we understand each other?'

Arthur nodded and then both men remained in silence, Arthur sitting down on the cold flagstones next to Will, his back against the wall, his knees drawn up and the doctor easing himself onto the low support around the font. He leant against it, readjusting his wig under his hat. A few minutes later Arthur sprang up as the door opened and Jim Cook appeared with Bartholomew Pinn and his brother Michael, who was carrying a wooden hurdle. They nodded briefly at Arthur and Bartholomew said to the doctor, 'I would have brought the wagon, but it won't make it over the snow.' He looked across at Will. 'He'll be safer us carrying him.'

Will was laid on the hurdle and Arthur, the two Pinn brothers and Jim Cook began to carry him the few hundred yards up the hill and across the track to the low farmhouse at the crossroads while John Bowra rode leading Cook's horse and Arthur and Will's mares.

'Gently with him,' Arthur urged, as Michael Pinn stumbled in the deep snow and Will was jolted on the hurdle. Arthur, his eyes almost constantly on his brother, said to Bartholomew, addressing his back, 'I'm grateful for this, Pinn, you know that.'

Pinn looked straight ahead, the wide brim of his hat keeping the worst of the snow out of his eyes and replied, 'I owe the doctor for my two boys and my Molly's life.' He briefly looked back down at Will.

'Besides, I've a brother myself.' He jerked his head back at his brother behind him. 'If it were Micky here laid out with a ball in his belly, I would want help where I could find it. So you're welcome to our assistance, Gray, but then we're quits I should say.'

'Yes, Pinn,' Arthur replied, 'That's as fair as I can expect from any man, I reckon.'

All the Pinn family had gathered for the Christmas feast and as the men with their burden approached the farmhouse, Molly Pinn was at the door. Behind her, various members of the family were pressed together, all waiting to see their unexpected guests. The twin boys whom Bowra had delivered safely into the world, stood hiding behind their mother's apron, curiosity written on their wide-eyed faces.

Molly nodded at the doctor and said briefly to her husband, 'Table's cleared and I've laid an old sheet over it.'

Bartholomew nodded at her and the family scattered as the men manoeuvred the hurdle through the kitchen door. John Bowra supervised while Will was lifted off the hurdle and laid on the table. The doctor had opened his bag of instruments and laid them out on a smaller table.

'Johanna, take the children into the parlour,' Bartholomew ordered his sister-in-law. 'And keep grand-da out of the way.'

'John, you must tell us who you want here to help,' Arthur said, keeping hold of Will's hand.

'Well, I must hurt him a great deal so take a leg each, Bartholomew and Michael. You, Cook, hold hard his right side and Arthur you must keep hold of his left arm. He will try to escape the knife, that's a sure thing.'

'Looks out of it to me, anyway,' Michael Pinn said peering at Will's seemingly lifeless form, but taking hold of his leg anyway.

There was an audible drawing-in of breath by the four men holding Will down, as the doctor cut away part of his blood-soaked clothing. He laid bare the gaping wound, with fresh blood now welling up and spilling over the table and onto the straw Molly had hastily put down as they arrived. Arthur who five minutes ago could hardly feel his limbs for cold, now felt the sweat running into his eyes, as he watched the steel in the doctor's hand catch the bright sunlight as it streamed through the large kitchen windows to their left. He looked away from the table to the peaceful scene outside. The snow had finally stopped and the gentle rolling hills towards Bilsington and beyond looked calm and beautiful and purest white against the pale sapphire of the sky.

As John Bowra had predicted, the treatment he was inflicting on Will roused him from whichever dark place he was in and he cried out and with unexpected strength tried to struggle up.

'Hold him hard there, lads,' the doctor called out, not looking up from the task in hand, up to his elbows in blood. The four men held Will down with more vigour.

As Will let out a string of obscenities, tossing his head from side to side, Arthur put his hand on his brother's brow. Will suddenly opened his eyes wide and looked straight at Arthur. 'Sweet Jesus! Have pity, have pity! Oh Jesus! Oh Fucking Christ! Let be, oh let me be!' His brown eyes met Arthur's and then his body went limp and his eyes seemed to roll upwards as his lids half closed.

'Fainted away,' Bowra said, satisfied. 'Now I can finish my work. Molly, you'll find some stout thread and a needle in my bag. Fetch it here and thread it, there's a good girl. And get your little sister-in-law to bring my patient a clean nightshirt and some warm water and rags to clean him up a little and he will be a new man.'

He looked at the four men still standing around the table, looking pale. 'What's this?' he said briskly. 'If you ain't got the stomach for the consequences, you shouldn't start the proceedings in the first place. Now, Mistress Molly, a cup of ale for me and if I may trouble you to put some bacon in the pan, for I was called away in the early morning light, by this man,' –with a nod in Cook's direction, 'before I had broken my fast.'

He looked at the Pinns and at Arthur and Jim Cook, still standing about, anxious and bemused at the speed and apparent brutality of the doctor's ministrations. None of them could look as Bowra started to sew up the flaps of skin on Will's belly that he had sliced open a few minutes previously. He was almost as quick sewing up the wound as he had been in opening it to remove the ball and very soon Will had been carried aloft to the back bedroom, as white as the nightshirt they had put on him.

Far from watching over him, the doctor followed the Pinns downstairs saying to Arthur, 'I've done my bit now. It's out of my hands. As I said he's young and he's strong, though I'll tell you straight - pieces of his greatcoat and shirt and the Devil only knows what other filth besides, were carried into the wound with the ball. It is always the case and he is in such a mess that I can't tell if it has all come out. So if he lives, he will live and if he dies, he will die. He will lie in a fever these next few days that's for sure. Now he has a wife, doesn't he? Can she be got here? Molly Pinn is a good girl but her hands are full with her boys and the farm.'

Arthur nodded, thinking of Beth waiting at home. It seemed long distant. But Beth had not long since miscarried. He didn't think she could undertake a journey in such bad weather. Days of nursing Will would tax her strength. He longed for the comfort of Beth's presence, but he knew he must send for Sarah to come.

'Yes, he has a wife,' Arthur began to explain. 'But she has been ill. Likely my own wife will come. But is there nothing more to be done? No medicine or physick?'

Bowra shook his head. 'There's plenty of quackery but none that will make a ha'porth of difference. I'll make up a couple of pills to try and fight the fever, but in my experience, it's down to the man himself to make his recovery or not. Your brother must fight his way out of it, or not at all. And now,' he said briskly, 'I'm ready for that bacon and then I shall make my way back to Canterbury.'

'Yes of course,' Arthur replied. 'I'm truly grateful to you, John.'

Bowra held up his hand. 'No more of that. I think we understand each other pretty well. I'll not call on Will again. My presence can make no difference one way or t'other now.'

Down in the kitchen, the two Pinn women were presiding over the meal at the table. The bloodied straw and sheet had been gathered up in a sack and had been burnt outside, while Molly had mopped the flagstones down. There was no sign now of the bloody events of the previous hour. The Pinn brothers were already seated and Jim Cook was demolishing a large plate of bacon and sausage and a meat pie. Arthur noticed there was a place set for him and the doctor. He realised he had not eaten or drunk, apart from the swig of brandy in the church, for almost twenty four hours, but as soon as he put a mouthful of bacon between his lips, he felt his stomach heave. He paused for a moment and chewed slowly but after a couple of mouthfuls, he pushed his chair back from the table, made his thanks to Molly and the doctor again and went back upstairs to sit beside his brother.

A few minutes later he heard the doctor's horse whinny as he mounted and looking from the window, saw him riding carefully away over the snow-covered track, his hat pulled low over his head. He went to the door and standing on the top landing, saw Jim Cook coming out of the kitchen and called to him. As Cook approached the top of the stairs, Arthur said, 'Jim, I must ask you to ride again. I need you to fetch my wife. Beth is staying at my house; you'll find her there too but don't alarm her. Make it clear that Sarah must come and not Beth. Don't attempt to come back tonight. I think you can ride back to Hawkhurst now and fetch her here first thing in the morning.'

Cook nodded and started down the stairs again.

'And Jim, find out how the land lies. If anyone has informed against us?'

'Aye,' Cook replied. 'I'll discover what I can.'

In Arthur's nightmare, Tom Carswell's face melted into Will's, both of them covered in blood. Arthur woke with a start, slumped as he was in the low chair he had drawn up beside the bed. His hand went automatically to find his pistol, but he remembered taking his holsters off though it took a moment for him to come to his senses and remember where he was. It was dark now, but someone had brought up a candle and placed it on the small table near the window. There was also a jug of ale and a tankard on a small tray with a piece of cheese wrapped in linen. Arthur brought the candle over to the bed and held it aloft. Will lay flat on his back, bathed in sweat, his head tossing from side to side, his eyes open but unseeing, his breathing fast and rasping.

From downstairs the ordinary everyday sounds of family life floated up to him. He heard men's laughter and a small child's squeal and even the crackling of logs as someone had heaped another onto the blazing fire in the Pinn's parlour hearth. Then he heard the cheerful tune of a fiddle start up and he remembered Micky Pinn was something of a musician and realised that a sick unexpected visitor wasn't going to spoil the Pinns' merrymaking on Boxing Night. He put his hands up to his face and rubbed his eyes. He drew out his watch and saw it was nearly nine o' clock. Jim Cook should have reached Hawkhurst. He wondered how he had broken the news to Beth. He felt a great longing for her and then looking at his brother, a great feeling of guilt. But the feeling of longing was greater than the guilt.

He poured a tankard of ale, raised it to his lips, then set it back down, reached into his pocket for the flask and drank a mouthful of brandy and then another and then tipped the rest of it into his mouth.

December 27ᵗʰ, Tuesday morning

The following morning, Molly Pinn came into the room carrying a jug of water, a warm woollen shawl around her shoulders.

'I thought you might like a wash, Mr Gray,' she said kindly. 'How is your brother?' She came to stand next to Arthur and peered down at Will. 'Don't look so well, does he, poor man? Bartholomew says your wife is coming to nurse him. Though I don't know when she'll be able to travel. Snowed all through the night something terrible. Micky says there are drifts five foot deep. Lucky they fetched the flocks in early this week. Bartholomew knew we would have wicked weather.' She looked up at Arthur rather shyly. 'I've fetched you one of my husband's shirts, yours being so stained. If you change it, I'll try and soak the bloodstains from it.'

Arthur took the clean shirt from her and went to the window. It was true. The snow had fallen steadily all night and the contours of the surrounding countryside merged into each other, forming a white blanket dotted with trees whose bare branches were bent almost double under the weight of the snow. Instead of the azure blue of yesterday, this sky was an iron grey, threatening, brooding, malevolent. It seemed impossible that Jim and Sarah would attempt to ride more than twenty miles in such weather.

'So you'll bring your shirt down to me, Mr Gray?'

'What? Oh yes. It's very kind of you, Mrs Pinn.'

'It will save your wife having to try to get the stains out.'

He nodded.

'I'll make up a truckle bed for Mrs Gray in the little dressing room beyond,' Molly was saying. 'We don't have another bedchamber for you to use but there's the small back parlour I hope will do for you – I've lit a fire in there and there are comfortable chairs. I can sit with your brother for some of the day and Micky's wife Johanna will too, then you could get some sleep. We heard you was up most of the night. You're welcome to sit in the front parlour with us but Bartholomew reckons you might not-,' she paused, aware of the ill feeling there had been between Arthur and her husband over the Wingham affair.

Arthur turned back, aware that these people were being kind, but all he could give his mind to was Will and at the back of his mind, like a bruise on his spirit, the lifeless body of Tom Carswell lying face up on the sand on Camber beach.

'No, the small parlour will suit me. I'm sorry we're putting you to such trouble, Mrs Pinn,' he said with an effort. She smiled but said no more and crossed the room to the stairs leaving Arthur to his thoughts and the care of his brother which became more difficult as the long day went on.

27ᵗʰ *December, Tuesday evening*

Beth pushed open the door of the small back parlour and then closed it shut behind her, but she remained where she was, with her hands at the back of her against the smooth oak. She leant against it for a moment, feeling her legs weak under her. Jim Cook had been reluctant to bring her, saying Arthur had insisted that his wife and not Beth should be fetched. But Sally and Susie had woken on Boxing Day morning with putrid sore throats and Sarah insisted she could not leave them. Beth had gladly come with Jim Cook. She felt fit and strong and she was Will's wife. She and Jim Cook had been on horseback nearly seven hours, with just one stop at Tenterden. They hadn't been able to set out until nearly noon. Though she had on a woollen cape lined with rabbit's fur, she had never been so cold in her life and throughout the journey her mind was troubled, wondering what news would meet their arrival.

Bartholomew Pinn had taken her straight up to Will, where Molly was sitting with him. She explained that Arthur had watched him all night and most of the day and she had finally persuaded him to try and doze at least in the chair in the small quiet room at the back of the house.

Beth nodded, hardly hearing what was being said, finding Will feverish and not aware of her presence. She was aghast when she saw him and now she needed to see Arthur and find out what had gone so terribly wrong on the beach yesterday morning.

As she leant against the closed door, the quiet babble of the voices of the Pinn family in the kitchen - brothers, wives, children, grandfather, was cut to a low hum.

Arthur was seated at the table, a single candle next to him the only light in the room, apart from the dying embers in the grate. She strained her eyes to see. He was slumped over the table, leaning on his right elbow, his hand across his eyes and his left hand over a tankard with a bottle of brandy next to it. Beth didn't know if he had noticed that she had come in to the room at first. She took three steps across the room, hesitated and then laid a hand on his shoulder. She felt his muscles tighten under her touch.

'How has this happened to Will, Arthur? Is it true that Tom Carswell is dead?'

He spun round hearing her voice, thinking it had been Sarah who had come into the room. 'Beth,' he said, hauling himself up and pulled her into his arms, holding her tightly, not able to say anything else.

'Arthur, is it true? Tell me what has happened.'

He put her from him and sank back down into the chair. He nodded. Beth drew up a chair next to him, looking into his face. He looked ghastly even in the kindly light of the candle. He still wore his greatcoat, the bloodstains dried out, though he had changed into the clean shirt that Molly Pinn had lent him. His face had a yellowish tinge, his eyes red as fire and great dark circles under them. His hair, which had escaped from its riband, hung in ragged skeins round his face.

'Chapman and I both fired, Beth. He fell at once. He should have put up his pistol. He aimed at Will. O God, O God!' He wiped his hand across his eyes, poured some more brandy into the tankard and drank it quickly. Beth said nothing, but put her hand up to his face and laid her palm on his cheek. He turned his face, so his lips were on her palm and pressed them against it. 'It's a punishment, Beth, ain't it?

A punishment because we've lain together, even though you're Will's wife, my own brother's wife.'

She shook her head and then said flatly, 'Why would God punish Will, then? I can't think any more about God. Of all of us, Will is innocent in this. Was God on Camber beach? How many more people will God punish, Arthur? Is he so vengeful he must hurt everyone else for our sin? An unborn babe and now Will? If you hadn't fired, what then? Maybe Will would be dead. Maybe your firing deflected Carswell's aim. Blame Carswell. Blame Collier's men for posting him back amongst his own. I don't believe this is God's doing. I can't believe in a God who wants to hurt people. This is just something that has happened, because if you all ride armed, someone will get shot. This time it was Will's turn.' Her voice which had started calmly, ended on a sob of fear and anger.

She stood up and went across to the fire, taking up the poker and stabbed the embers, so they blazed up momentarily, crackling and sparking.

'You shouldn't have come, Beth,' Arthur said at length. 'I told Jim Cook to bring Sarah.'

'Sally and Susie are ill. Nothing to be concerned about, I do assure you. They have the sore throat, but Sarah wouldn't leave them. Besides, it's my place to be here,' she explained, gazing at the shapes in the flames. She walked slowly back to the table and Arthur caught hold of her as she passed, pulling her towards him, his head bent at her waist. She put her arms around him, holding the back of his head, as great racking sobs shook his body.

'Hush, shh, Arthur, it will all come right, my darling.' She stroked the back of his neck and smoothed his hair, rocking him gently, wondering to herself which of the two men's pain was the greater – the physical pain of Will, her husband who was lying upstairs in a feverish state hovering between life and death, or the mental anguish of Arthur, her soulmate, the man she could not but love, who felt himself damned if his bullet had killed Carswell and damned if he had done nothing and Carswell's bullet had taken Will's life.

Beth sat with Arthur for twenty minutes and then climbed the stairway to the bedroom at the back of the house where Will had been laid. Molly Pinn was leaning over Will bathing his forehead with a piece of damp linen. He was muttering incoherently under his breath. Molly looked anxiously up at Beth.

'He's in a fearful fever, Mrs Gray and he will keep trying to roll onto his bad side.'

Beth came round to the other side of the bed and looked at her husband. 'Have you any more pillows or a bolster? If I lay them against his bad side, he won't be able to harm himself, nor even turn to that side'.

'Thanks be you're here. I'd never have thought of that. I'll go to the linen cupboard now. I understand you're this poor gentleman's wife. We thought it was Arthur Gray's wife was coming, for you had been poorly.'

'No, my sister-in-law had to stay to look after her little girls. They have not been well. And I'm quite fit myself now.'

Molly gave a little nod. 'I'll fetch those pillows. Have you persuaded your brother- in-law to rest?' she asked, crossing the room.

Beth turned her head away from Will to answer. 'Yes. I'm afraid he's somewhat in liquor,' she said apologetically.

Molly shook her head, her hand on the doorknob. 'He looked pretty near exhausted when he got here but he wouldn't leave his brother. I'm not surprised he has taken a drink or two. They are pretty close, I guess. My husband and Micky are the same.'

Beth nodded. 'Arthur has had the care of Will since he was born.'

'Trouble is, they don't have a lick of sense between 'em when it comes to all this sort of business,' Molly declared as she looked once more at Will and went to find the pillows.

Though Beth had assured Molly that she would be able to manage Will's care by herself, as the night progressed she began to despair. His nightshirt and the sheets above and below him became soaked with sweat. She tried to raise his head to give him a little ale from a leather tankard, but Will knocked it with a flailing arm and it splashed down Beth's bodice. She set the tankard down and resolved to fetch Arthur.

He was dozing in the low armchair, the candle almost guttered. She shook his arm, calling his name. He woke at once and looked at Beth startled, grasping her arm.

'Arthur, you must help me with Will,' she pleaded, the anxiety in her voice rousing him to full wakefulness.

He sprung up straight away, rubbing a hand over his face and licking his lips. 'Is he worse?'

'I think, yes.'

'You should have waked me sooner, Beth,' he exclaimed and he was out of the room and up the stairs.

Between them they managed to drag the sheet from under Will and replace it with another. Arthur pulled off his nightshirt as gently as he could and judged it easier to leave Will naked, than to struggle to get another on. He seemed to lie a little easier and as they were lowering him down onto the pillow, he opened his eyes. Whether he looked at Arthur or into the space beyond him, Arthur couldn't tell, but he said thickly, grasping his hand, 'Arthur? You must look after Beth. Look after her for me? Promise?'

His voice sounding so normal after his incoherent rambling, startled Arthur and Beth but after a pause Arthur said steadily, 'You'll look after Beth yourself, brother.'

Arthur's eyes met Beth's until a groan from Will showed them that if he had spoken for a moment in sense, he had now returned to his own world of fever and pain.

For two days Beth and Arthur and the two Pinn women and sometimes Jim Cook, when another man's strength was needed, shared the care of Will who lay feverish and unaware of his surroundings. Some hours he lay in such a sweat, with the linen soaked, his hair in wet strands, clutching at the thick bandages Bowra had fastened round his middle, that the women would call for Arthur to come and take hold of his arms and hold him still, lest he set his wound bleeding or suppurating again. He tossed and muttered mostly incoherently, but sometimes Arthur would recognise a reference to a childhood incident which Will in his fever, was reliving.

On occasions he seemed to be back on the beach at Camber for Arthur clearly heard him say *'I'll be damned if I do!'* and then he sighed deeply and pleaded with his brother to take him home. He spoke Beth's name often and called her his *darling* and his *dear wife*, but at other times his manner towards her was as it had been as a child, adoring and admiring, pleading with her to come home. *'Arthur is marrying Sarah,'* he sighed once and added, *'I thought he would marry you.'* Then he would mutter a string of unintelligible words that no one could decipher.

On the third day, his fevered outbursts grew less and he became quiet and still. Beth, grave and anxious for she thought the end might be near, sat beside him, her head in her hands. Arthur came in and touched her shoulder. Will moved his head on the pillow and opened his eyes. Arthur could tell looking into them, that they were clear and seeing reality and not the unfocussed eyes of his feverish state that saw shadows and phantoms.

'Will?' he said. 'Will, are you better?' He grasped his hand.

Will looked puzzled and seemed to stare at Arthur and then at Beth and then whispered, his voice hoarse, 'A drink, for God's sake!'

Beth, tears through her laughter, went to the pitcher and poured him some small beer holding it to his lips as Arthur supported his brother's shoulders.

The following day, Will managed to take a little beef broth which began to restore some of his strength. Arthur, anxious to get Will home, went outside with Bartholomew Pinn to discuss the likely weather for the day and the possibility of borrowing one of the Pinn's wagons to transport Will back to Hawkhurst. It had not snowed again since the day the Jim Cook had brought Beth to the farm, but the milder weather had produced a thaw and what had been frozen, snow-covered tracks on Boxing Day were now muddy trails. Pinn's wagon was newly wheeled and with two sturdy horses borrowed to pull it, Arthur felt sure it would make the journey home in safety.

Arthur and Cook carried Will downstairs, loosely clothed in his breeches and shirt, his boots on his feet and wrapped in his greatcoat and two blankets. He gripped his lip tightly as he was carried and looked pale and weak as they laid him in the wagon, a pillow under his head. Jim Cook tethered Arthur's, Beth's and Will's horses to the back of the wagon and mounted his own horse and Beth got up onto the seat. The whole Pinn family was ranged outside to see them go as they had seen their arrival. Arthur went up to Bartholomew Pinn and shook his hand warmly.

'I'll get Jim here to drive your wagon and pair back as soon as may be,' he said. Bartholomew acknowledged him with a nod.

'You have my thanks, as you know, Pinn,' he added, nodding at Molly and then climbed up beside Beth.

'I hope your brother does well,' Molly said shyly. Arthur smiled at her but said nothing, geeing up the horses and set the heavy wagon on its way.

Ruckinge, Hamstreet and Woodchurch came and went, Jim Cook riding on before and then coming back to warn Arthur of any particular difficult stretches of track where he thought the wagon might become stuck fast. Beth, her cloak wrapped tightly round her, sat mostly silent and grave, Arthur grim and determined and Will, most of the time, gritting his teeth, telling himself the journey couldn't last for ever, and clutching his side as every bump and pothole jolted him and he felt as though a hundred white hot pokers were stabbing into his wound.

Saturday, late afternoon December 31st, 1740

As they approached the neat frontage of the *Oak and Ivy* Inn, lights burning at its windows, Arthur slowed the horses down and called to Cook, 'You go in, Jim and see who's about.'

Jim rode on and tethered his horse as Arthur drove the wagon up the slight incline. As he approached the inn, Jim came out with several others, Pete Tickner, Sam Austin and the Kingsmills. Coming from behind them and pushing past them to face Arthur, was an old woman, dressed in black, a shawl around her head. The men looked grim.

'Arthur Gray, Arthur Gray!' she called, her voice thin and weak.

Arthur looked at her again and then recognized Elizabeth Carswell, Tom's elderly mother. 'Mrs Carswell,' he acknowledged, taking his hat off, barely knowing what he should do or say.

'Ain't ye got the decency to get down and face me?' she challenged him.

The horses whinnied slightly and the wheels ran back a little. He pulled on the brake and handed over the reins to Beth, getting out

328 • Mary-Elizabeth Thomas

and approaching the old woman. As he stood a foot away from her, she raised both hands to pull the shawl off her head. Her watery blue eyes met his and held them. No one spoke. Everyone's attention was suddenly diverted as a wood pigeon broke the silence and flew across the yard, arching up into the oak at the front of the inn, startling its companions into an eruption of silly chattering, fluttering the branches. Arthur looked up at them and then back to Mrs Carswell. He half raised a hand.

'I'm really very sorry for-,' he began but she interrupted him.

'Sorry? Sorry? Ain't you even heard the full story yet? Ain't you bothered enough to find out?'

Arthur started to speak and half turned to the cart indicating Will. 'My brother was badly wounded, Mrs Carswell-,'

'So he should be! If he died in mortal agony it wouldn't be recompense enough. Don't you know what Polly done?' She spat the words at him.

Arthur shook his head 'Polly? No, I knew she wasn't well-,'

'Hanged herself! Hanged herself in Newton's barn yesterday morning. And six months gone with their first child in her belly! And you did it! You did it! You did it!'

She began hitting him with open palms across his face and body and he tried to catch her flailing arms. He felt suddenly breathless, unable to bear this woman's terrible grief, desperate not to believe that what she had said was true. An image of Polly Carswell flashed into his mind, a sweet, simple girl with her red hair and freckles, Tom Carswell's sweetheart since childhood. Elizabeth Carswell crumpled, the fight gone out of her. He grasped her arms and she dropped to her knees. She shook him off and wrapped her arms around her body and let out a dreadful wail, animal-like, piercing – it seemed to reverberate around the trees. Arthur looked down at her and then catching Peter Tickner's eye, summoned him over.

'Take her home, Pete, for God's sake. Can one of the village women stay with her? She surely ought not to be alone?'

Tickner gently raised the old woman up. 'Come on, mother. Let's get you home.'

'I suppose it's true?' Arthur asked in a low voice.

Tickner nodded grimly and began to lead the woman away. She halted though and turned back to Arthur. 'Think on this, Arthur Gray. Polly can't lie in the churchyard. I can't even bury my boy and his wife in the same grave.' Her face crumpled and she let Tickner lead her away.

Arthur slowly went back to the cart. Beth was looking straight ahead but he noticed tears spilling down her cheeks. The men started to go back into the Inn. Arthur took the reins from Beth, released the brake, flicked the reins and started the cart forward. They drove in silence to the crossroads and then carried on up the gentle incline towards Seacox.

Will had gone through the worst of his illness at the Pinns and what he needed now was rest and good food and his wound dressed carefully. He was fretful if Beth was gone from his side for any length of time. He announced his intention of going downstairs on his third day at Seacox, but Arthur would have none of it, threatening to lock him in the room if he came up with any more absurd suggestions.

'Do you think Beth and I tended you so carefully that you can undo all our work by being impatient, Will?' he asked sternly.

'No, Arty,' Will said apologetically, looking up from his pillows. 'It's just so dull lying here, hearing you all going about your business downstairs.'

'Better to be dull than dead, brother,' Arthur pointed out. 'Do you want Beth to be ill again with worry if you have a relapse?'

Will looked pained. 'Oh no, Arthur. She ain't poorly is she? I thought I would be less trouble downstairs, that's all. But I see I'm wrong and I'll be less trouble to you all if I stay up here.'

'Well, make sure you do then,' Arthur said severely. 'Should Corker be on the bed covers?' he asked looking at the mongrel who was curled up happily snoring at Will's feet.

'Has Sarah said he may not?' Will asked meekly.

'No, I'm master in this house, Will. Let him stay if he keeps you happy.'

Will nodded, reached down to touch the dog's ears and then winced as the movement disturbed his healing wound.

'Just lie still and try to rest, Will,' Arthur said, closing the door behind him.

He had been shorter with Will than he intended but his mind was occupied. That morning Jim Cook had ridden out and come back with the news that George Chapman was in Lewes Prison. He had confessed to the murder of Thomas Carswell and would be tried at the next Assizes. Arthur had decided to lie low for the days following his return with Will to Seacox, until he knew more. There were wild rumours circulating but nothing certain was known. There were no witnesses outside the gang to what had happened on Boxing Day morning. He had a physical pain in his gut when he thought of Elizabeth's Carswell's words to him. He thought of attending Thomas Carswell's funeral but Beth took him to one side.

'No, Arthur,' she said taking his hand. 'You mustn't think of it. Mrs Carswell would be upset I'm sure and who knows that she might not lay evidence? We have to get over this as best we can. Let Sarah attend in your place. She's a regular churchgoer. No one will think it strange if she is present and in that way, she can represent you.'

'But it might have been my bullet that killed him. Don't you see how that haunts me?'

Beth put her hands up to her face. 'You mustn't think it, Arthur. You can never know for sure. That is the cross you must bear.'

'Another cross to bear, Beth?' he asked, uncertainly. 'I'm bearing a good few already, I can tell you.'

'You must stop this or it will drag us all down,' Beth demanded. 'Go and see George Chapman. See if he will retract his confession.'

He looked into her eyes and took her face in his hands. 'Beth, my wise counsellor,' he said softly. 'I couldn't go through this without you.'

He gently kissed her eyelids and her mouth and then dropped his arms from her as he heard Sarah's steps outside the room. He called for Jim Cook to saddle his horse, saying nothing to Sarah and leaving Beth to make whatever explanation she chose for Arthur's sudden departure.

January 19ᵗʰ 1741, Lewes gaol

Arthur was unwillingly reminded of his last visit to Lewes gaol two and a half years previously when he had visited Grayling in those dark days after John's arrest and before his transportation. It was as dark and forbidding as it had been then, more so, in the failing light of a January afternoon, a chill wind bringing flurries of snowflakes with it. He was led down the dank, echoing corridors by the same gaoler. If he recognised Arthur, he said nothing, but lifted up the great collection of keys and opened the cell door.

'You can lock me in with him. I'll call you when I'm ready,' Arthur said curtly. The gaoler nodded and sniffed, banging the door shut, the echoes ringing down the long passage and Arthur heard his footsteps shuffling away.

'Arthur!' Chapman was sitting at the table and he raised his head to look at his visitor. He looked shocked. 'What are you doing here? There's no reason for you to be here.' He looked back at the table and Arthur saw he had a bible open in front of him.

'I didn't know you could read, George,' Arthur said and then cursed himself silently for making such a stupid observation.

Chapman took no offence and shook his head. 'I can't. Gives me some comfort though to have it open before me. I remember bits of it, from my ma reciting it.'

Arthur rubbed a hand over his face and sat down on the narrow bed, looking at Chapman. He looked haggard, unshaven, unwashed, his eyes moving quickly in his sallow face.

'George, what are you doing here? No one can place evidence against you. No witness can place us definitely at Camber that morning. Retract your confession, man! You'll be home within the week.'

Chapman looked across at Arthur, shaking his head. 'I know it was my ball that killed him, Arthur. I knew it straight away, as soon as he fell. Oh God,' he groaned, anguished, crossing himself and began to mutter the '*Our Father*' under his breath.

Arthur was about to interrupt but then waited for him to finish. He got up and placed a hand on Chapman's shoulder. 'George,' he said eagerly, 'there's no need for this. You can't know for sure any more than I can, but what's done is done. Carswell should have put up his gun. We both warned him.'

Chapman stood up, clasping the bible in front of him. 'It's best this way. I couldn't live with myself anyway, knowing I killed him. When they hang me, it puts you and all the other men in the clear, don't it?' He touched Arthur's arm. 'I ain't got no family, Arthur. Only a sister married and living up in York. I ain't seen her since she wed eight years ago. Don't even know if she's alive, anyway. It's different for you, Arthur. You got a wife and them three little girls and all the men in the gang depending on you for their livelihoods and through them, their families too, all depending on you being around. Don't you see it, Arthur? I see it clear. I ain't shopped no one in my confession. Said I'd seen strangers landing goods the previous night and went back to fetch what they'd left behind. Said Carswell came upon me and I shot him. So you see, all's well and no harm done to anyone else.'

He suddenly dropped to his knees and tugged at the hem of Arthur's coat. 'You can read, Arthur, can't you? Read something for me will you while I kneel here?' He thrust the bible into Arthur's hands.

'Come, George, get up.' He helped Chapman to his feet and sat him back in the chair. 'Please think again about this. They'll hang you if you carry on, you know that.'

Chapman nodded. 'So long as my immortal soul is saved, I don't care about nothing else, Arthur. But please read something to me. That bit about the little maid, Jairus' daughter, who died and was raised. I always liked that story. My ma told it to me.'

Arthur looked about the miserable cell. 'George, I ain't read the bible enough to know where that bit comes from.' He flicked through the pages helplessly.

'It don't matter then, just read anything.'

Arthur, uncomfortable, found the Psalms, not knowing one from the other but simply read the verses at the top of the page. *'Cause me to hear thy lovingkindness in the morning; for in thee do I trust; cause me to know the way wherein I should walk; for I lift up my soul unto thee. Deliver me, O lord, from mine enemies; I flee unto thee to hide me. Teach me to do thy will; for thou art my God: thy spirit is good; lead me into the land of uprightness.'* Arthur's voice falterered and he said, 'Amen,' quickly.

Chapman's lips were moving slowly, his eyes closed. Arthur bowed his head and waited.

'Amen,' Chapman said simply. 'Thank you, Arthur, for that. It has brought me some comfort. And thanks for coming to see me but don't come again. I'm prepared for what must come.'

Arthur rose slowly and held out his hand to Chapman, not knowing what else he could say. 'Goodbye then, George,' he said falteringly.

Chapman gripped his hand, nodded and then let it fall. Arthur called to the gaoler and was led out into the cold January night.

Chapman was hanged four weeks later and his body gibbeted at Hurst Green where he had been born and lived. Two days later, Arthur rode to the gibbet at the crossroads. Looking up at the ragged figure swinging in the wind, he felt the bile rise in his throat as he recognised Chapman's haggard features under the tar coating his body. He thought he was going to vomit and he took several deep breaths, then got off his horse and thrust his hand into his pocket pulling out a small bible and turned to the place Beth had marked for him. He slowly read from the eighth chapter of Saint Luke, the story of Jairus's daughter. *'And her spirit came again and she arose straightway: and he commanded to give her meat. And her parents were astonished: but he charged them that they should tell no man what was done.'*

The wooden gibbet creaked in the light wind. 'Amen, George,' Arthur said softly and turned back to his horse.

CHAPTER THIRTY NINE

April 1741, Hawkhurst

Will slowly recovered his strength through the cold winter and early spring, but he had become thin and pale. Though he made light of his wound, Beth would often glance at him when he didn't know he was being observed and saw him hold his side and sit down where before he would have stood. Arthur hadn't let him go on any of the smuggling runs, saying that he had enough to do keeping the paperwork up to date, though in truth it was Beth who did most of this.

With the coming of the warmer days of the spring, the dark earth which had seemed dead and still all winter began to show the fresh green shoots of new growth and Will too seemed to regain his stamina and vigour. He took Corker out for long walks, all around Hawkhurst as far as Flimwell in the west returning by the Frythe woods.

It was towards the end of one of these long walks that he came past Robert Stone's strange old house by Upper Willow Pite fields and saw the doctor's gig and Parson Saunders' gig drawn up outside. Corker, ears flying, ran through the open door, as Will hurriedly went after him to call him back. He caught him just inside the porch and fastened the piece of rope he always took with him round Corker's collar. He was about to leave, when the tall thin manservant came out. Will recognised him as he and Beth had paid her uncle a courtesy visit after their marriage, to thank him for giving Beth away at their wedding.

'Good Day, Doust,' he said brightly.

Doust bowed his head. Will noticed that his shoulders sagged slightly.

'Is anything wrong?' Will asked.

'I'm sorry to be the one to tell you, sir, but my master died in his sleep last night.'

Will sucked in his breath. 'Well, I'm mighty sorry to hear it and so will Beth be. I don't know what to say, Doust.' Will scratched his head. 'I suppose my wife is his nearest relative. No doubt there's a load of business to deal with. And a funeral to arrange. I think I'd best get back to tell her.'

'Mr Stone's attorney resides in London, sir,' Doust explained. 'My master left instructions to inform him and I believe left instructions for his funeral with Parson Saunders who is here at the present.'

'Well, I'll leave it to him then, though I'm sure my wife will want to do all that is proper.'

He made his way down the wooded pathway which led back into Hawkhurst village letting Corker off his lead and wondering how this would affect Beth. He felt slightly uneasy. He imagined Beth would become very rich with her uncle's fortune and he supposed that this strange old house would come to her. He hoped she wouldn't want them to live in it, though. Perhaps she would rent it out. It never occurred to him that by marrying Beth, her inheritance would become his inheritance.

Beth was more shocked than saddened by the death of her uncle. He had never been warm or loving and shunned the company of people, but he was a link with the past that was now broken. Understanding from Doust that he had sent a carrier up to London to give the news of her uncle's passing to his attorney, she waited for a letter which she assumed would come shortly, if not a personal visit to discuss how her affairs stood. However she was not prepared for the letter which arrived from *Silitoe and Craven, attorneys-at-law*, some two weeks after the funeral.

It disclosed that her uncle had left her only a hundred pounds and asked, with the greatest respect, that she make arrangements to vacate the house she now occupied as the present owner wished to sell it, the present owner being Mrs Robert Stone. Beth's hand shook as she read the letter. Her uncle had a wife! She looked around at the room she was sitting in. She had lived here all her life. She assumed it had been given to her father by his brother but she had hardly paid attention when she had been visited by the man of business soon after her mother died and she had declined her cousin Nick's offer of help to manage her financial affairs. She called to Annie to say she was going out. Will had gone into Tunbridge Wells to see his tailor. She would call on Arthur at Seacox. He would know what to do.

'It's a typical attorney's letter, Beth,' he said, after reading it. 'Do you think it can be true? When did Robert Stone have an opportunity to meet any woman let alone marry one? But this will have consequences for you and Will.'

She nodded. 'I know, Arthur. It seems we may not even have a house to live in. I have some money from my father. But I don't know how much a house costs. What should I do?'

'There's nothing to worry about. Do you think I would let you and Will find yourselves in any sort of difficulties? You can come and live here. I'd planned to build a house for you here anyway. I should have started it sooner.' He smoothed down her hair, pulling her closer to him, aroused at once by the feel of her skin and the sweet smell of her hair. *This is where you should always be, Beth*, he thought to himself. *Always in my arms so I can take care of you.*

Arthur thought that for the first time in his life, he was in a position to offer Beth more than she had herself. As her fortune had diminished, so his had grown.

'Would you like me to go up to London and visit this *'Silitoe and Craven'* and find out what I can on your behalf?'

'Yes, Arthur,' she said gratefully. 'I know Will would prefer you to go'.

In the event, it proved unnecessary for the next day brought another letter.

Dear Mrs Gray,' it began, *'I cannot apologise enough for the clumsy way Mr Silitoe has written to you. Though I am wishful of selling the house, I do not wish to inconvenience you any more than is necessary and you must please take your time to find another house before you think of relinquishing this one. I have many times wondered if I should introduce myself to you, but since your uncle and I married, we remained on good terms for only a short time and chose to live apart thereafter,*

though he visited twice yearly to reacquaint himself with our son, whom I hope I may
have the honour of presenting to you when I visit. I intend to come down into Kent
next Monday sennight when I beg to make your acquaintance. I am, Madam, your
affectionate aunt, Emilia Stone.

On the appointed day, Beth had made sure that Annie had the
house as tidy and clean as it had ever been. Beth had brought in
armfuls of bluebells and placed them in vases all over the house, their
woody sweet smell pervading all the rooms. Arthur and Sarah came
over at ten with the girls who were sent to play in the garden. No one
knew what age Mrs. Stone's son might be as they had no idea how
long Robert Stone had been married. Lunchtime came and went and,
Sarah began to talk of going back home, when Will, looking out of
the window, said he rather thought Beth's aunt had arrived. A small
coach had drawn up.

'Come away from the window, Will,' Beth said, going up to her
husband and standing next to him, peering out as he was doing. She
hastily drew back her head, as a figure emerged from the coach. Beth
went to sit next to Sarah. They heard Annie open the front door and
she tapped on the parlour door.

'Mrs Robert Stone, m'am,' she announced with a nervous bob.
Even Annie realized the importance of this visit since she would lose
her position if her master and mistress lost the house. Beth and Sarah
had risen and were returning Mrs Stone's curtsey, as Will and Arthur
stood ready to make their bow, Will appraising the woman whom he
already disliked for having upset Beth.

Arthur, however, gasped inwardly in amazement, recognizing the
woman straight away but almost unable to believe it was she. She was
tall and had thick dark hair, neatly dressed with rolls of curls on top
and down her back, topped with a fetching lace cap also in black. Her
elaborate gown was of sombre black and standing next to her, equally
black-clad, was a fair-haired boy of about eight or nine. The last time
Arthur had seen her, he had known her as Mrs Gresham and he had
accompanied her to Robert Stone's house after John Stone had died.

He immediately felt himself awkwardly placed. To acknowledge
their previous encounter would mean disclosing the facts of Beth's
father's relationship with this woman, a fact which he had made sure
Beth had never known about. He wasn't even sure whether Mrs Stone

338 • Mary-Elizabeth Thomas

would recognize him after all this time. He needed to speak to her on her own.

Will had already gone forward, as host.

'May I present ma'am, my wife Mrs Gray, my sister-in-law Mrs Arthur Gray and my brother, Arthur Gray.'

Her eyes looked startled as she looked up into Arthur's face, but she said nothing, simply acknowledging his bow.

'We were all very sorry to hear of my uncle's death, Mrs Stone,' Beth said hastily.

Emilia Stone nodded her head. She gently pushed her son in front of her. 'May I make known to you, your cousin, Mrs Gray? This young man is Benedict Robert Stone. He will be nine next month.'

Beth held out both hands to the little boy. 'I'm very happy to know you, Benedict. Have you a kiss for your new cousin?'

He looked up at his mother who nodded and smiled. The boy then came over to Beth and kissed her proffered cheek. Beth's feelings were mixed. This was the child who, with his mother, had deprived her of an inheritance which although she had never given much thought to, had always been there at the back of her conscious mind. 'Benedict, my three nieces are playing in the garden. They have some new hoops. Should you like to join them if your mamma is agreeable?' Beth asked him.

He looked over to Mrs Stone. 'May I, mamma?'

His mother nodded. 'Yes of course, my love. Off you go.'

Beth called for Annie to take the boy out to Sally, Becca and Susannah.

There were a few moments of silence and then Arthur said, 'Mrs Stone, this is an awkward situation for my sister-in law and my brother to find themselves in. They've asked me to act for them in this. I wonder if you would allow me some moments of your time to discuss how things might best be arranged. Perhaps if you and I stepped next door?'

'If you will permit me to make a different suggestion?' Emilia Stone said. 'I have not yet been up to the house. If you accompany me there in my carriage, you may return in it and send Benedict back to me in it. If you're agreeable to keep him here for an hour or so, Mrs Gray?' she said looking at Beth.

'Of course, Mrs Stone'.

Beth did not call her new relative '*Aunt*' and Mrs Stone did not ask her to.

Will spoke quietly to Arthur as the ladies were making their farewells. 'I'm sure I can deal with this, Arthur. Shouldn't I at least come with you?'

Arthur shook his head. 'No Will, it's best left to me, believe me. I have both your interests at heart.'

'No I didn't mean that,' Will said hastily. 'I'm sure you'll manage it better than I could. But don't you think I should come with you?'

'No I don't. You can safely leave it with me.'

Once settled in the carriage, Emilia Stone turned to Arthur and smiled ruefully. 'I knew you at once, Arthur. You must think this a strange turn of events.'

He nodded. 'To tell the truth, Mrs Gresham, Mrs Stone I should say, I wish I'd never taken you to Robert Stone's house when you came here after John Stone's death. Because of you my sister-in-law has lost everything that would otherwise have come to her. Forgive me for speaking plainly, but I suppose you were in fact married to Robert Stone?'

'I can see how it must appear to you,' she said and shrugged. 'It's true, I had an irregular relationship with John Stone for many years, but my relationship with his brother was certainly sanctified by the church. I knew you would demand proof. Charles Silitoe knew it was the first question that would be asked. Well, we were married at St George's, Hanover Square in June '31 and Benedict was born and baptized the following May. You will find the records of both events in the parish books.'

The carriage had by now drawn up at the strange old house and Doust and another servant were waiting to greet their new mistress. Emilia Stone was polite but brief, to her late husband's servants whom she had met only once on the occasion that Arthur had brought her here those few months after John Stone's death.

She took off her cape and gloves laying them over the back of one of the heavy walnut chairs and looked around the room at the dark panelling, the small windows and the heavy dark furniture. 'Dear me,' she exclaimed. 'What a gloomy place! It is darker even than I remember it. This will certainly be no loss to me.'

'Then you plan to sell it?' Arthur asked.

'Sit down, please,' she said. 'I know you want to cut to the chase. I shall tell you how I came to be in this position.' She sat opposite Arthur. 'The fact is, Robert Stone fell in love with me, I think, the day I met him when you brought me here. I say it without vanity and I did not realize it at the time, but it is the only explanation I can offer. He called on me in London as he had undertaken. John had left no provision for me at all. I was not expecting him to, though I had been hoping for some remembrance of him. I had an adequate fortune anyway from my first husband. Robert found me a miniature of John as a boy and made arrangements to bring it to London to give to me himself. Why else would he bring it himself unless he had a partiality towards me?' she asked Arthur.

He nodded.

'Thereafter he called on me weekly and very soon asked me to marry him. I was not in love with him. I told him so, but it didn't seem to matter to him. He was insistent, forceful even on the point that we should marry. I had no wish to leave London and he was not wishful to leave Hawkhurst. It was a strange marriage from the start. He stayed in London with me two, three days at the most every fortnight or so. I never wished to come here. I think, even before Benedict was born, we both realized we had made a mistake in marrying. It suited us both to part. As I said in my letter, he came to London twice a year to see our son. He made over a small allowance to me and Benedict.'

'But didn't he ever wish to bring his son here?' Arthur interrupted.

'Apparently not,' Mrs Stone remarked. 'So you see my dealings with the Stone family have been, mixed – I cannot think of a better word. That is why I wish to cut all the ties with this place.'

'Will you not at least let Beth buy the house she is living in, from you?' Arthur asked. 'She's lived there all her life.'

Emilia Stone frowned. 'I think not. I want no further transactions with the Stone family. Call it a woman's caprice if you like. I am sure John provided for his daughter?'

Arthur nodded in assent. 'But he was the younger son as you know. He had no lands, only money invested.'

'Well, that's fair enough isn't it? I have my own son to think about,' she replied. 'I shall rent out this house and the land, for the estate will come to Benedict eventually and he must have the freedom to do whatever he wishes with them. I shall let my man of business deal with that. I am removing to Bristol. I have a sister there. As soon is my business here is finished, we'll be off.'

She stood up and offered Arthur her hand making it clear the meeting had come to an end.

Though Arthur he had no love for attorneys, he employed Matthew Pope of Goudhurst for matters of formal business and sent him up to St George's, Hanover Square where he verified the entries under marriages and baptisms for the months Emilia Stone had indicated. Arthur had no wish for Beth to be made aware of her father's relationship with Emilia Stone before Robert Stone had married her but decided to tell Will.

'So you see, brother,' he said, his arm round Will's shoulder, 'I think it better that Mrs Stone has gone away. Beth wouldn't want to know anything untoward about her father.'

'You're right,' Will agreed. 'And I've already started to look for a house for us.'

'There's no need, Will. I still have the lease on the house that Sarah and I used to live in just four doors away from you. It's been empty these last few months. There's a piece of land now beyond the garden where they knocked down old Chittenden's house. I've already made enquiries and the land may be purchased for just over one hundred pounds. That will give you plenty of room to expand the house. I think it'll suit you very well.'

Will started to explain that he wasn't sure that he could immediately lay his hands on a hundred pounds without asking Beth to use some of her money, but Arthur cut him short and told Will that he had in fact already laid down a deposit and had the rest of the cash ready whenever it might be needed.

Will, still discouraged by Arthur from going on any of the smuggling runs, spent his time going over the plans for bringing the house up to date by adding an earth closet, a new range, a run of new long windows at the side of the house giving onto the now extended gardens and four new rooms built on to the back. By July, Mrs Stone's business matters had been completed and her new aunt and cousin disappeared out of Beth's life forever as quickly as they had entered it. Though she still had her relations from Northiam, her aunt, uncle and cousins, it was Will and Arthur and to a lesser extent Sarah and the girls, who were fixed as Beth's family. Arthur was satisfied that Beth and Will's welfare were his concern, as much as Sarah and his daughters were. Beth's house was sold to a clothier moved down from Westerham. The strange old house of Robert Stone's was let to the younger son of a bishop and his family who chopped down the woods at the side and back, to let in plenty of light and this gave the house a different character altogether. And when the building works at the house at the top of Highgate Hill at its junction with the Rye Road, were completed, it was freshly painted and decorated and ready to welcome its new master and mistress.

CHAPTER FORTY

1741 early August, Rye

Arthur, working in the back parlour of the *London Trader* inn, that he often used as an office when he was in Rye, looked up from his writing to see Harriett Marshall standing in the doorway.

He put down his quill and smiled. He always had a soft spot for Harriett because she had been his first lover and they had remained friends even after they stopped sharing a bed. As his fortunes had risen, he had often helped her out with money or odd jobs to supplement the meagre income she made by barmaiding and taking in washing. She was thirty six now and looked her age. The years and the hard life she had led, widowed at twenty four with three children to bring up, had coarsened her features but he could still see the young woman he had first known all those years ago, in the large brown eyes and her thick brown hair now greying at her temples, even if her figure was thin and drawn, her stays hardly necessary over her flat bosom.

'Harriett, it's good to see you. Come in, sit down.' He poured her some beer. She sat down at the table, clutching her shawl around her thin shoulders.

'Will said I would find you here. You look busy.' She hesitated and seemed nervous, glancing at the papers spread over the table. He put the quill back in the inkwell and carefully placed a blank sheet over the rows of figures making it appear as if he were about to do so anyway and not having done so on account of her presence.

'Not too busy to talk to you, Harriett. How are the children?'

She smiled anxiously. 'Oh, Lizzie's fifteen and courting. Alice is thirteen and has just got a place as kitchen maid, Pembury way.'

Arthur nodded. 'I hadn't realised - of course they are nearly grown women. And how is James? He must be, oh seventeen?'

She half smiled and nodded. 'That's really why I've come to see you. I'm worried about him.'

'What's wrong?' Arthur asked, concerned, for Harriet really did look worried and had a pinched look about her cheeks. 'Has he got up to some mischief with a girl?'

She laughed nervously. 'N... no, he doesn't, that is he hasn't – what I mean is he doesn't lie with girls.'

Arthur put his hand over hers and gave a short laugh. 'Well, just because I was only fifteen when you took me to bed Harriet, doesn't mean that every boy is the same. Give him a couple of years and you'll be worrying that he won't stop bedding girls.'

She shook her head. 'You misunderstand me Arthur, or I've said it clumsily. He doesn't bed girls because he lies with boys.'

Arthur looked at her for a moment before answering. He saw there were tears in her eyes.

'I love him so, Arthur. I shouldn't say so, but he's dearer to me than my girls. He's my only boy and the image of his father. I think that's why it upsets me so, that he's so different in character from Samuel.' At this she did start to cry and pulled out a dirty handkerchief from her sleeve.

He let her cry for a while, always uncomfortable around a woman's tears and then said, 'What can I do, Harriett? I don't understand it but I suppose I don't object to what a man does in his own bedchamber.'

'That's just it, Arthur, it isn't just in his own bedchamber. He and his, *friend,* I will call him, hang around the inns together. People are beginning to talk, even his own sister, Elizabeth has asked me about him.' Her voice broke on another sob and then she looked back at him dabbing at her tears.

Arthur patted her hand. 'All right Harriett, I'll speak to him. There, all will be well. Dry your tears, there's no harm done and probably it's just a foolish thing with him and he'll soon meet a girl for you to disapprove of.'

She laughed in spite of herself. 'Oh Arthur, I was hoping you'd speak with him. There's no one else I could turn to. It's a weight of my mind.' She finished her drink and wiped the back of her hand across her mouth. She stood up and awkwardly held out her hand. Arthur took her in his arms however and kissed her on the mouth. 'Think nothing of it, Harriet, sweetheart.'

When he had seen her safe off the premises, he called Jim Cook to him and spoke quietly with him. Within an hour, Cook returned with the information Arthur had sought. James Marshall's 'friend' was Nathaniel Martin, a tall handsome youth from Lewes, a few years older than James. They had been seen, arms about each other, drinking at the *Rye Gally*, the *Ship in Distress* and various other hostelries in Rye.

Arthur had his 'spies' in Rye and left word for them to let him know what James Marshall got up to. A couple of weeks later, Jim Cook brought word to Arthur that things had taken a turn for the worse. James Marshall had been involved in some sort of incident at the *Rye Gally*. The man whom he had offended was the servant of Lord Avebury and he had gone to his master with his version of the incident. Lord Avebury had laid the whole before one of the Jurats. It wouldn't be long before Marshall was arrested.

Will and Beth's new house, Hawkhurst, August 18th 1741

Arthur tied up his horse in the recently enlarged stable at the back of Will and Beth's newly-modernised house and saw Will through one the large new windows at the back of the house. He pushed open the back door and stepped from the hallway into the handsome drawing room, where Will was looking over some handbills advertising a horse sale at Sevenoaks the following week. After looking over the handbill with Will and agreeing there might be some likely bargains to be had, he came to the point of his visit. 'I've some business to transact, Will. We must all be in Rye on the 25th of this month.'

'What's up?' Will enquired.

Arthur looked up at him. 'I want us all to be seen in the town this evening, so there's no question of anyone thinking there's a run going on. It's Pete Tickner's birthday. Let it be known we're celebrating hard.'

Will looked puzzled. 'Arty, what's all this about? Pete's a good enough friend, but we don't usually make such a bustle over a birthday.' Seeing Arthur's quizzical expression and half smile, he gave a knowing sigh and said, 'Ah, I see you've something planned. Well, are you going to tell me?'

'Yes and I want you to arrange things for me.' He went to the door and looked outside before closing it. 'Is only Beth in the house? I don't want anyone else to know about this.'

Will nodded. 'Annie has stepped out for the afternoon. Beth is in the kitchen, I believe.'

'Do you know James Marshall?' Arthur asked.

Will shook his head and said, 'No, I don't think so. Should I?'

Arthur in turn shook his head. 'No not really. It's before your time by a little while. His mother, Harriett and I – well, we were close a long time ago.'

'Now I know who your mean,' Will exclaimed. 'She's a washerwoman and barmaids at the *Dolphin*, don't she?' He gave a low whistle and eased himself back in his chair, balancing on the two back legs and grinning. 'I never knew you and she were – close? Is that how you put it?'

'You were too young to know,' Arthur said lightly. 'The fact is, she came to see me a while ago about her boy, James.'

Will's chair overbalanced and he quickly righted himself by grabbing hold of the table. 'God, Arthur, he ain't your son is he?'

'Hardly,' Arthur replied disparagingly. 'I might have been a stripling when I caught Harriett's eye but she was already widowed with three children. I believe James was already five or thereabouts.'

'How old is he now?' Will asked

'Seventeen.'

Will's lips moved silently as he did some mental arithmetic. Arthur waited for the inevitable.

'So you were fifteen when you took his mother to bed?' Will asked, impressed.

Just then the door opened and Beth appeared with a tray. Arthur stood up immediately and held the door for her.

She set the tray on the table. 'Here,' she said, pouring a pale liquid from the jug into the three tankards. 'Fresh lemonade made with the lemons you sent down from your glasshouse, Arthur.'

Will took a large mouthful and then winced, screwing up his face. 'Oh, sweetheart, surely it needs sugar?'

Beth looked doubtful. 'But I put masses of sugar in it. Is it still tart?'

Arthur gingerly tasted some, his lips making the same disapproving shape as Will's. 'Will's right, Beth. Have you enough sugar? I can send some down.'

'No, I'm certain there's plenty in the larder. I've probably read Sarah's recipe wrongly. What a shame, for I'm sure it's most refreshing on a day like today. Now what is this joke that Will was laughing at before my lemonade screwed your faces up?'

'No joke to speak of,' Arthur said quickly. 'Harriett Marshall in Rye has some trouble with her boy.' Arthur's tone became serious. 'The fact is, he's a catamite.'

As Beth looked puzzled, Arthur asked, 'Do you know what I mean, Beth?'

She nodded quickly. 'Yes of course I do.'

'It ain't up to me to judge him but his mother is concerned for him. I've found out that someone has informed against him. Apparently he spurned Lord Avebury's man, who is of a like nature, while they were staying at the *Rye Gally*. The man took it ill and went to his master, pretending to be innocent in the matter and Avebury has laid the information before the Jurats saying Marshall attempted - well, what he had no business to attempt.'

Will looked perplexed. 'And how are we involved, Arthur? I take it this is the business in Rye you were talking of?'

Arthur nodded and continued. 'I can't refuse Harriett's request for help. But the only way out of this for the boy is to take him over to France. The *Brown Wren* will collect him on the night of the 25th. But I don't want anyone to suspect that we have anything to do with it. That's why we'll all be seen at the *Mermaid* making merry. In fact I want us all to be seen up and down the town that night so that no one will suspect we have anything to do with his disappearance. I want you to round everyone up and make sure the gang members are there. Jim Cook and Pete Tickner will make sure Marshall is at the *Mermaid* too and then he'll be whisked away.'

'Who else knows of this?' Beth asked.

'None besides us. Jim and Pete know only that they have to make sure Marshall is in the right place at the right time but they don't know why.'

'What about Harriett?' Will asked

'Least of all Harriett,' Arthur exclaimed.

Beth looked doubtful. 'So she'll not know that her boy is being taken to France?'

Arthur put his hand over hers. 'She mustn't know; otherwise she won't be able to hide it from him, or even let him go.'

Beth looked uncertain and shook her head. 'I don't know what's worse – for her to know that he's going and that she'll probably never see him again, or for him to go, unbeknown to her without saying goodbye. That is indeed a difficult choice to make.'

She looked lost in her own thoughts, her face very grave.

Friday 25th August 1741, Mermaid Inn, Rye

Will had done his work well and by eight o clock in the evening, men began arriving, walking up the cobbled hill of Middle Street slipping into the front door of the *Mermaid*. It had been another warm, humid day and all of them were ready to slake their thirst with whatever liquid refreshment was on offer. Thirty of the gang were gathered sitting at two of the large oak tables.

Arthur had given a roll of banknotes to the landlord with instructions to keep the beer and spirits flowing. Christopher Cadman raised his eyebrows for there had been no word of a run in town and it was not the usual time for the company of men to be gathered together.

'We're just here to make merry, Chris. It's Tickner's birthday and I'm feeling generous,' Arthur explained smiling as he took his place at the table positioning himself between Pete Tickner and Will. At a raised eyebrow from Arthur, Tickner nodded and indicated James Marshall sitting a couple of tables away, a full tankard in front of him. He was sitting next to a fellow with fair, almost white hair with an undeniably handsome face, whom Arthur guessed to be Nathanial Martin. He was dressed much finer than any of the other men, in satin breeches and a fancy linen shirt with very full sleeves.

The ale and spirits flowed freely and although Arthur kept a full tankard in front of him, he drank very little but kept his eyes on

Marshall. Some of the men started singing bawdy songs amid shouts of encouragement and laughter to the discomfort of other patrons who looked disapprovingly but would not dare say anything. Arthur was wearing his usual three holsters and taking out two of his pistols, laid them on the table in front of him. James Stanford, who was sitting opposite Arthur, peered closely at one of the pistols. It had a curious engraving of a fire-breathing dragon in the brasswork along the body of the gun.

'That's a fine piece you have there, Gray. Can I take a look?'

Arthur nodded and Stanford took it up. 'Who made it for you?' he asked.

'Buckmaster,' Arthur answered, just as Cadman approached with another tray of full tankards. The landlord looked worried when he saw the pistols on the table. 'There ain't going to be trouble, is there?'

Arthur shook his head. 'None at all, Chris, none at all. Stanford here is just admiring my pistol. Ain't you, Stanford?'

Stanford nodded and took out one of his own pistols and laid it in front of Arthur for his inspection. 'I reckon you can't beat Henshaw for a good weight distribution, never mind all that fancy brasswork. Put that in your hand, Gray and give me your opinion.'

This led to a heated discussion by all the men on the merits or otherwise of the various gunsmiths, with pistol after pistol being laid upon the table for mutual inspection and comment. Eventually Arthur took to his feet and said, slurring his speech although he was perfectly sober, 'Come on then Stanford, my Buckmaster versus your Henshaw. Now we shall see who is superior. The target is the sign hanging at the *Red Lion*'.

'And what's the forfeit, Gray?' asked Stanford, standing up rather unsteadily.

'The loser to pay for the drinks for the rest of the evening,' Arthur suggested.

The men got to their feet and staggered along the street towards the *Red Lion*. Several of the younger patrons also came out of the *Mermaid* to see this display of target shooting. Arthur made sure that Marshall and Martin were amongst them. The men set to loading their pistols and cocking them ready to fire. Anyone who had a Buckmaster or a Henshaw could take part. The other men whose weapons came from other gunsmiths, looked on. Naturally bets were laid, most favouring Arthur and his Buckmaster.

'The target is the centre of the "R," in 'Red Lion', Arthur announced. 'Come on George, you take first shot.'

Kingsmill who had a Buckmaster and was therefore on Arthur's 'team' took aim and fired. As he was far gone in liquor, the fact that he hit the sign at all was something of a miracle. None of the other men were any more accurate, Dick Mapesden, for the 'Henshaws' making the best attempt by hitting the "d".

Several of the residents threw up their sashes, alerted by gunfire and the noise of the boisterous crowd. One of the locals, a crabby old gentleman, poked his head out of his window, his wig askew and croaked, 'You should be ashamed of yourselves, preventing good Christian folk from getting to sleep.'

'Go back to bed, granddad,' Sam Austin shouted, firing off his pistol into the air. The window was hastily banged shut.

'Come on, Gray, it only leaves you to fire,' Stanford declared.

Arthur took out his pistol, aimed and fired. His ball whistled through the air and left a hole clean through the middle of the "R".

His team erupted in cheers clapping him on the back and shouting.

Jeremiah Curtis, who hadn't taken part as he used neither Buckmaster nor Henshaw weapons, came up quietly and spoke in Arthur's ear. 'Good shooting, Gray. I always knew you was accurate.'

Arthur bridled but ignored the remark though it had hit home, just as Curtis knew it would.

'Reckon that's down to you to pay for the drinks then, Stanford. We'd better spend it here, as Thorowgood will need to pay for a new sign,' Arthur said, looking at the damaged sign swinging in the light breeze.

The men and their various hangers-on made their way into the *Red Lion* and sat down. Henry Thorowgood, the new landlord, came over to Arthur and said, 'I want no trouble here, no trouble at all. You're welcome to drink but I want no fighting.'

Arthur looked at him and something in his expression caused Thorowgood to nervously moisten his lips. 'Drinking is all we've come for, Thorowgood,' he answered quietly.

Arthur looked at his watch and saw it was half after nine. He put it back in his waistcoat and took a swig from the tankard noticing Marshall sitting at the next table, looking rather the worse for drink. Sam Austin, one of the younger gang members, brushed past his table and jolted Marshall's tankard, which spilt over his companion's elaborate sleeve. Nathanial Martin looked annoyed but remained silent. Marshall however got unsteadily to his feet and said, slurring, to Austin, 'Mind what you're about.'

Austin looked round and said, jeeringly, 'You can fuck off!'

'Why don't you fuck off, Austin – ain't you got any goods to run tonight?' Marshall taunted.

Nathanial Martin put his hands over his face and several other interested onlookers held their breath to see what would ensue. No one ever mentioned the business face to face with any of the company and certainly not in Arthur's presence.

Arthur stood up. 'That's enough, Austin. Come and sit down.'

Marshall, aware that he had an audience and full of Dutch courage and foolhardiness would not be silenced. 'We all know what you do, Arthur Gray.'

'I don't doubt it, Marshall, but all we're here for tonight is drinking,' Arthur replied trying to take the heat out of the situation. The last thing he wanted was for Marshall to bring attention to himself. Arthur sat down, but Marshall remained standing and swaying slightly.

'Think you're all above the law, don't you? Think you can get away with murder. But it only needs me to fetch one of the Jurats and you're taken, Gray, aye and all the rest of you – that includes you Austin.'

He jabbed at Austin's shoulder, but it was a boy's gesture and Sam was a well built young fellow of twenty used to hauling eighty pound bags of tea and more. Sam went for his pistol. Although it wasn't loaded, he held it with the butt out ready to dash it over Marshall's head.

Arthur sprang out and grasped Austin's pistol out of his hand pushing Marshall back in his seat Putting his mouth close to Marshall's ear, he said menacingly, 'No one's interested in your opinions, Marshall and unlike Austin, my pistols are loaded and cocked and as you seem to know, I ain't afraid to use 'em. Now just sit quietly with your friend there,' with a nod at Nathanial Martin, 'and I'll send a drink over to you. You'll raise it to me and acknowledge it. Is that clear?'

Marshall remained silent.

'Is that clear, James?' Arthur asked again and Marshall nodded.

Arthur did as he had promised and watched as Marshall accepted the brandy that Thorowgood brought over to him and raised it to Arthur, nodding. Arthur in turn raised his tankard and the moment of danger appeared to have passed. The drink started flowing freely again and one of the men started up another song.

Fifteen minutes later Marshall rose and stepped into the back corridor on his way to the necessary house. Arthur pushed back his chair and followed him out. He waited in the corridor and checked the time again to find it was five minutes to ten.

Marshall appeared at the end of the corridor, adjusting his breeches. He paused on seeing Arthur but then made a move forward. Arthur waited until he was about to brush past him and in a sudden movement pushed forward pinning Marshall against the wall with his forearm across his throat. Arthur's face was inches from Marshall's and he could see his eyes bulging as he maintained the pressure against his throat.

'Now listen well, James. I know what games you've been playing and who you've been playing them with and they're dangerous games to play especially if you turn a man down who has the power to harm you. Keep your mouth shut when I let you go but just nod to let me know we understand each other.'

Arthur released the pressure of his forearm and Marshall put his hand to his throat and croaked, 'I don't know what you mean!' He looked nervously along the corridor hoping that someone would come to his rescue.

Arthur immediately pushed his arm back against the youth's throat. 'Suffice to say, information has been laid against you to one of the Jurats you're so keen to talk to. You risk imprisonment or even hanging. So what's happening is this. You're making a journey tonight. Over to France. I've paid lodging for you for six months, after that it's up to you to look after yourself.' He slightly eased the pressure.

Marshall gasped. 'Why are you doing this? What's it to you? I can't go to France, I can't leave home. I won't go. You can't make me.'

'Do you really think I can't?' asked Arthur, saying the words slowly and with menace. They stared at each other and then Arthur added, in a softer tone, 'I'm doing this for your mother's sake, you're nothing to me. But your mother and me have been friends many years. You stupid boy, don't you know you've broken her heart with this behaviour? Look James, I don't know what the penalty is in France, it's probably thought less of than it is here. And you ain't known over there. You can make a clean start, find work. That Nathanial Martin, he's a doxy for sure. But maybe you ain't, James. You're only young. You've plenty of time to find yourself a nice girl.'

He looked into the boy's face and for a moment he looked so much like Harriett, that Arthur had half a mind to send the boy round to the *Dolphin* to say goodbye to her. But he knew she wouldn't be able to let him go. He hardened his voice. 'There's no time to waste. There's a boat waiting. Listen boy, your mother don't know about this arrangement.'

Arthur dug deep into his pocket and drew out a guinea which had been sawn in half. 'Therefore, you're to take this with you. When you've got a job, hand it back to the Captain of the *Brown Wren* at Boulogne, or get someone to hand it to him for you and he'll bring it to me to pass on to your mother. Then she'll pass her half coin to come to you. It will signify to her that you're safe, at least. You're to exchange half coins every six months and both of you will always know the other is well. Now step outside with me and you'll find two men ready and waiting to take you to the boat.'

Marshall seemed to hesitate and then burst into tears. Arthur, moved for the affection he still held for this boy's mother, patted him on the shoulder. 'Come here, James, give me your hand to signify you bear me no malice so I can tell your mother we parted on good terms.'

The boy could not look up but held out his hand which Arthur shook before leading him to the heavy oak door at the back of the inn. Sure enough, two men appeared out of the shadows. They had a heavy cloak with them which they wrapped around the boy's slight figure and Arthur watched them as they disappeared into the night. When they had gone from his sight, he turned back to the noise and merrymaking in the taproom.

CHAPTER FORTY ONE

Early October 1741, the Dolphin, Rye

Harriett sighed, pressing a hand to her back and wished the long evening shift would come to an end. It has been a long day. She had spent all day washing and a heavy rain had prevented her hanging any of it outside, so it was hanging indoors in her second room. She and Elizabeth shared a room now; Alice was working at a big house at Pembury and they only saw her on some of her half holidays once a month. She hadn't seen James or Arthur since August. She assumed Arthur had taken her son to another part of the country until things had quietened down. It was a sadness constantly in her heart, not knowing where her boy was.

Harriett took a tray of drinks over to one of the tables and glanced down as a man's hand caught her wrist as she passed on her way back to the bar. 'I want some service here, woman. Are your legs too old to move any quicker?'

She recognized Jeremiah Curtis's handsome face with its customary sneer. 'What do you want?' she asked quickly, pulling her hand free.

'Wine, woman and sharpish. There's plenty of other taverns to drink in. And I want some food. None of that pigswill you brought me last time I was here, do you hear me?'

'I'll bring you some stew,' she said. She had been a barmaid long enough to know it wasn't worth getting into arguments with customers who had taken too much liquor.

'Causing you any trouble, is he?' Thomas Beane, the landlord asked Harriett as she went into the back room to fill a dish with some of the stew from the cauldron hanging over the range.

'Nothing I can't handle, Tom,' she replied smiling.

'Why don't you go off, early, Harriett?' he suggested. 'You look tired, have done these past couple of weeks. It's quiet tonight, Anne and I can manage. And don't worry, I'll pay you for a full evening.'

'That's kind of you, Tom. Yes, I am tired. It's not like me.'

She carried the tray with the dish of stew and a bottle of wine over to Curtis's table. As she set it down, he took her wrist again. 'Heard from your boy, lately?'

She looked down at him quickly. 'What do you mean?'

'I ain't seen him around. Wondered where he's got to, that's all. Or perhaps he's set up home with his sweetheart. If that's the right word to use,' he sneered.

She shook her head. 'I don't know what you mean,' she said quietly.

'Funny how he disappeared after that row with Gray. Said something he didn't like, did you know that?'

Harriett's heart skipped a beat. She had no liking for Curtis but she wanted to hear what he had to say, in case he knew where James was. 'Tell me then, if you know anything.'

Curtis looked down at the stew. 'Oh I don't know if I can remember it now. Oh yes, wait a minute. We was all in the Red Lion. He accused Gray of murder, now I come to think of it. A murder that some poor bastard has already hung for. Don't see how Gray would let anyone get away with that, least of all some molly-boy.'

Harriett clenched her teeth. 'Is that all?'

'That's enough ain't it? Ask anyone who was there. Ask one of the barmaids. If you've murdered once, what's to stop you doing it again? Perhaps Gray's got a taste for it.'

'You must be drunk,' she said accusingly. 'You still work for Arthur, don't you?'

'Oh no, I don't work for him. I work with him now and again. I've never worked under him. Unlike you, until you lost your looks and he went panting after fresher meat. Which reminds me, your girl Lizzie, how old is she now?'

'You stay away from her.'

He looked up at her. 'Maybe I will, maybe I won't. Now, leave me alone, will you? I'll see if this stew is worth eating.'

She looked down at him and then stepped back to the bar.

'I'll be off now, then, Tom,' she called, wrapping her shawl round her shoulders, but instead of going home to Watchbell Lane, she walked up to the *Red Lion* and went to find Henry Thorowgood, the landlord.

'What can I do for you, Harriett?' he asked. 'Not come here to drink, have you?'

She shook her head and gave a little smile. 'No, I wanted to ask you something.'

He looked at her. 'Well? Ask away. Don't want a job do you? There's always a job here if Tom Beane throws you out,' he said, laughing.

'No, no. It's about my boy. About James.'

Thorowgood looked uneasy. 'I don't really know nothing, Harriett. I haven't seen him since, well, since, Arthur Gray and him had their disagreement.'

Harriett's mouth went dry. 'Then it's true? They did row?'

The landlord nodded. 'Thought James might have taken himself off to lie low for a while. He was slinging insults, you know.'

Harriett put a hand to her mouth. Could Arthur have done James some harm? She wondered why he hadn't been back to Rye or even explained to her where James might be.

'Are you all right there, Harriett? Why don't you sit down for a moment?'

Harriett put one hand out to the bar. 'No, I'm fine, thanks. I'll be getting home now.'

She made her way back to Watchbell Lane and into the bedroom at the end of the hallway. She undressed quickly and got in beside her elder daughter. Lizzie turned over in her sleep and opened her eyes. 'All right, mumma?' she asked sleepily.

Harriett smoothed her hair. 'Yes. Go back to sleep,' she whispered pulling the covers over her. 'Lizzie,' she said suddenly. 'You don't have nothing to do with Jeremiah Curtis, do you?'

Lizzie turned round. 'What? Of course not, mumma. He must be over thirty.'

Harriett smiled.

'Anyway,' Lizzie added. 'I'm walking out with Luke Dowdy.' She turned round to face her mother in the moonlight. Harriett looked at her daughter. Luke's father was the landlord of the *Two Brewers* where Elizabeth worked.

'He seems a nice enough lad,' Harriett said.

'Is anything wrong?'

Harriett sighed. 'No. I'm tired, that's all. Let's go to sleep.'

The next morning instead of sorting out the linen, Harriett set off to visit Rachel Spain, her best friend. She and her husband Robert lived in a small house in Coggles Lane with their four children. Robert still worked for Thomas Lamb and there was only Rachel and her two youngest children at home.

'Come in,' Rachel said, smiling her welcome. 'Shift along there, Peter. Here, take Robin and lay him in the cot while Mumma talks to Harriett.'

The little boy took the baby from his mother's arms and carried him along the tiny passageway.

'It's about James,' Harriett confided as they sat at the kitchen table. 'Have you heard anything, Rachel? I wondered if perhaps Robert had heard something. They say James rowed with Arthur Gray and he's not been seen since. I can't think Arthur would harm him but there are such wicked rumours, I don't know what to believe.'

'But Harriett,' Rachel said steadily putting her hand on Harriett's thin arm. 'You told me you had asked Arthur for help. He surely wouldn't have done James any harm. You said he had always been a good friend to you.'

Harriett nodded. 'So he has. That's why I don't know what to do.' She rested her head in her hands and Rachel was silent for a few moments.

'Can't you go and see him and ask him directly?'

'I shouldn't dare go to his home. How would I get to Hawkhurst? No, I've only ever seen him down here. But he's not been in Rye since August to my knowledge.'

Rachel pushed Harriett's cup towards her. 'They say the gangs have been working at Deal and Folkestone way this back end of the summer. It don't mean anything I'm sure, Harriett. Arthur will be back in Rye soon enough and you can have it out with him then. But I'm sure it's nothing to worry about.' Rachel looked at her elder son. 'No, get down from Harriett, Peter, you're much too big a boy to sit on her lap.'

Harriett smiled and pushed her chair away from the table to make room for the five year old. 'No, you're all right, Peter. Come and give me a cuddle.'

'It's true, Rach. There are lots of rumours flying. I don't know which ones Harriett has heard but they're saying young Marshall mouthed off about the gang, Arthur in particular and the boy hasn't been seen since,' Robert Spain said to his wife that evening. 'They were all drunk, they'd had some sort of shooting contest at the *Red Lion*. It's hard to know what to believe. It's true though, there are so many of them in Arthur Gray's gang, that if he did want to carry someone off, there's nothing could be done about it.'

'Well, he's always polite to me on the odd occasion I have seen him,' Rachel commented.

Her husband nodded. 'That's because he's never forgot our help. But if he's loyal to his friends, maybe he's a hard enemy to have. I don't think I would cross him, Rach. I know he's always armed. I think he must be the most powerful man hereabouts.'

'Well, I'll believe the best of him until the worst has been proved,' she said, serving out her husband some more of the boiled mutton and parsnips which was their evening meal.

The London Trader alehouse, Rye

Four days later, Arthur's business did bring him to Rye. He wanted to see Thomas Lamb and had got Jim Cook to drop a note round to his house.

Just after one o' clock, Arthur heard a commotion outside the little back room where he usually worked and the door burst open. Harriett Marshall stood there with Jim Cook right behind her, holding her arm.

'I told her you were busy, Arthur but she would burst in,' Cook said apologetically.

Arthur looked up from his writing and got up when he saw Harriett. 'That's all right, Jim. Bring us in some ale, will you?'

Jim Cook nodded and went out. Arthur drew Harriett into the room, closing the door firmly behind her. She looked at him, her face ashen.

'Where is my boy, Arthur?' She lurched towards him and grasped the front of his linen shirt in both hands. 'What have you done with him, Arthur? I've heard such terrible things. What have you done? If he was rude to you, he's only a boy. Only a boy,' she collapsed into tears, covering her face in her hands. He put his arms around her and sat her in the chair.

'Harriett, he's safe. That's all I can tell you.'

She raised her face to his. 'And you haven't harmed him?'

'How can you think it, Harriett? Perhaps I should have told you everything, but you wouldn't have let him go. I thought it would be safer for you if you could honestly say you didn't know where he was.'

'What do you mean, Arthur?'

He paused as Jim Cook knocked and brought in two tankards and a jug of ale. Arthur waited until he had gone. 'Let me tell you Harriett, how thing stood with James,' Arthur said and started to explain just why it had been imperative to carry James out of the country.

'I'm sorry, Harriett. It was the only way to keep him safe.'

'But France, Arthur! I shall never see him again.' She sobbed into her apron.

Arthur looked at her and squeezed her hand. 'Perhaps some day he'll be able to return, but the warrant for his arrest is still in force.'

He explained about the exchanging of coins as a way of knowing her boy was still safe.

'I've set him up for six months. He may be able to find work in Gravelines. There are lots of English there. At the moment he's in Boulogne, but no one else knows that. You see why it's important that you tell no one?'

She nodded and eventually her sobs subsided. 'When I heard the rumours, Arthur, I didn't know what to think.'

Arthur shook his head. 'I've got accustomed to any villainy being laid at my door, Harriett. It's true that because we're such a large company of men we can pretty much do as we choose. I try and keep order as best as I can when men are working for me, but it doesn't surprise me any more that people believe the worst of us. So if people are saying that I did James some mischief, that doesn't surprise me. At least that means the authorities will probably stop looking for him.'

Harriett nodded slowly.

'Who is it you heard the rumours from, Harriett?'

She wiped her eyes. 'It was Jeremiah Curtis first told me, but then I asked around and it seems everyone has heard something like it.'

Arthur slowly rubbed his chin. Jeremiah Curtis again. He would have it out with him one day soon, he thought. He looked across at Harriett. He felt he had offered her as much comfort as he could and as it was nearing two and he knew Lamb would soon be coming, he drew her to her feet and kissing her briefly, sent her on her way.

CHAPTER FORTY TWO

June 1742 , Folkestone then Aylesford

Although Folkestone Warren was an ideal beach to land on as there were many secret paths and tracks up the cliffs, it could be treacherous climbing up in wet weather. Arthur came to grief as he made his way up a path he had taken many times before. He lost his footing in a deep gulley leading his horse and swore as he felt his ankle twist. Will, behind him, heard him curse and called out, 'What is it, Arthur, are you hurt?'

It was a dark night and although there was a full moon, it had been obscured nearly most of the time by thick cloud and the men were using half blacked-out lanterns to light their way. Arthur didn't reply and Will realised his brother's horse had halted and called again but just as he did so, Arthur replied.

'No. Well, yes. I've wrenched my foot, Will. Give me a moment.'

Will came up to him to find Arthur leaning against his horse tentatively trying to put his weight on his injured foot. He gasped as he did so and lifted it up again. 'Damn and blast it,' he said through gritted teeth. 'It's no good. You'll have to help me until we get to the top. I can't ride Peg until we're on the flat.'

'Hold on then, Arty. I'll get Pete to lead both our horses while I give you my arm.'

He went back down the steep track and came back with Tickner. 'What's all this?' he asked.

'My own stupid fault, Pete,' Arthur said ruefully. 'But I can't put any weight on my foot. I'll be all right when I can ride.'

Tickner took the reins of both horses and watched as Will took Arthur's arm over his shoulder as they made their way up the steep track. At the top both men helped Arthur remount. They set off along the Pilgrims Road through Canterbury and then made their way past Maidstone, intending to cross the Medway at Aylesford.

It was about seven in the morning when they approached the sleepy little village placed like a jewel in the beautiful setting of the surrounding countryside and the winding river, the little church nestling against the river bank and the inn they used as a safe house next to it. A drenching rain had been falling most of the night, but it began to clear as they approached. They often stopped to breakfast at the *George* and Arthur pulled up and dismounted, gingerly trying his foot on the ground but the sharp pain shot through his ankle and up his calf. He would have fallen if he hadn't been able to steady himself against the mare. Will slid out of his saddle and came over to his brother. Arthur was shaking his head. 'It won't answer, Will. I'll need to get this strapped up I think. Help me inside and I'll give you the paperwork to take up to Stockwell.'

Arthur took his brother's arm again and hobbled inside. Henry French, the landlord, looked up as they came in followed by the rest of the men. Will helped Arthur to a seat.

'What's this then Arthur?' Henry said wiping his hands on his apron.

'I think I must ask you for a room, Henry,' Arthur said. 'And maybe even a surgeon. I've done my foot an injury. But bring the men their breakfast first and then they can get on their way.'

Arthur sat down with Will and Pete and he handed Will the paperwork. After about half an hour the men were mounted up again and ready to be off.

'Are you sure I should leave you, Arty?' Will asked anxiously.

Arthur laughed then winced as he twisted in the chair. 'Yes, I'm sure once it's strapped up tightly, it'll be fine. I'll see you tonight, but don't worry if I stay here the night. Go and explain to Sarah, will you?'

Will nodded, patted Arthur's shoulder affectionately and was gone.

'Well, Arthur,' Henry said when it was quiet again, with only a couple of customers sitting in the coffee room at the back. 'I think we had best get you up to a room. I'll just call Deb to go and open it up.'

'Deb? I didn't know your daughter was here,' Arthur said. 'Thought she lived Bexley way.'

Henry nodded. 'Aye, so she did when she was married to Jack Winton. Thought you knew, Arthur. He died these six months ago and more. Deb stayed on up there with her in-laws. They keep the '*Black Dog*' on Rochester Way. But I think they tried to manage Deb more than she likes to be managed so she decided to come back to her old Dad. Which pleases me very much as you can imagine.'

Arthur nodded. 'Yes, you did tell me your son- in-law had died and I was sorry to hear it. I forgot though.'

They had reached the top of the small winding staircase and a female voice called up from below. 'What is it, Dad? My word,' the slight young woman said seeing her father supporting Arthur who was leaning rather heavily against him.

'Bring the key to number five, will you, Deb. You remember Arthur, don't you?'

She came half way up the stairs and looked up. Arthur turned round awkwardly to look at her.

'Hello Deb,' he said. 'I'm out of action, as you see.' He indicated his foot which he was holding off the ground and then looked at her again. She smiled and a dimple appeared in her chin. 'Sprained is it, not broken I hope?'

'Well it hurts like the devil but I hope I ain't broken it,' Arthur replied. Deb squeezed past them and put the key in the lock.

'Let's sit you in the chair and we can see what's what,' Henry said, lowering him into a high backed chair. He knelt down in front of Arthur and cautiously began to pull off his boot. Arthur gripped the arms of the chair and then said rather sharply, 'Stop there, would you Henry?'

The landlord looked up. 'I'm sorry if I've hurt you.'

Arthur looked down at his boot again. Deb knelt down next to her father and took the boot in her hand round Arthur's ankle. 'I think we'll have to cut the boot off, Arthur,' she said.

Henry scratched his head. 'I think she has the right of it. Nice boots too. I'll go and get a knife.' He disappeared downstairs.

'I'm sorry about your husband, Deb,' Arthur said at length.

She looked up at him with a little smile. 'Thanks, Arthur.'

'At least your dad is pleased to have you back home.'

She nodded. 'I can twist Dad round my little finger,' she grinned. 'Jack's parents began to look on me as the unpaid help, I think.'

Henry came back in with a large knife and started to slice down the seam of Arthur's boot, going as carefully as he could. Arthur gritted his teeth because as soon as the restraint of the leather had gone, the damaged tissue began to swell up and the skin was already black and blue with bruising. Deb had fetched a small footstool which she placed under Arthur's calf so he could rest the leg without putting any pressure on the ankle.

'Do you think it's broke?' Henry asked.

Arthur sighed. 'Can't tell.'

Deb stood up. 'Well I think you should send Sam for the surgeon from Maidstone, Dad. I can make a poultice up but the surgeon should look at it first.'

'What do you think, Arthur?' the landlord asked.

Arthur leaned back in the chair. 'I suppose so, though it seems like a lot of fuss about nothing.'

'I'll bring you a bowl of rosemary water, Arthur. You'll find that soothing until the surgeon comes,' Deb suggested before slipping out of the room. Her father followed her, calling to the lad who ran errands and did odd jobs around the inn.

Ten minutes later Arthur was dozing when Deb came back in carrying a tin bowl which she set down in front of him. She had tied a large apron round her trim waist and as she knelt in front of him he woke with a start feeling her cool hands on his calf. She had pushed the stool to one side and lowered his foot carefully into the warm fragrant water. Arthur drew in his breath sharply and she looked up at him quickly, a frown on her brow. 'Is it hurting you?' she asked.

He looked down at her. A strand of hair had escaped from her cap and had swung down and nestled in the hollow of her collar bone. He wondered why he had never really noticed how attractive Deb was. He shook his head. 'No, it feels good.'

She went over to the window, undid the latch and pushed it open. The sounds of the little village wafted into the room. 'It's hotting up outside. I love days like this. It makes make me want to climb on a horse and just keep riding and see where I end up. I sometimes wish I was a boy, Arthur. I'd join your gang. Would you have me?' she laughed.

He smiled. 'I'm glad you're a girl, Deb.'

She came and stood beside him, smiling. 'Why do you say that?'

'I'd rather it was you putting my foot in a bowl of water than some great gawky lad.'

'Perhaps I could hide my hair under a hat and put on a pair of breeches and ride with you, then,' she suggested with a laugh.

The thought of her just so, took Arthur's mind off his injured foot. He was adding to the picture when they heard footsteps coming up the stairs and Henry came in with Dr Ashby, one of the surgeons from Maidstone.

He was very matter of fact with the injury, felt it carefully, pressing and prodding to find exactly where it hurt, much to Arthur's discomfort but finally pronounced it was not broken but very badly sprained. He recommended a clay poultice with stout bandaging. He charged Arthur ten and sixpence and bid him good day, warning him not to put his weight on the foot for three days and then to rest it for another week. Deb went off to make up the poultice. She came up half an hour later, wrapping it round Arthur's ankle and left it on with a towel wrapped round it which gave him much relief. Then she strapped it up. It felt well supported and the sharp pain was reduced to a dull ache.

He heard the church clock strike midday as Deb was clearing up the room. 'I guess you would like to go to bed, Arthur?' she said making it sound like an invitation but when he looked at her, she was looking quite solemn. 'I'll send Dad or Sam up to help you, if you like?'

'No it's all right, Deb,' Arthur responded rather quickly. 'I'll manage.'

In fact he was desperate to use the chamber pot and as soon as she was gone, closing the door behind her, he hobbled across to the bed using the chair as a support, pulled his breeches open and relieved himself in the chamber pot. It took him some time to pull off his breeches and drawers and then he pulled his shirt off over his head, manoeuvred himself back onto the bed, pulled one sheet over him and was very soon asleep.

He slept a full eight hours waking in the cool of the evening, when Henry brought him up a tray with some boiled mutton, a dish of buttered turnips, a bowl of apple dumplings and a jug of cream, the whole washed down with a tankard of Henry's home brew. He had also brought up a stick which he said Arthur might find useful for getting around.

The meal was delicious and now that his foot didn't hurt him so acutely, he found the enforced idleness somewhat tedious. It was his usual practice when coming off a night run, to rest for maybe three or four hours so that his sleep wasn't spoiled the following night but having slept so long today, he now felt wide awake with nothing to do. He used the stick to hop over to the window and looked across the yard of the *George* to the peaceful meadows beyond, the brown and white cows serene in the fields and the evening call of night jars floating through his window. He wondered idly how the run had gone.

He reached over to his jacket and took out a letter he had received from John Grayling two days ago. Grayling wrote twice a year. Although his first letters had been backward-looking reflecting on all he had lost and how lonely he felt in the strange land, they gave a detailed account of his progress. He had collected the fortune in gold moidores and pieces-of-eight that he had been sending out regularly in small packages during the two years before his transportation. He had installed himself in Queen Ann's County, Maryland using the alias *Joe Gardener*, buying a small house and had set himself up as, of all things, a wine dealer. Then this last letter had come:

'I love my Margaret as trew as any man ever loved his wife, Arthur, but I know we will never see each other again in this life. And knowing I have done my dutty by her and hearing from her now and again, I know she is settled in comfort with her sister and need never go short of any mortal thing with the money I put aside

for her. However, it can be dredfull lonely here in this vast land and I have had the fortune to meet a respektable widow woman, Dutch by birth, her name is Ans, but I call her Annie. She is about forty with a son and dorter, who is married with two babies and the son, Cornelius, lives with us. For we have set up house together, Arthur and in all things and to all people, excepting for the Parson, we are known as man and wife. If it is a sin Arthur then I am prepared to answer for it on the day of my judgment. I have not breathed one word of this to my Margaret, my true wife and know I can depend on you to do the same, dear lad.

God forbid you should ever come here but if you did Arthur you wouldn't dislike the country. There are flat parts not as good as the Marsh but remindful of it and our little house looks over a great river. I must have water and it has to do me instead of the sea. Some days I can look out of my back window and just for a moment think I am in Kent or Sussex –,'

Arthur folded the letter back up and put it away. Was it a sin, he thought, for Grayling to set himself up with a new life? Not in his eyes. Grayling had been sent away from the country of his birth, from his wife and friends. God made men to be needful of the company of women, Arthur thought. If men were not, then how would mankind continue? Who would say it was sinful for Grayling to find comfort where he could?

He dozed and daydreamed the evening away and at about eleven, hauled himself out of his chair and hopped back over to the bed. His foot was beginning to throb and he thought it might be eased if he lay down. He had put on his shirt whilst sitting in the chair but pulled it off again as the night was almost as warm as the day. He sat on the side of the bed and then heard a tapping on the door. 'Yes?' he said softly.

The handle turned and Deb stood in the doorway, holding a candle in a brass holder. Her straight light brown hair hung loose over one shoulder. She was holding a large fringed shawl around her, but her legs and arms were bare.

'I heard you stirring,' she said meeting his gaze with her light green eyes.

'Yes, I couldn't sleep,' Arthur answered.

'No, neither could I,' she said simply, pushing the door shut behind her and letting the shawl fall to the ground, stood naked before him. 'Shall I come in?' she asked with a little shake of her head.

Arthur, his eyes running up and down her body taking in with pleasure her wide hips, her small belly, her breasts seeming almost too heavy for the small frame of her ribcage, sucked in his breath. 'I think you'd better,' he said.

She stepped across the room, set the candle down on the little table beside the bed, pushed Arthur gently back on the pillows, sat astride him and pulling his hands up, placed them over her warm soft breasts. He drew her down to him and his tongue slid into her waiting mouth.

Deb crept out of his room at about five. Arthur lay back when she pulled the door shut behind her and fell off to sleep almost at once waking just after nine to the smell of smoked sausages frying in the kitchen below.

If he thought Deb might seem embarrassed at meeting him again in daylight, he was wrong. He hobbled downstairs and she brought him his breakfast. Henry sat down to share a tankard of ale with him and the three of them chatted away. Arthur said he felt able to ride the fifteen or so miles home. Deb came out to the stable with him and after Henry had helped him mount and wished him well, Deb remained.

'You don't have to worry, Arthur. I'm not going to be a bother to you. Jack taught me the pleasures a man and woman can enjoy and I've missed him and that pleasure, these last six months more than I can say. So any time you're passing, I'll be happy to share your bed, that's all. But I'm no whore, Arthur. You're the first man whose bed I've shared since Jack died, so don't think I do that with every man who finds himself laid up here.'

'I don't think that, Deb. I don't think that at all. How is it you're so worldly wise? How old are you?'

She laughed and patted his horse's neck. 'Twenty. Ride carefully, Arthur.'

Thereafter when he made runs up through Aylesford he would usually let one or other of the men lead the run into London or he laid the goods up in Henry's extensive cellars before running them up the next day. He started off by bespeaking a room but after a while Deb told him to come to her room for the night. He was anxious at first, wondering what her father made of it. But Henry never said a word about it and never made up a bill for Arthur. Deb was always pleased to see him and couldn't wait for him to join her in bed. She was always good humoured, passionate and tender and full of surprises. There were no demands from her outside the walls of her bedchamber and in some ways he was reminded of his relationship with Harriett Marshall, except for the fact that he had been a novice in matters of the flesh then; but there was the same easy acceptance of the relationship for what is was, to be enjoyed for the moment, its sole purpose the giving and receiving of pleasure, honest and simply defined in its purpose and its execution.

There was only one moment of embarrassment when a terrific thunderstorm and strong winds in the winter of '42 caused Arthur to abandon his intention of sending the gang with their goods up to London that night. Many travellers on the road had the same idea so that Will, going in to find Henry, could only bespeak one room, the rest of the men having to go on to the *Anchor*, a little way ahead. Will came back to find Arthur stabling their horses, the rain dripping off his hat and down his collar.

'I've bespoke a room for us to share, Arthur. It's the only one Henry has left.'

Arthur looked embarrassed. 'Oh. The fact is Will, that is, I normally sleep in Deb's room when I'm here.'

Will smiled at him, not fully understanding. 'Well it's mighty good of her to give up her room-.' He stopped as he realised what Arthur was telling him. He blushed. 'Oh. Oh, I see. Right. Right. I'll be off to my room then.' And he turned to go.

Arthur paused and then took two steps after him laying a hand on his shoulder. Will turned round. Arthur looked into his brother's face. 'Sarah doesn't know of course, Will. It don't mean anything. You know how it is.'

Will gave a half smile. 'Sure, Arthur. Anyway, it's your business. Nothing to do with me.' He looked uncertain and then said, a little awkwardly, 'Good night then, Arty.'

CHAPTER FORTY THREE

June 1744, Hawkhurst, then Ashdown Forest

'I've decided to run up from Eastbourne or Pevensey on Thursday,' Arthur said to Will and Beth as all three sat round the table in Arthur's study at Seacox.

'Any particular reason, Arty?' Will asked looking at the map that they customarily used when planning a run.

'I've six cutters coming over from Boulogne so we'll have plenty to unload and Stockwell is pretty full. It'll be easier to run up to Kingston from Eastbourne. I don't know why it's so slow to offload goods from Stockwell.'

'Do you think it's this war, or the rumours of the uprising?' Beth asked. Arthur often brought the London papers back with him and they were full of news of foreign affairs. They reported the disaffection of the followers of Prince Charles Edward. These supporters wanted to restore the man they considered the rightful heir to the English throne which had been so readily taken by the first German George and now by his son.

Arthur shook his head. 'It's beyond me Beth. Why should a war in foreign parts put our tea merchants off buying tea? Anyway whatever the reason, we'll take it up to the Kingston warehouse. They've plenty of room there.'

Beth twisted the map round so she could look at it. 'Heathfield and onto Tunbridge Wells, or Maresfield and on to East Grinstead?' she suggested.

'Let's try the East Grinstead road,' Arthur agreed. He looked across at his brother. 'It's up to you then, Will to put the word about. I can use a hundred and fifty men. I'll leave it to you to choose whom you will.'

Will went down to Rye and put the word about. He had no trouble in recruiting enough men. They were sitting in the *Mermaid* and Will was marking down numbers in the note book he carried. He looked over at Curtis. 'Are you in, Curtis?' he asked. Curtis studied Will's face for a moment. 'From Pevensey you say?'

'No, I said Eastbourne, Curtis,' Will replied, going back to his book.

'What and then across Ashdown Forest, East Grinstead, then where?'

'South Godstone, Croydon, Morden and so across to Kingston,' Will said impatiently. 'Yes or no?'

'Put me down as yes, then, Gray,' he answered and went across to the bar.

It was a cold night for June, more like March, Arthur thought as the last of the kegs were unloaded at Eastbourne. He had sent the first of his men off on the road towards Polegate heading for Kingston. He had entrusted Jim Cook with leading the first despatch of men and goods and he and Will would work together with the remainder to be laid up at their safe house at the *Crown,* East Grinstead, with its large cellarage and underground passages. Though Arthur knew Will was perfectly capable of leading a run himself, he remained anxious about Will's strength and health since he had been shot on Camber beach three and a half years ago. Though the wound had healed well, if Will got tired Arthur had noticed his brother's hand would be pressed inside his coat to his left side. Each winter he developed a hacking cough that could last months. At those times Arthur refused to let him on any of the runs, saying he needed Will to keep the paperwork in order.

'It's this cough, ain't it, Arty?' Will had asked point blank. 'You don't think I'm up to it.'

'I know very well you're up to it. It ain't that at all. I know you would carry on regardless. But why risk it? Your cough will be gone in a couple of weeks and then you're welcome to rejoin us in the rain and snow! Come on, Will,' he said encouragingly, rubbing the back of Will's neck affectionately and then putting an arm round his shoulders in a gesture he had used since they were boys. 'Stay at home for a while, go through the accounts with Beth, keep an eye on Sarah and the girls for me, go out riding on Saladin, eh?' he suggested referring to Will's latest acquisition, a huge black stallion.

Will nodded reluctantly. It would be pointless to try and withstand Arthur anyway.

However his few months enforced holiday was now over and Will was once again acting as deputy to Arthur. A choppy sea had blown up as the unloading progressed and it was some two hours after the first men had departed, that Arthur and Will finally sent the tub boat back to the cutters and the small boats made their way back across the Channel. It was nearly eight and although the sun was up, it was hidden behind the thick slate-grey clouds and a whipping wind ensured the temperature remained chilly.

It was two in the afternoon by the time they had ridden as far as Nutley and were approaching the heathland of the Ashdown Forest. Ever since passing through the tiny hamlet of Golden Cross, a strange drifting fog had stolen across the countryside, heavy and wet, the sun hidden away behind the blanket of rolling cloud. The fog seemed to deaden the sound of the horses' hooves on gravel tracks and the sparks that the horseshoes normally made on the cobbled streets of the small towns and villages were dampened.

The moist air seemed to affect Will's lungs and he started coughing. Arthur knowing that Will would hate it if he mentioned it, tried to ignore it but he had to comment when he realised Will had slowed his horse down as a coughing fit seized him. Arthur rode his horse up to Sam Austin telling him to ride on and that he and Will would catch them up.

They were so far up country from the coast and well hidden in these drifting mists that Arthur had no fear of Riding Officers or Customs Men. He reined back his horse and rode over to Will. He said nothing but reached into his pocket for the flask of brandy and undid it, holding it across to Will who took it and held it to his mouth. His eyes had watered from coughing and the brandy, strong and pungent, seemed to restore a little of the colour to his cheeks. Will looked across at Arthur.

'We'll lay up at the *Crown*,' was all Arthur said. 'That is, if we ever find it in this fog. I've sent the rest of the men on.'

'Coleman's Hatch must be a little to the north,' Will responded, when suddenly a shot rang out and then another. Arthur, looking round, just had the chance to see red-coated riders before he dug his knees into his horse's flanks, with a cry of 'Dragoons!'

Both brothers urged their horses to a gallop and rode deeper into the foggy heathland. Arthur reached into his belt and took out his clasp knife. He started cutting the half ankers and oilskins free from his horse and noticed Will doing the same. The wooden kegs thudded to the ground behind them and their horses, free from the weight and discomfort of the barrels banging against their flanks, opened their stride and covered the ground even faster. The shouts of the men pursuing them grew less, as Arthur and Will reached a stream. They crossed it and made off on the other side. The fog was even thicker by the water and they slowed to a canter and then a trot and finally drew their panting horses to a halt. Arthur put his head on one side to listen as did Will.

'Anything?' Arthur whispered.

Will listened a moment more, hearing only their own horses' soughing breathing and then shook his head. 'No, I reckon we've lost them.'

Arthur's mare circled round and shied a little. 'Well, I don't know where we are now,' he said. 'How the devil did they know where to find us?'

'Chance?' Will suggested.

'What, you think it likely that they chance upon us in the middle of nowhere, on a route we don't often use? I don't think so, Will,' he said, looking to right and left for a clue in the landscape as to where they might be. Arthur didn't think the Dragoons had a hope of finding them but he was no longer sure of the route they should take.

'If we go back to the stream it'll lead us eventually to the Hatch,' he said to Will. 'It'll give the horses a chance to drink. Peg is panting like anything.'

Will nodded and they turned back in the direction they had come from and heard the sound of the babbling water strangely flattened by the fog. Arthur dismounted and let Peg reach down to the water, grey and deep with the reflection of the slate sky in it. As he stood beside her, he noticed she was standing unevenly.

One of her hind legs was not as flat on the ground as the other and thinking she might have picked up a stone, he bent down to lift her leg. As he did so, his clasp knife, which he had tossed back in his pocket instead of thrusting it in the sheath at his belt, fell out. He reached to pick it up from under the large stone where it had rolled, when he felt a sharp stab in his hand and saw a slither of black and white convulse quickly from under the stone and curve swiftly away through the grass. He looked with a mixture of horror and fascination at the two bite marks on the fleshy part of his palm at the base of his thumb and saw the skin already begin to swell, red and shiny. 'Will,' he called, unsteadily. 'Will, come over here.'

'What is it?' Will asked walking across to Arthur. 'Has Peg taken a stone?'

Arthur turned to face his brother, holding his left wrist tightly with his right hand. Will looked down at Arthur's hand.

'A snake's bit me, Will.'

Will continued to gaze as Arthur had done, at the puffy flesh with the two clear teeth marks in it, two white holes surrounded by angry red. Arthur became uncomfortably aware of his heartbeat racing but whether this was from fear or from the effects of the venom, he couldn't tell. Will had pulled off his neckerchief and was wrapping it securely round Arthur's wrist, so tightly that the veins on either side of it stood out.

'Mount up slowly, Arty,' Will said uncertainly. Arthur did as Will suggested, Will steadying him as he did so and then he scrambled up on Saladin. 'We'll follow the stream, like you suggested, Arty. We'll be in Coleman's Hatch in no time, you see if we aren't.'

Arthur nodded instinctively holding his left arm across his chest against his body. His hand was throbbing and he felt his mouth was parched, but he still couldn't tell if it was fear making his body react this way.

After fifteen minutes, Will was sure they had taken the wrong route. For all he knew this wasn't the stream that led into Coleman's Hatch at all. He looked back at Arthur. He was upright but very quiet and pale. Will's eyes picked out shapes in the fog ahead. He pulled his horse to a halt and Arthur did the same. Will took out his pistols, held one and cocked the other placing it very carefully back in its holster flicking the skirt of his coat away so he had easy access to it.

He recognised the wagons by their bright colours though they appeared muted in the grey blanket enveloping them. They were gypsies' wagons. Local legend had it that they kept vipers as pets. Whether this was to keep people away, Will didn't know but he was willing to take a chance they might know how to deal with a snake bite. There were all sorts of myths about the way they used herbs and plants to heal any manner of ills, or even it was said, to cast spells.

There were two wagons and he saw only two horses, tethered a little way away. He slid off his saddle whispering to Arthur to stay put and crept his way alongside one of the wagons. He saw four shapes standing round a fire and the smell of a delicious stew wafted across to him.

'Turn around slowly,' he commanded. The four shapes spun round and Will found himself pointing his pistol at four girls.

They broke out into a language he couldn't understand. Arthur had ridden up. The girls looked from Will to Arthur and one of them began to laugh. The shortest girl at the front turned to her and shouted out a word of command. The laughter stopped and she looked at Will.

'What do you want?' she asked, in a low voice with a strange accent. 'What's the matter with your brother?'

'A snake's bit him,' Will answered and then thought to himself, *how does she know we're brothers?*

The short girl said something in her strange language to the other three girls and they moved forward towards Arthur. Will held his pistol up and the girl looked accusingly at him.

'Do you want us to help or not?'

He paused and then nodded. She said something to the other girls and one of them held Arthur's horse, while the other two helped him to dismount. They led him over to a wooden seat close to the fire.

Arthur noticed their strange language and their voices, low and sweet. They all looked very similar with olive skin, white teeth, and masses of thick dark hair. Although they wore sleeved and laced bodices, their full skirts ended just below the knee showing their green and white striped stockings and black shoes laced round their ankles and tied at the front.

His left hand was throbbing and his arm ached especially under his arm pit but he no longer felt his heart pounding so fast. The short girl who seemed to be in charge, was issuing commands to the other girls. She then knelt before Arthur and drew out his injured hand, stretching out his fingers.

'How long ago?' she asked Arthur looking up into his face.

He shook his head and looked across at Will.

'A half hour or so,' Will said.

She got up and disappeared inside one of the painted wagons.

'Can you help him?' Will called after her.

She didn't answer and he looked across at the other three girls who smiled back at him. One of them said something and the other two laughed. A few moments later, the first girl came out of the wagon. She carried a short knife with a thin blade, a small bowl, two heavy stoneware pitchers and a small leather bag. She thrust the blade of the knife into the embers of the fire, pulled the stoppers from the pitchers and undid the drawstring of the leather pouch. Then she emptied the contents which looked like a collection of old leaves, into the bowl and set it over the fire, pouring some of the liquid from one of the pitchers into it. She picked up a small dark blue cup from a wooden stool near the fire and pouring a little of the liquid into it, handed it to Arthur.

He took it in his right hand and lifted it to his nose sniffing it. It smelled very sweet, of cherries. 'What is it?' he asked.

She laughed. 'Wine.'

He looked at it, reluctant to drink. He looked across at Will who was also looking uncertain. She quickly snatched it out of Arthur's hand and took a mouthful, swallowing it down and wiping the back of her hand across her mouth.

She said something to the other girls who also took up some of the little cups pouring out some of the thick dark ruby red liquid and drank it. She handed a cup to Will.

Arthur took the cup she had offered him again and this time held it to his lips and drank. It had a rich thick texture smooth on the tongue and was very sweet, but when he had swallowed, the kick on the back of his tongue made him cough. The girls poured more of the liquid and this time both Arthur and Will drank freely. Arthur felt the warm liquid radiating heat inside his body. He began to feel relaxed and tense at the same time, relaxed in his body but tense in his mind, wondering what the girls would do. At the back of his mind, he wondered if they were anything to do with the Dragoons who had ridden up on them.

One of the girls sat next to Will, while two others knelt in front of Arthur and began talking to him in the strange language, touching his face with smooth hands, patting his hair and shoulders. He felt his left arm taken by the first girl and went to look, but one of the others turned his face back to her. He tried to stand but they pushed him back down and then out of the corner of his eye he saw the first girl take the knife from the fire, wrapping the handle in a piece of leather and bringing it towards his left hand. He saw Will rise to his feet but before he could do anything, the girl had plunged the red hot blade of the knife against the wound in his hand, searing his flesh with a hiss and he smelt his own flesh burning. Just as he thought he would pass out with the pain of burning, the girl had taken up the other pitcher and poured the liquid over the wound. It felt icy cold and his hand went numb and started to shake uncontrollably.

He thought he would faint but the girls held him upright and one of them pressed the little cup to his lips and tipped the liquid into his mouth. He looked across the flames of the fire to see Will staring at him, looking puzzled, the gypsy girl standing next to him holding his arm. Arthur felt very tired and closed his eyes.

Will looked on in amazement as the three girls picked him up, as if he had weighed no more than one of them and carried him into one of the wagons. Two of the girls came out closing the little wooden door of the wagon shut behind them. One of them went over to Will and Arthur's horses and began to take off their saddles. Will wanted to move but seemed rooted to the spot. He was sure Saladin would kick out when unknown hands approached him but the girl whispered in the stallion's ears and he whinnied and snorted, picking up his front hooves and then he dropped his head rubbing it against her hand.

One of the girls ladled out some of the stew and brought it over to Will, pushing him down on the seat. She sat beside him and touched his hand. The other two girls sat in front of him, bringing a brightly coloured blanket with them. They too had a dish of stew each. They all began to eat.

Arthur woke up, looking at a ceiling he did not recognise. A girl who looked familiar, was bending over him.

'You're all right, Arturo. You're with me,' she said in her low gentle voice.

He sat up, still groggy and then remembered the events of the previous day. Gypsies!

He looked about him. 'They're dirty,' he said thickly.

'Look about you. Is my caravan dirty?'

He looked at the neatly painted walls, crisp and white; the brightly coloured blankets, the gleaming pots and pans. He shook his head, knowing there was something he should remember.

'And me? Do I look dirty?'

He looked at her smooth olive skin, shining white teeth, mass of thick dark hair, large golden hoops in her ears, the white linen of her blouse, the fancy embroidery on her full skirts. He shook his head again and sat up cautiously. As he went to lean on his left hand, he felt a dull ache in it and looking down suddenly remembered what had happened to him. He hand was neatly bandaged, with some light padding over the base of his thumb. 'What time is it?' he asked.

She looked puzzled. 'It is time to eat the first meal of the day,' she answered. 'Stay here.'

When she was gone, he lifted the blanket that covered him. Though his coat and shirt had been taken off him, he was still wearing his breeches. She came back with a wooden plate, slices of hot meat and a hunk of dark soft bread. There was a mug of a hot drink which smelt like coffee. He realised he was ravenous and started to eat. She sat opposite him, watching.

'What's your name?' he asked, chewing the meat which tasted good, although he couldn't recognise what it was.

'Sidi,' she replied. 'Leave the bandage on your hand three days, and then wash it two days only in rain water. Then it will be good as new, Arturo.'

He frowned. He didn't remember telling her his name. 'The soldiers, did you see any soldiers?' he asked her.

She nodded her head, her earrings bobbing against her black curls. 'They were about all morning yesterday, from sunrise. Before even. But they have gone now.' She took the plate from him. 'A man brought them here.'

Arthur leaned forward. 'What man? What was he like?' he asked urgently.

She shrugged her shoulders and nodded at him. 'One like you. But dark. I will bring you your shirt,' she said.

He frowned. 'Where is it?'

She looked back at him over one smooth olive shoulder as her sleeve slipped down her arm. 'I washed it. It was dirty. I washed you. You were dirty.' She opened the little door and stepped down. Arthur looked out of the little window she had opened at the side of the wagon. He could see a blue, clear sky and the sun already well up.

He looked down at his hand again and tried to stretch out his fingers. He did so cautiously expecting it to hurt, but apart from a feeling of pulling, there was hardly any discomfort at all.

She brought back his shirt, fresh and dry and warm from the heat of the sun. He slid out of the bed and found he could stand up easily in the wagon. He pulled on his shirt and she handed him his jacket and holsters.

He stepped outside. He noticed two more wagons had drawn up and the horses including his and Will's were quietly eating the grass. There was a fire burning with a large pot hanging over it. Three men were sitting round the fire, eating and laughing, dressed in dark breeches and brightly coloured shirts, two of them with bandanas round their dark curls; the third, a very handsome fellow with dark flashing eyes, had his tied back with a coloured neckerchief. They turned round when Sidi called to them and all stood up. They had been speaking the same language as the girls. 'This is Arturo,' she said. 'My brothers Stevo, Panch and Branko.'

The men nodded and smiled and one of them pointed to Arthur's bandaged hand and raised his eyebrows enquiringly. Arthur taking it to be an enquiry after his welfare, nodded and smiled back.

There was a commotion from one of the other wagons and two of the girls from the previous night appeared followed by Will and the third girl. The brothers laughed and called out to the girls. Sidi touched Arthur's arm.

'These are my sisters, Pesha, Lela and Jofranka.' The girls smiled and said something to their brothers which caused them to laugh again and then they brought Will forward, sat him down and carried him a plate of food and some of the coffee-like liquid Arthur had drunk. Will looked across at Arthur. He nodded back at him. When all the men had eaten, Sidi came and stood next to Arthur.

'Stevo and Panch will take you to the track that leads to the little village you call Coleman's Hatch. It is quite close.'

She went back to the wagon. The men were kicking out the fire and Arthur and Will watched them carry over a rolled up piece of turf that they had cut out in order to build the fire. They pushed it back into its place and trod it firmly down, so it was hard to see that there had ever been a fire there. The wagons were hitched up to the horses. They saddled up Saladin and Peg and just threw blankets over their own horses before mounting. Arthur and Will mounted.

Sidi turned round. 'Good bye, Arturo and Gillaume,' she called out. 'Remember, only rainwater, Arturo.' And she started up her wagon in the other direction, the tallest of the sisters, Jofranka seated next to her and the other two in the other wagon following.

Arthur and Will rode in silence following the gypsy brothers until Will asked, 'Is your hand all right, Arthur?'

Arthur nodded. 'You know, it hardly pains me. I'm wondering now if it was a snake bite after all.'

They began to approach a wider track and Stevo and Panch waved their hands in the direction they should take. Arthur held out his hand but they clapped their own palms against his instead of shaking hands and did the same to Will. They turned their horses round and went back the way they had come. Arthur and Will watched them go and then urged their horses forward.

Will was very quiet and then he said hesitantly, 'Arthur did you, that is, did you and your gypsy girl, you know, do anything?'

Arthur shook his head and looked across at his brother. 'I can't remember, Will. Did you?'

Will shook his head. 'I'm not sure, either, Arty.'

'Oh,' Arthur replied sensing there was more to come.

'The thing is, Arty, I think I may have been unfaithful to Beth.' He hung his head. 'Several times.'

He sounded genuinely concerned, but Arthur had to bite his lip. 'What makes you think so, Will?' he asked, looking straight ahead.

'When I woke, I was, well, I was completely unclothed. And so were they.'

'All three of them?' Arthur queried.

Will nodded. 'I think it must have been that drink, Arthur. I don't remember any of it, I don't think. Well, parts of it, perhaps. They all look so alike; it's hard to be sure. What is worrying me,' he said looking across at his brother, 'is, how shall I ever explain it to Beth?'

'Well you'll say nothing, of course,' Arthur said quickly. 'You're not sure anyway, Will. Believe me, there's no reason to tell Beth.'

Will remained silent. 'If that's what you think, then I'll say nothing.' He rode on a few paces. 'They were fine looking girls, though, weren't they, Arty? And their horses! Did you see that chestnut?'

Arthur laughed out loud. Only Will could spend a night with three girls and speak about their horses the morning after.

Will, in a fever of guilt about his possible indiscretions, led the next run up to Stockwell and stayed over the next day, flying up and down the Strand and Fleet Street looking for some stockings Beth had set her heart on months ago, but had never been able to find in either Sevenoaks or Tunbridge Wells. Will, anxious to get the precious parcel home to Beth as soon as possible, sat in his room in the *Robin Hood* and wrote her a note to go in the parcel with the carrier who was about to leave:

I have bought you six pairs of white silk stockings and thereby exceeded your commission for me. They each have the clocks embroydered as you wished at the ancle two pairs with bright blue clocks, two pairs with green and two pairs (my favourites) with pink clocks. I am sure when you have them on, your dear legs will set them off" and then added, thinking of Beth, waiting at home for him, ' *the writing about your stockings and your dear, pretty legs makes me feel what is not to be expressed.'*

As Sidi had instructed him, Arthur kept the bandage on three days and when he unwrapped it, he found there was a padding of strange smelling leaves and what looked like moss pressed against it. He brushed it off and had to move over to the window to look for the faintest marks on his skin. He was sure Sidi had burnt him with the knife but there was no such injury. The tiniest marks that were there were so faint, they began to look just like the lines on his palm which had always been there. He collected rain water and bathed his hand as Sidi had told him. Within a week, there were no marks at all and if Will hadn't been with him, he might have begun to think he had dreamed the whole episode. There only remained the nagging uncertainty of the identity of the dark man who had brought the Dragoons into the Forest.

CHAPTER FORTY FOUR

16ᵗʰ July 1745, London

Arthur made his way to *Jonathan's* and asked the porter whether Sampson Gideon had arrived, wondering if he had been able to help with the request he had made in a letter to him a few weeks ago.

Smithson nodded, taking Arthur's hat. 'He's waiting in the back room sir. He's been here a few minutes.'

Arthur nodded and made his way through the crowded room. Even though he was familiar with most of the faces, he wouldn't be able to name more than three of four of them. He smiled to himself. It was strange, he reflected. He had been coming here now for eight years. He wondered how many of the men dealing in money and stock were receivers of the goods he ran into London and how many of them would acknowledge him if they knew.

He tapped the door once before opening it and Gideon looked up with one of his small smiles and stood to take Arthur's hand. Another man sitting next to him, taller than Gideon, stocky with fair hair and very blue eyes and about Arthur's age, also stood.

'Well, Arthur, I think I have the very man for you to help you in your mission. This is none other than Jacob Kirckman himself. In the world of harpsichords, I think you may rest assured that there's no name higher than Mr Kirckman's.'

The fair haired man smiled and said in a heavy accent, 'I think perhaps my friend and rival Shudi might disagree with you there.'

Gideon allowed himself a smile. 'It's having rivals that keeps us all on our toes, wouldn't you say, Arthur?'

Arthur nodded as he took the seat that Gideon was offering, opposite Kirckman and shook hands with him.

'Are you fond of the harpsichord, Mr Gray?' Kirckman asked.

'You would very soon find me out, if I pretended to know much at all,' Arthur laughed. 'But I would very much like to buy one. It's to replace a very old spinet for someone who is dear to me and plays it well.'

'Then you had best come and visit me in my workshop. Could you bring the lady with you?' Kirckman asked.

Arthur raised his eyebrows.

'I suppose I am right that it is for a lady?' Kirckman asked, with a half smile.

Arthur nodded.

Kirckman put his hand into his coat pocket and drew out a small card. 'This is my direction, Mr Gray - Broad Street, Carnaby Market, not far from here. I am generally there in the mornings and would warmly welcome you and your lady.'

Arthur returned home to find Sarah at work in her terrace garden, dead-heading the roses, Susie at her side holding a small trug. He watched her for a moment, thinking how he would feel if it was Beth standing here, if Beth were his wife and he was coming home to her.

Sarah was unaware of his presence until Susie looked up and ran across to him. 'Daddy, come and help me pick the roses,' she cried, tugging at his coat and clamouring to be picked up. He whisked her up. 'Oh I wouldn't know one end of a rose from another, Susie,' he laughed. 'Better leave it to your mamma.'

Sarah looked up and pushed her straw hat back on her head. 'I didn't hear you, Arthur.' She came over to him and raised her face to his. He kissed her lips quickly, holding Susie between Sarah and himself. 'I have to go out for a while,' he announced.

'But Arthur, you've just got back from London,' Sarah protested.

'I have things to do. I'll be back for supper.'

And before she could protest further he had swapped his heavy riding coat for a light summer coat and had gone round to the stables to saddle up a fresh horse.

He found Beth at home also enjoying the warm sunshine but she had taken a chair outside and was sitting with a book in her lap, Corker at her feet and like Sarah she was wearing a large straw hat. Arthur noticed her pretty bare feet showing at the hem of her dress.

Beth saw him looking at her toes. 'Yes, I am quite the gypsy, Arthur,' she laughed. 'It's so warm, I've taken my shoes and stockings off. I'd forgotten how delightful it is to feel the grass under my toes.'

He came and sat on the grass next to her. 'Beth, I want to ask you something. It was to be a surprise but it seems I have to involve you at the planning stage after all.'

She looked down at him. 'What's all this, Arthur?'

He took her hand and looked at her long fingers for a moment. 'I want to replace your spinet with a new harpsichord. I wanted it to be a surprise for your birthday, but the man who makes them wants to discuss it with you before he will do so.'

Beth didn't speak for a moment. 'That would indeed be a fine present, Arthur,' she said quietly. 'Does Will know?'

Arthur nodded. 'I told him a long time ago he should buy you another, but he said you always maintained your old spinet was fine. But I've often heard you speak about the new models.'

'I don't think I'm a good enough player to warrant a new model, Arthur.'

He looked into her eyes. 'But would you like it?'

'You know I would,' she replied.

'Then let me do this thing for you. It should have been my life's duty to do things to please you, so allow me to do this. It costs me no effort, only money.'

'But you put the effort into making the money. I know that.' She stood up, marking the page in her book with a ribbon. 'Who have you been talking to about the instrument?' she asked, expecting him to name the music sellers in Sevenoaks.

'Someone called Kirckman, Beth. I liked him. He's Swiss. You would think him the most sober fellow until he laughs and then he looks completely different.'

'Kirckman?' Beth breathed out. 'Jacob Kirckman? Arthur, he and his colleague Shudi are the best harpsichord manufacturers in the country, probably in the whole of Europe. He makes instruments for the King himself!'

'Oh, then he must be good,' Arthur said calmly. 'Trust Gideon to know the right man for the job. Would you come to London with me to see him? I think we should stay overnight. I'll write to Kirckman and ask him to bespeak rooms. You'd like to see the shops in the Strand and Fleet Street the next day and we could ride back at our leisure.'

Sitting so close to Beth on the grass in the shimmering heat of the afternoon filled Arthur with such a longing for her physically that he was unable to stay. He knew it was a weakness in him but he could not stop this need for Beth any more than he could stop his heart beating by choice.

His longing for Beth would not be appeased and he found himself riding to Aylesford in the late afternoon where Deb Winton welcomed him with such a simple and genuine pleasure that he felt guilty for using her body by proxy for Beth's. They strolled beside the river and Arthur pulled Deb to him, loosening the lace cap she had tied over her straight brown hair and then started to unloose her gown. They found a quiet bank beside the gently flowing river, surrounded by birdsong and crickets and made love, easily, companionably.

'Who is it you think of, Arthur, when we lie like this?' she asked. 'Not your wife I think. Someone else.'

He looked upset, anxious not to hurt Deb's feelings though what she said was true and he wondered again at her worldly wisdom.

She sat up, fastening her laces. 'Don't worry Arthur. It don't hurt my feelings, truly. I think of Jack when we couple, but it don't take away from the fact that it's you that is giving me the pleasure. What goes on in our heads, well that can't hurt either of us, can it?'

He leaned over and kissed her. 'You're a good girl, Deb.'

Will agreed it would be a treat for Beth to accompany Arthur to London and would have gone with them except that the day Arthur said that Kirckman had asked him to go coincided with a run. If the run was cancelled it would mean losing the favourable tide for two days. Arthur told Sarah there was business in London to transact and that Beth was going with him. He let Sarah think it was connected with Emilia Stone though in fact there had never been any further communication between Beth and her uncle's widow since the time Mrs Stone had come down to Hawkhurst four years ago.

It was just Arthur and Beth therefore who left Hawkhurst one beautiful sunny morning a few days later in late July mounted on their favourite mares and both enjoying the companionable ride on roads that Arthur knew very well. The good summer meant that the roads were dry and the going easy.

As Kirckman had said his workshop was situated a few streets away from Change Alley in a busy street at the sign of the *Kings Arms*. It was at the end of a terrace and there was an alley at the side leading to stables, store rooms and the small tavern from which Kirckman's workshop took its name.

Arthur stabled their horses after lifting Beth down and they made their way round to the front entrance. Arthur pushed open the door. They heard the tinkling sound of a harpsichord as someone was repetitively playing the same key, until he was satisfied with the sound. There were two complete harpsichords in the front of the shop and scattered around were various parts of instruments in different stages of manufacture.

'Good day, Mr Gray and Mrs Gray.' Kirckman greeted them with a neat bow. He was in shirtsleeves with a leather apron tied round his waist and his fair hair was neatly tied at the back of his head. He wore small round spectacles but he took them off as he greeted his visitors.

'I have made a few notes but perhaps you would like first to see how we make our instruments? Max, some refreshments for our visitors,' he called to a young lad at the back of the workshop. It was light and airy inside, the walls were lime-washed white and the large windows let in plenty of light. There was a fresh smell of new wood, cypress, spruce, conifer and mahogany.

'We use different woods for different purposes,' he explained, 'and their cost varies.' Kirckman spent an hour explaining the various processes involved but it soon got far too technical for the non-musical Arthur and at the end even Beth was struggling.

'Let me hear you play something, Mrs Gray,' Kirckman suggested at the end of the tour. 'That will give me an idea of your touch and your range.'

Beth looked anxious but took her seat.

Kirckman passed her several sheets of music which she looked through before selecting one. He bent over her shoulder to see the music she had placed in front of her. 'Well, if you have chosen Buxtehude, you must be a player worth listening to,' he commented, smiling.

Beth gave a nervous laugh. 'Please Mr Kirckman, remember I learned as a child and play only for my own pleasure and that of my close friends and family.'

Kirckman nodded. 'There is no finer audience to play for than those you love and who love you,' he said.

Beth started the piece and faltered at first, overcome by having to perform in front of such a knowledgeable listener, but she soon found her touch and the difference between her old instrument and this new one was amazing to her. The notes were sweet and true and had a lightness that her old instrument had lost. She reached the end of the piece, the final notes ringing out in the workshop. Arthur thought it sounded perfect.

Kirckman nodded and went to his notes. 'The left hand is stronger than the right and the little finger of the right hand sometimes loses its strength but that can often be caused by nervousness.'

'I think you're being kind Mr Kirckman, in attributing my mistakes to nervousness. I think they're more likely due to my inability.'

'Not at all, Mrs Gray,' he said. 'Not a virtuoso performance of course, but there is a good amount of technical mastery and a love of music which must always stand you in good stead, even when confronted with a difficult piece. I'll sketch what I think will work for you.'

He went on to describe at length some of the musical details and when he had finished he laid aside his quill with a decided movement and a nod of satisfaction.

'Now then, my friend,' he said, putting his arm on Arthur's shoulder. 'Come and meet my wife. We live above the shop, as you say. I think she has tea and cakes for you and then we'll take you out to dine tonight. I regret our rooms are not big enough for us to have guests to stay but the *King's Arms* in the courtyard at the back is clean and respectable and you will be comfortable. Now come, come and meet Dorti.'

Dorti Kirckman was plump and brown-haired and if Arthur was not mistaken, about fifteen years older than her husband. Later that evening, while he and Kirckman were standing at the bar of the *White Hart* in Covent Garden, his host explained to Arthur how his marriage had come about. 'I was apprenticed to her husband Herman Tabel when I came over to England in '31. He was a manufacturer of very good harpsichords. I always thought Dorti a fine woman. Herman died in '38 and I proposed to Dorti immediately. Some people thought it was indecent haste and it's true that by marrying her I acquired the business and all the stock in trade. I will not deny it. Why should I? But we are truly fond of each other, Arthur. It's a good marriage. Like yours, my friend. I see the affection between you and your wife.'

Arthur was confused for a moment and then realized that Kirckman thought that Beth, being introduced to him as *Mrs Gray*, was his wife. He opened his mouth to correct the mistake and then changed his mind. Perhaps for this one evening, he could appear with Beth by his side as his wife.

He didn't give a thought to any awkwardness that might ensue at supper with the Kirckmans, but Mrs Kirckman's only question about marriage was to Beth, asking how long she had been married and she answered with perfect honesty, 'Nearly six years.'

The rest of the conversation was about music and the making of instruments. Kirckman told them something of Switzerland describing the beauty of the mountains and the sweetness of the air and Mrs Kirckman spoke a little of Flanders. Then the talk drifted to the war and the uprising. The pleasant evening came to an end and they walked back to Broad Street.

When Arthur and Beth went into the *King's Arms*, only one room had been bespoken for them. Beth said nothing until the lad had shown them the room, turned down the covers, waited for his penny from Arthur and then left.

'Beth, this isn't my doing,' Arthur said quickly. 'Kirckman bespoke it for me. He has assumed because I spoke of you as Mrs Gray, that we are husband and wife. Believe me, I wouldn't uncomfort you.'

She looked at him. 'But you do uncomfort me, Arthur.'

She turned away from him and he put a hand on her shoulder. She spun round and in a moment she was in his arms.

He put a hand up to touch her curls. 'I'll go, Beth. I can find another room easy enough. Only don't be upset.'

She said nothing and he felt her heartbeat racing against his chest. 'No, don't go,' she said.

'What do you mean, my darling?'

Beth shook her head. 'I don't know what I mean. Only I don't want you to go.'

They stood a little way apart from each other. 'If ... if you would wait outside, Arthur, I need to use the chamber.'

He started towards the door. 'Yes, yes of course, Beth. I'll go down to the yard myself,' he said and opened the door softly hurrying down the flight of stairs. He went into the necessary house and relieved himself and came back out into the yard. He heard the soft whinnying of the horses in the stable and a few calls from revelers a few streets away. Above him were a starry sky and a pale half-moon. He walked about until he judged he had allowed Beth time to make whatever preparations she wanted to and then made his way back upstairs.

He opened the door softly. Beth was standing by the window, her hair down over one shoulder, wearing only her chemise which fell in soft folds half way down her thighs. The moonlight caught her hair. She crossed her arms and with one gentle movement pulled her chemise off over her head. Arthur could only stare. He hadn't seen her naked since they had made love in the half-built dining room at Seacox five summers ago. Her limbs and belly were more rounded now, her breasts fuller. He could see from their rapid rise and fall that she was breathing quickly. *If my soul is required of me this moment*, Arthur thought to himself, *I would gladly give it. Beth is here with me and the world is shut outside; Sarah, Will, Deb, my daughters, all, all forgotten.*

He started to pull off his clothes and went to Beth drawing her soft and yielding body against his. He carried her to the bed, kissing her throat, her breasts.

He felt her hands on his belly and lower and then, in a quick movement she pulled herself away and slid away from him and off the bed.

'Beth, what is it, love?' he asked sitting up and looking at the contours of her back.

Her curls shook. 'I can't do this. I want to, but I can't. Forgive me.'

He swung himself to the side of the bed near her, his need for her still obvious and acute. He covered his groin with his hands.

When he said nothing, she turned round. 'Arthur?'

He shook his head. 'How can there be anything to forgive?' He stood up and pushed one of her curls back behind her ear. 'I'll go and find another room.'

She touched his cheek. 'Would it be wrong of us to lie in the same bed? Would that be wrong? Just to lie next to each other and feel the warmth of our bodies?'

He looked at her again. 'I won't touch you, Beth, but I can't promise – well. You know what I mean. You can see what being close to you does to me.'

She looked down at his groin and then in a swift movement grasped his hand and placed it in between her thighs so he felt her warmth and moistness on his hand. 'It's the same for me, Arthur. It always will be.' She turned, picked up her chemise and pulled it on. She lifted the sheet and climbed into bed.

At first they lay side by side, each aware of their own space in the bed, two inches apart, wide awake. Then as Beth got tired, she relaxed and turned towards Arthur. He gently pushed his arm under her head and she nestled against him wrapping an arm across his chest. A shaft of moonlight fell across her face. He kissed her forehead and eventually slept.

Seacox Heath, July 25th 1745

Sarah, emptying the pockets of Arthur's light coat before she added it to her pile of washing, pulled out what she thought was a handkerchief and then feeling her knees go weak, lowered herself to the bed, holding the lace cap in her hands. She willed it to be one of hers but she knew as soon as she looked at it that it was not. It was a Brussels lace cap with thick lappets hanging down the back. Sarah with a short neck chose either thin lappets or none at all. But she knew very well who wore such caps. Beth with her thick curls and long neck knew that this style suited her and all her caps were fashioned like this.

Sarah's hands started to shake and she felt breathless. She raised the cap to her face and inhaled, trying to link its faint perfume with Beth. Though she suspected it, she never had any proof of Arthur's faithlessness until now. And now that it was lying in her hands, she wished she could undo it. All the time it was just in her mind, she could deal with it, bear it. She had wanted to believe Arthur when he said he was escorting Beth to London on business and reckoned that if Will had agreed to it, there could be no mischief afoot. But this small patch of Brussels lace had changed all that.

She heard a banging at the back door and remembered that Will was coming round to pick up one of Arthur's pistols on his way to the gunsmiths in Tunbridge Wells. The ramrod had broken and he wanted it repaired. She flew down the stairs carrying the wicker washing basket and thrust the cap into her pocket. She intended to think about what to do, how to handle this new situation, but as soon as she saw Will looking so carefree, she couldn't keep the words back.

'Don't you think it strange, Will, that your wife and my husband spend so much time in each other's company?' she snapped at him as soon as he came in. 'Don't you ever wonder what they do together? What they got up to in London last week? Don't it shame you, Will?'

Will looked Sarah straight in the eye. 'Beth could never do anything I would be ashamed of. And you should say the same about my brother,' he said steadily.

She stared back at him for a moment and then shrugged her shoulders, bending to the linen in the wicker basket. 'Oh, well, if you want to be blind, that's your business.'

'Oh I ain't blind, Sarah, I've seen many things.' He was looking at her keenly and she met his gaze and then felt uncomfortable.

'What things?' she asked. 'What have you seen?'

Corker came trotting into the kitchen and Will bent down holding out his hands. 'Here, boy. What's that you've got?' he said, pulling an old bone out of Corker's reluctant jaws and then said to Sarah though he kept his eyes on the dog, 'Oh, you know how you see something as a child and you don't make sense of it until you're older and then it dawns on you, just exactly what it was that you saw.'

A chill seemed to descend into the room and Sarah went to the back door that Corker had pushed opened and pulled it shut. 'Well, if you must talk in riddles, Will-,' she said eventually, turning back to her linen.

'It ain't a riddle though, not any more. Only –when I was a boy I used to keep a cat in Tulhurst's barn. She had kittens regular. And I used to spend as much time up there as I could. I would sneak off whenever I got a chance, nearly every Sunday when Arthur thought I was at church.' He looked over at Sarah's back and sensed how she had stiffened as he was speaking. 'And I saw things which didn't mean much to me at the time, as I said, but now I see things more clearly.'

Sarah's mind flew back over the years to Sundays spent between Goudhurst and Hawkhurst while she rode on a horse, a man's arms stealing round her waist. 'What are you saying, Will?' she asked in a frozen voice.

'I'm not saying anything and neither should you.'

'I'd rather you said it, Will. Say what you have in mind.'

He glanced at her and then said, 'It's just this - no one could mistake Becca for anyone's child but Arthur's, for everyone says she is the image of our mother. And Susannah has your looks. But, who does Sally favour?'

'Well everyone says how like her father she is,' she countered and then wished the words unsaid, having fallen straight into a pit of her own making.

'Oh yes, her father.' Will glanced across at Sarah, his face set and then he called to Corker. 'Come on, boy, we must get to the gunsmith's.'

Sarah watched him go, her hands trembling as she gripped her apron. She took the lace cap out of her pocket again and turned it over in her fingers. She sat there for an hour, twisting the lace, tying and untying the ribbons.

The back door opened and Arthur walked in, shaking the rain off his coat and placing his wet hat on the table. 'There's a rare storm blowing up, Sarah. I think I'll go and tether the new trees with Jim-,'

'Why is Beth here so much? I sometimes think she lives in this house!' Sarah snapped.

Arthur stared at her. 'What are you saying, Sarah? What's all this?'

Sarah raised her face to his. 'I know, Arthur, I know.'

He looked at her calmly. 'What do you know?'

She pulled the lace cap out of her pocket and flung it across the table to him. 'I know this is hers. It was in your pocket. That's why you took her to London. Now tell me it isn't true. Swear this isn't Beth's! Swear on Becca's life it isn't Beth's.'

Arthur looked at her silently. He thought back to just over a week ago, by the Medway at Aylesford, when he had loosened this cap from Deb's light brown locks pushing it into his pocket as he unloosed the lacing at her bodice, her hands running through his hair, her warm mouth pressing against his lips as he pulled her into his arms. 'I swear on Becca's life and on her soul, that this is not Beth's,' he said slowly.

Sarah looked shocked, stunned into silence. She knew Arthur would not falsely swear on the soul of his favourite daughter. 'Well, it isn't mine,' she flung at him, standing up.

'No,' he said quietly. 'It belongs to a barmaid.'

Sarah looked up at him. 'A barmaid?'

'Yes, Sarah. Are you happy now?'

'Who is she?'

Arthur went over to the chest and poured himself some small beer. 'I haven't the slightest intention of telling you.'

Sarah sank back down in her chair, her mind in turmoil. She had been prepared to hear Arthur defend his relationship with Beth; she had expected him to tell her that Beth was his soul mate or some such nonsense, but to hear that he had been with a common barmaid, - that could only be for pleasures of the flesh.

'Why do you – why do you go to another woman's bed? I don't understand,' she said slowly, pain in her voice. 'I never refuse you my body, do I? Ain't I always willing when we couple? I do what I know pleases you. Even when I was carrying the girls, I always made sure you got your satisfaction, didn't I? So why must you go to another woman's bed?'

Arthur didn't answer. He didn't know himself. All Sarah had said was true. She had never once refused him access to her body. But whenever they came together, there were always other issues crowding in on them. With Deb, it was simple gratification for them both. Deb was warm and comfortable in bed, endlessly inventive but with no demands on his life outside the bedchamber. With Beth, there was no comparison. With Beth it had been different. Beth was as far above any other woman, as the evening star was above the light of a single tallow candle.

'You can't love me,' Sarah said accusingly.

Arthur rubbed his hands over his face. 'I'm not in the mood for this, Sarah.'

'Say you love me then,' she said, her voice rising in anger and frustration at her inability to understand her husband standing so calmly in front of her.

He paused and then spoke. 'Of course I love you.'

'But not as much, not as much as you love-,'

'Say it then, - not as much as I love, who?' He leaned his back against the oak door of the cupboard and looked over at his wife. 'Beth is my dear sister-in-law. I've known her all my life. What more is there to say? Sarah?'

Sarah looked at him, a thousand words dying on her lips. Dare she say them? She knew she dare not cross the line again.

Susannah ran into the room. 'Mamma, Becca has taken my doll!'

The moment was past. The room became again one of simple domesticity. *We can all be comfortable again,* she thought. *At least she doesn't have this with him. He doesn't stand in her kitchen; she doesn't have children who call him father.* She suddenly looked down at her youngest daughter and reached out to smooth her hair.

Arthur went back several times to see Jacob Kirckman to find out how the harpsichord was progressing.

It was almost finished when Arthur visited some time in October. He went into the back workroom and was amazed and aghast at the same time; amazed at the beauty of the instrument, but aghast at the size of it, much bigger than he had imagined or allowed for.

'Come, come and look, Arthur,' Kirckman said enthusiastically. 'I am very pleased with it. I have used lacquered brass strap-hinges so the lid lifts easily and all on a stand of solid mahogany. Now what do you say to that, my friend? Will your lady like it? But what is it? You're looking worried. Is it not to your liking?'

Arthur quickly shook his head. 'No, nothing like that Jacob. Of course it's a work of art, but I didn't realise it would be so big. I've been stupid. You told me at the outset it would be nine feet long. It's just seeing it all put together – do you know, I don't think this will fit in Beth's house.'

Both men stood looking at the instrument for a while. Arthur rubbed his chin, trying to think how to get the instrument into any of the rooms in Beth's house. The only room he could think of where it would fit was his own dining room at Seacox, twenty five feet long and with glazed doors through which the instrument might be brought in.

'Jacob, let me go away and think about this. Perhaps I'll have it delivered to my house instead. How do you transport it?'

'By river as far as we can and then by a specially adapted wagon. It will be ready in two weeks. I know you wanted it for Christmas but I would recommend you take delivery of it before the winter when the roads can be so unreliable. You should have snow, like we do in Switzerland. Then we put them on a giant sledge and it glides easily, with no damage. But here you have rain and mud,' he said sighing.

Arthur returned home and went straight to see Beth. Will had gone to the horse fair at Horsmonden and would not be back until the next day.

'Well, I don't mind at all, Arthur,' Beth said when he had explained the problem to her. 'You're making too much of it. In fact, I was a little uncomfortable with the idea of such a lavish gift. It's enough that you will let me come and play on it. It doesn't have to be in this house.'

'But that's what it was meant for,' he said unhappily. 'So you would have it to hand whenever you liked.' He was looking round the room wondering if he might get one or two of the walls knocked down and a larger door created.

Beth guessed his intention and shook her head saying firmly, 'No, you've done enough for us in this house. If there's any enlarging to be done, I know Will would rather have larger stables.' She laughed. 'Don't look so miserable, Arthur. You always said that your dining room was meant to be a music room. Becca and Sally have lessons on the spinet, after all. Think how pleased they'll be.'

He shook his head, far from happy, though at the back of his mind he realised that having the harpsichord in his house meant Beth could always call round with good reason. He got up to leave, going out through the back door. 'I'll just have a look at the stables then, Beth, to see how we might enlarge them.'

Sarah, who had known nothing of the commissioning of the harpsichord, was surprised when Arthur told her of its expected arrival and asked her to tell Jim Cook where she would like the dining table and the beauset moved to, so that the harpsichord could be brought in through the glazed doors.

Sarah laid down waxed papers all over the carpets so that the men delivering it wouldn't bring mud onto the floor. There was great excitement when Sally saw the wagon pulled by four horses coming up the incline to the house just before noon. Arthur went out straight away and directed the men to bring it round to the back before sending them back to London giving them two shillings apiece for their trouble. He returned to the dining room to find his daughters standing by the harpsichord but not daring to touch it. Sarah was gathering up the waxed paper and setting the room to rights.

'Daddy, please may we try it?' Becca asked breathlessly. 'Please! We don't know how to open it.'

'I should think not,' Arthur said severely. 'What do you think of it, Sarah?' he asked looking across at her.

She shrugged. 'It's a handsome piece. I hope the girls have talent enough to justify its cost.'

'How much did it cost, Daddy?' Becca asked taking Arthur's hand.

'Never mind, miss,' he said bending over the lid and finding the 'S' shaped brass hooks in order to raise the lid. He did so and the girls peered in, Susie clamouring to be picked up so she too could see inside.

'Oh look, mamma,' Becca cried. 'An angel, there's an angel on the inside.'

'That's the soundboard, Becca,' Arthur said looking at the heavy gilt brass rosette, indeed incorporating an angel set in the lid.

Sally and Becca had brought chairs to sit at it and play. 'Mother, come and play with us,' Sally said insistently.

'I can't play, Sally, as you well know,' Sarah said sharply.

'Then is this just for us, Daddy?' Becca asked, looking from her father to her mother. 'But you could learn, mamma. Mr Gibbons could teach you, couldn't he, Daddy?'

Arthur looked at Sarah but said nothing.

'I expect Beth will like to come and play it,' Sarah announced meeting Arthur's eyes.

'Can she play, Daddy? Can Aunty Beth play?' Susannah asked catching his hand.

He looked down at his smallest daughter. 'Yes Susannah, certainly Beth can play. She had lessons for many years.'

The next day, Arthur went to fetch Will and Beth so she could try out the instrument. The girls had arranged the chairs in the dining room in a row so they could be the audience while Beth played. She and Will came into the room and Beth couldn't help but breathe an amazed 'Oh,' when she saw it. She ran the backs of her fingers over the smooth mahogany and walnut lid and then smiled as Arthur lifted the lid to reveal the beautifully engraved interior and the angel the girls were so taken with. Sarah kept back, holding Susie's hand.

'Do you like it?' Arthur asked casually but not quite able to keep the pride out of his voice. She didn't reply, but slowly put her fingers to the keys and picked out one chord after another. He pulled the stool out and said quietly, 'Please play something.'

She glanced at him and then at Will, who had already taken his seat. 'Yes, do, sweetheart. Delight us all,' he said.

'I have the music,' Becca said excitedly. 'It's the piece Sally and me are learning for Mr Gibbons but it's so difficult.' She held a sheaf of stave papers in her hand.

Beth smiled as she recognised the piece. 'Mr Handel's *Suite in E major* —"the Harmonious Blacksmith." Lucas Webb should be here to hear it.'

'Play it, Aunt Beth, do,' urged Becca. 'May I turn the pages for you? I'll try and keep to the right place.'

Beth nodded and arranging her skirts carefully, seated herself at the stool, with Becca on her left. She played a few scales, her fingers making themselves acquainted with the touch of the keys, at first slightly unsure and then growing in confidence as she became used to the timbre of the instrument. She paused, smiled at Becca and then began the piece. The first notes were slow and controlled and as she progressed and played with a surer touch, the music began to fill the room. Arthur watched as her body swayed slightly back and forward keeping the beat and her long fingers moved up and down the two manuals.

Susannah was sitting on her father's lap, but Arthur was unconscious of his small daughter's wriggles, with eyes only for Beth sitting at the instrument. As the piece progressed, it got faster with the notes up and down the keyboard and trills embroidering the melody. Beth nodded when she reached the end of each page and Becca, her face solemn with concentration, turned the pages as quickly and quietly as possible. Towards the end, the repetitative melody climbed higher and higher and filled the room with its tinkling high notes and then grave bass tones brought the tune to its end.

There was a moment's silence, then Susannah clapped her fat little hands together and cried delightedly, 'More, Aunty Beth, play some more.'

Everyone else joined in clapping and Beth who had seemed lost in the music, grew a little pink and stood up, gathering up the music sheets and handed them to Becca.

'Oh Aunt Beth, do you think I'll ever play half as well as you?' she asked breathlessly.

'Well you have the most beautiful instrument to practise on. I confess if it was in my house, I should scarce be away from it,' she said, half looking at Arthur.

'Lucky for Will then that it's in our house and not yours,' Sarah said with a short laugh, wishing the words unsaid as soon as she spoke them, but not able to stop herself.

'Yes indeed,' Beth said at once. 'You're quite right Sarah.'

'But Aunt Beth can come and play whenever she wants to, can't she, Daddy?' Becca urged.

In the moment's silence that followed, Becca was aware that the room was full of adult feelings and awkwardness that she barely understood but only sensed. She was at an age where blushes came readily and her cheeks flushed.

'Beth is welcome at all times in this house, as she knows,' Arthur said. 'Isn't it so Sarah?'

Sarah looked at Arthur and then at Beth. 'Why of course. Your own brother's wife? How could it be otherwise?' She smiled with her mouth, but her eyes were hard as iron.

CHAPTER FORTY FIVE

November 1745 Jonathan's Coffee House, London

In November while Arthur was up at Stockwell staying over the night, as the days were too short to ride back to Hawkhurst in any comfort, a note was brought round to him. He recognized Gideon's hand inviting him to meet with him on the next morning at *Jonathan's*.

He dressed early and set out and although he arrived by ten, Gideon was already there in the back room, clad as always in sombre black. He rose to greet Arthur and when he had called for coffee, he said in a low voice, 'I do not know how closely you have followed the fortunes of Prince Charles Edward?'

Arthur raised his eyebrows. This was the last topic he expected Gideon to raise. 'Hardly at all, sir,' he said politely. 'I know there was all that fuss in the summer when he arrived in Scotland and all the militia gathered in Finchley to defend London. Hasn't it all blown over?'

Gideon took a sip of his coffee, shaking his head. 'No, no, not at all. Oh, I've no doubt it will soon run its course. I have heard however from the most reliable sources that the Prince is on his way south towards Derby. It will come to nothing with only a handful of the English supporting him, mostly Roman Catholics from Lancashire, but it will cause panic in the City and there will be a run on the banks. Most men will follow their hearts instead of their heads and will try to sell, but with your permission, Arthur, I should like to buy on your behalf with the capital you have invested with me while prices are low. I believe I may achieve you a healthy profit.'

Arthur looked across at Gideon. 'As you know, Mr Gideon, I'm perfectly happy to leave all that side of business in your hands. Please do as you think fit. You haven't let me down yet.'

Gideon inclined his head slightly.

At this moment there was a knock on the door and Smithson entered with a note on a silver tray. Gideon took it with a small nod of his head and broke open the wafer reading quickly. 'Lord Lyttelton is without and begs a word,' he explained. 'However, it does him no harm for him to wait. Our political masters think they need only click their fingers and we all run.'

'And don't we?' Arthur asked, amused.

'No. I don't and neither I believe do you. The trick is to let them think that we do.' The Jew allowed himself a small smile. 'Now back to our business.' He explained the investments he planned to make on Arthur's behalf and suggested what the profits might be.

Arthur looked thoughtful for a few moments. 'Well, you've given me something to think over and I thank you for it. Now I must allow you to see your other visitor,' he said getting up to leave. Gideon also rose and held out his hand. They shook hands. As Arthur walked through the door into the main room, he passed an anxious looking man waiting to go in. He knew Lyttelton was a member of the Government and wondered, with a smile to himself, what he might say, if he knew he had been kept waiting until Arthur Gray, the leader of the Hawkhurst Gang, had finished his business with Sampson Gideon, before he could himself go in.

April 1746 the Mermaid, Rye

The advice Gideon had given Arthur concerning his investment turned out as always to be extremely sound and he had made a profit of some two thousand pounds by buying when nearly everyone else in the panic, thinking the Uprising might succeed, had sold stock at a loss. Arthur wanted to celebrate his good fortune with a small party. He invited Will and Beth and her uncle and aunt, Ann and William Pix, along with Thomas Lamb, to join them. Mrs Lamb, growing frailer, was unable to attend but it was a pleasant evening, the wine flowing freely, Arthur and Will in a buoyant mood, Beth looking beautiful, Sarah in an accommodating frame of mind as the girls were being looked after by Joanna safe back at Seacox, with Jim Cook keeping an eye on them all.

Will and Beth's uncle, William Pix, were enjoying a conversation about horses, when Arthur looked over to the door and saw Jeremiah Curtis enter with his arm about a young woman. He looked at her closely and then recognized her as Alice Marshall, Harriett's younger daughter who must be about eighteen, he thought. He frowned. He was quite sure Harriett wouldn't approve of her daughter walking out with Curtis, who was almost twice her age. Besides, Harriett was a modest woman in her dress and Alice who had a more voluptuous figure than her mother, was wearing low cut stays and tight lacing. Her gown was cut after the latest London fashion and was hemmed two or three inches above the ground, so that when her skirts swung, her ankles and feet were displayed. He was half listening to what Lamb was saying to him, when Lamb followed the direction of Arthur's gaze. 'What is it, Arthur?' he asked.

'Jeremiah Curtis,' Arthur replied. 'I just need to have a word with him.'

Lamb put a hand over Arthur's as he made to get up. 'Don't cause any trouble, eh?'

Arthur looked across at him. 'No trouble at all sir,' he said but just as he was about to get up, Curtis came over. He was not drunk, but he had certainly been drinking. He made an elaborate bow to the women. He nodded at Sarah, saying, 'Mrs Gray,' and then, 'Ma'am', bowing to Ann Pix. He took Beth's hand and kissed it, saying, 'And last but by no means least, Beth, the other Mrs Gray of course.' He nodded slightly to the men. Alice was holding his arm, looking uncomfortable.

'We're celebrating Arthur's good fortune, Curtis,' Will said. There was no love lost between the two of them. 'He's made a large profit on an investment.'

'Is that so?' Curtis said mildly. 'Then he has all the more money to spend on Mrs Gray,' he added looking directly at Beth, before turning to Sarah and smiling.

'A word with you, Curtis,' Arthur said getting up and going over to the bar. Curtis paused but then followed him, pulling Alice by her hand behind him.

Arthur looked down at Alice and said gently, 'Does your mother know who you're with, Alice?'

She looked disconcerted, but said nothing.

'What's it to you who she's with, Gray?' Curtis asked. 'You had the mother, I've had the daughter. Or perhaps you want a share? How many women do you want, Gray? Well, you've certainly got the money for as many as you want.' He looked down at Alice and pulled her head up by cupping her chin.

'How much would you charge Gray here, Alice?' he asked her. 'How much would you charge him, for a tumble with you? Three shillings, four? Or perhaps you'd just like a feel of her, Gray?' He pulled Alice in front of him so her back was pressed against his chest. He crossed his arms in front of her and cupped her breasts over her gown, pushing them together. 'There's plenty to get hold of here, isn't there, Alice? I daresay if you asked Gray for a guinea, he'd likely pay.'

'Stop it, Jeremiah,' Alice said quietly. 'You know I'm not like that.'

'Let me walk you home, Alice,' Arthur suggested. She looked anxiously up at Curtis.

He shrugged. 'Do what you like. I've other business to attend to.' He pushed passed Arthur and made his way into the inner taproom.

Arthur looked down at Alice. 'Would you like to sit with us for a while? I have a small family party here, that's all.'

She shook her head.

'Well, wait just a moment while I excuse myself to my guests.'

He came back to Alice, offered her his arm and they set off the short way to Watchbell Lane. Halfway down the Strand well lit with flickering flambeaux, they heard footsteps. Arthur tucked Alice's hand tighter under his arm and turned round.

'Changed my mind,' Curtis said. 'Don't fancy a cold bed tonight. Come here, Alice.'

Arthur pressed her hand and put her away from him. 'Leave off, Curtis. What is it with you?'

'I don't know, Gray. All I do know is that you always seem to come between me and my plans,' he said bitterly.

'I could say the same about you, Curtis.'

'Don't know what you mean.'

'I mean, Curtis, that the Riding Officers and the Dragoons seem to know an awful lot about my plans these days.'

Curtis shrugged. 'Well if you will run with five hundred men, that's five hundred tongues can run loose. I know you don't let 'em drink on a run, but that don't mean their tongues ain't loosened when they're on their own time.'

Alice looked from one man to the other. A sneaking wind blew round her ankles. She wished she had brought a shawl.

'Well?' Curtis asked. 'Are you coming, Alice?'

'No she ain't,' Arthur retorted. Curtis approached and Arthur thought he was going to take Alice by the arm so he stepped across in front of her, but then Curtis swung round, crashing his fist into Arthur's chin and knocked him back against the startled girl. Arthur righted himself and ducked out of the way of Curtis's second punch and countered it with his own right fist, with all his weight behind it, right into the side of Curtis's face. Curtis fell onto his back but quickly rolled over cursing. He dragged himself up and came at a run, his head aiming for Arthur's belly.

Arthur saw him coming and turned on his heel catching Curtis's arm and pulling him round to deliver another blow, his knuckles feeling Curtis's teeth through the skin at the side of his jaw. Curtis staggered back knocking into Alice as he fell and grabbing at her for support. His hand made contact with her arm and as he staggered back, he pulled her with him, the linen at her shoulder tearing and she fell in a heap at his side. Curtis remained half lying, half sitting, propped up on one elbow, holding the other hand to his jaw. Arthur stood over him catching his breath, bleeding from the old scar above his eyebrow. Alice was trying to get up, attempting to put her gown to rights, but under the light of the flambeaux, her naked back was illuminated and Arthur was horrified to see dark bruises, some obviously in the shape of a man's fingers over her neck and shoulders.

'Good God! Does he do this to you?' he asked Alice, who with shaking hands was trying to tuck the torn linen back into her stays.

Curtis looked at Alice and then hauled himself up. 'She deserves it. She's clumsy sometimes and too slow.' He leaned heavily on her shoulder and cupped her face with his hand. 'Ain't you?'

Alice looked up at him with her soft brown eyes and then looked across to Arthur. 'Yes,' she said softly.

'Are you mad, Alice? No one deserves this,' Arthur exclaimed indicating the bruises on her shoulder. He held out his hand to her. She hesitated, lifted her own hand and then turned back to Curtis and took the arm he held out. He pulled her to him, turned up her face to his and kissed her hard on the mouth, his hand on the back of her neck, pressing her lips hard against his open mouth, his other hand at her breast. He let her go and turned to Arthur, rubbing his swelling jaw.

'Til next time then, Gray?' he said and he led Alice back up the Strand, her gaze resolutely straight ahead as she passed Arthur.

Arthur watched them go and then put a hand to his bleeding eyebrow and felt the shoulder of his coat wet with blood. Feeling he couldn't go back into the *Mermaid* with a bloody face, he decided to go to Harriett's and a few moments later, she was opening the front door to him.

'I'm sorry I couldn't persuade her to come back here,' he said, as Harriett dabbed at his cut with a piece of linen, after he explained how he came to get it.

Harriett shook her head. 'She's taken up with him these last couple of months, Arthur. I can't do nothing with her. She gave up her job in Pembury on a whim. She sometimes helps me out with the washing but most of the time she hangs around with Curtis. That's when I miss her not having a father to keep her straight. Or even her brother,' she faltered.

Arthur quickly looked up at her. 'Have you heard from James lately?'

She shook her head, resigned. 'Not since you sent the last half coin from me over to Boulogne these eighteen months since. He never returned his half. Perhaps he moved away,' she said, sad and quiet.

'Lizzie is still with you, though?' he asked.

'Yes, she's a good girl. Still walking out with Luke Dowdy. I think they'll marry soon.'

She finished dabbing at Arthur's cut and put the bowl down and went to fetch Arthur's coat. She had sponged the blood off it and had hung it in front of the small fire. She sat at the table opposite him. 'Thank you for trying to bring Alice back, Arthur.'

He looked around the room for a moment, the washing lines still hanging across the room though there were only a few pieces of linen drying. It was just as he remembered it when Harriett has first brought him here as a young lad of fifteen after John Grayling had struck him round the face, that evening so long ago. He smiled at the memory. It was strange, he thought, that it was that same old wound that Curtis had split open tonight. His gaze rested on Harriett. She must be well over forty he thought and noticed how grey her hair was at the side of her face above her ears. He took a handful of coins out of his pocket and put them on the table. She looked at the small pile of silver, concerned and uncertain. 'What's that for, Arthur?'

'For friendship,' he said. 'And for making me presentable again, to go and face my party at the *Mermaid*.'

Part three

1746 –1748

CHAPTER FORTY SIX

August 13 ***th*** ***, 1746, Seacox Heath then Rye***

Arthur spread the London newspapers over the table in his study. He read one version, and then another to see if the editors showed any difference in their interpretation of the new Act. But in his heart he knew. It couldn't be made any plainer. The *Gentleman's Magazine* seemed to have it most succinctly – *"The Legislature made an Act, whereby it is enacted, that after 24*th *June 1746, if any persons, to the number of three or more, armed with fire-arms, shall assemble themselves together, in order to be aiding and assisting in running, landing and carrying away uncustomed goods, they are guilty of a capital offence. The only question will be, whether a person is guilty of that offence?"*

No matter how many times he read it, Arthur felt only one course of action was left open to him. He spent all day in his study, snapped at Sally when she came to fetch him for supper and had equally harsh words for Sarah when she followed Sally to find out what he meant by refusing to join his family for their meal.

An hour later realising he was hungry, he ordered Sarah to prepare him a fresh meal, calling her in from the evening cool of the garden shade where she was sitting fresh and pretty in a clean gown. He made her come in to stoke up the range again and reheat his dinner.

He was angry with himself, with fate, with the Government, with his daughters and his wife, for even though he knew what he must do, it was so far outside of what he wished to do, it made him feel uncomfortable, miserable, wrathful and ultimately helpless.

He told himself he would sleep on it and mull it over again in the morning. He allowed himself to respond to Sarah's lips and hands as they lay in bed and she planted little kisses all the way from his collar bone over his belly to his groin. Impatiently he quickly grasped hold of her hips and thrust himself into her bringing on his own pleasure as quickly as he could, without a thought for hers; and then swung himself out of bed and went down to sit in his study again, poring over the papers once more.

Once Arthur had made up his mind, he decided to go and tell Thomas Lamb. He went to the secure cupboards in one of the secret passages in the house and took our some papers putting them carefully into a flat leather bag. He was putting on his coat as Sarah came into the hallway.

Her eyes narrowed. 'Are you going out, Arthur?'

He nodded. 'I'm going to Rye.'

He was about to open the door when he turned round. 'What do you do all day, Sarah?'

She looked puzzled. 'What do you mean?'

'When I'm out on a run – what do you do?'

'Well you know what I do. I cook, I clean, I sew and mend, I like to be in my garden, I see to the girls.'

He nodded. 'Come here.'

She frowned but did as he said. He quickly put his arms around her and drew her against his body and kissed her temple. 'You're a good wife, Sarah,' he said gently and then just as quickly put her from him.

She looked up at him, pink with pleasure at this small compliment. 'Is anything the matter, Arthur?' she asked.

He shook his head. 'Nothing at all. I'll see you later tonight or maybe tomorrow.'

As soon as he got to the *London Trader*, he sent one of the boys round with a note for Thomas Lamb, who arrived about twenty minutes later. Arthur was waiting in the usual back room. He was standing up, his hands pressed deep in his pockets. Lamb entered and glanced at the table strewn with papers and books, the quill left on one of the pages and a blot of ink slowly forming a dark blue stain upon it.

They shook hands and then, glancing at Arthur's face Lamb asked, 'What is it, Arthur? What's amiss?'

Arthur looked at the papers. 'I'm stock taking, sir. I think that's what Gideon would call it.'

Lamb looked surprised. Arthur's voice sounded quiet, resigned, sad.

'Come, sit down and tell all,' the old man said, sitting down and putting his hat on the table.

Arthur reluctantly pulled a chair out, the seat towards him and sat astride it, leaning his elbows on the back of it. 'Those pages you see before you,' he indicated with a nod. 'They ain't anything to do with the next run. There ain't going to be a next run. I've decided to finish it,' he said quietly.

Lamb said nothing but continued to study Arthur's face. 'May I ask why? I think I know but let me hear it from you.'

'It's this last Act, Thomas,' Arthur began, using Lamb's Christian name for the first time ever. 'The Act that came out in June. It ain't a case of being transported if we run goods now – the penalty is hanging.' He rubbed a hand over his face in a gesture Lamb knew well. 'They'll hang us just for assembling together. They'll fine a parish for harbouring a smuggler and they'll hang you if you give yourself up and hang you if you don't and they have to come and find you. No, it ain't to my taste any more. Besides, since they took the duty off tea, our profits have come down as you yourself know. Not that that alone would have changed me in my course. No, it's these harsh penalties. They will have us, Thomas, the Government will have us. They want to make it impossible for any sane man to try his luck, by putting him at the mercy of so much potential treachery and betrayal!'

'So this is truly an account of your wealth, Arthur?' Lamb asked gazing again at the papers spread out over the table.'

'Yes,' Arthur assented. 'Do you know, Mr Lamb, I believe I am worth ten thousand pounds! Gideon's last piece of advice added even more to my wealth.' He gave a short laugh. 'Ten thousand pounds and I used to feel rich when I had a shilling in my pocket!'

'Arthur, I don't know what to say. Of course you will do what you think is right for you,' Lamb nodded, 'and for those around you.'

Arthur also nodded and began putting the papers together.

'Does anyone else know of your decision?' Lamb asked.

Arthur shook his head. 'No. All the time I don't put it into words, it don't seem real. I know I would be foolish to continue, but I can't think what I'll do to fill my days. I haven't known any other life since I was eleven. I don't know what the men will say. Most of them rely on it for the living they have got used to. It's different for me and for Will. We can live for the rest of our lives on what we have made.'

Lamb put a hand on Arthur's shoulder. 'Do you not think any of them will continue?'

Arthur shook his head. 'I've no idea, Thomas. Not if they realise the dangers. It's taken some organising, that's for sure. I don't know who else could do it.'

He said it without vanity. It was just a fact.

'I don't know quite where this places us,' he said looking across at his benefactor.

'Well, it's the end of a long and rewarding business association,' Lamb said calmly. 'I've no complaints. You've served my investment well.' He leaned forward and touched Arthur's arm. 'You know Arthur, there has always been affection too.'

Arthur looked into Thomas Lamb's eyes, a pale blue now with the dullness of age, something he had never noticed before. 'On my side too, sir,' he responded gripping Thomas Lamb's proffered hand and both men would have said more if their characters had allowed them to speak freely to each other.

Lamb held onto Arthur's hand a little while and then said, 'Forgive me, Arthur. I cannot stay longer. My wife is – well the fact is Dorcas is very ill.' He cast his eyes down and seemed to stare at the floor. 'I don't like to leave her on her own for very long.'

'Then I apologise for having brought you from Mrs Lamb's side,' Arthur said quickly. 'You should have explained. You can't have wanted to sit here listening to my plans.'

'Nonsense, Arthur, you've been in my thoughts a great deal of late.' He looked as though he would say more but instead he straightened his neckerchief.

'Well it'll be a busy time,' Arthur said at length. 'I have to close everything down. I'll have to travel to France a couple of times and then decide what to do with the rest of my life.'

'If I can help you in any way Arthur, you know you can rely on me.'

Arthur looked up and smiled. 'Yes, I've known that these many years.'

'So you see Beth, after all these years, I'm finally doing as you wanted.' Arthur had called round to see Beth and Will to tell them of his decision on his return from Rye. Will had taken two of his horses to Lucas Webb to be shod and he found Beth alone sitting in the garden in her favourite spot under the shade of the plum trees. She said nothing.

'Ain't you pleased?' he asked.

She nodded slowly. 'I'm pleased that Will and you will be safe, but I know you're not happy, Arthur. What will you do? I can't imagine what you'll do without having the planning or organising of the next run to be done.'

He took a step or two across the grass and sat down gazing up at the blue sky. 'I don't know. I can hardly play the country squire can I?' He half smiled. 'Perhaps I should have set Will up as a farmer. It would have been enough for him, striding over his fields, looking after his animals. I never gave him the choice.'

'He wanted no other choice. He's never wanted anything contrary to your wishes, don't you know that?' Beth replied, reaching over and taking his hand. He let her hold it and looked up at the sky again and then at the leaves on the trees beginning to rustle in a light breeze.

'Hear that, Beth? It will be good landing weather for the next night or two. A full moon, clear skies and a light breeze. Ah well,' he sighed. 'I'll make one last crossing over to France to settle up with Ducroix.' He laughed. 'Perhaps I should keep one boat. What do you say? We could sail off in her; see where she takes us, just you and me. Perhaps we should sail across the sea and go and find John Grayling.'

He stood up and Beth also rose. He put his arms around her and held her very close. 'Did you say Will was at Lucas Webb's?' he asked into her curls, after a while. 'I'll go and find him there and tell him of my plans.'

Will, leading his newly-shod mares out of the smithy, took Arthur's news with a calmness which took his brother by surprise.

'But you do understand what I'm saying, Will? No more runs, ever?'

'Well of course I understand, Arty, you're the boss. What will we do instead?'

'I don't know, that's just it. Is there anything you'd like to do?'

Will shrugged and stopped to tighten the girth on one of the mares. 'I'll do whatever you suggest. I'll be able to keep my horses, I suppose? When will you tell the men?'

'I'll try and tell as many of them as I can in person. I suppose word will get round once I've told a few of them. So you don't mind, Will?' Arthur asked again trying to be sure of Will's feelings.

Will smiled. 'I'll miss the excitement and the rides up to London. But I'm sure you'll think of something for us Arthur.'

Arthur put his arm round Will's shoulder and realised perhaps fully for the first time that it was just as Beth had said - Will would always accede to his wishes and had a blind faith in Arthur's ability to lead them in the right course.

CHAPTER FORTY SEVEN

Government Offices, Whitehall, October 1746

Thomas Pelham Holles, the Duke of Newcastle, looked once more at the sheaf of letters he was holding in his hand. They were from John Collier, the Surveyor General of Riding Officers for Kent and from John Simon, the Solicitor to the Customs. The main topic of their correspondence was Arthur Gray and the Hawkhurst Gang. Collier asked for more men, Simon asked for arrests.

'Who is he, this Gray? Do we know?' the Duke asked the assembled ministers. Though his brother, Henry, was First Lord of the Treasury, Newcastle as Home Secretary had jurisdiction over all matters of imports and exports and more importantly, over the revenue raised from such activities.

'He's a nobody, sir,' Lord Lyttelton answered, little knowing that he had stood behind Arthur at Jonathan's coffee house, waiting to see Sampson Gideon, only some months ago.

'A nobody? For a nobody he seems to be causing us a great deal of trouble,' the Duke said crossly, scratching his head under his large wig. 'Henley, what can you tell us about tea? We reduced the duty didn't we, but it ain't made much difference according to Collier.'

Lord Henley, one of the younger ministers, turned in his chair to face the Home Secretary. 'Our figures such as they are, are not quite up to date,' he said apologetically. 'You will remember, your Grace, that the Tea Dealers sent a petition to Parliament in '36, avowing that half the tea in England paid no duty-,'

'Yes, yes, we know all that Henley,' the Duke said impatiently. 'And we brought in the Act of Indemnity hoping to put a stop to these smuggling rogues and here we are ten years on and apparently in no greater control than Walpole was then.'

Henley looked down at the table.

'Well, Harrington, have you any more recent figures? Did I not tax you with this task some weeks ago?' the Duke asked.

Earl Harrington nodded and gathered his papers together. 'Yes, Duke and I'm afraid it ain't pretty reading. It's thought that one and a half million pounds of tea are drunk in England each year, yet the Exchequer received duty on only about 650,000 pounds.'

Newcastle pressed his lips together, got up from his chair and paced the floor with his customary quick step. 'Gentlemen, I assume we can all do our sums? Then you must all see that we have more than half that again coming in by the back door.'

'Harrington, can you possibly mean that 850,000 pounds of tea are smuggled into the country each year?' Lord Chesterfield asked, aghast.

Harrington nodded. 'In fact, some say that is a conservative estimate. The East India Company assert that they knew of someone who claimed to smuggle in half a million pounds of tea each year, with his gang alone.'

Lord Chesterfield looked uncomfortably at the large silver tea pot on the tray in front of them. Newcastle noticed his glance and pushed his wig back on his head.

'Good God, Chesterfield, I hope you ain't thinking that this tea might have come in by the back door?'

Chesterfield met his gaze and then said haltingly, 'How can we be sure, Duke? Do you know where the housekeeper buys our tea?'

'How the devil would I know that?' Newcastle snapped. 'By Jove, this is some business. And yet apparently carried out by a Nobody. What is his parentage, where was he schooled? I'm sure my brother would like to have him in our Administration as soon as hang him!'

'Yet hang he must,' Lord Chesterfield said briskly. 'For he makes fools of all of us, aye he makes a fool of you, Duke, with every cup of tea that is drunk!'

'His father kept an alehouse as far as I can ascertain and drunk himself to death. Gray went to a charity school. He can probably barely read or write,' Henley said with an attempt at a sneer.

'Can barely read or write, yet deals in thousands of pounds' worth of goods and no doubt speaks to the Frenchies in their own tongue as well!' Newcastle looked purple with rage. 'Gentlemen, evidence I need and evidence must be got, do I make myself clear?'

Lord Lyttelton shifted uncomfortably in his chair. 'We have been wondering Duke, whether to try for treason.'

The Duke raised an eyebrow. 'Treason? How so? I had thought we had done with that.'

'It is said the smugglers carried many spies and traitors across to France last year,' Lyttelton explained.

'Well he will hang for both or either. Any other ideas?'

Lyttelton cleared his throat. 'We might try to convict him capitally for consorting with gypsies,' he said uneasily.

Newcastle looked across at him. 'Have you taken leave of your senses, Lyttelton?'

'Your Grace will remember it has been made a capital offence. We have an anonymous informant who says Gray and his brother consorted with gypsy women.'

Newcastle raised his eyes heavenward. 'It is a capital offence to set fire to a hayrick, Lyttelton but I don't believe it will make an example of Gray to hang him for so doing. No, no, I think a man like Gray deserves to suffer at Tyburn. It would be of great service to the country. But he must go down for smuggling. Where can we get witnesses?'

'Your Grace, it might be something of a problem,' Henley acknowledged. 'For since we passed the new Act last June carrying a capital conviction for smuggling, Gray don't seem to be doing much at all. He built himself a huge house in Hawkhurst and seems to spend most of his time there now.'

'Pretty little village down in Kent,' Earl Harrington mused. 'Went there once on my way to Eastbourne.'

'Enough of that, George,' Newcastle fumed. 'Gentlemen, what we need are witnesses to say they have seen him running goods since June of this year. I don't want the jury to send him to America instead of Tyburn! It will be a shame if this fellow ain't hanged just for want of evidence. Let us meet in a fortnight, gentleman where I hope to hear better from you. Meanwhile I shall write to Collier to say we can spare no more men while we have so many troops in Flanders and Mr Simon must wait for some witnesses to be found before we can arrest anyone!'

CHAPTER FORTY EIGHT

November 1746, Rye

Early in November Arthur set out for Rye, just as he sometimes set out for Lydd, or Dungeness or Camber. He couldn't break the habit of visiting the places where so much of his life and his attention over the past twenty five years or so had been spent. It was good to meet up with former members of the gang although he knew that sometimes his appearance gave them false hope. He had seen many a face light up with expectation when he appeared in one of the inns or alehouses the gang had formerly used - faces of men who hoped he might be bringing them word of another run, another chance to earn good money and to feel once again the pleasure of working together as a team with a common purpose and goals. He knew many of the men had fallen on hard times, relying on rough labouring or repairing walls for there was little enough work to be had on the farms in the winter months. He suspected some of them had fallen into petty crime, burglary and receiving stolen goods as a way to make ends meet.

He went into the *Two Brewers* and found Ben Raven, Robert Bunce and Jeremiah Curtis sitting at one of the tables. Ben looked up at Arthur, his face breaking into a smile. 'What's to do, Arthur?'

He drew up a chair and joined them. 'Nothing, Ben.'

'No plans, then?' Ben asked dejectedly.

Arthur shook his head. 'No. I really have given it up.'

Robert Bunce took a mouthful of ale. 'Never thought I'd live to see the day, Arthur.'

'No, I never thought of it either Robert, but it's a different game now. Just the four of us sitting here could be construed as assembling together for the purposes of running goods and we could all find ourselves at the end of a rope.'

They all looked very thoughtful as they drank. Just then there was a commotion at the door and they all looked round. Arthur at once recognised John Henley, Ned Henley's youngest brother. He was flushed and untidy, his coat and boots splattered with mud. Arthur and Ned had often worked together on runs from Folkestone and Arthur had a continued respect and affection for all three brothers because Ned's assistance had been pivotal in helping Arthur's men while they had been pinned down on Sandwich beach when the Wingham men had behaved so treacherously.

'Arthur, they said I would find you here. I've been in every alehouse in Rye I think.' He pulled a chair up to the table. 'I knew you would want to know.'

'Know what, John?' Arthur asked, signalling to the landlord to bring over some more ale.

John took a long sip before he spoke again. 'It's Ned. He's been taken.'

The men round the table groaned. Arthur rubbed his hands over his face. 'Where is he?' he asked quietly.

'They took him to Dover gaol last night and he's been taken straight up to Newgate today. Taken my brother in chains, the bastards!' He downed the rest of his ale and poured another.

Arthur thought to himself for a moment how he would feel if he had heard that Will had been taken. 'Has he been charged?' Arthur questioned.

John nodded. 'Under the '36 act. He hasn't run for two years, Arthur, you know that. He's opened a grocery shop. Half of Folkestone buys from him.'

It was true. Ned had retired on the proceeds of his smuggling activity and had invested a good deal of it into his large grocer's store.

'I don't understand it,' Ben Raven put in. ' If they've had the Act since '36, why are they only starting to use in now, ten years later?'

'They think we're scum and it's finally got to them that a lot us have been making money out of free trading. That's what they think we are, scum,' Arthur said severely. He turned to John. 'Where's Patrick?' he asked, referring to the middle Henley brother.

'Gone up to London. Ned asked him to get hold of Kelly. He's a good Irish Catholic attorney. Reckon he has the best chance with him. Ned says we should do whatever Kelly asks.'

'What are you going to do?' Arthur asked.

'I've brought Jennifer round to our house. My wife is looking after her. I must get back to them. Jen has taken it hard,' he said, referring to Ned's wife of twenty years. He stood up and reached out his hand towards Arthur.

Arthur also stood, grasped John's hand and gave a half smile. 'If I can do anything, John-,'

John Henley nodded. 'I know, Arthur. I'll be sure to let you know.'

His exit and the news he had brought cast further gloom over the table. They finished their drinks and made their way out.

CHAPTER FORTY NINE

January 1747 Rye

Arthur, walking down Longer Street in late October saw Harriett Marshall on the other side of the road and crossed to speak to her. He hadn't noticed at first that she was with another woman. When he caught up with them, they turned round to face him on hearing his greeting, and he saw she was accompanied by her younger daughter Alice. Though Alice was wearing a heavy cloak, it was obvious that she was heavily pregnant.

'Arthur,' Harriett said, a smile on her pinched face. 'It's good to see you.'

'You too, Harriett and you Alice,' he nodded, not making reference to her pregnancy. 'Can I buy you some refreshments?' he asked. 'Let me at least help you with those bundles.'

Harriett and Alice had been collecting the bundles of washing that Harriett still took in. The women gratefully handed him the heavy burdens, Alice sighing with relief and putting a hand to her back. They turned into the *George* where Arthur went to the bar and ordered some ale and plates of hot buttered wheat dressed with cinnamon. He joined them in the little alcove they had chosen. 'I hear Elizabeth was married in the autumn,' he said, sitting next to Harriett.

She nodded and smiled. 'Yes, they have a nice room at the *Two Brewers*. I see her most every day. She's Mrs Dowdy now and expecting her first in the summer.'

'Though it seems as though you'll be a grandmother before then,' Arthur said gently, indicating Alice. Alice looked down at her plate.

Harriett touched her arm and turned to Arthur. 'Yes, God willing, this baby will arrive any day now, won't it Alice?'

Alice looked quickly at her mother and nodded.

'It's Curtis's child,' Harriett said. 'Left her as soon as she started to show.'

Arthur put his tankard down. 'But he surely acknowledges the child as his? He will be responsible for its upkeep?'

Harriett shook her head. 'He ain't had nothing to do with her since. She'll have to have a bastardy examination before the Jurats,' she said and then turned to her daughter, 'and then you must name him, Alice. Tell her Arthur, that it is so.'

'Don't talk about me as if I wasn't here, mother,' Alice said sharply.

'But what your mother says is true, Alice,' Arthur agreed. 'If it's Curtis's child, then the Jurats will expect him to make provision for it. He ain't a poor man, after all.'

Alice looked uncomfortable. 'He says he will deny it,' she said miserably.

Harriett looked shocked. 'You never told me that, Alice,' she said. 'How can he deny it? Any number of people knew you were always in his rooms. Enough people made it their business to tell me.'

'He never suggested marriage, I suppose?' Arthur asked.

Alice sighed and shook her head.

It was difficult to know what to say so they turned to other subjects and when they had finished eating, Harriett got up and helped Alice to her feet. Arthur picked up the washing and walked with them towards Watchbell Lane. Before they were halfway there, Alice stopped with a sharp cry and put her hand on her mother's shoulder. 'Oh Mumma,' she said. 'I think I have wetted myself, Mumma!'

Harriett moved her daughter a little way to the side and saw the puddle under her feet. She gave a short laugh. 'No, that's your waters broken, Alice. Should signify a quick birth, so come on, let's get you home.'

Arthur had looked away but turned back looking at Harriett.

'If you would kindly give Alice your arm, Arthur, we will get her home and you can be on your way. I hardly like to ask you. If you don't mind that is?'

'No, no of course not. Whatever you say. Alice, lean on me and we'll be home in a moment and your mamma can look after you.'

They set off again, but had to stop when another pain racked through Alice's body and she leaned against Arthur and her mother. Arthur was glad when they reached the house and Harriett quickly took out her key helping her daughter along the passage and into the bedroom as Arthur waited in the hallway.

'Can I fetch the midwife for you, Harriett?' Arthur asked, anxious to be off.

Harriett looked over at him and smiled. 'I can't afford the midwife, Arthur. No, I can manage. Rachel Spain said she would come. I'd be grateful if you would call on her and ask her to come round. She'll be at Mr Lamb's. Since Mrs Lamb died, she's been going in as a daily housekeeper. Her Robert still works for Mr Lamb. I'm sorry, Arthur, here am I assuming I can ask you to act as a messenger-,'

Arthur nodded and cut her short. 'Nonsense, we're old friends, ain't we? I'll send her round as soon as I can. Good luck.'

Harriett smiled as Arthur went down to the narrow hallway and she turned into the other bedroom, where Alice was groaning with another contraction.

Arthur, glad to be out of the house and away from the women's work going on inside, set off for Conduit Hill. He had only once visited Lamb at his house before and that was very recently, last September after Mrs Lamb's funeral. However today his business was with Rachel. Arthur had always had a respect and gratitude for Robert Spain and his wife for the way they had looked after him so long ago after John Turner had given him a beating. He hadn't seen Thomas Lamb since the funeral and for the first time on that occasion, he had realised that Lamb was an elderly man.

Arthur decided to go round to the garden door since his business was with Rachel Spain and not with Lamb himself so he was surprised when he knocked at the door and Lamb answered it.

'I'm sorry, sir,' he apologised. 'I didn't think I would disturb you. I've come with a message for Mrs Spain. I'm told she's here today.'

'Rachel? Yes she's upstairs sorting out my linen I believe, Arthur. There's no trouble for her is there? Come in,' he said holding the door open.

Arthur removed his hat and wiped his boots. 'No, no trouble. It's just that her friend, Mrs Marshall has asked her to call round. Harriett's daughter is in labour and Rachel has promised to assist. I'm merely the messenger.'

'Oh, everything must take second place if a new life is about to enter the world,' Lamb said and called up the stairs to Rachel. 'I believe she has set the teapot out on a tray. I would take it as a kindness if you would share it with me. Dorcas and I would normally take a cup at this time,' he said sadly.

'That's very kind of you,' Arthur replied, 'but let me carry the tray in, sir.' He picked it up and followed Lamb through to the back parlour and set it on a table as Rachel came down the stairs.

'Here's Arthur come with a message for you, Rachel.'

'My message is from Harriett Marshall, Rachel. Alice has stated her labour pains and Harriett says you had agreed to assist her,' Arthur explained.

Rachel looked across at Thomas Lamb. 'May I go, sir? I'll finish the linen tomorrow if I may?'

'Yes, yes, go along, quick as you can. Take as long as you need. I shall tell Robert where you are when he gets back.'

'Thank you, sir,' she said, pulling off her apron and disappearing into the kitchen.

Arthur turned back to the table and poured out two cups of tea and passed one over to the old man. 'It's a sad business, Mr Lamb. Alice is a good girl at heart but she's been let down. Not that I think the man ever promised marriage, but he's deserted her now.'

Lamb shook his head, looking thoughtful. 'Perhaps he is already wed to another,' he suggested.

'Oh no, I know he ain't. It's Jeremiah Curtis who's done Alice wrong. I wouldn't normally name another man, for it's his businesses after all and none of us is innocent, but I have a kindness for Alice's mother, Harriett. She's always worked hard and has had a difficult life.'

Lamb looked up, alert. 'Curtis? Are you sure?'

'Oh yes,' Arthur said, drinking his tea. 'Alice was forever in his rooms. He never tried to hide it at the time, but now he denies the child is his, so Alice will go up before the Jurats with her bastard, no doubt.'

Lamb shook his head. 'Poor child. And you're certain of Curtis's involvement?'

Arthur nodded again. 'But enough of that sir. How are you?'

Lamb took a sip of tea. 'Oh, missing my wife, Arthur. I was married at eighteen you know, a little like you, I think. At that age you grow up with your wife.' He looked around the room and nodded towards a portrait on the wall. It was of Lamb's wife when she was a young woman. 'I like to take my tea in here, with her portrait. You will think me foolish, but I find myself talking to her.'

Arthur shook his head and said gently, 'Not foolish at all, sir. You'd been companions many years, after all.' He finished his tea and rose to leave, Lamb escorting him through to the handsome narrow hallway and opening the front door for him.

As soon as he had said goodbye to Arthur, he went back into the parlour and looked up at the portrait of his wife. 'Well, my dear, it cannot hurt you now and I am going to do something I should have done a long time ago.'

With that he went back into the hallway, putting on his hat and coat. He picked up his stick and set out down the hill towards Longer Street.

Lamb tapped on the door of Curtis's lodgings with his stick. There was no reply and he stepped back into the street to raise his head to look up at the windows to see whether there was any sign of Curtis's presence. He tapped again and this time he heard the sound of the window sash being opened as Curtis's head appeared.

He looked down into the street and seemed surprised to see Thomas Lamb standing there.

'Well?' he asked turning back to the room and Lamb heard Curtis talking to whoever was in there with him. He put his head out again. 'What can I do for you?'

Lamb called up to him. 'Some moments of your time, if you please. A matter of some importance.'

Curtis withdrew his head and banged the window shut. A few moments later, Lamb heard footsteps coming down the stairs inside and a female voice. The door opened and a girl pushed passed Lamb, giggling as she called back to Curtis, 'Til tonight then, darling.' She pulled her cloak tighter round her and blew a kiss before turning down the street.

Curtis stood in the hallway, doing up his jacket and tying back his hair in its riband. He gave a nod of his head indicating that Lamb should follow him and Lamb found himself climbing a staircase that he had not climbed for some thirty six years. He followed Curtis into the larger of the two rooms on the first floor. There was a fire burning in the hearth and the bed was dishevelled. Lamb was in no doubt that Curtis and his latest paramour had vacated it in order to open the door to him. Curtis sat down on one of the chairs in front of the fire drawing one leg across the other and clasping the ankle. He indicated that Lamb should sit opposite him.

'I'm sure you have a good reason for coming here, Lamb but I ain't got a clue what it might be, so hurry up will you?' He opened a decanter and poured himself a glass of brandy, holding the bottle up to Lamb. Lamb nodded and Curtis poured another glass holding it out to him. The old man took a mouthful and then put his hand in his pocket and drew something out of it. He held it out to Curtis. Curtis looked at him for a moment, his interest caught and he lent forward holding out his hand. Lamb dropped into his open palm a gold necklace with a heavy pendant hanging from it.

Curtis held it and putting down his glass, turned the pendant over to reveal a miniature of a young dark-haired woman. He shrugged. 'So?'

'Look more closely, Curtis,' Lamb requested.

Curtis did as he was asked and then ran his tongue over his suddenly dry lips. He screwed up his eyebrows into a frown. 'Why have you a painting of my mother?' he asked.

Lamb looked at him for a moment. 'Maria Curtis rented this room when she left my employment in 1711,' he said, his watery blue eyes staring straight at Curtis's dark ones.

'I was born in 1711,' Curtis said.

'Yes. When she left my employment she was with child. I commissioned that miniature myself.'

Curtis looked at Lamb, not seeing the obvious.

'Your mother was a pretty woman, Jeremiah. You have her dark eyes, but I think the line of your brow and your nose come from me,' Lamb said his voice a little unsteady.

Curtis's mouth dropped open. He looked at the miniature again. 'Are you telling me that I am your son?'

Lamb nodded. Curtis sprang up and went over to the window. He stood there in silence for a while. 'And you have watched me these thirty six years and not once acknowledged me?'

Lamb flinched at his words. 'It is only because my wife is now dead that I am able to do so. I would never dishonour her while she lived. She could never have children. It would have been a double insult.'

'You thought nothing of dishonouring my mother, though.'

Lamb closed his eyes, reliving a moment so long ago when pretty dark-haired Maria Curtis, his maidservant, had stood before him in the front parlour of his house in Conduit Hill, weeping as she told him she was bearing his child.

He opened his eyes. 'I've done what I could for you, Jeremiah. I provided for you both while your mother was alive and have continued to provide for you since her death. Your allowance has been placed monthly with your attorney. As my wealth has increased, so has your allowance.'

'My allowance?' Curtis's eyes flashed in anger. 'You talk of my *allowance* when I am your only son? Everything you have should be mine.'

Lamb remained silent. Curtis continued to pace the room. 'I live in these two rooms and you have that large house in Conduit Hill! I've been known as a bastard all my life because of you. Why did my mother never tell me? Why didn't she make it publicly known?'

'She was a modest girl, Jeremiah. She was willing to accept what I could offer her and never berated me for not giving her what I could not. She never had to work after you were born. She chose to do a little sewing to fill her time, but you and she lived in comfort here, did you not?'

'Comfort?' Curtis flung at him. 'What is *comfort* compared to the riches you have surrounded yourself with?' He poured himself another drink as more thoughts crowded in on him. 'My God! You've bankrolled Arthur Gray above me. You've shown him preferment all his life. The son of a gin-soaked publican above your own son? By Christ, this takes some stomaching I can tell you! I never liked him and now I have another good reason to hate him. And you! Why shouldn't I shame you in this town now? I swear this story will be all over Rye by this evening. Where will your standing be then?'

'I've told you, Jeremiah, there is only one person I wished to protect by keeping this secret and she is now in a place where the truth can't hurt her. I'm an old man, Jeremiah. I'm not a young man anxious to set up in business and careful of my reputation. What information you care to put about in this town can't hurt me. But one thing I will have made public knowledge in Rye. At this very moment, your own child is being brought into the world. You have no wife that can be hurt by such a revelation. I wish you to acknowledge this child as yours, yes, and support it, too.'

Curtis gave a short laugh. 'By God, this is rich, coming from you. Perhaps in thirty-six years I might decide to pay a visit to my bastard. By what right do you think you can ask this of me? You haven't taught me morals for the last thirty six years. A bit late to try now.'

Lamb's hand tightened on the arm of the chair. 'I spared your mother the indignity of going through a bastardy examination in front of the Jurats, by setting her up financially so neither she nor you would ever be a drain on the finances of this town.'

'Yes and spared yourself the possibility of her naming you as the father,' Curtis put in quickly.

'I don't deny it,' Lamb said steadily. 'But I expect you to do the same for Alice Marshall and her baby.'

Curtis flung himself back down in the seat. 'Why should I acknowledge that little trollop? She couldn't wait to get on her back. She used to hang around my rooms all hours of the day and night panting for me to lift her skirts. She gave up her job on the off chance I might fuck her now and again. I've used her many times bent over that chair you're sitting in, with her waggling her arse in the air and begging me to take her. Or are you so old you've forgotten what it's like to have a woman hot for you like a bitch on heat?'

Lamb stood up stiffly. 'Can you never speak of a woman except in these disgusting terms?' he asked.

Curtis shrugged. 'Why not? They're all the same, ain't they? All got an itch they want scratching, but some are itchier than most and little Alice is one of 'em. If you were thirty years younger, she'd have caught your eye I've no doubt.'

Lamb remained silent and then picked up his hat. 'So you will not acknowledge the child?'

Curtis looked across at him. 'What will you do if I don't? Stop my allowance?'

Lamb shook his head. 'No, I don't deal in blackmail, Jeremiah. I thought I could appeal to your better nature. I promised your mother I would support you financially and I will. No, since you refuse to take any responsibility, anything I do for your child will be done in my own name not in yours.'

Curtis shrugged again. 'Perhaps it will die and spare you the trouble.'

Lamb shook his head sadly and crossed the room to the door. He looked once more at Curtis before he left. 'We could have done better than this, my son.'

Curtis sneered. 'Thirty years ago, perhaps. Push the door shut on your way out, won't you?'

Fifteen minutes later, Lamb reached his own front door and found his hand was shaking as he tried to put the key in the lock. He made such a noise pushing the key in this way and that, that Robert Spain, puzzled by the noise came into the passageway and was surprised to find his master there as he opened the door.

'Are you not well, sir?' he asked sharply seeing how pale the old man looked.

'A little wine, Robert, if you please, in the parlour,' he said in reply, passing his hat to his manservant.

Robert watched him with concern as he went unsteadily down the passageway and into the parlour. Robert heard him sigh as he sank into a chair and he followed his master in. He poured the red wine into a fine glass and watched as Lamb took a mouthful.

'Take a drink with me, Robert,' he said, 'and sit down a while.'

Lamb had often invited Robert to share a drink with him, since Mrs Lamb had died. He knew the old man missed her sorely. He poured himself half a glass and sat opposite his master, waiting for him to speak.

'Rachel has gone out,' Lamb said at length. Robert nodded.

'She was called to go to Harriett Marshall's rooms. Her daughter Alice is in labour and your wife is helping.'

Robert nodded again, wondering why this should affect his master so much.

'When your wife returns be sure to come and tell me about the babe, will you?'

Robert shrugged his shoulders. 'Yes, of course, sir if that is what you wish.'

'Yes, Robert,' Lamb said, closing his eyes as the effect of the rich wine on top of the glass of brandy began to have a soporific effect and was dispelling the hammering feeling in his chest he had felt since his distressing conversation with his son. It was time anyway for his usual afternoon nap. 'Yes, Robert,' he repeated, 'that is what I wish.'

After leaving Lamb's house towards ten at night Robert went first to Watchbell Lane to see what progress was being made. He tapped on the door and after a few moments, he heard the lock being turned and Rachel stood there, her sleeves rolled up, her hair escaping from her cap. He took her in his arms and kissed her. He nodded towards the two back rooms, as a groan sounded from one of them. 'How are things going, Rach?'

'Slowly, Robert. I shan't be home til morning I shouldn't think. This baby is taking its time coming. Still they all take their own time and there's nothing to be done about it. Do you remember our first three coming so fast, I was barely laid down on the bed before they appeared and then little Robin taking nearly two days?'

He smiled at the memory. 'So you're sure you won't be able to get back? All this talk of babies makes me want to make another with you tonight!'

She kissed him on the nose and pushed him towards the door, as another shriek came from the back room. 'Be off with you, Rob,' she laughed slowly.

He stepped reluctantly out of the door and turned back to his wife. 'Lamb wants to be told about the babe, Rach,' he said. 'Now why do you think that is?'

'I can't think. Maybe he likes babies,' Rachel replied.

'You don't think Harriett was one of Lamb's old paramours, do you?' he asked.

She gave a little laugh. 'No, Harriett's been my best friend for years. Apart from Arthur Gray, she never had any other lovers. I know she would have told me. Now get off home, Rob,' she ordered. 'There's a fish pie in the cupboard, for your supper. I'll see you tomorrow,' and she turned back, going into the bedroom and took over from Harriett, who was rubbing Alice's back to ease the pains, as she lay on her side clutching a pillow to her breasts when each contraction racked her body.

A week later, Harriett came back into her bedroom carrying a large bucket full of cheap coal. She pulled the door shut behind her for there was a cold draught blowing along the passage and she didn't want the baby to take a chill. She was about to tell Alice that it had begun to snow, when she looked down at the chair where her daughter was sitting in front of the fire, her feet resting on an old stool. She had evidently fallen asleep suckling the baby for she lay back in the chair, her head to one side, still holding the baby gently, her gown unlaced. The baby was asleep too, with the contented look of the infant who had drunk his fill at his mother's breast, the nipple pressed against his cheek, a drop of pearly milk still formed at its tip and another at the corner of the baby's mouth.

Harriett quietly lowered the bucket of coal to the floor and gently picked the baby up. He stirred softly in her arms, his small solid weight comfortable against Harriett's own breast. Alice woke and looked at her mother with confused eyes. Then they cleared and she was about to speak when Harriett put her finger over her daughter's lips.

'Shh, he's sleeping. I'll put him in the cradle. I've made some soup. It's ready in the other room. Go and eat it while he's quiet. You need to keep your strength up so you have enough milk for the greedy little man.'

Just then there was a determined knocking at the front door and the baby immediately woke, his face transformed from pink serenity to an angry red as he began to wail.

'Now who can that be?' Harriett said crossly. 'It's probably for someone upstairs and not for us at all. You go and see Alice and I'll see if I can get him off again. Do your laces up,' she said quickly, nodding at Alice's open gown.

She went into her second room, with its lines of drying linen, to the small table at the far end. She walked around the table jogging the baby gently in her arms and making up a little song singing it close to his soft pink ear. A few moments later she looked up and was surprised to see Alice come into the room looking rather nervous, followed by Thomas Lamb, his hat in one hand and a large basket in the other.

'Mrs Marshall, do forgive my intrusion. Ah, there he is.'

He was looking at the baby lying across Harriett's shoulder. 'A fine boy, I hear. Yes, yes, it's true, he is fine indeed. And so big.'

Harriett had no idea why he had called, thinking it must have something to do with the fact that Rachel was his housekeeper but she immediately warmed towards anyone who agreed with her that her grandson was the finest baby ever born. Lamb looked across at Alice and could see why Jeremiah had been attracted, for her full red lips were full of promise, a contrast with her soft brown eyes which looked frightened and as though tears might form in them at any moment. 'And you, my dear, how are you?'

She gave a little bow. 'I'm very well, sir, thank you.'

Harriett, aware that Mr Lamb was standing with a linen sheet almost flapping at his shoulders, drew out a chair. 'Would you like to sit down, sir?' she asked.

He noticed the two bowls of soup on the table and the hunk of bread. 'I've interrupted your meal. I'm sorry.'

438 • Mary-Elizabeth Thomas

'No, not at all,' Harriett said scooping up the bowls and pouring the soup back into the pan by the fire. 'Can I offer you some ale sir, heated with a little cinnamon?'

'Well do you know, Mrs Marshall, that sounds just the sort of thing I should like very much?' He took his seat and watched as Harriett handed the baby back to Alice who sat down with him. The baby, smelling his own mother, instinctively turned his small mouth to her bosom and started making sucking movements with his mouth. Alice laughed nervously and put her little finger in his mouth to comfort him. Harriett set the mugs of ale on the table and all three began to drink the spicy warming liquid.

At length Thomas Lamb put his mug down and looked across at Harriett. 'You must be wondering why I'm here.'

She said nothing but nodded slightly. Lamb looked at Alice.

'Forgive me for speaking plainly, Miss Marshall, or may I call you Alice?'

Alice nodded. She knew he belonged to the most influential family in Rye, brother to James Lamb who was the Mayor and she wondered if this was how the process of bastardy examination began, when she would be questioned under oath about her pregnancy and the identity of the father. She would likely be set to work somewhere in order to pay for the upkeep of the child.

'I believe the father of this child is known to you but that he denies it is his?' Lamb asked, scanning her face.

She nodded anxiously. Alice's hand went instinctively to her mother's and clutched it. Lamb hastily delved into the basket by his side and pulled out a small leather bound bible. He looked straight at Alice with his pale eyes. 'Do you swear to me on this child's soul and on the Holy Scriptures that this is Jeremiah Curtis's son? And that there is no possibility of it's being any other man's?'

Alice looked at her mother, her bottom lip trembling. Harriett nodded at her. 'Tell the truth, Alice.'

Alice nodded and placed her hand on the bible. 'He is Jeremiah Curtis's son. I have known no other man, whatever he may say. And I swear this on my baby's soul.'

Lamb continued to look at her and then he put his hand over hers on the bible. 'May I hold the little one?'

Alice again looked at her mother, still fearful that this was some official ritual and that Mr Lamb was planning to take the child from her and place it with some rich couple who could not have children. She cried out on a sob, 'Don't take him away from me, sir! I'll find work and support him. I won't become a burden on the town, only don't take him.'

Harriett catching her daughter's nerves, suddenly fearful, scooped the baby from Alice. 'I work, Mr Lamb, I've always worked hard. I can get another job, take in more washing. I can look after them both.'

Lamb, aghast at the unintended effect of his words looked at both women, pale and frightened, the one thin, pinched, probably old before her time, the other still with the beauty of youth, voluptuous yet vulnerable and both fearful that the most precious possession in these poor bare rooms was about to be snatched from them. 'Forgive me, ladies. I had no intention of frightening you. I have not come here to take this precious babe from you. But my visit does concern him. Please, sit down, Mrs Marshall. Make yourself calm, Alice.'

The two women faced him.

'There is nothing more innocent than a new born babe,' he began. 'Yet their arrival is often the end result of crimes or misdemeanours and I fear this little one is no exception. He has not the benefit of a father who is married to his mother and it was the same for Jeremiah Curtis. I do not know how much of Jeremiah's present condition may be laid at that door, but I would not wish it to happen again to this little one.'

Harriett and Alice were looking at him as though he were speaking in riddles.

'This little babe is my grandson,' he announced, a slight tremor in his voice. 'Jeremiah Curtis is my son. I have tried to persuade him to acknowledge this boy and provide for him, but he chooses not to. It is therefore my responsibility and my pleasure and would very much be my honour, if you would allow me to acknowledge him and provide for him.'

Alice let out a little sigh of disbelief. Harriett feeling her knees go weak, dropped to a chair.

'You don't mean to take him away from me sir, to live with you?' Alice asked in a small voice.

Lamb shook his head. 'Take him away from his loving mother? How would that serve him? No, Alice. I would like you, that is,' he corrected himself, 'I would count it a privilege if you and your mother would come and live with me.'

Harriett drew in her breath and her eyes narrowed. She was not clear what exactly was being offered or expected.

Lamb saw her concern. 'Forgive me Mrs Marshall, I've spoken clumsily. I mean no disrespect to either of you. Your friend Mrs Spain is a daily housekeeper to me. I've asked my brother James if he will take her on as his housekeeper and I should like to offer her vacant position to you, Mrs Marshall. Alice, I thought you might like to sew my linen for me. However, you may do as much or as little as you choose. I shall pay you the same whatever you do. But I would like this young man,' he indicated the baby in Harriett's arms, 'to be brought up as my grandson, legitimate or not. My will shall be changed in his favour, no matter what you decide but I do so hope you will both agree. What do you say?'

Mother and daughter looked at each other across the table. Then Alice crossed round the table and fell into her mother's arms sobbing. Harriett had to purse her lips very hard not to join her.

Alice started to shake her head. 'I can't believe it, Mumma. I can't believe it. My boy to be a gentleman? Yes, Mr Lamb, oh yes, please.'

At this Harriett also started to weep and Lamb too had to make use of his lace handkerchief to dab at his eye.

'May I hold him, now?' Lamb asked and Harriett passed the baby to Alice to give to his grandfather. For only the third time in his life, Thomas Lamb held a child to his breast that was his direct descendent. The baby, aware of a new strange smell and the hard press of a man's chest against him, where he was used to the softness of women, started to wail and emptied his bladder. Lamb started to laugh as he felt the warm liquid against his coat. 'That's right, little man. Wet your silly old grandfather's coat. I have another after all. What do you think of all this, my little lad, eh? Alice, if you please, open the rush basket I have brought with me. I have been shopping, hopeful of this outcome. I have brought my grandson some gifts.'

Alice, laughing and crying at the same time, lifted the basket to the table pulling out a silver rattle, a little silver cup and spoon, a soft wool blanket and a little white silk cap with lace strings. 'Look, Mumma. Look at all his things.'

As Alice held out her arms to take the wailing baby, Lamb smiled warmly at her. 'What have you called him? Has he been baptised?'

Alice shook her head. 'Not yet, sir. His name is James Marshall.'

Lamb nodded, gently touching the baby's cheek. 'Then I should be very honoured if he may be baptised James Thomas Lamb Marshall.'

CHAPTER FIFTY

February 11th 1747, Aylesford, then Hawkhurst

Arthur rode back to Seacox from Aylesford towards five in the evening. It had been a clear, bright day, with a watery sun doing its best to shine. He had spent the morning looking over some ploughing instruments, still intending to set Will up with a farm, but had found it difficult to raise much interest in the relative merits of one appliance over the other.

Then he waited at the *George* from noon onwards for it was the day of Ned Henley's trial and his brother Patrick had promised Arthur he would ride back from London as soon as there was any news, breaking his journey at Aylesford. Deb had gone visiting, so Henry French brought a chair up to Arthur's table and joined him in a mug of ale. Arthur's mind could not settle to anything and when they heard a horse canter up, Arthur pushed his chair away from the table and went out into the yard. As soon as he saw Patrick Henley's face, he knew the news was good. Patrick drew his horse to a sudden halt, took off his hat and waved it in the air, seeing Arthur.

'Praise all the saints! Acquitted! Acquitted! Jesus, Mary and Joseph, thanks be. Thanks be.'

He almost fell off his horse into Arthur's arms as he clapped him on the back. Henley had stood in danger of being transported for seven years if he had been found guilty.

Patrick's face was wreathed in smiles as they entered the taproom. 'Line up the drinks, Henry, there's a good man, for I've a powerful thirst on me. Acquitted! Free as a bird.' He kept an arm over Arthur's shoulder as they made their way to the table. 'Kelly, the attorney, he's a powerful good speaker Arthur. Had them in knots. Tied the other witnesses up so in the end they were all arguing against each other.'

'But where is Ned, Patrick? Is he released?'

Patrick nodded, looking up from his drink. 'Walked free straight away. Jennifer was staying up in London so she has taken him off. They'll be back tomorrow I've no doubt. There's sure to be some celebrating in Folkestone tomorrow night. Every Irishman for miles around will have free drinks, that's for sure. Will you be down yourself, Arthur?'

Arthur shook his head. He had promised Harriett as well as Thomas Lamb that he would attend their grandson's baptism down in Rye the following day and though he would have liked to celebrate Ned's freedom, he felt he could not let them down. 'No, I can't be there. But tell him I'll catch up with him as soon as I can. Now, let me buy you another drink.'

Back at Seacox, Arthur led Peg round to the stables and found Jim Cook there saddling up his own mare. Jim had stayed on at Seacox carrying out all sorts of jobs around the house and land. Cook was well wrapped up and Arthur greeted him. 'Where are you off to, Jim? You look as though you're dressed for the cold.' He indicated Jim's thick muffler and heavy coat and boots.

To his surprise Jim looked nervous. 'Oh, I'll be away til morning, Arthur,' he said.

Arthur turned to lead Peg into the stable then immediately swung round. It suddenly dawned on him that Jim was going out on a run. 'Jim, are you mad? You're running tonight aren't you? That's why you're dressed as we used to.'

Jim looked anxious and then his face changed to one of eagerness. 'Yes, Arthur, the *Old Molly*'s coming over from Calais full of brandy and wine, tea too. She's landing at Folkestone Warren. Why don't you come?'

Arthur paused for a moment, the hairs at the back of his neck bristling with anticipation. He thought of the anxious wait on the beach, the men's easy camaraderie, the relief when the blue flash signalled and then the business of unloading and running the goods across the county and up to London. Nothing in his life excited him as much. For half a moment he stood rooted to the spot and then he shook his head. 'No Jim, I've given up and I mean to stick to it. I thought you had too.'

'The word's got round already that Henley got off,' Jim said encouragingly. 'No one will convict us, Arthur. We're too strong.'

Arthur dug his hands into his pockets. 'Ned was lucky. He was charged for running under the Act of '36 because he hasn't run since this new Act. But if you're caught now Jim, they'll charge you under it, I've no doubt and the penalty is hanging, no questions asked.'

'But you got to be found guilty first, Arthur, ain't you?' Jim asked.

Arthur nodded, patting Jim Cook's mare as she shied a little. 'Yes, but it ain't like the local Assizes where our own people look kindly on us. You would most likely be taken up to the Old Bailey where the jurors are London men who know nothing of us. Come back inside, Jim.'

Jim shook his head. 'I can't, Arthur. It's the only thing I know.'

Arthur looked down at the ground and then up again at Cook. 'Who else is going?'

'Dick Mapesden, Robert Bunce, Sam Austin, Tom Fuller, the Kingsmills, about thirty of us. Are you sure you won't come?'

Arthur shook his head again. Bunce was nearing sixty. He had known no other life than smuggling. Arthur felt the burden of depriving so many men of the only way of making a living they had ever known, by giving up his effective leadership. 'No, I shan't ever run goods again. But you have a job here, Jim. You don't need another income.'

Cook nodded. 'I know that and I'm grateful for what you pay me. But I just can't stop. Nor can most of the others. What else would they do?'

Arthur sighed. 'If you're intent on going, I can only ask you to take care.'

Jim gave a little nod of his head, dug his heels into his mare's flanks and rode off.

Arthur set off the next day and rode into Hawkhurst to call on Will and Beth who were to accompany him to Rye for the baptism of Alice's baby. Sarah had chosen not to go. She was not a keen horsewoman at the best of times and the road to Rye in February could be muddy and wet. Arthur couldn't quite shake off the lowness of spirits he had felt since talking with Jim the day before. He despaired that his men were prepared to risk their lives by running goods. The elation he had felt yesterday at Ned Henley's acquittal had dissolved.

Saladin, Will's great stallion was snorting and pawing the ground, anxious to be off as soon as he felt the saddle on his back. Beth warmly dressed in brown and gold was already seated on her gentle Prue.

Arthur looked across Beth to Will. 'You won't go on any more runs, Will?'

Will, tightening the reins, looked up surprised. 'No Arty, of course not. We've finished, ain't we? Why do you ask?'

They set off down the Moor.

'Some of the men are still running.'

'Oh surely not?' Beth interrupted. 'Not with the risk of hanging?'

Arthur nodded. 'Yes, there was a run last night. Jim Cook went.'

'I ain't saying I don't miss it,' Will put in. 'But it wouldn't be the same, not if you weren't in charge and I wouldn't go without you.'

'Well I ain't going again, so that's settled.' Arthur sighed and then said more brightly, 'I looked at some ploughs yesterday, Will.'

'Did you, though?' Will asked.

Arthur grinned. 'Yes, for you. For your farm.'

'Oh, right,' he responded. 'Now the road is clear, do you fancy a gallop Beth? Arthur?'

Arthur looked at Beth and raised his eyebrows and then all three of them urged their horses faster and they went galloping down the wide track that would lead them to Rye.

An hour later, they were making their way from the *George*, where they had left their horses, to St Mary's Church. When they turned the corner of Longer Street they found themselves facing Jeremiah Curtis and a young woman, his arm thrown carelessly round her shoulders. Curtis stopped in his tracks.

'The Church is this way, Curtis,' Arthur said.

'Why would I want the Church?' he asked languidly.

'Alice Marshall's baby is being baptised,' Arthur replied meeting Jeremiah's gaze.

An annoyed flush coloured Curtis's cheeks momentarily. He shrugged. 'So? Ain't nothing to do with me.'

'How can you ignore your responsibilities, Jeremiah?' Beth asked indignantly.

'Why do you believe a little trollop's word over mine, Beth?' he questioned. 'That's what she is, however much she might protest her innocence. That's what a trollop is, ain't it, Will? A woman who don't care how many men she lets into her bed?'

Will took a step forward, but Arthur put his arm on his brother's shoulder. 'Lamb has accepted him as your child,' Arthur challenged.

The news that Lamb was Curtis's father had spread around Rye. It made gossip for a day or two, but it was felt to be old news from the past without much effect on the present. Though Thomas Lamb was part of the most influential family, he had never sought public office and his good nature and pleasant personality had won him many friends over the years who weren't prepared to criticise him for any folly committed in his younger days. They had seen his genuine sorrow at his wife's funeral and only the most die-hard moralists would condemn him.

Arthur had heard the news direct from Lamb himself a couple of days after Thomas had told Jeremiah. He was shocked at first and then felt even more gratitude for Lamb's kindness to himself. Lamb had never shown any favouritism to Jeremiah over himself and when Lamb explained that he had been financially supporting his son since his birth, Arthur realised why Curtis had never been as desperate to join in every run as Arthur had been. He could always depend on a secured income away from the gang.

He looked at Jeremiah's sneering face now and wondered why he had not seemed to inherit any of his father's affability.

'If Lamb accepts the child, more fool him,' Curtis said. 'He can afford to look after it. Come on, Evie,' he said to the young woman at his side. 'We've better things to do than gossip on street corners.' And he took her arm and guided her away.

After the baptism, as the little party made its way back to Lamb's house on Conduit Hill, Harriett shyly approached Arthur, walking next to Will and Beth. He offered her his arm.

'Well, Harriett, it's strange how things turn out, isn't it?'

Harriett looked up at him fondly. 'I would never have believed it, Arthur, not in a thousand years. Alice is still shy of Mr Lamb, but he is as kind as can be and dotes so on little James.'

Arthur laughed down at her. 'I've no doubt he'll be thoroughly spoiled.'

'No, it's not possible to love a child too much,' Harriett said, smiling. 'You don't know how good it feels to have a boy in the house again and such a fine house.'

'It's time you had some good luck,' Arthur replied warmly. 'I do believe you've put on some weight. Your cheeks are looking quite rounded. And surely that's a new way of doing your hair, with those curls at the front?'

Harriett blushed. 'I have more time, these days. I used to have my hair like this long ago when I was first married. It does take some time. It used to be easier just to scrape it back with a comb. But Mr Lamb isn't a hard taskmaster by any means. Sometimes all my work is finished by one o' clock and I'm at liberty to sit with Alice and the boy. I don't think I've eaten so well in my life.'

Arthur smiled again and patted her hand resting on his arm. 'Well the life suits you and I'm glad of it for you.'

'I never thought to have so many blessings. My only sadness is never hearing from James.' She paused for a moment. 'I like to think he is happy somewhere, Arthur, even though he never contacts me. Do you think that it is possible?'

'I'm sure of it, Harriett,' Arthur said swiftly. 'He probably found work further in land and so hasn't been able to return his half of the coin by boat.'

They both knew that if James wished to, he could easily have written a letter to his mother but such thoughts were best left unsaid. Better to think, as Harriett did, that he had made a life for himself somewhere.

They turned into the little path leading to Lamb's front door. 'I'm ready for some tea and cakes,' Arthur said changing the subject to a happier one. 'And Thomas Lamb tells me there's champagne to toast his grandson's health.'

CHAPTER FIFTY ONE

April 1747, Hawkhurst

Will came back from Goudhurst one afternoon in early April and rode over to see Arthur. Arthur noticed Will's grim face. 'What's all this then?' he asked, leading his brother into the back parlour.

'I've just come back from Goudhurst, Arty. There's bad trouble brewing.'

'What do you mean?' Arthur asked, frowning. 'What sort of trouble?'

'I was in the *Star and Crown* with Stanford. There were several of the old gang there, Tom Fuller, George and Tom Kingsmill, Bernard Woollett, oh, a few more. They'd been drinking all morning. A fight broke out – I don't know what it was about - something and nothing, I think. I think one of the men made free with Lizzie Doe and Bernard took offence. They're walking out together you know. Then the argument started to turn into something more serious. One of the Standing brothers made a comment about the gang trying to muscle in on all the labouring jobs now there's no runs going on. It turned bad after that. There was a stand up fight between some of them and in the end we all got thrown out, but I ain't sure if that's the end of it.'

Arthur sighed. There seemed to be no end to the consequences that had followed his decision to give up the smuggling runs. 'Has anything more come of it?' he asked.

Will shrugged. 'Well maybe it's nothing, but do you remember William Sturt? I think me and Jim Cook was at school with him for a year or so.'

'Sturt?' Arthur asked. 'Thought he joined the army? Wasn't he over in Flanders?'

'I don't know. He's back now anyway and talking about taking us down a peg or two.'

'What does he mean by that?'

Will shook his head and stood looking out of the window. 'I don't know, Arthur. But it didn't feel right.'

The trouble between the two rival groups of men would not go away. April was uncommonly hot. Day after day brought blazing sunshine, with the sun already hot by nine in the morning where only the month before it had been frosty and cold. No rain fell and the tracks around Hawkhurst and Goudhurst became dusty and dry.

By the 17th April word came via Lizzie Doe who overheard a conversation at the *Star and Crown*, that a band of a dozen or so Goudhurst men had formed themselves into the *Goudhurst Militia* under the leadership of Sturt. Their intentions were unclear at this time.

Arthur came back from Hawkhurst alarmed at the latest turn of events. He thought the newly-formed Militia might have set themselves up to inform against any of the gang members still running in order to take advantage of the bounties they might receive. He warned as many of the men as he could, not to continue. His words fell mostly on deaf or reluctant ears. Henley's acquittal seemed to have instilled in them a sense of invincibility. Arthur, more aware of the intractability of a Government sworn to stamp out smuggling, was less sure.

Lizzie Doe told her sweetheart, Bernard Woollett what she had overheard and the Kingsmill brothers had lain in wait that evening for William Hodgkin, one of the Goudhurst men who had signed up with the Militia. The brothers had taken him back to their house and beat him into telling them who the other members of the militia were and what they intended to do.

Hodgkin, nursing his bruises and cuts eventually gave them the names they were after. Tom Kingsmill held the blade of his hanger to Hodgkin's throat. 'You can go back to your band of twelve, Hodgkin and tell them that we'll meet them in Goudhurst and have this out with them once and for all. Understand?'

Hodgkin nodded, his eyes wide with fear.

'And you can swear on your children's' souls that you won't join them against us. If I see you there Hodgkin, I'll cut your heart out with my own hanger.'

'I swear then, whatever you say, Kingsmill,' Hodgkin pleaded.

'Get a bible, George,' Tom Kingsmill said. George brought the bible and laid Hodgkin's hand on it forcing him to swear as Tom had demanded.

'Listen Hodgkin,' George said. 'You can tell Will Sturt and your other companions that we'll see them here in Goudhurst at noon on the twenty first. Them against us, we don't want any Dragoons involved. This is our fight, no one else's.'

Rose Kingsmill, listening in the back room, bowed her head, wondering what would be the end of this for her brothers.

Arthur told Will to come over to Seacox with Beth on the morning of the twenty first. If the trouble was not confined to Goudhurst he wanted to be sure that all those he cared about were safe. The day was quiet until towards seven in the evening when there was a tremendous hammering at the kitchen door. Sarah got up to go to it, but Arthur caught her hand and stopped her. Beth, sharper-witted, knew immediately that something was wrong when she saw the look between the brothers. Arthur went to the kitchen drawer where his pistols were kept and handed one to Will.

'Will, open the door to the safe passage. Beth, Sarah, get ready to go in there with the girls if I give you the word.'

Beth looked from Arthur to Will. 'What's going on Arthur? Will?'

Sarah, white faced, gathered her daughters close. 'Who is it Arthur? Who is at the door?'

Arthur went to the kitchen door and called out. 'Who's there?'

A voice replied, unsteadily, 'Tom Kemp.'

'Are you alone?'

There was a pause. 'Yes'

Arthur slipped the bolt, throwing open the door. Tom Kemp, dishevelled and with a rough bandage tied round his head, stood on the threshold. Arthur looking to left and right as he drew Tom Kemp into the kitchen, rebolted the door. Beth, Sarah and the girls came forward from the passageway, looking alarmed. Arthur pulled out a chair for Kemp and poured him a mug of ale.

'Thanks, Arthur, thanks. I'm parched with thirst.'

Arthur sat down opposite him. 'Well, what's happened? It's this foolish fight with the Goudhurst Militia I suppose?'

Unexpectedly, Tom Kemp burst into tears, trying to speak but unable to while his heaving sobs made it impossible for him to utter a word. Beth put a hand to her mouth and Will looked uncomfortable. Sarah quickly pushed the girls into the back parlour, despite their protests and pulled the door shut.

'What's been going on, Arthur?' she asked.

'Tom will tell us in his own time,' Arthur announced. 'Come on Tom, whatever it is, you're safe now.'

Kemp took a deep breath and another gulp of ale and wiped his eyes with his sleeve. 'It was terrible, Arthur. Terrible. I never imagined anything like it. Two men dead and six of us wounded in one way or another. I been hiding up in the woods between here and Goudhurst all afternoon. I stuck to the woods for fear of being caught. Yours was the first safe house I come to. I didn't dare go to my Dad's yet.'

Arthur and Will both looked grim. Beth and Sarah in the background could not speak.

'Just tell us what happened, Tom,' Arthur said.

'There was sixteen of us. We thought that would be plenty.'

Tom wiped a hand over his face. 'We set out from the *Oak and Ivy* and met at Lizzie Doe's in Goudhurst. We rode up Back Lane. But they was waiting for us, all armed, most of 'em at the *Star and Crown* but others, I swear they was on the Church tower or in the belfry - otherwise they couldn't have fired on us so accurate as they did. George Kingsmill was leading us. He was mad when he saw their positions – I ain't never seen him so wild, and he led his horse right up to the front door of the *Star and Crown*. Then Bernard tried to break the door down by shooting through the lock. Oh Jesus! He was shot through the head by one of their men from high up on the Church tower I think. I saw his brains come spilling out all over his shoulders!'

He paused and his hand shook as he picked up his tankard and took a mouthful of ale.

'Next, George steers his horse towards the church and as he's about to leap over the churchyard fence another shot rings out and he falls forward over his horse, which carries on with the leap and goes galloping like it's driven mad with all the shots firing. Poor George is dragged by the stirrups right up to the North Door, then the horse rears up and George rolls away, a great hole in his chest.'

Sarah gasped and put a hand to her mouth. Beth looked across at her, knowing what George Kingsmill had once been to her, though not a word about it had ever passed between them since the day of Sally's birth.

'Killed?' Will asked horrified. 'Bernard and George both killed?'

Tom Kemp nodded. 'After that the rest of us fought our way out of it as best we could. They had the advantage see, firing from on high? We couldn't get our shots accurate from horseback. We all went off in different directions.'

'And what about the Goudhurst men?' Arthur asked.

Kemp shook his head. 'I don't think we killed any of em, maybe winged one or two.' He looked up at Arthur with scared eyes. 'What's to become of us now? Will they track us down?'

Arthur shook his head, rubbing his hands over his face. 'Christ, what a mess! And two men killed needlessly.'

Sarah had stumbled over to the table and pulled out a chair quickly pouring herself some ale.

Kemp looked across at her. 'I'm sorry Mrs Gray, to tell such a bloody story at your kitchen table.'

Arthur looked curiously at his wife. 'Sarah, perhaps you'd better go upstairs and take the girls. You too, Beth.'

'No, let me stay, Arthur,' Beth said. 'Tom needs his head attended to.' She went to the tap. Sarah slowly stood up and crossed the room in silence. Will and Arthur didn't speak as Beth bathed the wound on Kemp's head and applied some salve, dressing it with a clean strip of linen.

'You can stay here tonight, Tom. I'll ride into Hawkhurst tomorrow and tell your father you're safe and see what news is to be had,' Arthur said.

Kemp looked relieved and some colour started to creep back into his white face. 'I don't even know what the fight was about Arthur, to tell the truth. I though we was just going to knock some heads together. I didn't think there would be killing done.'

Arthur shook his head and met Will's eyes over Tom Kemp's bandaged head.

Riding out the next day, Arthur and Will found the townsfolk of Hawkhurst edgy and anxious. The only talk in the inns was of the skirmish and the disbelief that two of their men had been killed. The former members of Arthur's gang who had been involved were numbed and shaken by the realisation that they were not invincible.

Two days later, Arthur rode to Goudhurst itself and saw the bullet marks in the door of the *Star and Crown* and the broken fence at the churchyard where George Kingsmill had tried to leap it. He was saddened to meet Bernard Woollett's father, come up to take his son's body to Cranbrook for burial, accompanied by Bernard's sweetheart, her eyes red-rimmed, and her shoulders sagging. Lizzie had watched Bernard ride out from her home and had known nothing more until two of the victorious Goudhurst Militia, drunk with success, had come to tell her his body was lying in the *Star and Crown*, a linen towel wrapped round his head to hide the terrible wound which had killed him. He was to be buried on the 28th at Cranbrook. George Kingsmill was to be buried the same day at St Mary's, Goudhurst, the church in whose grounds he had died.

Soon after Arthur had set out for Cranbrook for Bernard's funeral, Sarah got her own mare out and saddled her, bidding Sally to mount behind her. 'You're growing so tall, Sally. I want to get some material to make you up some summer gowns,' she said as casually as she could.

'I'm growing taller too, mamma, can't I come and choose some material?' Becca asked, not wishing to be deprived of this treat and wanting a day out. She was aware of the tension in the house over the past week without fully understanding its cause.

'No, Becca, you stay with Susie and Joanna. I'll take you another day.'

They spent a little over an hour at the draper's shop, Sarah agreeing immediately to Sally's choice of the bolts of material spread out before them. When they came out, a lone bell at St Mary's was tolling. Sally looked up the incline to the church and then as they walked up the hill, she looked in the other direction and saw a funeral wagon being drawn towards the church. Sarah pulled her hood over her head and bade her daughter to do the same.

'It's not respectful to do our shopping while there's a funeral taking place. We'll just slip into the church and go home when it's over. Take my hand, Sally.'

Sally looked puzzled but didn't question her mother's decision and they slipped into the church and took their seats at the back. It was a small procession which followed the simple wooden coffin. Sarah recognised Rose Kingsmill and Tom Kingsmill at once, Rose weeping softly. They were following a short, dark-haired woman who clutched the hand of a small girl aged about five. Sarah knew this must be Sarah Kingsmill, George's widow and their only child.

The sermon preached over the coffin cannot have given his widow much comfort. '*The way of the transgressor is hard*', Isaac Finch proclaimed.

Even hearing this indictment from the pulpit, his widow kept her composure but when the coffin was taken back out for burial, her feet seemed to drag under her and she all but slumped to the ground. Her brother-in-law supported her and she stood swaying at the graveside, until the Parson snapped the prayer book shut and the gravediggers started to fling the earth over the coffin. Tom Kingsmill escorted her away.

Sarah and Sally had been standing further away in a corner of the graveyard. When the mourning party had gone, Sarah took her daughter's hand and led her over to the grave and looked down at it for a while.

Sally looked at her mother. 'Why are you crying mamma? He was nobody we knew especially, was he?'

Sarah looked at the heap of earth and then at her daughter. She pushed a strand of hair back behind Sally's ear. 'A little girl has lost her father today. That's always sad, isn't it Sally?'

Sally peered from her mother to the grave and shrugged. 'Can we take my material home now, mamma? I can't wait to show Becca.'

CHAPTER FIFTY TWO

Spring/Summer 1747, Hawkhurst then Newgate gaol, London

The spring and early summer of 1747 passed interminably slowly it seemed to Arthur. Time had seemed to fly when he had the gang to organise. There were always men to round up, routes to decide, and prices to be agreed. He was often away from home and the times he was at Seacox were rare enough to be taken with enjoyment.

Now his enforced idleness meant he was forever at home. Sarah and he rowed over the smallest matter and his daughters seemed to fill each room with chatter and squabbles. His patience short, Arthur often shouted at them to go to their rooms and leave him in peace. Sarah, trying to comfort Susannah who had fled to her mother in tears after one of Arthur's outbursts, confronted her husband.

'You were happy enough for us to make our own pleasure when you was out most days! We aren't acting any different. It's you Arthur, you who've changed. You never used to hang about the house under my feet all day,' she stormed.

'Under your feet, Sarah?' Arthur thundered. 'How dare you, woman? I think you've forgotten who provides this house for you and your daughters. What other woman in Hawkhurst do you know who enjoys a house of this size and convenience? Have you forgotten that when I married you, you were living in three rooms with your father and grandmother? The dining room here would swallow up those piddling three rooms!'

'Yes, and you were living in two rooms with your drunk of a father!' Sarah snapped.

'I was but I never asked you to live there,' he flung at her. 'I made it my duty to provide for us from the day we married.'

'It was your duty,' Sarah retorted. 'I was carrying Sally.' The words tripped off her tongue before she could think about them.

'That was the start of our problems,' Arthur hurled back at her and paced about the room.

Sarah, who had been prepared to brazen this row out, began to feel fingers of anxiety stabbing at her heart. 'What problems? What do you mean, Arthur?' She looked up at her husband, but his expression was closed against her.

He reached for his hat and his light jacket. 'I'm going out.'

She stepped over to him and touched his arm, looking up at him with troubled eyes. 'Where are you going?'

He paused for a moment and looked at his wife. 'Just out,' he said and opened the door.

Sarah followed him round to the stables. 'You'll come back for supper, won't you, Arthur?' she asked in an anxious voice.

He shrugged without looking at her. 'I don't know.' He mounted Peg and rode away.

Five minutes later, he reined in his mare from his furious gallop up in the woodlands and slowed her down to a walk. He was uncomfortable with himself. He hadn't meant to argue with Sarah. It was a pointless argument. What she said was true. He had changed, not she or their daughters but he couldn't fit into this new way of life. He turned Peg round and rode towards Will and Beth's house. Will had been in Maidstone again, adding to his stables. He might get an hour alone with Beth. Just being alone with her, talking to her, would salve his spirit, he knew.

But when he got there he found that Will had returned from Maidstone, with news that cast Arthur's troubles into insignificance. Information had been laid against Jim Cook, to the Local Justice of the Peace on the oath of two credible persons, that he was guilty of carrying away uncustomed goods since the act of June 1746, the penalty for which, if convicted, was death.

The news flew around Hawkhurst. Jim was well liked and he was the first local man to be charged. Arthur went to see Jim as soon as he was allowed, at Maidstone Gaol. Jim was distraught, unbelieving about what had happened, but still talking of Henley's acquittal and believing the same would happen to him.

Worse still, the two 'credible persons' who had brought the charge before the Justice were Robert Worthington and Christopher Barrett, two part-time former member of Arthur's gang. They were the first two to betray one of their own. Arthur's fury spilled over when he went to try to find them in Folkestone but they neither of them were to be found at home, their wives and children disappeared and their homes shut up. Someone, either working alone or as an agent of the Government, was prepared to pay a substantial amount of money to keep these witnesses out of the way.

The evidence sworn was that Jim Cook had run goods, with several others not yet taken, on the night of 11th February earlier that year. Arthur could not argue with the facts and felt his heart race when he thought of that night when Jim had tried to persuade him to accompany the other gang members to Folkestone Warren. If he had gone with them, Arthur himself might be one of the *others not yet taken*. What was appalling was that the gang' s central belief that each man worked as part of a team, had dissolved into treachery and betrayal and from now on none of them could tell who could be counted as friend or enemy.

One sunny afternoon in July within five weeks of being charged, Jim Cook stood trial for his life. And two weeks later he was hanged.

Two months later, Pete Tickner was taken from his farm early one morning and charged with running goods in September 1746 under the terms of the Act of '46 and faced the same death as Jim Cook.

Every former gang member now feared the early morning or late night knock at the door. Some of them packed up their possessions and set out for the west or the north of England, where they weren't known and they could try and build a new life.

It came as a relief therefore, when Pete Tickner's sixteen year old son, rode to Seacox from his father's farm in Sandhurst to tell Arthur that his father had been acquitted under the '46 Act, as the witness's evidence was thrown out as being unreliable. But their relief was only temporary as Tickner was to be tried again, on a different indictment, under the '36 Act, for running goods in December 1744.

He was found guilty and sentenced to transportation to Maryland on 2nd February aboard the convict ship *St. George.*

Arthur, visiting Tickner in his miserable cell in Newgate, the great brooding fortress-prison, felt all the horror at his friend's confinement but also relief that Tickner wasn't facing execution.

'Grayling has made a life for himself in Maryland, Pete,' Arthur said, encouragingly.

'Yes, but he had laid up money there, Arthur. My money is all tied up in my farm. Besides, I don't want to make a life out there. Ann and the children are here. No, Tom will have to take on the farm and look after his mother and Lizzie. God willing, I can return when I've done my seven years.'

He stared into the distance. 'Lizzie will be seventeen when I return and Tom a man of twenty three. Did we do wrong, Arthur?' he asked looking up at his old friend. 'I been thinking while I've been in here - I get plenty of time for that,' he said with a short laugh. 'It didn't seem wrong while we was doing it, did it? It wasn't like stealing from an honest shopkeeper, was it? We was just taking from the Government.'

Arthur shook his head. 'I don't know any more, Pete. God knows where it will end.'

He stood up taking hold of Tickner's hand and shook it warmly, then clapped him on the back. 'I'll come up again before Christmas in a couple of weeks,' he said.

Tickner stood awkwardly in his leg irons. 'My boy is coming then. He says his mother wants to come but I don't think it's fit for Ann to see me like this. We sail from the Downs you know, from Deal. I don't think I'll be able to stop her from coming then.'

Arthur nodded not knowing what to say and then called to the gaoler through the little grating, to let him out.

As they walked along the dark passageway, the meagre daylight only reaching it from small grilles set in the ceiling, he stopped and turned to the gaoler. 'You look like a reasonable sort of fellow to me,' Arthur began. 'What would it cost, if such a thing might be bought, to have Tickner's leg irons removed?'

The gaoler looked at Arthur and then stroked the stubble on his chin. 'Well, let me see. If such a favour might be bought, which I ain't saying it might, I suppose it might be bought for ten pounds.'

Arthur said nothing but waited until they had turned out of the passage into the little room at the end furnished with a table and chair and where there was a small fire burning, which constituted the gaoler's office. Arthur put his hand in the pocket of his waistcoat and drew out some gold coins placing them in a small pile on the rough table.

'Here then. Let them come off as soon as I've gone,' he said.

The gaoler said nothing but as soon as Arthur had turned and left, he picked the coins up and dropped them into a small leather purse tied round his middle.

CHAPTER FIFTY THREE

Tuesday 28th December 1747, Will's house, Arthur's house

It was towards nine in the evening and Beth was sitting quietly with a book on her lap. Will, pleasantly tired after an energetic ride, stretched out his long legs in front of the fire, Corker dozing with his nose on Will's left foot. They could hear Annie clattering about in the kitchen with pots and pans and singing as she usually did, not quite in tune, but very merrily all the same. There was a sudden loud commotion in the kitchen and a heavy hammering on the door. Beth looked up startled and anxious. Will sat up slowly and even Corker raised his head, a low growl in his throat.

'Shh, boy,' Will said warningly, getting up and going into the kitchen. Beth saw him take his pistol out of the drawer.

'Let me find out who it is before we answer the door,' Beth whispered, clutching Will's hand. He hesitated for a moment and then nodded.

Beth went to the door and as she approached she called out, 'Who's there?' in a voice as normal as she could keep it.

'It's Colonel Brotherton, Mrs Gray. Would you open up please?'

Beth gave a sigh of relief and looked across at Will. Will had bought several horses from the Colonel and they had supped with him and his wife occasionally. She started to unbolt the door, just as Brotherton called out, 'We've come for Will, Mrs Gray. I have men at your front door. There's no escape.'

Beth tried to push back the bolt but the door had already been thrust open and the threshold was filled with Dragoons, standing

461

behind the Colonel, all of them with carbines drawn. As soon as they pushed into the room, they pointed their guns at Will.

He gave a half smile and put up his hands allowing his pistol to swing from the middle finger of his open palm. 'Have you come for me so soon, Nathan?' he asked the Colonel.

Colonel Brotherton looked uncomfortable. He drew out a piece of paper from his pocket and began to read: *'William Gray, I have a warrant here for your arrest charged by the oaths of Richard Standing and Benjamin Snelling with riding with divers other persons armed with firearms and other offensive weapons and aiding and assisting in the running of uncustomed goods in the parish of Goudhurst in the County of Kent since the year of our lord 1746 in contempt of the King and his laws and am charged to carry you before the Justice of the Peace at Maidstone.'*

The Colonel dropped his shoulders. 'I'm sorry about this Will. I had no alternative. Put up your pistol and come along with us and my men will put away their carbines.'

Beth ran to Will's side. He put out an arm to catch her to him, laying his pistol down on the kitchen table as he did so. They could hear Annie sobbing in the background.

'Get word to Arthur. Try to warn him.' Will whispered in Beth's ear. 'Tell him it was two of the men of the Goudhurst Militia who've sworn against me.'

'Hurry along, Will,' Brotherton urged.

'Annie, fetch my husband's coat and hat if you please,' Beth called out. Annie, glad of something to do, scurried out to the passageway.

'Shall I get my horse, Nathan?' Will asked uncertainly, pulling on his coat and hat and not able to stop his hands from shaking.

Brotherton shook his head and pulled out some hand chains.

'We'll mount you, Will. I regret I must ask you to put out your hands,' he said, holding the chains out in front of him. Will drew in his breath, but then put his hands forward and was silent as the Colonel fastened the chains around his wrists and thrust him out of the door. Beth and Annie could only follow in silence as one of the Dragoons held the horse while Will mounted, Corker running between his master and Beth, barking and whining alternately. The rest of the men mounted, surrounding Will and he had time for one last glance round at Beth before he disappeared into the night.

Beth felt for a moment that she might be sick or faint. She looked up at the night sky, calm, peaceful, a backdrop of dark blue studded with the lights of hundreds of thousands of stars, just as they had been five minutes before. *How can they be the same*, she thought to herself, *nothing will ever be the same, don't the stars know that?* Then she felt strangely calm.

'Bring me a lantern quickly, Annie, I must saddle Prue.'

Annie muffing her sobs in her apron, raised her tear-stained faced to Beth. 'Oh, mistress, what's to become of Mr Will? What will they do to him? They won't hang him, m'am will they, not like they done to poor Jim Cook? Oh no, oh no!'

'Stop it Annie,' Beth said sharply, though the hair at the back of her neck bristled at her words and she felt sweat break out under her arms even in the chill night air. 'Of course they won't hang Will. How can you even think it? But I must get word to Arthur. Now, hurry and fetch my cloak and hood.'

She stepped across to the stable door. Prue whinnied as she heard Beth approach and Annie came hurrying out with a lantern and Beth's outdoor clothes.

She wrapped her cloak round her and pulled the hood over her hair, hastily heaving Prue's saddle on and within moments was on her way across the yard and out of the stable gates.

Beth had never ridden alone at night before and even with the lantern held aloft on its holder, she felt nervous as the lights of Hawkhurst were left behind and she rode up the incline leading to Seacox. Thoughts started to crowd in on her but she pushed them aside, allowing herself only to think that Arthur would know what to do and would make it all right again.

She was relieved to see the candles still burning at Seacox. She stopped at the front of the house and dismounted, tethering Prue to the post and stepped up to the front door tapping firmly on it. She heard the heavy bolt being drawn aside and then instead of seeing Arthur or Sarah in the light of the passageway, Beth was sunned to see a red coated Dragoon. He pulled the door open and Beth saw Sarah standing behind him looking small and frightened, with several more of the soldiers around her. One of them came forward.

'It's Mrs William Gray, isn't it?'

She ignored him and looked at Sarah, wanting to ask if Arthur was there but not wishing to give anything away.

Sarah said in a small voice, 'They've come for Arthur, Beth. But he's not here. They won't go away, though. They say they'll wait until he comes back.'

Beth looked up at the Dragoon who had addressed her. 'By what right do you stay here?' she asked, with a calmness she did not feel.

He tapped his pocket. 'By right of this warrant, Mrs Gray. It is Mrs Gray, I take it? Captain Shaw at your service,' he said, pleasantly enough.

Beth took off her cloak and hood, shaking out her curls.

'Come through into the parlour, Beth,' Sarah urged.

'I take it you've no objection to my sister-in-law and myself having some private conversation?' Beth asked indignantly.

'None at all, madam,' the Captain replied. The passageway seemed very full of men, tall in their high hats and scarlet coats, their long carbines menacing. Beth pushed past them and followed Sarah into the parlour where Sally and Becca were sitting. They scrambled up as soon as they saw Beth.

'Aunty Beth, it's so horrible! The soldiers won't go away,' Becca cried. Beth held out her arms to her and sat with her on the silk-covered sofa.

'Where is Arthur?' Beth whispered to Sarah over Becca's head.

Sarah shook her head. 'I don't know. He went out yesterday and hasn't come back yet. He said he might not return until tomorrow. Perhaps he's in London.'

Beth looked down at her lap.

'What is it Beth? Where's Will?' Sarah asked suddenly.

'Colonel Brotherton came for him with a party of Dragoons. He's been taken, Sarah.'

Sarah pressed a hand to her mouth, as Becca's voice caught on a sob.

'Oh not Uncle Will? Will Daddy fetch him back, mamma? Perhaps that's where he's gone.'

Sarah looked at Beth closely. 'Do you know where Arthur is, Beth?'

Beth met her gaze and shook her head. 'I've no idea, none at all. Perhaps he knows about this and is planning a means of escape already. What does Captain Shaw say?'

'He says they'll wait until my Daddy comes home,' Sally interrupted. 'They've hidden their horses away so he won't know they're here. Can't you go and find him, Aunt Beth?' she pleaded.

'Sally, I don't know where to go,' she replied, trying to think where Arthur was likely to go if he knew of this trouble. There were so many safe houses he had used during the smuggling runs, and Beth knew that he might have chosen any one of them to hide up in and plan his next course of action. Beth tried to think of the gang members he could have called on - Thomas Kemp, John Watts, any of the Hawkhurst men or perhaps he had gone down to Rye to see Thomas Lamb. She stood up.

'Well, the Dragoons can't stop me from riding out, Sarah. I'll ride to as many places as I can think of.'

As soon as she had made a decision she felt better, stronger, calmer. She went back out to the passageway, Sarah and the girls following. She made her way to the door but Captain Shaw stood up and barred her way. She looked up at him, anger in her grey eyes. 'You will hardly prevent me from moving about at my will?' she asked sarcastically.

'No, Mrs Gray, but two of my men will accompany you wherever it is you are intent on going so late at night.'

Beth's spirits sank. If they followed her, she might lead them straight to Arthur. She looked back up at the Captain and then turned on her heel and went back to the parlour, shaking her head silently at Sarah and the girls.

Meanwhile at the *George* in Aylesford, Arthur shifted onto his back and tucked his arm around Deb. She laid her head on his chest and he could tell by her rhythmic breathing that she had soon fallen asleep. He looked over at the window where the open curtains revealed the starry night sky through the small panes. He had spent a long day in London with Gideon, who had converted a few of his investments back into gold coins. Arthur had brought some back with him and they were lying safe in Henry French's cellars. Tomorrow he would take them to Seacox and lay them up in one of his own secret passages there.

He hadn't really intended to stop off at the *George*, but the welcoming lights as he crossed the little bridge made him realise how tired he was. He decided to stop off for something to eat and drink before making the last few miles home, but Deb was there, fresh and pretty in green brocade. She had such a smile of welcome on her pretty lips, that it seemed the most natural thing to go up to her bedchamber after she had brought him his food and drink and as always, he found pleasure and release in her arms.

It had been a terrible year, he thought, gazing out at the stars. The horror of Jim Cook's swift trial and hanging woke him in a cold sweat some nights; the recent events of late - the pointless skirmish at Goudhurst with George Kingsmill and Bernard Woollett killed and just lately Pete Tickner awaiting transportation at Newgate, hung over him like a black and lowering cloud. Surely if the authorities were going to act against himself and Will, they would have done so by now, he thought.

He sighed and shifted slightly as Deb stirred against him. Perhaps if they got through this winter, the spring might bring happier times for them. He would use the money to buy more land. He felt sure Lamb would sell him more and maybe he would set Will up with a farm. He moved the pillow under his head with one hand, tucked his other arm around Deb and fell asleep.

Beth woke with a start, stiff and cold, sitting in the chair where she had eventually fallen asleep. Sarah had taken the girls up to bed just after midnight and had come back downstairs to join Beth in the parlour.

Beth looked across to the table where Sarah had fallen asleep sitting in the chair, her head resting on her arms propped on the table. She also woke and they both realised that it was a horse's hooves on the gravel track that had woken them. Beth rubbed her hands over her face and stood up but Sarah was already in the passageway. The Dragoons were already alert, barring the way from the two women in case they shouted out and gave a warning to their intended captive.

One of the Dragoons had taken Beth's horse and hidden it with theirs a little way off from the house, so that Arthur, leading Peg round to the stables had no idea anything was amiss. He put his key in the lock but the door was drawn open and he found himself staring down the barrel of a long carbine. He was vaguely aware that Beth and Sarah were standing some way back in the hallway, their faces white and strained. He opened his mouth to speak, but two of the Dragoons pushed passed him and seized both his arms pushing them behind his back, as Captain Shaw read out the warrant.

Arthur half shouted to the two women but he was bundled onto a horse his wrists chained like Will's had been. Casting his head back, he heard Sarah's cry and saw Beth's expression as she raised a hand and then dropped it, mouthing words to him that his disordered senses couldn't interpret.

CHAPTER FIFTY FOUR

Tuesday 18th January 1748, Rye

After Arthur and Will had been taken, the gang members were fearful and in a state of disbelief. Some of them expected both brothers to walk through the door of the *Mermaid* or the *London Trader* at any moment. Others said it was all up with them. It was known they had both pleaded not guilty and that they were going to be taken up to Newgate for trial at the Old Bailey at the next sessions.

Curtis was sitting at a table in the corner of the bar room at the *Mermaid* with Ben Raven, Tom Kingsmill and Tom Dixon.

Thomas Lamb was also at the *Mermaid* sitting alone at a table a little way away from them.

'Is it the end, would you say, Curtis?' Ben Raven asked. He had little liking for Curtis, but habit drew him to the inns where the gang were used to meet.

Curtis shrugged his shoulders. 'It's the end of the Grays, ain't it? The end of a rope for them.'

'The end for all of us, I reckon,' Raven said as he picked up his tankard. 'Can't see anyone else taking over. Ain't worth it no more is it?'

'Gray got too big for his own good,' Kingsmill mumbled. 'Left us to get on with it, when he'd had enough. Where was he when we needed him at Goudhurst last April? George would still be here if he'd stuck with us.'

Raven shook his head slowly. 'I ain't got no quarrel with Arthur or Will. They always done right by me.'

468

Curtis finished his drink and summoned the landlord over to the table. When he had poured another tankard, Curtis picked it up and put in to his lips. 'They'll both be leaving rich widows behind them. Have you thought of that, Kingsmill?'

'Why would I think of that?' he asked. 'They'd both be too much trouble. One with three daughters and the other - well she's too high and mighty for my liking.'

'Oh, I think she might be brought lower,' Curtis suggested. 'I think Beth Gray would be only too willing to find herself another husband.'

'And you'd take her on?' Tom Dixon asked.

'Well, she must be worth a bit. Her father had money, didn't he? And she's all alone now. I reckon she'd be grateful for another man in her life and in her bed.'

Raven shook his head as he put his tankard down on the table in front of him. 'I don't reckon it's right you talking as if Arthur and Will was dead and buried. I don't reckon it will come to trial. Who would bear witness against 'em?'

'Money can jog a man's memory, I reckon,' Curtis said.

'Then we're all at risk and we don't know who is friend or foe,' Raven put in. 'Well, I'm away. I hope you ain't in the right about Arthur and Will, Curtis. It would do me a power of good to see 'em both walk through that door right now.'

With that he pushed his chair away from the table and got up, pulling on his coat and made his way out. Shortly afterwards, Dixon and Kingsmill also left. After a while Lamb made his way over to Curtis.

'You don't object if I join you?'

Curtis looked up at him. 'No, come and join me, honoured sir,' he said sarcastically.

'I was hoping to have some private conversation with you. Perhaps you will walk with me to your lodgings?' Lamb asked.

Curtis looked as though he was going to refuse but he quickly tipped the last of his beer down his throat and clutching his coat, made his way out followed by Lamb. Neither man spoke as they made their way to Longer Street. Curtis made his way upstairs, not waiting for the older man's slower progress. He pushed open the door throwing his hat and coat over a chair. Lamb stepped towards another chair and looked across at Curtis who waved his hand absently signifying the old man should sit down.

'Well, what has my father to say to me now?' Curtis asked, seating himself in the opposite chair and pouring himself a glass of brandy from the decanter on the small table next to him.

'You were speaking of Beth Gray,' Lamb began.

Curtis shrugged. 'What of it?'

Lamb rubbed a hand over his chin. 'I heard you speak of marriage with her?'

'Don't you think I'm good enough for her, Lamb?' Curtis asked defiantly. 'Like I said, she'll be glad enough for any man to take her on when they hang the Grays. She'll be the widow of one hanged felon and sister-in-law of another! I ain't sure she's good enough for me, now I think of it.'

Lamb's eyes looked troubled. 'What makes you think you won't be taken, Jeremiah? None of you is immune.'

'Oh, I reckon I'm safe enough. It's the ringleaders they're after and now they've got 'em, ain't they? No, I reckon I'm pretty safe and when it's all died down, I'll be ready to take her on as a wife. Perhaps you'll come to our wedding?'

Lamb looked solemn. 'There has been no trial yet. It's likely they'll both be acquitted. But in any case, there will never be any marriage between you and Beth Gray,' he asserted.

'Oh come on, Pa,' Curtis sneered. 'Got an eye to her yourself, have you?'

'By God, Jeremiah, if I were twenty years younger I would beat some manners into you!' Lamb said, his voice rising in anger. Then he stopped himself and took a deep breath. 'I will tell you why you will never marry Beth and this is for your ears only. Your word on it, sir.'

Curtis looked at him, questioningly. 'Oh, for what it's worth, my word on it then.'

He looked across the room, only half paying attention to the old man's presence.

Lamb paused and then said quietly, 'Beth is your half sister.'

Curtis's head snapped round, total disbelief in his face. *'My half sister?'*

Lamb nodded. 'If you breathe one word of this, Jeremiah, you will never receive another penny from me. I swear it in spite of my promise to your mother.'

Curtis had stood up, twirling the stem of the brandy glass in his hand. 'You? Beth's father?'

Lamb nodded again.

'So you and, what was her name, Jane Stone? You and she made a cuckold of John Stone! Well, you old goat,' he said. 'And there was I thinking I got my dissolute ways from my mother, when it seems I got 'em from you as well. So she is my half-sister! Well, Jesus fuck Magdalene! Are there any more of your bastards I should know about?'

Lamb winced at his blasphemy and ignored the question. 'Beth knows nothing and will know nothing of this. Is that quite clear?'

Curtis shrugged his shoulders. 'Well, it does spoil my plans. My half sister!'

He threw back his head and began to laugh. Lamb looked puzzled and uncomfortable.

'My God,' Curtis said at length. 'That makes me Will Gray's brother-in-law. How exquisitely funny! And kinsman of sorts to Arthur! Well, I salute you, father. You have put the cat among the pigeons. But tell me more. Did her father, John Stone, never suspect? And Beth is what, a couple of years younger than I am? You must have gone from my mother's bed to her mother's bed and then back to your wife's. I think you have me beat there. I don't think I've ever dispensed my favours separately to three different women. Well, all in one bed maybe, but never behind all their backs!'

Lamb chose to ignore his son's comments. 'No word to Beth. I have your word on it, remember. And your allowance will end if you break it.'

Curtis looked at the old man. 'It's a pity I can't tell her,' he said sarcastically. 'You know I'm tempted to forego my allowance just to see the look on her face. How we should all enjoy playing happy families!'

Lamb looked angry. 'You will not tell her.'

Curtis gave his sneering smile. 'So now I have the upper hand with you?'

'I don't think you will give up your allowance so easily,' Lamb opined.

Curtis shrugged. 'Well, I have to admit, I would miss getting the portion of your wealth you allow me.'

Lamb rose to go.

'No, wait, Lamb. Tell me more. Why are you so keen for Beth Gray not to know of this? Oh, I can see it's embarrassing to admit you've been dipping your wick in so many different candle holders. But her mother's been dead a long time, her father too.'

'Beth has troubles enough, now. I would not add to them. She has happy memories of her parents. Why should I spoil that? I have only told you so you will stop imagining that you could ever marry her.'

Curtis rounded on him. 'What if I'd asked her to marry me years ago? I nearly did. I think she would have said yes, after Gray married Sarah Allen. She was all to pieces then. What then, Lamb? You would have had to confess to us both and shamed your dear wife. She would have found out the dirty tricks you had been playing.'

Lamb shook his head. 'Since it never happened, there is little point speculating what I might have done.'

Curtis poured himself another brandy.

'I wish you wouldn't drink so much, Jeremiah,' Lamb said, his hand on the door knob.

'And I wish you had been married to my mother,' Curtis countered, pouring another. 'We none of us get what we want, Lamb. You should know that.'

CHAPTER FIFTY FIVE

Saturday 29th January 1748, Seacox Heath

It was early evening, a cold night after a dry, bitter day, icy winds blowing down from the north. Beth, Sarah and the girls had eaten and Joanna was clearing the dishes away. Susie had asked Beth if she would play some music for them. Though she had no heart for it, Beth had gone to the harpsichord and started to tune it for she hadn't played since Christmas Eve, the last time they had all been together. Sarah and Sally were sitting by the fire. Sarah had some darning in her hands and though her sewing box was on the floor at her side, she did not open it and but sat with the stockings in her lap, staring into the fire.

There was a sudden knocking at the door. The women looked at each other, frozen with apprehension. Joanna came into the room looking as white as her apron, wondering whether she was supposed to answer the door.

They were all aware of the rumours around Hawkhurst that Arthur's money was hidden away at Seacox and they lived in apprehension that robbers and villains from miles around might attempt to break in and ransack the house. Beth kept Arthur's pistols ready. She had sometimes watched Will cleaning his pistols and knew how to load and cock them. She had already got used to the heavy weight of them and the feel of the smooth wood and brass in her hand. She went to the drawer in the kitchen table and took both of them out and nodded to Sarah who went to the back door.

The knocking continued and then the last voice they had expected to hear, called out, 'Sarah, let me in. It's me, Arthur.'

On a sob and with hands trembling so much she could hardly slip the heavy bolts or turn the key, Sarah pulled open the door and fell into Arthur's arms as he stood in the threshold. Their three girls ran to him and all tried to press themselves against him as his embrace pulled them all in. Beth longing to share in his embrace forced herself to hold back, unconscious that she was still holding the pistols. At last he looked over Sarah's head, his eyes meeting Beth's.

'Put up the pistols, Beth,' he said softly and held out one arm to her.

She nodded slowly, laying the pistols carefully back in the drawer and crossed the room into his embrace. He kissed her on the cheek and then put everyone from him.

'Daddy,' Susie called out, wrinkling up her small nose. 'You smell horrid.'

The child's comment broke the tense atmosphere and Sarah and Beth both laughed through their tears. The kitchen which had been quiet and unhappy before, broke into busy chatter and laughter, everyone trying to talk at once. Joanna was dispatched to fetch water to boil up for Arthur to wash in. He looked terrible, thinner in the face with two weeks' growth of beard, dark circles under his eyes and just as Susie had said, he smelt bad. He hadn't ventured any explanation and both women, though desperate to know how he came to be free, didn't want to ask until he was ready to tell. Beth longed to ask about Will and why he wasn't with his brother.

Sarah poured out some fresh tea and dished up a plate of the stewed pork left over from dinner. Arthur tearing a hunk of bread from the loaf, ate ravenously. The five females sat round watching him, Sally and Becca taking it in turns to replenish his cup with tea each time he drained it.

He paused for a moment and met Beth's gaze. 'Will is being taken up to Newgate tomorrow.'

At this Beth paled and put a hand over her mouth.

'Don't worry, Beth,' he said quickly. 'I was released for lack of evidence and now I'm free I can make myself busy on Will's account. He'll soon be out.' He reached across and put his hand over Beth's and pressed it. Then he looked at his three daughters. 'You go and choose me some clean clothes to put on while your mother sponges me down. Don't worry, Susie, I'll soon smell better.'

The girls chased upstairs as Arthur pushed his plate away from him and stood up. 'You can have no idea how good it feels to be able to move around at will,' he said, stretching.

Sarah was at the sink, busy with bowls of steaming water. 'Wait in the dining room, Beth,' she said over her shoulder, 'while I bathe my husband.'

Beth could only look at Sarah's back before opening the kitchen door and leaving husband and wife together.

Arthur stripped off his clothes and threw them to the floor. 'These are only good for burning, Sarah,' he said.

Sarah, her head bent over the large tin bowl, couldn't stop the tears welling up in her eyes and splashing down her cheeks into Arthur's washing water. He touched her shoulder and she turned to him, pressing herself against his naked body and sobbing into his chest. He put his arms about her and touched her hair. 'Come, Sarah,' he said gently. 'I don't want you to get the taint of the gaol on your clothes.'

She had noticed the red raw skin at his wrists and ankles and took his calloused dirty hands in her small ones and carried them to her lips. 'Did they keep you chained hand and foot, Arthur?'

He nodded. 'It's all right, Sarah. I'm safe now. It don't bother me at all.' He patted her shoulder. 'Fetch me the water, there's a good girl.'

She carried the first bowl over to the table and set a thick linen towel on the floor for Arthur to stand on and as he dipped his head and hands into the hot water, she took another fold of linen and started to scrub his body.

A half hour later, he was clean and shaved, with salve dabbed on his limbs where the irons had chafed him. He was dressed in clean linen, wearing an old pair of breeches, comfortable soft boots and a warm jacket. His face was gaunt, pale after a month's confinement in gaol when he had been used to being outside almost every day of his life.

He explained that the parcels of food and other comforts that Sarah and Beth had taken to Maidstone Gaol were soon used up; and there being no washing facilities, the spare shirts they had taken their husbands had been worn over and over again. Beth could hardly bear to think that Will, so fussy about his clothes was still there in such conditions but Arthur took her hand again and reassured her that Will would soon join them.

'Beth, don't worry. One thing I have learned is that money will buy you almost anything. I had hardly any with me so I wasn't able to do very much. But people are very uneasy about our imprisonment. Colonel Brotherton has been extremely kind - it was a horse lent by him that carried me home tonight. Though they indicted me under the '46 Act, they admitted today that no reliable witnesses have come forward. How can they? I haven't run any goods since the Act. Neither has Will, though they say they have witnesses. That means they're false witnesses and if they've been bought once, they can be bought again. I just need to offer them more to withdraw their evidence than whatever they are being offered to speak against Will. All will be well, believe me.'

Beth looked at him, her lips tight. She nodded slowly.

'And you're in no danger, Arthur?' Sarah asked, touching his arm.

He shook his head. 'No, not at all.' He paused looking at both women. 'Now, I'm hungry again. Is there any of your seed cake, Sarah?'

The house began to feel almost normal again with its master's presence in it once more. They retired to the dining room. Beth played the harpsichord while Sally and Becca sang a piece of nonsense which had been all the rage over Christmas in London, while Beth accompanied them, its silly simple lyrics enabling them all to join in and almost forget the late horrors of their existence. Sarah brought in a tray of tea and pastries and the seed cake Arthur had requested.

'Are you staying here, Beth?' he asked as he settled back in the chair close to the fire. 'That's a good idea.'

Beth nodded. 'I go back to our house in the daytime. But I sleep here.'

'We've been so worried Arthur, about your money,' Sarah explained.

'That's why I kept the pistols ready,' Beth said. 'We were worried someone might break in.'

Arthur looked concerned. 'I hadn't thought. How stupid of me. But who would harm you? No one from Hawkhurst. Has anyone attempted anything?'

Sarah shook her head.

'Perhaps you should go and stay with someone else, all of you. I'll have to be out and about a good deal these next few days and weeks,' Arthur said.

'Don't be silly, Arthur. Where would we go?' Sarah asked doubtfully.

'To anyone not connected with the gang – Lucas and Martha would take you in, Sam Terrell, Bill Bishop,' he suggested.

'No I shan't leave, Arthur. You're safe now. You can look after us,' Sarah said decidedly.

The girls were sent up to bed a little later and shortly afterwards, Arthur, Sarah and Beth followed. Beth said goodnight at the door of Arthur and Sarah's bedchamber and lay in bed for a long time, trying not to think about the conditions Will was suffering. She heard in the adjoining room, the low murmur of Arthur and Sarah's voices and then the unmistakeable sound of their lovemaking, as they sought comfort in each other's bodies.

The following morning, Arthur woke with a start and couldn't think for a moment where he was. In his head he heard the sounds of the gaol where he had wakened for the past month; the constant clanging of the heavy iron doors, the shouts of men, the groans of others who had succumbed to gaol fever, the curses of the gaolers as they did their rounds.

He lay back on his soft clean pillow, hearing nothing but the early morning sound of birds in the far distance beyond the window panes and their shutters and nearer to him Sarah's soft rhythmic breathing. He turned towards her and smelt her clean hair and touched the soft skin of her shoulder peeping out from her nightgown. She smiled in her sleepy state and reached her arms around him. Arthur felt the welcoming softness of his wife next to him, as he pulled up her nightgown and felt her thighs open as he gently pushed one leg over them, his hands seeking the comfort of her breasts, so soft against his calloused fingertips.

After breakfast when Arthur ate eggs, bacon, sausages and hunk after hunk of soft white bread spread thickly with butter and the girls had been sent into the dining room to practise their music, he pushed his plate away from him and faced Sarah and Beth.

'I must set off as soon as I can. There's a lot to do. I must go to London and Rye. Sarah, you, Beth and the girls must go to your brother Joseph in Goudhurst. I'll take you there first.'

Sarah shook her head. 'Arthur, please don't make us go. We'll keep the doors locked and we can hide in the safe passages if there's trouble. But this is my place. You won't want to come back to an empty house. You were glad enough of my company last night and this morning,' she said casting a sideways glance at Beth.

Twenty minutes later, Arthur came down dressed for riding and carrying a small leather bag crammed with the few things he might need. Beth met him in the hallway and took his arm.

'Shouldn't I come with you, Arthur, since you ride on Will's business?' she whispered, her mouth close to his ear. He took her hand, warm and small in his own and sighed.

'No, I can do this better alone and faster.' He looked into her troubled grey eyes and quickly pulled her to him. 'Beth, about what Sarah said-,'

'I understand it, Arthur. You're husband and wife. What would be more natural than that you should comfort each other?'

'It doesn't mean that I love you any less,' he said, pressing her towards him, but then he heard Sarah in the kitchen and they sprang apart.

CHAPTER FIFTY SIX

Late January 1748, London

Arthur rode first to London, taking his usual room at the *Robin Hood* at Stockwell out of habit gaining some comfort from the familiarity of the place. He sent a note to Sampson Gideon, asking him to meet him at *Jonathan's* that evening if possible. A note came back late afternoon stating that a meeting that evening would be impossible but that he would be pleased to see Arthur the following morning at nine.

'I want to raise in cash, every penny I am worth and as quickly as possible, sir,' Arthur explained as soon as they were seated in the back room at the coffee house.

Gideon, pressing his fingertips together, nodded gravely. 'That was exactly as I had anticipated, Arthur and I have already begun this process.'

'You know my brother is held at Newgate?' Arthur asked anxiously.

Gideon nodded. 'I've been at the coffee house in Ludgate Hill several times these past weeks. It's the place where they accommodate the juries from the Old Bailey when they are unable to reach a verdict. I find it's the best place to discover the latest happenings at Justice Hall.'

'Then you'll know that Will has been unjustly charged under the Act which could hang him. I'll lay out every penny I have to gain his release,' Arthur said forcefully.

Gideon nodded his understanding. 'Your total wealth in cash will be an immense quantity, Arthur. In what form do you want it?'

'In English gold coin.'

'Then I shall place it in a safe house known to me. It's in an area of London where many of my race make their homes. You may have every confidence in it,' Gideon said, allowing himself a small smile. 'In order to realise your assets into cash, Arthur and quickly, you understand I may be selling some at a loss?'

'Yes I understood that but I'll still be able to raise a considerable sum?'

Gideon took a sip of coffee and pulled out a small notebook from his pocket. 'I believe after calculating your assets and investments and the likely price I shall be able to get for them, that I'll be able to raise for you something in the region of nine thousand pounds.'

Arthur rubbed a hand over his face. 'Yes, I had thought as much myself. I believe I've sent almost half that sum to Maryland over the past ten years in Spanish pieces-of- eight and Portuguese moidores.'

Gideon nodded.

'Can I lay my hands on the money that's in America?'

Gideon considered the point and then frowned. 'Not in a time scale that would be acceptable for your desired outcome.'

'I thought as much,' Arthur sighed, then frowned.

'Go on,' Gideon encouraged.

'In order to have Will released, I need the charge against him to be dropped entirely. I need to pay off the man at the very top of the process. I don't know who that may be or how high I need to look. I'm hoping that nine thousand pounds will buy him off.'

Gideon looked very keenly at Arthur before replying. 'As I warned you previously, there are men at the very highest positions in Government who have made it their business to break your gang. However, applying to them would be pointless. All the money you could raise would be a drop in the ocean of their wealth, believe me. But there are some officials further down the line that might be more amenable to suggestion.'

'Then how should I go about it? I'm in your hands completely as far as this goes.'

'I'll do my best to arrange things for you.'

'Fix up whatever you can for me. I'll be in London for the next three days but I can return at any time.'

Gideon nodded. 'Very well. Leave it in my hands and I'll send you word when I have arranged something.'

They both stood.

'I can't thank you enough, sir,' Arthur said.

Gideon nodded but did not speak and pressed his hand warmly.

Arthur's next appointment filled him with a mixture of relief and dread; he was going to Newgate to see Will. As he approached the vast building, its menacing presence seemed to overshadow the alleyways and passages around it. The huge grey stone walls and gatehouse towered over every other building. Above the great iron doors, on a stone ledge cut into the walls were displayed larger than life-size models of the leg irons, chains and shackles that the wretched inmates might expect to wear for their detainment.

Arthur was escorted down endless passages and stairwells until he felt he was going into the bowels of the earth itself. At last the gaoler led him to the door of a cell halfway along a passage and gave him the now familiar option, of having the gaoler in with him, or being locked in with the prisoner.

'Lock me in with him, man,' Arthur said impatiently and waited as the gaoler lifted his great collection of keys and turned the lock pushing the door open. Peering into the semi darkness, Arthur became aware of Will's form lying on the small bed pushed towards the side of the cell. He stepped in, hearing the door clang shut behind him and before he had time to speak, Will turned towards him and in a second, despite being hampered by his leg irons, he was in Arthur's embrace. Both brothers clung to each other, Will unable to speak.

Arthur, his throat tight, clutched his brother to him. 'It's all right, Will. It's all right. You'll be out in no time, little brother, my little brother.'

Arthur sat at the rough table opposite watching Will eat the hunks of bread, cheese and meat that Arthur had brought with him and swigging mouthfuls of ale from a leather bottle. Arthur had pulled out the purse of gold he had brought in with him and Will hid the coins beneath a loose stone under his bed.

'There are shirts and breeches and some linen towels in the bag and two blankets. I'll come back tomorrow with a wicker basket with more food. Sarah says if I wrap some cheese in muslin, it will last longer. But you'll be out of here soon, Will,' he added quickly.

Will, pausing between mouthfuls looked at his brother. 'Will I, Arty? I think I'll run mad if I have to stay here long.'

Arthur looked round at the miserable cell. Though it was small it had a very high ceiling which made it feel even colder and the small barred window some fifteen feet high, gave hardly any light. There was straw on the floor and patches where the floor was wet. Arthur feared that Will's habitual winter cough would trouble him severely once it took hold in this damp miserable place. He already looked pale, thinner, his face covered by a beard, his shirt and clothes dirty and creased. Arthur's heart ached to think of Will's wardrobe full of clothes.

'Is Beth all right, Arty? You've seen her?'

'Of course I've seen her, Will. She's staying with Sarah and the girls. They're keeping up their spirits.' He didn't tell Will how they were armed with pistols when he first went home.

'Don't let Beth come here, will you Arthur?' Will asked anxiously. 'I couldn't bear her to see me like this. This is no place for her.'

'No, but you'll soon be reunited with her. Everyone sends their love, even Corker. The girls are looking after him,' Arthur said.

'And my horses? Saladin will go mad for want of a gallop if he's locked up in his stable.' His eyes seemed to look into the distance. 'What I wouldn't give for a gallop on the Upper Wish, Arty.'

Arthur stayed an hour. 'Pete Tickner is still here somewhere, Will,' he said rising to go. 'I'll try and see him before I leave. He is being sent for transportation the day after tomorrow.'

Will looked puzzled. 'Oh of course, I've lost track of time. What day is it?'

'The last day of January, brother,' Arthur replied. 'I'll come tomorrow, but I don't know when I can come back after that. I have to make myself busy getting you out of here so don't worry if I don't come for some time. You know I'll be working for your release every moment of each day.'

Will nodded. Arthur stood up and took Will in his arms. Will couldn't speak his goodbye and Arthur pressed his hand on Will's shoulder, hugging him close. He called to the gaoler to let him out and followed him back to the gaoler's small room. 'What's the price to remove my brother's leg irons?'

'Twenty pounds,' he said shortly.

Arthur slipped his hand into the purse he had tied around his waist and drew out the coins. 'Take them off tonight,' he said shortly. 'I'll be back tomorrow so make sure of it.'

CHAPTER FIFTY SEVEN

1ˢᵗ February 1748, London

Arthur called again briefly the following day with the basket of food as he had promised. He thought that Will looked slightly better, having been able to change his clothes, though he admitted he was longing for a shave.

He had no further news for Will apart from telling him he had seen Pete Tickner for a few minutes the previous evening after leaving Will's cell. He had only time to wish his old friend a safe passage and to promise to keep an eye on Tickner's wife and children over the next years. He encouraged Tickner to make contact with John Grayling and before he knew it, he was shaking Pete's hand and clapping him on the back, neither man sure if they would ever see each other again and each remembering countless occasions over the past twenty or so years when they had shared the excitement, the anxiety and the camaraderie of a run across the Marsh or up through the Kentish countryside.

Arthur had to leave Will after an hour as he was anxious to get back to his lodging in case word should come from Gideon. He heard nothing for a day and a half and then a servant rapped on the door of Arthur's room and pressed a sealed paper into his hand.

Arthur tore it open. All that was written was an address with brief directions and a time.

Arthur began to get ready at six, pulling a dark greatcoat over his clothes, a muffler ready to hide most of his face and pulled his hat down low. His leather purse heavy with gold coins was tucked inside his shirt next to his skin, and he wore a holster with two pistols round his waist. He took a hackney cab to Fleet Street and then made his way on foot down Bouverie Street as directed until he heard the river lapping nearby. He made his way cautiously towards Watermans Stairs and looked for the third house from the end as the directions had given.

It was quiet and very dark. In the distance he could hear sounds from the alehouses and taverns he had left behind in Bouverie Street. It looked as if the crumbling houses near the Stairs were uninhabited for there were no lights at any of the windows. He was about to knock on the door of the appointed house when it was thrown open. Arthur couldn't see into the unlit passage and a cloaked figure stepped out, his hat pulled down so low that Arthur couldn't see any of his features except his mouth. The man said nothing but held out his arm indicating the short walk to the Stairs leading down to the wide dark river.

Arthur stepped in front of the man and approached the top of the stairs. He stepped down about twenty steps which were steep and narrow with no rail to hold onto, only the slippery wall. Bobbing about on the bank of the river was a small boat tied to the iron bolt attached to the last step. The boat had a small lantern set in its side. Arthur stepped down to the bottom step and clutching the side of the boat, lowered himself into it. The man followed and taking up the oars, pushed the boat away from its mooring, pulling the rope in. He started to row into the middle of the river and Arthur felt for the first time the great power and pull of the tides in the Thames and its great width. A chill wind blew across from the south side. The man stopped rowing. He drew the oars in and Arthur felt the little boat being drawn along by the prevailing current and felt the familiar discomfort in his stomach.

The man lowered his head and Arthur waited for him to speak. 'I believe you wish to make a transaction pertaining to a detainee at Newgate?'

Arthur nodded and said, 'Yes.'

'Then the sum required for such a transaction is five thousand pounds.'

Arthur's instinct was to agree straight away but he paused. If the man felt he answered too readily, he might think that such a sum was a piddling amount to Arthur and raise it beyond his capability of paying. 'That's a lot of money,' he said.

The man sighed. 'And having your neck stretched is a painful way to meet your end,' he said flatly.

'When would this money be required?' Arthur asked.

'Two nights from now in this same place. There'll be a horse and cart waiting at nine. Agree?' the man asked.

'Have I your word that the transaction will be successful?' Arthur asked.

The man sighed again and said impatiently, 'The money guarantees that the man in a position to obtain the outcome you require will be offered your money to do so. No one can vouch for his word, until it is given.'

'But I understood you were the man who could obtain the outcome I require,' Arthur said shocked at the realisation that even this amount of money couldn't guarantee Will's release.

The man picked up the oars again. 'You can decide while I row back to Watermans Stairs,' he said impatiently.

Arthur's brain worked frantically in the few minutes he had. Was it worth casting nearly half his money on such an uncertainty? Yet if he did nothing, he had no where else to turn. The little boat was approaching the stairs. The man manoeuvred the boat next to the wall and tied the rope to the iron eyebolt. 'Well?' he asked.

'The money will be here,' Arthur replied.

The man said nothing and waited for Arthur to leave the boat and mount the stairs. At the top the man turned back to him. 'At nine then. Two nights from now.'

'Yes,' Arthur agreed.

The man turned and walked away into the night crossing a passageway and disappeared into one of the alleys running back up to Fleet Street. Arthur turned back into the night and retraced his footsteps back to Bouverie Street and managed to get a cab to take him back to Stockwell.

Arthur spent the next two days in frantic activity. He had to hire a horse and cart and several wooden chests. He had a note carried to Gideon telling him when and where he needed his five thousand pounds in cash.

A note from Gideon came back to Arthur, giving an address in St Giles and Arthur made his way there. A man opened the door and ushered Arthur inside. The man opened a locked door to an inner room and there on the floor were several chests. Arthur lifted the lid of one and saw heaps of gold coins massed together, the light from the small lamp the man held, catching their glint and sending out shafts of golden lights into the room. They manhandled the chests onto the cart and Arthur covered them with a tarpaulin. The man disappeared into the night.

Arthur, feeling alone and nervous, climbed up in to the driver's seat and set off. He was glad he had his pistols inside his coat. The roads were quiet as a heavy rain had started to fall. He passed a few lone horsemen and a couple of other carts. Fleet Street was busier, its many taverns noisy and smoke-filled, though the revellers paid him little attention. They probably thought he was a labourer on his way home with his tools in the back of his cart.

As he made his way down Bouverie Street he heard the river lapping louder than last time he was here, the rain and a stiff breeze making it much choppier than it had been two nights ago. Sure enough another wagon was drawn up at the stairs and the same man dressed as he was before, stood next to it, waiting. Almost in silence they transferred the chests of cash.

'It will be counted and if it's short, there's no deal between us,' the man commented.

'It's all there as agreed,' Arthur said quietly.

The man climbed up to his wagon, flicked the reins and Arthur watched him disappear with his five thousand pounds.

He waited for the next two days in a fever of anticipation. He half expected to see Will appear in the *Robin Hood*, but when he had heard nothing by the third morning, he sent again a note round to Gideon and they met at *Jonathan's*.

'Arthur, I can tell you no more. These processes cannot be hurried. You may not hear anything for a month or so.'

'A month?' Arthur said exasperated. 'Will may be tried within a month.'

'If your bribe was accepted, he will not be tried at all. Believe me, you would do better to go home and wait for news there. I'll send word to you if I hear anything.'

Arthur reluctantly left the coffee house and did as Gideon suggested after visiting Will once more. Will looked dejected when he heard nothing had yet happened. Arthur, worrying that his money might have disappeared without trace, didn't tell him any details of the transaction he had made or how much money he had ventured.

Back at Seacox, Arthur grew more frantic as each day brought no word from Gideon. He hardly slept and when he did, the great brooding prison that held Will, haunted his dreams. He dreamed he was running down Newgate's endless damp echoing corridors deeper and deeper into the subterranean passages looking for Will and never finding him. He would wake in a sweat with a start, jolting Sarah awake.

He decided to take Will's stallion, Saladin, out for a gallop and the great stallion was eager to be off as Will had known he would be. Arthur could feel the horse's pleasure at being out of the confines of his stable.

Beth rode with him. They rode off in silence but Arthur soon confessed to her the transaction he had made. She looked solemn, despairing that such a vast sum hadn't yet brought any results and returned Will home to them. 'I want to go and see Will,' she said quietly as they paused at an open space looking down towards Seacox.

He reached across his horse and touched her cheek, shaking his head. 'No Beth,' he said emphatically. 'It isn't fit for you to see him. Will doesn't want you to go. He doesn't want you to see him there.'

'But I feel so helpless doing nothing.'

'If there was anything you could do, I'd ask you to do it. You know that?'

She nodded.

'I'll go back up to London tomorrow and see what I can find out,' Arthur said, turning Saladin round as they made their way back.

Sarah was waiting for them at the door and when Arthur saw the piece of paper in her hand, he slid quickly out of the saddle and tore the sealed note open. Both women looked at him expectantly.

'What is it, Arthur?' Beth asked tremulously. 'Is Will free?'

Arthur shook his head, trying to keep the disappointment out of his voice. 'I don't know. This is just a note from Gideon asking me to meet him tomorrow.'

Beth caught his hand and looked at him with troubled eyes. 'I must come with you. I must be there to hear whatever news you get as soon as possible.'

Arthur looked at Beth and then at Sarah. 'Yes, all right. We'll both go.'

They set out an hour later for Stockwell and arrived at the inn just before five. As they shared supper in one of the small booths set aside for dining, Arthur looked anxiously at Beth. 'I shouldn't have brought you with me,' he said. 'I can't take you with me tomorrow. I'll have to leave you here. If Gideon's message – well if it means I have to transact more business, I may have to leave you here alone.'

Beth gave a little impatient shake of her head. 'Do you think that will worry me, Arthur? I'll keep to my room and wait as long as need be. I'll take my meals there. You must do whatever is necessary.'

They parted outside the door of Beth's room.

CHAPTER FIFTY EIGHT

Thursday 17^h Feb 1748, London

Arthur hardly slept and rose at six anxious to meet with Gideon and find out what had happened. Though it was just after eight when he stepped up the familiar steps to the coffee house, it was already busy bustling with life, the merchants and traders eager to do business as early in the day as possible before their rivals had the opportunity to make better deals.

He stepped into the usual back room and a servant brought him a tray of coffee. A half hour later the door opened and Gideon entered. Arthur stood at once trying to read his expression. 'What's happened? Your note was so brief.'

Gideon nodded and sat down. 'It's not the outcome you have wished for, Arthur-,' and at his words Arthur felt a sensation as if the floor underneath his feet had given way.

'Sit down, my friend and let me tell you what has transpired.' He pushed Arthur gently down into the chair and sat opposite him. 'Your brother is no longer charged under the '46 Act but he hasn't been released. Your money was sufficient to change the indictment to a charge under the '36 act. It means he cannot be convicted capitally, he won't be hanged.'

Arthur put his hands up to his face and covered his eyes. 'God be praised,' he said, his throat dry.

'Indeed,' Gideon agreed quietly and waited for Arthur to compose himself.

Arthur felt a sudden surge of relief flooded because Will no longer faced hanging. But then he felt alarm as Gideon's words began to register. 'It means he faces transportation,' he said, his face in his hands.

'If found guilty,' Gideon reminded him.

Arthur stood up and paced across the room. 'You said my outlay was only sufficient to change the charges. What if I ventured the rest of my money? That might be enough to throw out this new charge.'

Gideon turned round in his chair to face Arthur, shaking his head. 'Arthur, I do not think that will be possible no matter how much money you lay out. Intractable forces are working against you. My information leads me to believe that they as determined in their course as you are in yours.'

Arthur continued to pace the floor shaking his head. 'What are the charges exactly?'

'They relate to running goods in Kingston in '43,' Gideon began.

'Five years ago?' Arthur fumed. 'What witnesses can they have they dragged up from five years back?'

Gideon shook his head. 'I know no more than this. There's nothing more you can do for your brother but you must realise that you are yourself in danger? My advice is to see your brother once more and then take what money is left and remove yourself and your family into another part of the country or to France where you will be safe.'

'And leave Will to face his trial alone?' Arthur asked defiantly. 'I've always looked after him. I won't leave him now.'

Both men were silent for a while and then Arthur sighed and looked across at Gideon. 'Thank you, sir for what you've done. I know you've done your best. Believe me, I know how true a friend you've been to me, but the rest of this business is now up to me.'

Gideon nodded. 'I have realised the remainder of your assets into cash. I was surprisingly able to redeem most of them for their face value so I do not believe you have sustained a loss.'

He did not tell Arthur that it was Thomas Lamb himself who had bought Arthur's investments and bonds at their cost price so allowing Arthur to maximise his redemption value. Lamb had asked Gideon to keep the transactions secret.

Arthur rose to leave and Gideon also stood. The two men faced each other and shook hands. 'I wish you luck, Arthur. You know how to contact me when you need the rest of your cash. But I do urge you to consider my advice.'

Arthur nodded, shook Gideon's hand once more and left.

His mind was in a whirl as he tried to take in the news. He remembered how easily he had told Pete Tickner to make a new life for himself in Maryland. He had never envisaged the possibility of having to say the same to Will. He thought of the money had had laid up for himself in America thinking that he himself might face transportation one day, never imagining it would be Will and not himself in that position. He found himself walking towards Newgate.

Will was standing the other side of the iron door when he heard the key being turned in the lock and then Arthur stepped into the cell. He could say nothing but embraced Will pulling him close, rubbing the back of his neck in an old affectionate gesture. But then Will was seized with a fit of coughing and held his side. Arthur picked up the leather bottle on the table and held it out to his brother. 'You're not well,' he said.

Will shook his head, waiting to catch his breath. 'I'll be fine, Arty,' he gasped.

Arthur could only wait until Will took another mouthful of ale and sat down.

'I don't face hanging any more, Arty,' he said at last. 'It's your doing, isn't it?'

Arthur nodded. 'But who's laid evidence against you on the new charge? Do you know?'

'Two of the servants at the *Druid's Head* in Kingston. The 27th December 1743! Huh!' Will gave a short laugh. 'I can't remember what I was doing then, so how can those two fellows?' he asked. 'I've pleaded not guilty, of course. I'm due for trial in the April sessions.'

Arthur nodded. 'Then I'll go to Kingston and buy off these witnesses. They can hardly have come forward of their own accord after all this time. Someone has sought them out and paid them, that's for sure. I'll buy them out, Will. If the bastards can be bought once, they can be bought again by a higher bidder.'

Will looked at Arthur, who had always got him out of scrapes when he was a child. 'I know you'll do your best for me, Arty. I can never repay you.'

'There's nothing to repay. You're my brother, aren't you?' Arthur looked at him again, trying not to let his concern for Will's condition show in his expression. His beard made him look older. His complexion was pale against the dark growth of his beard and his eyes seemed to have sunk deeper into his face

'I'll be off to Kingston as soon as I can and then I'll go and tell Beth the news.'

'Is Beth here?' Will asked.

Arthur nodded. 'At Stockwell. She wanted to hear the news as soon as I got it. Do you want to see her, Will?'

Will shook his head. 'Not like this, Arty. Give her my love and tell her I'll see her soon, anyway. She mustn't worry about me. Don't tell her how wretched I look.'

Arthur gave a little smile and rose to leave. As he hugged Will close, he wondered how many more times he would have to visit his brother before he was released.

Arthur collected Peg from the stables behind *Jonathan's* and made his way through the streets towards London Bridge intending to ride from there into Surrey and Kingston. It was towards three in the afternoon when he reached the little town and passing the gilded statue of the old Queen Ann, made his way into Market Place. It was still busy with stalls and traders, all seemingly able to ignore the pungent smell coming from the tannery and candlemaker's close by. He stopped at the *Castle Inn*, where he and Will had often stayed on their runs up to the warehouses a mile outside the town.

The landlord, Jack Evans recognized him at once. 'Hello, Arthur,' he said cheerfully. 'Ain't seen you up this way for a long time. How are you and that brother of yours?'

'Will's in Newgate,' Arthur said grimly.

The landlord's jaw dropped open. 'Never?' he exclaimed. 'On what charge?'

'Running uncustomed goods, Jack. Can we talk for a moment? I need to ask you something.'

Evans put the tray he was carrying on a table nearby and took the seat next to Arthur and looked expectantly at him. 'What's all this then, Arthur?'

Arthur lowered his voice. 'Two men, servants at the *Druid's Head*, names of John Godard and Gyles Taylor. Do you know them?'

Evans nodded slowly. 'What about them?'

'They placed evidence against Will for a run five years ago, the fucking bastards! Are they still at the *Druid's*, Jack?'

The landlord looked thoughtful. 'Well I can't be sure. They were certainly there six months ago for I was a man down and Taylor came and worked for me, when he'd finished his shift there. But I don't know that I've seen him lately.'

'What do they look like? I can't remember either of 'em. I only wish I could,' Arthur said fiercely.

'Well, there's nothing particular about either man. Godard is dark, about average height, Taylor a little above average, about your build,' the landlord replied.

Arthur sighed. 'Thanks for your help, Jack. It seems I'll have to go to the *Druid's* and ask directly for them.'

He rose to go but Evans caught hold of his arm.

'Hold on a moment, Arthur. Kate Hammerton, one of my barmaids does a few shifts there. Let me send her over. She'll be able to tell you more.'

Arthur saw Jack go back to the taproom and have a word with a woman carrying a tray of drinks. They both looked across at Arthur and the woman put the tray down and came across to his table. He stood up and offered her the chair opposite.

'Jack says you want to ask me something?' she questioned, tucking a stray curl back in her cap as she sat down.

'I understand you work at the *Druid's Head*?' Arthur asked.

She nodded.

'Do John Godard and Gyles Taylor still work there?'

She looked interested. 'Well that's a queer thing you should ask,' she said. 'Both of them left about a week ago without a word and nobody's heard from either of 'em since. Do you know where they are?'

Arthur shook his head slowly. This was a blow indeed. 'Do they have family here Mrs Hammerton, wives or children?'

'No, they was both single men,' she said, 'and both had rooms at the *Druid's*.'

'How did they seem before they left?' Arthur asked. 'Did they seem any different?'

Kate drew in her breath and paused. 'Well, John Godard said to me the last shift we worked together, something about having had enough of waiting on other men and it was time to move on. I never give it a second thought til you asked me just now.'

It was a small enough clue, Arthur thought, but just the sort of thing a man might say if he had come into a substantial amount of money. 'There's just one more thing, Mrs Hammerton,' he said. 'Were they both working here in '43?'

She thought for a moment and then answered. 'Yes they was, for my little boy was born that year and both of em' worked my shifts for some of the time I was off when I had him.'

'You've been very helpful, Mrs Hammerton,' he said putting his hand in his pocket and drawing out a few coins. 'Perhaps you'd like to buy something for your little boy?'

She held out her hand, her face breaking into a smile at this unexpected gift. 'Why thank you, I didn't know it was that important to you.'

He nodded again. Someone had paid both men enough for them to walk away from their jobs and set up elsewhere. Someone had also ensured they were well enough hidden away so they could not be approached by anyone else offering a larger bribe.

Arthur arrived back at the *Robin Hood* at about seven, tired and dishevelled from the activities of his day. He took Peg round to the stables and made his way up to his room but first knocked on Beth's door. She flew to open it and he stepped inside.

'Arthur, I could hardly wait for you to come back. Tell me what's happened. Have you found out anything?' she cried.

'It's as we already knew, Beth,' he said flatly. 'Will was charged on the evidence of two paid witnesses. I tried to track them down but they've been paid off and have moved away or they're being kept out of the way until the trial begins.'

Beth looked cast down at this blow. 'Have you seen Will?'

'Yes, he sends his best love and says he will see you soon. As indeed he will. You must believe that.'

'But what can we do next?' Beth asked. 'I've been thinking – I can apply to my aunt and my uncle William Pix for money. Since Jeffery Pix died, my Uncle William has inherited all his money and estate.'

'I don't think that's a good idea,' Arthur replied shaking his head. 'Gideon tells me that no matter how much money I lay out, Will goes to trial. But if he's found not guilty, he'll go free. They surely won't bribe a whole jury to find him guilty?'

As soon as he said it, he realised that if the men in power were determined enough, anything was possible.

'Will's trial is fixed for the April sessions. Thank God that gives us some time. I'll take you home tomorrow and then return. I can't leave you here. It may be a while before there's any news.'

CHAPTER FIFTY NINE

Thursday 3 March 1748, London then Sandgate

Two weeks later Arthur, despondent and dejected, rode back from his abortive trip to London. He had not been able to gain any further information about Will's trial. He knew who the judge was likely to be, but not the jurors.

As Arthur rode home he tried to mull over what his last options might be. He could keep the remainder of his money in the hope that he could bribe some of the jurors at the last moment when their names were announced. He had to admit to himself this was a forlorn hope. Or he could hope to discover where Taylor and Godard were lodged just before the trial date and try to pay them off. Both these options depended on so many variables that their success seemed unlikely.

He could elect to do nothing and hope that Will was found innocent at trial. This left so much to chance that Arthur felt he couldn't consider it as a possibility.

Or he could accept the fact that Will would be found guilty and sentenced to transportation, in which case he would make himself busy as he had done ten years previously for John Grayling and buy a comfortable cabin for Will.

But then what? Will could never return to Kent or Sussex. Would he have to stay in America? And then there was Beth. He knew Beth's loyalty. She would go with Will if he had to stay in America. Arthur didn't know how he could live if both Will and Beth were lost to him.

As he approached Sissinghurst, Peg went lame. There was a forge in the village so he dismounted and led her the last half mile to the forge and went into the *Bull Inn* to wait. He was just about to sit down when a voice called him and turning round he saw John Henley sitting at one of the tables. It was good to see a familiar face and he took his drink over to the table. 'How are you, John?' he asked

John Henley smiled. 'I'm well, Arthur, but this is bad news about Will. Ned was shocked to hear it.'

Arthur nodded and then his face broke out in to a smile as he cursed his stupidity for not thinking of the solution sooner. Seeing John Henley made him realise that there was hope yet. 'John, where can I contact Kelly, the attorney who got Ned off? I can't think how I've been so stupid.'

'Is Will going to trial then?' Henley asked.

'Yes, in April.'

'Kelly is down in Folkestone next week. He and Ned are good friends. Why don't you come over and talk with him?' John suggested.

Arthur nodded. 'I will.' He shook John's hand. 'This is a piece of good news. I feel more hopeful now.'

Beth insisted that Arthur allow her to accompany him on Will's business in Folkestone. They arrived at four and went to the *White Horse* in Sandgate Road. Mr Kelly was waiting in the coffee parlour. He was of short stature and stocky build with a shock of red hair. He had pale eyes and a small pair of spectacles perched on his nose. He shook hands with Arthur bowing to Beth and indicated they should join him at the small table.

Arthur came straight to the point. 'You know my brother Will is in Newgate charged under the 36 act, the same as Ned was, and faces transportation? You got Ned off and I'm hoping you can do the same for Will.'

Kelly nodded. 'Yes I have made myself familiar with the case, Mr Gray. But I have to say the situation is somewhat different.' He pushed his spectacles back higher on his nose. 'Things have changed somewhat since Ned was released. The Government doesn't want to waste time bringing men to trial unless they're reasonably sure that they'll be found guilty. So they're making sure that they have witnesses who will give evidence under whichever of the two smuggling acts a man is charged. The two witnesses against Will have sworn their evidence on oath. I've found out what I can about them, the two men Godard and Taylor, and there's nothing out of the ordinary about either of them. Everyone speaks of their generally satisfactory characters; they've never been accused of any transgressions and seem to have lived fairly blameless lives.'

Arthur's disappointment showed in his face. 'Are you saying that he will be found guilty on their evidence?'

'I'm saying more than that, Mr Gray. The longer your brother stays in gaol, the more likelihood there is of further witnesses being paid to swear on oath that they have seen Will smuggling since July 46' and then the charges will revert to the original one, which you know would lead to hanging if found guilty.'

Beth let out a cry of disbelief.

'I'm sorry to say this, Mrs Gray, but you must face facts. You know that the powers currently controlling this country are making it their business to stamp out smuggling by whatever means possible. They're ensuring that anyone who is taken is tried under the Act most likely to bring about a guilty verdict. You will remember Mr Tickner's case. The case against him under the '46 act was weak, so they re-tried him under the '36 for which the witnesses were more vehement in their evidence, or better rehearsed,' he added drily. 'Unfortunately in your brother's case, it could work the opposite way, with the charge reverting from the '36 Act back to the '46 Act. Believe me, I have reason to think a case is currently being got together for that very purpose.'

Arthur groaned out loud thinking that all his efforts, all the money he had laid out had been in vain. 'Is there no hope? Is that what you're telling us?' he asked despondently.

Kelly shook his head. 'Let me explain a little of the law to you, Mr Gray. The authorities like a man to plead *not guilty*. It enables the case to go to trial and they can hear the evidence for and against the defendant. If however the man charged pleads *guilty*, there is no trial, merely a sentencing according to the requirements of the law.'

He paused to let this sink in. 'It's my earnest advice that you tell your brother to change his plea to guilty. Although it means he will be immediately sentenced to transportation, it closes the door to any further uncertainty and he will very likely be out of the country before another charge could be brought against him. His neck will be saved.'

Arthur and Beth both sat in silence absorbing this information. If Will elected to go to trial, there was a very slim chance he might be found not guilty and he would be freed. But if whilst waiting for trial, the charge was changed to prosecution under the Act of '46 –then Will would face hanging if convicted. By pleading guilty he was automatically consigning himself to transportation with no chance of freedom. Arthur rubbed his hands over his face.

Beth looked up, her hands clasped in her lap. 'There's only one option. Will must change his plea to guilty. It will save his life,' she said in a low voice.

Arthur nodded slowly. 'I agree, Beth. We can't risk him staying in gaol any longer.' He looked across at Kelly.

'I believe it's the right decision,' the attorney affirmed. 'You should see your brother as soon as possible and get him to change his plea.'

Arthur waited a moment in silence and then said quietly, 'Thank you for the effort you've made on Will's behalf.'

'Ned Henley asked me to do all in my power to help you, Mr Gray. I'm happy to do so. And now if there's nothing further I can help you with, I'll make my way to Ned's.'

Beth and Arthur watched him go. He took both her hands in his.

'Beth, I believe all will be well. I've three thousand pounds left. It will ensure a cabin for you and Will. You know I've laid up money for years in America thinking I myself might be transported. It'll be there waiting for you. Will can bribe the convict traders and buy his freedom.'

'And then what, Arthur?' she said dejectedly. 'I know he won't be able to come home, even if he does that. He can only return in safety if he serves seven years as a convict.'

Arthur looked down. 'Yes,' he said softly.

'Then I'll go with him and we'll stay there forever.' Beth looked at Arthur, biting her lip.

He took her hand and when he spoke, his voice was hoarse with emotion. 'John Grayling has made a good life for himself in Maryland. There's no reason why you and Will can't do the same. You'll be able to buy a farm. The land is fertile, Grayling says. Many men have become rich from growing tobacco. I don't want you to go, but there's no other option that can keep Will safe.'

'You did everything possible Arthur,' Beth said in a small voice and wiped a hand across her eyes. 'They can't hang him. You've saved him from that.'

They ate a meal in silence, neither of them very hungry and sat together in the back room of the inn in front of a small fire. 'I'll ride to London tomorrow and see Will and do what is necessary. I'll take you home first,' Arthur said gently.

Beth nodded, standing up. 'I'm so tired but I don't know if I'll sleep.'

Arthur stood up facing her and then put his arms around her.

'How did we come to this?' she asked.

'I don't know, Beth,' he murmured into her hair. 'I don't know.'

Arthur followed her an hour later, knowing in his heart now that he would lose them both; Will, his beloved brother and Beth, the woman he had loved all his life. He thought back over the years of a thousand different memories. As Beth had asked, so he himself wondered – how had it come to this?

He lay in bed, looking out of the window he had left ajar, hearing the sound of the sea a little way across the road. Its rhythmic lapping had lulled him to sleep eventually, but he had woken with a start remembering the events of the day. He knew that the ship that carried Beth and Will away from him would also carry away all the happiness he might ever have hoped for in the future. He sighed and got up, pulling his shirt round him. There was an urgent tapping at the door. He stepped across to open it and Beth fell in his arms.

'Arthur I can't bear it, I'm so afraid! That long crossing! Will is not always well. How will we live there Arthur, how will we live?

How can we leave everything we have known and loved?' she cried, white-faced.

'Shh Beth, you mustn't worry, you mustn't. You must be strong, as I must be. I must live without you,' he said, stroking her hair. 'I'll never see you again Beth, my darling, my love.'

She turned her face up to him and he quickly pressed his lips to hers kissing her fiercely, drinking in the scent of her skin, the softness of her hair, wanting to absorb it into himself, knowing she would soon be lost to him forever. He pulled her closer, feeling her heart beating against his chest and as her arms reached for him, he slipped his hands inside her nightshift feeling again the silkiness of her skin, running his palms over her belly, her waist, her breasts, burying his face in her neck. He pulled his own shirt off and pushed her shift down over her shoulders letting it slip to the floor. He lifted her over to the bed. She cried out his name as he pressed himself against her, feeling her thighs open to him, waiting for him. They both knew it was wrong and neither of them could stop.

They fell asleep, their arms and legs entwined as the pink dawn broke, its rosy fingers stealing across a navy sky.

Thursday 10th March 1748

Arthur woke and looked across at Beth curled up against him, her hair a halo of brown and gold on the pillow. He sighed at her beauty and gazed at her, wishing he had a painting of her, fearful that he might one day forget what she looked like. He noticed the pink curve of her mouth, her dark lashes, her smooth pink cheeks, the gentle line of her neck and the soft rise and fall of her breasts as she slept. He moved his arm slightly under her and she stirred and then woke. Her soft grey eyes opened and she whispered his name.

'I have to go now. I have a long day,' he said softly.

She nodded and put her arms around him. 'Just hold me again for a little while, Arthur.'

He took her in his arms. They both knew this was the last time they would ever lie like this, lovers in each others arms. He gently put her from him, kissing her forehead and left the bed.

It was a beautiful day, a pale clear sky with the warm sunlight sparkling on the dew as they set out for home. They stopped once

503 · Men of Sorrows

at Tenterden to water the horses and then got on their way again, sometimes silent, sometimes talking of past times. To talk of the future was too painful. They rode into Hawkhurst towards one in the afternoon and as they rode up the gentle hill to Seacox, they were both aware that their time together was ending. They would never ride like this again, neither as companions or lovers. Arthur saw the soft red brick of his house, smoke rising from the chimney and thought of the time he had brought Beth here long before it was built, when they had all their hopes in front of them on that summer morning so long ago.

They rode round to the stables to attend to the horses, Arthur lifting off the saddles and hanging them on the iron hooks.

'I'll rub down the mares, Beth. You go in,' he said as brightly as he could turning back to the stable as Beth walked up to the kitchen door. Her cry brought him running back out and looking to the house, he saw her at the door, a stricken look on her face, a Dragoon holding her elbow and a white-faced Sarah and their daughters standing behind her, as more of the Dragoons came out of the house.

Time appeared to stand still. His first instinct was to jump back on Peg and gallop away but his legs seemed rooted to the spot. He dropped his shoulders and walked towards Colonel Brotherton.

'Arthur Gray, I have here a warrant for your arrest-,'

'Yes,' Arthur said simply. 'I understand. Who has sworn against me?'

The Colonel looked disconcerted. He looked at the paper in his hand. 'Humphrey Haddon, John Pelham and John Polhill.'

Arthur let out his breath in a sigh of disbelief. Haddon worked as a servant at the *George* in Lydd, Pelham was a rough labourer and sometime fisherman from Lydd and John Polhill was one of the Riding Officers. Arthur hadn't seen any of them for a couple of years.

'Which Act am I charged under?' Arthur asked, his voice hoarse.

'The '46,' Brotherton said briefly.

It had happened then. This was the end. There was no one to work for his release on the outside once he was imprisoned as he had been able to do for Will. Jim Cook, Pete Tickner and Will were now all beyond his reach; and besides, all his money was gone. It would be paid out to take Will and Beth to safety and a new life. He let out his breath slowly. 'Colonel Brotherton, will you allow me time to say goodbye to my family?'

Brotherton seemed to hesitate and then nodded. 'So long as you do it outside where my men can see you, Arthur. We know there are hidden passages in your house. You can't escape now.'

Arthur turned towards Beth, Sarah and his daughters. He walked up to Sarah and took her in his arms. She was weeping softly. 'Hush Sarah, there's a good girl.' He rocked her gently in his arms and whispered in her ear. 'There's a chest of money in the passage leading from the false chimney place in the front parlour, about eight hundred pounds. You can be comfortable.'

Sarah shook her head, raising her tear-stained face to his. 'No I can't Arthur, not without you.'

'Yes, yes you will,' he said soothingly. 'Listen, Sarah, you're not to come to Newgate. Promise me?'

She nodded, her face hidden against his chest. 'Arthur,' she said in a tremulous voice. 'Arthur!'

'Shh, there's nothing more to say, Sarah,' he whispered soothingly. 'You've been a good wife, better than I deserved. Now you must look after our girls and try and be happy again.'

He held out his arms to his daughters and they embraced him as he kissed them all and whispered his love for them. 'Look after your mother and your little sister Susie,' he said to Sally and Becca, crying in his arms.

'I must ask you to hurry, Arthur,' Brotherton called out.

Sarah handed Arthur a leather bag. She wiped her tears with her apron. 'There's some food, Arthur, cheese, bread, a seed cake and clean shirts and a blanket.'

He kissed her again. 'You've looked after me to the last, Sarah,' he said gently, as she clung to his chest again. 'Come, you must let me go.' Arthur disentangled himself from his family and looked across to Beth. She stepped into his arms and he lowered his mouth to her ear, whispering.

'Beth, you know what I intended to do today. You must get word to Will somehow, to change his plea.'

She nodded, tears streaming down her cheeks.

'Don't fail me,' he continued in a low voice. 'Ask Lucas, or Lamb. Ask anyone who you think may help. Ask Lamb how to make contact with Gideon. He holds the last of my money.'

Brotherton approached and put a hand on Arthur's shoulder. 'It's time to go,' he said.

Arthur pulled Beth to him and pressed his lips to her cheek and then the top of her head, whispered his goodbye and let go of her. Then he turned to the Colonel, holding out his wrists for the chains to be fastened.

After being charged before the Justice at Maidstone just before seven in the evening, Arthur was put into the holding cell at Maidstone gaol with six other felons, various wretches who had committed minor crimes and who would receive their punishments the following day. It was inevitable that the Justice of the Peace would commit Arthur to Newgate as the severity of the charges was beyond his jurisdiction. After a sleepless night, Arthur was taken out again, his wrists still manacled and was mounted on a horse surrounded by the party of six Dragoons who would escort him to Newgate.

They approached the great prison towards ten in the morning, the clock of the gloomy church of St Sepulchre's opposite, tolling the hour. The gaol's forbidding towers and battlements cast a deep shadow across the street. Arthur raised his eyes above the huge iron doors, looking at the fetters displayed there and the great dial set in the wall bearing the words, '*I come as a thief*'. He was bundled off the horse and the great doors were opened.

The foul gaol stench made him almost gag as he was taken to the Keeper's Lodge to be formally entered as an accused felon at Newgate. The Keeper asked him if he wished to make a deposition naming anyone he wanted to appear as a character witness for him at his trial. Arthur hesitated. He dare not name Lamb or Gideon so he named Sam Terrell and William Bishop, Hawkhurst men, both tradesmen who had known him all his life. They were not involved with the gang in any way and they would surely swear that Arthur had been honest in his dealings with them.

Though the chains were removed from his wrists, they fitted leg irons to him and then he was taken, stumbling through the long dark passageways until they came to a cell at the far end. He was pushed in, the leather bag Sarah had packed was thrown onto the floor and the door clanged shut behind him; he heard the key turn in the lock.

He looked around the cell. It was like all the others he had been in - a square room with high walls, twice a man's height, with only a tiny barred window to let in any light, a table with one candle on it and a jug, a chair, a bucket in the corner and a low narrow bed pushed against the wall which was wet with damp and a green mould. He moved towards the bed and forgetting he was fettered, took too long a step and fell forwards into the damp straw, its foul smell invading his nostrils. He hauled himself up and pulled the bed away from the damp wall, dragged the leather bag over to it and sat down.

He unwrapped the bread that Sarah had wrapped in linen and tore off a hunk, chewing hungrily. He paused, needing to quench his thirst and reached over to the table pulling the jug towards him. It was half full of foetid water. He hesitantly took a sip but as the rank liquid filled his mouth, he felt himself heave and spat it out. He reached back inside the bag and pulled out the wool blanket, carrying it to his face. It smelt of home. He wrapped himself in it as best he could and lay down turning on his side, pulling the edge of the blanket to cover his face, the choking feeling of despair and helplessness washing over him.

He must have dozed because the clanging of the door woke him and for a moment he was unaware of his surroundings, expecting to find himself in his bed as Seacox. The dream vanished as a voice called out, 'Ho there, prisoner, on yer feet.'

Arthur turned over and recognised the gaoler as the same man who had charge of Will and to whom he had paid several amounts of money to try and ensure a little comfort for his brother.

The gaoler didn't seem to recognise him at first, but as Arthur stepped forward into the meagre light, the bulky man raised his eyebrows. 'Oh, if it ain't you, mister! Got yourself banged up then? Or have they took you in his place?' he asked, tipping out the water from the jug on to the floor and refilling it from a large earthenware bottle.

Arthur looked puzzled. 'I don't know what you mean. Whose place do you think I've taken?'

The gaoler looked up from his task. 'That brother of yourn. Excaped last night. We had some trouble. Hawkins, the night gaoler must've been far gone in liquor. Two prisoners knocked him on the head, took his keys and lets theirselves and the prisoners either side of 'em, out - one of 'em being your brother.'

Arthur could hardly believe what he was hearing and was filled with elation that Will was free. 'And they got away?' he asked the gaoler anxiously. 'Have they been retaken?'

The gaoler shook his head. 'Ah, that I don't know. Ain't nobody seen any of 'em since, though. Who knows?'

Arthur allowed the feeling of joy and relief to stay with him, trying not to think beyond it for as long as he could and in his mind's eye pictured Will galloping on Saladin over the tracks and fields of home, dressed in fresh linen and clean clothes.

The feeling of relief lasted for about ten minutes and after the cell door had been clanged shut again and he was sitting on the rough chair, the blanket still around him for warmth, he realised that by his escape, Will had committed himself to a life on the run. He could never ride freely again, he could never go back to his home with Beth. Arthur had no doubt he would be hunted down with a price on his head.

CHAPTER SIXTY

Newgate Gaol, early March 1748

Will, dozing in his cell towards midnight one moment, was, fifteen minutes later, running for his life down Newgate Street, his heart hammering inside his chest as if it would burst, his old wound giving him a painful stitch in his side. He hadn't had time to think beyond the fact that his cell door had been flung open and three men whom he had never seen before in his life stood there carrying lanterns, telling him to follow them and run. And run they did, along endless passages and up and down flights of stairs until they came to a barred grille leading along to another passageway.

'This is the grille that Charlie swears he's loosened,' one said in a breathless voice. It was soon obvious why the two escapees had brought Will and his fellow prisoner from the next cell with them. It needed the combined strength of the four of them to ram their weight against it. They heard the scraping sound as the iron loosened from where it had been set in the wall, but whoever Charlie was, he had been chipping away at the joints to some purpose for on the third onslaught as all four men hurled themselves against the grille, it gave way and they fell through tumbling over each other on the wet floor. They ran up the narrowing passageway which led to a hatch. It lifted easily and they stumbled out to moonlight and fresh air. Looking around at the rough ground strewn with heaps of earth, some marked with rough wooden crosses or markers, Will realised they were in a graveyard.

'Newgate burial ground,' one of the men said with a rough laugh, holding up two heavy iron keys on a chain, 'and here are a set o' keys!

Our brother Charlie digs the graves, only he's been digging a bit further than usual of late. Don't know who you two are, but thanks and good luck. It's each man for hisself now, ain't it, Dan?'

The other man, apparently his brother, gave a quick nod. Will glanced at the other escapee who looked as surprised at his good fortune as Will. The four men ran to the heavy iron barred gates. They all held their breath and then sighed with relief as they heard the key turn in the lock and they were free.

'Run like the wind,' Dan advised as he and his brother ran off into the night. Will glancing over his shoulder, set off in the opposite direction and soon lost himself in the maze of alleys and passageways around the gaol. He knew he needed to find the Thames and within a short time he could hear and smell the great river. He made his way to Westminster Stairs and paid the boatman with the one of the coins he had on him, to row him to Vauxhall on the other side where he knew the South Lambeth Road would lead him to Stockwell and familiar territory.

A wagoner carried him for sixpence all the way from Stockwell to Sevenoaks and then a farmer driving a cart pulled by two oxen, took him to Lamberhurst. By keeping to the woods all the way, Will finally got to the outskirts of Hawkhurst and home towards ten in the morning. He didn't dare go to Seacox or his own home though he longed to surprise them and thought of the look on Beth and Arthur's face when they saw him but sense told him it was the first place the militia would come looking for him so he skirted past Hawkhurst and made his way to James Stanford's home towards Etchingham.

Will approached the newly built square-fronted house with caution, hiding behind a chicken coop. He heard the back door open and Mary Stanford came out with a basket of linen followed by her four-year-old son James. Will heard her laughing with the little boy as he passed her the clothes pegs to hang up her linen. He waited a few minutes. Everything seemed normal with no sign of any militia. He took a deep breath and stepped forward into the yard. 'Mary!' he called.

He saw her spin round. She looked puzzled and Will realised that with his beard and in his tattered state, she didn't recognise him.

'Don't you know me, Mary Stanford?' he asked laughing and she looked closely at him and then broke into a smile.

'Will, Will! Have they freed you?' she shouted, looking surprised and puzzled.

He came up to her, still looking around nervously. 'Is James here, Mary? Is it safe?'

'James is within. But how is this, Will? James!' she shouted into the house. 'James, come out quickly.'

James Stanford came to the doorway and he smiled broadly as he recognised his boyhood friend and hurried over to Will, embracing him. 'Have they freed you, man?' he asked, clapping him on the back and drawing him into the house.

'It's a long story James,' Will replied. 'I escaped. I need you to get word to Arthur and Beth. Can I stay here a while?'

Will saw the smile on Stanford's face turn to puzzlement. 'Ain't you heard, Will? Don't you know? Arthur's been taken. They took him to Newgate this morning.'

What colour there was in Will's face, drained out of it. 'No! Say it's not so, James!' He put his hands over his face. 'I can't believe it.'

'It's all over the village, Will. Brotherton came for him yesterday afternoon. But sit down,' he said, pulling out a chair at the large kitchen table. 'Mary, get Will some ale and food. He looks as thin as a rake.'

Will sat down holding his head in his hands, propping his elbows on the table. All his elation at his freedom turned to ashes in his mouth. Mary Stanford carrying her six month baby in one arm, brought him over a jug of ale and bread and meat while young James and his little sister Mary came and stood by Will, looking solemnly at the tall, bearded man who smelt bad, sitting at the table.

An hour later Stanford escorted Beth, as they rode back along the road from Seacox towards Etchingham. Beth was at first unable to take in what Stanford told her, that Will was free and was at that very moment eating breakfast in the Stanfords' kitchen. Crying with joy, she had wanted at first to go home to collect some things for Will but James warned her that this was where the militia would come looking for her husband, so she and Sarah hastily packed a bag with some of Arthur's clothes for Will to wear. Beth carefully placed Will's pistols in the bag. Beth rode next to Stanford anxious to meet her husband; her joy doubled because if Will had escaped, Arthur could too.

Will stripped himself naked standing in the Stanfords' yard, the two eldest of the Stanford children watching from the door giggling, until their mother swept them away back into the kitchen. Will bent over the pump swinging the handle many times until he felt he had got the smell of the gaol out of his body and his hair. Mary lent him her husband's razor and he shaved off his beard and putting on some of Stanford's clothes that Mary brought out to him, waited for Beth to arrive. She swung herself down from the saddle straight into Will's arms crying and laughing at the same time, as Will pulled her close to him burying his face in her hair.

'What are you going to do Will? What's your plan?' Stanford asked as they all sat around the kitchen table.

Will shook his head. 'I don't know. Now Arthur has been taken, it's all changed. I have to work out a plan to get him free. I can't think straight right now. I'm so tired.' He coughed raspingly rubbing his eyes with his palms and drew his hands down over his face.

'Is Will safe here?' Beth asked James and then looked across at her husband. 'Surely the militia are looking for you, Will?'

Will nodded. 'Bound to be.'

'You're safe here for a night or so. After that, I'm not sure. It depends how many Dragoons they can spare, I suppose,' Stanford said encouragingly. 'Why don't you rest, Will? Take our room. Mary and I have to go out, don't we, love? The house will be quiet.'

Mary Stanford looked confused for a moment and then seeing the warning look in her husband's face, agreed. 'Yes, indeed we do.'

'We're visiting Mary's father in Heathfield. We'll be gone all afternoon,' Stanford explained. 'In fact we're late already. Get the children ready, Mary.'

Mary bustled about after the children and twenty minutes later as her husband pulled himself up next to her in the driving seat of the wagon she looked at him anxiously. 'Why are we going, James?'

He met her look with an amused expression. 'What does a man want when he comes out of gaol, Mary? Food and drink, a wash and his wife. We've given him the first, now we can give them a few hours together without them worrying they'll disturb us.'

Will and Beth watched the Stanfords leave and walked back into the kitchen. Beth gathered the plates and mugs from the table and set them on the dresser, but Will walked over to her and turned her round, drawing her against him. 'Beth, my darling wife, I've longed for you so much these past months,' he murmured into her hair. 'I dreamed sometimes I was holding you, running my hands over your beautiful body, making you mine. When I woke and found myself in my cell, it nearly drove me mad.'

'Oh don't speak of it, Will,' Beth said softly. 'I can't bear to think of you, or Arthur, in that place.'

Will nodded. 'If only Arthur was free, I could be perfectly happy. I'll get him out one way or another and we can all be together again.'

He started to loosen the laces at the front of her gown, his hands seeking the softness of her breasts. He drew in his breath at the touch of her skin against his fingertips. 'Come to bed with me, Beth,' he breathed. 'Don't ask me to wait any longer.'

He put his arm about her shoulders, caressing her neck and they mounted the staircase together.

CHAPTER SIXTY ONE

Saturday March 12ʰ 1748, Etchingham near Hawkhurst

The next morning dawned bright and sunny. 'I don't know how long it will be safe to stay here, Will,' James said anxiously, later that morning.

Will looked up gazing distractedly out of the small panes of the kitchen window. 'I long to be in my own home, James,' he said.

James shook his head. 'That's not possible, you know that.'

Both men fell silent as Beth came into the kitchen.

'Have you thought about settling in France, Will?' Stanford asked. 'There's many a Kentish man with a price on his head has made a home for himself there. They say you can hear English spoke as readily as French in Gravelines.'

Will looked solemn. 'I have to get Arthur free before I go anywhere. He'll know what to do.'

Stanford looked at Beth as she pulled out a chair and sat next to Will. 'What do you think?'

'I know Will can't ever stay in Kent. You can't stay anywhere you're known, Will,' she said despondently.

'Are you certain of it though?' Will asked, scanning her face. They had spoken of it last night, curled up in the little bed, whispering in the dark.

'Arthur is sure they'll never give up looking for you. You know his plan for you, for us.'

'Well, if the choice is America or France, I would sooner go to France, but I'd rather stay here,' Will said sadly looking around him. 'I just can't imagine living any where else.'

'As Beth says, I don't think it's an option. You must see that,' Stanford put in.

They were all silent for a little while, mulling over the possibilities.

'Arthur has some money laid up in London. He wanted to use it to buy a safe passage for Beth and me to America,' Will explained. 'But that was while I was still banged up. Now I'm free, I can use it to secure Arthur's freedom.'

'I'll go and see Thomas Lamb,' Beth said decidedly, after a short time. 'Arthur asked me to speak to him.'

Stanford smiled encouragingly but Beth looked thoughtful. She had heard from Arthur how much money had been needed to get the charge against Will changed. She didn't think three thousand pounds would secure such a deal for Arthur. But she had another plan. Lamb was very wealthy and had always shown a particular fondness for Arthur. If she begged him, surely he would use some of his great wealth on Arthur's behalf?

'Do you plan to ride together to Rye?' James asked them both. 'Surely not? I can escort you Beth, while Will stays here.'

'No James, I ain't such a coward to hide behind my wife's skirts, or put your wife in any danger by staying here while you ride off. No, we'll keep off the main road. It's been a dry spring, ain't it, the road should be dry.'

'Well, no one will recognise you,' Stanford said, trying to make a joke. 'Apart from when you showed up yesterday in your prison filth, I ain't ever seen you look so shabby.'

Will looked down at Arthur's old coat, too broad for him and with the breeches belted tightly to stay up.

'No,' he agreed ruefully. 'Beth brought me some of Arthur's clothes. You know he ain't got time for tailors.' He paused almost as if waiting for his older brother to come back with a smart reply but of course there was none.

Ten minutes later, Will and Beth set off towards Rye. As they approached the north end of the little town, Beth drew Prue to a halt. They were hidden in a thicket of trees some half mile outside the town. 'Will, I can't think it wise for you to be seen here,' she whispered. 'Anyone might see you and inform the Dragoons.'

Will looked up at the town.

'I'm safe here,' Beth continued. 'Let me go on my own.'

Will looked uncertain but then he nodded. 'I'll go to Bexhill, to the *Swan* just a little way out of town. I'm not so well known there. I think I'll be safe and there ain't Dragoons there.'

'I'll come to you there, Will.'

'No, I'll come back and meet you here, Beth. I don't want you to ride alone to Bexhill. I'll be back here at six just before sunset, in this same place.'

Twenty minutes later Beth was tapping on the front door of Thomas Lamb's handsome house in Conduit Hill. Harriett Marshall opened the door to her and looked surprised and worried when she saw who her master's visitor was.

'Oh, Mrs Gray,' she said looking anxiously at Beth. 'Is there any news of Arthur? I beg pardon for asking you, when you've come to see Mr Lamb. Excuse me indeed.'

'Of course you may ask about Arthur, Mrs Marshall. I know you're very old friends,' Beth said stepping into the hall. 'But he's still being held. I know nothing more.'

Harriett shook her head, her eyes sad and downcast.

'Beth, this is a pleasant surprise,' Thomas Lamb said, putting his head round the door of his drawing room. 'I thought I recognized your voice. Come in, my dear.'

He walked up the passageway leaning heavily on his stick, Beth noticed. He took her hand in his thin one and kissed it. She heard the soft wailing of a baby upstairs. Lamb smiled. 'My grandson. He's fifteen months old. Such a fine little lad. He took his first steps last week. Harriett tells me nothing in the house is now safe.'

Beth smiled back at him. 'I don't believe you mind that in the least, Mr Lamb.'

'No, indeed,' he said, as he ushered her into the drawing room and a comfortable chair. 'But I know you haven't come here to talk about my grandson. It's about Arthur Gray, isn't it?'

Beth met his gaze with her clear grey eyes. 'It's more than that, now Mr Lamb. Will has escaped.'

Lamb looked shocked. 'Escaped? And is he here?' he asked looking around as if he expected Will to walk through the door.

'No we thought it too dangerous in Rye.'

'Yes, I believe you're right.'

'Mr Lamb, I understand from Arthur that you know how I may contact Mr Gideon? I know he has Arthur's money, what's left of it, in safe keeping. I know I may speak to you in confidence. It was to buy a safe passage for Will and me to America.'

Lamb did not look at all surprised to be hearing this.

'Do you know of this then?' Beth asked.

Lamb nodded. 'There are those of us who are fond of Arthur who have been working on his behalf where we can. I can put you in touch with Gideon. But I don't think you should go up to London alone, Beth. If I weren't such an old fellow with gout in both knees, I should come with you. I'll ask William Pix, your uncle and my kinsman to accompany you. Robert Spain can take you there at once.'

Alice Marshall brought in a tray in with a silver tea pot and fine blue and white cups. She was a very different Alice Marshall from the one who had caught Jeremiah Curtis's eye, with her long dark hair now tied neatly back, wearing a dark gown, high cut and with a neat lace cap on her head.

They waited until Alice had left before continuing their conversation.

'There's something else I must ask you,' Beth said. 'I know there's only three thousand pounds of Arthur's money left. I know how much it cost him to get Will's charge changed. I am asking you, Mr Lamb,' she faltered, looking down and then met his eyes again. 'I am asking you sir, if you will use some of your money to secure Arthur's release, or at least, use it to attempt to have the charge changed to the '36 Act. Neither Will nor I, could bear it if he, if he-,'

Lamb took her hands quickly in his. 'Beth my dear, if I thought money could secure his release, he would be free as we speak. But there are men in the very highest positions in the land who want to keep him in Newgate. The Duke of Newcastle himself, the brother of the First Lord and himself the Home Secretary, has made it his business to have Arthur brought to trial.'

'Then you won't help him?'

'Beth, it can't be done,' the old man said sadly shaking his head. 'I have tried, many of us have tried.'

She got up stiffly.

'My dear, I'll do anything else I can. Come and stay with me here when you come back from London. Have Will's horses brought here and anything else you wish. Let me help where I can.'

Beth nodded slightly but was grave and solemn as she let herself be led out to the stables where Robert Spain was getting out the lumbering old coach to take them the short way out to Northiam and William Pix's farm. On his return, having left Beth there, Spain was despatched to the thicket just outside Rye to meet Will and explain why Beth herself could not meet him there. Will had no choice but to return alone to Bexhill.

CHAPTER SIXTY TWO

Newgate Gaol, Monday March 14ᵗʰ 1748

Two days later just after noon, Beth and her uncle turned into Newgate Street. She insisted on going in alone and though her uncle said he would not allow it, she simply dismounted and joined the ragged, rowdy crowd who were waiting to be let in. William Pix, flinging a shilling at a ragamuffin to hold their horses, hurried after her. 'Beth I can't let you go in alone. It isn't fitting,' he protested.

'Uncle, wait for me here. It's my wish to go to his cell alone,' she replied bluntly.

The great doors were opened and as William Pix was left in Keepers Lodge, Beth was escorted down dark corridors and stone passageways. She felt a cold chill creeping into her bones. It seemed to rise up from the bowels of the dark, miserable, foul-smelling place. It would be hard to keep your spirits up in such a place, Beth thought and she reflected on the places where Arthur had grown and lived, the sweeping expanses of the Marsh, the windswept shore of Dungeness, his beloved Seacox with its vistas down over the green woods of Kent and Sussex. And here men had confined him in a cell, iron fetters on his legs.

The gaoler pulled aside the iron shutter and called in to Arthur's cell. 'Visitor for you,' he said thrusting the key into the lock as he did so and pushed open the heavy door.

'Call me, when you wants to come out, Miss,' he said dismissively and pulled the door shut. In two steps Beth was in Arthur's arms, unable to speak, dry sobs in her throat, unaware of the stench in the cell, the damp dripping walls or Arthur's dirty clothes and stubbled chin as he pressed his face against her hair. 'Beth, you shouldn't have come, but I'm so glad you have.'

He turned from her, shaken by the way his hands seem to tremble. He wanted to say so much but all he said was, 'I can offer you some ale, Beth. My last sixpence bought it.' Then with a tremor in his voice, asked, 'How is Will? Have you seen him?'

She sat at the table as he went to fetch the jug from the small ledge under the high barred window. 'Will is well, Arthur. But you must tell us what to do.'

He turned around. 'Thank God! I was so thankful when I heard he had escaped. But it can't last. He can't stay out.'

Beth looked at him with frightened eyes. 'What do you mean Arthur? We thought of going to France. It's closer, easier to come back, if-,'

Arthur shook his head slowly. 'It's too close - France, Holland, Austria. They're all too near with too many English regiments about. It is easy to get there, sure but easy too for someone to bring Will back. There's a bounty on his head now and some men would give up another man's life for just a few pence. Sweetheart, I can buy you both a new life in America. But Will has to give himself up. If he does anything else, I can't be sure of his safety. But you must persuade him. Can you do it?'

Beth took two paces across the floor, shaking her head, 'I don't know, Arthur. This place is so terrible. It will be so hard for Will to come back here – to allow himself to be brought back now he has tasted freedom again.'

Arthur got up and caught hold of Beth's hands. 'But it can't last, you must see that. They won't let Will go free. You must do this for me. Promise me.'

She looked up at him in distress. 'Oh Arthur can't you work as hard as this for your own freedom? I can't bear to know - to think of what might happen to you.'

'Shh,' he said soothingly. 'I'm resigned to what will happen to me if I know that you and Will are safe – that's all I ask. Where is he now?'

'At Bexhill. I think he's trying to arrange a boat for France.'

'Who does not know him at Bexhill? Young fool!' Arthur looked distraught for a moment. 'You must get James Stanford to help you persuade Will. Or Lucas Webb. Everything is arranged. Gideon sent word to me. He's used my money as I asked him to furnish you and Will with the Captain's own cabin on the *Justitia*. She sails on May 10th, the first ship after the April Assizes. But Will must give himself up. Beth, you've never failed me. Don't fail me in this.'

Beth shook her head in despair.

Arthur undid the little bag she had brought him with fresh supplies and a leather purse with fifty pounds and then called to Jupp the gaoler to let Beth out.

'Let me stay longer, Arthur,' she begged.

He shook his head holding her close before putting her from him. 'No, you must go. I should be a villain to ask you to stay longer in this place.'

'I'll come back when I've spoken with Will.'

He nodded as Jupp swung open the door and banged it shut almost as soon as Beth had stepped out, leaving Arthur in his cell with just the faint impression of her soapy scent that had first attracted him when they were children.

Her Uncle William Pix looking anxiously around the corridor from Keepers Lodge sighed with relief when he saw Beth. They rode their horses back to the inn at South Audley Street where their coach was left and they travelled back to Rye almost in silence.

CHAPTER SIXTY THREE

Tuesday 15th March, 1748, Rye

The next day, Robert Spain was dispatched to Bexhill to leave a message at the *Swan* telling Will to meet Beth outside Rye that evening at six. She would tell him what Arthur had said his brother should do. Arthur had always known best. She would have to persuade Will that he still did.

She set out down Conduit Hill at about a quarter before six. She knew she would be able to persuade Will. She knew he would do this terrible thing if she asked him. He would allow himself to be taken back to the dreadful place from which fate had allowed him to escape. As she walked down Longer Street, she saw Jeremiah Curtis going into his house. He didn't seem to notice her at first but then as he recognized her, he stood in her way. 'Well, Beth Gray, what brings you past my door?' he asked looking her up and down.

She attempted to pass. 'Let me by, Jeremiah,' she said quietly.

'I'm just wondering how you're filling your time Beth, what with both Arthur and Will banged up.'

She sighed and turned to cross to the other side but he took her wrist, saying in a softer tone, 'I'm really sorry to hear your troubles. But I may be able to help. Step inside for a moment or two and I'll tell you.'

She looked up at him but for once there was no sneering look in his eyes. 'You mean you know something? You may be able to get Arthur freed?'

He nodded quickly.

She turned into his doorway. 'Then tell me quickly, Jeremiah. I'm in a hurry.'

He followed her up the stairs, noticing the sway of her hips under the panniers of her full skirt. 'Then step inside with haste, Beth.' He drew out his key pushing the door open and followed her inside.

Once in his room, Curtis caught hold of her sleeve and pulled her towards him, a wild look in his eyes. 'Arthur and Will, Will and Arthur! They're all the same to you, ain't they? You didn't seem to mind bedding two brothers, how about a third?'

She wrenched her arm away, leaving the ripped lace from her sleeve in his clutch. 'What do you mean, Curtis? Why have you brought me up here? You said you had something to tell me.'

'Oh I got plenty to tell you, Beth. How about this? I know you went from one brother's bed to the other or for all I know maybe all three of you shared the same bed. Or maybe you had a rota? Arthur on Mondays, Will on Tuesdays. Who got you on high days and holidays? You seem to like brothers. How about me?'

Beth raised her hand to hit him but he caught her wrist and said venomously, 'I said, how about me?'

'I don't know what you mean,' she said, her breath coming in gasps. 'Do you mean you're Arthur's brother? Is that what you're telling me? That Lamb is his father too? I sometimes wondered if Lamb's kindness had a deeper reason.'

He laughed. 'How can Gray's whore be so innocent?' he taunted. 'Ain't you ever looked in a mirror, Beth?'

He pulled her by the arm over to the large mirror above the fireplace and pushed her in front of him forcing his elbows over her shoulders and squeezing her face between his palms, holding her head upright so she saw both their reflections in the mirror. 'Do you see anything of John Stone there?' he challenged. She looked bewildered.

'Look harder Beth. Whose face do you see there looking back at you? Thomas Lamb is your father as well as mine! Welcome to the family, little sister.'

She looked at him, all the colour draining out of her face feeling that her world had somehow been tipped upside down and all reality was falling out of it. 'What? Why are you saying this? It's a lie, a lie!'

Beth looked at her own reflection and then allowed her eyes to travel to Curtis's reflected image and then back at her own. She was breathing so fast, she began to feel light-headed, the blood singing in her ears, Curtis's breath hot on the back of her neck. He pulled all her hair back from her face and held it on top of her head, so her forehead was bared. 'There, my little sister, you must acknowledge we come from a damned handsome family?'

Looking back at her face next to his, she knew on the instant that what he said was true, even though her mind was trying to reject the awfulness of it. The line of their brow, the shape of their eyebrows, the straight nose was the same. Even though Curtis's hair was dark, almost black and had none of her golden highlights, the resemblance was so acute, that Beth wondered how she could have missed it all her life. Her thoughts were in turmoil. Everything that she thought she knew about herself had changed in that split second. John Stone was nothing to do with her. Her mother – Beth could hardly believe it. Her mother must have taken Lamb as a lover. It was too much to take in. She needed to be alone to think. She pulled herself out of his grasp, realising that this man in front of her was her brother.

'Then why do you hate me so? Why are you treating me like this?'

'Oh I don't hate you, Beth. In fact, I quite like you. Admired your balls, if you'll excuse my vulgar expression. But I can use vulgar expressions because I'm only a bastard, ain't I? Whereas you, you've had the benefit of having a mother who made sure she had a husband before she opened her legs for Lamb. But she was just as much a trollop as my mother.'

Beth put a hand over her mouth. It made her feel sick to hear him speak about her mother like that. But her mind was tormented because what he said was true. Or perhaps it wasn't. Perhaps Lamb had forced her mother? But as a hundred images flashed through her mind, she knew her mother had been a willing partner. She thought of the occasions when Lamb had been in her mother's presence. Though she hated to admit it, there had been something deeper than mere acquaintance.

'Oh, it hurts, don't it Beth, facing the truth? Well, I faced it for years. I always knew my mother was no better than a whore. Long before Lamb made his dirty little confession, I'd been hot for you. Then when I discovered from our venerable father that he had dipped his finger in John Stone's pie, so to speak, it added piquancy to my lust. But Gray had to have it all, didn't he? How do you think I liked knowing that my own father had favoured him above me, bankrolled his gang and sold him land to build that vast palace of a house? And Arthur had you as well, Beth. Both brothers had you and I could only wait in the wings.'

'You're a fool Curtis! I should have welcomed you as a brother at one time. With both of us being only children, we could have gained comfort from being brother and sister. But you're pathetic. You can't hold a candle to either brother. Lamb may have bankrolled the gang but it's Arthur kept it together all these years and allowed Lamb to make his profits while Arthur and Will took the risks.'

Curtis laughed again. 'You don't get it, do you? You think Arthur is so clever, don't you? Then explain why he's in gaol when I'm standing here, free? Who do you think has been paying off witnesses these last couple of years? Do you think Haddon and Pelham had the brains enough to come up with their evidence? The funny thing is that it's the allowance Lamb paid me that enabled me to pay them off. Believe me, Beth, Arthur will hang. I might have paid to procure the evidence, but Gray has made enemies of people in very high places by his success. They can't stand to see someone like him rise above himself. I do believe if I hadn't helped things along they would have managed it themselves eventually. My money may have bought their evidence, but it's their power that's keeping Gray in Newgate.' He looked at Beth as he walked towards the door and turned the key in the lock.

Beth was stunned, reeling after both these revelations. 'You mean you're the traitor in the gang? You betrayed Will and Arthur?'

'All of 'em. Shopped Arthur to the Dragoons when they ran goods from Eastbourne, but the idiots got themselves lost in the fog on Ashdown Forest. Anyway it turned out for the best. He'd only have been transported then. Now I know both the Grays will hang. I started with Jim Cook. Once I began I couldn't stop. Took me some effort to track down those two witnesses against Will. I've been up and down to Kingston these many times. You wouldn't believe how well paid I have been for it. I tell you, men in high places are determined to have Arthur walk up Holborn Hill to Tyburn.'

Beth put her hand to her mouth as she heard his words, all the colour again draining out of her cheeks, her legs turning to water.

'I'll make it my business to be at his hanging, Beth. Perhaps you'd care to accompany me? I'm told some women find it rather arousing. We could console each other afterwards and then go and wave goodbye to your husband.'

She raised her hand again to hit him, but he caught it with one hand and slapped her across the face with the other, knocking her sideways across the room.

'That's how to do it, Beth,' he said scornfully, dragging her back in front of him. 'Raise one hand, but hit with the other. The man don't expect it then, see?'

He kept hold of her arm twisting it painfully behind her back, as he forced his mouth onto hers. She felt his hand at the lace of her gown, trying to poke his fingers under her stays.

Beth twisted her head away from him and his open mouth trailed across her cheek to her ear and then slid across her throat and down to the swell of her bosom. His hand had pushed under her stays, his fingers pinching her nipple and squeezing the tender skin around it. With a forceful movement he pushed the top of her stays down, the whalebone snapping as he tore at the delicate lace of her chemise and pawed at her breasts, drawing his head back to look at her. She cried out and he pushed a hand over her mouth, but she turned her head quickly and bit his hand. He yelled, slapping her cheeks again, one then the other and struggling to pull off his neckerchief, he stuffed it in her mouth.

'Oh yes, that's better,' he said, holding her by the shoulders and giving her a shake pinning her arms to her sides. 'You don't look so high and mighty now,' he taunted, running his eyes over her reddened cheeks, her eyes wide with fear, the cloth in her mouth forcing it wide open and making her gag, her breasts half exposed, the jagged line of her torn and broken stays pressing into the tender skin underneath them.

In a sudden movement, he pushed her onto the table and bent her backwards over it, pinning one of her arms behind her, knocking a jug and tankards flying, a small wooden box pressing painfully into her back as he pressed the top half of his body over hers and pushed one knee between her thighs.

With her free hand Beth grasped his hair and pulled as hard as she could tearing some of the strands away in her fingers, feeling the nausea rise as the cloth pushed at the back of her throat. He swore at her, trying to seize her breasts in one hand before pinning her across the throat with his forearm, pressing down hard on her windpipe crushing the breath out of her, his other hand unfastening his breeches. She clutched ineffectually at him with her one free hand while trying to breathe in air through her nose feeling the blood pounding at her temples. She could feel her heart thumping in her chest and a rasping in her lungs as she became short of air. She became aware of the cool air on her naked legs and belly and realised that Curtis had forced her skirt and petticoats up around her waist. She was trying to beg him to stop but her voice was just a gurgle of choking sounds through the cloth that was thrust into her mouth.

'What's that you're saying, Beth? I can't quite make it out,' he taunted. Then she felt her body beginning to lose its strength and the room seemed to darken, Curtis's forearm like an iron bar across her throat. Her muscles relaxed, the hand that had clutched at his arm dropped away. Her legs, which she had been trying to press together, lost their tension and fell apart. She felt Curtis's knee pushing them wider still, giving him access to whatever he chose to do to her. In her half-conscious state, she was waiting to feel the invasion of her body, unable to do anything about it.

She became aware of the chiming of the clock on the mantelpiece and thought, stupidly, to herself. 'Six o'clock and Curtis is going to rape me and watch me die. Will will be wondering where I am.' She gave up trying to breathe. She thought of Arthur and Will, playing in Hawkhurst as children. She half smiled as she remembered Will as a happy toddler. She wished they could all be children again. But it was night now. Everything was dark. Everything was peaceful. She could sleep.

She slowly became aware that the pressure across her throat had eased and she inhaled through her nose, the air painful as it coursed down the back of her dry throat. She lay still, unable to move, her whole body feeling heavy as if her limbs were made of lead. She opened her eyes to see Curtis still above her. She felt his hand on her thigh, the fingertips pressing into the soft skin where it joined her body and saw him peering at his own hand resting on her flesh. He moved his hand across to her other thigh and then trailed his fingers upwards pressing the flat of his hand on her lower belly. He gave a short laugh and took his arm away from her throat and his hand away from her belly as he started to re-fasten his breeches.

She lay still, not knowing if he would let her move not even knowing if he had taken her, for her body seemed numb. She cautiously raised her head. When he didn't try to stop her, she pulled the cloth out of her mouth, coughing, choking, her eyes watering. She quickly pushed her skirts down over her legs and pulled up her bent stays to cover her breasts, the bruises already forming on her bosom and throat. She hauled herself up, feeling sick.

He looked at her scornfully. 'Oh I'm all the devil you take me for,' he said shortly. 'It seems the spirit is willing, but the flesh is weak. In my head I want to ravish you and use you as cruelly as you expected me to. You can't imagine half the things I had in mind to do to you! I wanted you bruised and bloodied, naked on your knees before me, begging for mercy, telling me you want me more than Gray. But it seems that even I ain't quite villain enough to fuck my own sister! Strange ain't it? The thought of it has driven me mad these many years, ever since I saw you when you were a prissy ten year old, mincing up Middle Street as if you had a carrot stuck up your arse! You only had eyes for Gray then. And then, when I have you at my mercy, with your breasts spilled out and your legs pushed open as wide as I choose, I find I no longer have the means to drive into you. I might want to fuck you Beth, but my cock don't!'

He started to laugh and Beth, her eyes never leaving his, slowly pulled herself off the table and backed away from him, towards the door. He walked towards her and she pressed herself up against the wall shrinking away from him. He stood over her and she could feel his breath on her face. With a sudden movement he snatched the key out of his pocket and pressed it into the lock and Beth heard it click as he unlocked it.

'You're evil, Curtis,' she said, her voice a hoarse whisper as she clutched at her bruised throat, her head spinning. 'And you can make only evil, where good might have been.'

She tugged on the door handle, took one last look at him and then turned quickly making her way unsteadily down the stairs and out into the street, her lungs filling with air as she inhaled deeply. She dropped to her knees and was sick in the gutter, again and again as if her body was trying to rid itself of some foul poison.

'Oh my good God! Oh my dear lady!' Rachel Spain almost fell over Beth as she turned the corner. At first she thought the woman was one of the town hussies, drunk and disorderly and had half a mind to call the Constable but then she recognized Beth Gray and put her basket down. She threw one arm around her shoulders, pulling her own shawl off and wrapping it round Beth's half- nakedness. 'Can you get up, Mrs Gray? Yes, that's right, lean on me. Oh my good God, lady, what's happened to you?'

Beth could not speak and hardly knew where she was being led but leaned heavily on Rachel who walked as quickly as she could to Conduit Hill, habit leading her to the garden door. She banged heavily on it and after a few moments her husband came running to open it, exclaiming when he saw Beth, 'Jesus, what has happened to her?'

Rachel shook her head. 'I don't know. I found her like this not five minutes since. For pity's sake Rob, fetch her some brandy.'

Beth slowly coming back to herself, recognised where she was. She took a sip of brandy that Robert held out to her. She stood up holding the table for support. 'Where is Thomas Lamb?' she demanded shakily. 'Is he still here?'

'Why, yes, Mrs Gray he's in his parlour where you left him,' Spain replied. Beth shrugged off Rachel's arm from her shoulder, but wrapped the shawl more tightly round her and stepped unsteadily into the passageway. She thrust open the door of the parlour banging it shut behind her.

It woke Lamb from a pleasant dream and he looked about him in surprise and then horror as he saw Beth's dishevelled appearance and torn clothes and the bruises on her neck. 'Good God, child. What has happened? Who has done this to you?' he exclaimed rising up as quickly as he could.

Beth looked at her father with wild eyes. 'Your son, Mr Lamb, he has done this to me. My brother has done this to me!'

Meanwhile Will, leaning up against a tree in the thicket where he was supposed to meet Beth, patted the flanks of the horse he had borrowed from Stanford. He had waited all day in his room at the *Swan* and now strained his eyes against the gathering darkness, as the sun set over the hills towards Hastings.

'Where is she then, eh?' he said gently to the horse rubbing its ears. The horse whinnied softly. He looked around him for a while and then tethered the horse to the nearest tree. He pulled his coat tighter round him, rammed his hat low on his forehead and made his way into Rye.

He was too well known in Rye to make his way openly into any of the taverns or alehouses. He hardly felt safe walking on the streets. He stole along Longer Street pulling his collar up and wearing his hat low on his forehead. He turned up into Conduit Hill, slipped round the gardens along the backs of the houses and brushing past the shrubs and trees, approached the garden door and knocked.

There was silence at first and then a commotion indoors. Robert Spain opened the door and Will, seeing Spain's troubled expression, edged past him into the back hallway. He went to push open the door of the parlour as Thomas Lamb had risen to open it. Lamb's mouth dropped open to see Will standing there but Will looked over his shoulder and saw his wife, white faced, her gown ripped and Harriett Marshall daubing a salve over the bruises on her throat and bosom. Will's face turned as white as Beth's as their eyes met and in two paces he was across the floor and had her safe in his arms.

'Leave us,' he called out fiercely pulling Beth closer to him and Lamb nodded at Harriett, who quietly put down her pot of salve and linen swabs as they left husband and wife alone.

Twenty minutes later Will stepped out of the parlour and found Lamb in his study looking anxiously towards the door. 'She's told me everything,' Will said quickly, his expression icy. 'You're her father, apparently and she's in your care so tell me how she's come to such harm when it was your responsibility to look after her?'

Lamb nodded, his expression pained. 'I know Will and I do take the responsibility. It is clearly my fault. I never thought Beth would come to harm here in Rye. I can hardly believe it of Jeremiah.'

Will snorted. 'I can believe anything of him. He's hurt Beth knowing she's his sister! And he's betrayed us all. Because of him, my wife has come to harm and my brother is in prison.'

Lamb nodded again, a haunted look in his lined face. He leaned forward in his chair putting his elbows on the small table in front of him and covered his face with his hands. 'What will you do?' he asked quietly.

Will stared at the wall, behind Lamb. 'I'd like to rip Curtis's heart out with my bare hands! But Beth has told me Arthur says I must give myself up.'

Lamb paused a moment. 'If you're going to do as Arthur says, then let me speak to my brother first. You know he is the mayor here. If you give yourself up to him, he will make things as comfortable for you as he can.'

Will shrugged. 'Do you think I care for my own comfort?' He turned around hearing the rustle of silk skirts behind him and Beth stood there, a little more colour in her cheeks.

'Will, what are you going to do? Please give yourself up. If you're seen, the Dragoons will shoot to kill you! Please Will!'

He turned round and took Beth's hand and kissed it. 'Beth, my darling wife,' he whispered. 'Never forget how much I adore you.' He drew her to him once more and kissed the top of her head. 'I have something to do first,' he said grimly.

Both Lamb and Beth looked alarmed at his words but Will fastened his coat, picked up his hat and with one last look at Beth, crossed the hallway and let himself out the front door.

He made his way to Longer Street to the house where Curtis lodged. The front door stood ajar. He pushed his way into the passage and flew up the stairs to Curtis's two rooms. He heard laughter coming from inside and put his hand on the door knob throwing open the door. Curtis was seated at one of the low chairs. A girl wearing only her chemise which was pulled down to her shoulders, sat sprawled on his lap. They both looked up in alarm to see Will standing there. The girl hastily covered her breasts with her hands pulling the chemise around her shoulders. Will hardly glanced at her. 'You girl, go!' he snapped.

She looked up at Curtis as if to get his approval.

'I said, go!' Will snarled and without further ado she sprang up with frightened eyes, gathering her clothes from the floor and flew out of the room. They heard her feet on the wooden stairs as she hurried down and banged the front door shut behind her. Will kicked Curtis's door shut.

He remained seated. 'So you're out of Newgate are you? What do you want, Will? Come to visit the scene of the crime?' He jerked his head in the direction of the window. 'That's where I had your wife – flat on her back on that table. She was hot for me, Will, whatever tale she has told you. She couldn't pull her skirts up quick enough. She's a noisy whore when she's being had, ain't she? I liked to hear her squeal. She couldn't get enough of me. Well she's been deprived, ain't she, with you and your brother banged up? She was like a bitch on heat.'

Will, his fists clenched in his pockets, looked across at Curtis. 'Before I've finished with you, you bastard, I'll ram those foul lies back down your throat!'

Curtis looked around him and laughed. 'Oh yes? I don't see your big brother here, Will. He ain't here to fight this battle.'

'Oh, I don't need Arthur for this. This is my battle, just between you and me.'

Curtis looked at Will again. There was a deadly serious cast to his face. If he didn't know that he could easily beat Will in a fight, Curtis might have felt a moment's anxiety. They were of the same height, but Curtis had more weight to him and Will had never been completely fit since his wound; besides he had spent the last three months in prison or on the run. Curtis got up slowly out of the chair. He shrugged. 'What's it to be then, Gray, pistols, knives?'

Will shook his head. 'I don't need any weapons. I'm going beat you with my bare hands, Curtis.'

The two men began to round on each other and then Curtis made a sudden lunge for Will with his left fist. Will, quick on his feet, ducked out of the way and brought his right fist up under Curtis's chin. He staggered back taken by surprise at the weight and force behind Will's punch but gathered himself together enough to swing a punch catching Will on the shoulder. He reeled back almost loosing his footing but came running back at Curtis, his head low, catching him with all his weight in the belly. Both men tumbled on to the floor, sending furniture flying in all directions and the bottle of brandy which had been on a small table by Curtis's chair, spilled its contents all over the floor.

Curtis snatched hold of the neckerchief round Will's neck and started to pull it tight as both of them lay sprawled on the floor. Will caught hold of his opponent's fist and slowly twisted the fingers back, so the pressure on his throat was released. He sprang to his feet followed quickly by Curtis who came running at him jamming his fist into Will's left side, right over the site of his old wound.

Will swore with the sudden pain and drew in his breath, doubling over. Curtis grabbed his head in a neck lock pulling Will round the room trying to choke the air out of him. Will stumbled around dragged by Curtis and then he slipped on the brandy. Both men crashed to the floor. Will swung himself out of Curtis's grasp and as he made to rise, Will caught hold of his ankle, twisting it and bringing Curtis crashing to the ground on his back. Will quickly got astride him and rammed his left fist, then his right, bringing his punches crashing into Curtis's face; the blood started to pour from a cut over his eye and then from his nose. He tried to lift his hands to protect his face from the fury of Will's well-aimed blows but Will sensing he had the upper hand, continued to beat Curtis's face to pulp.

'Take back your lies, Curtis,' Will snarled between gritted teeth, his breath coming in quick gasps. 'I believe my wife and you will admit to me you have lied, if it's the last thing you say!'

Curtis said nothing and then smiled, the blood oozing from his mouth, through his teeth. 'No lies, Will, I had her!' he croaked.

Will grabbed hold of Curtis's neckerchief and pulled the ends tight, his face inches above the other man's. 'Tell me the truth, you fucking bastard, you fucking, fucking bastard!'

Curtis face started to go blue, his eyes widened. His lips started to move again. 'For Christ's sake, man!' he gasped. 'Let go.'

'Tell me the truth!' Will thundered.

Curtis moved his head, choking, as blood from his nose ran down his throat. 'All right! I tried to but –couldn't. She's as pure as she was when she entered my room.'

Will loosened his grip on the neckerchief and drawing his arm back, delivered his last punch to the side of Curtis's jaw, sending him senseless.

Will got up slowly and held on to the fireplace for support, feeling the room spin. He put a hand to his side and rubbed his jaw, looking in the mirror to see his face reflected, his eyes wild, his hair dishevelled, blood oozing from a cut on his cheekbone. He made his way out of the room and stumbled down the stairs and out in the street.

The question of whether or not he would give himself up was now academic, as at either end of the street, there was a small party of Dragoons, their carbines raised. He looked at one end of the street and then the other. At the end of the street nearer to him, he saw Beth and Thomas Lamb standing behind the Dragoons. He walked slowly up to them raising his hands high in the air.

Beth pushed through the soldiers and ran to Will's side. He nodded to her, as she put her arms around him. 'It's all right, Beth.'

CHAPTER SIXTY FOUR

Friday 18th March 1748, Curtis's rooms, Rye

Lamb made his way up the staircase at the house in Longer Street. He had felt his age these past weeks, felt the weariness in his bones and the tiredness in his heart. But he was undaunted in his mission. He rapped on the door to his son's rooms with his stick and when there was no answer, he put his hand to the door knob and pushed the door open. Curtis was sitting at his table and looked across at Lamb. Curtis's expression changed from surprise to disdain. Lamb noticed the bruising on Curtis's face, the black eye and swollen lip. 'No wonder you're keeping to your rooms, Jeremiah,' Lamb said quietly.

Curtis said nothing but turned back to his papers.

Lamb remained standing. 'I have never offered violence to any man Jeremiah, but believe me, you're the only man to arouse the desire in me to do so.'

Curtis snorted. 'Have you come here to say anything useful?'

Lamb seated himself stiffly in one of the chairs at the table. 'I have certainly come to say something.'

Curtis remained silent.

'You should hang, Jeremiah! Two good men are in gaol, one awaiting transportation and the other awaiting trial for his life. Both of them are better men than you will ever be. Can you imagine how it hurts me to say that to my own son?'

'And you're saying I should hang? You want your own son to hang too, do you Lamb? You really want that?'

Lamb paused a moment and shook his head. 'No, I am too weak. I am not man enough to allow my own son to hang. But I can no longer allow you to live here, to be a constant reminder to me of all I will lose. I am sending you to France, Jeremiah.'

Curtis gave a short laugh. 'And how in God's name do you propose to do that, you fool of an old man?'

'Quite simply, if you refuse to go or try to escape, I will lay information against you, as a smuggler,' Lamb said steadily.

'And won't that defeat your own purpose, Lamb? By doing that, you put my neck in a noose. No,' Curtis said shaking his head. 'I know what store you set by family. You won't do it.'

'And would you gamble your life on the fact that I would not, Jeremiah?' his father replied, waiting to see what effect his words would have. 'Ah, I see that takes some thought, when it's your own neck that might be stretched and not another man's.'

Curtis pushed his chair away from the table and stood up. 'You stupid old goat! I could counter that by laying information against you, your connection with Gray all these years.'

'Oh Jeremiah, whatever failings I have, you can be sure I have been a very careful businessman. There's nothing to connect me to Gray, nothing in writing anywhere. I have been nothing if not meticulous. I despise myself for it now. I let other men take the risks so I might accumulate more wealth. But it does put me in a position whereby I need fear nothing from you or what you might threaten. It's bad enough that you betrayed the Grays and all the other men but when you sought to harm Beth, I knew I must put an end to your treachery.'

Curtis looked out of the window and then back at Lamb. 'Oh, she took no harm from me. What is she anyway, but a piece of skirt? Never could make up her mind which brother she wanted. You know, we're all of a kind, you, me and her. We all want what we can't have. I don't think any of our motives have been pure.'

Lamb shook his head in despair. 'You don't understand do you? You're my son and despite all, I love you but Beth is my daughter and I cherish her, I adore her. You have a son whom you won't even acknowledge so how can you know how a father feels for his daughter? A father would give up his life easily for his daughter. It is simple, Jeremiah. You will go to France and that's an end of it. You will never come back; I will never see you nor hear from you again. You may take a thousand pounds with you. I daresay that will tempt you. There is however, a condition attached.'

'What is your condition? An undertaking that I won't return?' Curtis asked, sneering.

'You won't come back, Jeremiah,' Lamb said mildly. 'I have lodged a letter with William Pix to be opened if you return, subsequent to my death. It lays sworn evidence against you, sworn and witnessed. No, this is another condition entirely. Before you go, you will marry Alice Marshall and give her child a father, such as you are. I have a licence for your marriage and on the day that you marry her, you will be taken to France.'

He leaned forward and rose to his feet. 'There is no more to say.' His met his son's gaze, turned slowly and left the room.

It was a very small party that gathered at St Mary's Church, Rye, to witness the solemnisation of the marriage between Jeremiah Curtis and Alice Marshall. As soon as the register was signed Lamb accompanied his son down to the small boat that was to take him to France. Lamb's face was set as Curtis reluctantly climbed aboard in silence and Lamb waited by the water's edge as it set sail. When the departing sails became a blur to Lamb's sight, he took three quick breaths and pulled a handkerchief out of his pocket to wipe his eyes. He watched the boat for a little while longer and then made his way wearily back into town to his own house, to greet his new daughter-in-law and her family who had now become his.

CHAPTER SIXTY FIVE

Sunday 20th March 1748, Rye then Newgate

To her surprise and almost her shame, Beth slept soundly each night at Thomas Lamb's house. She kept the window open and heard the gentle lapping of the sea at night and the calling of seagulls first thing in the morning. Her sleep was dreamless; it was her days that were filled with anxieties and horrors. She had seen Will taken again by the Dragoons with no time even to give him a bag of clothes or food. Lamb promised he himself would escort her to London the following week insisting she recover fully from her ordeal at Curtis's hands.

On Lamb's return from Church, he came into the parlour to find her sitting quietly. He looked down at her brown hair with the golden lights and momentarily saw Jane Stone's posture in the straight back, the womanly shoulders. Lamb took hold of the back of one of the chairs. 'Beth,' he said unsteadily. 'Let me embrace you once as my daughter.'

She stood up and the old man took her closely in his arms and held her to him. She felt him tremble with emotion.

'My mother-,' she began shakily.

'You have no reason to think badly of her, my child,' Lamb said quickly. 'Your mother always loved your father, even though he let her down. She sent me packing almost as soon as she knew she was carrying my child. She wanted nothing from me. John Stone provided everything for you. All she asked was that I look out for you and I tried to do that, Beth, tried to keep you from harm. But I failed you in that, this last week.'

Beth dropped to her knees, the tears pricking her eyelids. She took hold of Lamb's hands with hers. 'Since my mother never asked you for anything, let me ask. Let me beg. I beg you, I beg you as my father, please save Arthur. Please use what power you have to save him. I can't bear it, I can't.'

She raised her face to his, as he tried to bring her to her feet.

'Get up, child. Get up. This isn't fitting. Not fitting at all. My dear, you must get up.' He drew her to her feet with difficulty for she was taller than he. He led her back to the chair.

'I shall do whatever I can my dear, when we go up to London but you must prepare yourself for the worst. Will is to be sentenced at the same Session as Arthur's trial. You must prepare to leave with him. I can hardly say it myself, Beth, but you and Will must sail to America whatever Arthur's fate.'

On the same morning that Beth was begging Lamb to save him, Arthur attended chapel at Newgate. Jupp, the gaoler, had told him that Will had been brought back in chains. Arthur knew his only chance of seeing Will would be at chapel and sure enough Will, in leg irons joined the rest of the prisoners in the chapel and filed into a seat four rows in front of his brother. Their eyes met. The service lasted nearly two hours and at the end Arthur hurried forward and caught Will's arm. 'Will, stay behind. Say you want to pray a while,' he whispered hastily.

Will nodded and spoke to the chaplain on his way out and was allowed back in. He made his way awkwardly to the back pews where Arthur was waiting and they both knelt down bowing their heads, Arthur's hand grasping Will's.

'Are you all right, Will?' he asked urgently. 'You've done the right thing. You know that, don't you?'

Will looked across at Arthur. 'I know you wouldn't have told me to give myself up if it wasn't my best chance, Arty. But what about you?'

Arthur nodded and then they both bowed their heads quickly as one of the gaolers came up to them. They remained silent for a moment as if in prayer. Will pulled Arthur's sleeve. 'You'll get the charge against you changed Arty, won't you? Then we'll all go together to America, won't we?'

Arthur sighed. 'I don't know Will. I may have to take my chance at my trial.'

'It's Curtis!' Will whispered urgently. 'Curtis who betrayed us! He's been paying off the witnesses. He tried to, he tried-,' Will stopped suddenly not wanting to tell Arthur what Curtis had tried to do to Beth.

Arthur who had spent many hours going over the events of the past two years, heard Will's words without surprise. Since Curtis had found out that Lamb was his father, his antagonism towards Arthur had increased and when Arthur thought back over the years, he could see Curtis's hand in all the bad luck that had befallen the gang. But his mind was too occupied with Will's fate to think of trying to exact revenge on Curtis.

'That's enough praying,' the gaoler said sternly. 'On your feet you two.'

'Next Sunday Will, be sure to be here,' was all Arthur could manage to say as they were ushered off in different directions and Arthur heard Will's chains clanging on the cold flagstones of the chapel as he was led away.

Newgate Gaol, April, 1748

Arthur saw Will at chapel for the next three Sundays. They had the opportunity to exchange only a few words. At first Will kept asking eagerly what news there was of dropping or changing the charges against Arthur but on the third Sunday he didn't ask. Arthur kept up the pretence with Will that there was a good chance of the charges being dropped; but Beth visiting Will and Arthur each week, never brought him any such news. She had somehow become immune to the horrors of the gaol. If the two men she loved could bear to be there, she could bear to visit them. Arthur noticed with despair the dark circles under her eyes, where none had been and for the first time saw a furrowed line in her brow.

The following week Beth visited and told Arthur that the names of the jurors for the April Sessions had been published and Lamb was working hard to find out as much as he could about them. Lamb himself visited Arthur a week later. Arthur lying on his bed, climbed to his feet when he heard the familiar sound of the iron grating at the window being drawn back and Jupp's voice call, 'Visitor for you.'

He and Jupp had developed a tolerable level of understanding and whenever Beth visited he brought two earthenware mugs and the ale or wine that Arthur had purchased from the supply in the gaol itself at extortionate prices, for those who could afford it.

Expecting to see Beth, Arthur was shocked to see Lamb enter the cell. The old man was looking very distressed and immediately took hold of the back of the rough chair to steady himself.

'Mr Lamb, I had no idea you would visit. Are you sure it's safe for people to know you are connected with me? Have you any news?'

Lamb who was breathing heavily, held up his hand for a moment as he caught his breath. Then he sat down. He nodded briefly. 'What harm can come to me now, Arthur by acknowledging that I know and like you? I have hidden behind other men for too much of my life. But yes, I have some news for you. I only wish I had more.' He paused and looked around. 'I had no idea the conditions were so bad, Arthur.' He shook his head. 'I thought I was descending into Hell itself.'

'You get used to it,' Arthur said shortly. 'I've almost forgotten what fresh air smells like.'

Lamb shook his head again and then spoke. 'I have found a Counsel to act on your behalf. It was difficult to find anyone prepared to act for you.' He sighed. 'However you have one friend on the jury. I have known him these forty years and more and I've already spoken with him. He will speak up for you when the jury comes to discuss the case. Your trial is scheduled for the first day of the Sessions on Wednesday the twentieth.'

Arthur nodded. 'Yes, I was told. And Will is to be sentenced at the end of the Sessions.'

'I've used my best endeavours to find Haddon and Pelham, the prosecution witnesses, but they are being held somewhere most secure. I don't believe they will surface until the day of your trial. I never thought it would come to this, my boy,' he said shaking his head. He drew out his handkerchief and wiped his eyes. 'I'm sorry, Arthur, so sorry. It distresses me so much to think that your dealings with me have led you to this. And that my son should betray you!'

'Don't think that, sir,' Arthur said quietly. 'I would have taken this path anyway. In fact I did take this path, long before I knew you were connected with it. Jeremiah always begrudged me your patronage. I can hardly blame you for thinking that I was worth investing in. I suppose none of us thought the Government would take such a harsh line.' He paused. 'I want to ask you about Beth. You will be able to see that she boards the *Justitia* with Will and that she has every comfort available?'

'Of course my boy, you need not ask. I shall take her down to Deal myself. I will not fail her again,' he faltered, not knowing whether Arthur knew what Jeremiah had attempted.

Arthur looked quickly across at the old man. Lamb's watery blue eyes met Arthur's. 'There was some – unpleasantness, between my son and Beth,' he said awkwardly.

'Unpleasantness?' Arthur exclaimed.

'She came to no harm, Arthur. Will took Jeremiah to task over it.'

Arthur looked puzzled. Will had not mentioned anything to him.

'In what way – *took him to task*?' he asked.

'There was a fight. Your brother was entirely the victor,' Lamb explained as best as he could. He rose slowly, leaning on the table for support. Arthur remained seated and then looked up at him. 'You know I've always loved Beth?'

Lamb nodded. 'Yes. As have I. Her mother once told me we each have a cross to bear. How right she was.'

Arthur also rose and stood facing the man who had been his benefactor for so many years. 'Thomas, don't come again,' he said quickly. 'I can see how it distresses you. You've done as much for me as you could.'

Lamb unexpectedly put his arms round Arthur and clung onto him. 'My boy, my dear, dear boy,' he said tearfully. Arthur held onto him until he heard the old man's breathing become steady again and forced a smile as he took his arms from him. They shook hands as Arthur called for Jupp. Lamb pressed his hand to Arthur's shoulder, but could not speak further and bending over his stick, made his way out of the cell leaving Arthur to his thoughts.

CHAPTER SIXTY SIX

April 1748, Arthur's cell, Newgate

Two days later, Patrick Kelly, the Irish attorney called to see Arthur at Ned Henley's request.

'I can't speak for you, Mr Gray. You know I have been de-barred on a malicious lie. It was because I helped Ned get his acquittal, but I can tell you what to expect at your trial if you would like me to.'

Arthur nodded. He had heard about Kelly's fall from grace and the reasons supposed for it, coming as it did a few months after Ned's acquittal. 'Any advice you can give me will be helpful. I've tried to imagine what it might be like.'

Kelly seated himself and took out a notepad and a pen and started to sketch a diagram of the Court room. 'You'll be taken through the passageway from the gaol to the Sessions House. The Court room is not a place built to put heart into any man or woman on trial there, Arthur. It's as well to know that. The whole construction is designed to emphasise the conflict between you as the accused and the rest of the court. You will have to stand here, at the bar,' he said turning his sketch round to show Arthur. 'In these stalls to your right, that's where the jurors sit. At the end of your case they'll huddle together and come up with a verdict. Directly facing you, that's where the prosecution witnesses and your defence witnesses will stand. You have called defence witnesses?'

Arthur nodded, raising his eyes from the drawing. 'Two tradesmen from Hawkhurst. Nothing to do with the gang. We were all boys together. I think they'll vouch for my good character.'

'Good, good,' Kelly said encouragingly. 'If the prosecution witnesses' case is thin, your character witnesses will stand you in good stead. The judge sits behind the witness box and next to him the clerks and writers who take down everything that is said. After the witnesses are called, your Counsel will speak for you and you will be asked to state your case.'

'But how can I prepare it, Mr Kelly? I don't know what the witnesses will say.'

Kelly nodded. 'Aye it's an awkward position for any man to be in. That's why you must pay close attention to what evidence the witnesses put forward, so you can dispute it. You have only one chance to do so, remember. There's also a sounding board, here, placed above your head, which amplifies your voice so there's no doubt that the jurors can hear all you have to say. When it's finished, the jury will announce their verdict.' He paused for a moment. 'Those that are found guilty are brought forward at the end of the session to hear their punishment.' His eyes, unwavering met Arthur's. 'Of course, if you're found innocent, you leave the courtroom there and then.' Kelly turned the piece of paper round and pushed it across the table to Arthur. 'That's as much as I can do for you, Arthur. I wish you the best of luck.'

Arthur took his hand and shook it. 'I thank you for it, Mr Kelly. And my brother, he'll be sentenced at the end of these sessions, as I understand it?'

Kelly nodded. 'Indeed he will. I'm certain of the sentence. By pleading guilty he'll be sentenced to transportation. No further witness has come forward. It's a certainty as far as I'm concerned and I understand you've undertaken the arrangements for his safe passage.'

'Yes,' Arthur replied. 'It has kept me sane, knowing that Will will be safe.'

There seemed no more to be said.

Tuesday 19ᵗʰ April, 1748

Arthur could tell from Beth's expression as she stood before him, that something was wrong. She had put down the small basket of food and clean shirts on the table but didn't meet Arthur's eyes.

'What is it Beth? What's wrong? Is it Will? Oh God, tell me! It's not Will?' He clasped her wrist and put a hand under her chin making her look at him.

She shook her head. 'No, I've just seen Will. He's all right. Perhaps a little better. His cough bothers him less. Oh Arthur, I don't know how to tell you though.'

He looked straight into her grey eyes. 'Just tell me Beth, whatever it is.'

She looked at him for a moment. 'Bill Bishop and Sam Terrell your witnesses-.'

Arthur nodded. 'What of them?' he asked sharply.

Beth shook her head. 'They won't appear for you.'

A groan escaped Arthur's lips. He rubbed his hand down over his face, exhaling. 'Why not?'

Beth took both his hands in hers. 'I saw Bill Bishop yesterday and made some comment, about how he was getting here on Wednesday. I saw it in his eyes at once. He wouldn't answer, tried to fob me off, but then he simply said, he wouldn't be able to come. He wouldn't say any more but I could tell he was afraid. I went to see Sam Terrell. I got it out of him eventually. They have both been visited by men – I don't know who they were but Arthur, I fear they were agents of the Government! Sam said he was advised not to make the journey. They said it would be all the worse for Sam's wife and children and his very livelihood if he came to London. It must have been the same for Bill Bishop. I can't believe such wickedness exists!'

He quickly put his arms around her, his chin resting on her curls. He was reeling under this blow. Without any character witnesses, he had only his own wits and his own voice to put his case, to dispute the evidence without knowing what that evidence might be. A rage inside him wanted to give voice to every oath he could think of, but he pushed his face further into Beth's curls, waiting for his heart to stop hammering so wildly inside his chest. 'It's a blow Beth, but Kelly has given me some useful advice. Don't worry, sweet. Who brought you up to London today?'

'William Pix,' she answered. 'He and my aunt are being very kind.'

'Then go back with them tonight. I don't want you to attend my trial. Yes, I mean it. It would distract me too much. I must have a clear mind to do what must be done.'

She gazed up at him for a moment. 'If that's what you want, Arthur.'

'Yes,' he nodded kissing both her hands. 'That's what I want.'

CHAPTER SIXTY SEVEN

Wednesday 20th April 1748, Courtroom, Old Bailey, London

Jupp fixed Arthur's leg irons back on and he was led along the covered passageway leading from the gaol to the Court house. As Arthur looked around him the Courtroom appeared just as Kelly had drawn it. He looked up at the large windows and saw that it was a beautiful morning, the sun advancing across a clear blue sky. Two birds swooped into view crossing the sky in a perfect arc and disappeared to the west. For a split second he was lifted away from this oppressive courtroom and imagined himself standing somewhere on the Marsh looking up at this same blue sky, surrounded by hundreds of birds and the low bleating of the Marsh sheep with their silly quiet faces.

He blinked and returned to the present. Kelly was right that the courtroom made the distinction between the prisoner at the bar and the rest of the court, very obvious. He felt very much alone. He glanced at the twelve men on his right and wondered which of them was Lamb's friend, ready to speak for him to his fellow jurors when they considered their verdict. They all rose when the presiding judge entered, dressed in sombre black and as soon as he was seated, a tall thin man with spectacles perched on the end of his nose, whom Arthur understood to be the clerk of the Court, read out the charge accusing Arthur of running goods at Lydd.

The spectators in the public gallery fell silent as the words were spoken. Arthur heard them and found himself thinking of many runs he had made at Lydd. He thought of the *George*, of the tall spire of the church and the peaceful little houses. He forced himself to listen to what was being said - that on the 13th August 1746, he along with seven other unknown men, had assembled at Lydd for the purposes of running uncustomed goods *'to the evil example of all others; against the peace of the King, his crown and dignity,'* the clerk read out.

Another man short and dapper, stood up. This was the Counsel for the King, the chief prosecutor. He began his evidence. 'May it please your lordship and you gentlemen of the jury? The prisoner, Arthur Gray, is indicted upon an Act of Parliament made in the nineteenth year of his present Majesty-,'

Arthur found himself thinking of Seacox, of the first time he had gone there with Beth. He had to force himself to return to the present. *Get a grip on yourself, man,* he chided himself. *You must concentrate on every word that's said, you know that.*

'The Prisoner at the bar, as you will hear from the witnesses, has made himself extremely famous in this way. There is a gang known as the Hawkhurst gang, which has terrorised the neighbourhood for miles around and Gray has been the principal leader of this gang. There are several witnesses to these facts, which cannot be contradicted and I believe it will appear to you that he is guilty and likely to be brought finally to justice. Call John Pelham.'

Arthur looked at John Pelham whom he had known for many years. He had worked as a fisherman, not very successfully and Arthur had seen him in and around Lydd for many years. Pelham was sworn in and looked about him nervously, his tongue darting over his dry lips.

'Look at the Prisoner. Do you know him?' Counsel asked him.

Pelham forced himself to look directly at Arthur. Arthur lifted his chin and fixed his gaze on Pelham.

'Yes,' he answered in a hollow voice. 'I've known him to be a smuggler these many years. Him and many others.'

'Did you ever see him concerned in running and landing uncustomed goods?'

Pelham took several deep breaths and then started to speak in a low voice. 'Yes sir. I was fishing and saw him on the 13th of August 1746. I saw him between Denny Marsh and Jews Cut.'

Arthur almost laughed. It was so much like a child reciting the lines he had learned at school, that it was transparent he had been coached.

'I saw eight or nine men but of them, only Gray was known to me,' Pelham declared. 'He was armed with a blunderbuss. They loaded tea and brandy onto fourteen or fifteen horses and ran them towards Lydd.'

Arthur's Defence Counsel then took the floor. Arthur had never met him. He was an elderly man, Arthur guessed near to retirement and possibly that was why had had been willing to take the case. He asked Pelham how near he was to the place where the goods were being unloaded.

'Can you say for sure the Prisoner was among them?' he asked Pelham.

Pelham looked directly at Arthur. 'Yes, because the Prisoner rode by me as near as I am to that gentleman.'

'You mean, my Lord Chief Justice?' the Counsel asked, indicating the judge some ten feet away.

'Yes,' Pelham replied

'How do you know that this was on the thirteenth of August?' he asked.

'Because when we sell our fish, we write down the day of the month.'

Arthur almost laughed again. If every fisherman wrote down every day he went out fishing, he would be very surprised to hear it. He doubted that Pelham could write, let alone maintain detailed records and then keep them for two years.

'Have you your book here?' Arthur's Counsel asked.

Pelham shook his head. 'No'.

Arthur sighed in disbelief; surely he wasn't going to be found guilty on the evidence of a non-existent book?

'Why did you not report this before?' The Defence Counsel was getting into his stride now and posing questions to cast doubt on Pelham's evidence.

Pelham looked doubtful and his tongue darted again over his lips. 'I didn't realise it, then.'

'But you must have known this before. How came you to keep this a secret for a year and a half? Did you not think it your duty to give an account of this to a Magistrate as soon as you knew it?'

'Y...Yes,' Pelham stammered. 'But I had no opportunity - I couldn't get anybody to take my information.'

Arthur's Counsel looked satisfied and took his seat. The Judge nodded at Arthur. 'Now it is your time to make your defence.'

Arthur's mind went blank. He had been listening so intently, he had forgotten that he would be asked to speak. 'You say you have known me many years?' he asked Pelham.

'Yes.'

'You say I'm a smuggler?'

Pelham nodded.

'Is that a sign of assent?' the judge asked. 'You must speak, man, not nod or shake your head so we are in no doubt of your evidence.'

Pelham looked nervously at the Judge. 'Yes, my lord.'

'So you say that you know me, and that you saw me pass within ten feet of you but yet you didn't recognise any of the men I was with?' Arthur continued.

'No,' Pelham said nervously.

'What clothes had I on?' he asked Pelham.

Pelham looked unprepared for such a question.

'You say I was close to you. What clothes had I on? What horse was I riding?' he repeated.

'I cannot say exactly.'

Arthur shook his head and then looked directly into Pelham's pale eyes. 'Didn't you write it in your book?' he asked scornfully. 'Where is this book of yours? You never saw me there, Pelham.'

The Judge indicated Pelham should leave the box and Humphry Haddon was called to be sworn in; the same Haddon with his long greasy locks and thin face who had taken charge of Arthur's horse many a time at the *George* in Lydd, but not once since June 1746, as Haddon surely knew.

'How did you come to know the Prisoner?' the Prosecution asked.

Haddon leaned forward. 'I lived as a servant at the *George Inn* in Lydd.'

'Can you mention any particular time when you saw the Prisoner?'

'Yes, on the 13th August 1746, I saw him with seven or eight more and there were fourteen or fifteen horses.'

Arthur exhaled loudly. Haddon and Pelham had learned their lines from the same book, so it seemed.

'What time of year was this?' the Prosecution asked again.

'I was driving a load of corn in a team so it was high summer. I was forced to get out of the way by them and I think they went further inland. He, Gray, had pistols and passed close by me. I've known him to be a smuggler many years. I had goods from him –.' Haddon stopped, aware he was swimming into deep water.

The Prosecution Counsel returned to his seat, also realising that his witness was beginning to incriminate himself.

Arthur's elderly Defence stood up. 'How can you be so precise as to the date when you allege to have seen the defendant? You could have driven with corn any time in July and August. Do you remember the day of the week?'

'No.' Haddon shook his head, his thin locks of hair swinging round his face and he was stood down by the Judge before Arthur had a chance to question him.

Arthur cursed under his breath. Why was he not allowed to question Haddon? His evidence seemed even less well-rehearsed than Pelham's had been.

John Polhill, a Riding Officer whom Arthur had had dealings with on many occasions, was being called to the stand. Polhill had always seemed a reasonable man to Arthur and had turned a blind eye on many occasions in exchange for a few bottles of brandy or lace and silk for his wife and daughters. He looked flustered, uncomfortable to be here.

'Give an account of when you saw any smugglers,' the Prosecution urged.

'On the thirteenth of August 1746, I saw a gang of smugglers go through Lydd.'

'Which way did they go?'

Polhill looked resigned. 'I think they went further up into the country.'

'Did you see their faces?' the Prosecution Counsel questioned.

Arthur held his breath. Would Polhill also lie as easily as the other two witnesses had done?

Polhill looked from the Counsel to the Judge and then to Arthur and paused before making his response.

'Did you see their faces, sir?' he was asked a second time.

Polhill shook his head. 'No, sir, I did not.'

Arthur allowed himself to feel a grain of comfort. If the Riding Officer could not swear to Arthur's identity, surely the jury would not be swayed by the evidence of two such apparently unreliable witnesses as Pelham and Haddon.

'But you saw a gang of smugglers on the 13th of August 1746 ride from Lydd further up country. You know it was the thirteenth of August. How?'

Polhill looked resigned. 'Yes, I saw a gang. I did not see their faces. I know it was the thirteenth of August because we have to minute it in our book.'

But not me, Arthur said to himself, *you cannot swear, Polhill, under oath, that you saw me on that date.*

The Prosecution Counsel looked satisfied, not wanting to question Polhill further. He looked at the Judge and bowed his head. 'My Lord, we rest it here-,'

The Judge nodded. 'The prisoner has made a deposition that William Bishop and Samuel Terrell of Hawkhurst were material witnesses for him.' He looked around the Court. 'Are they here?'

Arthur's Defence Counsel rose before the Judge. 'My Lord, I regret they could not be here,' he said.

The Judge raised his eyebrows and looked at Arthur. 'Now is your time, then, to address the Court.'

Arthur looked across at the members of the Jury each studying his face intently.

'I have not been at Lydd these three years for the purposes of which I have been charged,' he said calmly, his voice sounding loud to his own ears as it was amplified by the wooden sounding board above his head. 'Why would I risk my life, knowing the penalties attached to smuggling? The evidence given by Pelham depends on a book he cannot produce. Haddon can only guess the date he alleges to have seen me because he was driving a wagon of corn. One man says I had a blunderbuss and the other says I carried pistols. I believe even they would be able to tell the difference between two such different weapons if their evidence was true. Mr Polhill cannot swear under oath that he saw me at all. I swear that none of them saw me there, because I was not there in Lydd on that day. Both these men Pelham and Haddon would rather take a man's life away for anything, for any bribe, than do an honest day's work.' Arthur looked at the Judge and then the jury. 'That is my defence, gentlemen.'

There was a muttering amongst the spectators' gallery at Arthur's words especially when he said the word *bribe*, and some of the jurors looked uncomfortable.

'Consider your verdict, gentlemen,' the Judge ordered.

Arthur watched as the twelve men huddled together, their voices hushed. He couldn't make out a word that was being said. The voices of the jurors became quieter and finally ceased. The Clerk of the Court rose.

'Gentlemen of the jury, have you reached a verdict on which you all agree?'

The elected foreman rose. 'No.'

The judge leaned forward. Did Arthur imagine it, or did he look rattled?

'Then have you reached a judgement on which a majority of you agree?'

The foreman spoke. 'Yes.'

The Judge fixed his eyes on the two rows of men, before speaking. 'Then I ask you, Gentlemen of the jury, how say you? Is the Prisoner, Arthur Gray, standing here before you, guilty or not guilty?'

There was a moment's silence. Arthur's eyes were drawn again to the sky beyond the windows. A skylark, he was sure it was, circled round and disappeared. He looked back at the ordinary face of the foreman, whose next words would mean life or death for him. The foreman looked straight ahead and opened his mouth. He closed it and then swallowed as his Adam's apple bobbed up and down. He coughed and then spoke one word.

'Guilty.'

Arthur had the queerest sensation that the courtroom was spinning round. He took hold of the bar in front of him and momentarily closed his eyes.

'Arthur Gray, you have been found guilty as charged. You will be brought back at the end of the Sessions for sentencing. Take him down.'

The Judge's words were meaningless. There was only one possible sentence, as every man in the Court room, Haddon, Pelham and Polhill included, knew. The only possible sentence was death.

Arthur was taken out of the courtroom and back through the passageway to his cell. As he was being led away, he did not see Thomas Lamb at the back of the spectators' gallery, rising stiffly and leaning on his stick shaking his head, the tears flowing freely down his pale, lined cheeks.

A half hour later, Lamb made his way into the inn in South Audley Street and ordered a small glass of brandy which he swallowed in one mouthful before making his way slowly up the staircase and tapping on the door of Beth's room. It was opened in a flash. As soon as she saw his red-rimmed eyes, Beth's own face crumpled, a cry on her lips as Lamb caught her in his arms.

'No! Oh no! Oh no, no no no! Oh please God, no,' she wailed, almost dropping to her knees.

'You must be very brave, my child. We must both be very brave.'

Towards six in the evening, Jupp came for Arthur again. He was taken with the other prisoners who had been tried that day to hear their verdicts. The Judge read from the prepared list. A woman who had been tried before Arthur for theft was sentenced to death and dropped to the floor in a dead faint when it was announced, her manacles clanging on the stone floor as she fell. Several others were sentenced to whipping or branding, two for transportation. The Judge looked at his list and turned to Arthur.

'Arthur Gray. You have been charged with an offence which carries the death penalty if convicted. You were found guilty as charged and I therefore sentence you to be taken to a place of execution on the next date assigned for hangings and there to be hanged by the neck until you are dead. Thereafter your body to be hanged in chains as an example to others who might be tempted to your evil ways. And may God have mercy on your soul.'

Arthur had a sudden vision of George Chapman's tarred body hanging in chains at Hurst Green all those years ago, as he had stood reading George's favourite bible story. His hands began to shake uncontrollably and they shook all the way back to his cell. Jupp told him he would have to have his wrist chains put back on, now he was a condemned man. Arthur nodded blankly and as soon as the door banged shut behind him he stumbled over to the bed, pulling the blanket round him holding it to his face desperately trying to find a small square of it that still carried the faintest aroma of his home, but as he breathed in portion after portion, all he could smell was the foul, damp odour of the gaol.

CHAPTER SIXTY EIGHT

Thursday 21ˢᵗ April 1748, Newgate

Beth could not stay away. She could not sleep. Though Lamb begged to be allowed to take her back to Hawkhurst, she shook her head. 'Leave him? Leave him here alone?' She was astounded that he could think it. 'I'll have to tell Will. I don't know how he will bear it.'

Will felt it almost as a physical blow when Beth, white-faced, told him that Arthur had been sentenced to death. He took three deep breaths and then turned away from her. She looked at his back and then she saw his shoulders heave and heard two great gasping sobs. She quickly stepped round in front of him and pulled him into her arms, as they both wept. She stayed with him an hour. Will hardly spoke. Every time she thought he had stopped weeping, his tears welled up again. She poured him some brandy with shaking hands and forced him to take two glasses.

Jupp then escorted her down into the basement cells. Arthur could not even take her in his arms, his wrists chained a few inches apart. She could only cling to him, saying his name over and over. He thought she might faint.

'Beth my darling, you'll make yourself ill. Come and sit beside me on the bed.'

She allowed herself to be drawn down next to him. He took one of her hands and held it to his cheek. 'There's something I want you to do. I asked Lamb not to come again but I need to see him once more. I need to ask him to use his influence one last time for me.'

Beth turned to him, her cheeks blotched, her eyes brimful of tears. 'Is there some hope then, Arthur? Some chance he may secure a pardon for you?'

He saw the sudden hope in her eyes. He shook his head and smiled. 'No, no. It's not for that. There's something I must ask him, that's all.'

Saturday April 23rd

Two days later, Lamb, looking frailer than ever, took his final leave of Arthur, after listening to Arthur's request. 'My boy, I swear by God and all His saints, I will use every last piece of influence I have to secure this promise for you. You may have every faith in me.'

He left the cell with a heavy heart but a determination that he would do this last thing for the man who had come to mean so much to him.

Arthur had asked Lamb to do whatever he could to prevent them taking his body back to Hawkhurst to hang in chains there. Lamb shuddered at the thought. He spent two long days in London calling in every favour he was owed, laying out large amounts of money amongst the judiciary, the justices and magistrates in the City. He sat down in the evening of the second day and drafted his letter to Arthur. He had secured a firm undertaking that after hanging, Arthur's body would not be taken to Hawkhurst. His body would hang in chains at Stamford Hill in London. Arthur reading it clutched the paper to his chest. 'Thank God, thank God, thank God.'

He had only to wait now for another hour for the last piece of news. William Pix had promised Beth he would attend the spectators' gallery when the final sentences of the Sessions were passed. He listened to the list of those sentenced to be hanged, of which there were three; and then those sentenced to be transported for seven years to Maryland, of which there were twenty one - case number two hundred and ninety three, William Gray, being one of them.

Arthur, hearing the news from William Pix, stumbled to the chair in silence. All his efforts had paid off. Will was saved. Will and Beth could make a new life. He looked up at Pix. 'Transportation? God be praised,' he said softly.

'Arthur, I can't stay. Beth's aunt wants to get her home. She has taken it badly, all of this, though she knew it was inevitable. Now she knows she must leave all that is familiar to her.'

'Yes of course. Yes, you must get back. Thank you for your care of her.'

Pix nodded and was gone.

He hurried back to the Inn. This time Beth did faint when she heard the news. Her aunt Ann was with her and between them they carried Beth to the bed and laid her upon it, her aunt loosening her stays, her uncle chafing her wrists. Her aunt looked thoughtfully at her, as she lay there and shook her head with disbelief once more, at the events of the past few months.

CHAPTER SIXTY NINE

26th April 1748, Newgate

Jupp pushed his face against the peep-hole in the door and called through, 'Visitor for you, Gray.'

Arthur unclasped his hands from behind his head and rose from the hard wooden bed. He rubbed his face and approached the door. 'Who is it Jupp?'

Jupp grunted. 'A lady!'

'Mrs Gray?' Arthur questioned urgently.

Jupp shook his head. 'No lady I seen here before. But a very fine lady, very fine indeed.'

Arthur wondered who it could be. 'Well bring her in Jupp. What can I offer her?'

'I reckon we can run to a bumper of brandy, seeing as how it's such a very fine lady,' Jupp said and Arthur could hear his shuffling footsteps as he went off up the stone passage. Then shortly afterwards he heard him return, with another pair of quicker, lighter footsteps and the swirling rustle of silk skirts. The lock was turned as Arthur heard the collection of keys jangle and the door was thrown open. Arthur looked at his visitor with no idea who she could be, except it was very obviously true that she was an extremely fine lady, dressed as she was in a wide panniered gown, frothy white lace of the finest French variety at her neck and a velvet cloak and hood of deepest royal blue. Her powdered wig was elaborately trimmed with ribbons and jewels. The sparkle of diamonds at her throat and her wrists glittered, even in the poor light of the single candle and the meagre daylight from the window.

'Beggin' your pardon, milady, but I has to lock you in, or stay in there with you. Do you feel safe to be locked in?' Jupp asked apologetically.

She smiled across at Arthur. 'Ooh, I don't know. Arthur Gray, am I safe in here with you?'

He looked blank and she let out of peal of warm rich laughter, which immediately carried him back to a balmy July night eleven years ago. 'My God, it's Nell Villiers,' he said. He glanced across at Jupp. 'Of course Lady Villiers is safe with me, Jupp.'

Jupp looked at the lady for confirmation and she gave a little nod of her head.

'I'll be back with your refreshments then,' he said, dragging the door shut behind him.

Arthur continued to gaze at her. She was like a being from another world standing there in all her finery.

'Well, Arthur Gray, what an exciting life you do lead! I have been following your escapades these many years in the *'Gentleman's Magazine'*. None of my friends would believe me when I said you had shared my bed! I had no idea you were such a great villain. You are a great villain, are you?'

'They say I am,' he said, half smiling.

She took a turn about the cell. 'Dear me, this is very grim. And the stench!' She drew a lace handkerchief out of her sleeve and held it to her nose. He at once smelt the perfume, the same as she had been wearing all those years ago and he was transported back to the tented room at Vauxhall Gardens and the vast proportions of her bedchamber in Grosvenor Square.

'Why have you come to see me?' he asked and then paused for Jupp was opening the door again and entered carrying a bottle and surprisingly, two glasses and not the broken earthenware tankards he usually provided. He set them on the small table, bowed slightly to Nell and went out of the cell banging the door shut and turning the key in the lock. Arthur poured them both a glass of brandy and handed Nell's to her.

She raised her glass. 'To old friends,' she said.

'Old friends,' Arthur repeated and tipped the liquid down his throat.

'I suppose it's idle curiosity has brought me here,' Nell said at length. 'I confess I've never been inside Newgate. And so they are hanging you for smuggling tea,' she added. 'It don't seem quite fair to me, I must say.'

'Nor to me,' Arthur replied.

'Well if you had killed a man, I could understand it.' She fingered the diamond pendant at her throat. 'Have you killed a man?'

Arthur inclined his head slightly.

'Oh,' she said doubtfully, 'well in that case, I suppose you do deserve it.' She was silent for a moment and then asked, 'the man you killed, was he too a great villain?'

Arthur looked into the distance behind her, seeing Tom Carswell's face as he lay face up in the sand at Camber, as he had seen it almost every day of his life since. He shook his head and sighed. 'No, he was not many years more than a schoolboy, I think and no villain at all.'

She looked at the rough wooden chair next to the table. 'Is that safe to sit upon?'

Arthur wiped the chair with the corner of his coat and offered the seat to her. She sat down carefully, spreading her skirts. 'I'll take another glass.'

Arthur poured them both another. There was a silence and then she asked, 'Are you scared, Arthur?'

He remained silent and wondered if he should tell this woman how afraid a man could be faced with his inevitable hanging. Should he tell her he was afraid of losing his nerve when the final hour came and having to be dragged crying like a baby, to the scaffold; that he was scared of wetting or soiling himself at the last moment; that he was scared of the pain when his neck broke; scared of the slow agony of suffocation if his neck didn't break; scared that he wouldn't be dead when they cut his body down and dipped it in tar before hanging him in chains; scared of the nightmares he had, when he woke in a sweat having dreamt he was still alive but hung in chains at some God-forsaken crossroads.

But all he said was, with a forced laugh whose falseness he hoped she would not notice, 'Not as scared as I was when you mentioned your husband that morning, when I stood naked as a baby in your bedchamber.'

She smiled and played with the lace at her sleeve. 'Did the watch keep good time?'

He nodded and tapped the pocket at his chest. 'It's been with me all these years. And did your husband get his waistcoat back?'

She smiled. 'He wore it but a handful of times. He grew too fat for it. I believe it hangs still in his cupboard.' She finished her drink and poured herself a little more. 'Will your woman be there, when they hang you?'

Arthur looked grave and shook his head, his thoughts of Beth and not of Sarah. 'No, I wouldn't have her there for the entire world.'

She looked at him, her expression serious for a moment. 'It's supposed to be easier if you can see a friendly face in the crowd. Will no one be there for you?'

He shook his head. 'I hadn't thought of it.'

'Would you like me to be there? Someone on your side? The crowds can be very boisterous, I've heard.'

He shrugged his shoulders. 'I'm not sure why you've come. You can't pretend to have any feeling for me?'

She shook her head. 'No, but I liked you well enough for one night eleven years ago and nobody should stand on the scaffold bereft of a friend.' She stood up and turned away. Arthur waited in silence. She faced him again. 'Well,' she said, 'I have something to show you.' She pushed her hand into the lace at her bosom and pulled out a locket on a fine gold chain. She held it out and Arthur put out his hand. 'Open it,' she said.

The necklace was still warm from her body and he prised the locket open with his nail. It sprang open and he looked at the likeness of a young boy and on the other side under the glass, a lock of light brown hair. 'Who is it?' Arthur asked.

She paused a moment. 'That is Alexander John Villiers, my only son. He was ten last week.'

Arthur drew in his breath, but could say nothing.

'On my husband's death, he will inherit the title and all his wealth.'

Arthur looked again at the miniature, at the boy's solemn smile, his frank blue eyes and brown hair. Though he wanted to, he couldn't speak.

'He's very enterprising, a handful at times. Like his father,' she said looking him straight in the eye. 'I love him with a kind of insanity. He's my only boy; perhaps all mothers love their sons like that. I have two daughters that I love – differently,' she finished. She took the locket back from him and thrust it among the folds of lace at her bosom. 'So Arthur, shall I be in the crowd for you?'

He paused before answering, staring into his glass. 'Yes then, I should like you to be there,' he acknowledged and they were both silent. 'I believe they are to hang my body in chains afterwards.'

She paled. 'I shall spare myself that sight,' she said fiercely. 'What needs them to do that to any man?' She downed the rest of her brandy and said, more brightly, 'I shall come with unpowdered hair, and then you shall be sure to find me in the crowd.'

He smiled. 'Yes I couldn't miss that halo. Are your curls still so red?'

She nodded and with a quick movement pulled several pins from her wig and pulled it off fluffing out her hair which immediately sprung out surrounding her face with a mass of auburn curls just as he had in mind. 'There!' she said.

'Yes, it's just as I remembered – except you're wearing rather more clothes.'

She laughed. 'Aye and so are you. Well Arthur Gray, is there anything else I can do for you? Do you have enough food? Perhaps I could send some wine?'

Arthur shook his head. 'Thank you but I have enough for my wants.'

She stood facing him and held out her hand. 'Until we meet again.'

He took her hand but she quickly raised her face to his and kissed his mouth. She pressed the little lace handkerchief into his palm. 'There, perhaps it will take away some of the stench of this awful place.'

Arthur went to the door and called to Jupp, who came shuffling along the passage, keys jangling.

She turned back and said diffidently, 'I don't know what I believe, Arthur, but I hope your God will go with you.'

He said nothing but nodded slightly as she left the cell and when she had gone and he could no longer hear her footsteps, he held the lace handkerchief to his nose and breathed in its heady aroma.

Nell's goodness extended even further for two days later Jupp flung open Arthur's cell door and told him to follow him. Arthur in a sudden panic thought he was being taken on his final journey and felt his legs turn to water, but Jupp laughed. 'Takin' you up to that young brother o' yourn. That fine lady paid handsomely for you to visit him.'

Arthur could hardly follow him fast enough as he stumbled along corridors and up a flight of stairs and at last found himself outside Will's cell. Will was standing immediately inside the door and the brothers fell into each others arms. Arthur held him from him a while though, looking at Will's sunken eyes and the two high points of colour on his cheeks. Arthur rubbed the back of Will's neck, not able to speak anything beyond his name.

Arthur looked about the cell. 'Once you're on board, Will, you and Beth, in the Captain's own cabin, I think you will regain your strength. You'll have the best of the food and drink. You'll be able to be on deck as much as you want.'

Will nodded and then burst into tears and sat with his hands covering his face. 'Arty, is there no hope for you? I can't bear it, I can't lose you. You've always been there.'

Arthur pulled Will's face to his shoulder. 'Will, Will! Come on little brother! There's always hope. A pardon may come down from the King himself. There are people still working for my release.'

Arthur was surprised how easily the lies tripped off his tongue, in his desperation to offer some comfort to Will. A hundred images of Will as a little boy come flooding through his mind and at the back of them like a bruise that would not heal -the knowledge of the betrayal that he had carried against Will all these years through his helpless love for Beth.

The cell door was flung open and Jupp ordered Arthur to his feet. There was time for one last embrace and then Arthur was stumbling back to his own cell, his mouth set and his features rigid.

Arthur knew they would meet for the last time once more on the following Sunday, the first day of May, for Will was due to be taken to Deal on the Sunday after ready to board the *Justitia* two days later. Arthur knew, but tried to set it beyond his conscious awareness that the next Hanging Day was the day after the *Justitia* sailed.

On the first day of May outside the forbidding prison fortress the day dawned blue and perfect, puffy little clouds scudding gently across a caressing sky. The brothers sat two rows apart in the little chapel, Arthur's eyes drawn the whole time to Will's back and Will often looked round at Arthur with haunted eyes. When the service came to an end, Will stood to one side waiting for Arthur to shuffle out of his pew. They were allowed to walk together to Arthur's cell and Jupp locked them in together. Arthur held out his arms and hugged Will to him neither able to speak. At last Arthur put Will from him and they sat down on the bed together.

'I don't think I can board the ship without you, Arty. How can I leave you here?'

Arthur put his hand on Will's head and ruffled his hair. 'You know you must go, Will. You and Beth will be safe. I thank God for it.'

Will shook his head. 'I never thought it would come to this. I'd give it all up to have you safe, Arty.'

Arthur patted Will's shoulder. 'No, don't say so, Will. What times we had, eh? Remember your first run from Hastings? How you soothed Ben Raven's mare? Remember our fight with the Winghams? I've thought often of the smell of the sea on a frosty night, going by moonlight up through the Marsh, a hundred men behind us. How many men can have such memories?'

Will nodded. 'Arthur, Beth is, she is – she's the finest woman in the world, ain't she?' He looked across at his brother.

Arthur looked straight back at him. 'Yes, brother, she is. You will ... you will look after her, won't you?'

Will met his brother's eyes. 'Until my dying breath. Arthur, I know-,'

If Will was going to say more, Arthur would never know for the door was thrown open and Jupp stood there. Arthur quickly put his arms around Will and kissed his cheek. 'God keep you safe, little brother,' was all he could say as Will clung to him.

'Come along there, Gray,' Jupp said and urged Will forward. Both brothers stood and Arthur pulled Will to him once more for the last time, and then quickly dropped his arms. Will had time for one more glance round and left the cell, leaving Arthur alone.

CHAPTER SEVENTY

May 4ᵗʰ 1748, Will's house, then Arthur's house

Beth had been pacing the floor unable to settle to anything. She had hardly slept though her body ached with tiredness but as soon as she laid her head on the pillow and closed her eyes, she was haunted by a picture of Arthur and Will. The dreadful prison, dark and forbidding, stalked her dreams, waking her with a start. Her heart ached and she felt sick whenever she thought of Arthur's fate.

She was filled with a black despair that she and Will had to sail the day before the execution was to take place. They would never know peace again. At the same time, she knew there was a new life within her. She had reflected with wonder that she might be pregnant and the last few weeks had confirmed her suspicions. Once again she did not know whether this was Will's or Arthur's child. She told no one. Who could she tell? She felt a black and shameful guilt knowing that she would willingly give up this baby in exchange for Arthur's life and then fell to her knees shocked at her attitude, trying to find the God of her childhood and despairing when she felt her empty words reverberate around the room.

It was kind of Lamb to take her in and once she got used to the idea that he was her father, she found the old man's presence a comfort; but today she felt a great longing for familiar things, for things that Will and Arthur had touched. She decided to ride back to Hawkhurst.

She hardly paid any attention to the road. Prue seemed to be aware of her mistress's lack of attention and picked her way carefully over the cobbles and then Beth urged her to a canter as they left the town and reached the open road. The roads seemed very quiet. She couldn't help but think how it contrasted with the days not long since past when two hundred men and horses ran goods up this same road on their way to London.

An hour later, she turned in to the stable yard at her own home. Lamb had asked Robert to bring the rest of the horses including Will's beloved Saladin to his own stables and there was a stillness and quietness in the stable yard that brought pain to Beth's heart. She went into the house and the familiar smell of it and the sight of Will's boots in the passageway and his coat hanging on the peg brought her lower than she could remember. She leant against the coat and breathed in its smell, rubbing the material of the sleeve against her face. In her imagination she heard Will calling to Corker, heard again his cheerful tenor accompanying her as she played the latest songs from the music sheets sent down from London, felt once again his lips drop a careless kiss on her curls. She wrapped Will's coat around her and went into the chill parlour, sliding into a chair, unable to cry and feeling she was all alone in a world she no longer understood.

An hour later she went back out locking the door shut behind her. She mounted Prue and set off up the incline. She would go and see Sarah and the girls. Seacox held a shadow of Arthur's presence. At least Seacox wouldn't seem so empty and bare. As she crested the hill and caught sight of the house she frowned as she saw a wagon loaded up outside with two of Arthur's horses hitched up in front of it. As she approached nearer she gasped in amazement and disbelief to see Sally seated next to the driver's seat and Becca and Susie sitting in the back with great piles and packages and Corker sitting between them. 'Sally,' she called out. 'What on earth are you doing?'

She brought Prue alongside the wagon. Becca looked up at her and Beth saw she had been crying. Just then Sarah came out carrying a wooden chest in front of her, which she hoisted up at the back of the wagon. She was wearing a travelling cape and hood.

'Sarah? Where are you going? I don't understand.'

Sarah looked up at Beth, tight-lipped and pale. 'We're leaving, Beth,' she said shortly.

Beth looked again at the wagon. 'Leaving Seacox? But where are you going? When are you coming back?'

Sarah looked up at Beth again and turned back to the house. 'I have one more chest to bring,' she said.

Beth hastily dismounted and followed Sarah into the house. Dismayed, she saw pictures and mirrors taken down from the walls, some drawers emptied and left open. She had never seen the house so untidy. Sarah went into the kitchen and picked up another wooden chest from the kitchen table and held it in front of her. Beth stepped forward and grasped Sarah's wrist. 'Sarah, tell me.'

Sarah looked as though she would push past Beth but then she put the chest back on the table and faced her sister-in-law. 'Don't you understand, Beth? I can't bear it, can't you see that? I can't bear the shame of it. I can't face walking down the street any more. I can't bear the thought of the girls walking in Hawkhurst and everyone pointing at them knowing their father was hanged.'

Her face crumpled as she said the word. 'I can't do any more for Arthur. I always loved him, you know. He was all I wanted. I know I wasn't enough for him. I wasn't clever, but I tried to make him comfortable. That was my way of loving him.' She suddenly thrust her chin forward. 'I'm... I'm going away with Josiah Colvill.'

Beth started to protest in disbelief. She knew the carpenter had worked for Arthur at Seacox but had no idea he was any more than an acquaintance to her sister-in-law.

Sarah went on steadily. 'I don't love Josiah but I think we may be able to live a tolerable life together. I'm not like you, Beth. I can find no pleasure in reading or music. I like to cook and clean and look after my children and my man. Josiah's wife has been dead these many years and his children are all grown. He has a sister in Lincolnshire; no one will know me there. I'll be Mrs Colvill and no one will connect me with Mrs Gray, the widow of the hanged smuggler. Josiah will be able to get carpenter's work. And one day I might be able to forget all this.'

She flung her arms up. 'This great house, this great fortress, it was never mine, Beth. You were here all the time in every room, your step on every floor, your hand at every window, your face in every mirror.'

Beth put her hands to her cheeks slowly shaking her head. 'I can't believe it, Sarah. I can't believe you can leave it like this. To run off with Josiah Colvill while Arthur is still in gaol!'

'What difference will it make if I wait until they hang him?' Sarah asked on a sob. 'I've been his wife for sixteen years. Do you think this is easy for me? Do you think I can ever be comfortable again?'

She bent forward over the kitchen table spreading out her arms, her cheek pressed to the smooth oak and cried out, sobs shaking her body. Beth looked at her. She had never understood Sarah and she did not understand her now. There were sudden footsteps at the door and Becca ran in, looked at her mother sobbing at the table and ran into Beth's arms. Beth smoothed her hair and held her tightly, Arthur's favourite child pressed close against her breast. None of them spoke.

Eventually Sarah pulled herself up, wiped her tears and picked up the chest again. 'Come along, Becca,' she said quietly.

Beth followed as Sarah pushed the last case on the wagon. She turned round and Beth bent and kissed her cheek. 'Goodbye then, Sarah,' she said. 'I hope you find contentment.'

Sarah nodded slightly and then returned Beth's kiss.

Becca hugged Beth again, tears streaming down the young girl's face. 'Tell Uncle Will, I'll look after Corker for him. And I'll take him for a walk every day. Oh Aunty Beth,' she sobbed again, 'you will come back from America, won't you? One day?'

Beth said nothing but held her closer.

'Will you see my Daddy again? I know what they're going to do to him,' Becca whispered.

Beth gave a nod.

'Give him our best love, will you, from all of us?' Becca sobbed.

Beth whispered, 'Yes', the lump in her throat making it painful to speak. She couldn't answer further and hugged her niece again and then helped her up into the wagon. She reached up and kissed Susie, sitting solemn-faced, holding a doll with all the calm acceptance of a nine year old. Beth smiled up at Sally through misty eyes. She reached up to kiss her. 'You're fifteen, nearly sixteen now Sally. I've known you since the moment you were born. You look after your mother and your sisters, won't you?'

Sally gave a little nod, just as her mother did. Sarah took Sally's hand and pulled herself up into the wagon. She gave one last look back at the house and Beth stood back as the wagon rolled away. She watched it until it disappeared out of sight towards Flimwell and their new life. Beth turned round to gaze at Seacox, shuttered and quiet. She mounted Prue and rode off in the opposite direction back to Rye.

CHAPTER SEVENTY ONE

Monday 9th May 1748, Arthur's cell, Newgate

Beth came for the last time to visit Arthur in his cell, to spend last precious moments with the man she had loved since they were children. She had taken care to dress in the gown which Arthur had brought back the first Christmas they had all spent at Seacox. Even in the poor light in the cell, the shimmering gold of her petticoat seemed to spread a halo of light on the straw-covered floor. She entered the room in silence and Arthur simply took her in his arms.

He paused a few moments and then murmured, 'Now I finally know what life is for, Beth. The house and all my money would have been nothing without you. If the world ended now, with you and me together in this cell, I should die a happy man. You were the best thing in my life. I should have married you. Do you remember that summer before you went away? It seems so long ago now.'

She nodded, pressing her face into his coat.

'My only regret is leaving you and Will,' he said at length.

'Don't talk of regrets, Arthur my darling. I can bear anything except that, I think.'

He drew Beth down to sit beside him and looked eagerly at her taking her face in his hands. 'Will needs to be in the open air when you're on board ship. He's never been strong since he was shot. And he outgrew his strength even as a lad, too lanky, taller than me,' he smiled.

Beth couldn't help smiling back. 'How that inch bothered you.' She looked into his face and then said, 'Arthur, I'm bearing a child. It might be yours or Will's. It makes no difference, does it?'

He looked anxious and almost unbelieving. 'A child, after so long?'

She gave a short laugh. 'It's strange, isn't it?'

He took her hand and kissed her fingertips. 'Are you well? You look well. I don't know what to say. I can't look after you. But you must take care on that long voyage-'

'Oh I know I will be well. I can't see the point of the child coming at all after all this time, if it was going to be lost. I long for it to be your child, Arthur. You can't know how I have envied Sarah your daughters.'

'Allow Sarah her daughters, Beth. You always had my heart, you know that, don't you? And you'll look after Will? He's not always wise. He needs you. I've always been there to look after him and now I won't be able to do that.' He took her face in both his hands and brushed a strand of hair from her eyes.

'I think we did great wrong,' Beth said at length.

'Do you, my darling?' he asked. 'I don't know. How can it be wrong to love someone as much as I have loved you?'

'Will knew.'

Arthur shook his head.

'Yes he did. I tried to tell him on our wedding night, but he stopped my mouth with kisses. He said you and I were the two people he loved best in the world. He knew, but he never let me say it. He's worth the pair of us.'

Arthur took her hand. 'Then you must love him well for the rest of your life.'

She looked around the cell for a moment. 'How has it come to this Arthur?' she asked, a thousand memories of their life crowding in on her thoughts. 'We were just ordinary people, living in a little village in Kent.'

He looked at her and smiled. 'You were never ordinary, Beth.'

He stood up. 'I'm glad Sarah didn't come. I said goodbye to her the day I was taken. She would go to pieces if she came here. She's not strong like you, Beth. I've never known such courage as yours. Sarah will move away when I'm gone. She should remarry. She'll be a rich widow. Some comfortable merchant will snap her up I'm sure. I hope Becca will do well. I think she has something of cleverness in her. Sally and Susannah, well they are their mother's daughters,' he finished, shrugging his shoulders.

Beth hung her head, not able to tell him Sarah had already left.

'I sometimes think of Carswell,' Arthur said, a little while later, looking into the distance beyond Beth. 'If it was my bullet that killed him, I have the blood of four people on my hands. He and Polly, their unborn baby and Chapman. Oh God!'

Beth raised her eyes to his. 'You mustn't think it, Arthur! Please don't say so. You've given so much. How many men were able to give their families better lives because of the money they made through you? That's what you must think of, Arthur, nothing else.'

He remained silent. 'The child, Beth? When is it due?'

She gave a small smile. 'At Christmas-time I think.'

Time moved on. They sat, they sometimes stood. They embraced or held hands. At last he spoke. 'Sweetheart, you must go now.'

Beth clung to him as if she could not let him go. She couldn't tell how long they embraced. Seconds, minutes?

At last he took her hands from his shoulders and cupped her face. 'Now let me look at you once more.'

He gazed at her as if he was seeing her for the first time. Then with his right hand he touched her eyelids, her brow, her nose and her mouth and pulled her to him, burying his face in her hair.

'My Beth,' he whispered, his mouth close to her ear. 'I'll think of you at the end. I would have endured it all and can endure what is to come, for just one precious hour of knowing you. And yet I've been blessed with knowing you all my life.'

He tightened his grip around her and then he slowly let his arms drop. He kissed her forehead and called out in a voice that was not quite steady,

'Jupp, Mrs Gray is ready to leave.'

Jupp unlocked the great iron door, and standing next to Arthur and with unexpected understanding, left it open so that Arthur could watch her go.

His last sight of her was her proud, swinging walk, shoulders back, head aloft, her wonderful hair glinting gold just as he remembered it, even in the dim light from the grating above the passageway. She turned at the last and said his name once finally and then she was gone from his sight into the pale sunlight of the May afternoon.

LaVergne, TN USA
04 August 2010

192100LV00008B/44/A